Raves for Do[illegible] series:

"The Gate Of Ivory is an engaging first novel . . . thoroughly enjoyable . . . the feisty Theodora's narration reveals a charming and gutsy female with whom its's a pleasure to share these adventures."

—*Isaac Asimov's Science Fiction Magazine*

"Egan brings a fresh attitude . . . Theo's reactions to the contradictory world she finds continually ring true in entertaining ways." —*Publishers Weekly*

"A fine blend of fantasy and SF themes, and her world and society could become serious rivals to the popularity of similar books by Marion Zimmer Bradley and C.J. Cherryh."

—*Science Fiction Chronicle*

"This tale of high adventure offers a great deal of entertainment to both science fiction and fantasy readers, but it is the highly original characterization, as well as a pervasive thread of quirky humor, that makes this foray into imagination so very memorable." —*Rave Reviews*

"It's great fun . . . this sequel manages to stand well on its own, going off in new directions to provide a satisfying, high-spirited adventure."

—*Locus*

THE COMPLETE IVORY

THE GATE OF IVORY

TWO-BIT HEROES

GUILT-EDGED IVORY

Doris Egan

DAW BOOKS, INC.
DONALD A. WOLLHEIM, FOUNDER
375 Hudson Street, New York, NY 10014
ELIZABETH R. WOLLHEIM
SHEILA E. GILBERT
PUBLISHERS
www.dawbooks.com

Cover Art by Richard Hescox.

DAW Book Collectors No. 1197.
DAW Books are distributed by Penguin Putnam Inc.

First Paperback Printing, September 2001
2 3 4 5 6 7 8 9

THE GATE OF IVORY

For Yu Wen, who has always know
that which of us is the tymon
depends on where we are

For Sam, the unseen critic

And for Mary Lou Egan, wherever she is—
don't say I forgot

TWO-BIT HEROES

For Robert F. Murphy, whose twice-weekly
show"Introduction to Cultural Anthropology"
is still a legend in the minds
of armies of graduates

GUILT-EDGED IVORY

With appreciation and thanks to
the spirit of Cao Xuequin

THE GATE OF IVORY

Chapter 1

I was laying down cards in the marketplace when I got the latest job offer. "Here comes money," Irsa, the vendor next to me had said and moved out of the way so as not to scare him off. So I'd given him his fortune, all the usual sort of nonsense, and out he came with this. I hadn't expected it of him; he looked too respectable. True, he hadn't mentioned the exact nature of this job. But I'd been in the Square long enough—I thought—to know what that meant.

"I might want to hire you," he repeated, as though he expected a dim-witted foreigner like me might need it said twice.

"Move on," I said, picking up my Tarot cards. "Your fortune's been told."

"I'm serious," he protested.

"Please, noble sir. I'm well aware that people hired by Street of Gold Coin procurers are never seen again. Unless you want me for one of the Great Houses?" I smiled with polite rudeness. It was obviously out of the question. By Ivory standards, I'm not even pretty. Eight centimeters shorter than everyone around me, hair auburn instead of black—they wouldn't let me into a Great House as a domestic servant. Not that I felt I was really cut out for prostitution.

"I'm not talking about Gold Coin *kanza*." The word he used was Ivoran, and meant rotten flesh, animal dung, scum to the tenth power. I looked at him in surprise, as he'd intended. "I like your card-reading."

"Thank you, noble sir." I was as phony as any other market fortuneteller.

"I'm not a noble sir. 'Gracious' will do."

So he wasn't part of the nobility, although he dressed like it. More and more interesting. And it hadn't been easy to read his cards. Usually the marks responded, gave you answers, hints, facial expressions. "Someone I know has had an accident? Why, you must mean my great-uncle Hobar." Not this man. Total silence as I interpreted the pictures. It was unnerving.

He said, "You're not Ivoran. How did you end up here?"

I shrugged. "If you really want to know, pay me." To my surprise he brought out another coin and laid it on the ground before me. I shifted position on my rug. "Know, oh gracious sir, that this humble person who is I was born on Pyrene, far from—"

"You can skip the formalities. I'm not paying you as a storyteller."

I sighed. "I left Pyrene and went to Athena as a student. A classmate of mine had a father who was first mate on the *Queen Julia*, one of those big luxury liners out of Tellys. One of his wealthy passengers had reserved a suite for the full run, from Tellys to Athena to Ivory, and left at Athena. My friend talked his father into letting him use the suite—it was booked round trip—and take some friends along. It seemed like a great opportunity. You know—I mean, the gracious sir must be aware of what starship passage costs. If I hadn't gotten a scholarship to Athena, I'd never have gotten even that far. So I came along. That was two years ago."

When I stopped he said, "But you're still here."

"The gracious sir asked me how I came here. Not why I remain."

He dropped another coin. I scooped it up and added it to the others in my pouch. "I spent a happy month on your lovely planet, which is how long the *Julia* was in orbit. We went to the Lantern Gardens, the Great Obelisk, and the Lavender Palace. I'd heard about the sorcerers and magicians of Ivory, and while I knew they were fakes, I still wanted to see them. How many chances would I get to play tourist? My friends weren't interested in phonies, though. The night before we were due to leave they wanted to visit the Lantern Gardens again—they were fascinated by the naked floorshow, we don't have things like that on Athena. So I left them and went off to the Street of Gold Coins by myself—"

"Why the Street of Gold Coins?"

"Well, I didn't know where else to find a sorcerer. And I'd heard you could buy anything there."

He nodded. "Go on."

"I wish I could; unfortunately, I don't remember a lot of what happened next. I don't even know which building I went in. I have a vague memory of a small woman in a green robe, with black hair down to her knees, opening a door." I began shuffling my cards. This next part was embarrassing. "I woke up the next afternoon in an alley. My money was gone."

He laughed. "You were rolled."

"I was rolled." Because it's an old story doesn't make it funny. "The *Julia* was gone, my friends were gone—I did have some money, because they'd left it for me at the hotel. I've spent the last two years trying to make enough money to buy passage back." And barely making enough to live on. But if I let myself see how impossible it was, I'd go crazy.

"Have you made friends here?"

"I don't see that that's any of your business, gracious sir."

He brought out another coin. This was a good day for me.

"No real friends, no relatives, no guildmates. No one to care if I live or die, which was a problem when my tourist badge expired." Among the higher classes of Ivory, murder is considered a practical craft, rather like needlepoint. A noble who wants to keep his hand in might pick off a passing stranger on the way home from a hard day in government. Tourists are exempt, by Imperial decree; they wear large red badges, prominently displayed. When mine expired, flickering to a burnt-out black, my spirits went out with it.

"I want to hire you," he said, a slight variation on his first statement: I *might* want to hire you.

"For what?"

"To read cards. Not these," he said, seeing my eyes go to the Tarot deck in front of me, and dismissing it with a contemptuous gesture. "I have my own cards. Come with me and I'll test you on them."

This could get too deep for me to swim out. "Gracious sir, I'd better tell you right now that I'm as phony as any other magician on Ivory. I can't read cards. I just make them up."

"You think our sorcerers are fakes." He smiled. "You've been here two years, but you still haven't learned much about Ivory. Rest easy, your lack of talent doesn't matter. The virtue is in my cards, not in the person using them."

He put out his hand and helped me up.

And so I met Ran Cormallon. His office was a house in a street I had never seen before, in a quiet part of town. The furnishings told me he was wealthy, but I had known that much from the way he was dressed. There were six beautifully appointed rooms—tapestries, paintings, computer screens in cabinets of inlaid marble-wood—all empty of people. We walked over wine-colored rugs embroidered with intricate calligraphy.

The innermost room of the top floor contained one large marble-topped desk with one chair behind it. I thought that Cormallon would sit, but he motioned me to it. "Open the drawer." I did so, slowly. A corner of gold caught my eye—a case for a pack of cards? Seeing my hesitance, Cormallon reached in and brought it out. He opened the case and spilled the cards on the desk. "Shuffle them," he said, "stack them, do whatever it is you do." When I had them shuffled and stacked neatly on the marble desktop, I looked at him. "Now read them," he said.

I turned over the top card. It showed a man sitting in shadow, bound and gagged. It was very realistic, with gradations of shade I'd never seen before in a deck of cards. "I don't even know what they're supposed to symbolize," I protested.

"When you're more used to them, you can tell *me* what they symbolize. This one is The Prisoner. Go on; you're doing better than you know."

I turned over the next one. It was an ancient water ship, with a smokestack; as I put it down a picture flashed through my mind of a different ship, a modern pleasure vessel. I touched the card again, and this time I was looking through a porthole into one of the cabins. Ran Cormallon was stretched out on a bed, reading a notebook; a young woman sat cross-legged on the carpet, her dark hair held back by a red jeweled pin. I couldn't see what she was doing. I took my hand away from the card and looked at Cormallon. "I don't suppose you've been on a boat recently."

He smiled. "Go on. This time see if you can tell me something new."

"With a woman," I said slowly, "who pins her hair up with a red pin."

"Go on," he repeated. "The next card."

I turned over the next card and dropped it hastily. It felt hot. I looked at the picture and saw an Ivoran house on fire, flames shooting up around the white stone.

Cormallon was watching me closely.

"It's hot. I can't touch it."

"Try the next one."

I put my hand on the deck, then drew back in pain. "They're all hot, gracious sir. I can't get near them."

He nodded, replaced the three cards in the deck with no apparent difficulty and returned it to the drawer. "You can drop the 'gracious' . . . since I'm to be your employer."

"You're taking it for granted, aren't you, that I'll accept the job?" Though there was no doubt in my mind that I would. The money alone would have decided me, and I was overwhelmed by what had just happened.

"If you hadn't already decided to take it, you wouldn't have been able to do what you just did."

"I didn't get very far, though." When he didn't reply, I said, "Why did the cards become hot? And what about that building on fire—"

"A temporary problem, I'm sure—it may have something to do with your predecessor in this position. She was involved in an accident, which is why I had to find a replacement."

I was ready to ask more questions when he brought out my advance. It was more money than I'd seen in the last six months.

"Thank you, gracious—ah, Ran."

He blinked. "A plain 'sir' will do. I know Athena makes less use of formality than we do, but there's no need to go overboard."

"Yes, sir." I took the money.

On the way back to the market I realized what the

woman on the ship had been doing. She had been dealing out cards.

Trade Square Marketplace is the loudest, busiest, and most dangerous corner of the Imperial Capital, which is the loudest, busiest, and most dangerous corner of Ivory; which is not a planet known for its peaceful style of living. But it was the only place lawless enough to let a stranger earn a living, and the only place well-organized enough to protect me while I earned it. The Square only *looks* like chaos cubed; those of us who sold there knew it was as carefully run as a Pyrene military maneuver. I paid a weekly fee to the Merchant's Association—a non-official, profit-making organization—and was not disturbed by thieves, cutthroats, pickpockets, or policemen. Irsa sponsored my membership in the Association; she was the closest thing to a friend I had here. I went straight from Ran Cormallon's office to her fruit stall in the market.

"Cormallon," she said thoughtfully. "They're big fish. Not one of the six Houses, but one of them that claims to be seventh. Specialize in sorcery, I hear, and other things less respectable. Lots of money there. Didn't I tell you when I saw him?"

"But how much of that money am I likely to see, do you think? Can I trust him to let me stay around when the job is over? Burial fees are so much cheaper. And I didn't like—" I paused. I hadn't liked the way his offer of employment came hard on the heels of my admission about my lack of family. I may be a dim-witted outlander, but I was well aware that I was probably the only person in the market that day who wasn't protected by some sort of kinship web.

"If you ask, I'd say the Cormallons are rich enough to be able to afford a little honesty. They've got their good name to consider, too—they've always honored their contracts. I'd work for them myself if they made the offer. For certain, if it was that young sparklehawk who was here today doing the offering." She grinned. Irsa was fifty-eight; she had nine children, and about as many teeth. "I don't ask questions," she went on, "no, I was well brought up. But if he's paid you already, that's a good sign."

I'd trust Irsa's judgment about the ways of Ivory before

my own, or in fact before anyone's I'd met so far. I said, "What about my membership in the Association? If I let it lapse, will I be able to get in again?"

She shrugged. "It's a risk. If you—" A man in a red embroidered robe leapt suddenly on an older man in brown who had been fingering the bronze cups in an adjoining stall. The two fell, pushing Irsa's cart back and upsetting one of her piles of fruit. She pulled the cart back farther as they scrabbled on the ground. She was standing perfectly still, her eyes following two rolling pellfruit across the dirt. The man in red had a hotpencil, which he pressed against the other's temple. The victim's face contorted. "It's not fair," he said, in a shaking voice. "You weren't—supposed to—"

"I was within touching distance," said the man in red.

The other was dead. Irsa went to pick up her pellfruit, stooping with a look of disgust on her face. "Aristocrats, both of 'em," she said as she returned to me, one large round fruit in each hand. She raised an arm to wipe sweat off her face with the back of her robe. "You'd think they had better places for that sort of thing. Why, dear," she said to me, "you look a bit scretchy. It's all this sun, makes everything seem more important than it is. I know you weren't brought up to it, dear, but so what if two fools choose to end their quarrel in front of us? It's happened before, it will happen again. Ishin na' telleth!" She looked around for something to give me to cheer me up, and ended by giving me what she gave anyone in distress: a piece of fruit. It was all she had to offer.

I asked the innkeeper where I stayed for the name of a reliable bathhouse. I usually carried jars of water from the well in the innyard up to my room, but I felt I deserved a treat.

"Asuka baths are good," he said to me. I'd just paid my last week's bill, and I could see him wondering.

"A good day in the Square," I said, smiling. He'd been patient about my not knowing the customs when I first came here. I could have paid him the next three months in advance, but I didn't want him to wonder *too* much. At that time I still had to carry all my money in the belt around my waist. No Ivoran bank would accept me, since I wasn't on the Net.

"Well, it'll make up for the fluteplayer. He's off."

"The fluteplayer's gone?" I'd heard him play every evening since I came.

"Dirty kanz skipped without paying for the last two weeks. Said he had a job in the north, and the next thing I know his room's empty." He shrugged and spat into an engraved copper vessel behind the counter. "Ishin na' telleth. It's too hot to get excited about." He went back to his record book. "Try Asuka," he called to me as I headed for the door. "Good family."

Asuka was expensive, but well worth it. It was one of the tallest private buildings in the capital, over twenty stories high, with grayglass walls and an aviary garden in its inner courtyard. I was met at the doors by two female guards, both dressed in gray, who gave me a rather perfunctory weapons search and handed me over to the people inside with a friendly slap. "Facial, massage, manicure, body painting?" they asked me.

"Just a bath." The man behind the desk handed me some towels and a woman took me up the grav to the tenth floor. We walked down a long hallway, the woman first with a gun in hand. She coded an alphabox in the wall and a steel door slid aside. "All steel walls and floors," she said, stepping inside. "Weapon-proof glass—good view of the park. Soap and extra towels here; this controls the temperature. The rooms on either side of you are empty. Please note that Asuka personnel all wear gray. If anyone in gray is harmed for any reason, we hold the client liable. If you have any questions, this will call the desk." She bent over, twisted the taps on and off, then straightened up and looked at me. "Is everything to your satisfaction?"

"Fine."

"How long will you want the room?"

"Two hours, I think."

"Should we notify you when that time is up, or wait for you to call?"

"Ah, no, you can call me."

She nodded and stepped into the corridor. "Enjoy your time with us." The walls closed seamlessly behind her. I threw the towels down on the floor and stepped into the bath. It was almost two meters long, and wonderfully deep. If I filled it all the way, it would go past my head. I faced the window and let the water run over my feet. Oh, this was more like it. I hadn't had such a bath since Athena—no, I'd *never* had such a bath.

In the park below it was spring, all green and white and budding. A hot day for spring, though, a reminder of how bad a summer in the capital could be. I wondered how many more summers I would have to spend here before I made my passage money. I'd begun to think it was impossible, and now here was this Ran Cormallon, dripping gold coins, providing me with hope and this lovely soak in the tub. "As long as it's not too dangerous," I said aloud, swishing about in the water. My voice echoed off the walls.

I was just a scholar, trying to get my degree. I hadn't planned on a two- or three- or five-year hiatus, but I was handling it, I thought, in the true spirit of Athenan rationalism. Mmm—they should have tubs like this on Athena. They wouldn't dream of having them on Pyrene, my birthplace; nonutilitarian, a waste of time and space. I had no kind memories of Pyrene, not of my crèche-guardian, my teachers, my classmates. It was years before I could acknowledge that anyone could be happy on Pyrene; that, in fact, most citizens were. The best thing they'd done for me was to give me my scholarship to Athena at the age of twelve. They had expected me to come back with my degree, of course, and revise municipal sewer systems, or some such. I changed my citizenship as soon as I touched ground on Athena and never looked back.

Brian Lonii, a guide for new students, met me at the port. I told him what I wanted to do, steeling myself for his contempt; and wonder of wonders, he did not speak of my debt to the state, but only laughed and took me to the top of the Scholar's Beacon, where I could see the parks and buildings and labs of North Branch spread out to the horizon. He took a picture of me there, with the railing and the sky behind me. I wish I had thought to bring it with me when I boarded the *Julia*.

Within a week I'd moved in with Brian's cluster. In two weeks I changed my field of study from technical administration (Pyrene's designation for me on my application) to cultural anthropology; and a year later I changed it to cross-cultural legends and folk literature. I spent half my waking hours getting language implants—I was the only undergraduate I knew who spoke Ancient English, Chinese, and Hebrew. I completely overlooked Ivoran. But then, it was a living language, and what folk tales can be gotten from contemporary life?

One day Brian came to me with the news there was a suite free on the *Queen Julia*. I took a hasty implant of the spoken (but not the written) language of Ivory, and here I was, two years down the path—Ivoran years, which made them even longer—an illiterate fortuneteller for the world at large and Ran Cormallon in particular. Well, ishin na' telleth, as they said here, being the strongest way of saying "I'm not about to care" that it can be said. I had heard of monasteries in the hills nearby where the men and women spent their days thinking and tending gardens. "Saying 'ishin na' telleth' to the world," it's called. I doubted I could ever match their fine and careless composure.

It was too bad about not being able to read, it had made life difficult for me—though it was not all that unusual on Ivory, not the badge of shame it would be on Pyrene or Athena. But I *had* picked up some compensatory skills along the way.

Those cards, now, those were unusual. . . .

Chapter 2

"Welcome, noble sirs. Can I get you some refreshment?"

The bald man harrumphed, returning Ran's bow. He ignored me, which was understandable, since he didn't know I was there. I was in my alcove, well within earshot, behind a satin curtain. The alcove was just big enough for me to sit comfortably, spread my cards, and get a good view of the office from the automatic projection on the curved wall. The more I knew of his affairs, Ran kept telling me, the more specific I could be in my card-readings. I found I had no more trouble with the deck; in fact, it was a joy to me to have this sudden, sure skill, to see the rich pictures and feel the new emotions tumble into my mind, and, to be truthful, to be able to look through a window into the lives of strangers and know there was nothing they could do about it.

The three officials sat themselves on raised platform cushions that tended to put their eye levels just below Ran's. The woman and the younger man took silver cups from Ran and sat holding them mechanically. The bald man ignored his cup. He folded his hands over his chest, just where his robes parted to accommodate his bulging stomach.

"I don't think this need take too much of your time, gracious sir. Our request seems pretty straightforward, as I understand these things."

"So it is. I just want to make sure you know what you're asking."

"I'm asking for a simple removal. And if I may speak plainly, your fee seems a bit high for a service we could easily perform ourselves."

"You're free to perform it, noble sir." When the bald man didn't answer, Ran went on, "What you are paying for in this case is untraceability. Two of you belong to a particular house, no need to mention names, and you want that house to remain uninvolved in this. All of you are colleagues in the Department of Water and Power, and all of you will be advanced through this action. You don't want to anger your victim's family or alienate your own. Very well. His death will not only appear to be a natural death, it will *be* a natural death. Stroke, heart attack, whatever you like. Sorcery partakes of nature, after all. And if you considered my fee too outrageous, you wouldn't be here."

The woman's bracelet tapped the cup in her hand. She seemed startled by the sound. The bald man looked at his two colleagues, then back to Ran.

"How long would this take?" he asked.

When they had filed out, Ran pulled back my curtain. "Well?"

"I don't like them."

"I'm not pleased by their company myself, but that wasn't the question I had in mind."

I sighed. "The cards don't like them either, Ran."

"Sir."

"Sir. There's something funny about them and their designated victim. Something to do with a blood relationship. Necessary information we haven't been given—"

He was already going to his shelf of hand-held books, pulling down the current year's volume of the *Imperial Rolls*. "Hideo, Hideo . . . here it is. What a victim our victim is—no major family support, no powerful relatives. A gift from heaven, apparently. You're sure of the cards? Could it be that a blood relationship with one of our three visitors is what you're seeing?"

I ran the cards again. He was always patient at this point, almost deferential. "I can't explain it, but I get the same answer both ways. Our target or our clients: a powerful person involved, a blood tie. And possibly illegitimate—it's on the left side of the configuration."

"Huh. Well, I'll put them off for a day or so while I make inquiries."

"I'm sorry."

"Why apologize? That's what you're here for, to warn me off dangerous ground." He went over to the small round window behind his desk, unscrewed the locks, and pulled it open. The smell of late-flowering cinnatree came in with the summer breeze. It's strange how deeply smells go in the memory; the antiseptic smell of my crèche when I was small, the smell of old books in the artifacts library of Athena's North Branch. The Square was always filled with the aroma of food cooking. Cinnatree is a wonderful smell to enter a tiny room, it seemed to pull down the walls to the world outside. I stretched and let my legs dangle from the alcove niche. "This is the first negative report you've given me," Ran went on, "and I'm glad. You're coming more into tune with the cards. Are you doing as I said, keeping them with you and sleeping with them at night?"

"They're always in my pouch," I said, patting the leather bag I had slung beneath my outer robe.

"The more you do, the more you'll be able to see." He unlocked a drawer in the desk and pulled out a green candle and a small plastic packet of dried leaves. "There's no need for you to wait around, I won't be seeing any more clients this afternoon."

"Well, I was wondering if I might use one of the terminals in the other rooms."

"Go ahead; you don't need my permission. Polite of you to ask, of course."

"The problem is, I need an access code."

"Why can't you use your own code?" His voice changed. "Are you involved in anything you didn't tell me about?"

"No, no. I don't *have* a code . . . I'm not on the Net."

"That's impossible."

"No, a lot of people in the market aren't on the Net. They don't like to be kept track of, and when I started to work the Square they told me not to register. It's not compulsory, you know."

"Great bumbling gods in heaven!" It was the first time I'd seen him surprised. "How do they *tax* you, woman?"

"Oh, they don't. The Emperor sends census takers into the market every now and then, but they never get very far. I saw one get pretty badly beaten, and he was one of the lucky ones."

After a moment of wonderment he said, "I knew the Emperor always has notices up for census takers willing to travel out to the Northwest Sector to try and register the outlaws, but it never even crossed my mind they might also be trying to register people in the very shadow of the capital. I've been leading a sheltered life." He took out a scrap of paper and wrote down a number. "Here. Since it's a family number, I've got to know what you'll do with it."

Feeling my face get a little hot, I said, "I want to learn to read and write."

He shook his head. "Theodora, I have ceased to be surprised. Memorize it, burn it, and use it as much as you like."

So I took it to one of the other rooms. It was the first time since my classmates left Ivory that anyone had called me by my name.

It was a silly thing to be so pleased about, I thought, especially as I had rarely heard my full name anyway, not since childhood. It was a nice enough name but nothing special; we only used one name on Pyrene, so we dug deep for variety. My crèche-guardian named me from a random-historical program, after an ancient empress. On Athena I was usually Teddy, or even Teddy Bear, which latter I left behind as one of the few advantages of my exile. (It's hard enough looking small and cute—and in a totally asexual way, I might add—without having your nose rubbed in it.) But this casual human contact had warmed me more than anything else on Ivory.

Sentiment, however, did not stop me from making my usual daily cash-count, as I walked back to the inn:

Third class passage to Athena:	520,500 dollars
520,500 dollars =	140,166 tabals Ivoran
Weekly salary =	760 tabals
which makes today's earnings =	108 tabals
My total savings to date =	9,120 tabals
140,166 – 9,120 =	131,046 tabals still to go.

I could save the necessary in about three years, provided I remained the single-minded miser I had become.

It was odd: When I was pulling in two or three tabals a

day in the market, I was never so obsessed with money. Now that I was making a higher salary than I could ever make on Athena (where even the most honored scholars saved for decades to make their one trip on a starship), now that my goal was a serious possibility, I regarded every spent coin as an enemy.

I stopped to buy a bag of apples in the market, mentally subtracting the price from my savings:

9,120 tabals
– 63 kamb. (rounded to one tabal)
9,119 tabals.

Which increased, you will see, my tabals-still-to-go amount by one. This may not seem like much, but when you figure in this same amount every day it comes to quite an unfortunate total per month. I decided against getting any meat or rice with the apples.

I found myself doing calculations like this one all the time, and I didn't like it. I also found myself lying awake at night, worrying about my money belt, wondering the best way to approach one of the nonNet bankers who operated so informally in the market. They charged a ridiculous interest rate for the "favor" of looking after your money; but I'd heard they were reliable. Of course I could have used Ran's access code to get a legitimate account; but then the account would belong to Ran, and I wasn't quite that naive.

One of my ancient literature texts had been a piece called *Moll Flanders*—an English story about a woman making her way in a hostile, male-dominated society. I remember that this woman couldn't pick up a pewter tankard without reappraising her general net worth. She was beginning to look more and more sensible.

Anyway, I took my apples home and had them for supper. It seemed to me that they'd tasted better in the days before I reduced them to numbers. But then, maybe they were just off-season.

The next day Ran met me at the door. "Good news," he said, "in a manner of speaking. Your report on our threesome of yesterday checks out. They failed to tell us that their chosen victim is the illegitimate son of our Noble District Magistrate. It seems to be an open secret, that's why he's rising so fast in the department, and why our friends are so nervous." He took a bite out of the piece of fruit in his hand. "Have you had breakfast? Have a plum." He tossed me one. "I've already warned the magistrate about them, and he's sent us a reward. Not what we would have gotten from our almost-clients; but not ungenerous, I think. They'll be in the Imperial Prisons by lunchtime."

"Is that a good idea? Won't you be making enemies?"

He shrugged. "Nothing we have to worry about. Hardly anybody ever comes out of the Imperial Prisons. It's not like the army." (The army being where most Ivoran criminals end up.) "There's not even a trial." He grinned happily, a row of perfect white teeth in a brown face. The level of physical beauty I encountered on Ivory was depressingly high; if I hadn't kept in mind that my stay was temporary, I might have gotten an inferiority complex.

"That's not why I'm so pleased, though," he was going on. Or possibly I was just showing the effects of two-plus years by myself.

"Sorry," I said, into a pause in the stream, "I missed that. Who are 'they'? What do they want?"

"It's a lovely idea. One of the Great Houses, of course. Who else would own prostitutes? Do you think I'd take a commission from some Gold Coin rattrap? An advisor at the Yangs' has come up with something new. Something new!" He practically sang it. "You don't know how boring this job can be, Theodora. Nothing but routine, day in and day out. Everybody has the same three or four problems. 'Cast me a curse, gracious sir, I need a luckspell, gracious sir,' —I'm tired of hearing it. We sorcerers can be creative enough for ourselves, but nobody knows how to make use of us. I only get about three halfway interesting assignments in a year."

"But what *is* it?"

He looked sheepish. "Sorry. I don't usually let myself get enthusiastic. Well, ishin na' telleth. Here's what they want—"

One of the Great Houses had come up with the idea of using sorcery in their business. Every boy and girl in the House was to be given what we decided to call an *over-*

texture, a sort of double tactile image. A client who stroked a girl's breast would feel that, in addition to warm flesh, he was touching something else—silk, perhaps; or leather, or steel, or the petals of a rose. Ran was intrigued, but before he accepted he wanted me to run the cards. There was to be some small trouble, I reported, but with people rather than the assignment itself. That was good enough for him.

The next few weeks were busy ones; it was a complex project. Each of the House entertainers had to decide what image he or she wanted to project and, proud egoists all, none of them wanted to repeat another's sensory texture. It was a new concept, and Ran had to work out the spells from scratch. Our house suddenly became filled with people using vidiphones, using computers, running back and forth between our office and the Yangs'.

That was how it happened. The overtextures were to be attached to the entertainers themselves, rather than planted as an illusion in the minds of the customers, and so lengthy spells had to be placed on every one of them. It was time-consuming, and since Ran charged a high fee for his time, the House hired another, cheaper sorcerer to assist him in the actual placing of the spells.

I was on a terminal in an empty room, practicing my reading, when I happened to look up at the spy projection of Ran's inner office on my wall. His new assistant was there, measuring one of the boys from the Great House. I was so engrossed with the boy—as I said, the level of physical beauty on Ivory is high—that it took me a moment to notice the woman. Ran's assistant looked very familiar. I wasn't sure why, but I had a very uncomfortable memory associated with her . . . then I got it, and the surge of anger that went through me was a new experience.

I linked with the room, voice but not visual; this is not considered strange on Ivory, where no one gives away any information if they can help it. "Is Ran Cormallon around?"

"He's in another room. Shall I call him?" That was the voice, all right.

"Yes, please. Tell him it's a private call." In a minute Ran was there. "It's Theodora. I don't believe it myself, but I've met your new assistant before. She's the one who rolled me when I first came here and made me miss the *Julia*."

"Are you sure?" I could see him in the spy projection, turning to look thoughtfully at the door. The door itself was out of my line of sight, but I knew it was closed, since I had said the word "private." "I don't suppose," he said wistfully, "that you would be interested in revenge."

There's nothing a well-brought-up aristocrat likes better than the chance at a good bit of vengeance-taking. As an Athenan, I should have been beyond that sort of thing.

"The hell I'm not," I said. "Two years of my life—I could be a Master of Arts at North Branch by now."

"Leave it to me," he said with delight. "You'll allow me to participate, won't you? I mean to say, as my employee, it's as much an offense to me as to you."

That seemed rather convoluted to me; if not for her, I wouldn't *be* his employee. I wasn't about to object, though. I said, graciously. "I'd be happy to hear any ideas you have."

"Thank you." He cut the link. On the projection I saw him smile.

The Great House commission took a few more days. Ran worked closely with his new assistant—Pina was her name, I learned—then told the House he had to take care of family business for an afternoon. He left her to finish placing the spells by herself.

When Ran got back to the office there was a message for him on the Net. The House was not pleased. Somehow it had happened that one of the girls our new assistant cast her spell on—a nice girl who thought it would be fun to feel like polished mahogany—ended up with skin of dragon hide. And a boy with the look of a statue of some ancient god, who had asked for the texture of marble, found that he had sprouted thorns. His first customer actually bled.

"Let's go," he said. "I hear the Yangs can be very rough on people when they want to be."

A Yang representative met us in their public room. "Something will have to be done. Curran—" (the boy with the thorns) "—is scheduled to sing at Lord Degrammont's birthday party tonight."

"Oh, it shouldn't affect his singing," said Ran calmly.

The man glared at him. "And who is this person? You can't bring strangers into our House."

"A member of my own House," he answered politely, "although not my family. Theodora, this is the gracious sir Tyon Yang. Theodora is my assistant. I usually like to choose my own, when I get the chance."

The man's mouth tightened. "Please come with me, gracious sir and lady."

I was moving up in the world. I hoped I would be around long enough to enjoy it.

The Yangs had a disciplinary chamber in the private section of their House. It was shaped like a pit; old-fashioned, trite, psychologically formidable. Pina stood in the pit's center. There were only four other people present, aside from Ran and myself. Three men and one woman, in formal robes with the circled Yang "Y" on their chests, sat in the front row. Empty seats rose behind them. I wondered what they filled them for.

"Madame Pina," said one of the men, when we had been seated, "this hearing is to determine whether your actions today stemmed from simple incompetence or were a deliberate attempt to sabotage the reputation of this House." A ring of fire sprang up around Pina, knee-high. "All questions are to be answered truthfully, on peril of your life." Like all entertainment Houses, the Yangs went for a good show. They knew how to go about it, though, and I speculated on what Ran's and my roles were to be in this.

To give her credit, Pina's voice didn't even waver. "I will, of course, answer truthfully, my lords. I have nothing to conceal. Ask your questions." The circle of fire blazed up a bit, but that was all. A good sign for her.

"We will first hear testimony from Ran Cormallon, a witness and possible co-defendant. Please enter the ring."

Oh-oh. Ran went down to the pit, and the fires parted to let him through. He ignored Pina. "At your service, gracious sirs."

"Sir Cormallon, please give us your estimate of Madame Pina's capabilities as a sorcerer."

"I can only answer for what little I've seen. She did the jobs I gave her well enough. Passable, I would say, but little creativity or style."

"Could she make such an error as this, in your opinion?"

He shrugged. "It's possible, gracious sirs. I really couldn't say."

The Yang woman spoke. "Did you have any inkling when you left that she might be planning this?"

"No," said Ran carefully, "when I left, I had absolutely no idea that she had anything like this in mind."

"Thank you. Please return to your seat. We may have other questions."

He sat down again beside me.

They questioned Pina for about half an hour. She denied having intended any harm, protested that she didn't know what had gone wrong with her spells, and speculated that some lesser, and jealous, sorcerer was trying to make her look bad. She asked for mercy. The four Yangs debated for several minutes.

"Madame Pina," said the first questioner finally, "we are willing to grant that your harm was probably accidental. However, regardless of intent, you have damaged the reputation of our House. We rely on the trust of the public. You will have to restore our integrity in their eyes." He looked around at his colleagues, who nodded, and turned back to Pina. "To redeem ourselves and show we had no connection with this unfortunate incident, we must condemn you professionally. We will make it clear that you are a risk, and that anyone who hires you does so at our displeasure. Most of your clients are not the sort who could afford to annoy us, and we regret ending your career in the capital."

Pina looked white.

The man went on, "But we have no wish to be vindictive, and though we may claim otherwise publicly I assure you we will not pursue this matter beyond the city boundaries. I would recommend a change of name. Thank you for your presence—"

"No, wait! My lords, please! I've spent years getting a name in this city—I won't go back to the provinces! Please, give me another chance. I can remove the spells, I know I can. Please." To my discomfort, she started to cry. The Yangs were filing out. I felt a tug and realized Ran was standing beside me.

"It's over," he said. I stood up.

"Wait, please!" called Pina. "Listen to me! How could I know this would happen? Please! Oh, please!"

The Yang judges were gone. Ran and I were at the chamber door. I looked back, and my last image was of her standing in the empty pit, an old man in green standing beside her, waiting patiently for her to finish so he could show her out.

We walked back to Ran's office, scuffing through the cinnaflowers that were all about on the sidewalks. The breeze ruffled through my robes with an unexpectedly cool tang, and I realized I had been sweating.

"It wasn't the way I thought it would be."

Ran was disappointed with my response. "It wasn't as severe as some would have made it," he said defensively, "but I thought you foreigners didn't like that sort of thing."

"Maybe we went too far."

"*Too* far?" He sighed. "If there is one thing I'll never understand, it's outplanet thinking. You people start fights as much as anyone, kick and claw as much as anyone, and then you pick your enemy up out of the dust, brush him off, and send him away with gold coins and 'Better luck tomorrow.' If Pina hadn't cried, you wouldn't be acting this way."

"She did cry, though, and I feel rotten."

"What have we done that was so terrible? All right, Pina won't be living her life where she planned on living it. How is that different from what she did to you?"

"She didn't know that what she did to me would be so serious—"

"When you interfere in someone's life you have to take the consequences."

"—and at least, with me, it's not for life. I'll be going home eventually."

He was silent for a while. My robes swished over the white cinnablossoms. I stepped on one, deliberately, and as I lifted my foot the petals sprang back into place. Hardy flowers, the cinnas. They last until the autumn rains carry them down the gutters.

When Ran spoke there was a trace of anger in his voice. "You foreigners have no concept of honor—not to mention self-defense. You think you can forgive your enemies.

That's crazy. One day your new friend is going to bring you down with your own knife, and serve you right." He muttered something under his breath. It sounded like "ishin na' telleth." "Look," he said, "I'm going out to celebrate. You can come if you like. Otherwise I'll see you tomorrow."

"Go on ahead, then. I'm tired. I'm going home."

So he went on to the office and I turned to go through the market to the inn.

I lay on the bed, soaking in nothingness. This room was valuable to me, the closest thing to peace in the city. I looked at the ceiling of plaster and wood, the discoloration under the beam that showed when the light from the high slit window ran over it. It was quiet. I missed the fluteplayer.

A restless night followed. I got up for the third time to use the privy down the hall. By the hall window I stopped to feel the breeze; this window faced the courtyard, rather than the street, and so was cut bigger than mine. Moonlight shone on the well and I saw lights in the windows across the way. I made my way back to my room. Outside the door I stopped.

I was usually far from intuitive, but the sudden and compelling feeling pricked at me that something was wrong. I reached out hesitantly to touch the door. It was red-hot.

I backed away, stood for a moment in confusion, and ran down the stairs to wake the innkeeper.

I left them pouring water over what was left of my possessions. My money was gone; I'd locked the door and left the money belt under the mattress (the first place anyone would look but my choices were few) and the last I saw of it was as a charred heap of metal among wet ashes. Whatever was salvageable from it my neighbors got to before I could. After an hour or more of people rushing through with buckets—there are better ways of fighting fires on Ivory, but the protective association my inn belonged to couldn't afford them—I decided to slip out before the innkeeper thought to stop me. It had just occurred to me that I might be held liable for the damages.

I found myself stripped down to my skivvies on a dark

street, without money, my card pouch still dangling by my waist. I was never without the cards, at any rate; being cautious to the point of fanaticism, I literally wore them everywhere. ("Detail-oriented," my advisor used to say on Athena. I just looked at it as avoiding trouble in advance.)

But I hadn't been quite as fanatic about my money, which was strange, but this wasn't the time to analyze the matter. I needed clothes and shelter, meaning more money. I naturally thought of Ran. He would be out celebrating somewhere by now; looking at the moons I saw to my surprise that it was only about the fifth hour. I found a quiet corner and began laying out the cards on the pavement.

The Lantern Gardens are not the sort of place where one goes in one's underwear. On Athena—although somehow I couldn't see the situation rising on Athena—I would have blushed and hidden behind a bush. But since then I had spent two years in Trade Square, where anyone can do anything, and shame has yet to be invented. The manager told me that sir Cormallon was not there (I knew he was from the cards) and said I simply *could not* walk through the restaurant like this. I told him he'd better supply the tablecloth to wrap me in, because I planned on going through. Really, I thought, how can this man be so upset? And the Lantern Gardens famous for their naked floorshow. Unless he felt the sight of my particular body would ruin his patrons' appetites, and I couldn't argue with him there. On Ivory, at least, I'm not to everyone's taste.

Ran was at a table with a woman, which did not surprise me; he'd had me run the cards several times on matters dealing with his private life. She was exotic by local standards; blonde hair piled up with a jade pin, slant black eyes. She caught sight of me first, making my way to their table, and the black eyes opened wide. I suppose I did look rather alarming, in a red-and-black studded tease-gown belonging to one of the performers, and far too big for me.

Ran turned to see what his companion was staring at. To my disappointment, there was no surprise at all in his face. "Something come up?" he inquired laconically.

I told him about it. "So I need an advance, for clothes and food and that sort of thing—"

He was getting up. "Sorry to cut things short, my dear,"

he said to the woman. "I'm afraid I'll have to be leaving." He started to count out some coins onto the table. "Please feel free to continue the evening as my guest. I hope I can ask for you again?" He turned to me. "Let's go."

"What? Look, you don't have to leave. I just need some money. I left the inn before there could be any trouble, you don't have to worry about my being arrested, or having to pay anybody off. . . ." He was drumming his fingers on the table. He gave me a few seconds to realize that there might be more going on than I knew about, and he might not want to explain in front of someone else. "All right," I said, shifting gears. "Let's go."

In an attack of upper class formality, Ran took my arm. Necessity had carried me beautifully through the evening up till now, but all at once I became acutely conscious of what I was wearing. Ran didn't seem to notice.

"Let's go out that way," I said, pointing to a shadowy area of the restaurant.

"Nonsense." We started down the main aisle. By the time we were halfway to the door I had to stop myself from laughing. The manager was staring from the side with a horrified look on his face. Some patrons stared openly, while others studiously looked around their winecups and over their forks and just past me. My partner was serenely oblivious. I was taken by a great feeling of fondness for him at that moment.

Near the door I spotted a face that looked familiar, a face that didn't seem to belong in the Gardens. I recognized the Athenan embassy officer sitting at a table. He ought to know me, as well; I'd practically camped out in his office for weeks after the *Julia* left, begging for a loan, either official or personal; at least a subradio check with Athena so he could know whether to extend me credit. Surely his budget covered that, I kept saying. The bastard—the *kanz*—claimed he couldn't do anything without my I.D.—stolen, of course, along with everything else.

I waved at him as we went out.

"What's going on?" I asked outside.

"I'm not making the same mistake twice," he said, and shook his head because the carriage he'd been hailing pulled up. The horse was six-footed, but rather old, and I could sense Ran straining to hurry the driver on. We got out at the office, where we climbed briskly up the four flights of stairs to the roof. I'd never been up there before. Under an overhang in the corner of the empty cistern was a small aircar.

"*Where* are we going?" I asked, climbing in.

He fiddled with the controls. "Home," he said, leaning back in the seat with a sigh. For the first time since I'd known him I saw him relax.

Chapter 3

We flew until the sun came up. All around us I saw the shadows of what by day were sun-browned fields, irrigation channels, small groves and lakes, followed by vineyards, followed by hills covered with trees at the height of summer growth. We had come far to the northwest—far, at least, to me, who had never been more than three kilometers from Trade Square.

"It begins here," said Ran, and I opened my mouth to ask *what* began there, when the air shimmered, wavering before my sight like the capital on a hot day. Then it straightened again, and I knew we had just passed a sorcerous barrier.

More hills then, and trees, and in the midst of them, fast approaching, an expanse of greenery that flaunted human attention: streams, gardens, arched bridges, and small houses tucked away here and there. In the center of all rose a huge house of white stone, with steps leading to the front doors. I caught a glimpse of the inner courtyard and then we were down.

Ran sat for a minute tapping on the controls. No one came out to greet us; the early-morning quiet felt very strange after everything I had been through. "This is going to be awkward," he said. "Getting you inside, I mean."

I knew what he meant. It's not that members of one family never visited another; if your families have been allies for the past five hundred years, and nobody has offended anybody in all that time, you might be asked over. My own position was less clearly defined.

"Well, waiting won't help," he said. So we got out and climbed the steps to the high green doors. He rested the palm of his hand against them and said, "I've come home."

The doors opened, gently, with an inward swing. As we

passed through, I saw they were at least ten centimeters thick. A long, wide corridor led to the heart of the house; at its end a man appeared, jogging down the length toward us. He was gray-haired but vigorous, in a short green robe, bare-armed, with a gold band around his wrist. He stopped and stared at me.

"Don't panic, now," said Ran, not to me but to the man. "In fact, Jad, don't pay any attention at all. She's not really here yet."

"I, ah, see," said Jad, recovering. "I was sent to tell you breakfast is being served. Your grandmother is aware that you're back, and expects you at the table."

"She would."

"She also wants to talk to you about the—foreign object—you brought through the barrier." He carefully did not look at me.

"Mmm. Yes. Tell her I'll be right there, that I have to wash first."

"I will." He turned to go, but looked back again for a moment. "Best of luck, youngster," he said to Ran, and then he vanished quickly down a passage.

"Better hurry," said Ran, pulling my arm, and like Jad before us we were jogging down the corridor. It ended in a staircase; we trotted up without even a pause. A woman passed us coming down, a gold band on her wrist. She halted in shock. "Never mind, Herel. She's not really here," said Ran, hustling me past. I looked back and saw her staring up at us, her mouth an O.

We entered a small room on the second floor. I sat on the bed while he paced. "All right," he said, "there's no need to worry. I'll go down first and explain to Grandmother why you're here. She'll understand; she's very radical, in her way. I should have gotten you clothes. Never mind. I wonder where Tagra is." He stopped pacing, which was good, as I might have gotten violent. "All right. Wait here, don't go out, and I'll be back in a few minutes." The doorway had a red curtain over it; he flung it back and left.

I waited. And to think that just a few hours ago I had been sleeping in my own room at the inn, refuge and symbol of whatever peace Ivory had to offer me. I decided there was no reason not to lie down while I could.

Someone was trying to wake me up. "Here," said Ran's

voice. He let a white silk robe slip from his arm to the bed. "I found some clothes for you."

"I look stupid in white."

"Wake up, come on. It's all I could find, anyhow, so it will have to do. Grandmother's waiting."

I got up and slipped it over my head. Ran was pacing again. I unhooked the absurd Lantern Gardens gown underneath and it fell around my feet. They were still dirty in their sandals from the fire.

He said, "Be polite, I don't have to tell you that. You don't have to mention why we're here—"

"Good, because I don't *know* why we're here." We started down the staircase.

"And Grandmother is nobly born, so remember to address her that way. I'll show you where to sit. And don't hesitate about taking any of the food, it would be a mortal insult."

"Why would I—oh."

"And don't speak to anybody until I've introduced you. And don't—never mind, here we are. No time for anything else." He squeezed my shoulder. "Don't worry, you'll do fine."

We were in a high hall flooded with sunlight. Screens were open at intervals in the arched ceiling above. Four people sat at the long table, leaving most of it empty. They watched me enter with noncommittal expressions that reminded me of Pina's inquisitors. Ran steered me to the old woman at the head of the table. She wore an old-fashioned gown of midnight blue, and above the neckline I could see her pale, smocked skin. Her white hair was done up in a braid that encircled the top of her head. She wore it like a crown, holding her neck stiffly as she turned to me. Ran bowed and said softly. "Grandmother, this is the one I was telling you about. Theodora Cormallon."

I was too startled for a moment to move, to take the outstretched hand she offered me. Then I realized that of course he was using Cormallon as my house name; as an employee I was entitled to it, and he wanted to play down my outsider status for his grandmother.

"My dear Theodora," she said, quite easily. "Welcome to our table. I hope you like hermit's eggs?"

"Thank you, noble lady. I don't know, I've never had them."

"Then it will be a treat. Ran, will you show our guest to her seat?" She unwrapped her napkin.

Ran looked toward the three others at the table. "Grandmother, I'd like—"

"I have every intention of introducing Theodora. Sit *down*."

He did so, motioned me to my cushion first. I learned later than Grandmother was committing a slight breach of etiquette; as Ran was technically the first in the family, it was for him to introduce me to those he felt I should know. However, as he had said, she was radical in her own way.

"Theodora, please recognize Kylla, my granddaughter; and Ane and Stepan, my great niece and nephew, Ran's cousins."

Ane and Stepan nodded. Kylla smiled and said, "I'm pleased to see you again." It was nice of her to join in the pleasant fiction that I was not a stranger invading their home; she didn't have to be that polite just for me. And Grandmother's use of the word "recognize" was more appropriate to a second meeting than a first, implying that I already knew everyone. For the first time in my entire life, as I sat among these courteous people, I felt that I was out-bred. It made me more nervous than Ran's earlier hints of physical danger.

Kylla's seat was across from mine, and I decided to copy her table manners with whatever came up. It was prickly-strange watching her. On Pyrene siblings are brought up separately, and I wasn't used to seeing people the same age look so similar. She was very like Ran. Yet somehow what on Ran was quietly masculine, on Kylla was flamboyantly feminine. Her eyebrows were thin and upswept. Two dove-pins held back a mass of black hair, showing delicate ears with gold shell earrings. Gold shine covered her eyelids and swirled on her cheeks. She smiled at me and picked up her fork with her left hand.

I picked up my own fork with my left hand and had to stop, because there was nothing on my plate. But Grandmother must have already given orders. A gray-haired man appeared beside me with a platter of eggs and some sort of meat; he began spooning out the eggs, the gold band on his wrist showing beneath the sleeve of his robe. Two slices of meat followed onto my plate. Everyone seemed to be waiting politely for me to begin eating. The servingman crossed over to my left to pour tah into my cup. As he bent over, I saw the blue tattoo of a "C" on his leathery right cheek.

"C"—Convicted criminal.

Only a small minority of Ivory's criminals actually go to prison, as did the three officials we sent up not long before. Most are taken care of quite simply with an induction into the Imperial Army. In realistic terms this is as much a life sentence as prison would ever be; the blue tattoo never comes off. All deserters and even dischargees from the army were criminals through necessity, severed from re-entering society by a mark on the face. It was common knowledge that in the Northwest Sector many of these deserters had banded together, robbing and plundering travelers and small villages. The Emperor could have cleaned out these pockets of bandits, had he troubled to do so, but no one lived in that sector anyway but a few farmers and small ranchers, hardly worth bothering about.

So I did not miss the significance of the fact that Ran's family chose their servants from army deserters. They were people whose loyalty was assured. They had no ties with the outside world, and nowhere else to go. I realized how lucky I was to be admitted to the house and still be sitting here alive. The Cormallons were breaking at least ten different laws.

I also realized what I had in common with the deserters, why Ran had chosen me. I had no friends, no relatives, and no ties with any other family.

Grandmother tapped on her glass. I looked up and saw her watching me. "You must try your tah, my dear. Our neighbors to the south, the Ducorts, grow the tah plants themselves, and the leaves are quite unequaled." Ran was watching me, too, his eyes tense. *Don't hesitate about taking any of the food.* But I hadn't known my position was this dangerous when he told me that.

I picked up the cup of cool red porcelain. The tah steamed gently pink inside. It wasn't fair; I had avoided ever drinking tah, no mean feat on Ivory, because it was physically addictive. I now felt it would be nice to live long enough to become addicted. I took a few sips.

It was delicious.

Thus began one of the most awkward meals of my life. Ran's grandmother would occasionally initiate a line of conversation, which one of the other four would try to pick up, only to have each topic trail off into silence after a few minutes. At one point Stepan tried to bring up something about a sorcery assignment he was working on at his home in the north. Grandmother looked at him benignly and said, "Family business, Stepan." No one said anything after that.

At the close of the meal Grandmother said, "Ran, I'd like to speak with you in my room." She was struggling to rise off the cushions, and he came forward at once and took an arm. She said, "It's this business of a personnel exchange with the Ducorts." They were leaving the hall. I started to get up, uncertain about interrupting. Kylla caught my eye and shook her head. I let them go.

Ane and Stepan were leaving as well. Kylla came around the table to me. "Grandmother's been waiting to pounce on him about this particular business for days now. She'd have been annoyed if they were interrupted. If there's something you want or need, let me help you."

"Right now all I need is a bed, and about twelve hours alone."

She smiled. "I'm glad it's something easy. There's a room connected with mine, you can sleep there. It was just cleaned this morning, so no one will bother you."

"If Ran asks for me—"

"If Ran asks for you, I'll tell him you've got important business of your own. Don't worry about Ran. In any case, knowing him, he'll probably be snoring himself within five minutes after Grandmother is through with him."

She took me to the room, another small but pleasant place with green hangings on the walls and a window facing east. A bar of light crossed the bed. "If you want anything I'll be in my study. Just ask one of the goldbands, they'll take you to me. Pleasant dreams."

She was gone. I pulled off the robe and dug in under the coverlet. There was an early morning chill in the room and the bed was more comfortable than I remembered a bed could be.

The bar of light was gone. There was a sound somewhere, like bare feet on stone. I swung my legs down and went to look out the window. It was still light; the sun must be somewhere on the other side of the house. The hanging in the archway across the room swung back and a head appeared. "Sorry. Did I wake you?" It was Kylla.

"How long was I asleep?"

"It's almost dusk. You haven't missed supper, though." She came in. "Do Athenans all sleep during the day?" she asked curiously.

"Only the eccentrics." I looked around for my sandals, found them under the bed. I felt the grime against my fingers when I picked them up. "Sorry, Kylla, I don't wake up very well. Thank you for the bed." I really looked at her for the first time, and was astonished.

The makeup and bangles of that morning were gone, and it was the first time I'd seen a respectable aristocrat without her public robes. She wore a short tunic and wide blue trousers, and her hair was tied in a thick braid. There was a dagger in a decorated sheath in her belt. One foot was in a short furry boot, the other still bare. She sat down on the bed. "I'm going night hunting," she explained, "anything to get away from doing the records, and the kitchen needs game. If you and Ran aren't going to be busy, maybe you'd like to come along. You can't get much hunting in the capital."

Great Plato, that incredible fringe of eyelash must actually belong to her. "Er—no, I don't really get to hunt in the city. I don't know what Ran has in mind, though. He might want me for something."

"Too bad." She got up and went into her room again. I could hear her rummaging around. "I haven't seen Ran since breakfast," she called to me. "I don't know where he is."

"Oh."

"If you get bored, try the gallery, or the library. Or there's a bath in the courtyard that's big enough for swimming."

"Thanks."

"I'll see you tomorrow." Her footsteps faded away. I went to the narrow window and rested my chin there on folded arms for a while. I saw Kylla's figure appear below with a bow slung on her back. She walked steadily out past the trees, over the hills, until she was too small to follow. Less light was coming in the window now.

No sense putting it off.

I made my way downstairs, not sure where I was going. The dining hall was empty. A man with a gold band passed me in the main corridor and as he went by I tried to look without staring for the "C" on his cheek. "Excuse me," I called after him.

"Yes?" He turned. It was there, all right.

"Do you know where I can find Ran?"

"No, I'm sorry, I don't know where he is."

"Thanks." He went on.

Well, there was the gallery—whatever that was—and the library. There was also the bath, but I didn't feel like stripping in front of people I didn't know. Especially since sitting with Kylla just now had reminded me of what a comparative ugly duckling I was around here. That's what I would leave Ivory with: an inferiority complex, and chronic back pain. Why were there so few chairs on this damned planet? For the moment my worries about money, dealing with corrupt officials, and murderous aristocrats paled before these two considerations.

My bad mood ended, to my relief, when I saw Ran through the open doorway of one of the rooms I passed. I went in.

"About time you became conscious," he said. "Take a look at this."

I looked. It was a rather basic Net linkage terminal, small screen.

"This is one of the first pieces of the Net to come to Ivory. They brought it straight here off the ship from Tellys, and my grandfather put it together. The cabinet's Ivoran, of course."

That went without saying. It was a complex, over-ornamented border of marblewood, with stars, moons, leaves, faces, and fish all leaping and tumbling together. Though perhaps I was being unfair. The last time I had walked on Foreigner's Row, the Athenan embassy, which I used to find in perfect taste, had seemed rather bare and pathetic beside the carved and decorated exterior of Merchant's Bank.

"Nice," I said politely. "Ran, I'm starving. Is it too early for supper?"

He pressed a button on the set. "Could somebody there bring me some food? I'm at the terminal in Grandfather's study . . . seed-bread, I guess, and cheese and fruit." He looked at me for each one, and I nodded. "Thank you." He released the button and grinned at me. "The first thing Grandfather did was set up a link in the kitchen."

There was something . . . *easier* about Ran, here on his own territory. I sat down on a tasseled pillow to wait for the food. "Would you like to tell me why we're here now?"

"Oh." He looked uncomfortable. "I suppose you mean here on Cormallon, not here in this room. . . ."

"Yes, that's what I mean. What's so special about a fire that we had to run off like this?"

"All right." He swung out of the terminal seat and dropped down on a cushion beside me. He had eyelashes just like his sister, I noticed. "I told you that you weren't the first person to hold your job."

"I remember." And I knew more than he thought, too. I'd had a lot of time to experiment with the cards. Ran's previous card-reader had been connected with Ran's fortunes, and was therefore accessible to me through the deck. She was twenty years old, beautiful, clever, with a bluestone pendant she never took off. She came from somewhere in the mountains. She was somehow related to Ran. And she was dead.

"My cousin used to run the cards for me," he said slowly. "She died in a fire. It started quickly, but there was no reason to think it wasn't an accident. I was suspicious, of course. You're *supposed* to be suspicious. But time went by, I found my replacement . . . I was very careful with you, you know. You stayed in the alcove and nobody saw you. But nothing more happened, and I decided I was being over-cautious. This matter with Pina came up; it seemed a shame to deprive you of witnessing your revenge. I let us be seen together. But when your room catches fire that very night, it's hard to think of it as a coincidence."

"You think it was deliberate."

"It's possible. A sorcerer can easily cause fire from a distance. Spontaneous combustion: it's one of the first tricks one learns."

My stomach was beginning to feel a little queasy. "Why should anybody care about me? I haven't offended anybody . . . not anybody important, at least."

"Nobody does care about you," he said, not conscious of any brutality, only describing the rules of Ivory. "But Cormallon has plenty of enemies, like any Great Family. I've even got a few of my own. By now you must know that without the guidance I get from the cards I wouldn't be able to function. There are too many twists, too many enemies—just too many variables in each case to try to work without the edge the cards give me. I'd have been dead my first month as a sorcerer without them. And of course I've never told anyone that I have to depend on someone else to read them for me. If the wrong person became suspicious, wondered why I always take an assistant with me when I travel—well, they might want to test their theory, and leave me without a reader. I'd be working blind, open to any attack—"

"That's what I've never understood. Why don't you read them yourself? Other sorcerers do."

"I wish it were possible. I did a stupid thing once, and now I'm paying for it."

"I don't understand."

He looked pained, and even a trifle embarrassed. "When I was ten, they took me to see my grandmother. She'd been ill for several years—most of my life at that point—and I barely knew her. It was a formal interview, held right after my tenth year initiation. There was to be a party afterward and I was impatient to get to it. I stood there in my best clothes while she asked a lot of questions and tested my learning in sorcery. Then she made the remark that, since I was the last male to be initiated in the immediate family, she supposed she wouldn't have another boy to test until I got married." He coughed. "I was something of a brat in those days. I told her I didn't like girls, and I was never going to get married. She passed it off as a joke, but I insisted. Even a ten-year-old in our family is supposed to know his duty."

He paused, and smiled wryly. "I had a curse put on me. Grandmother said that I didn't have the proper familial respect for women, but I was damn well going to learn. She got out the pack of cards that belonged to my grandfather—the pack you have in your pouch there. She said that when I was given these cards at the age of sixteen I wouldn't be able to read them. I would never be able to read any deck. If I wanted to have the cards read for me, I would have to find a woman to do it. And I would have to keep her happy doing it, because no one else would be able to read for me while she lived."

Unpleasant thoughts were going through my head. This was to be a lifetime job? But what about Athena?

Ran was still talking. "I tested it, of course, when I turned sixteen. The cards were dead to me, their pictures turned up randomly and showed me nothing when I touched them. The first woman I tried was in the terminal ward of the city hospital. She could read them, but no one else could. When she died, I hired Marla. Marla was a distant cousin of mine who wanted to visit the capital and make some money."

"Ran—"

"She stayed with me for five years. She hadn't planned on it being that long, although I warned her when I gave her the cards. We ended up hating each other. I had to have her information, and I had to trust what she told me. What could I do? She was family." He took a deep breath. "It was a relief when she died. Then there was the problem of a replacement. I saw you in the marketplace, reading that ridiculous Tarot—no Ivoran, that was clear. I thought my luck had turned."

"But Ran, what—"

"Sir. Not Ran."

I let it pass. Considering the circumstances, it might be best not to annoy him too much. After all, the only people Ivorans were honor-bound not to kill were members of their own families, and that only because there had to be *someone* they could trust. "Tell me the truth. Just what were you planning to do when I saved enough to book passage home?"

"Well . . . I had a few ideas." He grinned. "Raise your salary, for one thing. Force you into debt—that was my second idea—or arrange to have your money stolen. Or prevent you from reaching the ship on time. They're not in port that often, you know, and passage money isn't refunded, so that would really slow you up for a while."

What fine, nonviolent scenarios. Although if all else fails, the way would have to be cleared for the next reader. . . . "Do we have any work to do right now?"

"No. Why do you ask?"

"I'd like to be alone for a while. I've got a lot to think about."

"Certainly." He helped me rise like the well-brought-up gentleman he was. He was so damned charming about everything, so sure I knew all the rules of the game, it's all in fun, so sorry if you almost got killed.

A young woman appeared in the doorway with a bowl of cut fruit and cheese. Her hair was brown and tied back, and her face was lovely in a very clear and young way. I stood up. My stomach was still whirling and standing up made it feel twice as hollow as before. "Thanks," I mumbled as I pushed past her, taking a piece of melon from the bowl. Perhaps I could get it down in a few minutes. I looked into her face when I thanked her.

Some people are allergic to the ink they use in the tattoos. From the midsection of her cheek back to her ear, the right side of her face was a hideously swollen, red-purple mass. She saw my eyes widen, and for a moment I thought she would run away. Then she turned away from me and walked inside, her head high. She set the bowl down with a thud. "Do you need anything else?" she asked Ran.

"No, thank you, Tagra," I heard him say. "This is more than enough." I fled down the corridor.

Chapter 4

I wandered blindly around the house for a couple of hours. Suppertime must have come and gone. I passed few people in the halls, though once I saw the serving-man from breakfast puffing up a flight of stairs with a loaf of bread. Twice I found myself in the inner courtyard, and the second time I sat down on a bench in the colonnade. The water in the pool rippled softly.

No cinnatree scent here, although the air seemed fresher and cleaner than in the capital. There's something about moving water . . . I began to wonder just why I'd been upset. My life had been up for grabs since the morning I woke up in an alley. Naturally Ran would take advantage of it; that was what he was. And the game remained to be played out. By the time an Athenan-bound ship touched ground I planned on being ready for it.

Torches flared up under the pillars. No warning, no one to light them: Cormallon household magic. I went over to inspect one, cupping my hands around the flame. It was almost completely dark now and the courtyard looked suitably barbaric, with the torches mirrored in the black water.

Across the yard an electric light snapped on and the sound of two women arguing came clearly out the window. There goes the mood, I thought wryly. True, electric light is also quaint . . . but when you think of torchlight you think of ancient armies, processions, banquets. Electricity, on the other hand, is more likely to bring to mind turbine generators.

A slight attack of culture shock, I told myself, that was all it was. It was bound to recur every now and then. . . . Well, if I was still in the game, it would help to learn the rules. I wondered where the library was.

* * *

It was in a cavernous room on the second floor, densely carpeted, softly lit. I had passed it by before, and the goldband I pestered into leading me there had to insist before I would go in. "There are no books, no tapes, no terminals. How can it be a library?" I asked him. He shrugged. Like all the goldbands, he didn't say very much; at least, not to me.

The room was lined with shallow wooden shelves from ceiling to floor, with sliding ladders against each wall. The shelves contained everything except books. There were pieces of pottery, necklaces, pendants, and rings, odd bits of stone, and miscellaneous specimens of daily life, some of which I could identify and some I could not. On a shelf nearby I saw a brass shoehorn.

By far the greater number of pieces were stone, and most of them were the milky red or bluestone found in Ivory riverbeds. Stone has always tempted me; I picked one up.

"Would you like some makel?" asked my host. "No, thank you," I answered, cleaning the sauce in my bowl with a piece of bread. We were gliding on Lake Pell on a late summer evening, the lanterns on the prow swaying gently over the water. "More wine, then," said Bakfar. "More wine, by all means." I was well content. My business with Bakfar was almost concluded, and the profits for Cormallon should be substantial. My girl from the Great House handed me a cup, and I kissed her as I took it. Her hair was warm and fragrant. Bakfar provided for his guests like a gentleman, a good omen for our future association. All at once I was stabbed by a searing pain in my side. I looked down, expecting to see a knife, but there was nothing there. The stabbing came again. I gasped for breath. The cup rolled out of my fingers and struck the boards of the boat. The girl stared at me. The night sky framed her white face. I looked with effort to Bakfar. Poison or sorcery, I didn't care. I would kill him.

I dropped the piece of stone. It hit the carpet soundlessly and I turned to look for a chair. I needed to sit *now.* You fool, I thought, seeing none, there are only about ten chairs on all of Ivory. Sit on the floor if you must.

It's not easy to stop being a fifty-year-old man, let alone one who has just been murdered, in the space of a minute. I needed to sort things out. I sprawled pretzel-fashion in the position I dropped, not bothering to get comfortable. I remember paying a great deal of attention to the feel of the carpet on my fingers.

After a while I looked at the shelves. If every one of them held something like *that* . . .

That man had really existed, nobody made him up. Sitting in that boat on Lake Pell I'd been conscious of the unbroken memory of Seth Cormallon, stretching back through childhood. That was fading now, but I still had the central incident, the one I'd lived through—his murder.

I ought to put the stone back, I knew, but I didn't want to touch it again. I started to get up when my eye was caught by a bronze plaque in the base of the wall. It said, in simple lettering: "Immortality is a privilege to be won and not a right. Rest in peace knowing you will live in honor and love as long as Cormallon endures." The stones, the jewelry, the random flotsam of several hundred lives—this library was Ran's family.

There was a sound to my right, a whirring, mechanical sound. I leaped to my feet.

"Didn't mean to startle you," said the voice. "But you really should pick it up. We can't leave relatives on the carpet. People would step on them, and how would we explain it to Grandmother?"

He rode out into the dim light—rode, on a floater horse, the kind I'd seen used in Athenan hospitals for nonambulatory patients. His legs were strapped to the sides. "Eln Cormallon, at your service."

I supposed I would have to get used to seeing echoes of Ran's face in the people here. But the resemblance was strong in him—if not for the lines around the eyes and mouth, if his hair were black instead of brown, he would be Ran's reflection.

"And you must be my brother's mysterious guest. Is your name really Theodora?"

I nodded. I had never thought of myself as mysterious before.

"But what's your family name? Ran's keeping it a deep, dark secret."

"Cormallon, I guess, at the moment. I don't really have one."

"Amazing." He maneuvered the floater to just above the carpet, reached over, and picked up the stone I'd dropped. He could just reach it with the tips of his fingers. "But Theodora is far too long. I'll call you Theo . . . in case there's a fire or something, and I have to shout for you in a hurry." He leered with melodramatic wickedness.

I couldn't help laughing. At the same time I wondered what Ran had told him about fires.

He reached behind the floater and pulled out a bottle. "Will you join me? Vintage Ducort. For your christening."

"Some other time, thank you. I couldn't handle it on an empty stomach."

"Empty stomach? What happened to breakfast, lunch, and dinner?"

"There was a breakfast back there somewhere . . . and I've got a piece of melon in my pocket."

"But this is horrifying. What will happen to our reputation for hospitality? Still, no need to panic, we'll fix it right away." The floater carried him off toward the door. I followed.

"Look, you don't have to—"

"Just how weak are you? Are you going to faint? I'll dismount, noble lady. You can ride and I'll walk."

I wasn't sure if he was kidding or not. Rather than put it to the test I accompanied him to the kitchen.

It was a big room with a central plank table where a substantial, broad-shouldered woman was rolling dough. It was clear from the air that she was already responsible for something wonderful baking in the oven. "Hello, Herel," Eln said to her. "Just thought I'd ride through. Where are you hiding the good tah? And didn't I see some hermit's eggs here this morning?"

"Now, Eln—you know supper was hours ago. Grandmother wants you at table with everyone else. You can't keep showing up here at all hours—"

"Herel, Herel, you misunderstand me. We have need of your noble talents. Our guest here is about to collapse from lack of nourishment. Have pity. —Theo, look pale, or Herel might not feed us."

Herel shook her head, a broad, involuntary grin on her

face. She began pulling out bowls and cutlery and laying them on the long wooden table. Eln brought his floater over to the table and I took a seat on the bench. My feet didn't quite reach the floor. The table was huge, the room was huge, Herel—pretty huge herself—was dealing with pots and pans of a suitable size for mass cooking; all in all, I felt as though Eln and I were children who had wandered into a giant's kitchen.

Eln took up a paring knife and started peeling an apple. "Have you been on Ivory long?"

"Over two years now." He finished the apple and handed it to me.

"And from what fantastic planet did you come?"

I told him my story, in a general sort of way. He listened closely and asked questions about Pyrene and Athena, my friends and what I did there. "And you've been working in the capital for two years. Doing what?"

Well, it would be easy for him to find out, if he wanted to. "Telling fortunes. In Trade Square."

"But I've never known foreigners to have the talent . . . ah. A light begins to dawn. You're Ran's new card-reader, true?"

I said nothing. He laughed and said, "You don't have to worry. It's an open secret, at least in the family. Poor Ran . . . and Grandmother's so easy to deal with, if you don't get her angry. Well, I hope you're charging all the freight will bear. You're irreplaceable, you know."

I remained silent, shifting uncomfortably. I watched Herel's broad, workmanlike hands deftly kneading bread dough. Eln said suddenly, "Have you heard the Emperor's latest speech? It's priority one on all the terminals. Every time I punch for the racing scores from the capital it keeps popping up . . . 'In view of the, er, dipping balance of the trade situation . . .' "

I had to laugh. It was the Emperor's favorite phrase, and Eln had captured the pompous tones with cruel precision.

Herel fed us royally. Eln made her sit down and have some wine with us while he told the story of the flyer he had backed in the last Imperial races. "Came in last in a field of forty-three. Do you know what the odds are for that? If only I'd known, I could have bet the other way."

He imitated the flyer's owner making his excuses; he had a gift for imitation.

Other stories and talk followed. I lost track of time. It must have been near sunrise when the door opened and Kylla came in. She looked tired and disheveled, and was unslinging her quiver as she spoke. "Herel, I'm glad you're up. Can you give me a hand? I've got three groundhermits outside, they'll need to be plucked . . ." She saw Eln and me at the table, looked from him to me and back again. "Oh, dear," she said.

"It's not a good idea to spend much time with Eln," Ran said to me later that afternoon. We were in the study, where he was searching through the files on his heirloom terminal.

"Why not?" I asked.

"Eln is . . . a very moody sort of person. He gets upset about things sometimes. No, not exactly upset . . . he's unreliable."

"You don't trust him?" For I wasn't very clear on that.

"Of course I trust him. He's my brother," he said, with an air of self-evident logic. "But he's not reliable, and you shouldn't spend your time with him."

I shrugged, a response I often found useful in the face of Ivoran thinking, and changed the subject. "Why are you always on the Net now? You never used to spend much time on it back in the city."

He watched the screens flick past on the terminal. "I'm making sure there aren't any enemies lying around that I've forgotten." He halted the flow of data and made a note on a pad beside the terminal. "It's incredible that the people we've got investigating this haven't come up with any strong possibilities. They keep *eliminating* suspects. It's very irritating of them."

"What if you don't come up with anybody? Do I stay here for the rest of my life?"

"I've thought about it," he said seriously. "I suppose we could handle the business by vidiphone for a while, with me in the capital and you here, but I don't think it would work in the long run. You really need personal contact to make your judgments. You'd have to come back with me."

Praise Wisdom for that.

"Meanwhile, I almost forgot—see that book on the table? The one with the red binding. Yes, there—take a look through it."

I picked it up; the cover showed a single symbol in white against a blood-red background: ᛉ. I remembered Ran had a crystal block in his office etched with the same symbol.

"It's a book of sorcery," he said. "The Red Book, for beginners. Start studying it."

"Ran, you know I've got no talent for sorcery."

"True, but the more familiar you become with technique, the better your understanding of our work will be. Besides, there are some things anybody can pick up, and they might do you some good. How to avoid certain spells, for instance."

"How?"

"Read it and see." He went back to writing in his pad.

I read in the shade of the courtyard until dinnertime. Grandmother wasn't there for the meal, nor had she been present at lunch or breakfast. Ran said that she was often ill and ate in her room. For the Cormallons dinner was a meal of many tiny courses; the whole thing together didn't make up their usual breakfast, but was somehow very satisfying to the mind and palate. Kylla passed me a tiny seedcake, the dessert, and poured me a little bellglass of white wine. "Are you coming with us tomorrow?" she asked.

"With you?" I looked around at Ran. "Where?"

"We're going on our jaunt," he said. "It's a family custom, at least with Kylla and me. We ride out into the hills and camp for a couple of days. We do it every year."

"If you're sure I won't—" I cut it off. Inappropriate response. These were Ivorans; if I were in the way, they would not have asked me. "Thank you . . . we'd still be within the barrier, wouldn't we?"

Ran smiled. "We'll be within the barrier. It's a jaunt, we're not looking for trouble. Think of it as a long picnic."

"Will Eln be coming along?" I asked. As usual, he was not at the table with us. Ran's cousins were gone as well, I didn't know where; so the three of us were alone.

Kylla looked at her brother, who was silent. "Will he?" she asked.

He got up and walked around the table. A servant began gathering up the plates. Ran brushed by him and left the room.

Kylla watched him go with a worried look on her face.

"I'm sorry if I said the wrong thing," I told her.

"It's not your fault." She started to pile the plates at one end of the table, where the servant was scraping them into a large wheeled bucket. "Eln used to come with us . . . until a few years ago." A slight tremor appeared in her voice, so faint that I could not be sure if I imagined it.

There was only the scrape, scrape, scrape of knife against plate, and the sound of food hitting the bucket.

Ran reappeared in the doorway. "If you want him to come, then ask him," he said.

Chapter 5

Kylla handed me a pack. I slung it over my back and then staggered under the weight. "I hope you don't expect me to walk very far with this," I said.

"Don't be silly," she smiled. "You don't have to walk at all with it. It's a jaunt, not a hike."

I followed her out the door and down the front steps. "Then how are we going to—Great Plato, what's that?"

Ran came up to the edge of the lawn leading two huge animals. "Olin will have yours in a minute, Ky," he said. He slapped one of the creatures on its flank, a move which alarmed me but which the beast seemed to tolerate. "This one's for you," he told me.

The hell it was. "What *is* it?"

"It's a horse," he said, "the old-fashioned, unmodified kind: straight Terran stock. Her name is Patch."

Well, in an intellectual way I was delighted; so these were the guardian animals so often mentioned in Terran legends, partners of battle and adventure. I had imagined them to be about four feet tall, and covered with armor plate.

I approached the creature very slowly. It stamped its hard front foot onto the ground and made an ominous noise through its snout.

I stepped back. It was so *big*. "It doesn't like me."

"Nonsense. You just have to get to know her."

"I'm not getting up on one of those things."

"Then how are you going to keep up with us? A dead run all the way?"

"Can't we take the aircar?"

Eln's voice came then, startling me. Apparently he had joined us while my attention was, well, focused on the monster. I've noticed before that fear makes me overly attentive. "Ran, I could get her my other floater. It's modified for speed."

"If she won't mount a horse, why would she mount a floater?"

"No, it's a good idea," I said quickly. "I'm willing to try it." It was at least mechanical, not a huge unpredictable beast with teeth the size of my fist. Machines are different.

So it ended with two of us on mechanical horses and two on flesh and blood. Cormallon, I found, covered a lot of territory. There were brooks, streams, woods, even the beginnings of mountains. Ran and Kylla kept a slow, sightseeing pace, and Eln showed me how to match my speed to theirs. But when Kylla broke into a gallop over a meadow flecked with white hearthwhistle and golden violets, and Ran laughed and went after her, Eln put out his hand to the front of my floater. "Don't try it," he said. "They're going too fast. You're new to this, and your legs aren't strapped in like mine." It looked as if it would take us a while to catch up. As we rode after them, he said, "Are you having a good time? Nature can be horribly boring, if you're not in the mood for it."

"I'm having a wonderful time. I never realized there were so many different plants here," I said, for while I'd been aware intellectually there was a whole planet around me, until then I had only seen the more cultivated flowers for sale in the market, cut to uniform length and with thorns removed. "That's hearthwhistle," I told him, pointing. Kylla had been telling me names all morning, far too many to remember, and I was proud of the handful I had managed to retain.

"So it is."

"It's beautiful."

"It's a weed, and it's everywhere." He looked the meadow over with a jaded, supercilious air, a connoisseur searching for the truly fine, and not finding it.

"Aren't you having a good time?"

"I tend to prefer my entertainment on a more verbal level." Seeing my disappointment, he said, "But I agree with you, it's beautiful. Beauty's cheap on Ivory . . . the weather, the sky, the hearthwhistle . . . that doesn't stop it from being a weed, though."

I was tempted to ask him why he had stopped coming

on these expeditions with his brother and sister, but knew it was forbidden territory. Besides, he might answer, and I was already more involved with these people than seemed good for me.

We camped by a lake that afternoon. Ran and Kylla busied themselves tending to the horses and setting things out for the night. I thought that for people who were used to a troop of servants in their house, they seemed perfectly content to take care of themselves.

The idea of servants had bothered me, scratching at the corner of my mind, since I arrived at Cormallon. Pyrene is a fiercely egalitarian place, and Athena likes to think of itself as a meritocracy; neither system had prepared me for where I was. And it puzzled me that the Cormallons would want so many people not-of-the-family in their home. Only after much thought did I realize that they *needed* servants. It was a big place, on a technologically backward world. They could hardly set dustcatchers loose in the rooms—I hadn't seen one on the entire planet. Naturally they could have imported them from Tellys, but if it was the first time the import fees would be astronomical. (They explained this to us on Athena: Tellys knows it can't hold onto its technological lead forever. But when it runs out, they'd like to have a good bank account to fall back on. So the very first model of any item imported by any planet from Tellys is stamped with a fleur-de-lis, meaning "new and copyable technology." For that fleur-de-lis you pay two thousand times the actual price of the item. It's a nice system, for Tellys.)

Ivory wasn't a poor planet, but they didn't seem to import much. I remarked on it to Eln as I unwrapped the bedrolls. Ran and Kylla had gone off to collect wood for the campfire.

"Well, what do you expect, Theo," he said. "You know aristocrats. A century ago the emperor managed to bully us into pooling our resources and bringing in the Net. And the aircar. And a few other things. But how long can you expect nobility to cooperate? Not to mention semi-nobility." He grinned.

Eln had a more detached way of looking at things than most Ivorans, a more historical perspective. History to anyone else I'd spoken to seemed to mean their immediate family tree. I told Eln so.

"It's the way I was brought up," he said, rather cryptically I thought, and taking his bedroll off the back of the floater he dropped it at my feet. "Don't forget this one."

"Thanks a bunch." I put it with the others. "Don't you import anything from Tellys these days?"

"One or two things, privately bought."

"What sort of things?"

"Theo, darling, why this fascination with our balance of trade? The Emperor talks about it all the time, but you don't have to."

"I'm interested," I said, a little hurt. "I get interested in things."

"Well, try to get interested in something else. It's not a subject I long to pursue." He was silent for a moment, then said, "Let's find a topic more in common. Your situation, for instance. One can't help but notice that you and Ran arrived here rather precipitously. I hope you're not in any trouble?"

I couldn't tell if he was genuinely concerned or not, or how much he knew already. "It's not a topic *I* care to pursue," I said.

"Ouch." He reached into his sidebag and pulled out another in his never-ending supply of wine bottles. It was amazing that he never seemed to be drunk. "Will you join me? We may still find a lawful subject for conversation, after a few swallows."

"Why not?" I took the bottle. "May dawn follow night." It was a toast I'd heard in Trade Square.

"And night follow dawn," he said, taking it back. I'd never heard that one before, but it had the ring of " 'ishin na' telleth' " about it. "Did I hear Ran questioning you about sorcery this morning? It seemed a little odd. I was under the impression he knew more about the field than you."

"He's teaching me." I took another swallow. "It's not going well."

"Oh? What seems to be the problem? I can imagine my brother isn't the most patient teacher."

"It's the book. It just isn't very clear about some things. I've memorized all I could—"

"Aah, now that's always fatal. Rote memorization. You have to pick up the patterns, the reasons for things. Then you won't have to memorize."

"There *aren't* any damn reasons," I said, more sharply than I'd intended. But trying to fight my way through that vaguely written mishmosh of a textbook was very frustrating. They seemed to have a whole other way of looking at scholarship here.

"There are always reasons. Look, what part are you reading?"

"Part One." There are only two parts to the Red Book. Part One's title would translate as: Things Tend to Become More Diverse. Part Two reads: Things Tend to Become the Same. Neither of them made a lot of sense.

"How would you find someone who wanted to remain hidden?"

"Location spell," I said, glad to have something easy.

"What's the hierarchy of search in a location spell?" When I didn't answer he said, "Outside to inside? Or vice versa?"

"The book doesn't say. I couldn't find it, anyway."

"All right, break it down. What are 'outside' traits?"

"Outside traits are those most liable to change," I parroted. "They would usually include color of hair and eyes, name, and clothing. And inside traits," I went on as he opened his mouth, "are more fixed and less easy to change. These are often intangibles, and would include hobbies; entertainment preferences; handwriting; and height, which is hard to change without surgery." I took a deep breath.

Eln applauded. "So now," he said, "which does the spell search for first? Inside or outside traits?"

"I don't know! The book doesn't say."

"Oh, Theo, this isn't like you at all. Is this how they train Athenan scholars? You're letting yourself be thrown by the strangeness of it all. Think of it as a problem in logic."

"What's the answer?"

"I'm not going to tell you. Think about it tonight before you go to sleep."

"And you criticized Ran's teaching methods!"

"Getting testy? It doesn't become you. Have some more wine."

"Thanks." I always get a nice glow from alcohol. I

thought about location hierarchies, and Eln sang a song about "a girl of the open sea," who had apparently had an interesting life. It was about then that Kylla came out of the trees with an armful of dry sticks.

"Oh, no, he's singing," she announced. "Theodora, you shouldn't encourage him. His mouth will be open the rest of the night."

He raised one eyebrow and took out a harmonica for the refrain.

We were camped that night near "the very skin of the barrier," as Eln put it. Perhaps the Cormallons liked to go as far as they could, when they had the chance, without actually crossing into strangers' territory.

Kylla passed around cups from the pot of tah she had resting over the fire. "Temple's not far from here, is it? We could visit. Theodora's never been there."

"It's about a mile over the hill," said Ran, with a slight tilt of his head toward the northeast. "But aren't you tired?"

"Well, I was thinking of tomorrow."

"Let's go now," said Eln, poking at the fire. "I'm not tired."

Kylla said, "Oh, yes, Ran. Can't we go now? Theo, you want to come, don't you?"

"I'm willing," I said, not to disappoint her.

Ran looked tired himself, but he let the majority rule. We went to see the temple.

It was more like the ruin of a temple. Moonlight cast a bluish tinge on the light stone at the top of the hill. We came in through the gaps in the circular wall and stood on a marble floor that still showed a clear picture of a burning torch at its center. The torchfire was inlaid red and yellow strips of stone, its smoke black and gray. Part of the flooring around the picture had been pulled up, and grass grew high there.

"Ishin na' telleth," said Ran softly.

I was surprised. I thought there was still enough beauty here to be worth caring about. Then I realized he was paying respects to the purpose of the temple.

There must have been a dome once. Now we stood under

naked starlight. "It was damaged," said Ran, seeing my glance run over the broken masonry where the roof should have joined the walls, "during one of the wars of succession. Which dynasty was that, Ky?"

"The Prian," said Eln. "Eight centuries ago."

A historical mind. "Who won the war?" I asked him.

"We did. At least, our candidate won the throne. Otherwise we wouldn't be here."

There had been no war on Ivory for the past two hundred years. They still kept up the barrier, of course.

"Let's sleep here," said Kylla.

Ran said, "All our things are back at the camp."

"We can get them tomorrow. Who's going to take them?"

He shrugged. But the marble was too cold for sleeping, so we laid our cloaks down on the grass. Kylla offered her cheek for her brothers to kiss. There was a pause, then Eln, followed by Ran, kissed me good night as well. I lay down near Kylla. She reached out her hand and took mine. "Good night, Theodora," she said. It was a long time before I went to sleep.

"Where is everybody?" I asked Kylla when I woke. The sun was well up, and Ran and Eln were nowhere to be seen. Our camping gear had been deposited in a pile nearby and her horse was contentedly chewing the grass beside the temple wall. "Won't that stuff hurt him?" I asked her, pointing it out worriedly.

She laughed. "I'm glad you're here, Theo. Everything seems new and different when you're around." She handed me a jar that proved to be berry-flavored tah; the smell when I unstoppered it was heavenly. "Grandmother said I could have an outbuilding of my own, for when I want to be alone. Eln and Ran have gone to argue over where it should be."

"Shouldn't you be there, then?"

She shook her head. "It's men's work."

I knew that the great families were old-fashioned, but it was the first time I'd heard *that* phrase. I was shocked.

"Kylla, it's going to be *your* place."

"I know," she said, unruffled. "I'll veto anything I don't

like. Meanwhile, it's a nice morning, and I'd rather sit on this hill with you."

There was nothing I could say to that. She broke off a piece of bread and handed it to me. "Just a minute," she said, going through her pack, "there's jam in here somewhere."

I munched and thought. I found myself remembering the story of Ran's curse, and exactly what his grandmother had said: He was the last male in the immediate family to be initiated. And Eln had said that he was Ran's *older* brother. So why was Ran ranked first in the family? Shouldn't it be Eln? How had he lost the rights of inheritance? Unfortunately it was not the type of question one could ask.

I said instead, "Is there some reason I shouldn't talk to Eln?"

"It's an awkward subject," said Kylla, "but I suppose it's made no less awkward by confusing you about it. Eln can be . . . difficult, sometimes. It's hard to explain unless you've seen it happen. He gets hurt, and he doesn't hold back. Well, I suppose it's not easy for him, being the most intelligent of us and seeing all the rewards go to other people. He can't even be sure he'll have a place in the library when he dies. . . . He *is* the brightest of us," she said, seeing my look. "If you'd grown up with him you'd know. He has Cowper's Disease. He got it when he was ten . . . a side-benefit of Tellys' contact with us. It doesn't affect them the way it does us. You've wondered about the floater, naturally. Artificial limbs wouldn't do any good. The nerve damage goes too far." She put her breadknife jam-side down in the grass, not noticing. "Our father couldn't stand it. We have high standards in the family . . . and I found out later he'd had Eln's cards read at his birth. I don't know what they said, but this seemed to confirm everything. He tried to trade Eln to another family, but Grandmother wouldn't hear of it. After that . . . he just paid no attention to Eln at all. It was horrible. Father died a couple of years later, but meanwhile. . . ." She was silent, then said very quietly, as though sharing a great shame, "Eln declared ishin na' telleth on the family. He moved away to the capital. After Father's death, Grandmother had him brought back. He was very ill. Cowper's Disease makes you vulnerable, you know, it does something to the part of your body that fights sickness."

"The immune system."

"I suppose. When he was himself again, he just stayed on. Grandmother never lets anyone remind him he declared ishin na' telleth."

That was the shame, not that he declared it but that he went back on it. When done sincerely—not just as an expression of discontent, the way I'd heard it a thousand times in the capital—you were not supposed to be able to care again. The object of your declaration was no longer part of your world. The man who went back on ishin na' telleth had never done it properly in the first place. He was beneath contempt, a buffoon, worthy of whatever happened to him now. Because such things could never work out. As sure as the moons rose and fell, he would be hurt again.

"Ran reminded him once," she said softly. "He was first in the family by then, and Eln said something to him. Things were very bad." She repeated, "Things were very bad."

We ate bread and jam. The sun rose higher.

When the brothers came back, we packed up and began riding again. Ran decided school was back in session and started to quiz me on what I'd learned of sorcery.

"How do you find someone who doesn't want to be found?" was his third question.

"Do a location spell," I said, and added, when he did not seem disposed to question further, "the hierarchy of which is, of course, from inside to outside."

"Why 'of course'?"

"The spell works by elimination. Inside traits are less liable to change, so the subject pool is more likely to contain the person you want. For example, say you're looking for a man with blond hair who likes classical music—and lives in the Northwest Sector. There would be more variables, but I'll just use those three."

Ran was looking at me. I went on smugly. "The blond hair would be easiest to change. If you began with an *outside* trait like that, the spell would isolate, say, a few hundred people in the Northwest Sector with blond hair, and then begin eliminating those who don't like classical music.

But the man you're looking for probably isn't even there among the ones you've isolated—he's most likely changed his hair color and moved out of sector. If you start from the *inside,* the odds are much higher that somewhere along the line you'll find the one you want." I paused. "It's also easier to recast—"

"All right, you've made your point." He turned to Eln. "What's so funny?"

"Nothing," said Eln.

Since I seemed to be getting the hang of things, Ran let his questions go for the rest of the afternoon, and time passed pleasantly. That evening he and Eln went off to look over another possible site for Kylla's outbuilding. When they came back, they weren't speaking.

"I'm sorry the jaunt tuned out so badly for you," Kylla said to me.

We were in the dining hall of the main house, setting up for supper. Kylla was gathering hearthwhistle into vases for the table. "I'm sorry it was spoiled for *you,*" I replied.

The last night out had been awful, the tension between Ran and Eln unable to be ignored. We all tiptoed around it, Kylla speaking to Ran, Ran to me, Eln to Kylla . . . pretending things hadn't changed. It was no use, we cut things short the next morning and came back. I did feel partly responsible; I was the one who brought up Eln's coming along in the first place. Ran and Kylla, at least, might have had a good time alone. "I'm not looking forward to supper with them, either," I added.

"Perhaps Eln won't come," she said. "He often doesn't."

But he did come. He came and seemed totally unchanged, his attention bent on keeping Grandmother and Kylla and me amused. The fact that he never addressed Ran might well have gone unnoticed had we not known the way things were.

Grandmother looked brighter than she had when we left. She let herself be charmed by her older grandson, who seemed to be her favorite. She allowed him to help her up when the main meal was complete, so that she could take dessert in her room.

She grasped her cane with one hand and Eln's shoulder

with the other, and peered at Ran. "Have you given thought to your problem?" she asked him.

"Yes, Grandmother. I've decided that we'll be returning to the city tomorrow."

It was the first I'd heard of it.

"You'd best take care of Theodora, now," she said sternly, in the tone of one who says, "these things don't come cheap."

"Yes, Grandmother."

"Kiss me good night, then; and come see me tomorrow morning."

He did so. She and Eln left the room.

I looked at Ran.

"I was going to tell you after supper," he said.

"You said that you hadn't been able to find out who did it."

"Maybe no one did it. The fire could have been a coincidence, you know."

"You don't believe that any more—" I began, and Kylla said, "If she's really in *danger,* Ran—" when Eln walked back into the hall.

"I certainly know how to quiet a room, don't I?" he said. "Pass me the wine, will you, Ky?"

She handed him the bottle. He didn't bother to pour it, but wiped off the lip with the palm of his hand and took a swallow. "Sorry to hear you're leaving, I should say. I should say it, brother, but I won't. Don't feel you have to hurry back for my sake."

Ran touched the rim of his fragile crystal wine bowl, gently twirling it a half-circle. There was a thimbleful of red wine inside that raced after the tilt of the bowl.

"Don't feel you're under any obligation to answer me, either," Eln went on.

"Why should I answer you?" Ran said idly. "Ishin na' telleth."

Eln's face grew very red. " 'Ishin na' telleth' is a good refuge for the incompetent," he said. "For the sort who can't afford to care if he succeeds or not, because he fails so often. The sort of person, I'd say, who annoys someone enough to have a curse put on him. Who loses his card-reader, the life of a family member, through his own negligence. Who's probably about to lose another reader the same way. Don't tell me about ishin na' telleth." I *knew,* from what he said and how they took it, that Ran's problem had never been spoken of before, and that Eln was trampling on a Cormallon taboo in order to inflict the greatest hurt with the least amount of effort.

Kylla said, "Stop it, Eln, please. You're going too far. You know what happened last time—"

"I don't need advice from someone who's admitted strangers into her bed within the very bounds of our property."

A servant who had come out to scrape and clear away the dishes dropped a knife. It clattered into the bucket. We all looked over at the sound. The man bowed stiffly and walked away, leaving the dishes out and a wine bowl balanced on top of the bucket.

I wanted to make him stop. I felt hurt for Kylla's sake, and acute embarrassment at being there at all. But if he could hurt *Kylla* . . . if I spoke, what would he find to say to me? I didn't want to know. And it was none of my business anyway.

She said hoarsely, "I'm not fighting with you. Listen to what I'm saying. I love you. Haven't I always loved you?"

"And you've always supported our brother. Don't change now."

"I'm *not* going to fight you, Eln," said Ran. "Give it up. I'm older now."

"Then tell me you don't care—" "Na' telleth" was the word he used, "—*really* tell me. Declare me out of your life. Why put us through all this?"

Ran said nothing. After a moment he stood up. His hands tightened on the wine bowl; he seemed about to speak. Then he lifted it up over his head and brought it crashing down on the table. Crystal shards and wine spilled over. He left the room.

Eln looked as though he were trying not to cry.

In the cool of early morning I packed to leave. I'd brought nothing with me, but now I had three robes, undergarments, belts, a bracelet, and a spare pair of sandals—all presents from Kylla. When I'd tried to give them back she had said, "Don't be silly, Theo," in her best aristocratic manner. She had her brothers' highhandedness, sometimes.

I put it all in a canvas pack—that was from Eln, another present; he gave it to me for the jaunt.

There was a knock on the door-post, and someone pulled the curtain back. It was Tagra, the lovely girl with the spoiled face.

"Grandmother wants to see you." She spoke tonelessly.

"Ahh . . . I think Ran's expecting me outside."

"He knows he has to wait." She lounged against the wall and looked contemptuously over my possessions. "Are you coming?"

I left the pack on the bed and followed her through the halls. I was uncomfortably conscious of her dislike, and found myself wanting to explain . . . but explain what? How can you apologize for a look? No words had actually passed between us. There was nothing I could take hold of.

She stopped at a door with a violet curtain. "Here." She pulled it back for me.

The room was blue, diffused with morning sunlight from the latticed window at one end, where Grandmother sat on a wooden bench in her nightrobe. The window was the largest I'd ever seen on this planet, almost as tall as I was.

"Come in, dear. No need to be shy." She put her hair-brush down on the stool by her feet and held out her hand.

I took it. "Good morning, noble lady."

It seemed strange to see her without her braid pinned atop her head; it hung down like a sculptured chain of ivory over her right breast. "How long have you been reading the cards for my grandson?"

"Almost half a year now, noble lady."

She nodded and took down an inlaid marble box from the bureau beside her. Her fingers played with the lid. "You didn't know Ran when he was a child." I shook my head. "That was no loss to you; he was insufferable. He has improved since then, but he still has a long way to go." She wore the ghost of a smile. "I have plans for the boy, and I want him to be able to meet them. Tell me," she said suddenly, "I've heard that you come from Athena. What is it like there?"

So I told her about the university, and the people I'd known, all the while wondering why I was there. No Ivoran does anything without a reason. What did this woman want from me? Presently she said, "Thank you, my dear, I never had much opportunity to hear firsthand of other worlds. And now I'd like to show you something." She grasped a corner of the bureau and pulled herself up, groping for her cane. I handed it to her. She led me slowly from the sitting room into her bedroom. I had never before seen anyone walk with the care and concentration she put into the act.

I stared about in surprise. The bedroom was covered with maps. Star-maps, land masses, continents, city plans—they filled the walls. One half of the wall nearest the door was covered with pictures of places I'd never seen—though one of them, I recognized, was the Scholar's Beacon on Athena. A carved wooden bed pushed into one corner was the only concession to conventionality. A long marble table cut the room in two; it was piled with maps and charts, and an ornate astrolabe stood in the middle.

She smiled at the look on my face. "It's just a hobby, child. Cormallons are curious about things, and I haven't been off the estate in more than forty years . . . yes, it's true. Don't look so surprised at everything, Theodora. Not everyone is brought up the way you were. See, this is where I was born." She pointed to a dot on a large map displaying five great land masses; on a peninsula in the southern hemisphere were the tiny words "Ducort estate 3." Looking further along the map I saw written "Imperial Capital" and "Cormallon main estate." I felt my own ignorance wash over me. I had not had much time for research before I came to this world, and after I arrived my time had been taken up by more immediate concerns. I hadn't even known that I was living in the southern hemisphere! But then, shouldn't it be warmer here at Cormallon than it was in the capital? I studied the map's notations and realized that Cormallon was much higher above sea level, as was most of the Northwest Sector not too much farther on. I had not known, either, that Cormallon was so close to the sector—was that why it was so easy for the family to find deserters to put in their employ?

Grandmother went on, "Times were different then. I grew up on a Ducort tah plantation and only left it when I married into Cormallon. I only left *this* estate when I went to family gatherings with my husband. From what I hear, young women in the cities—those not of the Great

Families, anyway—are very free indeed in what they do and the jobs they hold."

"People without money can't afford this sort of chivalry," I said boldly, for the sake of Irsa, whose cart was next to mine for two years. It did not seem to displease Grandmother.

"It is not quite . . . chivalry," she said. "It is custom, which is much more important. You may be surprised, by the way, that I know the word 'chivalry.' The home tongue of my first people—I mean the Ducorts—is French. We lost much during the settlement of this world, but the families cling to their ways."

This time I tried not to let the surprise show on my face. I had heard of French and knew that it had not been spoken as a native tongue anywhere for more than five standard centuries. Custom *was* important to the families.

"Let me tell you a story," she said.

"I am the only one old enough in Cormallon to remember the days before we made contact with Tellys and the other planets of this sector. In those days there were no aircars, there was no Net . . . and women of respectable families were never seen by outsiders. Women criminals could not even be held guilty for violation of the law; their families were assumed to be responsible for everything they did. For me, you understand, this does not seem so long ago.

"The tah plantation where I lived bordered the sea; there were five other families to the north and south of us, all allies of long standing. And far to the other side of us was a road, parallel to the sea, which led inland in time to the capital. We sent our tah to market along this road.

"But the road was difficult to get to. Our workers carried sacks of tah by foot over the kilometers of undergrowth that separated us from it. All the families agreed it would be a good thing to build a road of our own, to connect us with the Imperial road, and we would send our wagons of tah along it. It would be a major undertaking, but we could all share the expense.

"So they made the agreement among themselves and then said, through whose property shall we build this road? No man wanted it to be through his own property, for then strangers would see his women. The arguments over this took many weeks, and at last our family was forced to agree to have it built on our land.

"They sent for builders from the capital and these builders brought a great machine with blades and a huge wall on its front, to clear a way for this road. We saw it drive up and sit near our house, ready to work the next morning.

"We women knew what was happening, and much as our men did not want the road, we wanted it even less. You know, my dear, that we are often rather free in our way of dress when here on the estate."

If Kylla was a sample to judge by, this was certainly true. I nodded.

"We knew that if the men of other families would be passing through our property, we would be made to wear veils and robes from head to toe. No one wanted that. So the next morning the women of the household all filed out to the construction site, led by my great-grandmother. She sat down in the dirt just in front of the great machine, and we all sat down around her. I was perhaps five or six years old. The construction manager was horrified. He had to pretend not to see us . . . but he could hardly start up his machine and crush us all. He begged and pleaded with thin air, and cursed his luck. 'If there were women of the house here, I would ask them to be kind to me!' he cried. 'I have my job to do! I would ask them to take pity on a man with children to feed!' My great-grandmother did not move. He went to my great-grandfather, who did not want the road built there either, you will recall. My great-grandfather said mildly, 'Women will have their way in these things.' And he went inside to smoke his pipe, and did not come out again. This went on for five days, until the construction manager took his machine and went back to the city.

"So you see, Theodora," she smiled, "Custom is a weapon as well as a disadvantage, and women of Cormallon and Ducort have ways of accomplishing what they want."

I never doubted that for an instant, Grandmother. "Yes, noble lady."

She looked about and took the inlaid box she had been holding all this while and put it on the table. "The mortality rate of males in the Great Families is regrettably very high. That is why women still are not often risked outside estate boundaries. We keep the records, run the family councils, bear children to replace the ones lost in inter-family disagreements; so we are far too valuable to risk. Did you know that while the men of the Great Families keep the businesses going, much of the art and literature of the past four centuries has been created by women?"

I shook my head. If it were not absurd, I would think that she was trying to convince me of something. But what could my opinions possibly matter to her?

"But all this does not necessarily apply to you, my dear. You are precious to us in terms of the safety of our family, but your role requires a certain amount of risk. You could never be bound by the confines of an estate."

Now, why did she want to reassure me of that? And just what did the noble lady want from me?

"Well, enough," she sighed. "You must be going, and we come to my purpose in asking for this visit. I am grateful for your telling me of other places; and I'd like to give you a gift in return." She reached again for the inlaid box and played with the lid a moment, thinking. Then she opened it. She removed something shiny and black, about the size of a ripe plum, and held it in her fist.

"You see, dear . . . I know that you may be facing some danger now, with no family to look out for you, and it may be hard to know whom to trust." She showed me what she held in her hand. It was a plump black cat, carved of onyx. "In old-fashioned times, girls would take these to dances and hold them to cool their hands. This one is special. Give this to someone to hold, and when you take it back you will know his thoughts concerning you. Wear gloves when you touch it, or else pick it up with the sleeves of your robe; otherwise it will betray your own thoughts." She placed it in my hand gravely, flesh against flesh.

I looked at her, startled. Grandmother liked me. She wanted something from me, yes, something complex that I couldn't grasp, but she liked me. She wished me well.

"Good-bye, child."

I hesitated. "Noble lady? What happened to the road?"

She had to recollect for a moment. "Oh. They never built it, after all. We went on sending the sacks of tah by foot. Of course, now they have aircars, so perhaps we saved them some expense. Run along now, child, my grandson must be waiting and I'm feeling tired." She took my hand. "Good-bye, cherie."

"Good-bye, noble—good-bye, Grandmother."

I went downstairs in a daze. Eln was waiting for me at the doorway.

"How's Grandmother?"

"All right. A little tired." I wasn't sure how to act with him; I hadn't seen him since last night's dinner.

"I wanted to say good-bye." He leaned over from his floater and kissed me on the cheek. "Theo, if you *are* in any trouble . . . I'm willing to help."

"I'm all right, Eln."

He nodded, and said, "We're bound to meet again. Safe journey."

I was wondering if I were being a fool, refusing help when it was offered; when Eln maneuvered his mount around in the corridor and the sunlight that streamed through the open front doors hit the niche just under his seat. I saw the shining outline of a fleur-de-lis stamped on the black metal.

A fleur-de-lis: new and copyable technology.

How much had that cost the Cormallons? I would have given a lot to know when Grandmother bought it for Eln—before he left the family, or afterward, as a bribe to come back. We have high standards in the family, Kylla had said. Ran hadn't been exactly gentle with my life, but he did me the honor of assuming I could play the game without any help. But someone had loved Eln too much, had made exceptions for him. And that was what he couldn't forgive.

I went down the front steps into the sun, where Ran sat playing with a white puppy. He stood up. "Ready?" he asked me.

Chapter 6

It was dark before we passed over the crumbling line of the old city wall. Ran stopped several times to call ahead and make arrangements for us. It seemed like pointless dawdling to me; he could have called from the car just as easily. I had plenty of time to think about Eln. Whatever his problems—and it was clear I had no real understanding of what they might be—I couldn't get over the feeling that, somewhere along the line, Eln and I had hatched out of the same misfit egg. The country of his birth made no place for him that he could accept, a feeling I knew something about. What would I have been if I'd been fool enough to stay on Pyrene? As pathetically vicious as Eln, perhaps, but without the saving grace of Eln's wit.

I longed to turn the car around, go back and tell him there were other places he could go to, other things he could attempt and win, planets where he would be respected. All he had to do was let go of the game he was playing here and learn new rules. Fine, Theodora! Tell that to an Ivoran, who believes in his heart that all foreigners are barbarians, and that the Imperial capital and his native estate are the twin centers of the universe. Tell that to Eln in particular, who couldn't even loosen his grip by the rules of his own people long enough to make his ishin na' telleth declaration respectable.

There was something else, too.

"Eln reminds me of somebody," I said to Ran somewhere over the foothills.

He grunted, which meant that he was either acknowledging my remark or thinking of something else.

"I can't seem to pinpoint it, though," I went on.

"Maybe someone from Athena," he said. So he was listening.

"If I'd met anyone like him on Athena, I'm sure I would remember."

"An actor, then. Or a politician. Or a picture you saw once on a terminal." He spoke with Olympian disinterest, swerving to avoid a startled hawk.

So I followed the thread of memory in silence, not getting very far. Soon enough we saw the yellow square of Ran's house and were parked on the roof, under the lip of the cistern.

Once inside, Ran stalked about making sure all the shutters were closed. As soon as I entered the office, I saw that a cot had been set up alongside the desk; I went over and bounced on it tentatively.

"I'll be sleeping in the room outside," said Ran, appearing in the doorway.

"I thought you said we were being too cautious and the fire was a coincidence."

"I said it *could* have been a coincidence."

"What's to stop this hypothetical pyromaniac from starting a fire in here?"

"Watch." He took out a match and twisted the bottom. Nothing happened. He twisted it again. "Try it yourself. This room is so well protected, even an ordinary fire can't get started. Ane and Stepan are in the house across the street, they'll be keeping an eye on the place. They spent the day setting up a monitor in here—the slightest whiff of any sorcery but my own and they'll be over immediately. Other than that, the business goes on. I'll screen the clients and you stay locked up at night."

"I stay where?"

This was my first argument with Ran. Hitherto I had silenced all thoughts of disagreement with the private incantation: Well, he's paying you. If the disagreement was strong I added: And he's paying you a *lot*.

I had many occasions to repeat these chants over the next few weeks. In Ran's eyes I was simply too valuable a commodity to risk out on the street, at least until we had a better idea of where things stood. I passed the time observing clients, using the Net, and going through Ran's sparse collection of hand-held books. In the evenings he brought home dinner for us from market cookshops and we ate on the rug in the office. There are about twenty cookshops in and around the Square, and he varied his choice randomly every day. I mean that literally. Since the human brain is incapable of generating true random patterns, he assigned each shop a number and pulled the numbers from the Net. I began to understand that Ran was nothing if not thorough.

Sometimes Ane or Stepan joined us for dinner; never both. One always remained across the street, in touch with the monitor. We played cards and drank great amounts of cherry wine; sometimes Ane sang or played the kitha. Ran was trying his best to keep me entertained. Unfortunately the effect was too premeditated. Ane seemed a nice young woman, but she and Stepan were both naturally quiet and the effort involved in their good fellowship was painful to watch.

I might at least have had the satisfaction of knowing that Ran's social life was as curtailed as mine; but since he was doing it of his own free will, to be polite, it just made me uncomfortable. I told him so, and after that Ane or Stepan would occasionally come over with dinner for one and a message from Ran saying he would not be home that night.

And sometimes in the middle of the night, alone in the office, I would lie down on the inconceivably expensive carpet and beat it with my fists and pull up tiny tufts of shadowy crimson. I had been freer in the marketplace.

It was Anniversary Day, the anniversary of the founding of the current dynasty, and cooks and bakers throughout the capital were making the stuffed rolls and green tah, sticky cakes and sugared fruit that were customary on the occasion. The Square will be a madhouse today, I thought; and I unscrewed the window a bit so as to look down disapprovingly on Ran's quiet, residential street.

I could hear horns and cymbals, very faintly, in the distance. Ran was out somewhere, probably enjoying himself; no clients today. They were all off celebrating instead of scheming. Schemers without peer. When you think about it, I said to myself, why does a man come to a sorcerer but to gain an unfair advantage over someone else? What a lousy business we were in. I made a face out the window—take it any way you like, Ane or Stepan; I'll bet you wish you were outside, too.

It was perhaps symptomatic of my state of mind that I saw everything in the worst possible light. I knew well enough that plenty of our clients came to escape trouble, not to cause it. Sometimes we attacked, but sometimes we defended, like any warriors; and Ivory found us honorable enough. I pulled down a book, flipped through it, put it back, and heard Ran come in downstairs.

He was carrying a box of stuffed rolls and swinging a jar of green tah. He set them on the floor. "Happy Anniversary Day, Theodora," he said.

"Ran, I'm bored."

"Sir," he corrected.

I glared at him. He cleared his throat. "Well, uh, let's see. How much farther have you gotten with the Red Book?"

"This isn't going to cheer me up, I'll tell you in advance."

"How does one cast a love spell? People always seem to find that topic interesting."

"There's no such thing, as you know perfectly well. We can't make people fall in love, it's too complicated. We can only make them fall in lust."

"And just how is that accomplished? Not the casting, just the effect on the victim."

"A lust spell creates certain physiological effects in the victim when he is in the presence of the person in question. Increased heart rate, sweating, pupil dilation, and a long list I didn't bother to memorize. Since these are symptoms of sexual attraction, the victim interprets them as meaning he's attracted to this person and behaves accordingly."

"And that's why—"

"That's why the victim can't know he's under a spell, or it won't work. He'll feel the same symptoms, but he'll just interpret them as a bunch of artificially caused metabolic changes. And we can do similar things to convince someone that they're afraid of something, or that they're hungry, or angry, or whatever. And come on, Ran, can't I just go out for a day?"

"You know, it's rather charming," he said, "But although the book won't tell you this, the effects of these spells can be quite long-lasting. A few years ago a rather plain young woman came to me—daughter of Benzet, the architect—and asked me for a love spell for a certain young man. I explained why I couldn't help her, but she said she was willing to take anything I could give. Well, by the time they'd made love a few times and talked together and spent their afternoons together . . . she told me I could lift the spell, that she had enough memories to comfort her, and she didn't want to tie him down when he might be happy with someone else. So I lifted it. They were married a week later, have a nice farm out on the Ostin road. Didn't seem to make a bit of difference in their relationship, as far as she or I could tell."

I sighed. "All right, so you don't want me to go out."

"The effects of a fear spell can also build to such a pitch that, even when removed—"

"We can celebrate here, I guess."

"Now, that's a good idea. The smell was beginning to drive me crazy." He popped a stuffed roll into his mouth. "It won't be much longer, you know. Take heart."

"You've found our pyro? Or have you decided there isn't one?"

"I've decided that if nothing happens in the next three days, there isn't one."

"Fine. Send me out to get killed."

"There's no pleasing you either way, is there? Please, have a roll."

"Thanks." I *was* hungry. "Are you going to open the tah or leave it there as a conversation piece?"

"Sorry." He pulled out the stopper. "Sticky cakes are in the bottom of the box."

I gave myself over to gluttony for a while. By the time I'd gone through half the provisions I was feeling a little sheepish. "Sorry I've been so short-tempered," I said.

"Quite understandable," he said politely. "More tah."

"No thanks. I'll be pissing all night." I was glad I could match his politeness. It is considered good form, in the better circles of Ivory, to give a physical reason for refusing a host's food. Otherwise it might be interpreted as a lack of trust. That didn't apply to Ran, but still—good manners.

"That's what holidays are for." He finished the jar. "Kylla should be by later."

"Tonight? She's in the city!"

"Tomorrow—she's attending a dance here tonight, she'll

be staying as a houseguest of the Ducorts. I may drop in on them later myself, so don't be surprised if you wake up tonight and I'm not here."

"Stop worrying, I'm not going to panic. I can take care of myself." And so I can, except where the people I'm dealing with are bigger, stronger, more numerous, or carrying weapons. That covered just about everyone on this planet, but I was damned if I was going to let it affect my peace of mind, such as it was.

I turned in early that night. Lying on the cot it suddenly came to me whom Eln had been reminding me of. Not a professor or a politician, either—although, in a sense, it was on Athena that I met him. It would be pleasant to tell Ran how wrong his guesses were, but he wouldn't get the reference anyway. Eln reminded me of Loki. Red-bearded, resentful, entertaining Loki, an aspect of the Terran trickster god. That's an Athenan scholar for you—track down our associations and you'll find they all come out of books.

I suppose it was something about his sense of humor, and the way he was-part/was-not-part of the family. I thought of Ran sleeping in the next room. If Eln was Loki, who did that make him? Thor, I supposed, but he was really too sophisticated for Thor.

It was a pity, I thought, as I settled sleepily into the mattress, that these metaphors never quite worked out.

Too much tah can keep you awake, just as everyone says. I woke up twice, the second time apparently irrevocably. I was annoyed with myself. Ran had clients coming in the morning and I would be falling asleep over the cards—the alcove niche was warm and stuffy and lent itself to that kind of thing. A quiet check of the outer room showed me that Ran was gone, doubtless to Kylla's dance. Lack of sleep never seemed to bother *him* in the morning.

I resolved to lie motionless on the cot until sheer boredom sent me under. This had never worked before, but there was always a first time. I lay down accordingly.

Within minutes I began to hear creaks, rustlings, and the other night sounds that are reserved for empty houses. That one was *almost* like a door opening . . . that one *almost* like a footstep . . . It went on for the better part of an hour. I refuse to give in to this, I thought; I refuse to put on the light.

Then a hand reached down and grabbed me.

I don't know when I woke up, but from what I learned later I must have been unconscious for at least half a day. I was in a small, steel-walled room whose metallic anonymity reminded me of the Asuka baths, except that here one could not even begin to guess where the door was. Plato, Athena, and all gods of scholars stick by me now, I thought; I had no idea what was going on but I knew I was in for it.

It is a tribute to the habit of months that the first thing I did was check to see if I still had my cards. I did. Then I looked around at the drab walls. There might easily be observation equipment, but if so, it was hidden. I took stock of myself—no headache, nausea, or needlemarks. Athena was with me so far. But how had they put me out? Sorcery? No form that I had been taught—it had happened too quickly. I felt the walls, searching for the door; nothing.

There was a low table on casters nearby. The only other object in the room was the bedroll I'd awakened on; I went over and sat on it.

After about an hour a seam appeared in the wall opposite. The metal parted and a man came in. Tall, broad, middle-aged, with carefully curled beard and ruby earrings. His robes were plain and white, and his belt was brown leather. He walked like a wrestler.

"Don't worry," he smiled. "We haven't taken your cards."

I didn't say anything.

He motioned to the table. "Won't you sit with me?" There was a cushion beside it; he sat, and I took the floor. His perfume was strong in the tiny room. I recognized the scent—it was one Ran used at times, and it cost more per centiliter than I made in a month. "I gather that you *are* Cormallon's advisor," he went on. "Either that or his lover, and I tend to think it's the former."

When I still didn't answer, he said, "You may as well admit it. Why else would you be holding the pack of cards?"

I said, "I'm Cormallon's pupil. He's instructing me in

sorcery and he gave me a deck for my own guidance. What does that have to do with you?"

"It's a rich deck to give a beginner."

"I paid a lot of money for it."

"I see. Well, I'm going to test my theory." He took out a pipe, a rather gaudy one, no different from the cheap synthawoods on sale in the market but for the silver plate on the stem. Possibly it was a signal, for a boy came in then in short gray robe and scraped knees. He carried tah, one cup, which he set in front of the man. It was insultingly rude. I was his guest, albeit an involuntary one, and there should have been two cups. I ought to have been grateful for one less thing to worry about, but I felt anger, and it surprised me—before this I had only been scared. "It would stand to reason," he said, "that if Cormallon has to depend on one specific person to give his readings, then the power can't be transferred until your death." He was watching for my reactions. I hoped I wasn't giving any.

"So," he went on, "you're not going to be touched. For the moment. We'll give Cormallon a little time to get nervous, notice he's lost something. Then we'll make our offer: a slight payment to me, the nature of which doesn't concern you, and we'll send back his cards. And we'll kill you, so he can be free to get a replacement. I mean no offense by the last statement; but after all, we can hardly return you. You've seen what I look like."

"Then why," I said, "did you let me see you?"

He smiled.

I thought, Ran, if you ever decide to take revenge on this man, I swear I'll never give you a hard time about it.

He said, "There isn't anything you'd like to tell me?"

"About what?" I asked sincerely. He seemed to have the whole story, and he'd be proved right soon enough.

"Well, then," he said courteously, and stood up, a host taking his leave. I put my palms on the table, shifting my weight to rise also.

He lifted his sandaled foot and brought it down on the back of my right hand. I rocked back, gasping. I could feel a tear starting down one cheek, and I turned my face aside.

"Perhaps I'll come back later," he said cheerfully, "and you can run through the cards for me. That would be very enlightening, I'm sure." He paused at the door. "You don't really believe, I hope, that Cormallon won't agree to these terms?"

I clasped my right hand. Any revenge you want to try, Ran. I set no limits, use your fine imagination. But I wasn't fooling myself. Of course he would agree to the terms. He was an Ivoran. There was no reason not to.

It felt as though at least a day, and perhaps more, had gone by. My hand was bruised but not broken; it throbbed only when I paid attention to it. I expected my captor hourly, but he had not returned. One meal had been served by the boy with scraped knees, a bowl with an impersonally tasteless grouping of meat and rice. The meat was unidentifiable. I tried smiling at the boy. He smiled back, rather shyly. "You have a name?" I asked. "I'm Theo." He shook his head nervously, his eyes looking toward the door. He never came back for the empty bowl.

I ran the cards four or five times; there was nothing else to do. They told me that Ran was in danger, which irritated me. *I* was the one in danger. Ran had a few problems, certainly, stemming from my kidnapping; but nothing he couldn't handle. The Prisoner card kept turning up. "How helpful," I murmured, finding myself talking to the deck. Why not? I'd become obsessed with these painted pieces of cardboard. I ran them daily, ate with them, slept with them, and half the time dreamed about them. I'd been so relieved to find they hadn't been taken. Identifying their safety with mine . . . it wasn't healthy. And this was what I was, in Ran's eyes, in the eyes of the man with the vulgar pipe. They paid me in gold or they stamped the back of my hand for it, but here my profession was what I was.

I picked up the cards and threw them against the wall. Let them lay there. Eventually someone, maybe the boy, would come and put them carefully together and send them off to Ran with a note saying I was dead. And Ran would find someone new to test them and know it was true. It was a pity I couldn't burn them, but I had nothing to start a fire.

Time passed, and finally I gathered them up and put them back in my pouch.

The lights had gone out. I got up quickly, not knowing what to expect. There was only dark, and silence. Then a seam of gray light appeared where the door ought to be; I moved to a diagonal position across from it. My heart was pounding as though it were about to leap out of my chest. It was lighter outside the door—I could see a man's silhouette on the threshold. Before his sight could adjust to the darkness I ran the space between us and rammed him, head first, in the stomach. He gave a breathless groan. As I did I was thinking, "the eyes—you've got to find the eyes." I was no match for an adult Ivoran and my only chance was to fight dirty, a choice I felt Ran would have approved.

"Oof," said Ran's voice in the darkness. "Enthus . . . iastic, aren't you."

"Ran! What—" I dropped my hands from his face.

"Never mind. We've got five minutes before the lights come on."

He grabbed my hand and we started running down the corridor. It was lit with a ghostly gray luminescence, some kind of secondary power source, I guessed. We rounded a corner and ran into a man coming from the other direction, in a gray tunic and cap that seemed vaguely like a uniform. He blinked, startled. His hand went to his side. I kept running, straight into another tackle, and Ran got an arm around his neck as he went over. (I learned this art of the tackle as a child on Pyrene, where we played a game called football. At the time I hated it, but now saw that it did indeed prepare one for life.) "Very nice," said Ran to me, polite as always. He had the man's weapon and was holding it against his cheek. I turned away, not wanting to see how my employer handled the matter.

I closed my eyes and tried to concentrate on something else. This man was wearing a uniform, but I was not well-educated enough to recognize the colors of a family livery. It must be a powerful House, though. Where were we? The Shikibus'? The Degrammonts'?

I opened my eyes. To my surprise it was hard to do. Hadn't he finished yet?

He was whispering—no, chanting—in the man's ear. He held him by the shoulders, his head in the crook of an arm. The corridor seemed to waver; I put out a hand to the wall to steady myself. "Theo!" Ran hissed. I shook my head fiercely. He lowered the man gently to the floor and stood up. "Come on!"

"There's a grav bank," he got out as we pounded on, "at the end . . . but we need the power . . . to come back . . . on time." I could see it in the distance. Suddenly the corridor lit up to full brilliance. "Too soon," he said. "Hurry."

We reached the end and the grav opened. Ran punched the speed float and we shot up to the roof.

It was dark and windy. I could see row upon row of aircars—the building must be enormous, I thought. Some of them were huge shapes, like freight trucks. One of the cars had an open door, and Ran motioned me into it after him. "Wait a minute," I said. "This is a—"

"I know," he said, pulling me in.

We took off. "Ran," I said, "You're stealing a *police vehicle*."

"What other kind of vehicle could I steal? Theodora, don't you even know where you are?" He stopped fiddling the controls and turned to me in disbelief. "We just broke out of the city detention units, under police headquarters."

We flew out of the city, through the night. I never seem to travel in the daylight anymore, I thought. I looked over at Ran, sitting at the controls; he wore the rough-weaved uniform of the Imperial jails, gray shorts and overtunic. But a sweet smell was in the car, a scent much like the one I'd recognized on my interrogator. That was a Cormallon for you. He would wear the uniform, but he refused to wash off his perfume.

"Are we going home? Your home, I mean."

"No." He punched in the automatic. "That direction wouldn't be safe for us right now. We're going to another city. You've cost me a fortune in bribes, you know."

"I didn't expect you to come."

"I don't know why not," he said, sounding hurt. "When it was my fault you were picked up. I was so damn careful to watch out for sorcery, I forgot about brute force."

"Why was I picked up? Why should the police care about me? Or you either, for that matter."

"Well, sorcery *is* illegal. There are conventions. Painful though following the law may be, sometimes it is enforced—"

"Don't joke," I said, sounding as irritated as I felt.

"Where have you been for two and a half years? It's the truth."

"But everyone uses it. Some of your clients were policemen."

He was smiling, I suppose at my naïvetè. It's a strange universe—magic illegal on the one planet where it's known to exist.

"Still," I said, "If they never arrested you before—"

"And they haven't arrested me now, not as Ran Cormallon. No, there's just one person behind this. The only one who could have the power to lock you in a holding cell and keep it a secret would be the man who runs the place—the Chief of Police. He keeps too tight a rein on his people for it to be anyone else." I described the man who had spoken to me in my cell. He nodded. "I can see his point of view. It would be a three-way success for him: putting a Cormallon out of business and impressing his superiors; getting blackmail payments from me; and using me to ruin other sorcerers. Still, he's taking a lot upon himself . . . if he is. Maybe it's arrogance, but I don't believe anyone would take on the Cormallons all alone. Damn. I wish I could question him, but as my late father used to say, the one thing you never do is dance around with the cops. Father had a quaint way of expressing himself."

"So what do we do?"

"We'll kill him. Safest thing under the circumstances."

I remembered my promise and said, "Good."

He smiled, surprised but pleased by this rare evidence of my good sense.

I said, "But Ran, how did you find me?"

" 'Sir,' not—oh, never mind. Call me Ran. Stepan picked up that there was something wrong in the room and followed the men who took you. He called me at the Ducorts. Then I had to make a lot of bribes." He began listing them on his fingers. "To get myself arrested under a false name. To make sure my cell was unlocked. To find out where you were—it was sheer luck I got to you so fast, I knew what level you were on but not what cell. To have the power and the first back-up power cut off. There was an extra fee to see that your level was unpatrolled at the right time, but they did tell me that might not work out perfectly. No amount of bribery would let me bring in a weapon, though.

That's a death offense, for the guard and the prisoner both."

"I'm sorry about all the money."

"That's all right. I can take it out of your salary." He said it quite seriously.

We stayed that night in a branch house of the Cormallons in Braece, the only town on an island about two hundred kilometers off the coast, and a good five hours' travel from the capital in a direction just opposite Cormallon itself. The family here lived in a tall gray tower near the ocean, with dull reddish-brown waves breaking on dull brown rocks at the cliff beneath the tower's base. Mournful birds, as seem to fly over every ocean on every world, soared past the windows. The family was a small one, father and mother and aunt, little boy and girl. They were far removed here from the intrigues of the capital, seemingly quite content to be so. They also seemed the slightest bit in awe of Ran, but not in any uncomfortable way. They took us to a suite at the top of the tower, gave us clothes and towels, and left us alone.

Ran went to the Net as soon as they had left. I ran water for a bath and laid out my clothes from what they had given us. The water was too loud for me to hear Ran as he spoke to whomever was at the other end. I knew what he was doing anyway. He was arranging the police chief's demise. The details were just business; I had no interest in them. "All done," he said, when he came over to the tub. I sat on the edge, my legs dangling in the water, half in and half out of my robes. It was a family-size bath, deep enough to stand in, with enough room for six or seven people. A waste of resource in this case. "I'll turn off the water," I said. "Unless you want it deeper." I got up to do so, dropped back down into a cushion and took a deep breath, hearing my heart beat like the tide outside the windows. I felt hot and weak, as though I hadn't eaten in days.

Ran swung down beside me. "You look *awful*," he said. He put his hand on my forehead. "Shall I get you water? Should I have our hosts bring you some food? When did you last eat?" He sounded genuinely concerned, and it was more than I could bear.

"I'm not hungry. I'm all right." To my embarrassment I

heard my voice shake. Theodora of Pyrene, jailbreak-artist, ruthless criminal mastermind. And my hand still hurt. I turned my face away and got up, a little unsteadily, to go to the taps.

"Wait a minute," he said, taking hold of the sleeve of my robe.

"I'm sorry. I guess I've been more worried than I thought—"

He unhooked the top of my robe and started to kiss me. It was so startling I forgot I was upset.

I had thought about this happening since the first day I read the cards and long ago decided that I could not afford to get any more entangled in Ran's life. I was still going to leave as soon as I could, save myself, and ruin his career. This sort of thing was what we referred to on Athena as a conflict of interest. Not to mention it was a violation of the employer/employee relationship. . . .

Luckily Ran continued to take the initiative, because it might have taken me years to work out the ethics of the situation. He pulled me back down on the cushion and I slipped off what remained of my clothes, holding onto him as though I were drowning.

"What's digging into my back?" asked Ran some time later.

I investigated and found that I still had Grandmother's onyx cat lost at the bottom of my pile of robes; I was glad no one had taken it from me. "It's a present from your grandmother," I said sleepily.

"Present? Show me."

I pulled aside the robes and held it out. I heard his breath draw in. "Where did you get *this?*"

He took it gently from my hands.

"I told you, it's a present from Grandmother."

He was looking at me strangely, and I suddenly realized what I had done. I tried to take it back, but he held it out of my reach and, wrapping it carefully in his cloak, said, "I think I'd better give it some time to wear off first." It was late, and I decided I was too tired to try to understand.

A shrieking bird outside the window awakened me. Ran's cloak was tangled around my legs, and I had a panicked moment when I couldn't find my card pouch. Then I saw it on the floor across the room. I must have been in a confused state of mind, I thought. I heard Ran's voice from the other room; he was on the Net again. I dressed and went out just as he was logging off. "It's been taken care of," he said, "we can go home." As easy as that.

Well, it wasn't that easy for me. He made no move to touch me, or kiss me, or wish me good morning, as my Athenan lovers (none of whom had meant over-much to me, or vice versa) had been polite enough to do. Last night had clearly been erased. Granted, we had both been running on adrenaline since leaving police headquarters; there had been more of physical reflex than anything else in the timing of what happened; but there had been something else, too. I wanted it acknowledged.

I walked over to him. "Good morning," I said, more like a challenge than anything else, and I kissed him. He returned it, impersonally. Then he picked up my onyx cat from the Net counter, grasping it in a towel, and held it out to me.

"Better hold onto this," he said. "Grandmother doesn't give out gifts casually."

I took it from him and jammed it into my pouch, beside the cards. I went into the other room, found my outer robe and belt and made sure there was nothing I'd forgotten.

He was closing up the Net when I came back in. "Shouldn't we be running along?" I asked.

"Give me a hand with the cover? It's a guestroom Net; it will only get dusty if we leave it out."

So we closed it up, like courteous guests. He led the way down the circular staircase and I followed, with savage politeness.

We said good-bye to the family group downstairs. The aircar was perched on the hill above the rocks and the winds blew up around us. The little family was lined up outside the tower, red-faced in the wind. The father bowed nervously and the others followed suit. When we reached the car, there was a flash of blue smoke. Ran pulled me by the arm and we both fell onto the hardpacked dirt, rolling out of the way.

Nothing happened. I'd landed on my bad hand and sat

up, blinking with pain. Ran jumped to his feet. "Just who is responsible for this?" he said angrily.

They looked at one another. The little girl's face puffed up a dark reddish tan, and she began to bawl.

Ran stopped glaring immediately and went over to her. "Here, here, darling, it's all right. I'm sorry. I was just surprised, that's all." He knelt down and hugged her. "You wanted to show us what you could do, didn't you? You wanted to make an illusion?" She nodded, her face buried in his shoulder. Clearly words were still beyond her. "Well, and it was certainly a good show you put on, wasn't it? It took our attention."

She heaved, between sobs, "There—were—supposed to be—d-d-doves."

"Oh, darling." He kissed her. "There'll be doves one day, I promise." He reached to his shoulder and ripped off the silver clasp on his cloak. "Here, look." He showed her the diamond-shaped clasp with its long pin. She sniffled. He put it into her hand. "Keep it, now, be very careful with it; it's a magic talisman. You keep it with you when you work your spells. And if you study hard and practice long enough, I swear to you, one day you'll make beautiful doves." Magic talisman, indeed! The clasp and the cloak both had been supplied to Ran by her own parents to replace his jail uniform.

She stared at the clasp. "But don't you need it?"

"Not any more, honey. It's a gift, from one sorcerer to another."

A smile broke out on her face. She threw her arms around him and clung to him. I turned away and looked out to the ocean.

The sun was high over the water as we flew west. We ate as we flew, a boxed meal the Braece family had put up for us. A sea blossom wrapped in a piece of red-striped silk was in the box beside the food. I opened the card case from time to time and flicked through the deck.

"You're pretty quiet," he said.

I shrugged. "Sorry."

It took us several hours to near Cormallon territory. Ran bypassed the capital and took a straight line for home.

We had often been silent with one another, but where

before it had been companionable, now it grated. He shifted in his seat and would tap the controls, make an effort to stop, and then tap again. The green and brown hills, the vineyards, passed away beneath us.

"Look," he said, and stopped. When he spoke it was to state the obvious, and I felt that it was not what he had meant to say. "Look, at least we won't have to worry about any more attempts on your life. The police chief seems to have been the active figure, and he's out of our way."

We reached the Cormallon barrier. The air shimmered obediently around us, and the car caught fire.

Chapter 7

Time passed. It was dark and I was asleep. One dream kept recurring, the time when I was three years old in the crèche kitchen on Pyrene, and I spilled boiling water on my hands. I yelled and screamed and dropped the container I was holding, and the kitchen worker went to get my crèche-guardian, who sat and held me until they came with salve and painkillers, and took me to the infirmary.

I hadn't thought of her in years. The dream-memory of her face was sharp and clear, and didn't go with the voices I heard, familiar voices, but somehow removed from the place where I was dreaming.

Kylla's voice. I tried to open my eyes and couldn't. "Kylla!" It came out a croak.

"Theo, sweetheart, don't move. We've got you all strapped in."

"I can't open my eyes."

"You're wearing a bandage. Don't worry about it, it doesn't mean you're blind, we just can't take it off yet."

"Ran—"

"Ran's fine. He generated a personal shield right away. He extended it to you as soon as he could, but it was a few seconds too late. He's just downstairs, wait a minute." Her footsteps went away and I heard her talking outside the door. She returned to my bed. "He'll be right up. How do you feel? Any pain?"

"No." There was a delayed surprise to that realization; shouldn't I be, in fact, in a great deal of pain? Or how long had I lain here? Long enough for burns to heal? "Ky, how long—"

"Not too long. Don't worry about—"

Running footsteps. "Ky, is she awake? Theodora?"

"Hello, Ran."

I heard a released breath. "Theodora. How do you feel?"

"All right. I guess. I wish I could see you."

He sat down on the bed. "Tilt your head forward."

Kylla's voice was sharp. "Brother, what do you think you're doing?"

His fingers were loosening the bandage around my eyes. "Come on, Ky, it's almost time for it to come off anyway. Another day or two won't make any difference."

"Theo, if the light hurts your eyes, you speak up right away. Understand?"

The bandage came off, all of a piece, and I blinked. Ran sat blurrily before me, looking anxious. Kylla came over next to him and swung back the bar that held in my legs. She said, "Can you see me?"

"Yeah. Your hair looks nice up."

She smiled. "So much for Tellys medical advice," she said airily to Ran, and went over to the little table by the door. The top was covered with jars and white cloths.

Ran kept looking at me.

"Is there something wrong with me?" I felt my face; it seemed all right.

"What? No. You look fine. How do you feel? Can you sit up?"

I tried it. "It seems I can."

"Good. You don't know how worried I've been." He reached into the pocket of his robe. "Do you feel well enough to run the cards?"

"Damn you, Ran!" Kylla looked as though she were very close to hitting him.

He looked faintly surprised. "I'm sorry," he said to me, and inclined a head to Kylla. "Of course we're glad to see you recovered, and of course I hope I convey our relief and happiness. But there's no need to be impractical. In fact, Kylla, if we want to avoid such incidents as these in the future, we'd better get to work on them now." He fiddled with the pocket of his robe and brought out the familiar deck.

Ran and his priorities, some things never change. Suddenly it struck me as funny, and I began to chuckle.

He was taken aback. "Have you been tranking her up?" he asked his sister.

"No, no," I said. "Sorry. The cards, by all means." Lay

'em down, read 'em out, I almost added, but then I would have lost all credibility as a rational human being.

I ran the cards. It was odd; it was as if they were any pack of cards. No visions, no intuitions . . . at any rate, no intuitions that felt as though they carried any weight of truth. I didn't panic over it; already the power seemed so natural to me that I assumed it was bound to come back. I missed it, though. "I'm sorry," I said. "Maybe I'm not well enough yet."

"Don't worry about it," he said, as he gathered them up. He laid the pack on a tray beside my bed. "We'll try again later."

"Do you feel like eating?" asked Kylla. "The healer said you could have soup. Nothing stronger, for a few days."

"Yes, thanks."

She went away. Ran looked at me speculatively. "Kylla had a hill-healer in, as well as a doctor trained on Tellys. She sent to Perbry Monastery for the healer. One of the ishin na' telleth monks."

"Oh?" I bent an arm experimentally. Whatever they'd done, I seemed to have survived it. "What did he say about my injuries?"

"He didn't say anything about them. He said you don't get enough exercise. He also said you don't live in your body enough."

"What's that supposed to mean? Where the hell do I live, if I don't live in my body?"

"I wouldn't know. Anyway, one shouldn't take these ishin na' telleth people seriously. They don't even take themselves seriously."

"What did the doctor say?"

"He said you had a concussion and second-degree burns."

"Good for him."

"Yes. But when he left, you still had second-degree burns, and when the healer left, you were all right."

I thought about it. "He must have been some kind of sorcerer, then."

"Apparently. I thought I knew what could be done with sorcery and what couldn't. I always assumed these hill-healers lived on superstition . . . I don't like feeling like a novice."

He got up and walked around the bedroom. "There are too many mysteries in my life right now. I'm tired of this siege business, I don't want to lock us both in again and wait for something else to happen."

"So."

"So I'm leaving you here at Cormallon for a while. If you're safe anywhere, it's here. I have research to do."

"I just woke up, so I'm sorry if I'm slow . . . research?"

He smiled. "Know Thy Enemy."

That wasn't the way they taught us Socrates on Athena. But I guess each society finds the path that suits it.

I was in and out of consciousness several times after that, but the basic thing was, I felt fine and healthy for someone who by rights ought to be dead. It was a pretty shaky thought. *I* hadn't done anything to save myself (nothing I could have done), and the idea that I'd been plucked out of harm's way and nursed back to strength by people and forces outside of me was not really a pleasant one. Suppose I hadn't been saved? It took your innocent notions about having some control over your own life and trashed them rather ruthlessly.

Kylla said later that in a way my rescue was my own doing; in that, if I weren't a good enough person no one would have gone to the trouble of helping me. She meant that as reassurance. However, it struck me more as black humor, since it suddenly brought back a childish illusion of mine from about the age of six or seven: that if I was nice enough, I would never have to die. Teams of doctors would work round the clock to save me, donations would pour in from around the planet. . . . What a charming thought—had I really ever believed that? Obviously my world-view had undergone a material change since then. I was much closer to the Ivoran ideal of keeping myself to myself, and assuming that any time you let other people "help" you it was more likely to damage you than anything else. I wasn't going to try to explain all this to an Ivoran, though, and let Kylla think that my muffled laughter was some kind of physical reaction. She brought me more soup.

I spent a week in bed. Eln played chess with me, at least for two games, until we saw I was so bad in comparison with him that there was no point. We talked about a lot of things, things I had no chance to go over with Ran or anybody else—most Ivorans having no inclination for scientific or philosophical speculation. They're too intensely concerned with daily profit and loss, or in the case of the ishin na' telleths, too intensely *un*concerned. (Well, they would always make time for songs and plays, they liked the dramatic arts. But why make time for what won't bring you any juice personally?) So these hours were a vacation, a return to late-night sessions with Athenan friends, a chance to play with concepts which would never affect my life directly.

I said, "Magic bothers me."

Eln sat on the edge of my bed that afternoon, his floater hovering beside him, laying cards on the blanket. Not my cards, regular playing cards; it was some form of solitaire. Like an old Earth painting: the heavy sunlight through the window, the slender, tanned fingers tapping the ace of spades, dark eyes following the deal-out, and on his face the look of mild interest which was the closest he came to revealing full concentration. I wondered how I ever could have thought he and Ran looked alike.

He finally acknowledged my remark with a grunt.

I said, "Yes, Ran gives me these helpful explanations also."

He smiled. "Magic bothers you. Does this mean you're under a spell? Or does the concept itself bother you? Or are you implying your sorcerous education leaves something to be desired? Specific questions, Theo, are what lead to specific answers."

"You do this to annoy me, don't you."

"Yes. All right, you were trying to open a conversation. 'Tell me, Theo, what bothers you about it?' "

"Take me seriously, Eln. I can't talk to you when you're this na' telleth."

He said, not entirely happily, "This is as serious as I ever am. If you can manage to separate the content from the style, I don't think you'll have any complaints."

I thought about that for a while, then said, "I beg your pardon."

He smiled, not a teasing smile this time. He lifted my right hand and kissed my fingers with gentle courtesy. To cover my surprise I started to talk quickly. "Magic works;

that's obvious. I'm not going to waste my time debating the reality of what I've already perceived. I outgrew those sorts of arguments when I was twelve."

"All right," he said, promptingly.

"But so far as I can tell, it only works *here.* Surely if it worked anyplace else, I would have heard about it. And yet I can't believe the laws governing the universe were changed for this one particular planet. That's just . . . ridiculous."

"I agree. Although 'ridiculous' and 'impossible' aren't the same thing. Still, I don't like the idea either."

"So how do you explain it?" I folded my arms and stared at him.

He began picking up his cards. "How do *you* explain it?"

"I don't. I just use it."

"A good Ivoran answer. As I understand it, the human race did the same with electricity for a long time."

I wriggled with frustration under the blanket. "That isn't good enough!"

"No. Well, there are theories."

Now I froze. "There *are?* Ran never told me."

He shrugged. "I doubt if he's studied them; he's very practical."

"But you have studied them?"

"Well, I am the theorist of the family—it makes up for having no talent of my own, I suppose."

Was I hearing right? "Are you telling me you're not a sorcerer?"

"My dear, not in any shape or form. What gave you the idea I was? I'm someone who studies sorcery and designs new ways to use it. I can't use it myself, though."

In a family like the Cormallons it must be like being crippled twice over. "I always assumed . . . when you helped me study, you knew so much about it. . . ."

He smiled. "I know more about it than anyone you're likely to meet on this planet. Which makes it lucky for you, Theo, that you come to me with your question. Not that I can actually answer it, mind you, but I can recite more unproven theories than you or any sane human would really want to hear. Shall I start? If you don't stop me I will. Number One:—"

"Wait a minute. You're not making any of this up, are

you? It wouldn't be a funny joke." I saw his face and said, "I'm sorry. I would like to know these theories. Please go ahead and tell me."

He said, "The most popular one for the last couple of centuries is the genetic engineering explanation."

"Genetic engineering? Come on, Eln, Ivory hasn't been capable of anything that technically sophisticated, not ever. And I don't see—"

"Theo. Darling. Lately when you talk your brain seems to disconnect from your vocal cords. Possibly a side effect of your injuries."

I shut up.

"What do you know about the Pakrinor?" he asked.

"I saw a picture of one once," I said cautiously. "But they didn't photograph well. It was pretty blurry." The Pakrinor: the one and only alien species ever encountered by humanity. Date of encounter, somewhere around 100 or 200 post-Spaceflight. A fleet of fourteen ships, first sighted past Jupiter; as they put it, "just passing through." "They only stayed on Earth for a few weeks, as I remember. Not long enough for any good information on them, anyway. And as I understand it, the communication level between them and us wasn't all that reliable."

"So the books say. But they gave us the first practical star drive. Not as good as the present one, but enough to change history. Communication was reliable enough for that." He started dealing cards onto the blanket again.

"What does this have to do with magic? Are you trying to tell me—"

"I'm trying to tell you that Ivory is a hitchhiker planet."

I said, finally, "I've heard the phrase . . ."

"The star drive," he said, "was not free of charge."

"No, I understand that quite a few museums were gutted. They traded it for works of art."

"Works of art, yes." He gave a short laugh. "Not only canvas and stone."

"I don't know what you mean."

"Surely you've read that the aliens took riders along with them. Colonists, who agreed to be set down at the first habitable planet. Nobody wanted to wait for the twenty or thirty years it would take to build the first human starship. Pakrinor ships are *big*. Freighters, with huge holds. Several thousand people went, not to mention the records and tools and livestock."

"Yes, I think I did read about it. Wait, you're saying Ivory is one of those lost colonies? You mean people have been here since 200 PS? Great Plato, no wonder there's been genetic drift—we might not even be the same species anymore," I said, and stopped dead.

Eln didn't notice; his thoughts were less personal than mine. "I'm not talking about *drift,*" he said. "Our stories of that time are very explicit. The Pakrinor regarded one-tenth of their passengers as part of the payment—they kept them, never let them disembark. We don't forget things like that here, no matter how long ago they happened. As for the other nine-tenths . . . there was a great deal of medical experimentation."

"Experimentation—"

"It's too late to prove anything now. Maybe the government really did agree before we left." He paused. "I wonder sometimes what they did to the people targeted for the other hitchhiker worlds."

We were both silent. Magic as a force to be accessed only by beings of certain genetic background . . . that took some thinking about. Probably several days at least. I said finally, "I can wait to hear the other theories."

He laughed. He picked up my hand again and dug his knuckle in playfully. "So be it." Then he said, "Still. If the Pakrinor ever come back . . . I don't think they'll be made welcome. Quite the opposite."

"I get that impression. I'm glad we're on the same side, Eln."

He grinned. "I feel the same way. It's the quiet ones you have to watch out for." He cut one of his card piles to two and balanced the second one on my left shin. "Hear anything from Ran? He's been gone a week now."

"He calls Kylla every night. I've spoken to him a few times."

"Any news?"

I said, "Why don't you ask him the next time he calls?"

"Why don't I?" he said. He patted the bump in the blanket that represented my knee and slipped off the bed onto his floater. "Get lots of sleep tonight, Theo-my-darling. We start your exercise program tomorrow."

"We do, do we?"

"Forgive me if I presume. But your healer did suggest it. And you need to live more in your body."

The way I heard it, Eln had not been present when that judgment was made. I said, "You always have to know everything that goes on, don't you?"

"Lots of sleep, Theo."

"Right. Lots of sleep."

He waved and left. Several piles of cards remained perched just out of easy reach. The hell with them, I thought, and decided to start on that sleep right now.

In fact there wasn't any useful news from Ran. Or if there was, he wasn't about to reveal it over the Net link. I tabled the matter for the time being and concentrated on the present.

Which included the matter of exercise. Eln appeared at my door next morning with towels and two wooden staves. It was a shock to me—I hadn't thought he got up before noon.

"We're going to do sa'ret," he announced, and he handed me a staff.

Sa'ret: The River. "I think I've heard of this."

"Good," he said. "I'm glad Kylla got you a pair of trousers. Put them on, bring your staff, and meet me outside in five minutes."

"I haven't even had breakfast!"

"Ah. I'd almost forgotten." He reached into his pouch and pulled out a small loaf of bread. "There's more later if you work hard. Chew as you dress, I hate to be kept waiting." He gave me a mock salute and went out. I glared at him as he went. Was this any way for a hedonist to behave?

The River. That was my first day, my introduction to the way of movement that was sa'ret. We did the Old River first, the flowing stretches and bends of a river that wound over well-known lands. And we did the Middle River, the balancer; you use the staff most in Middle River. We finished with the Young River, the current with wild leaps over rock and down canyons. I was sweating hard by that time. It was clear that Eln was not only a better chess-player, he had a lot more endurance. Particularly since he had to modify the movements so they could be done solely with his arms, using apparatus he had set up in the garden. His verbal instructions to me about what to do with my feet were quick and clear, even as he was twisting on a set of movable bars several meters over my head. His staff rested, an unused talisman, on a perch nearby, while he grasped the bars in its place. His legs were strapped together at the thighs and ankles, giving him a merman look from below.

He was graceful on those bars, as if he were flying. It made me feel clumsy. Nor did I really understand what The River meant. It was several weeks before I came to realize that it didn't mean anything, and that that fact didn't matter. I came out every morning after that with Eln, and struggled and sweated while he flew gloriously overhead. But I did learn; at least I had the basic postures and positions down, after what seemed like an eternity but was only a week. A few days later Eln told me to close my eyes while I did it, and stop watching him. Another week went by. Then he put up mirrors all around the practice area; so what was the idea, I asked, am I supposed to watch or not? No answer from Eln, he just smiled and pulled up on the bars. So I did watch. How appalling—I *was* clumsy. What of it, I was a scholar, wasn't I? I didn't have to do this, did I? I could go in the house right now . . . I sighed as I shifted to Middle River; what was the use of trying? I closed my eyes and twirled the staff, opened them and watched the mirrors from the corner of my eye.

I was as graceful as anybody! I stopped utterly short.

"What's the matter?" His voice came down through the dappled morning sunlight.

I looked up through the shadow of the bars. I shrugged.

"Well?" he said.

I hesitated. "I don't think I was bad that time."

"You haven't been bad," he said, "since the sixth day."

We regarded each other. "Well," I said. I returned my feet to Middle River Seven position. As I did so, a leaf let loose from one of the garden trees and floated to the ground. "It's almost autumn."

"So it is," he said.

* * *

It was over a month since Ran had left to do his "research." It bothered me that he wasn't letting me know just what he was trying to find out. And when I was honest with myself I knew that that wasn't all that bothered me. Grandmother never came to meals anymore, and between her absence and Ran's, and Eln ignoring proper dinnertimes, the dining hall was a sad place. Kylla seemed busy and abstracted. Grandmother was ill, although just what the sickness was was never made clear to me, and from something Eln said I gathered that she didn't even know I was at Cormallon. This was somehow more shocking than anything; I'd been under the illusion that Grandmother knew everything that went on, at least where her family was concerned.

One afternoon I passed by Grandmother's sun-washed doorway, watching Tagra hand Kylla an empty lunch tray. "I'm glad she's eating, at least," I said to Kylla.

"Yes, but not much." Kylla swung back her hair out of her eyes, balancing the tray as she moved. Usually she put her hair up when there was work to be done, but she seemed to have little time for amenities these days. She looked tired and worried.

"What do you care?" said Tagra. She frowned at me and went down the passage.

"Sorry," said Kylla.

"I haven't even said anything to her this time."

"She's probably upset at the time you're spending with Eln. Don't know why—she's got him most nights."

"What?" I said.

She leaned against the stone wall. "Could you hold this for a second?"

"Sure—of course." I took the tray. "You look done in."

"I'll rest. But first I need to go down to the kitchen and talk with Herel. Come with me?"

I carried the tray. " . . . Tagra and Eln?" I said, cautiously, as we went down the stairs.

"For years," she said, resignedly. "And you'd think she'd relax by now. She's the only person at Cormallon who fits Eln's requirements."

Which brought up a lot of questions which were none of my business, but which I was quite interested in. While I was thinking how to phrase them we reached the kitchen, and the thought of continuing the subject in front of Herel was just beyond the limits of my indiscretion. Later during my visit I could find no way of slipping into the topic gracefully.

So there we were: Tagra hated me, Kylla was too busy to talk to, and Eln made me work. I also felt a bit of a fraud. After all, I wasn't *doing* anything. Just The River for two hours in the morning, and rooting through the library in the afternoons. And for this I was pulling down an enormous salary? Not that anyone else even hinted at such an attitude; on the contrary, they treated me more like a soldier honorably wounded, which just made me feel more uncomfortable.

So it came as a relief when Ran finally showed up, over a month after he disappeared. Even if I had to leave the safe cocoon of the estate, it was better than marking time in this strained atmosphere . . . although just why the atmosphere was strained, I could not have said.

I looked up from a new set I was trying of Young River Six-Three-Two and there he was, standing under a tree in the garden. I wiped the sweat out of my eyes and threw down my staff. The garden seemed to tilt for a minute; I knew I really shouldn't stop so suddenly.

"I didn't mean to interrupt," he said.

"Too late," I said cheerfully, "you have." And I walked out from under the bars, feeling as though a pressure had been lifted.

I was not the only one who had stopped suddenly. I'd forgotten Eln. "Theo," his voice came down. I looked up and saw that he'd swung himself over to the platform with his rest-seat. "Cut off my timer," he said, nodding to the floater down below. He usually had it set to rise to the platform after a certain span of time had passed.

I looked over at Ran, and back up to the platform. "You don't have to stop," I said, "we can leave."

"Cut off the timer," he repeated.

I went over and switched it off. When the floater reached platform level, Eln swung into the seat. He pulled off his sweatband and let it fall to earth. Then he took the floater down to safety level and rode it back into the house; without saying another word.

Ran chose a good-sized boulder off to the side of the practice area and sat down. "We need to talk," he said.

Was he going to give me a hard time about my being with Eln? I was annoyed with them both. I was beginning to feel that the Pyrene crèche setup made more sense than all this family intensity, and I was tempted to say so. Luckily I did not; for, as I found, it was not what was on his mind at all.

"I've been checking into this sabotage," he began. It was just another example of a moment I was glad I'd kept my mouth shut. "And I can sum up my findings by saying I have no idea who is behind it or why. It's not that I don't have enemies . . . but what would they have to gain by it? At least twice the attacks weren't against me at all, but focused on my card-reader. Why?"

I said, "Why? You've said yourself that eliminating me would be a neat way of making you vulnerable."

"That motive only works if the person doing this *knows* about you. I've been very careful, Theodora. And I've spent the last month checking everywhere and everyone I could think of. The secret is still a secret."

"The Chief of Police knew . . . suspected, anyway."

"And someone had to tell him. I know. And yet, I swear, it's not general knowledge."

"Eln and Kylla know, I think."

"Eln and Kylla," he said, dismissing them. "I'm talking about a threat."

"So this month was wasted effort, then," I said.

He spoke reprovingly. "Elimination of wrong data is never wasted effort. And there is another possibility I've been considering."

"Oh?" I had the impression that I wouldn't like this possibility.

"Someone tried to kill you because someone doesn't like you."

"I'm a likable person, Ran."

"Yes, of course you are. But let's look at—"

"Besides, that assumes the death of your cousin was accidental."

"Accidents happen. Let's look at—"

"And the Police Chief's actions were unrelated."

"Theodora. Try to think about this possibility rationally

for a moment. Don't talk. Just think about it. Yes, the Police Chief's actions could be unrelated. He could have been making a move on his own—these things happen, you know, they happened before you came here and they'll go on happening."

I was silent.

"Well?" he said.

"I'm thinking, all right?"

He cleared his throat. "I would like to hear what you're thinking."

"It's a nice theory, except for one thing—I don't have any enemies. I keep a low profile. I'm polite. Even in the market I always addressed customers by the highest title possible. I don't like to be noticed."

He said, "You've got at least one enemy, and so do I. Her name's Pina."

Oops. That was another story. I said, slowly, "She didn't know we were behind her being blacklisted. She knew it was a trick. But she didn't know about us."

"Possibly she found out. There's no reason to think she's an idiot."

I was quiet for a moment, then said, "I'm thinking some more."

"Good. I've been doing that for the last week. After I finished, I asked some questions. Pina's not in the city any-more. Her friends—of which she hasn't many, I might add—think she returned to her birth village."

"And you've got the name and location of the village."

"Yes."

I paused. "Have you been there?"

"Not yet," he said. "I thought we'd go together."

Chapter 8

I was glad to be leaving Cormallon. It was beautiful, it was peaceful, everyone was very nice to me; and there was something wrong with it. Something in the undertow that I couldn't identify and therefore irritated me. I hadn't felt this way on my previous visit, and didn't know why. Perhaps I'd simply been too unfamiliar with the family to be sensitive to these nuances. Anyway, I was more than willing to accompany Ran on this "business trip." That was the phrase we used to the captain of the *Summer Ice* to describe our reason for wanting to travel down to Issin at this time of year—and I suppose it really was business, although not, as we claimed, the export business.

We spent a couple of days in the capital waiting on the ship's schedule; and I used the time to ask a favor of my old market-mate, Irsa. She approached a couple of the illegal market bankers on my behalf, and we discovered that the ones who'd claimed they had to charge interest on handling my savings were taking advantage of a foreigner. They made profits on that money, illegal or not, and they were supposed to *pay* interest. I gave Irsa a split on my last week's pay, most joyfully, and made the necessary arrangements. By the time I boarded ship for Issin I'd made three payments into the account.

Issin is a good way down the continent, three days for a little freighter like the *Summer Ice.* Autumn was coming on, the captain pointed out, and we'd have slow going down Issin-way, watching out for the first ice. We had a good cabin, he said, and it was true. Of course it was the only passenger cabin on the ship.

I slung my pack under the narrow bunk and said to Ran, "Which of us gets the floor?"

"You do," he said.

"I was thinking we would match for it."

"I was thinking I'm senior to you."

"I was thinking how I hate rolling over onto the cards in the middle of the night. With a mattress it's not so bad. . . ."

"All right, all night." He threw some of the blankets on the floor. I bent over the bunk to hide my grin and offered thanks to Grandmother Cormallon. Ran *hated* to be reminded of my nonexpendability.

I did the cards that night; again they were unhelpful and I was left wondering if I were reading things into them. There was no clear sense of what was coming from them and what was born of my frustrated imagination. I joined Ran on deck afterward.

It was a cool night. Moonlight spilled in twin trenches over the water. I looked blankly up at constellations I didn't recognize; usually I saw that I was safe indoors after sundown.

"Where's your coat?" asked Ran.

"I left it on the bunk."

"You should be wearing it."

"You hate that coat," I pointed out.

"It's a secondhand disgrace," he said, "and unfitting for a member of our house. You ought to have gotten a new one when we were in the capital."

I shrugged. In the capital it was only cold for a few weeks anyway. "New coats cost too much. This one's cheap."

"And I assume it's warm. You should go down and put it on."

I decided to get him off the subject. "Ran, when you were at Cormallon, did you get the feeling everything was not quite right there?"

"Grandmother's ill. The house routine was thrown off. Is that what you mean?"

"I don't think so. Or maybe it is, I don't know."

"I was only there for a couple of days."

"And I was there for a month, and I still don't know what I'm talking about." I shivered.

"You should—" he began.

"I know," I said. "I only planned on staying here for a minute. I'm going to bed, don't wake me up when you come in." And I went down to the cabin. A long time later it occurred to me that I was nervous about Cormallon because it had come to represent, for me as well as Ran, a safe haven in a paranoid universe. The thought was upsetting when it came; I didn't want to rely on anything Ivoran.

We came into Issin harbor on early morning of the third day. Not a sign of ice anywhere, and I was beginning to think that the captain had ice on the brain. It was autumn, after all, even if we were pretty far south. It was go-through-your-bones chilly, though, and I wore my old blue coat on deck, wrapping the straps of my pack over the thick shoulders. Underneath it I wore a long wool robe, and underneath that a thin silk one.

Ran was already at the rail, looking over the harbor. "Not a land of excitement," I said as I joined him. A half-circle of rippling gray water, old wooden boats bobbing at their moorings, and maybe twenty or thirty stone houses on the hills around the bay.

"Every house there belongs to Cormallon," he replied. "And they do their share. You wouldn't think they could, just from fishing, but every year they send money into the treasury instead of taking it out. I only wish some of the flashier branches could do as well."

Hooray for them, I thought, and was immediately ashamed. This wasn't the most hospitable spot I'd ever seen. If they could wrench a good living from it, they were doing better than I'd been doing before I hooked up with Ran. I said, "Why do they call this ship the *Summer Ice*, anyway? It's a cold autumn, and I still haven't seen any ice."

"The captain and crew are Andulsine. It's summer up there when it's winter down here. That's where their regular route starts—comes by way of the capital, by Sebral, and down to Issin. I guess it's sort of a message to their Andulsine customers about their route. Anyway, even if they weren't from above the equator . . . icebergs have crumpled up a few ships in these waters even at high summer. *Our* high summer."

I was glad I hadn't known.

Ran looked toward the shore. "Our welcome," he said.

A rowboat was heading out to us. A man and a woman sat in it. The man had his back to me but I could see the woman's scarf blowing on the wind, rippling above the ripples on the bay. They both wore scarves wrapped around their heads, covering their ears, with green caps pulled over the scarves. At last the boat bumped against side of the *Summer Ice*. "Sir?" the man called up.

"Ran Cormallon," said Ran, as though answering a challenge. He added, one hand on my shoulder, "Theodora Cormallon."

"Welcome," called the woman. She looked up with a red and wrinkled face.

"Welcome, and come down," echoed the man. Ran glanced over at the captain, who motioned to have the ladder lowered. It was a rope affair, not at all like the elegant way we walked on board from the pier in the capital. I hitched the ends of my robes into my belt and felt them balloon out as the wind bit my legs, and tried not to picture what the Cormallon representatives below thought of the figure I must cut. Still, I had no intention of taking a tumble in that cold gray water for the sake of decorum.

They said nothing about it, though, as they helped me in. I noticed as I sat down that they both wore trousers.

"Beth and Karn, happy by your presence. It's a fine time for you to honor us," said the man. He was solidly built, on the late side of middle age, and his face was as ruddy as the woman's. He smiled at me as he said, "Luck for us all, the timing. We've a wedding at the house."

"My son," said the woman, Beth.

"Fine food and drink in plenty," said Karn.

"We only hope you remember all the words of the service," said Beth, and they both laughed.

Ran looked taken aback. " . . . Service?" he said, in a voice that was the pattern of noncommittance.

Beth and Karn exchanged glances. Some of the light left their faces. "We assumed," said Beth, "that as first in the family you would do the ritual yourself."

They looked at him warily, like children waiting to be told there would be no birthday gifts this year.

"Well, of course," said Ran.

"That goes without saying," I agreed, and though Ran's eyes flicked past me he gave no other sign.

"Is it today?" he asked.

"This afternoon," said Beth. "When we heard you were coming, we postponed it."

"I'm honored," he said, as gracefully as possible.

The wedding proper took place in a long, low stone hall attached to Karn's house. The bride and groom seemed about twenty years old; they both wore long red silk tunics with woven belts, and looked shy and silly. Everyone present was dressed up. I hoped I wasn't disgracing Ran with my own clothes, but probably not; the outer robe was from Kylla, and I had great faith in her judgment.

In some ways it was more like a night club than a wedding. I sat at a round table with half a dozen strangers, and the half of the table not facing the couple had to crane their necks for the service. The hall was filled with similar tables. Not that anyone had to crane for long; whatever Ran was mumbling over the bride and groom only lasted about a minute, the two exchanged their bluestone pendants, and everyone sat down for the main event, which seemed to mean: food. And there was food. One course after another of the most amazing, wondrous, deliciously prepared food it has ever been my privilege to partake. I didn't know what any of it was, and I gave up trying to ask and remember all the names of the dishes. Where had they been hiding this stuff while I was in the capital? I sat in a glow of calories and thought how mad I must be to consider leaving this fine planet.

Ran had to sit at the bride and groom's table, but I was in an expansive mood after the first two courses, and more than willing to try small talk with the people on either side of me. The girl on my left was Cara, the bride's cousin, and she told me that the exchange of pendants was temporary and took place so that "there would always be a little of them mixed together," come what may. That seemed a bit messy, I thought, considering that (for all I knew) they might not even be acquainted yet.

The boy on my right was more interesting. He was eighteen, and a medical student. Medical studies on Ivory cover a wide range, depending on where you do the learning; and since about half of it was secondhand knowledge from Tellys and the other half from a tradition of folklore, magic, and consmanship, it made for a fascinating topic. He held forth for quite a while, until I interrupted him by dropping the latest small dish of delicacies I'd been handed.

I'd been staring down at the dish, wondering if I were imagining the *eyes* I thought I saw there . . . not to mention the . . . *beaks?*

"Those are *heads*," I said to him.

"Yes," he said.

"Those are birds' heads," I said.

"Yes," he said again, and taking the one I held frozen in a pair of tongs away from me, he proceeded to pull the skin off the top of the skull. Then he pointed to the quartered brains inside and began explaining some neurological experiments he had been performing recently. Afterward he popped the brain into his mouth and smiled happily.

"They've done some excellent food, haven't they?" he said. "I came all the way from South Port when I heard they were planning to use the traditional dishes."

"Yes, I can see why you would." I hoped I hadn't eaten anything too strange underneath all the sauces. Perhaps I shouldn't get a list of the ingredients after all.

After a good deal more wine and more courses than I thought possible, the party started to break up. I parted amicably from my dinner partners and went to join the line of people waiting for their coats. Ran found me there. "We're to stay the night at Beth's house," he said.

"Yes, I know."

When the line reached me, Ran took my tattered and disgraceful blue coat and held it for me to get into. It was a gesture no one else on the line had yet made. He held it, I thought, no differently than if it had been the most expensive tanil-lined fur available in the Imperial stores. As I turned to put my arms in it, I saw the face of the woman behind me. Her eyes widened and she seemed impressed. Her glance flickered toward her own escort, a short, balding man who was looking at his watch. As I turned back to Ran, from the corner of my eye I saw her elbow jab out viciously, though not lethally, into her escort's side. "Hey!" he said suddenly. Ran and I headed toward the door. "What was that all about?" the short man went on. The door closed before I heard her answer.

* * *

The next day was clear and bright. Ran borrowed a land-car for us, the ferocious, hill-climbing, snow-ignoring, rock-crumbling kind they use around Issin. A closed car with internal environment—they like having that kind of option at Issin, too. We headed west toward the hills. Not many villages out there, the Issin people said, and what there were were definitely *provincial.* Ran let that pass, since in the capital Issin would be provincial.

It was dull. Two days' ride into the real hills, nibbling packed food and water and exchanging conversation about the environment, mostly on the order of "should we stop and ask questions at this village" and arguments over which direction we should be taking. The hills were pretty much dirt and grass, the sky was uniformly gray, and the occasional sheep herds only served to remind me how far off the beaten track I was. I entirely reversed my pleasure-induced estimate of Ivory made at the wedding banquet. This place *was* provincial. I passed the time recalculating the interest I should be earning on the last payment I made to my nonNet banker.

Some of these villages didn't even have names; they were just six or seven houses clustered together. We had reached the foothills of the Skytop Mountains when a local informant told us he had indeed heard of the village we were seeking, and we were on the right track. Just keep going *up*, he pointed; and the looming range of mountains shivered in the heat from the car's system.

Well, there was a pass, more or less, where he was pointing, and we could take the car most of the way. "*Most* of the way?" I asked Ran. He got that grim look I was beginning to know, and we climbed back into the car without further discussion. Anyway, it wasn't as if I had other plans.

So we walked into Pina's village. It really was Pina's village, too, and one could see why she'd been in no hurry to return to it. In fact, I began to seriously think that she probably hadn't. Sod huts and a lot of clotheslines seemed to make up the main portion of the place. We walked past rows of damp, flapping laundry, while a gaunt woman with a sheet in her hand turned her fixed, unhappy gaze from the clothes to us. "I'd look unhappy too," I said to Ran, my hands in my coat pockets. Her hands were red and worn-looking. "Can we leave her a pair of gloves?"

His mind wasn't on secondary considerations. "If this isn't the right place," he muttered, as though it were a complete sentence. Thematically, it was.

There was a group of men in open fur jackets sitting by a fire. They were playing a game with tablets. "We're looking for Pina," said Ran, into the silence our appearance brought.

"I'm Pina," said a man's voice. He came out of a nearby hut, stooping to get through the door. About fifty to sixty years old, stocky, with a huge knife stuck through his belt. There was fresh blood on his hands. "Beg your pardon, gracious lady," he said, seeing my glance. "I was skinning a jack." He looked to the men at the game and back to us. "Can I offer you mountain tea? We haven't got any tah, it's hard to come by here, strangers prefer it, I know."

"Excuse me," said Ran, "You're Pina?"

"Tregorian Pina, headman of this village."

Ran and I looked at each other. Was this whole thing a mistake? I said, "We're trying to find a woman named Pina. About twenty-five, dark hair—" of course she has dark hair, you idiot, I thought, and went on desperately, "she worked as a sorcerer in the capital for a while—"

"My daughter, you mean."

I hoped very much we meant it. I found myself smiling at the man and he returned the smile.

"You're too late, gracious lady. I welcome you if you're friends of my daughter's, but you've made your trip for nothing, and I must tell you unhappy news. My daughter Katherine died last summer."

The silence seemed to lengthen, and I found that I was uncomfortable and even a little embarrassed. I was ready to leave immediately, but I'd forgotten that Ran never took anybody's word for anything.

"Last summer?" said Ran. "She was not home long, then. It's a pity, since we came all the way from Issin to offer her a contract. We'd heard that there was a sorcerer from the capital here, and thought it would be better to deal with her than with the local talent. Local Issin talent, I mean."

"Yes, I understand she had a fine reputation. I know very little of the trade, myself. I'm sorry you came all this way for nothing, are you sure you wouldn't like some tea?"

"What did she die of?" Ran went on.

There was a long silence. One of the players by the fire grunted. Tregorian Pina said, "It was very quick. Merciful for us all that way. If you don't want to stay—"

"Tell him," said one of the players.

"That's right," said another. "Tell him what your fine daughter who was too good for her village did."

"Tell him," said a third.

The headman's face screwed up. "She was very unhappy. She never thought she was too good for the village, I swear she didn't. She was just unhappy."

"When she came back she talked different," said the first player.

"Had clothes that wouldn't last a season."

"Did you see her shoes? Made of paper, I swear to you."

"Didn't want to do real work."

"Enough!" roared Tregorian Pina. The comments cut short. He glared at them until they sullenly returned, or pretended to return, to the game. "She hanged herself," he said to us. He looked down at his bloody hands. "I've got to get back to work," he whispered. He turned and went back to the hut.

Ran and I stood there for a minute. Then we started the long walk to the car.

It was much longer going back. "When you interfere in someone's life, you have to expect the consequences," Ran had told me a long time ago in connection with this same Katherine Pina. Maybe he was thinking it over in those terms. Or maybe not; maybe he thought that she'd started this chain of events and it was up to her to take care of herself. I can only speculate because we did not talk about it at all on the way back to Issin. Nor did we ever talk about it.

When I wasn't thinking about Pina, I was thinking what a relief it would be to get out of that whole part of the world and offering thanks that we would be back in the capital in a few days' time.

As it turned out I was wrong about that, too.

A siren started to wail as we came in sight of the Issin buildings. Our car rolled onto the dirt road that led to the pond just west of town. As we took the road east, men and women spilled out and lined up just outside the circle of houses. They stood in a knot on the road, about a dozen of them. A good portion, I noted, were tall and male.

I said, "Something's wrong, isn't it?"

Ran did not dignify this observation with an answer.

I said, "I mean, this isn't some quaint custom I haven't heard of . . . is it?"

"I haven't heard of it either," he said quietly.

We rolled to a stop at the knot of people. Ran opened his door and leaned out. "What's wrong?" he yelled, over a strong sea wind. "What happened?"

"Get out of the car," said one of the men.

Ran hesitated. Then he jumped down, slamming his door.

"Both of you," said the man.

I found myself pausing as well. I looked at Ran, he nodded, and I didn't have any better ideas. So I got out.

"We repossess this car in the name of Cormallon," said the man, and he motioned to the others. Two of them climbed in and started throwing out our belongings.

"Hey!" I said. None of this made any sense. Wasn't Ran Cormallon entitled to use Cormallon property? Certainly more entitled than minor-branch provincials! Who did they think they were?

Ran just looked blank. He scanned the faces there and called, "Karn! What's going on?"

Karn hung back, looking embarrassed. Someone said, "Karn doesn't have to talk to you, he's disgraced himself enough by accepting you before."

"Have the decency to leave him alone!" called a woman.

Ran looked at Karn for a moment, then turned and climbed up on the front of the landcar. "I *demand* an explanation," he said.

"Demand? Who are you to demand anything from respectable people?" cried the woman who had spoken before.

"Cheat!"

"Thief!"

"No-name!"

He looked angry at that. "I'm the first in this house and family, and you'd better have a very, very good explanation, because right now I'm wondering how much Cormallon will lose by cutting out a few fishermen."

"First in nothing!" said the woman.

"I'll tell him," said Karn suddenly.

"You don't have to—"

"No," said Karn, "I'll tell him." He came to the front. "We know about you. We know about your cheating the treasury—"

"What?"

"—about your private bank account—"

"There is no private bank account!"

"—against all the customs and laws of the family."

The woman said, "Taking money away from all of us who earn it!"

That met with muttered agreement from everybody.

Ran said, "Listen to me. I don't know where you got this idea, but it's a lie. Why should I have a private bank account? I can take money out of the treasury any time I want."

"We got the idea," said Karn, "from our message-taker, who got it straight from the message-taker at Cormallon main estate."

Ran went pale at that.

"I have to get back there," he said to me. "Now."

"Not in our car," said a man.

Ran said, "I don't want your kanz car. Freighters call in every morning—"

"None that will take you as a passenger—not unless you've got enough gold in your bags. Cormallon won't pay for it."

"If he has gold in his bags, we should take it out. It's ours by right."

Karn said, "Enough—"

Ran was picking up our bags, throwing mine to me. "I don't know what's going on, but I have a right to be heard at Cormallon. I can't believe anything could happen without my being there—"

"Unless the evidence were overwhelming," said Karn. "And they say it was. Do you think Cormallon *owes* you something? Do you think we have to go through needless forms, like the Imperial Courts? When something is clear enough to see in the dark, we don't need to file a report on it to take action. Action's been taken. The disowning ritual's been read—by your own brother and sister—and only a fool would say that could happen without cause."

Ran had been growing paler and paler as Karn spoke. When he said, "disowning ritual," Ran looked as though he'd been punched in the stomach.

"You come here," said the woman who'd done the talking earlier, "in your fine clothes. You disgrace us by reciting the wedding service. You take our property off to who knows where—"

"Enough," said Karn again. His voice was weary.

"In the company of a notorious foreign assassin," went on the woman.

"What?" I said. I glanced at Ran, who still looked sick.

"Poisoner," she said, and spat at my feet. I had the feeling she would have liked to spit higher up.

"I don't—"

"Brin almost *died,*" she said. "He might still."

Brin? It came to me suddenly. The young medical student who sat next to me at the wedding feast. But that was impossible. Poisoning isn't that uncommon on Ivory, but practically everything at the feast had been passed around in communal bowls. It was probably *because* of poisoning that shared dishes were such a tradition. Why blame me . . . then I remembered the little delicacy dish of bird's heads. Little individual plates. I remembered his taking one and popping it into his mouth. . . .

He'd taken a couple of others from my plate, too, when he saw I wasn't going to touch them.

I looked around at the faces of the Issin folk. Someone was probably trying to kill me again, and there was nothing I could say to these people. They were all closed up against me.

"Leave," said Karn very quietly.

It seemed like a good idea. I strapped on my pack and grabbed Ran by the hand and pulled him away. We went toward the north. It was warmer that way.

It was all rather depressing. First Pina, now this Brin. I'd liked him at the feast; he was nice about being seated next to the eccentric foreigner. And then there was Ran. Ran hadn't said a word since we walked out of Issin. I'd never seen him like this, with all the fight taken out of him. It was frightening. Particularly since we were a long way from anyplace I knew how to get to, and minus his endless store of gold coins.

If we just went north, we should end up on the same parallel as the capital, eventually. Maybe in months or years.

We'd tramped a couple of hours when I heard a faint whine behind us. It was the damned landcar. Two Issin men, vaguely familiar, got out and approached. I wondered if killing us without witnesses would save Issin paperwork. "Ran, maybe we should run?" I said. Ran paid no attention. Of course, I'd always been the lousiest runner in my Healthful Sports class on Pyrene, and sometimes when you run it gives people ideas they didn't originally have. . . .

"Theodora of Pyrene?" said the taller man.

"Yes," I said, only because there was no point in denying it.

"We're here," he said, as though he didn't like the words, "to give you a safe ride back to Issin and provide you with passage money for the next northbound ship. When you're in the capital, a Cormallon representative will meet you. I'm to tell you specifically that your services have not been terminated. Cormallon still wants to employ you. Legally it does still employ you. All measures will be taken for your safety and comfort."

Well! I looked at Ran, who continued to be unhelpful. So I considered every aspect I could possibly think of for about ten seconds. But what did this really change?

"I'm sorry," I said. "My employment wasn't from Cormallon proper, but from Ran Cormallon in particular. So I'm ethically bound to stay with him. Thanks anyway. . . ."

He shook his head. "We were told you're a house member, a family employee—"

"Thank you for all your trouble," I said as firmly as I could. "But I'm afraid I have the best understanding of the circumstances of my employment. Safe trip back to Issin."

It must have come out as strongly as I meant it. He shrugged to the other man and they both climbed into the landcar, turned it awkwardly about, and drove away.

I watched them go unhappily. Maybe it was a mistake, but between an unknown reception in the capital and sticking with Ran, I chose Ran. Besides, he was acting pretty strangely—I wasn't sure he could make it without help.

"Well," I said. And started walking again.

He matched his strides to mine. He said the first words he'd come up with since Karn said "disownment." And they didn't sound like a compliment to my intelligence.

"Crazy foreigner," he said.

Chapter 9

Crazy foreigner I may have been, but I know a long walk when I see one. The next few months were an entirely new way of life, and if I made them seem as long in the telling as they were to live through I would have to go on for volumes. The routine was monotonous enough, yet soon the routine was all I thought about, all I anticipated, all I dreamed about. The walk through the southern woods all morning, the rest at noon; then walking till late afternoon, then the stop at the closest village. We kept near the coast, where most of the towns and villages are. Nor did we actually sleep in the villages, that would be asking for trouble—we just showed up at the town hall steps at sunrise, pretending we'd spent the night. Then the hall servants would give out the "indigent's breakfast," and we got our one meal of the day.

It's a custom of the southern towns to discourage vagrants. Anyone who chooses can appear on the town hall steps and get a free meal . . . provided they leave town immediately after. If the village is small enough, the breakfast is whatever was left over from the communal supper the night before. I preferred that; there was usually rice and fish and eggs in the bowl then. When it was a larger town, the hall cook would make up the breakfasts himself, generally tired vegetables and undercooked rice. Seagrass was a big favorite of the town hall cooks. I hate seagrass.

I say "we"—but I was mentally alone in this journey. Ran may as well have been a ghost. It scared me. I'd always had the impression of massive energy in Ran, of a mind with clear purpose, sharp and ready for anything. He'd always been so sure of himself—annoying, but you could forgive it since he was generally right. Now it was as if he weren't there at all. I had to make all the decisions—where to stop, what village to head for, when to rest. I didn't even know where I was going. He was supposed to be the expert, I was the barbarian outlander.

I just didn't understand how a thing like this could throw him so hard. He'd been disowned. I'd walked out on a crèche-family on Pyrene and lost an academic family on Athena, and it didn't mean anything to me. I hadn't even liked the former. Did the simple fact of shared genes make such a difference? It was eerie. It was as if the engine for all that energy and purpose had been Cormallon, and now he had no motive power.

That was Worry Number One. Worry Number Two was the cold. Winter was coming; already the wind was blowing in off the sea and we had to stay well inland, among the trees. The lining of my coat was nothing but tattered strips. I didn't know how we would sleep when it snowed, nor did I feel that one meal would keep us warm and moving through the day. I told Ran everything I was thinking about. (I usually did, during the noon rest stop, and as usual he said absolutely nothing.)

Teshin Village was on a peninsula that extended into a good-sized bay. There were some hills just to the north, and the ocean was about eight kilometers to the east. The village wasn't too big, which was good; I'd picked up some bad feelings about towns because of the lousy breakfasts they served. So one bright morning when the water birds were making an enormous racket, Ran and I walked across the muddy flats by the bay and into Teshin.

And here at last was our one piece of luck: it was the day before a holiday. Tomorrow was Imperial Guardian Venrat's Birthday—which no doubt meant as little to the people of Teshin as it did to myself, but it did mean a day of no work, feasting, and drinking. Which made the day before the feast a day of a great deal of work, planning, and preparation. The village hall was in chaos.

I was rebuffed and insulted by several busy people (a barbarian outlander learns to expect these things) before someone pointed me to Hall Manager Peradon. He was an elderly, stocky man seated at a chipped wooden table in the back of the hall. There was a line of people waiting to talk to him, so I just joined the line. From what I overheard the sole function of these people was to explain to the Hall

Manager why what he had ordered had not been done. By the time I reached him I felt quite sympathetic to the old man.

Still, I hadn't expected to be seized on like a long-lost friend.

"My child," he said to me, "I have just the place for you. Five bakras for the day, and all you can eat."

"I was really looking for something long-term," I said.

"Long-term! This *is* long-term. As long as you like. And if you decide you don't like it, we'll try to move you into something else." As he spoke a little boy with a blue cap was tugging on his arm. "I know, Piece-of-My-Heart," he said to the boy. "Don't joggle me. Tell your mother we have just the person." He looked up at me. "Sign your name here in my book, right next to '5 bakras'—we like to keep everything honest and on record here."

"My feelings exactly," I said, and signed "Coral Passuran."

He turned his book around and peered down at it. "That's a good, sensible name for a barbarian," he said.

"Thank you," I said.

"Just go with little Seth here to the kitchens—tell the Kitchen Chief you're taking Dana's place."

"Thank you," I said again.

Seth led me off to the back of the hall. "Hold on a minute," I said to him. I stepped up onto a bench and peered over the heads in the hall. There was Ran—still waiting by the door. Well, he wasn't going anywhere.

"Mother's in a hurry," said Seth, looking up at me distrustfully.

"Fine," I said. I climbed down.

The kitchens seemed to have even more people in them than the hall itself. Seth led me to a woman in a white apron, a sensible middle-aged woman who reminded me a little of Herel. "Here she is," said Seth.

"Here who is?" said the woman, frowning at me.

"I'm taking Dana's place," I explained.

"Ah!" she said at once, and the frown was replaced by relief. "About time Peradon found someone. The food has to go in the hot-pots *now*. Come over here . . . now, I'm Berta, the Kitchen Chief for the hall. We have three meals a day in the hall, but not like tomorrow, believe me. We're making Cream Hermit Soup, Wine-Steep Runner Stew, good dishes that they don't see too often here, but that'll keep in the pots. I'm sure you're familiar with them."

"Well, not *very* familiar."

"No matter. And the cakes and pies we'll get to later. This is the ledge where we keep the pots . . . the servers will bring them over here to you."

"And I put the food in the pots."

"No, no—Penda and I will do that ourselves, it has to be done right or it won't keep properly." She paused. "You don't know how to do it, do you?"

"No, I'm afraid not."

"Well, then. Stick to your job, stranger, that's all we ask." She raised her voice and yelled at a young man over by a table. "No, no, the *soup* first! The stew can wait! Bring the soup!" She sighed. "You have no idea what it's like," she said to me. "Oh, if you get tired, we can bring over a chair for you."

Just then the first shipment of soup arrived. "Penda!" she yelled, making me wince. A girl in her teens rushed over and they opened the first hot-pot. Berta ladled out a bit of the soup and handed it to me. "Here," she said.

I tasted it. It was a little gamy, but I suppose you have to expect that from groundhermit. "Very nice," I said.

"Thank you," said Berta. "Into the pot, now. Careful, sweetheart." They tilted the huge bowl just far enough, and when the pot was full they pulled down the hinged top and adjusted the metal braces that kept it airtight. "Mark it 'one,' " she said. She raised her voice and turned her face toward a woman seated across the kitchen, on a high platform against the wall. "We're marking it 'one,' " she yelled. The woman waved back.

"Who's that?" I asked.

"The observer, of course." They filled another pot. "We should really put stew in this one," she said to her helper. "It's too big to waste on soup." She filled her lungs and yelled "Stew!" to the world at large, and soon enough someone brought over a bowl of stew. She ladled around in it, sniffing. "Let's get some nice vegetables on it for you," she said. Then she handed me the ladle and I tried the stew.

It was delicious, and I said so. Berta said, "My own recipe. Bet you can't tell there's seagrass in there."

"I couldn't. I usually don't like seagrass."

"Sensible child. Hold the pot, will you? Gently now."

A few bowls later Berta set down her pot and put her hands on her hips. "Are you making fun of me?" she said.

I was taken by surprise. "Who, me?"

"You—tymon—is this your sense of humor, stranger? Why do you keep telling me about the dishes? Are you passing judgment on my cooking?"

"I, uh, no, of course not. But you gave it to me to taste—"

"Of course I gave it to you to taste! You're taking Dana's place!"

A voice called, "Is there a problem?" It was the woman on the platform against the wall. She was standing up now, looking over at Berta and me.

Berta said, "Now we'll have the observer staring at us the rest of the day!"

"Look, I'm sorry," I began. Then I stopped. All right, I can be stupid sometimes—but remember, I'd been on the edge of exhaustion for days. Here I was, in a communal kitchen among the population of the most suspicious, paranoid planet I'd ever heard of—why would they want somebody to taste the food, now? And pay hard Ivoran money to someone to observe the kitchen workers and see that the pots stayed locked and nobody did anything they shouldn't? I said, slowly, "Do you get much food poisoning here?"

"You *are* trying to insult me!"

"No, please, believe me. It's just that I'm a stranger. Peradon didn't say what my job was, that's all. It's not a problem, really. I don't think. *Do* you get much food poisoning here?"

The girl helping Berta said, "She's just nervous, is all. Well, really, how can we criticize? None of us volunteered to take Dana's place."

Berta said, mollified, "I suppose that's so. I'll overlook it, stranger," she said to me.

"Thank you," I said. After a pause I asked, "What happened to Dana?"

"She's not feeling well," said the helper.

"Oh?" I said.

"But don't worry. She'll be up and around in a few weeks."

"I see."

"Next pot," said Berta, "and try to look casual. I can't stand having the observer watch over my shoulder."

I sought out Ran several hours later. He hadn't moved from the hall door. "Five bakras," I said, jingling the contents of my pocket. He did not appear impressed. In fact, he didn't appear totally conscious.

"Now what we need is a place for the night," I said. "There's no inn, but the Kitchen Chief told me about a family who might have some extra rooms."

He stood up, which suggested he must be paying attention to what I said on *some* level. It didn't seem to interest him, though. Damn. We followed Berta's directions easily enough and they took us to a large house overlooking the village square. I knocked.

The door was opened by a girl of about twelve. She looked at me, then looked at Ran. "Yes?" she said. It was not a proper greeting, even if we did look a shade disreputable. Anyway, we'd washed in the bay that morning.

"Your mistress, please," I said.

"What?"

"Gracious lady Coral Passuran to see your mistress. Please tell her I'm here."

She closed the door gently and went away. A moment later it was opened again, this time by a more matronly figure in a good woolen robe. "I'm the mistress," she said, "Karina Mullet. May I ask your business?" The tone implied that she did not seriously expect us to have any.

"The Hall Kitchen Chief recommended you to us, gracious lady." (It was an adjective I felt it never did any harm to throw in, although she really wasn't quite up to it.) "We're looking for a place to stay."

She seemed faintly disbelieving.

I said, "We can pay three bakras in advance. If it suits, we'll probably want to make a longer arrangement with you."

She said, "Please give me a moment, uh, gracious visitor. I must consult my husband."

Again the door closed. There was no one in the street to watch, so I put one ear up against it. A brief but intense argument was going on inside. I couldn't quite catch most of it, or tell who was on what side, but the word "tymon" was used. Also the word "bakras"—that one mostly by the wife. Probably she was the one on our side, then. "Tymon" was spoken by a male voice. "We'll kill him later," I said to Ran, knowing he wouldn't pay attention. "Tymon": not only a barbarian outlander, but a Barbarian Outlander With No Manners. Most unfair.

I pulled my ear away from the door just in time. Karina Mullet swung it open and stepped back, waving us in. We were greeted in the inner entranceway by respectable husband Mullet, in his houserobe and socks, tobacco falling out of the pouch he was gripping in one hand. He was round-faced, middle-aged, and either a little bit drunk or very ruddy for someone of his dark complexion. Well, if you can't do it at home, where can you do it? I bowed, and jabbed at Ran to do the same—I wasn't sure he would, but his training in courtesy ran deep. I said, "Your hospitality honors us, gracious sir." Take that, name-caller!

He blinked. "Uh," he began.

"You must forgive our appearance, sir, we've had a long journey. We're greatly fatigued. I wonder if we might impose on you to let us see our rooms at once?"

"Certainly we can," said his wife. "This way, up the stairs."

I bowed again to her husband, just to rub it in. "I regret the postponement of our acquaintance until tomorrow."

"Oh. Yes. Me, too." He finally made his return bow. About time, too.

Madame Mullet said, as we went up the stairs, "Will you be wanting one room or two?"

"I suppose two rooms cost more than one," I said thoughtfully.

"Oh, yes, of course." She seemed amused.

"We'll only need one. This is my br—my husband," I said, remembering in time that we looked nothing alike.

I saw her thinking: your br—, your husband—fine. Maybe I should collect the money now.

Sure enough she said, "I wonder if you could give me

those three bakras before you retire? Then we won't have to worry about it in the morning."

I went down an hour later to ask if I could buy a meat pie from her, the market being closed. I still had two bakras left, and Ran hadn't eaten all day.

"Certainly," she said, and heated it up for me as well. "Your friend—I mean, your husband doesn't talk much," she remarked as she set the pie in the oven.

"He's been very ill," I said. "Affected his vocal cords. Nothing catching," I added at once.

"Ah," she said noncommittally. A moment later she said, "Would you like some tah to go with it? No charge, of course."

"Thank you, no," I said. I'd been as addicted to tah as any Ivoran. It had been hard enough getting my body to accept the decline to the one cup a day that went with the indigent's breakfast. If I got used to it again, how would it be later? And Ran's withdrawal pains had been worse than mine.

It's not the addiction; it's the expense. Still, I felt badly, since I knew Ran would have liked a cup.

My hostess took the meat pie out of the oven and wrapped it in waxed paper. Then she put two glasses on a tray alongside the pie. "Water, at least," she said. "The pie's too spicy."

"You're very considerate," I said, and found myself yawning.

She chuckled. "I can't get over your accent." She steered me to the stairs.

"What accent?"

"What accent, indeed. You talk like one of those high-toned nobles that come over the Net from the capital. That's why my man's eyeballs were popping when you said hello."

"I haven't *got* an accent."

She laughed. "Good night, gracious visitor. Don't bother about the tray; you can bring it down tomorrow."

I went up to our room and found Ran sitting on the bed. I handed him the pie and put one of the glasses on the night table.

"If I have an accent," I said, "it's *your* fault."

He raised his eyes to my face briefly, then started eating the pie. He did that sometimes; it could drive you crazy wondering if it meant anything.

I said, "When we've got a few more coins in our pockets, we'll see if there's a healer in this village. I mean, I guess you've noticed that you've got a problem." He went on eating and I pulled off my outer robe and sat down on my side of the bed. "If you've got something to say about seeing a healer, you'd better say it now."

After a minute I said, "I didn't think so."

Sleeping with a ghost is a very chaste experience. In case you wondered. The next morning as I washed at the basin, I heard sounds from out in the square, a voice raised in command and the tap of wood on stone. I looked out the narrow window that faced the street (like all well-planned houses, the good, wide windows of the house faced in toward the inner courtyard, not out on the dangerous world) and saw a dozen villagers, young and old, standing in the square holding wooden staffs. They were doing The River.

I hurried down to see if I could join them. I didn't have a staff, of course, but for Young River and Old that's not so important. I had a pair of trousers I'd not slept in more than twenty or thirty times; they would have to do.

I crept in on the far left of the group, hoping no one would object. The practice leader stopped everyone at once.

"What's going on here?" he said. He was about thirty, light-skinned for an Ivoran, with unexpectedly blue eyes that looked out from under a head kerchief that reminded me of Eln. Like Eln, there was something "off" about him; perhaps it was the coloring. Unlike Eln, he stared at me coldly.

"I'm sorry," I said, since I was the invader, after all. "I was hoping to join you. If this is a private group, I didn't mean to presume."

Someone muttered something that sounded like "tymon."

"Well," said the leader, with pure sarcasm in his voice, "Maybe our gracious visitor would like to lead the group this morning. We'd be honored, wouldn't we, friends?"

I said, "Thank you, but I'd rather not."

"Oh, come now, you can't be so rude. We'd love to see how it's done in the outworlds, am I right?"

There was general agreement. They were enjoying themselves.

So I walked to the front and stepped up to the practice leader's place. "I'll need a staff," I said, and he grinned and gave me his. Then he joined the other villagers.

There was a Middle River set I'd done perhaps five hundred times in the garden at Cormallon, trying for at least one set to achieve grace rather than simple memorization of movement. I could do it in my sleep . . . or I could if I weren't nervous.

I cleared my throat and said, "Middle Six-Eight-Eleven, Six-Eight-Two, Six-Two-Two, and repeat for a dozen. Staff horizontal to begin."

They looked at each other and shuffled around and held out their staffs.

"Now," I said, and went to position Middle Six. I felt stiff and mechanical as I moved through the set. Of course, they were probably surprised to see me do it at all, they may as well see an ape dressed up leading their sa'ret. The hell with them. I closed my eyes and pretended I was back in the garden, with Eln moving over my head. I closed them all out. Third set, fourth set, fifth set. I stretched the movements farther, just to see if it would work that way, and it felt right. I counted eleventh set and twelfth, mildly surprised that we were so far along. Maybe I'd left something out, but never mind, this wasn't as bad as I'd thought.

"And twelve." I opened my eyes. They were standing in a semicircle, sweaty and bright-eyed—probably the way I looked, too.

"Woh!" said one of the men. He laughed.

"I agree," said the woman next to him. She stamped her foot and started to clap. The others took it up and now I felt my face really get hot.

"Hey-oh," said the woman when it died down, "we should have outlanders lead us more often. Tanit always does Young River because he likes it."

Tanit, the practice leader, looked sour.

She called, "So what's next?"

"Yes, what's next?" a few others called.

"I'm just a novice," I said. "I'd really rather learn than lead. If Tanit doesn't mind, I mean."

Tanit shrugged, but I thought he looked rather relieved. He came back to the lead position. I held out his staff, but he said, "Keep it. I can lead without it, and I'll bring you an extra one tomorrow."

He stepped up into place. "Back in line, tymon," he said, but he said it ironically, like someone who's just had the joke on him.

From then on I heard the word "tymon" a great deal in Teshin Village, but it was no longer an insult, it was just a nickname. I didn't mind. By then I'd lived in a lot of places, and been called a lot of things.

Chapter 10

The practice session made me late for the hall breakfast tasting. Luckily not that many people showed up for breakfast on the morning of a holiday; they sleep late and save their appetites for later, or have something cold at their own homes. (The house where I was staying was one of the few in the village with an oven, and the Mullets were pretty snobbish about it.)

I went to Hall Manager Peradon, who was surrounded by even more people than yesterday, and tried to get his attention.

"Manager Peradon," I said finally, "you didn't tell me yesterday what my position was."

He smiled pleasantly. "I'm sure I must have, my dear, you probably weren't paying attention. But I hear you've been doing a splendid job, so just keep it up."

I launched into my speech. "You said that if I didn't like it, I could change to something else. That sounds like a good idea. So I've been thinking: I know I'm not a cook, I know the best jobs go to people who are related to other people. I'm not fussy. I can do scut work, I can sweep the floors—"

"Sweeping floors is only two bakras a day," he said regretfully.

"I'll take it."

The hall master looked down around his feet. "It seems to me the floors are clean enough already—I don't think we need any more sweepers. In fact, I believe the only opening at the moment is the one for Dana's position. And you've been doing such a fine job of it."

I looked at him, unimpressed. He went on quickly, "Although, if you want to expand your duties, help out in the cleaning and such—we could probably find a way to raise you to six bakras a day."

"Seven," I said, to my surprise. I really hadn't planned on keeping this job. But still, seven a day . . . and a clean bed. And I really should get Ran to a healer, the sooner the better.

"For you, flower petal, we'll make it seven."

I couldn't help returning his smile, the old crook. But I remembered to add, "Paid each night in coin."

"You can't wait till the end of the week like everybody else? Trust your Uncle Peradon. You can't have any safe place to keep it, staying at a place like Mullet's, and I'm the village banker."

Did everybody in the village know where the tymon was staying? Probably. "Once a night," I said. "Be reasonable—I might not be around at the end of the week to enjoy it."

He grinned—probably just what he'd been thinking. "So be it, child, but you're tearing the meat from my heart."

"Thank you, Uncle. Meanwhile, I was wondering if there's a healer in Teshin?"

"Not in Teshin," he said, "but in the hills just outside. It's not a half hour's walk to his house, and he's as fine as anybody in the capital. Have little Seth show you the way this evening after work, if you like."

"I will. Thanks."

"My pleasure. Seth won't want more than a bakra, either."

Peradon went back to his account books, probably a very different set from the one he kept on the Net—if he kept any on the Net at all, which was a doubtful matter.

Seth took us out to the hills that evening. It was a clear, starry night, with one moon showing as we circled the edge of the bay and made our way north. Wind blew through the grass.

"He cured my mother of arthritis," announced Seth.

I looked over at Ran, his face lit by moonlight, and wondered if the healer could do anything with a case like this. Maybe I was expecting too much. A Tellys psychiatric ward was the more likely place to go for help, but under the circumstances that was a little far away.

"What's the healer's name?" I asked Seth.

"Here we are," he said, and pointed to a hut in a clump of trees, halfway up the hill, facing the bay.

We climbed up to the door. Seth knocked. "His name is Vale," he said suddenly, pulling off his cap.

The door opened. A man of about fifty standard years stood there, thin, balding, looking like a breeze would carry him away. Delicate and birdlike, as though his bones were hollow.

His glance took in Seth, the tall stranger in the expensive but tattered clothing, the short female barbarian. An eyebrow was raised very gently and a smile passed over his face so quickly I was never sure if I'd seen it or not. "Can I help you, travelers?" he said.

"I don't know," I answered. "My friend . . ." I made a vague motion toward Ran.

"You'd better come in," he said.

Inside there was a clean wooden floor and a brick hearth. A striped cat was sleeping by the fire, and I paused when I saw it. "What's the matter?" asked Vale. Sharp eyes, I noted, and I wasn't sure I liked that.

"It's nothing. I'm allergic to cats," I said.

"Not this one," he said.

I'd had to use the Ivoran phrase "I have an aversion to," since they had no word for allergy, and I wasn't sure that we'd managed to communicate here. Possibly he only meant that his own cat was a likable creature. However, in all the time I spent in that hut—and as it turned out, I spent a lot of time there—I never sniffled or sneezed. And the last time I'd had to stay in a room with cats I'd felt my nose turn into an ever-expanding faucet, my eyes tear, and I'd left the home of my Athenan friends wishing I could bury my head in the dirt and just die.

Vale led Ran to a mat beside the fire and offered him a cup of tah. Then he watched Ran while he drank it. Seth and I sat in a corner and waited.

The firelight flickered over them. Vale helped Ran to lie on the mat, then knelt beside him. His hands moved quickly, lightly, over Ran's chest, shoulders, legs, feet. He cupped a hand on Ran's forehead. He pulled his ears and peered inside. Then he tapped him affectionately on one shoulder and helped him up again. That final touch was not diagnostic, but meant as reassurance, and was my first inkling of the many differences between healing outworlder style and healing Ivoran style.

Then he pulled off Ran's boots and examined the soles, leading me to wonder if I'd brought Ran to a sane man.

"Yes," he said. He turned to me. "Now, please tell me why you've come."

"He doesn't talk," I said.

"Maybe he has nothing to say."

"Look," I said, and started to get up. Vale raised a hand.

"Please humor me." He smiled. For the first time I realized that this was a being of great personal charm, when he cared to exercise it. No wonder the Teshin villagers thought he was great stuff. Take care, Theodora, I thought.

He said, "This happened all at once? The not talking?"

"Yes. He'd had a shock. He heard something bad, and the next thing I knew he was like this."

"No words at all?"

I flushed. "Well, he called me a name. But he hasn't said anything since."

Vale nodded. "He is a sorcerer, is he not?"

Taken by surprise, I said nothing.

Vale said, "Seth, you will wait outside."

The boy left. Vale came over and knelt in front of me. "He is clearly a sorcerer."

"Probably. You're the expert."

He said, with a touch of irony, "I am if you will let me be." The cat came over from the hearth, and Vale leaned back on his heels to make a lap for him. He stroked the cat's fur and said, "This is more than shock, I think. Does your friend have enemies?"

"Doesn't everybody?"

"Some of us more than others. I think that someone may have tried to hurt your friend. It may be worse than you know . . . it's hard to say. It's good that he called you a name, at least. A hopeful sign, that."

"Can you do anything for him?" At last the question. I wasn't sure I wanted the answer.

"Maybe. I'll need to make an examination."

"I thought you just did that."

"I just introduced myself. He knows I'm here and I'm a friend. He learned a little about me and I learned a little about him. The examination will take longer, about an hour."

"All right."

"In private."

I said, "No."

He knelt there, petting the cat. Then he said, "Would you like a cup of tah?"

And one cup of tah and some polite conversation later, I found myself waiting outside on the hill with Seth.

Seth said, "Do you know any stories?"

"No, do you?"

We sat in the grass under the trees. The wind shook the branches, and I wrapped the coat around me tighter. Luckily it was warm for the time of year, and the wind wasn't the enemy it would become in a month.

"I know lots of stories," he said. "I thought you'd have a new one. Being an outlander."

"Well, I can't think of any right now. You tell me one."

I said it because I wanted to think, but he went ahead and told a wonderful, harrowing, magical story about Kata the Mother of Soldiers and the evil Emperor of the tenth dynasty. I wished I had a notebook with me. From time to time I looked back at the hut where a suspicious-looking green glow seeped through the door frame.

"He'll be all right," said Seth once, interrupting the fight between the Clay Soldiers and the Emperor's griffin.

"I hope so."

"Vale's the best, everybody says. He's been here as far back as I can remember."

Seth was maybe all of ten. "Don't stop the story," I said.

He finished the story, and I applauded and stamped one foot against the side of the hill. Seth ducked his head. "You're a prince of storytellers," I told him.

"Don't make fun," he said.

The door to the but opened. "Come in," said Vale.

We went inside. Ran was sitting by the hearth, the striped cat leaning against him.

"I don't know," said Vale. "I'm sorry to give you an answer like this. I do know that it will take time."

"What's *wrong* with him?" For the first time I felt ready to cry.

"Shock, as you said. But that was just the stimulus. His life-force has been blocked."

" 'Life-force'—oh, really, what garbage! I didn't come out here and sit on your damned hill to hear about kanz like a life-force. I thought you could help." I grabbed Ran's hand and pulled him up. "Come on, Seth."

Vale stepped in front of the door. "*Listen* to me. He's a sorcerer. He draws on magic for his energy. Now he can no longer touch that source of power."

I said, "Get out of the way."

"Think a minute. I haven't even mentioned a fee yet, have I? Do I have something to gain by lying to you?" He said, in despair, "What is it about you foreigners that you can't see magic when it's in front of you?"

That made me pause. I remembered the jokes my Athenan friends and I had made about magic on the liner voyage out. My judgment of the situation had changed a great deal since then. I'd had to accept the reality of a lot of things I hadn't quite approved of . . . was I going to maybe wreck Ran's last chance because I didn't like the way Vale talked?

Then it hit me. *Blocked.* Ran's source of magic was blocked—and it was really Ran's ability to read cards that I used for his benefit, thanks to the curse. Except that I hadn't been able to read the cards for months.

Vale was watching me. He stepped away from the door. "I can help him," he said, "maybe."

"What do you want to do?" I asked.

"Bring him here every day. I'll work to wear away the blockage—it has to be done little by little, and he has to help me."

"He can't even help himself. He's been like this for months, he doesn't care what happens to him. I could have left him in the woods and he wouldn't have lifted a finger to stop me." What's more, he seemed supremely uninterested in this conversation now.

"Oh, he's not quite as na' telleth as all that." Vale smiled. "He cared enough to call you a name. And you cared enough to remain hurt by it for months."

I could really learn to dislike Vale.

"Need another cup of tah?" he asked pointedly.

"All right, you win. I'll bring him back tomorrow evening."

"Morning," said Vale. "Drop him off on your way to work." And as I left the hut with Seth and Ran, he added, "And if you experience any abdominal pains connected with your new job, see me immediately."

I hadn't mentioned my work. Apparently even the recluse outside of town knew what the tymon was doing.

Winter on Ivory is officially equal to five standard months. Which is really just saying that five standard months is equal to one-quarter of the Ivoran year. In real life, winter defines itself, and along the southern coast it blows in fiercely and stays for half a standard year, at the very least. I was glad to have settled in Teshin before it came in earnest.

I dropped off Ran every morning and went by after work to pick him up again, jingling my seven bakras all the way. (Seven bakras minus two bakras a day for rent and one for food—since I got all the food I wanted on the job, I only needed to pay for Ran—left four bakras to accumulate under the loose floorboard in our room. Which came to a total of three tabals profit per week, not bad compared to the nothing we had before entering Teshin.) As I waited for Ran in the evenings, I saw that a number of villagers made their way to and from Vale's hut.

Most of them seemed pretty healthy. I passed Hall Master Peradon once on the way down the hill, and asked him about it. "Well, of course," he said, "you don't want to climb up this hill when you're sick, do you? The whole point is not to get sick."

I thought Peradon was the last visitor of the day, so I went right up to the door and knocked. Usually I respected Vale's wish not to be disturbed when he was with someone.

"A moment," called Vale. He opened the door. "Oh, it's you, tymon. You'll have to wait a bit, I'm with someone right now."

Behind him, on the mat by the fire, I saw one of the young fishermen lying with his shirt off. His head was resting on his arms. As I stood there he turned his face to the door and called lazily, "Oh, she can wait in here if she's cold. I don't mind."

Vale bowed and motioned me inside. I sat down in a corner where Ran was waiting for me. The cat was in his lap.

Vale knelt down by the fisherman and placed his hand gently in the center of the man's back. Then he closed his eyes and breathed quietly. A moment later he knelt up higher, bent over the body on the mat, and began moving his hands down the sides of the back, a few inches from the spinal column. It was some form of massage. I watched the procedure for about forty minutes. He did the back, the legs, the rump, the feet; then rolled the man over and worked up from the feet to neck and face. He did not spare the area around the pelvis, which caused me to look away into the darkness of the hut for a few minutes and try to stop the redness I was sure was covering my cheeks. He worked cheerfully but quietly, and I didn't know what to think; it was by no means impersonal, but it wasn't sexual either. I wasn't used to seeing physical contact that didn't fit into one of those two baskets.

When he was finished, the man just lay there on the mat for a few minutes while Vale brewed tea. "Not tah," said Vale to me, when he offered me a cup, and the fisherman sat down beside us with his. "You shouldn't have tah just after a session. It overstimulates the system. And as for you, little tymon, you've drunk more tah in your time than is good for you—I can tell from the color of the whites of your eyes."

I peered into the shininess of my cup, trying to make out the whites of my eyes. As far as I could tell, they were fine. "That was interesting to watch," I said to Vale.

The fisherman—his name was Pyre, and I came to know him very well over the next few months—grinned at me and said, "Interesting to do, also."

I asked, "You really liked it?"

"Why would I come three, four times a week if it were boring?"

"Pyre is one of my more enthusiastic clients," said Vale. "But given the things he asks of his poor body, it's no wonder."

"I'm a chakon dancer," explained Pyre.

"I thought you were a fisherman."

"I'm a fisherman the way you're a poison-taster, tymon.

It pays me through the winter." He finished his tea and poured another cup, topping mine off as he did so. Pyre was of middle height, brown-haired, and wiry-looking. It was only when his shirt was off, as it had been a few minutes ago, that you saw the well-defined muscles of his arms.

When he'd left, I said, thoughtfully to Vale: "I wish I could do something like that. It's a simple thing, but he left happier than he came in, I'll bet. And when it comes to really helping another person, it's usually a pretty hopeless task."

"You could do it if you wanted to."

"Ha."

Vale said, "Yes, it is a simple thing, and like many simple things it takes years to learn. But it's like The River that way; you can learn the basics quickly, and then you let your clients teach you. That part only takes a lifetime."

"I've got several months."

He laughed. "It will have to do, then," he said.

"Come on, Vale, don't sell me kanz instead of a calf. I'm clumsy, that's just the way I am. I accept it. I can do other things."

"You can do this thing, if you want to."

"I'd better be taking Ran home now," I said.

"Wait," said Vale, and he called out, "Ran, would you mind picking up the dishes and helping me carry them to the bucket?"

Ran got up, came over to the low table, and began lifting the cups. I stared. ". . . Ran?" I said, tentatively.

"Not yet," said Vale. "He's not all the way back yet. But he's watching. I think it does him good to be here when the different clients come. The fluctuations in the energy fields draw him out."

Vale would *say* things like that just when you thought he was beginning to make sense.

"Think about it," he said as we left. "I haven't had a student in two decades, and it would do some of my clients well to have a different touch."

"Different, yeah," I muttered, as I led Ran down the hill. He almost tripped over a groundhermit hole, and I said, "Fluctuations in the energy fields, my maiden aunt."

* * *

But in fact he did seem better, and could respond to simple requests although he still wouldn't initiate anything. I thought about that, and I thought about not living enough in my body, whatever that may mean, and decided that a course with Vale might be good for me. It's hard to explain; it's not that I was looking forward to it, it's not as though I thought I would enjoy it; it was more like going for a blood test because it's a necessary thing to do.

So I knocked on Vale's door a few days later and said, "Maybe I'm interested in learning from you after all. Let's talk about money, Vale."

He said, "Sir or Teacher, not Vale."

I said, "You like to keep your relationships clear on this planet, don't you?"

He smiled and gestured me inside.

Chapter 11

Money was, of course, the first concern. I found that Vale expected me to appear on his doorstep first thing in the morning, and work through the evening. "It's the only way," he said. "You told me that you have just a few months."

"It's the only way to starve," I said. "What am I supposed to do without the coin I get from the kitchens? And how am I supposed to pay you?"

"You can't afford me, so don't worry about it. When I see a penniless barbarian working her way up the coast in clothes like yours, I really don't expect her to meet my tuition."

I said, suspiciously, "So you're not charging me? This is free?"

"It is not. It's only deferred. When I see a penniless barbarian in the company of a high-level sorcerer—in clothes that must have cost him a great deal once—I suspect she may one day come into better fortune." He added, "Especially when the sorcerer is Ran Cormallon. I saw him in the capital once."

I stared.

"A most impressive young man. We'll speak no more about it, though. Here is your mat—you see I've gotten you your own, and I expect you to keep it clean."

"You never said anything."

"I had nothing to say. On the floor now, and I'll show you the proper beginning positions. Kneel down, back straight, weight even—"

I did so. By the time the day was over, my knees and arms and calves and buttocks all knew they had been through a great deal more than they had ever expected. I had also settled with Vale that he would pay four bakras a day to me to make up for my loss of income, at an interest rate of twenty percent, compounded weekly. He said it would be unethical for me to charge money to any of the clients I would be working on, since I was only an ignorant apprentice. I asked if twenty percent interest struck him as unethical, and he said no.

I ate, breathed, and slept work for the next few months. When I wasn't practicing at Vale's, I was studying body charts in the room at Mullet's. I had to give up The River in the morning, I was too exhausted; studying with Vale was more physically demanding than I'd dreamed, and a second workout on top of it was more than I could handle. But I learned what I set out to learn. I'd come to this place a well-trained scholar, with, as Vale later said, a soul that needed a good turning-out; and had spent my time studying the crueler arts of Ivory instead of the kind ones. I had barely noticed there were kind ones. And if I had, I wouldn't have expected them to be this complicated.

Tinaje was what I was studying; Vale gave me a choice from three forms of touch healing: Bratelle, Perthes, and Tinaje, in descending order of roughness. Tinaje was the gentlest. That other stuff *hurt.* "They're very popular," said Vale. "Not with me," I said.

So Vale let his clients know that he had a tinaje apprentice, should they want free sessions, and many of them did. The most accommodating was Pyre, who showed up every day, and sometimes twice a day.

As he lay there on his stomach, Vale would walk around me while I worked, pulling my legs back and tapping my back unexpectedly with just enough force to make me bend the way he wanted.

"That's better," he said.

"But this way all my body weight will be on him!"

"Exactly," he said.

I said to Pyre, "Doesn't it hurt?"

"Nooo," said Pyre smugly.

"You're a feeble little barbarian," said Vale. "He's a big healthy boy. Don't be so timid."

After Pyre had left, Vale got out his charts and lectured me on the incomprehensible nature of Ivoran energy-flow theories. As far as I could tell he considered the body as practically imaginary, a convenient peg for dealing with the actual human condition, which he called "energies in flux." ("We'll save the muscle groups and rib counts for later," he told me. "Were you Ivoran, I'd begin with those. But we start with the most alien system first.") I really didn't know how to accept this sort of thing, which seemed firmly grounded in folk-belief. But I decided that Vale was the Teacher, I was there to learn, and I'd make up my mind later when I'd gathered enough experience. Meanwhile, if it worked, it worked . . . an acceptance system which had weathered me safely through Ivoran thought to this point.

I sat there thinking despairing things about the length of time it would take to learn these theories. Each chart was full of complex diagrams, and there were dozens of charts. I'd thought I was doing well to get the strokes and pressures down.

"All right, tymon, lie down," said Vale.

"What?"

"On the mat," he said patiently. "I'm going to demonstrate the fire lines and the major points. We'll do legs and back tonight."

"On me?" I lay down and pulled up my shirt. Mostly tinaje is done clothed, but the lower back is often bare-skin.

"Who else is here to demonstrate on? Besides, you look as though you haven't been touched very much."

"What's that supposed to mean?"

"My, look at those back muscles tense up. Now: Fire line one, the Point of Gathered Thunder."

He did it, he said, a little deeper than was necessary, almost perthes rather than tinaje, and when I got up I could see why. I could still feel the pathway tingling down my back and legs. It would be hard to forget, at least for the rest of the night, and I could review the points on my way home. Or so he suggested.

But in fact on the way home I ran into Seth, who'd come up the hill earlier on an errand for Hall Manager Peradon, and I let him tell me another story about Annurian the Outlaw and his band in the Northwest Sector. There seemed to be a lot of stories about Annurian, he was a popular legendary figure in the provinces. There were at least three Annurian tales in my new notebook (purchased for half a bakra after much soul-searching) and Seth said he knew dozens more. When I got back to Mullet's rooms, I should have studied the tinaje points, but instead I scribbled down Seth's tale and then lay awake dreaming about an adventurous life in the Northwest Sector. But doubtless such are the dreams of all provincial apprentices.

I was a few weeks into my training when one unusual thing happened. Vale sent me to see a client of his who was too old to come to the hut himself. But he was a connoisseur and hard to please, said Vale, so I was to do my very best.

"Won't he mind taking tinaje from an apprentice?" I said.

"Not at all," said Vale, which surely had to be a lie.

So I found myself on the ferry that made the once-a-week crossing to Kado Island, in the middle of the bay, on my way to see Curran Lormer . . . which was his name, I found after much digging, although the only thing the villagers ever called him was the Old Man of Kado Island.

The ferry was an actual little steamer, down-at-the-heels and elderly, but still a cut above the boats Teshin usually used. There were about fifteen people on it besides myself. I hadn't expected so many would have business on the island, but there were twenty or thirty families living there, and I suppose many of them had weekly errands. The boat would make two trips back, one at noon and one at sunset, taking care of everyone, inbound to out and outbound to in. But if I missed the sunset run, I would be stuck for a week.

We docked in the little inlet at the foot of the hill. A long series of wooden steps led up the hill to the blue sky above, and that was all one could see of Kado Island. As I stood on the dock, I saw two men in fisherman's trousers and jackets making their way down the steps, the wind whipping the trousers against their legs, scarves tied around their caps to keep them on. As they came closer, I saw they were gray-haired, with wrinkled, leathery faces. They smiled and nodded to me in passing, and headed for the boat. "Excuse me!" I called. They turned and bowed, their hands stuffed in their jackets. "Can you tell me where to find Curran Lormer?"

They looked at each other. "I am sorry?" said one. They

seemed polite but faintly off-balance, as though to say to each other, well, one can't expect a foreigner to make sense.

"Curran Lor—the Old Man. The Old Man of the Island."

The smiles broke wide. "Yes, of course," said the first man, relieved I spoke the language after all. They directed me over the hill and down to the island settlement. I thanked them and they bowed and hurried off to the boat, talking excitedly to each other about this encounter with the cosmopolitan.

I couldn't have missed it anyway. There were over a dozen cabins in this settlement, with wells, livestock, dogs, and children. Everybody knew the Old Man; they were thrilled to show off their knowledge to an outlander. An old porch with peeling paint and soft floorboards led up to the door of the cabin. Wooden wind chimes hung from a string above the doorpost.

I knocked. "Gracious sir?" I called. He might be hard of hearing.

He opened the door slowly. He was indeed very old, and pale-skinned. He was stocky, with alert black eyes, totally bald, and wearing a thick green robe with an orange undertunic. And he was short! He wasn't much taller than I was. "Curran Lormer?" I asked.

"Yes. And you are the little tinaje artist?"

Little, indeed—that was nice, coming from him. "Coral Passuran," I agreed.

So our relationship began with a lie. However, at the time, I thought I was the one who was lying.

He was a restful person to do tinaje for. He knew exactly what he wanted and needed, having dealt with Vale for at least ten years, and was willing to direct me when I asked for it. He was very tolerant. Looking back on how little I knew at that time, I realize that he must have been. He told me that he was in the last stages of hemgee poisoning, given him by an old enemy many years ago. He kept it at bay through herbal treatments and touch healing, but it was gradually winning.

"So my fire lines need especial attention, little one," he told me from the mat on the floor.

Poor man, I could see why he chose tinaje rather than

the other arts. For all he looked so stocky and vigorous, I could barely lean against him without feeling the delicacy of his bones and seeing him wince. His skin had the texture I came to associate with the very old, at least on this planet; it was gray-looking in the cabin, under the two candles that were our only light source.

"Where are you from, little one?" he asked.

I pulled his pendant out of the way. "Here and there," I said. I didn't like the idea of putting this much force on his body. Vale had taught me to lean over and let my weight to do the work, and not be afraid . . . but he also said that every case was different. Well, this was my decision then: I put one foot on the floor in a genuflection position, and rested some of my body weight on my own knee.

He didn't seem in as much pain after that. "Do they do tinaje differently in the land of Here and There?" he asked.

"Oh, much the same." I worked down the dorsal fire lines. "How could it dare be different, when Ivory is the center of the universe, and Teshin the center of Ivory?"

There was a rumble in his body, like a subdued chuckle. "You're not content in the provinces, are you?"

I grunted. An honest answer to that would be insulting. I said, to change the subject, "Do you know any stories?"

And he told me a story, and because it will tell you a little about how Ivorans regard the hill-healers, I will repeat it here.

The Tale of Two Families

There once was a healer named Old Kenthik, and he was a member of the family Solovay. They were enemies with a family named Davis, a very old and respected family indeed, who lived just next door. The Solovay men came to the Davis house and said that they wanted to make peace, because they all lived in a town on the coast (but bigger than Teshin) and wanted to combine their shipping line with the Davis one. So they agreed to pay the Davises a face-price of two hundred bolts of silk and eighty oil jars. After the Davises collected the payment, they called peace and invited the Solovays to a feast. All the important Solovay men came to the feast, including Old Kenthik, who was invited down from the hills. After the first course was served, Old Kenthik became ill and vomited on the floor, which was embarrassing because they had an Andulsine carpet of intricate design in the banquet hall. So he apologized and went out to be sick in the garden. But one of the Solovay women was walking in the garden next door, and she looked over the wall because she was curious about what was going on at this party she hadn't been invited to. And she saw Old Kenthik being sick under the rose bushes. And she said to herself, Old Kenthik's done The River every day of his life for the last fifty years, and his body is a friend of his. So she sent a note over to her young husband that said, "Husband, you've been poisoned." And her husband went carefully around to his relatives and told them so. One by one they excused themselves for some air, and went into the garden and made themselves vomit out the poison, and the young wife passed their knives and short swords to them over the wall. And when each one came back to the party he was armed. Then the young husband gave the signal, and they fell on their hosts and killed them, and set fire to their house. When the neighbors heard the noise, they came to investigate, but seeing the bloody weapons in the hands of the men, they were too timid to say anything. And the men said, "Go back to your homes, good neighbors. This is not because of anything you've done, and it's not because we're angry with you. It's just one of those things that happen because we are in this world."

"Well," I said to the Old Man, "that's a good story. I'll write it down when I get back to Teshin."

"It's not the real ending," he said. "The real ending's that the Imperial Police used to collect bribes from the Davises every week, and they resented the Solovay family for what they'd done. So every male in the family cleared out of town overnight and ran off to the Northwest Sector."

"Northwest Sector . . . say, do you know any Annurian stories?"

"Dull stuff," he said, and then he said "ahh," because I was going to work on his feet.

"I like them," I said, disappointed.

"I like true stories . . . I'll bet *you* have a story," he said. He grinned and wiggled his toes.

I gave the soles of his feet a gentle slap. "Dull stuff," I said.

"Dull," he repeated lightly. "You know, that's why I like the provinces. Someday when you're old and white-haired, you'll be glad for a place where nothing happens."

When the session was over, I thanked him as was customary for being so good as to trust me and took the sunset ferry back to Teshin.

"Name," Vale would say to me these days, as he demonstrated a certain point on the tolerant corpse of Pyre. "Soft Rain," I would say. "Line," Vale then said. "Earth," I replied. "Organ," said Vale. "Liver," said I. "Poisons which affect," said Vale. "Hethra, genroot, tiril . . . that's all I can think of." "Treatments," snapped Vale, who didn't like to see hesitation. "Liquids. Red tah and crushed tannis seeds. No purgatives." Then he would either make me do it all again, while I wondered what I'd missed, or he'd move to the next point and say: "Name."

We did anatomy at the same time, which at least I understood. Vale would have me count down the ribs and show what point was at what intercostal space, where the pericardium was, what to look for where the rib cage ended. By now I firmly grasped the fact that I'd gotten into a lot more than I'd bargained for when I decided to study with Vale. Before this I had never considered the knowledge of five hundred kinds of poisons and the proper treatment of stab wounds to be part of general health maintenance, whereas in Vale's mind it seemed to be what every young girl should know.

It was a relief to have the stories to look forward to. The clients always offered to leave me money, which I had to refuse, and I often said, "But if you have a story to tell, I'd like to hear it." Vale didn't mind, because he got to listen. There's nothing an Ivoran likes more than a story, and the blank pages in my notebook were growing few. I was beginning to think: This could get you a doctorate back on Athena . . . there's no point in thinking of your years here as wasted.

As for Ran: I saw no difference, but Vale told me to keep close to him at all times. He was heading for some kind of crisis, and it was important—so Vale said—that he come out of it in as gentle a fashion as possible. So I even took Ran with me on the ferry to Kado Island once a week, and let him sit on the porch while I did tinaje for the Old Man.

It was very late in the winter on one of my weekly visits, when I stood on the dock and saw the two gray-haired polite men who'd directed me to the cabin on my first trip. They were making their usual way down the steps, trousers flapping back from their legs, smiles for me and Ran as they passed. They had to wait for one of the ferrymen to do something with the plank, and as they hung back one of them approached me. "You know," he said confidentially, "he's Annurian."

"I beg your pardon?"

"Our Old Man," he said, with the same insane smile. "He's Annurian."

"*Vathcar* Annurian?" I said, for lack of anything else.

He nodded. "He thinks we don't know. But everybody knows."

"Annurian is a historical figure," I said, although actually I wasn't sure. Maybe he was a legendary figure. But in any case, he certainly lived a long time ago.

"He is, of course, historical. He retired thirty years ago. It was thirty years, was it not?" He appealed to his companion, who nodded.

Seth had never actually told me when his stories were supposed to have taken place. I'd only assumed it was a thousand years ago.

"It is, of course, an honor," said the other man, and they both hurried onto the boat. I wasn't sure what was an honor, talking to me or harboring a famous fugitive on their little island.

If he was, technically, a fugitive. Annurian: The leader of a raider band in the Northwest Sector that drove the Emperor crazy for years. That was the time that most of the stories were set in, the outlaw years. Later he was captured and sentenced to the Imperial Army. He worked his way through the ranks and, very likely, arrested many former colleagues; ending as Chief General and later Prime Minister. It was a Cinderella story, bloody but Ivoran.

"Gracious lady!" called a voice.

I turned. A few feet away, over the water, the man I'd just spoken to called, "Don't mention it, gracious lady! I don't think the new Emperor likes him."

It was probably just a story. I told myself that as I walked up the hill with Ran. Suddenly I froze. I remembered moving the Old Man's pendant out of the way when I worked; I didn't have time to think about it at the time, my mind being mostly concentrated on the tinaje and partly on the Old Man's stories; but I remembered the feel of it now as though I were holding it at that very moment. It was warm, warmer than body heat should make it; and it was carved from that favorite material of the Cormallon library, the material that best held psychic memories—what was an old man living in poverty doing with a bluestone pendant?

What did that prove? It proved Curran Lormer was a very suspicious fellow, that was all. It proved he had more of a past than the rest of the people on Kado Island. As for anything else, it was impossible to say . . . no, it wasn't. He couldn't be Annurian. Where was his tattoo?

At once I was relieved, reality was restored. Although, when I started to think about it, I realized I'd never seen him full-faced in the sunlight. Only by the light of two cheap candles in a dark cabin . . . and we could assume that his tattoo would have faded over the years.

"Come in, little artist," said the Old Man when I knocked.

"Who's little?" I asked, because he liked that kind of thing. But I was sad to see when I entered that he was even more tired and shrunken looking than usual. That was the way it was over the last few weeks; the poison eating away at him.

I had to do the tinaje more softly and carefully than ever. His skin was unnaturally warm. As I finished the neck and head I tilted his face gently to the right . . . and there it was, in the flickering candlelight, a faint gray over the lighter gray-white of his cheek: the letter C.

His eyes moved up to meet mine. "Well, little artist," he

said calmly. Upside down like that, the friendliest face can look threatening. "Did you see what you wanted to see?"

"Pardon?"

"Didn't anyone tell you, tymon of mine, that a fine intuition develops between people who work on tinaje together? I felt what you were thinking then, like a cold gust of wind."

"What I think is dull stuff," I said carefully.

He said, "You're a novice. It takes years to learn the craft, but you show promise or I would have sent you back to Vale. Let's not cut your career short, you and I, with a misunderstanding."

By all means, let us not.

He went on. "I'm an old man, the oldest man on Kado Island. But I sleep with a knife under my mat, and a short sword over the door post, and if you think you could get to either of them faster than I could, I can only say—you are wrong."

"I see."

The neck muscles under my hands were very tight. I wondered what would happen if I closed my fist around his throat. The outcome looked uncertain; he was old, but I was a feeble barbarian. "So the question is, my friend, are you going to go back to the capital and tell anyone where I am?"

"Would you kill me if I said that I would?"

"Most certainly."

"In that case," I said, "I won't mention it."

The neck muscles relaxed, and he laughed. "Oh, my dear barbarian. If we can't trust someone who's done tinaje with us through the whole cold winter, whom can we trust?"

I made the ferry crossing in a daze. When we docked, I took Ran with me to the market to pick up some supper, and that's when I got my third shock of the day.

We were walking down the narrow street that ran behind the village hall when I heard voices just around the corner. There was something both out-of-place and familiar about them. I frowned, feeling there was something about these particular voices it was important I should know; then I got it, just as they came round the bend and we were face-to-face with a dozen tourists. Of course they had to be tourists; they were speaking Standard with Athenan accents! They ranged in age from about eighteen to sixty, wearing Athenan clothing with the occasional robe thrown over their thermal suits, and they were talking the sort of non-stop, interested, meaningless jabber that made me home-sick. What could they possibly be doing in a backwater town like Teshin?

By the looks of things they wondered the same about me. A couple of them caught sight of me and halted their arguing colleagues, mostly by pulling forcibly on their clothing, and we stared at each other. "Hello," I said, in Standard.

"Hello," said the youngest, a girl—probably a first year student. Very likely these were her topic relations, and a wealthy group they must be, to afford the Grand Tour. But then, the retirement-age adults outnumbered the younger ones. I'd planned on saving up myself, and taking the sector round to Ivory and Tellys when I was retired; I was willing to save the money and skip Pyrene, the usual third point on the tours.

So here we were. About half the group didn't want to give up their argument, something about provincial art forms, but the other half clustered around me. "Are you Athenan?" asked the girl. She sounded uncertain.

"Legends and Folk Literature," I said, extending a hand.

"You must talk to Clement. He's Cross-Cultural Myths," she said. "I'm Annamarie, and I haven't decided yet."

"We're on a tour of the provinces," put in a boy who looked not too much older than Annamarie. "Clement wants to study the mental structure of the provincials."

"Oh, does he?" I said.

"Their world-view, you know. It's what he's famous for."

Annamarie said, "We're very lucky to have the opportunity of traveling with him."

"Who's your friend?" asked the boy, nodding to Ran.

Meanwhile the man Annamarie had gestured toward when she said "Clement" was raising his voice to his companion.

"Let's face facts, Tom," he was saying. "Our hosts in the capital are one thing, particularly the aristocrats. Abysmally ignorant, of course, but that's hardly their fault. They know how to behave, at least. But we're among primitive people here—you can't expect sophisticated visual expression from them. Of *course* the murals in the hall are representational. Do you think they've heard of Kohler dual-effect abstractionism here? Maybe we should ask one of them. How about that young savage over here?"

He was clearly referring to Ran.

I said to the boy with Annamarie, "He's my guide." Meanwhile I wondered how "Clement" would look staked out on the shore during high tide, when the clickers come out of the water looking for food.

"Oh," said the boy.

Annamarie said, "But listen, this is wonderful! Who would think we'd meet someone from home out here in the middle of nowhere? You *must* come and have dinner with us—we'll be here for three days, you could come any night."

"Where are you staying?" I asked, knowing very well there was no inn in the village.

"We've a boat docked on the bay side of the harbor. It's a wonderful thing, we rented it in the capital. It's got cabins and a kitchen and a big dining room, and it's all *luxurious*," she said in happy awe. With reason; things tend to be a bit more functional back in the schoolroom.

"Clement, really," said his debating partner, "You tell me these things as though you're teaching me something new. I don't expect children to fly. But many of the people here have quite modern minds. Look at the trade suggestion put forth by that fellow in the city—I forget his name, the head of Cormallon."

I felt Ran stiffen beside me.

The man went on, "Quite a sophisticated plan. If we got together privately, I think we *could* pry a few new designs out of Tellys before they got wise to us and cried monopoly. He's right, these things shouldn't be in the hands of governments; governments can't keep secrets, it's not in their nature. And my department could surely use that new scanner system."

"If you say so," said Clement tolerantly. "I stay away from technology, it's not my field. I'll give you this, though, Eln Cormallon puts on one colossus of a welcome party. My insides are still quivering. I'm just not sure," he said, lowering his voice, "that we should have brought the youngsters."

Ran was walking quickly up the street. I started after him.

"Wait a minute, friend!" called Annamarie. "Will you come to dinner?"

"Tomorrow," I said.

"We don't know your name!"

"Coral Passuran," I called, without stopping to think.

Ran was sitting on the bed at Mullet's, muttering. "Eln," he said. "I knew it was Eln. It had to be. I knew it all along."

I was alarmed. Vale had told me specifically that when Ran came out of it, it should be in "an atmosphere of gentle reassurance." This did not seem to fit that description . . . if he was normalizing at all, which was still uncertain.

"Ran? Do you know where you are?"

He looked up irritably. "Mullet's house, in Teshin, a long way away from where we ought to be. You know Eln is behind all this, don't you? I don't know about Kylla."

"Uh, are you aware of how things have been for the last few months? You remember?"

"Naturally." He emptied my pack on the bed. "We'd better start getting ready to move. There's a lot to be done . . . the important thing is not to trust anybody."

He was scary this way. When an Ivoran closes down that circle of trust to exclude his family, it gets awfully confining.

He said. "Take out the cards."

"I haven't been able to get anything from them. I haven't run them in ages."

"They'll work now," he said.

I started to take them out, then stopped. "Look, can we wait a little while on this? It's just . . . they make me nervous right now."

He was alert. "Nervous how?"

"You make me nervous, too."

He relaxed. "Just the jitters. No wonder you're scretchy. Never mind, we've waited this long. Where are your weapons, anyway? They're not in the pack."

I said, "Well, I've got a knife. And there's a hotpencil I stuck under the mat, but it de-energized on the way here."

"Contact weapons," he said with scorn. "I'm talking

about the real thing—the Issin people confiscated my pistols."

"I never had a pistol. They're expensive."

"Really, Theodora, I paid you a high enough salary—"

"I was saving up!"

He raised his hands. "All right, all right." He laid back on the bed, thinking.

After a while I said, "Are you going to lie there thinking all night?"

"Probably," he said.

"Yeah, well, it's good to talk to you again, too." I crawled under the blankets. After a minute I added, "If you can think in the dark, you'd better put out the candle. We pay the Mullets extra for those."

And he put it out, without another word.

When I woke up, he was already gone. There was a note on the bedtable that said: "Running errands. You'll find your wallet two bakras lighter." No signature, because discretion as well as courtesy form the two rivers that run deepest in a Cormallon. In truth I could not actually read the whole message, but I recognized the symbols for "errands" and "bakras" and the rest was self-explanatory.

I washed and went out to the square, where The River was breaking up. I waved to the participants. As I turned the corner out of the square, I looked down the street and saw Ran standing in the shadow of the village hall, talking to a man I'd seen from time to time in The River sessions. He was one of the more disreputable citizens of the village, and I'd picked up the idea (although no one had specifically warned me) that I should avoid his company.

I put it out of my mind and went out to the hills to do my class with Vale. I was at a difficult time in my training; I was somehow supposed to synthesize all the modes of thought and all the physical techniques and anything else I'd picked up on the way into some glorious whole.

"You shouldn't even have to stop to think about it," said Vale, grinning like a shark.

"I can't stand much more of this," I said. "It gets more and more impossible. Each time I think I've made progress you spring something on me that I see at once will mean months of study. I can't win. There's too much to absorb, it takes *years,* Teacher, and you knew that when you let me start."

"Well, well," he said.

"I'm not even a novice! I'm not even qualified to be a novice! I'm still at the beginning of the beginning!"

"Well, never mind that," he said. "I've been doing this for half a century, and I'm just at the beginning of the middle."

"Is that supposed to cheer me up? If you're not an expert, what does that make me?"

"That's not for me to answer," he said. He knelt down beside me. "You have to begin somewhere, tymon, or you'll never begin at all. I don't know what this obsession is with *expertness* you foreigners have. You're not a machine. None of your clients have complained to me, let that be enough for you right now." There was a knock on the door and he sat back on his heels. "That's someone I asked by to test you on. I can ask him to come back later, if . . . is there something else bothering you? You didn't bring Ran today, and you say he's normalized. . . . "

"He is." I sniffled. For a moment there I'd felt the threat of tears, but it was gone now. "Let him in, Teacher. Do your worst."

So he let in the client, age forty to forty-five, dressed like a fisherman but not anyone I recognized. "Where would you begin to work?" asked Vale, so I knew there was a trick somewhere. I looked the client up and down and watched the way he walked—there was something off about it—and asked him to lie down, and observed how his limbs fell when he relaxed. Then I picked up his boots and saw from the soles that he avoided putting weight on the inside of his left foot. So I said to Vale, "Tinther arthritis?" And Vale said, "Don't ask me, ask him." I thought about that and said to the client, "Excuse me, gracious sir, is there anything you would like to tell me before we begin?" And he smiled and gave me a beautifully classic description of tinther arthritis. I traced the twist in his muscle up the leg, and did a little extrapolation to figure where he would have to shift his weight to compensate. I moved up to the shoulders, and put my hand on the knot of muscles by the right side of the neck. "Here," I said.

Vale applauded and stamped his foot on the floor of the hut.

The client grinned at me, upside down. "Not bad for a tymon, I guess," he said.

Vale put me through a lot that day. I was glad when my old friend Pyre came in, last of all. Pyre was tolerant, he would take anything, and I wasn't sure I was up to much. But as I knelt over him something occurred to me. Vale was always telling me to "de-energize my telleth" before I began a session, and I'd always listened with a straight face and thought: De-energize, indeed. I'll begin when I begin.

But I felt wrung out, and didn't want to shortchange Pyre. So I knelt there and calmed myself down and cleared all the trash out of my mind, and told myself to just concentrate on the session. And as I put my hands on Pyre's shoulders he said, "Oh, *tymon*." I felt distant surprise but went on with it and when it was over he said, "You're really getting good at this, aren't you?" With just enough surprise in his voice that I wondered what his previous opinion had really been.

Pyre asked me to work on his hands afterward, because he'd been practicing the hand-walk scene from *Clerina,* the classic chakon theater dance. Vale was sweeping the floor, as he did once a day, trying not to hit the cat. I'd pulled my outer robe off along while back, and Pyre had his shirt still off. We were sitting there on Vale's hearth, laughing comfortably over a story Pyre was telling about his dancing partner, as I held his hand in my lap, putting pressure on the palm muscles. Ran walked in.

We'd been laughing too hard to notice the knock, and anyway my mind was focused on the session. Ran looked us over, and I let go of Pyre's hand. It was the first time since the beginning of training that I felt embarrassed to touch somebody. Ran said, "I came to talk to Vale." I resented his attitude—if anyone ought to understand tinaje, it was an Ivoran—at the same time I wanted to let him know that if Pyre had sexual interest in anybody it was not in women.

Pyre said, "I have to go anyway." He put on his shirt and fisherman's jacket. "I'll see you tomorrow, tymon."

"Tymon?" said Ran, raising an eyebrow. He turned to

me. "You'd best go as well. I want to speak with Vale privately."

If his edict about not trusting anybody was going to extend to me, he was going to hear about it. "Look, if you've got something to say—"

"You'll hear about it soon enough," he said.

Vale spoke up. "I think it's for me to decide if I want to speak privately to your friend. Why don't you wait outside, tymon?"

"Wait at Mullet's. This will take a while." Ran didn't look at me.

Well, so be it. Later he would have to listen to me.

When Ran hadn't shown up within an hour, I went to the Athenans' dinner without him. It would have saved the price of a meal if he'd come along, and that, I told myself, was the only reason I was annoyed.

Their boat was as opulent as advertised. Annamarie met me at the top of the plank. "I'm so glad you came, we're all dying to talk to you."

She took me into the dining hall, which had a long table (high enough for foreigners) and dining couches with satin covers. "Must be hell for the servants to clean," I said, and she responded with a look of puzzlement.

"We've put you next to Clement," she said.

"Thank you," I said, keeping sarcasm out of my voice.

It was a good enough dinner, not half the meal I'd enjoyed at the wedding at Issin, but a few notches above village hall kitchen fare. Wine was passed around freely, but I kept at one glass. Clement did not.

I thought I would have to bring up the work I was doing on Athena, and it had worried me a bit, as many of the details had faded in my mind. However, this was not required of me. Clement told me about his planned article on provincial myths and mind-sets. He told me about his last three articles and last two promotions.

He told me that his wives didn't understand him.

Eventually his chin rested on the pillow of his couch. One of the pleasanter aspects of horizontal dining was that it lulled people like Clement to sleep long before they started sliding one hand up your thigh. After that I could join in the general conversation.

And it wasn't bad. They were pleasant people, on the whole, and I even remembered a couple of relevant points from my experiences on Athena that added to the conversation, and we exchanged anecdotes about traveling on the *Queen* liners. I liked them.

Someone brought up the topic of the University Extended Research Institute, which was trying to open up a branch on Ivory to add to the ones on Tellys and Pyrene. But they couldn't seem to find a building of the proper size for sale, nor could they get a permit to build one of their own.

"Can you imagine," said the man who was telling the story, "the last time they applied, the official at the permits bureau wanted a *bribe?* He wanted five hundred tabals—god only knows what that comes to in dollars."

There was shocked murmuring around the table.

"Not only that," said the man. "The official before that one wanted six hundred tabals."

"They should have taken the second one, then." I finished off the sip of wine left in my glass.

A silence descended on the table.

"Well, they're not going to do any better if they wait," I pointed out.

The man said to me, as though repeating for a child, "It's a *bribe,* you see. He wanted a bribe."

"Yes. I understand the word."

"Are you saying," said a woman slowly, "that we should encourage corruption? Be a party to extortion of this sort? I must say, that's a strange view for an Athenan."

"On Athena it would be a bribe. On Ivory it's business as usual. I don't see the point of sticking to one's personal customs if it means you can't do business with anyone else—I mean, do they want to open a branch here, or not? Because without a bribe—without a lot of bribes, actually—they're just not going to."

Someone said, "But it's *wrong*."

"I don't know," I said. "On Athena you have to tip waiters for good service, and on Pyrene they consider that blackmail. It's just geography. Face it, nobody goes to the bathroom on Ivory without paying somebody else off."

I looked around the table. Annamarie was staring at her plate, embarrassed. Nor was she the only one who seemed uncomfortable. I saw their faces and I just knew that there was no way, no way in the world I was going to get through to them.

I got to my feet. "Excuse me," I said. "I'm afraid I have to leave early. Thank you for the excellent dinner."

There were a number of "you're quite welcomes" and "not at all, not at alls"—but nobody tried to stop me.

I walked down the plank and stood on the dock under the starlight and the crackling torchlight from the boat-deck. Water slapped the side of the dock. I took a long, deep breath of the crisp night air. Then I started back to Mullet's.

Chapter 12

Ran still wasn't back by the time I got to our room, so I went to bed. Nor was he back the next morning. I rose feeling a vague grudge against Ran, Vale, and all Athenan tourists, and tried to deal with a mind and a stomach equally unsettled. By rights I should have gone straight up to Vale's, but some contrary stubbornness kept me in the village. I worked on my notebook, did The River by myself when I thought I could handle it, and talked to Seth about his Annurian stories. I wondered about going back to see the Old Man when the next time came; I'd like to show him how my abilities had improved, but at the same time it didn't seem particularly safe. On the other hand, it would look strange if I didn't show up when I was expected . . . and there was no law that said the Old Man had to stay on the island if he didn't want to. He was probably good with a short sword anywhere.

I remember that day with special clarity. When evening came I went to the early supper at the village hall, saying hello to the kitchen staff before I sat down. Dana the food-taster was back on the job, and better her than me, I thought. The table I chose was already occupied by five women in fisherman's trousers and jackets, but they made room for me courteously.

They were strangers to Teshin and we stared at each other with mutual curiosity. They drank an enormous amount of wine, and spoke and moved with the wide, free gestures of the lowest-class trading families. One was only fourteen, but the others were in their thirties and forties.

I asked them who they were, and they told me they were boatwomen from the Kiris River (in the west) but they'd brought their barges down the Silver to the bay and thence to Teshin. "And what about you, outworlder?" asked the oldest. "Farther from home than we are, I think."

"What makes you think I'm an outworlder?"

There were chuckles at that, and I told them a little of my story—the high points, at least, and I changed Ran's name. There were clucks of sympathy in the right places, and a couple of the women made the gesture disassociating themselves from bad luck.

"Now," I said, "What brings five boatwomen from across the mountains to run the Silver River?"

And they told me, amid much mutual promptings; but since it is not part of my story I will not repeat it here. Anyway, bits of their explanation were highly personal, albeit highly interesting, and I suppose you can take the scholar out of Athena but you can't stop her blushing after you've done so.

It was a more successful dinner, socially speaking, than my previous night of Athenan hospitality. The upshot of it was that the boatwomen gave me their trading address in Bentham City and told me to look them up if things got too hot for me in the capital. Apparently life was a bit looser over the mountains; or, as the oldest said, "It's not the Northwest Sector, but it's as close as you can get and still be legal."

I left the hall feeling less of a clod and idiot than I had since the unfortunate events of yesterday. But as I walked down the street outside I saw Annamarie and the Athenan boy (whose name I never did get straight) walking toward me. It was too late to duck around a corner, so I went on hoping they wouldn't notice me.

"Oh, hello," said Annamarie.

"Hello," I said, still walking. But she stopped, so I had to stop or be openly rude.

"I'm sorry about last night," she said. "I hope we didn't seem too impolite. There was a lot of wine, you know."

"Yes, there was. I'm sorry if I offended anyone."

"No, no, it's we who should apologize, you were the guest. Free speech is the cornerstone of Athenan progress," she said primly, "and Clement was very annoyed with us when he came arou—when he woke up. What I was wondering, was . . . people asked me, you see, and I'd forgotten . . . what I mean to say is, what *is* your name again?"

I caught the reflex in time and said, "Actually, it's Theodora."

Her eyes widened. "Theodora of Pyrene?"

"Why, yes—"

At that moment Seth came running down the street. He barreled into me and grabbed me by the hand. "You must come at once," he said. "Ran sent me. You must come at once." He was panting.

"What, what's the matter?"

"You must come," he said. "Vale's been arrested."

"Two Imperial cops," said Ran. We were in our room at Mullet's, stuffing things into our packs. "They were on Vale's doorstep over an hour ago. They've got him in the basement under the village hall—for interrogation, I assume."

"Imperials? In Teshin? That makes no sense."

"No point in staying to figure it out. See if you can get food from the Mullets before we—no. Cancel that. We say nothing to the Mullets and we leave through the window."

"We're on the second story."

"There's a ledge over the downstairs window. We can reach there and drop from it. Anyway, the street outside is just dirt."

I thought about it. "Ran, it might not be us they're asking about."

"What do you mean?"

"Vale is the known friend of a fugitive who lives over on Kado Island. They might have heard . . . no. It still doesn't explain the timing." Annurian had lived on the island for years. Ran had broken out of his trance just yesterday, and one day later the nearest healer was brought in for questioning.

Still, what about Vale? Maybe if I got word to Annurian, he would able to do something for the healer; over the past winter I'd developed a lot of respect for the Old Man of Kado Island. If I could hitch a ride over on one of the fishing boats, I could warn him . . . try a little logic, Theodora. With two Imperials in the village you would leave a trail leading to Annurian's door? The Old Man really would kill you for that one, and you would deserve it for stupidity of such magnitude.

"Well?" asked Ran, waiting for me to continue.

"Never mind. We go out the window."

"Right." He handed me my pack.

"How did you find out about the arrest?" I climbed up on the sill. This narrow slit was going to be hell to get through, and even if a dwarfish barbarian could do it I didn't see how Ran was going to. I threw the pack down first.

"Manager Peradon sent word with Seth, right before I sent Seth to find you. I don't know if Peradon knows anything, or if he just decided on principle that Imperials and foreigners shouldn't come together. Just think, if the Imperials had offered him a split of their juice we'd probably be in the basement instead of Vale. Save the cops a lot of trouble. Are you ready to go?"

I looked down. "Maybe."

"But they were typical Imperials. Rudeness never pays, Theodora, remember that."

First thing Grandmother ever taught you, I was about to say. But Ran said, "Try to roll when you hit," and gave me a friendly push.

I hit the dirt. It was like being smacked by a giant fist. All the breath left my body and I was paralyzed for minutes.

"Theodora? Are you all right?" Ran was kneeling over me, fear in his voice. I *was* all right, although in pain, but I couldn't get my breath back to tell him so. "Theodora?"

After a bit I said, "M'okay."

"What?"

"I'm all right," I whispered. "Just give me a minute."

He sat back on his heels. "I told you to roll when you hit," he said.

"You said . . . there was a ledge, too."

"Oh, that—I realized as soon as you got up that that window was too narrow to get through without being pushed from this side. You would never have been able to get into position. But it's not that far up! I told you to roll!"

"Yes, well . . . when I can move again, I will."

A few minutes later I got up and started moving stiffly after Ran, heading out of town. "How did you get through that window?" I asked.

He smiled. "There's no point in being a sorcerer if you can't cheat," he said.

There was a clearing in the woods a few minutes' walk north of Verger's Ford. We dropped our packs and sat on them. Ran said, "We have to wait for somebody."

So we waited. I was still stiff and careful about jarring my back. I thought about a lot of things: Vale, first of all, and Seth and the Old Man and the people I used to do The River with and the kitchen workers. I hadn't said goodbye to anybody. Now it was too late.

Hours went by. "Who are we waiting for?" I asked.

"Friends," he said.

More time passed. Then there was the sound of rustling, and Ran stood up. He looked as though he wished I'd bought a pistol, and I was beginning to have similar thoughts. Then somebody broke through the trees.

It was Seth! He ran over and hugged me. "Tymon," he said. He lifted his face to Ran. "I brought them," he added.

Two men followed, one of them the disreputable character I'd seen speaking with Ran earlier. He was about forty, bearded, with the bead-rim cap of a follower of the Quiet Way (a na' telleth organization, a contradiction in itself which made one wonder about the logical faculties of the man wearing such a cap). He lived alone in a small house in Teshin and had a reputation for being able to get you cheap beer when the hall was closed. The other man was much younger, in his late teens, but tall and well-muscled; I didn't know him. "My uncle and cousin," said Seth to me, bowing.

"Peradons?" I asked.

"Somerings," he said.

"But perhaps not for long," said the older man, as he bowed also. "I'm Karlas, and this is my nephew Tyl. Seth and Tyl are both my nephews, from different lines." He smiled as he struck Tyl's lower back, and Tyl bowed uncertainly.

I should have known; everybody in these little villages was related in some way.

"Not for long?" I repeated.

Ran said, "I've promised them membership in Cormallon if this works out."

"I see."

"For my brother Halet as well," said Karlas, "but he'll have to join us later."

"I see," I said again.

Ran took my arm and pulled me aside. "Vale says they're all right. That's why I went to see him, to consult him about which villagers might be suitable."

"Ah," I said, not wanting to say "I see" anymore.

"Look, Theodora, what's the problem? What do you want from me?"

I said, "I want to know everything that's going on and everything you're planning."

He gave a short laugh. "Is that all?"

We looked at each other. "As soon as I get the chance," he said. He turned to Seth. "Thank you, and say thank you to the Hall Manager for me. You'd better get back and get a little sleep."

"Wait a minute, Seth," I said. "I think that they'll let Vale go once they find out we've left—"

"They already have," he said.

"He's all right?"

"I heard that he was."

"Good." I pulled out my notebook and tore off a sheet of paper. I wrote "Good-bye" and handed the page to Ran. "Put the symbol for 'Teacher' next to that," I told him.

He took the pen. "Vale will know it's not your handwriting," he said.

"But he'll get the message."

Ran wrote and passed the sheet to Seth, who folded it and stuck it in the pocket of his robe.

"Good-bye, tymon," he said.

"Good-bye, Seth. You're a prince of storytellers."

"You make things up, tymon," he said, and vanished into the trees.

Ran picked up our packs. "We've stayed here long enough," he said. "We're better off out of this whole area." He handed me my pack. "Well, tymon? Want to stand here all night?"

Tymon, eh? "It's almost morning," I pointed out.

"So it is."

And so we started walking north. All four of us.

* * *

Karlas and Tyl pulled their weight, I had to give them that. In fact they pulled more than their weight, for they often passed my pack between them, and after the first few hours I stopped offering to take it back. (Would Grandmother offer to take it back? Would Kylla offer to take it back? Certainly not. Anyway, as time passed the aching in my shoulders and lower back made abstract ethical considerations seem more irrelevant.)

That inglorious tumble from the Mullets' window had jarred me more than I thought. I was thrilled when we finally sat down. We stopped that afternoon for a rest and I didn't wake up again until the next morning.

Ran woke me just before sunrise. "There's a town just a quarter hour away. Karlas is going to get us some supplies, is there anything you need?"

"Uh, I'd better go with him."

"Are you joking? You're too recognizable."

"Come on, Ran, I'll wrap a scarf around my head and I'll just be a short, pale person." I got what I needed from my pack; it would be less noticeable if I left it here.

"It's not a good idea," he said.

"I've seen blonds and lightskins every day in the capital."

"This isn't the capital. It's the back-end of nowhere."

Karlas said, "It *is* a fairly large town. I mean, if the gracious lady has her heart set on going, I think she could blend in. As long as she kept on the scarf, you know."

Ran shrugged. So Karlas and I set off for Jerrinos, which was a fair-sized river town over three times as big as Teshin. Karlas was impressed with it—the streets were paved, at least in the center of town, and the lighting around the square was modern. He told me that he'd always dreamed of going to the capital, that it offered more opportunity for a man of scope, and he saw from Jerrinos that it was just the sort of place that would suit him. Then he went off to buy some new cloaks, shoes, and, I assumed, pistols. I thought about getting boots, but it was nearly spring and my present pair were still sturdy. Then I toyed with the idea of getting a pistol of my own . . . but they *were* expensive. If the prices for the ones on display in the market were firm, I'd clean myself out, and for what? I wasn't experienced in using them, and if anyone pulled one on me it would be too late to do anything about it. Possibly I could get one secondhand, but I didn't know whom to approach. In the end I compromised by getting a new energizer for my hot-pencil, a covered warming bowl for food, and a larger canteen.

Then I sat down on the town hall steps and waited for the indigent's breakfast to be handed out. No point in wasting money on a meal. It was rice and meat, with celery and ground tasselnuts sprinkled over the top, not bad for a place like Jerrinos. I put half of it in my new warming bowl to share with Ran. Then I met Karlas back at the square and we returned to the woods.

"No problems," I said to Ran when we got back. Karlas handed a pistol to him, and one to Tyl. There was a new green cloak for Ran, lighter than his old winter coat. He rolled it up and put it in his pack to wait until the weather got a little warmer.

"Are we going?" asked Tyl, standing up.

Ran said, "In a few minutes." Then he took my arm and pulled me off to one side.

"What's the matter?" I asked.

"Nothing," he said. "You wanted to hear my plans."

I grinned. "And you're actually going to tell them?"

He said, "I never know what you think is funny. Listen, this is what I want to do: First, I want to get to the capital as soon as possible. I know the territory there, I have contacts there, and I think there's a better chance of protecting us both in the city than in some little village where nobody feels any obligation toward us. It only took two Imperials to get all of Teshin on good behavior. All right so far?"

"So far, yes, the capital is a good idea. I was heading there anyway before Teshin."

"All right. Once in the capital I can look up old friends, do some research, see what I can do about fixing things with the family council. I can't make any specific plans until I see just how it looks. Satisfied, tymon?"

I said slowly, "But look, Ran, assuming Eln is responsible for our troubles—and I guess he has to be involved—I don't think he's going to let you get anywhere near the council. Or anybody else who might help."

He didn't say anything.

I said, "This must have occurred to you."

He said, "Don't worry about it," and picked up a twig and scraped mud off the bottom of his boot.

"Look," I said.

"Here's the problem." He took the twig, squatted down on his heels, and scratched a vague map on the earth. "We can go all the way around Mountain's End, and up through the pass along the coast. That's the way everybody goes, and it'll take us a good three months by foot. Or we can take a straight line through the Simil Valley, and be in the capital in six weeks. The problem," he said, "is the timing. Every spring the ice along the range melts and turns Simil Valley into a lake. It drains into the Silver River, that's why they've got dikes all the way from Verger's Ford northward to the valley."

I said, "It's almost spring now."

"Yes, that's the risk. We'll have to walk very quickly. I've spoken to Karlas and Tyl about it, they're willing to take the chance."

"I see."

He waited. I said, "Well, if everyone else wants to go, I may as well go, too." He looked pleased. "I mean, why get picked off by Imperials all by myself when I can die in company? I'd rather be done in by the forces of nature anyway."

"I appreciate it, Theodora, I really do. How are the cards coming?"

"Oh, wait." I took out the warming bowl. "I got this in town. May as well start on a full stomach."

He opened it and swept up a mouthful with his fingers. "Mmm. Good tasselnuts." He ate some more and said, "But this is supper-food. Are they serving dinner for breakfast these days?"

"Well, in a way. It's leftovers from the hall—it's the indigent's breakfast."

He stopped chewing and for a second I thought he was going to spit it out. For another second I thought he was going to dump the bowl. "What?"

I said uncertainly, "The indigent's breakfast?"

"Are you trying to insult me? What can you have been thinking? Are you begging on provincial steps now—a Cormallon house member?"

I found coldness creeping into my voice. "Look, friend,

you may have been the First in Cormallon, but that doesn't buy you a dinner roll out in the sticks. If you'll think back to your recent *incapacity*, you'll remember sitting on a lot of hall steps between here and Issin—and you wouldn't be alive today if we hadn't. Just what do you mean by criticizing me? I'm an outlander. How am I supposed to know you've got a fetish about free breakfasts?"

Ran was staring at me. It was the first time I'd ever told him off. What's more, I couldn't seem to stop.

"And as for today, I got us a free meal. Do you want me to apologize for that? Do you know how many bakras I've got left in my wallet right now? Not very precious many, I'll tell you that. And where do you think our finances are coming from? Do you think your two new allies are going to throw their life savings into the pot—not that it would amount to much, I'm sure? Not if they've got any brains they won't. They'll be holding most of it in reserve in case we fail. Which leaves you and me, and I don't know how much you've got on you, but . . . "

I found myself trailing off and starting to sniffle. Ran looked horrified.

"I'm sorry, Theodora. I beg your pardon." He put another handful in his mouth and chewed. The look on his face suggested he was chewing sawdust, and not very good sawdust either. He swallowed manfully.

"Oh, gods who watch over scholars." I no longer could tell if I were sniffling or chuckling. Ran finished the bowl and wiped it clean with a cloth.

He handed it back to me. "Thank you very much," he said. Then he said, "I'm sorry for my behavior. But, Theodora—we're not going to do this again."

"All right," I said.

We rejoined our two allies, who tried to look as though they hadn't heard anything of the last five minutes. We took up our gear and started moving. Try to look at it as a camping trip, I told myself as we walked.

Chapter 13

As it turned out, our new ally Tyl was almost neurotically shy, so it was some time before he brought himself to tell us that he'd turned his ankle. Even then he mumbled the information to his uncle Karlas, who passed it on to Ran and myself. I didn't appreciate it at the time, but this was the best thing that could happen to me—already I was having difficulty keeping up with the others. Not surprising; the three men I traveled with were all taller than I was, their legs coming up well past my waist, so that I had to jog to keep pace. Nor was this good jogging country. But we all had to slow down for Tyl, who made shift with a stick to try and keep the weight off his left foot.

That first night after Jerrinos I took out the cards. Ran saw what I was doing from across the campfire, but he went on arranging the undertunic he'd just washed so that it was closer to the heat. I started the configuration with a center-card for Ran, not something I usually did, but I suppose his condition was still bothering me. The card that turned up was the Aftermath, a scene of people running down a city street, one woman holding a baby while others crawled out from the rubble of destroyed buildings. It symbolized rebirth. As I touched it the buildings recoalesced into the house at Cormallon, the street became a hill, and the woman with the baby was Kylla holding a torch. She joined Eln on the hilltop under a night sky and they began reciting something. Like all my pictures it was silent, but I knew they were enacting Ran's official disownment.

No new information here. But as I kept my fingers on the card it occurred to me that perhaps I wasn't going far enough. I treated the cards like Net transmissions, I took what came over the lines and assumed that was all there was. What if there were more? Studying with Vale had meant finding level after level . . . now there was a thought. I still felt that "de-energizing my na' telleth" was so much double-talk, but calming down and opening up had seemed to help my performance at tinaje. Perhaps it would help with this as well. I took a few deep breaths and made myself as still as possible. I tried not to think about anything at all, and after a bit I let my mind creep up slowly on the card, gently, not grabbing for information but more as if I were just wondering. . . .

At once I was pulled away. It was like falling down a well. I was on the hilltop again, but this time it lacked the air of solid reality it had held earlier; strange, since now it felt as though I were actually present, not simply watching a picture. But present at what? Kylla was holding a torch again—or was it Kylla? Her face was older, and not as kind. She took Eln's torch away from him and handed it to someone standing behind her. Then she lit the kindling in the huge marble bowl on the crest of the hill. Eln said—and I could hear him!—"I'll light the rest of the funeral fires." She said, "It's too late. You don't have a torch." She sounded angry with him. I remember thinking that it hardly seemed fair of her under the circumstances.

The card was jerked out of my hand. Ran was bending over me, looking unhappy. "Theodora? What are you doing, are you all right?"

"Yes, of course. I was running the cards, what's the idea of interrupting me?"

He said, "I *couldn't* interrupt you. You didn't hear me. What were you doing?"

I told him. I thought he would say at once, "Try it again"—he was fond of information, and he'd been after me to run the cards for days. But he just looked thoughtful and said, "I don't know if this is a good idea."

"It was working all right until you pulled the card away."

"Working how? I never heard of card-reading like this. You say it didn't feel like a real event—"

"No, more like something symbolic, or something from the future—"

"I don't like it. How sure can we be about that kind of information? I've never thought much of oracles—and it might not be safe for you."

"It felt all right. I wasn't scared."

He said, "No. We don't know what would have happened if I hadn't been here to take the card away from you."

"Presumably the scene would have finished." I sounded a little irritated even to myself, like someone whose terminal shorted out at the end of a mystery story.

Ran said again, "No." So I put the cards away for the time being. Karlas had been squatting on the other side of the fire, waiting politely for us to stop talking; now he came over to me.

He said, "My nephew would like to ask you to give him tinaje. He hopes to ease the pain in his ankle."

I looked over at Tyl. He sat with his face averted, one hand clasping the ankle in question. I said to Karlas, "There's no guarantee the pain would be reduced. It's possible, but not certain." According to Vale's teachings, I wouldn't touch the ankle itself tonight, even if I did full tinaje, but direct the energies around it instead, which might or might not be of help.

Anyway, that's what Vale would have said to do. Karlas said, "I know. This is why Tyl wants to know something of your moral character."

"I beg your pardon?"

"Your character. Obviously the success of a tinaje session depends heavily on the moral character of the practitioner. This is well known."

The mind reeled. "It is, is it? Look, Karlas, you've got it backward. If it has anything to do with personality, it depends more on the attitude of the person receiving the tinaje. If he can relax and participate, it's reflected in his body and his body receives the benefit. But that's as far as it goes."

Karlas went on, "But I've already reassured him that your character is exemplary, or you would not be on this journey with us. I'm sure that the sir Cormallon would not have brought anyone into this who is not of the highest sort."

"Well, thank you," I said, as I gave up on achieving communication. "That's kind of you to say."

"So will you have a look at my nephew? He is a fine boy, I know he doesn't complain, but he is troubled by this."

"All right." I got up and went over to Tyl. "Hello," I said.

Tyl shifted his hulking shoulders and mumbled back. I assume it was hello.

Ordinarily I would talk to a client, to learn about him and put him at ease. It would probably have the opposite effect here, knot up all those hard-gained muscles. "Turn over," I said, making it an order.

He turned over gratefully.

Ran came by as I worked. "Can I watch?" he asked.

"If you like."

Working on Tyl, I could see what Vale meant when he said that people who built up their muscles had a different energy flow than dancers like Pyre. Both had trained their bodies sternly, but Tyl's energy was in separate pools, while Pyre's had leaped along like a river. "It doesn't hurt, does it?" I asked Tyl. I was going in more deeply than I ever had.

"I barely feel it, you're like a butterfly," he said. My goodness, he really could talk. I gave his back an affectionate slap when I was through, and he smiled. There was a pleasant feel to Tyl, like a large family dog.

Ran said, "You've studied hard, haven't you?"

"Yes, I have."

He nodded, as though figuring something out. Later he brought over a blanket from his pack. "I know you're too cheap to buy an extra one for yourself. Still, it's not spring yet."

"Thanks." I took it from him. It was dark red wool, Karlas must have picked it up in Jerrinos. "Well, good night."

"Yes, good night." He paused a moment. "Do you still have that onyx cat?"

"Yes, it's in my pack. Do you want it?"

"No. I just wondered. Never mind, tymon, sleep well."

Tyl's stride picked up over the next couple of days. They tried to slow down for me, but after keeping pace for half an hour or so he and Karlas would pull ahead, and Ran and I would meet them much later, sitting on a log or a boulder, waiting for me. "Sorry, my lady," said Karlas. "It's difficult to hold back."

I resented them for it, and it felt bitter to think of Ran going slower for my benefit. Not that he said anything about it—and I resented that, too. My feet ached and my back ached, in one continuous pain. One night I sat dully by the fire, thinking unhappy thoughts, when Ran sat down beside me. "You look more miserable than anyone I have ever seen," he began.

"Thank you."

"It's not you, it's the expression on your face. You should see it."

I grunted.

He said, "I know it's difficult for you, but . . . do you want to talk about it?"

I scuffed up some dirt. "I have," I said, "no physical endurance at all."

He seemed to be waiting for something more. "What of it? It's never bothered you before."

"I never *knew* it before!" And there I was, yelling at Ran. I said, "I'm sorry. Please excuse me for a little while." I went off a short distance into the trees where I could be alone in misery.

I hadn't known it before. I'd always done pretty well at whatever I tried to do, always comfortably in the top twenty percent of my class—and anything I hadn't done well at I'd figured wasn't all that important anyway. I hadn't known that my body was designed along such unheroic lines. Nor had I had any inkling of the shameful way one's mind would follow the physical state—making me resentful and short-tempered with people who hadn't done me any wrong.

When I'd told myself off sufficiently, I got up to rejoin the others. Then I had a major scare. There was blood on the boulder I'd been sitting on. I quickly checked my robes and found blood on my undertunic and between my legs. I was shocked and frightened, sure that I was hemorrhaging internally. Could I get to a doctor quickly enough? And was there a Tellys-trained doctor anywhere between here and the capital? I was shaking.

I'd taken a couple of steps back to the camp when I suddenly remembered there was another and less harmful cause of bleeding in a female. It would be hard for an Ivoran to understand that I'd forgotten about it, but after all I hadn't menstruated since the first time, when I was thirteen. I'd had the usual implants to inhibit ovulation, right on the dot, every three years. The implants were supposed to last from three to five years, but I liked to be prudent. My last one must have just worn off. Great Plato, what was I supposed to do now?

It occurred to me that besides the inconvenience, I was now capable of becoming pregnant—*involuntarily* pregnant. What a concept! I was capable of screaming my way through childbirth on a planet where the nearest medical facility I would trust was geographically and financially way out of my league. And what about Ran? Not that I was thinking, specifically, about Ran—but what if Ivory and the rest of the universe had indeed gone their separate ways, and we were different species? The definition of species was that they were able to mate and produce fertile offspring. But there were plenty of separate species that could mate and produce, well, *something*. There was no guarantee what. It might require sophisticated medical technology even to bring such a child to term.

Well, there was no point in thinking any further on that topic, or I would lose heart entirely. But, gods who are supposed to watch over scholars, this was really the final straw. I climbed back up on my rock, avoiding the bloodstain, and thought about crying. I just felt numb, though.

I didn't have the faintest idea what to do about menstruation, either. I wasn't sure about bringing up the problem to the others; maybe it was a taboo topic on Ivory; I'd never paid any attention to it before. Why doesn't anybody ever warn you about these things? I thought about all those marvelous stories I'd read back on Athena, the legends I'd fallen in love with—the heroes setting off to seek fortune and adventure. Knights and damosels rode forth to do battle at castles perilous, and the damosels never had this problem. And hobbits and tall elves strode swiftly over the earth, and the hobbits never had any trouble keeping up. Of course, hobbits were supposed to have great endurance.

If only I were a hobbit. A *male* hobbit.

Oh, well, I was just going to have to go ask. If they thought it was an unrefined topic to bring up, they would just have to live with it. I couldn't stay here on this rock forever.

I went back to camp and told Ran about my problem. He looked blank. "Don't you have an idritak?" he asked.

A what? "No," I said.

"I assumed you picked up some in Jerrinos," he said. "Well, it's late, but we can't avoid it. I'll have Karlas go into Spur, it's just a couple of miles away, and he can get you some. Really, Theodora, I would have thought you'd anticipated this."

"How can Karlas pick me up anything? Are we talking about an implant?"

"A what?"

Some confused exchanges of information followed. Eventually Ran shook his head and went over to talk to Karlas, who shrugged and left the camp. He came back in an hour with a small pouch containing a lot of little white things. They seemed to be made of absorbent cloth.

"What do I do with these?" I asked.

Karlas looked blank. "Whatever it is you women do with them," he said.

"You put them inside," said Ran.

"Actually inside me? How many at once? Are they sterile?" I looked at them distrustfully.

Ran and Karlas were at a loss. Apparently this was something they had never given much thought to, either.

Tyl spoke up. "If I may," he said quietly. Then he gave me explicit instructions. Ran and Karlas looked at him. "I have five sisters," he said, shrugging.

So I took the idritak pouch and went off to "do whatever it is we women do with them." It was more difcult than it sounded. I told myself as I worked at it that it was all part of being a primate. But since that day I have often thought I would rather be a marsupial.

I believed that I had reached the low point of my life so far. I was wrong. The following morning we arrived at the lip of the Simil Valley.

It was a long, narrow, bare-looking place; filled with undergrowth in the summer, they said, but just muddy now. We were lucky, they said, that it wasn't summer and we didn't have to pick our way through it. I didn't join in these congratulations, saving my breath for the descent. We went down the long hillside trail, boots on in spite of the warm weather.

"Almost spring," said Ran quietly to Karlas.

"Um," said Karlas. His expression was serious.

The valley looked long to me—too long to get through in three days, which was the schedule we were working on. But we tramped down into the heart, and I swore to myself that I would keep up, regardless of how I might have to run through the muck. Being too slow here would put all our lives in danger.

I had said I would ask for no more rest periods, and I didn't. I knew I wasn't going as quickly as the others could, but I went on. And on. Soon the pain in my feet and back spread to my neck, my calves, and my chest. I pushed a fist into the small of my back to try to minimize it, and walked that way. I didn't complain—but that was small credit to me. I didn't have the wit or the energy to complain after a few hours. Speech was beyond me. At first I thought longingly of the trip up from Issin, when I set my own pace and rested whenever I liked; it was another world. Soon enough I stopped thinking at all. It was one long dreamlike horror, step after step after step. I no longer moved to wipe away sweat. One foot after the other, that was enough to deal with.

Ran's hands were on my shoulders. "Theodora," he said. "You can stop now. We're stopping here. Do you hear me?"

I dropped down into the mud and lay there.

At once he knelt beside me. "Are you all right?"

"Yes. Go away."

He seemed to sense that I meant it, and went away. After a while, I don't know how long it was, he returned with Karlas. "Help me get her up," he said. They each took an arm, and we went on. That was how it was in the daytime. At night I took no part in setting up the fire or cooking. They left me alone, for which I was grateful. As for my body, it ached through the night; there were blisters on the soles of my feet and there were rashes on parts of me I had never known about before. It itched terribly, but when I saw the effects of scratching I tried to stop.

One day, two days, three days. We were still in the valley. Ran and Karlas were worried, always listening now for the sound of rushing water, but I was beyond that. In fact, I was the only person in the party who wasn't frightened. But something gave out on that third day. I had no notion it was coming; if I'd been asked before I entered this valley, I would not have thought that one's limits could be reached so quickly. Between one step and another it happened: I stopped. I sat down.

I said nothing to anybody, and it was several minutes before they realized I wasn't with them. Then they came back and stood around me.

Ran said gently, "Theodora, we have to get on. We can't even go back, it's too late. We're in danger here. We could be flooded out at any time, and it's a vicious flood, I've heard about it. Theodora? It'll cut through here like a knife through paper. We couldn't possibly survive."

"Go," I said.

"What?"

"Go. Save yourself."

They looked at each other.

Ran said, "Theodora—"

"Go. It's all right. I don't care." And I didn't. It's hard to enter now into my feelings on that day, at that moment, but I really didn't care. Things had simplified for me enormously: I couldn't continue. Therefore everything else had to follow from that point. Death just didn't seem like the thing to be avoided it was when I was in my right mind.

They went away and spoke to each other for a few minutes. I could hear them, but I wasn't interested. After a bit Ran came back.

"I've sent them on ahead," he told me.

"You go, too." Conversation was an effort but it had to be said. I didn't want the responsibility for his death. On top of everything else it was just too much. If he stayed, I might try to get up in a while, and I didn't want to.

"No."

"Please."

"No. Listen, Theodora, sweetheart, you don't have to talk. Lie down if you want to. Pretend I'm not here."

I sat there dully, resenting him for making me deal with his presence. After a few minutes—or maybe it was longer—I realized he'd pulled off my boots.

"What are you doing?"

"If you won't lie down, this will at least help." He poured water from his canteen over a tunic he'd pulled from his pack; then he started washing my feet with the tunic. He was crazy, but it would take too much effort to stop him. "Your feet look horrible," he said conversationally. "I didn't know a person could have this many blisters and rashes in such a small area. Athlete's foot, too. My, my—sensitive skin for a barbarian." When he'd finished washing off the sweat and grime he lifted one foot and began pressing against the sole with his thumb, using a tinaje grip.

"I didn't know you knew that," I found my voice saying.

"I watch and learn," he said, "much like yourself."

We sat there like statues for several hours. I said, finally, "I'm very sorry."

"Sorry about what?" He seemed genuinely blank.

"I've slowed everybody down. I'm not the stuff heroes are made of, Ran. I'm not even the stuff Karlas and Tyl are made of. I'm not worth wasting your time over."

He was quiet for a minute, then he said, "I have often had difficulty understanding you, Theodora, but never more than right now. I don't see what the question of how quickly you can travel through the Simil Valley has to do with how good you are. You're not a hiker, at least not with these people and in this terrain. Too bad, but I always took you for a city kid anyway, tymon. I'm strictly urban, myself, and when I go to the country—as you've seen—I bring plenty of comfort along with me. You'll probably never be called on to do something like this again, you know. And in the capital, who's going to care if you take shorter steps when you walk?"

I hadn't thought of it that way. Still, it was easy for him to be polite about it—he hadn't failed.

Then he was going on. "I know you have no reason to listen to me. I fell apart just when you needed me. When I found out that I wasn't going to have every move I made backed up by the family, I just gave up living. Yes, Vale claims that it was an attack by sorcery; but I know, myself, that I wouldn't have been vulnerable to it if I hadn't given up first. You had to take care of everything. That wasn't what you signed on for, was it? Don't think I haven't thought about it every day since Teshin—"

"Are you crazy?" I don't know how long he would have

gone on with that nonsense if I hadn't stopped him. "Look, I understand that this family business means more to you than to a tymon from Pyrene. Your world was hammered down in front of you, Ran, how were you supposed to react?" He looked so miserable. I raised his head. "I was irritated, of course, when you checked out like that. But I get irritated by a lot of things. That's all I thought about it. Really."

We sat there holding onto each other for a while. Eventually I noticed the particular aches and pains that had receded for the past few hours into generalized misery were making themselves known. I sighed. "We'd better go," I said.

He got up and held out a hand. We went limping off into the mud. I felt pretty miserable, but I really didn't feel too bad.

I must have thought I heard the sound of water a dozen times before we reached the halfway point on the trail up the pass out of the valley. "We're safe at this height," Ran said. When we got to the top of the ridge, I turned around.

"I wish I could see the water come through," I said. "After all that trouble, I'd like to see what could have killed me."

"Well, there's no hurry now," said Ran. "Do you want to wait?"

We sat for a time looking out on that lousy valley. I felt as though I'd spent a lifetime in it. The sun swung behind the mountaintops to our left. "I guess we should go on," I said.

He shrugged. "Sorry, tymon, it doesn't come on cue."

"Yeah, all things being equal I suppose I should be glad we missed it."

He laughed and helped me up. We crossed over the ridge. On the other side I stopped.

"What is it?" he asked.

"I thought I heard water. Never mind," I said, as I started walking again. "It's probably all in my mind."

Behind me the roaring got louder. Ran looked at me questioningly.

"No, thank you," I said. "We're out of it now. Believe me, Ran, you haven't got enough in the family treasury to get me in that valley ever again. That sound," I added firmly, "is in our minds."

"As you say," said Ran; "Grandmother taught me never to contradict a lady of Cormallon."

Chapter 14

We met up with Karlas and Tyl in the town of Tenrellis, a few days away from the capital. There were a lot more towns now, and a lot more traffic on the roads. They'd booked themselves into an inn—the sort of place that was as inexpensive as we could go without offending Ran's sensibilities. It was all right by my standards, anyway; which is to say, vermin were kept to a minimum. I ask for little else.

Ran agreed that we could stay for a couple of days and rest up. While he was eager to move, he didn't want us staggering into the capital in rags, too tired to deal with whatever we might find there. The morning after our arrival I went out to the market, leaving Ran behind with Karlas and an old, battered chessboard they had dug up somewhere. Chess has never interested me, probably because I'm such a bad player, and I wanted to buy something good to eat and sit under the striped awning by the market and think about how I didn't have to do any walking today. It was a beautiful springlike morning.

I was sitting under that striped awning, licking a lemon ice, when I heard a voice I knew very well. "Have you shrunk," it said thoughtfully, "or have I gotten taller?" It was Kylla, standing over me in her best go-to-the-city robes, hair demurely braided but with wide gold hoops in her ears and a hint of gold swirl on her cheeks. I looked down at the sandals that peeped out from under her robes and saw her toenails were painted gold, too.

"I'm sure I've shrunk," I said, blinking up at her face in the sunlight. "I really don't think there's much left of me."

"My, my," she said, and sat down tailor-fashion by my side. "We'll have to do something about that. How's my brother?"

"Well."

"And yourself?"

"Shrunken, but otherwise unharmed."

"Good." She played with the hem of her robe. "Theodora, I think we should talk. How would you like to check into the local Asuka baths with me? We could order in food and masseurs and anything else we like, and make a day of it."

The idea of hot water in bulk was very tempting. "Uh, you would be paying for this, Kylla?"

"Naturally."

I took perhaps a second to make up my mind. "Done. Let me leave a note for Ran at the inn."

She shook her head. "If you don't mind, I'd rather you didn't tell him about it. I'm not supposed to have any contact with either of you . . . and very likely he wouldn't take it well if he learned you were talking to me."

"I gather Eln doesn't know you're here."

"You gather accurately. But let's not destroy a beautiful day by digging into all the decaying details, all right?"

"Whatever you say—you're the one paying."

So we went down a few streets until we came to a cave-like entrance built into the hill on the north side of town. This branch of the Asuka business was very different from their glass-and-steel tower in the capital; it was built into a real cave, and much of it had been cleaned, but other than that left in a natural state.

"We'll take a suite," Kylla told the woman in the front. "The best one on the women's side. What's your security like?"

The woman, a burly, middle-aged top-sergeant sort, raised an eyebrow at the coins Kylla was counting out on her table; but she appeared otherwise unimpressed. "Solid rock, as you can see for yourself, gracious lady. At least two feet thick in every room, usually thicker. We've put steel reinforced entryways to each room, too. No windows." She took out a pipe, lit it, and added, "We're bonded against listening devices. There's a sorcerous sweep once in the morning and once in the evening to see that it's clean of tampering. And, I will say that we're the best in this town or any other—face paint if you're going out tonight, masseurs, you name it."

"Tinaje?" I asked.

She hesitated a moment, then said, "Of course. My girl Celia is a tinaje specialist. Have you tried her before?"

"No," I said, "I've never had a full professional tinaje session. She's specifically trained?"

"Of course, or she wouldn't be here. Will you be wanting her before or after your bath?"

Kylla looked at me. "After, I think," she said. "We'll be letting you know."

We were taken to a large room carved out of rock—by nature or man I couldn't tell, nor did it seem important. The important thing was the pool in the center, a thing of beauty with stone steps leading down to a steaming, rock-heated bath that came past my chin when I stood up at its midpoint. It was wide enough for eight or nine people, and you could sit against the walls and have the water lap up to your chest. Which of course I lost no time doing.

"Mmmm," I said to Kylla, when I felt the urge for conversation.

"Yes," she said. We were leaning against a wall of the pool, arms up on the sides, floating out straight from time to time and dropping back down. It was nice to have that as the sum total of my responsibility for the day.

"You want to talk about Ran and Eln?" I asked eventually.

"No," she said.

"Neither do I," I said, and floated some more.

After a while I said, "So what did you look me up for?"

"Well, actually . . . " she wrung out her braid and pinned it atop her head. "Grandmother told me to come."

"She did what? How did she know? I thought she was sick."

"She is sick. But she holds on, Grandmother does. She called me in last night and said, 'Cherie, our Theodora is going to be in Tenrellis market tomorrow morning, and she's going to be very tired, and she's going to need cheering up.' So I sort of borrowed an aircar, and here I am."

"My. Grandmother stays on top of things, doesn't she?"

"She tries."

I felt around the stone below my arm. "There are some switches here. Do you think we can make this a whirlpool?"

"You want everything, don't you, Theo?"

"I wasn't complain—"

"Of course we can make it a whirlpool." She lifted the casing and pushed a button. A current started to run clockwise through the water. "So, do you need cheering up?"

"Maybe. It wouldn't hurt, I guess."

She clucked and picked up the housephone by the steps and called for lunch. When it arrived, we climbed out and dried off on the enormous gray Asuka towels. We ate on the couches beside the pool, tiny meatpies and bread and cakes, and a potful of green tah. Then she clucked over the state of my body, which was still fairly blistered and rash-ridden, and sat down at a low, mirrored desk in the corner of the room and began pulling boxes and vials out of the drawers. "Here we are," she said, and started handing them to me.

So I put powder on all the parts of me that tend to get too damp, and oil on all the parts of me that tend to get too dry, and it was glorious beyond literary expression. Some of the itches I had picked up in the Simil Valley even faded away, and I vowed never to leave urban civilization again.

"Now let's play," said Kylla, and she got out yet more vials from this miraculous desk, this time tiny containers of face paint and nail colors and body designs. "Just hold still," she said. "Believe me, I can do this better than the house designers."

I could well believe it, and I held still. When she was finished, a full hour later, the mirror showed me a total stranger. This person was taller than me, and more fine-boned, with larger, darker eyes; and she obviously knew no fear, because she was wearing face and body swirls that I myself would never have the nerve to put on. I stood up and walked over to the floor-to-ceiling mirror on a nearby wall. "Wait a minute," said Kylla. She went to the pile of jewelry she'd discarded before entering the bath, picking up here a hoop of gold and gems, tossing aside there a handful of tiny I-don't-know-what's. "Hmm, your ears aren't pierced, are they? Well, try these." And she hung the hoop around my neck, and pushed two wide, delicately banded bracelets up my arms, and clipped a twisted strand of gold to my earlobe. Then she stood back and said, "No, you need symmetry." And she pulled the strand of gold off again. "Now look," she said. I turned to the image in the mirror.

It gave me an odd feeling. I could see that I was still at the bottom of this theme Kylla had created; but maybe because she had done so many changes, I could see things I usually missed in my own reflection. It was a shivery experience, half strangely objective and half not knowing what to think. I was lightly tanned, darker than I'd ever been, and I'd lost my baby fat somewhere on the northward trail; probably in the Simil Valley. No more Teddy Bear nicknames—it was quite possible they wouldn't recognize me on Athena. They certainly wouldn't recognize me with this pirate booty draped all over—I'd had no idea I could handle jewelry this gaudy and not appear a fool. I looked as though I could pass for one of the sophisticated ladies I'd seen coming out of private dining rooms in the Lantern Gardens, with wealthy, family parties.

"Oh, *Kylla*," I said finally.

"Not bad," she said, as she appraised the finished canvas. "We ought to outline your eyes in blue or green next time—better for unusual skin like yours, make you look more exotic."

Exotic was not a word I had heretofore thought of in relation to myself. I looked back at the image in the mirror. It was lovely, I had to admit, although the idea made me nervous somehow; but it wasn't, well, *Athenan*.

I said, "It bothers me a little."

"Think of it as a play," she said. "You can scrub it off and leave the role any time you like; this just expands your options."

They would read me out of the Ethics in Scholarship Group if they ever found out about this back on Athena, where it was a well-known fact of good society that a single black or gold ring, with perhaps a simple necklace for special occasions, was all a person of taste should require. Still, how likely were they to find out? I said, "How about the tinaje? It'll mess up the body paint, won't it?"

"Not unless the girl uses oil. I don't think they use oil for tinaje, but I'm not sure."

"They don't," I said. She looked at me. "It's just one of the things I happen to know in this life," I explained.

"Ah," she said, and she rang for the manager and asked if the tinaje specialist was available.

A few minutes later Celia came in. She looked like the daughter of the manager, and perhaps she was. She asked me no questions—which Vale would not have approved of, but not all systems are the same—and simply told me to lie on my stomach on the couch. Then she started on my upper back, without preliminary.

"Ow," I said. "That hurts."

"Some people like it hard," she said, pouting.

"I know some people like it hard. I'm not one of them."

She went back to work and I tried not to groan. But courtesy has its limits and after a few minutes I stopped her. "You're not a tinaje specialist, are you? You're perthes-trained, maybe even bratelle."

She knelt back on her ankles and looked at me suspiciously. "You said this was your first session."

Kylla got up from her couch. "Never mind, dear." She gave the girl a coin and dismissed her. "I didn't know I was dealing with a connoisseur," she said, and she sounded amused. She was probably thinking I'd come a long way from the stranger Ran brought home grimy from an inn fire and stuffed into his sister's robes. Well, it doesn't hurt to remember our beginnings.

So we just lay back on the couches and talked, about the latest scandal of the Emperor's wives, the rumors of the Emperor's impotence, and the accusations about the Emperor's progeny. A corrupt government at least provides food for conversation, particularly if personal topics are too painful to bring up on a pleasant day at the baths.

I told Kylla I would be glad to get back to the capital, and would be just as happy never to look up through the trees at the winter constellations again. She laughed—by then she had brought out a bottle of wine, which we were making use of without glass or wine bowl—and declaimed, "Too long, too well I know the starry conclave of the midnight sky; too well, the splendors of the firmament, the lords of light whose kingly aspect shows, what time they set or climb the sky in turn, the year's divisions, bringing frost or fire."

I applauded. I wanted to stamp my feet, but it would have meant getting up off the couch. She said, "Thank you.

That was the play I was in at Lady Degrammont's School for the Sage and Cultured Upbringing of Most Valuable Young Ladies. I was just the watchman," she added. "I wanted to be Agamemnon, but they gave it to Edra Simmeroneth because her family paid for the new wing."

Some things in academe are the same all over, I thought vaguely; then it caught up with me and I said, *"Agamemnon?"*

"Yes, it's a play about a king who comes home from a war—"

"I know it, I know it. It's in partial form at the Antiquities Library on Athena. How do you know it? I thought Ivoran history had gone its own way, I thought all that material from the past was lost—"

"I don't know how old it is," she said, and the thought didn't seem to interest her. "But it's a good story, Theo. You don't think anyone would forget a good story, do you?"

I said, "If you had that translated into Standard, the classics branch on Athena would pay you hard money for it. I don't think they have the least idea it exists anywhere."

She shrugged. "A lot of trouble to go to," she said. Then she said, "Before I forget," and pulled a piece of paper from the pocket of the robe she'd thrown over the couch. She wrote on it and handed it to me.

It was an address. "What is it?" I asked.

"In case you need to get in touch with me. This is a friend of mine in the capital. He'll see that any messages get through to me quickly."

A friend? The name above the address was Lysander Shikron. Not a Cormallon name, or any ally of the Cormallons that I had heard of before. I remembered Eln taunting her that night at dinner, when he said that she'd brought a lover within Cormallon boundaries. I decided not to ask.

Kylla looked, for the very first time, just a little guilty. She said, "Theo, take good care of that address. It's something that neither Ran *nor* Eln should know about."

When I got back to the inn later, I found Ran and Karlas still on their third game of chess.

"I'm glad I didn't stay," I said.

They looked up at me. "What happened to you?" Ran asked.

"I went to the Asuka baths, and the house designer painted pictures on me."

"You look beautiful, my lady," said Karlas.

"Thank you. What's the matter, Ran, don't you like it? It didn't cost all that much."

"I don't know," he said slowly. "You don't look like a barbarian any more."

"Is that bad?"

"I don't know," he said again. He looked down at the board and frowned.

Three days later we were in the capital. It was the first month of spring, a full Ivoran year since the day Ran sat down across from me in Trade Square and asked me if I wanted a job.

Chapter 15

We rented a house in one of the cheaper quarters of the city. The first thing Ran did after signing a false name on the rental agreement was to circle the building, squeezing his way down the narrow alley between our place and the tavern next door, and then crossing round back and inching through the crawlspace by the clothing store on the other side, all the while with a look of fixed concentration. The rest of us stood just inside the entryway while he worked. It gave me the feeling you get late at night, when lightning has flicked brilliance into your room and gone again, and you wait for the rumble to follow.

Then he put a neat printed card on the front door that read: "TRADESMEN AND VISITORS UNWELCOME. This constitutes fair warning that the first person to violate this property will accrue seven years of ill luck."

I said to him, "Sorcery is still illegal, isn't it? Should we be calling attention to the fact you've put a spell on the house?"

"Everybody does it," he said. "Anyway, the cop on the beat isn't going to cross the property line to arrest us—not unless he's an idiot. And he won't be an idiot if we pay him regularly."

So we moved in. It was good to have a roof over my head again, even if it was the rotting one we'd gotten here. During the first rainfall I put a pan down on the floor under the most major leak and said to Ran, "What are we going to do when the real spring rains hit?"

"We'll need a lot more pans," he said calmly.

And that was the spirit of the season. Ran went first to the Street of Gold Coins to see if he could set up shop as a sorcerer. He used the name he'd put on the rental agreement, and was arrested the first day. Arrested, he described later, by two very bored policemen who had no interest in pulling in one minor lawbreaker on a streetful of minor lawbreakers but who claimed they had no choice. An anonymous informant had lodged an official complaint against him with the Bureau of Urban Affairs. A bored judge, who sat court in an extra room at the police station to save time, pronounced him guilty, levied a fine, and apologized to him in one sentence.

Ran tried it all again two days later, under another name. He was arrested again and fined. We were running out of money.

The next day Ran went to Trade Square, rolled out a blanket on the ground, set down Karlas' battered chessboard, and offered to take all comers. He came home with three tabals.

"You should charge more per game," I said. "Considering how long a game takes."

"My dear tymon," he said, in one of his less acceptable flights into aristocracy, "it's not a question of *charging*. This is a wager. When you make a wager, you have to have the cash on hand to back it up. We are in no position today to risk more than three tabals. Now, logically, as the days go by, we will accumulate enough capital—"

"All right, all right." It was true, and I ought to have thought before I said anything, but his tone was irritating. I had been playing rather guiltily with the thought that I should open up the coffers I'd squirreled away with my nonNet banker before the trip to Issin, and make the coin generally available to the household. I felt some obligation, but at the same time it would mean consigning the homeward trip even farther into a murky future. Already Athena was becoming too abstract for comfort.

However, I knew I ought to be bringing some money into the house. So I went to Trade Square myself next morning, with a length of rope and some green cloth, and looked for my old vendor-mate, Irsa.

"Hello, youngster," she said when she saw me. "Wondered when I didn't see you—wasn't sure if you were too high-rung now, or if you were dead." She put down the fruit she was holding and hugged me properly.

"How are the kids, Irsa?"

"Trouble. Big trouble. Never get married, believe me."

Which is what she always said. "How about you? Lost a little weight, haven't you? You've not been sick?"

"Well, Irsa, as you say, the wheel always comes around. Which is why I wanted to ask you about renting a few feet off your market space, and what the Merchants' Association would do if I asked for my old membership back."

She shook her head. "It's the way it always is, isn't it? Well, sweetheart, I wish I could say no charge on the space, but times are hard, so . . . ten percent of the take?"

That was steep—steeper than I expected from Irsa. She'd only charged three percent in the old days, and sometimes not even that when things were bad.

I was in no position to bargain, so I said, "If that's how it has to be."

She grinned that broken-toothed grin. "But don't let the Association bother you, sweetheart, you're still a member in good standing."

"What?"

"I kept up your dues, is what I'm saying to you. I thought, well, if things go wrong, and they always do, why try to talk them into letting you rejoin? And they're a mess since the chairman resigned, the committee members all want separate bribes. Too much trouble, my dear."

"You mean you've been paying them for me right along, all this past year?"

She nodded. I was overwhelmed. What she must have paid out covered far more than the ten percent she was asking. "Irsa, I don't know what to say. You're a lifesaver. Thank you."

"Well, let's not dwell on it. Go on and set up your cards, you're losing customers."

"Actually, I didn't plan on doing the cards. I lost that old deck anyway, a long time ago."

"So what then—"

"Tinaje."

She blinked at me. "How—"

I said, "I figure I can set up a sort of tent if I run a rope from the top of your cart to the pole over there. I've got enough cloth and I'll just put down a mat inside."

"I didn't know you were healer-trained," she said.

"I've spent part of the last year studying tinaje with one of the best healers I know."

She frowned. "I thought you went off with that good-looking boy with the fancy clothes."

"It's a long story, Irsa."

She sighed and said, "Well, the wheel comes around sometimes and doesn't leave you in the same place. I don't know." She turned back to her cart. "Tinaje . . . at least we'll be getting some tone in this part of the market."

That's how we started the spring, with Ran and me in different corners of the Square. He never bothered with the Association, preferring to defend himself from thieves and cops. Nor did they bother him about joining, or anyway not after the first two representatives they sent. I knew that he was busy in other ways, too, but I didn't nag him about his secretiveness, mostly because when I remembered my own private bank account I didn't feel in a secure enough moral position.

It wasn't too bad in Trade Square. I'd been pretty hesitant about charging money for tinaje; Vale never had given me permission, but then, I'd left Teshin in rather a hurry. I told myself I was better than the girl at the Tenrellis baths, and the Asuka people had been willing enough to charge. And it seemed to work out; if a client looked too scruffy I simply turned him away, and I kept my knife in easy reach. Anyway, one yell from me and Irsa would have had the curtain down and the Association running our way. And in fact I had far less trouble than I anticipated. Dancers are big customers for tinaje, and dance students had a hard time affording the more reputable practitioners; they were always on the lookout for a new one. I found in a short time that I was developing a reputation with the Imperial Dance Academy.

Soon after I set up in the Square, a client came to see me. He was about thirty standard, tall and well-dressed, and I mentally raised my fee a bit when I saw him. He sat down on the mat, and I said, "Is there some particular problem you want to tell me about?"

"Not unless you count deceit as a problem," he said, and handed me a piece of paper. "I didn't come for tinaje. This is a message for you."

I read it. It was the address Kylla had given me at the Asuka baths, with a date and time underneath. I looked at the visitor and said, "You wouldn't be Lysander Shikron, would you?"

"Your servant, gracious lady."

He was good-looking, with sharp, dark eyes and a wry smile. Kylla didn't seem to have chosen too badly; maybe he didn't have the family's approval, but so far he had mine. "This is today's date," I said.

"Today is when you're wanted."

"All right," I agreed. "I'll be there, unless something goes wrong."

He rose to leave. I said, "I assume you came in here to divert suspicion. You didn't want to hand me a note in full view of the market."

"Yes?"

"Well, don't you think it will look strange if you leave after a couple of minutes? Tinaje usually takes at least half an hour."

"Maybe I changed my mind," he said.

"And that won't look good for my reputation."

"All right, what do you suggest?"

I pulled out my notebook. "Do you know any good stories?"

The address was in a better residential section of the capital. As I expected, Kylla was waiting for me there. She didn't have much time, she said, but gave me thirty tabals (all she could get away with at the moment) and told me Grandmother was about the same and that Eln was spending a lot of time on the Net lately. She also had a basketful of groundhermit, red eggs, and a bottle of Ducort wine. We moved these hurriedly to a sack for me and exchanged a good-bye kiss, followed by a different sort of kiss on her part for Lysander Shikron. I spent at least a full minute looking through my sack while this was going on. Then we left the house in separate directions, me back to Ran and Kylla off to the relatives she was supposed to be staying with.

When I got home, I found Tyl cooking a supper of vegetables and fried bread. "Fine as a side dish, but we can do better than that," I told him, and handed him my sack of goodies. His face lit up.

"How did you do it, my lady?"

"Foreign barbarians with no manners," I said modestly. "We have our methods."

"I haven't seen wine like this since the Emperor's Anniversary. Ah, lady, I was wondering—my shoulders have been hurting since I did the extra set on my stretch bars this morning—"

"No problem, Tyl, do you want me to work on you now or after supper?"

"Food first," he said, surveying the riches.

Later when Ran and Karlas came to table they stared at the array disbelievingly. "Tyl?" said Karlas. Tyl looked to me.

"Theodora?" said Ran.

"A lucky day in the market," I said.

Ran picked up his wine glass, took a sip, glanced at what he was holding, put it down and raised an eyebrow at me.

I did not choose to respond. It was difficult enough trying to figure some way of explaining our new possession of thirty tabals. And I did have to bring it out somehow; Ran could make much better use of it than I could to achieve our mutual goals, and besides there are some ethical lines I will not cross. I really didn't believe Kylla had meant the thirty tabals to go into my Athena fund.

When dinner was over, I still hadn't mentioned it. I did some tinaje work on Tyl's shoulders and helped him clean up the supper dishes. Ran would look at me from time to time, but not in any way that let me know what he was thinking. Finally he said, "You do tinaje for everybody else, but not for me."

"I'm sorry," I said. "I didn't think you had any interest in it." Which was better than coming out with the truth, that doing tinaje for Ran would just confuse me. I had come to accept, back at my start with Vale, that tinaje was a nonsexual form of art. In that definition, I understood it. I require consistency in my life, I don't like to blur definitions, I keep mental categories separate . . . in short, I didn't want to do tinaje with Ran.

"Well?" he said.

"Sit on the mat," I said. "I'm too tired for a full session."

He sat down obediently. I knelt behind him, took a minute to gather concentration, then went into the ritual for partial tinaje. I focused my attention on the necessary movements only. It was going well, I'd done the shoulder muscles, the arms, the upper back, when I moved to the head. There is a movement to help loosen tightness in the neck, where the person doing the tinaje places one hand on either side of the head, just above the ears, and rotates it. I placed my hands in the proper position and suddenly I forgot the whole session and thought: What nice, soft hair you've got.

As the thought crossed my mind I felt his neck muscles tighten.

Vale had warned me about the occasional telepathic experiences one has in tinaje, but I'd discounted it. I finished the session in professional manner, ruthlessly trampling on any personal thoughts and concentrating on the ritual.

"All done," I said, thinking, damn it, just what is it about my thoughts that annoys you so much? He'd closed all up after he took the onyx cat away from me, too. Evidently telepathy was overrated as a means of bringing people together.

Well, enough of stepping softly. I said, "I have something to show you," and I went upstairs to my room and got out Kylla's bag of coins. I brought them down and emptied the bag on the floor in front of Ran. He stared at them.

"Thirty," I said, when he started to count. He looked up at me.

"Pieces of silver?" he asked. Ivory is not a Christian planet, but I should have known they wouldn't forget a good story. I got up to leave. He reached out an arm and held me back. "I'm sorry," he said.

I waited.

"I would like to know how you got them," he said.

"Are you sure?" The only time since Teshin that I'd said Kylla's name, he'd told me never to mention it again.

He considered the matter. Maybe we were still in sync from the tinaje; I could almost see her name rising in his eyes. "Not necessarily," he said. He picked up a few coins and let them dribble through his fingers. "All right, tymon, we'll leave it alone."

I got up to go to my room. He called, "Theodora."

I turned. "Yes?"

"Whose side are you on, anyway? I never asked."

I wanted to say, why do I always have to be on somebody's side? But to Ran that would be as good as saying "not yours." I said, "I'm going to bed now. If you think of any other interesting questions, hold them till morning."

Traditionally, rudeness is an acceptable answer to having one's loyalty questioned. Ran said, "Good night."

I woke up next morning knowing that I'd had bad dreams, but not knowing what they were. I stood at the wash basin, not moving, trying to remember; something about a dripping sound, and an echo, and being in a bad place. Nothing else. I dismissed it and went on to the market.

It was an uneventful morning, not many customers, so when Irsa asked me to watch her wares for her I did so. It started to rain soon after she left, and I put up the sides and top of her cart and went and sat under my tent, keeping an eye on things as best I could through the narrow opening. One of the flash rains of early spring, it probably wouldn't last more than ten or fifteen minutes. Meanwhile the market emptied like an overturned cart.

I felt the tent shake and stuck my head out front to find the cause. Eln Cormallon was there. He was seated on his floater, dry and perfectly turned out in the midst of the downpour, and standing beside him was cousin Stepan, holding an umbrella over his own head and looking silly. The floater was dry, too; it must have been a spellshield.

"Hello, Theo." Eln smiled, the same look of gentle complicity he'd always shared with me, as though we'd just done a practice set in the garden only yesterday. "Put your head back in, you'll get wet."

"If I put my head back in, I won't be able to see you."

"True. Stepan, can we raise this rope, so I can get the floater inside the tent?"

Stepan appraised the situation with an expression of dutiful misery. "I don't think so."

"Well, then," said Eln, "I'm dry enough, so if I lower to the ground I can talk to our Theo comfortably, and you can hold the umbrella over her head."

"I don't have an extra umbrella," said Stepan.

"Yes, I know," said Eln.

So he lowered the floater, and Stepan squatted grimly beside me with his umbrella.

"Long time," I said.

"Yes, I'm sorry about that. You've often been in my thoughts, though."

"Same with me."

He said, "I never thought to see you doing tinaje. Kylla would approve, she likes the old ways. I don't mind tradition myself, when it's not at the expense of profit. . . . " He hesitated, thinking his own thoughts. "Theo, here's the problem. You shouldn't be here."

"I've been in Trade Square before. If you don't mind my saying so, Eln, your family is more than a little snobbish about the ways people can make a living."

"I meant," he said, "that you shouldn't be on Ivory."

I froze. "Oh."

"You ought to be on Athena, getting your degree."

I relaxed, a very little. "You have a point there."

"And it's my family that's mucked around with your life, so I feel some responsibility. I've done some checking. There's a liner due from Tellys in a couple of weeks, one of the *Queens*. It'll be in port for ten days, and then go on to the next leg of its run."

"To Athena."

"Yes, to Athena."

"Well, I appreciate your notifying me of the schedule, Eln, but if I could have afforded passage on a starship I would have left here quite a long time ago."

He laughed gently. "I had that impression. What I've come here to tell you is that your passage is already paid."

"What?" It came out as a choke.

"Your ticket and your ID are registered with the Port Authority. All you have to do is show up." He paused, and when I didn't say anything he went on. "What I would suggest is that you wait till the last day it's in port, less trouble all around that way. Now, the thing is, darling Theo, fond though I am of you, I can't afford to buy passage on every Athenan-bound liner that puts into this city. So this is a one-time deal, this ship only." He turned suddenly to Stepan. "I forget the name."

"The *Queen Emily*," said Stepan. By now he was thoroughly soaked.

"The *Queen Emily*," Eln repeated. "So there you are. By the way, if you're feeling especially grateful to me when you get back home, you might talk to a couple of people I've been dealing with on the faculty there. Let them know what a fine and trustworthy person I am, see if you can get them to stop dragging their feet." He paused again, but I still couldn't seem to come up with anything to say. "Well, there's no need to go into all that now. I'll leave you some notes on the subject in the Net link in your cabin, and if you feel like giving me a hand, that's fine; if you don't, that's fine, too. Theo?"

"Yes."

"You're getting all this information, aren't you?"

"I'm getting it."

"Good." He seemed uncertain. "You know, I would have paid your fare a lot sooner, if you'd just gone with the Issin people back to the capital. Still, no harm done, I suppose."

I said, "No, no harm done. Eln—"

He looked attentive. I don't really know what I would have said at that point, because that was when Stepan shot to his feet, rainwater started to pound me in the face, and I heard Ran's voice say, "Theodora, are you all right?"

I called, "Yes, I'm fine."

Through the sluice of heavy rain I saw Ran standing with Karlas and Tyl. They were standing warily, rigidly, by Irsa's cart, and if they were in anything close to the same mood Stepan was in, their nerves were stretched taut. Stepan's knuckles were by my face, and they were white. I hoped no one was armed. What was I thinking? They were all armed, I only hoped nobody was too nervous.

I said, "I think they were leaving."

Ran started to walk slowly toward us, followed by Karlas and Tyl. Eln raised his floater. He said, "As a matter of fact, we were just about to go." Ran kept walking. When he reached the floater, he stopped.

"Well, then," he said, "go."

Eln regarded him. Finally he said, "Don't blame Kylla for any of this. I didn't give her a choice."

"Everybody has a choice."

A funny sort of half-smile raised itself on Eln's lips, as though he couldn't keep it off. He looked down at me. "It must be nice," he said lightly, "to believe that."

The rain was starting to slacken. Followed by Stepan, he rode slowly out of the market, the only dry person among us.

Chapter 16

"What did he want?" Ran waited until we were home and the door was shut before he turned to me. His green cloak dripped on the floor. Tyl tried to take it from him, but Ran waved him away.

"I don't know exactly," I said. "We didn't have long to talk before you showed up. He was suggesting that I leave Ivory."

"I'll bet he was," said Ran. "Talk about nerve." He paced a few steps over the parlor floor, then pulled off his cloak, rolled it into a ball, and tossed it to Tyl. Tyl shrugged at me and took it away to dry.

I didn't know why I wasn't telling Ran about the ticket arrangement. I needed time to think . . . my impulse was to ignore it, try to pretend the ticket wasn't there. Was that because I was looking for an excuse to stay on this planet? Had I been kidding myself the past year? That didn't feel right either . . . no, it was the circumstances . . . the feeling I got from my talk with Eln was that I was perfectly free to go, provided I left my honor behind when I boarded.

I didn't plan to leave that way, and yet I felt guilty about the whole scheme. Why? And why was it dishonorable to leave now, and not later? Even if Ran got through this crisis, he would still be in a semi-lethal position without a card-reader. Didn't the argument that I'd been tricked into all this still hold?

Ran went to his room, presumably to brood, and I did the same. I have never liked ethical complexity.

That night I had more bad dreams. I woke up with the feeling that I'd been through a recurrent nightmare, one I'd had before but couldn't remember. Probably just as well, I thought; there was enough to deal with in my conscious life.

I met Kylla a few days later at Lysander Shikron's. We

sat in the servants' pantry, off the main kitchen, surrounded by shelves of sealed jars. She was jeweled and painted, no doubt for his benefit, but underneath it all she looked tired and drawn. She brought more money, twenty-five tabals.

"Eln spends his life on the Net terminal," she said, "and when he's not there, he's with Stepan. I never gave much thought to Stepan one way or another before, but now he gives me the creeps. He follows Eln around like he's waiting for raw meat."

Lysander was out of the room just then, and Kylla pulled aside her robes and put her perfect, bare legs up on a bench. She leaned back against the wall. "Oh, how I wish I could get out my pipe right now. But I'm trying to introduce Lysander to my vices gradually." She glanced at me and added, "I think we'll save some of this knowledge till after the wedding."

I was surprised. "You're planning to get married?" Implied in my tone was, you can pull this off with the family?

She smiled. "Give me some time, Theo. So far, the lead role in *Agamemnon* is the only thing I've ever wanted that I didn't get."

I shook my head and she suddenly gave a guilty start and dropped her legs. "Is that Lysander?" she said, as there was a thump on the door to the kitchen. But no one came in and she returned the legs to their former royal seat. "One of the house servants," she said. "I see that giggle, Theo, you may be holding it in out of courtesy, but you ought to keep your eyes down. You don't think I should be keeping these habits from my future husband, do you?"

"It's really not for me to say, Kylla."

She laughed and lit an imaginary pipe. "Isn't this the best way to break it to a beloved? Wouldn't you give him time before you exposed your, well, more unfortunate character traits?"

"No."

"What would you do?"

"I'd print out a list, and tell him to speak now or not bother me about it later. Then I'd have him initial it."

She really laughed at that point, not the ladylike silvery laughter she usually produced, but sheer guffaws. She put a hand over mine as she let go. "Theo, sweetheart," she said finally. "I can see why you get along with Ran."

I waited till she'd calmed down. "How's Grandmother?" I asked.

Her expression faded like a doused candle. "She never leaves her bed. And the only people she'll let into her room now are me and Tagra." She stared at the wall. "I wonder sometimes. It's frightening to think of Grandmother as powerless. Does getting old scare you, Theo? It does me."

"I don't know," I said honestly. "Death scares me. Getting old, the loss of beauty—I never had that much beauty to begin with. And getting older in an Ivoran family means gathering more power . . . anyway, up until near the end. Your people treat it with respect. Ivory is a good planet to get old on, Kylla, at least if you have a family like yours."

She went on staring at the wall. "Thank you," she said softly. "I'm glad to know that."

Lysander came back, and she put down her legs hastily.

Kylla had told me some things about that period of Eln's life no one at Cormallon wanted to talk about, the time when he declared ishin na' telleth on his family and went to live in the capital. Apparently he'd been here for two full years, longer than I'd somehow expected; how had he made a living? There were ways, I knew, and at least he could read and write—but without family connections it was damned hard. And he'd had no Tellys-imported floater then, something difficult to imagine, and which I didn't want to imagine. Kylla said he'd made do with a jerry-rigged board on wheels when he was in the city. It was an insult to Eln to think of him looking eye-level at people's knees.

I wanted to see the place where he'd lived. Kylla told me that he'd been retrieved from a room above a store on Marsh Street, on the other side of the business quarter. It was a store that sold secondhand jewelry, halfway a pawnbroker's, she said; there were two on Marsh Street. I chose the less prosperous looking one.

Inside there were bins of cheap trinkets, foreign-made necklaces of the sort tourists don't mind parting with, false gold and tarnished silver. The counters edging the walls held the better stuff. They were locked. There was one man behind the back counter, reading through some papers. No

Net terminal was in evidence; it was a place that dealt in cash.

I walked up to the man. He was young, perhaps twenty-four or -five; which made him a couple of years beyond me, but somehow I felt the elder. He was light-skinned, more gold than brown, with blond hair and gray eyes. He put down his papers when I approached.

"Can I help you?"

No "gracious lady" here, although the tone was quiet and polite. Perhaps I should try to dress better. "I don't know," I said, wondering what in the world I would say next. "I'm looking for something for a friend."

"Male or female?" he said.

"Male."

"We have a good selection," he said, gesturing to a nearby case. We moved over to it. "Rings, necklaces, ear-rings, belt-ends . . . did you have something particular in mind?"

"Not really." How unfortunately true that was. He wasn't a bad salesman, directing me at once to the more expensive material. But maybe he assumed I wouldn't have bothered him if I just wanted junk from the bins; I could have rooted through them by myself.

"Well, this belt-end is unique. A diving gryphon, you won't see many like it." He pulled it out and laid it on the counter for me to examine.

"Yes, it does appear unique." The gryphon looked as though it had eaten something that disagreed with it. "What about those gold things over there?"

"These?" He laid them beside the gryphon. "Spurs, shaped like salamanders. Ornamental, of course. You wouldn't have much use for them in the city."

"Oh, I don't know. They might strike my friend's fancy."

"He rides?"

"In a manner of speaking. Perhaps you know him—Eln Cormallon."

The hands over the spurs froze, then a tremble went through it, convulsively, like a ground tremor. I stared. I had never seen anything like it. He seemed tightly controlled, distant, unaware of his own reaction. His face remained impersonal.

"Eln Cormallon?"

"Yes," I said carefully. "He might like the spurs. He has an unusual sense of humor."

"Did he send you?" His face raised from the jewelry, his eyes looked into mine. "Do you know where he is?"

"I don't know. I suppose he's at Cormallon." Now I was the one who looked down. I was wrong about the control; I didn't want to see eyes like that.

"He's not in the city, then."

"I don't really know."

"And he didn't send you."

"No. I'm sorry." I wasn't sure what I was apologizing for, but I was sure that I owed it to him somewhere down the line.

He put the pieces back in the case, moving stiffly. "No. Of course he didn't send you." He looked up suddenly from what he was doing. "I'm sorry. Were you really interested in the spurs?"

"No. No. Put them away." I waved them back. "Pay no attention to me. I'm leaving anyway." I started edging down the main aisle. Interfering in people's lives—you'd think I would have learned my lesson from Pina. I felt as though I'd just broken into this store with two large men and had him beaten up.

"Uh, gracious lady?"

I paused, unwillingly, by the door. He stepped out from the dim light behind the counter, and I saw that his left arm, the one he hadn't used, was made of metal. I noted, for no reason, that there were rings of gold and gems on the metal fingers, and none on the biological arm. "Gracious lady, if you see Eln, would you tell him that . . . tell him that he's always welcome here?"

I nodded and went out the door. I wasn't two steps down the street when the door opened behind me and his voice said, "Gracious lady!" I turned.

"Never mind, gracious lady, please don't say anything. All right?"

"All right."

I turned back and started walking very quickly, before he could follow me and tell me he'd changed his mind again. I had the feeling he would have given me twenty different messages if I let him.

* * *

I went home that evening to find that we had a visitor. It was Karlas' brother Halet, a middle-aged, middle-class, slightly more respectable businessman in a striped cotton robe. He ran two stores back in Suttering, the town nearest to Teshin, and had stayed behind to arrange their new management. Now he was here to throw in with our cause.

"Honored," he said, as Ran introduced us. "I have the best hopes for our success."

We traded a few flowery compliments, and I said to Ran, "How did you get him over the property line?" Saddling an ally with seven years of bad luck seemed not in our best interests.

Ran sighed. "I had to break down the whole spell, get him inside, and then redraw it."

I frowned. "Then how did I get in? I wasn't inside when you redrew it."

"Trust me, Theodora, I'm a professional."

I hoped so. Halet pulled on my robe at that point. "My lady, I have something of yours."

"What?"

He opened his wallet and took something out. He placed it in my palm; it was small and hard, wrapped in tissue paper. I opened it and stared.

He said, "The Old Man of Kado Island is dead."

It was the pendant, the piece of delicately lined riverbed stone on its thin silver chain. The lines were like blue veins on skin of alabaster.

Halet said, "It's a bluestone pendant, isn't it? I've never seen one."

"How did you get it?" I asked.

"It was brought to me by Vale the healer. The Old Man sends it to you."

I didn't know why he used the present tense, he seemed to have good grammar—it made me nervous. "Why didn't he give it to Vale?"

Halet shrugged. "I can't say. Perhaps he didn't want it to stay in Teshin."

I snorted at that. The Old Man waits until he's dead, to leave Teshin the only way he can. I kept the paper between my hand and the stone.

"He must have known someone else, somewhere, that he could have sent it to."

Halet said, "You're a tinaje artist, I understand. No doubt he wanted it in good hands, with someone of high moral character."

That was even sadder and funnier. And it was the first time someone ever entrusted me with a responsibility based simply on my profession. That was even more of an ethical burden to bear than the pendant.

I said, holding the stone carefully, "Can I send it back to Vale?" Knowing the answer already.

Halet, and even Karlas, looked shocked at such a suggestion. Ran said, "Yes, you can. You can do anything you like, Theodora. Do you want me to send it back?"

"No," I said. "If he wanted Vale to have it, he would have given it to him."

Halet relaxed, and gave me an approving look. No doubt he was glad to share a house with an unregistered alien of high moral character.

It was a responsibility, but it was also a comfort. I took the pendant out that night (still wrapped in tissue paper) and placed it under my pillow when I went to sleep. I don't know why I did it. But for the first time in a long while I didn't have bad dreams.

I was afraid of losing it, so I made up a little bag of red silk (Tyl did the sewing) and tied it around the stone; and I wore the pendant that way, under my tunic and robes. After a few days I almost forgot it was there.

Ran came to me one night and said, "I want you to run the cards."

I said, "You didn't like it the last time I ran them."

"It has to be done," he said. "Look, I'll be with you the whole time."

"Oh, it doesn't bother me. I was just wondering why you changed your mind."

He looked uncomfortable. "Everything's dangerous," he said. "You can walk down the street and get kicked by a cart-horse."

"Yeah, no doubt."

"All right, something's very wrong here. I put on a mirror-spell not long ago—"

"A mirror-spell?"

He gestured impatiently. "Back-reflex. So physical harm

done to me would be reflected back, duplicated on the person doing the harm. Well, on Eln actually, he's the one I designated."

"And?"

"It didn't work." He started to pace. "It doesn't make sense. It was as if he were already in a mirror himself."

"So, maybe he is. He had someone cast a spell, got in ahead of you. Everybody keeps telling me how bright he is."

Ran looked at me, and I shrugged. He said, "He can't be in a mirror. That can only be self-cast, by its nature. Only a sorcerer can do it, and he's not a sorcerer."

"All right, explain it, then."

"There *is* no explanation. Are you carrying the cards on you?"

"Ah." I took out the deck. Ran settled himself on the floor and I did likewise.

The center card was the Charioteer with paired horses, one black and one white. Well, that was an identity card for Eln, if one existed. Then I thought again, and wondered who I was kidding—it could really stand for anyone in this schizophrenic family. I took another card without dwelling on it. This one was the Water-Drawer, a young man, bare-chested, with a bucket of water from a brick well. He was pouring the water into a jar, and there were more jars by his feet. I placed it beside the center card, keeping one finger on it, and let myself go.

I was in a room walled in ancient, jagged stone, with a flat stone floor. There were no windows. I felt somehow that it was underground, there was something dark and earthy-smelling about the place. It was damp and rooty, like wet flowers. In the center of the room were two couches, low and without sides or arms. A person lay on each couch. They lay like corpses, faces turned up, arms limp. I moved closer to the couches and looked down on them: One was Stepan, the other was Eln. Somehow I'd known that. There was a plastic tube running between them, one forearm to another, and as I watched the tube turned from transparent to red. Then there was a dripping sound that echoed off the stones. Suddenly I remembered my dreams, my recurrent nightmares of the last few weeks, and I knew that in the nightmare I was in this room.

I didn't want to be there any longer, and somewhere far away I took my finger off the card and gazed up at Ran. He said, "You looked upset for a minute."

"It wasn't important." I described the room, the people on the couches.

He said, "It sounds like the cellar at Cormallon. But what was it? A blood transfusion? Why?"

I shook my head. "It's not like the regular pictures, remember. It may not be literal."

"When you drew the cards," he said slowly, "you were thinking about the problem I just gave you? The mirror-spell?"

I said, "Trust me, Ran, I'm a professional."

He gave a half-grin. "All right. Thank you, Theodora. I'll go away and think about it until it drives me crazy." Then he picked up my right hand, kissed it, and went upstairs.

Well, well. I got up off the floor, made my way to my own room, hit the bed like a felled oak and slept heavily till dawn. It had been a confusing night all around.

The next morning Ran walked into the kitchen happily. Tyl was serving me more fried bread; it was cheap and one of the few things he knew how to cook well. I hoped Kylla would send me another message soon, we could use more eggs. "I've got it," said Ran.

"Oh?" In the morning my verbal ability is limited at best. Things would improve mentally after breakfast . . . if only Tyl would use butter instead of oil. . . .

"Theodora, you're not paying attention. This is it, I've figured it out."

"I'm glad, Ran. Tyl, can't you get butter at the Square? There must be a market for the tourists—"

Ran walked over to my place and lifted my plate. "Hey!" I said.

"Are you listening?"

I put down my fork. "All right, you have my full attention. But I'm telling you now that I'll make better sense if you let me take in some food."

He handed me the plate. "Eat, and listen." He sat down next to me. "Logically, why would a mirror-spell not work? The answer is because the target is already protected. All right, logically, how could the target already be protected?

Because he cast his own mirror-spell." He was spilling out the words quickly and cheerfully. "It's the only answer."

"You already explained to me last night why that can't be," I said. "Eln would have to do the spell himself, and he's no sorcerer."

"He's a theorist. He knows everything there is to know about sorcery on a theoretical basis. He's not a sorcerer because he has no talent."

I finished my last bread slice. "That's a major obstacle, isn't it?"

"All right, but listen. He's got a mirror-spell, and that can only be set by oneself. It's the very nature of the spell, it's part of the basic fabric of the way things work in magic, it's just . . . indisputable. It's easier to believe that Eln could get what we call 'talent' from someplace than that all the laws of magic no longer apply. That would be believing that stones fall into the sky and water runs uphill—" He stopped. "I'm starving," he said, as though he'd only just noticed. "Is there any more of that? Tyl—"

"In just a minute," said Tyl.

I said, "You can't just walk into the market and buy talent in a jar."

"Exactly, that's where your card-reading comes in. You know what Grandmother did when she cursed me? She shifted my ability in that one area from me to you—not you specifically, I mean, but someone who fit your parameters. Well, that's not so strange, in a way all she really did was link us up using a physical common point, the deck of cards. No different really from shifting good or bad luck from one person to another by seeing that an object that was in the first person's possession passes to the second person. You remember all this from the textbook, don't you?"

"Vaguely." Extremely vaguely. It was really Eln who used to explain all that sort of thing to me—Eln the theorist.

"It's been said for years that there must be a way to shift sorcery itself from one person to another. But until now no one's been able to do it."

"Eln? I don't see why you should think that he could—"

He shook his head impatiently. "If anybody could figure it out, it would be Eln. He's the best mind working in sorcery. Think what it could mean for the family! People interested in joining Cormallon could buy into the family and be trained, and we could guarantee them to be sorcerers when we finished. People born into the family and talent, but who want to be, I don't know, traders, could sell their talent to someone more interested in developing it. It would change the whole face of the business, and we would control it—it would still be the Cormallon specialty."

"Eln doesn't seem eager to make his knowledge public. If that's what he's really done."

All the animation seemed to drain out of Ran. "No." Tyl brought over a full plate to him, and he stared at it with uninterest. "No, he hasn't made it public. Why would I expect him to? I wonder when he worked it all out." He looked at me. "He hasn't bought his talent, he's stealing it."

"How do you figure that?"

"Well, stealing it in some sense anyway. I can't believe Stepan would agree willingly. No real sorcerer would."

"Ah. The transfusion tube. I begin to see where you're going."

He got up and started pacing, the way he always did when he was on the trail of something. When he was after an answer he was a walker, a hunter; all that energy had to come out somewhere. In similar circumstances I became a go-sit-in-the-corner-and-think-things-over person. And I don't talk about it till I've got it straight.

He said, "We have to know. We have to know how he's doing it. There's no way around the problem; we need to cut him off from his source, and to do that we have to know how he accesses it."

The word "access" brought it to mind. I said, "I understand he's been spending a lot of time on the Net lately."

Ran looked at me. "How would you have heard this?" he asked.

"How do you think?" I said.

He drummed his fingers on the table. "If only I had five minutes with his terminal! If I were at Cormallon—"

I said, "I think we can safely assume he put a confinement on his work so that only his own terminal could access it, and a lock on the terminal so only he can get in."

"If I were there . . . " His voice trailed off. "Money," he said, in a new voice. "We need money."

Well, that was something I always agreed with. The connection with Eln's Net work escaped me, though. Ran picked up his cloak and started off immediately for the Square, apparently eager to accumulate tabals as swiftly as possible. I followed, more calmly, but in much the same spirit.

Given Ran's new state of mind, it was only a matter of time until I broke down and told him about my nonNet account. In fact it was that very evening.

"How much?" he said, at once.

I told him. His face fell. "Well," he said politely, "I'm sure it's a fine amount for the purposes of one person."

"You always told me I was saving too much and spending too little!"

"Naturally I said that, I didn't want you to buy a ticket offplanet."

Here we were both silent, for different reasons. I was thinking of the ticket registered in my name, waiting with the Port Authority. The *Queen Emily* was due to touch down the next day, not that that should hold any relevance for me.

Ran said, "But you've got a banker. Presumably you've both checked on each other."

"I can't speak for him. But I asked around, and he was okayed by the Merchants' Association. And Irsa said he had a good reputation. That's all these unregistered bankers have to go on, their reputation; they don't play around with it if they want to last in the business."

He nodded, and held out a hand. "Come on," he said. "I want you to introduce us."

"You want me to introduce you to my *banker?*"

He pulled me up, and we left the house and went off toward the Street of Gold Coins. I said, as we walked through a spring evening in the capital, breathing in the scent of cinnablossom from every gutter, "Why the sudden obsession with coin? I thought we were doing all right."

"We need backing," he said. "More backing than you've got in your personal account, and more than Karlas or Halet have to give—or anyway, are willing to give, if they're sane."

"Just what is it you've got in mind? And why should my banker be willing to contribute?"

"They do loans."

"Yes, but the loans they do aren't anything we want to be involved with. I don't consider my body as collateral, Ran."

He smiled. "Relax, tymon. Under the right circumstances, they do loans on a noninterest basis—business loans, for a percent of the profit. Let's say, Theodora, that we wanted to rob that little office at the foot of Marsh Street that does Athenan-Ivory money exchange. And let's say that the office wasn't insured by the Merchants' Protective Group. We'd go to your banker, then, and show him all our plans, and if he thought they were feasible he'd put up the money to carry it out. Simple as that."

"And if he didn't think it was feasible? Why shouldn't he turn us in?"

"As you say, tymon—their reputation is all these people have." He laughed. "That, and a whole lot of money."

We reached my banker's office in the Street of Gold Coins. There was no emblem on the door, nothing to say this building was any different from the houses on either side. Ran knocked. He said to me, "After you introduce us, wait out here while I talk to him."

I said, "You're willing to tell your plans to a perfect stranger, and not to me?"

He looked surprised. "He has the money," he said reasonably.

Chapter 17

"What we want you to do," said Ran to me, "is break into the house at Cormallon."

We were sitting in the parlor: Karlas, Tyl, Halet, and Samanta, the wife and partner of my banker. I gathered she was here to safeguard their investment and see if we showed signs of doing anything stupid. I was tempted to behave stupidly then and there, but I managed to hold it back.

"Uh," I said, "are you craz—I mean—what do you mean?"

Ran said, "This is how I see it. We need to access Eln's information. Now, *I* can't go through the barrier, I've been ritually disowned. Nobody else here can go through the barrier, they're all strangers to it. That only leaves you, Theodora."

"It's always possible the barrier was set against me, too," I pointed out.

"Not likely," he said. "It's not set anew each time someone passes—it recognizes what's been defined as a friend, that's all. My definition changed when they read the disownment ritual. Your definition *could* have been changed. I'll admit it, but it's a lot of trouble to go to; and for what? To stop one little tymon from coming on the grounds? The goldbands could put you out just as well."

I saw the reason in that. And Eln didn't think me much of a threat anyway. He probably expected me to be on the *Queen Emily* any day now.

I said, "The goldbands certainly will put me out. Assuming they don't kill me on the spot."

"It's not probable." He gave me a level look. "Eln likes you."

"How long will he like me when he finds me breaking into his house?"

"Yes. Well, it's not without danger."

I said, "And the barrier isn't the only thing in the defense arsenal."

"True," he said, surprised. "How did you know?"

"I know the Cormallons."

Ran leaned over. "I guarantee that I can coach you through the rest of the ground defenses. If you're caught, it won't be through them."

I glanced around at them all, waiting; at Karlas and his relatives, looking tense, at Samanta, looking uninvolved.

"All right," I said.

Karlas smiled. Halet bowed his head to me. Tyl frowned.

Ran said, "There's still the lock on the terminal data."

"There's a lot more than that," I said. "But it's all right, we'll work it out."

Right, here we go—warrior queen Theodora of Pyrene sets out with lance and steed to storm the castle of the green knight. I felt stupid quite often the next few days, wondering how I could have agreed. I found I was checking off the days the *Emily* was in port, too, adding fantasy treachery to fantasy heroism. And while I was wandering around the house in mental turmoil, Ran was always out *buying* things.

"You're running through that loan like water," I said, when he came home with the aircar. We were standing on the roof.

"Just get a tarpaulin," he said. As I helped him to cover it, he added, "Wait till you see the other one."

"Other what?"

"Other car."

He didn't sound as if he were joking. "I beg your pardon?" Aircars are enormously expensive on Ivory because of the tax. They're still trying to get back what they had to pay to Tellys for the first model.

"We'll need two, Theodora, this and a one-seater for you to take through the barrier. It'll be easier to maneuver, and Karlas and I will be just outside Cormallon territory in the larger one."

I stopped fooling with the tarpaulin. "Ran, I don't drive."

He stopped, too. "What do you mean, you don't drive? You come from a highly industrialized planet."

"Yes, it is highly industrialized—with big, crowded cities. If everybody had their own aircar it would be chaos. That's why we use mass transportation." He kept staring at me. "I've never had to fly one of these in my life."

"I don't believe it." He said down on the rim of the aircar.

"I hope you're starting to see why it's better to let me in on your plans at the beginning."

He said, "Never? In your life?"

"Never."

He stood up. "Get in," he said.

"Look, Ran, it's a little late to start teaching me now—"

He said, grimly, "Our bankers will understand failure—intellectually—but they won't understand it if we back out now. Unless you want our bodies used as collateral after all—get in."

I got in. He sat in the other front seat. He'd named half a dozen controls and their functions when he stopped and said, "If I weren't letting you in on my plans at the beginning, this would be the night of the break-in, and it really would be too late."

"You're right. For you this is an improvement. I beg your pardon."

He nodded, and went back to the controls.

The ground defenses were next on my worry list, but Ran refused to talk about them. "There's no need," he'd say, whenever I brought it up. "They're very simple."

Fine, if that was the way he wanted to play it. Meanwhile I was becoming a real whiz at the aircar; Ran had to dive on the controls twice to keep us from crash landing in the meadow outside town. He didn't yell at me, though, he just got very pale.

The *Queen Emily* touched down in port, and we set the date for my exercise in thievery. Ran gave me lists of potential passwords to try on Eln's data lock, and at my insistence Tyl took apart a couple of my robes and made me a pair of new trousers. "You look like a provincial," said Ran when he saw them. "You're not going fishing, you know."

"I'm the one doing this," I said. "I'll set the dress code."

I thought, I'll bet he never gave Kylla a hard time about her hunting trousers. But then, Kylla is the sort of person who gets away with a lot.

The day came. Ran made a big point about not allowing there to be any witnesses for the operation; we didn't want the Cormallon council officially on our backs. I didn't ask him what I was supposed to do if there was a witness—I had a feeling he expected me to know.

We'd fixed on two hours after midnight as the proper time. Cormallon wasn't really an armed camp, despite indications to the contrary; basically it was a country home, and practically everybody went to sleep at night. There were no patrols, no guards as such—they left the defenses to sorcery and their reputation. And why not? No one had been silly enough to try to break in for at least two centuries.

"Eln might very well be awake," I said. Ran and Karlas were sitting with me in the kitchen after sunset, checking their gear and finishing up the bowl of rice and vegetables that Tyl had just made. I couldn't eat more than a couple of mouthfuls, and they lay like lumps of mud in my stomach. "Either I'm very nervous, or Tyl should stick to fried bread."

"Both," said Ran, as he slid a pistol into the holster on his belt.

"Eln has a reputation for roaming the halls at night," I said.

"He used to," said Ran. "But that was before he became the—before he had to handle all these new administrative duties. No doubt he keeps more normal hours now."

"You used to leave the administrative duties for days on end."

"Grandmother and Kylla could pick up the slack then." He handed a pack to Karlas.

"But if he *is* awake, he's very likely to be . . ."

"Right in the room with his Net terminal. Yes, I was going to mention before you left that you ought to enter that room very carefully. Thank you for reminding me." He glanced at Karlas. "Have you got the material?"

Karlas said, "Right here." He took a small vial from his robe. "Took the last of the money," he added.

"Reliable?" asked Ran.

"Believe me," said Karlas, "I checked very carefully."

"All right," said Ran.

He put his elbows on the table and leaned over toward me. "The ground defenses," he began.

"Oh, the oracle speaks," I said.

"Do you want to hear this before you go in? The ground defenses. There aren't any."

"Now, wait a minute—that isn't what—"

"Not any that are really there. The defenses are strictly illusory. There are set traps at various places on the property, and they're tripped by trespassers. They present sensory illusions of danger—things that inspire fear in the person receiving the illusion. The victim's fear is then fed back into the trap on a positive circuit, projected at them at a higher intensity, over and over until they lose their mind. With me so far?"

"More than I want to be. But look, if they aren't really there, why can't I just ignore them and walk straight into the house?"

"The feedback circuit," he said. "You're walking through some trees at night, you hear a roar just behind you—your first reaction is panic. A second later, true, you'd say to yourself that it's just a trick. But it's a second too late, you're already hooked into the circuit."

I thought it through. "Then why are we contemplating this merry expedition? It sounds impossible."

"Not impossible. For instance, if you could turn off the fear first at your end, not let the circuit start, there would be no danger. Unfortunately, you're not na' telleth enough."

"Who says? I'm as na' telleth as anybody here."

They exchanged looks. "So that's why," said Ran, "we got this for you."

He handed me the vial. It contained a great many little white pills. I inspected it, then Ran and Karlas, with narrowed eyes. "I don't know what this stuff is."

"Anarine," said Karlas. "Very good quality. I used to deal in some of it in Teshin—not as good as this, though."

Tyl came in then, carrying a bottle. "Is this what you wanted?" he asked Ran.

"Ducort ninety-nine," said Ran, pleasantly. "If this doesn't work, we'll have gone out in style." He took down glasses from a shelf and set one in front of me. "It has more of a kick with alcohol."

"I'm sure. Will I wake up tomorrow?"

He poured one for himself, then filled glasses for the others. "Concentrate on getting through tonight," he said. "We'll worry about tomorrow then."

A half hour and a half dozen little pills later, things were pretty fuzzy around the edges. There were only two glasses of wine, though; I think. Anyway, when Karlas tried to fill my glass again, I glared at him and said, "Do you want me to stop in the middle of this highly complex robbery and ask to use the toilet?"

"No," Ran answered, "we wouldn't want that." He took the bottle away from Karlas. "I think she has the basic concept," he said. "We'd better get into the car. Anarine is supposed to wear off quickly, isn't it?"

"The alcohol will keep it going a little longer," said Karlas.

We all went up to the roof. "Are you coming, too?" I asked Tyl.

"Sure I am," he said, and went over to the one-seater parked in the corner. There wasn't much room left on the roof.

"Hey!" I yelled. "You don't know how to pilot these things either."

Tyl grinned and went on. Ran said, "Get in the car, Theodora."

I did so, and said, "He doesn't know how to work that thing, Ran."

We took off, Tyl following perfectly. I don't recall most of the trip, except that periodically someone would hand me another little white pill. We must have been cruising at extremely high speed, though, because I remember going "Wooooh!" at one point, when we were crossing over a village.

We set down near a stand of trees just outside the barrier. Karlas took out another pill, but Ran said, "We want this to wear off, don't we?" and he put it back. We got out and stood between the two cars. Ran said, "Are you all right?"

"I'm fine," I said.

"We're going to be right here," he said. "That's directly south of the house. Just aim in this direction when you take off. See those hills over there?"

"Sure."

"Use them to steer by if you have to. I mean, I've preset the auto to return here, but it's better to be ready in case anything goes wrong."

"Fine."

"You can fly for about five minutes after you cross the barrier. You don't want to have to walk too far. But you want to put down *out* of line of sight of the house."

"Right."

"You remember all the passwords I gave you?"

"Uh-huh."

He seemed worried, but I wasn't. "Well," he said. Then he kissed me and said, "Good luck, Theodora."

"Queen Theodora, to you," I said.

He frowned, confused. "Hand me my trusty lance," I said, gesturing to the back of the aircar. He took out my data-case and handed it to me. I strapped it over one shoulder. Then he paused and took off his holster and put it around my waist himself, pulling the belt taut. He stepped back.

"Do you know where you're going?" he asked uncertainly.

"North through the barrier. Straight arrow to the main house: Land out of direct line of sight. Be careful going in the Net link room. Use the auto when I take off or else line up with the two hills."

Karlas said, "I told you it doesn't affect intelligence. Much."

I started toward the barrier. Ran said, "Don't you think you should use the car?"

"Right," I said.

He was looking pale again.

The one-seater wasn't that hard to maneuver. I set down behind the south hill outside the main house, on the other side of the front garden. The front garden was a massive project of streams, tall hedges, tiny bridges, marble benches, and pavilions. I'd always preferred the back garden, where things grew up wild and tangled, and the sa'ret equipment was set up. I started on the pathway through the maze that led up to the lawn. The night air was bracing, head-clearing, direct, and sharp; all I didn't want to be at this particular moment. I noticed a little white pill caught in the cuff of my tunic. "What the hell," I decided, and swallowed it.

It was more enjoyable after that. I decided I was glad to be there. I was thinking how lovely the garden was by night, when I noticed that the entrance to the Crimson Bridge was blocked by a giant with a scimitar. It was eight meters tall, and stood waiting for me menacingly, tapping the blade on the wood of the bridge. It growled, low in the throat, as I came nearer. I started to giggle; it was clean out of period with the rest of the garden. "Atrocious taste," I commented as I walked through it and went on to the Center Maze of Flowers. Rooting among the flower beds, snuffling up the path toward me was a gray rat about the size of Ran's aircar. It followed me through the Center Maze, occasionally nipping at my heels, and when I reached the entrance to the Path of Many Stones I turned and pretended to thrust with an imaginary sword. "Take that," I said, but it vaporized. "Damn," I said.

I went down the Path of Many Stones, looking for the door Ran had told me about. Somewhere around the quartz boulders, wasn't it? I counted them off, lost track, and had to start again. Seven, eight, nine. That must be the one. Hell, there was another huge rat, sitting on the boulder and baring its teeth. How annoying. I began to declaim, in a louder voice than was wise, "Why are your traps so barren of new pride, so far from variation or quick change? —Hey, I didn't know I remembered that. It must be the pills." We regarded each other. I went on, "All your best is dressing old rats new, spending again what is already spent." It licked its neat white teeth. "Move," I added. It sat there. I took out my pistol and rapped it on the snout with the butt. It vanished. I pushed the boulder over, grunting, and examined the damp earth beneath. Using my forefinger I drew a pentacle in the ground, and covered it with the sorcery symbol. A second later there was a large hole in its place, with steps leading downward.

I descended into a dusty, foul-looking tunnel. The floor was lit with greenish luminescence, showing the cracked stone and remains of vermin. Ran said the emergency exit to Cormallon hadn't been used in generations, and it smelled like it. I followed the tunnel to a wooden door at the end, opened it, and found myself in the back of a garden-supply closet, among rakes and hoes. I opened the closet door very slowly.

I was in the cellar. I looked around at the jagged stone walls, the floor with its carefully fitted blocks, the ceiling. I almost expected to see two couches there, but there were none. Nevertheless I was nervous simply being in the room and I wanted to get out. I reopened the closet, just to check my potential exit, and saw that there was no door visible at this end. I put my hand against the far wall—it felt like wall.

Still, I wasn't worried. I'd taken too much anarine for that. I headed for the cellar steps, walking as quietly as I could. The stairs came out in the kitchen; huge, deserted, and dark. It was another country entirely with the lights out, a different place from the friendly pocket of food and conversation I'd found when Herel the cook was holding court. I tried not to knock anything over.

Nobody in the passageway, nobody on the main stairs. My heart was beating faster, I noticed. Given my present rate of pulse, who knew what state of nerves I'd be in if I hadn't gotten blessedly tranked up ahead of time. Eln's Net link was on the second floor; I'd never been in the room, but Ran had drawn a map . . . here we were. There was just a curtain in the doorway, and no sounds coming from inside. Of course, some people can be awfully quiet when they use a terminal. There's no law that says you have to use the audio switch; if you're doing math, it's easier not to. Would Eln be doing math? I dithered in the doorway for a couple of minutes, getting up the nerve to look inside. It was the idea that someone could come along the second-floor passage at any time that finally pushed me to stick my head in and take the risk.

Empty. I hadn't realized I'd been holding my breath. I walked in and steadied the curtains behind me.

Now, let's see. His keyboard was covered with dust. Evidently he did use the audio switch, or else the screen pad and pencil. Not surprising—this was another heirloom terminal, first-generation import, and the keys were Standard letters. Tellys had gone to a lot of trouble to get the Net to accept phonetic renderings of Ivoran words in Standard letters. Ivoran just had too many damn characters, it drove the Tellys technicians crazy. As a result hardly anybody on Ivory used the actual keyboard, they preferred to talk or write on the screen pad. Ran was one of the few people I knew who punched the keys. Probably something to do with his aggressive instinct.

I needed the keyboard. I would leave dust tracks if I hit the keys, and Eln would know someone had been there. I actually stood there for a moment wondering if there was any way I could put the dust *back* on the keyboard after I was finished, before I realized I was being an idiot. It was the anarine, I would like to think. I activated the terminal, sound off.

-CAN I HELP YOU? the screen said. At least, I assume that's what it said. I typed, in Standard, PLEASE USE STANDARD.

-CAN I HELP YOU? it said, obligingly, in readable letters.

-YES, I said.

-PLEASE IDENTIFY YOURSELF.

I typed, ELN CORMALLON, 53462.

-ELN CORMALLON, YOUR NET MATERIAL IS ALL PASSWORD-PROTECTED. TO ACCESS ANY SPECIFIC INFORMATION, YOU WILL HAVE TO PROVIDE SPECIFIC CODES. WHAT AREA DO YOU WISH TO GO TO?

-ACCESS BY SUBJECT.

-VERY WELL.

-SUBJECT IS SORCERY-TRANSFER.

-VERY WELL. PLEASE GIVE ME A SPECIFIC CODE.

-HOW MANY INCORRECT CODES CAN I TRY BEFORE THE SIRENS GO OFF?

-I BEG YOUR PARDON?

-HOW MANY TRIES FOR SPECIFIC CODE DO I HAVE BEFORE SECURITY PROGRAM KICKS IN?

-THREE. BUT YOU CAN TERMINATE YOUR SESSION AND TRY AGAIN AS OFTEN AS YOU LIKE, SO WHY BE COY ABOUT IT.

-I LIKE YOUR SECURITY INFORMATION PRO-GRAM.

-THANK YOU. FOR AN ADDITIONAL 86,000 TA-BALS IVORAN A TIGHTER SECURITY PROGRAM MAY BE PURCHASED FROM SOFTSTAR OF TEL-LYS, AND INSTALLED FOR YOU AT NO EXTRA COST.

-SUBJECT IS SORCERY-TRANSFER.

-VERY WELL. PLEASE GIVE ME A SPECIFIC CODE.

I typed, STEPAN.

-INCORRECT. PLEASE GIVE ME A SPECIFIC CODE.

-I typed, BLUESTONE.

-INCORRECT. PLEASE GIVE ME A SPECIFIC CODE.

-I typed, RAN.

-INCORRECT. CODE "RAN" IS NOT A SORCERY TRANSFER SUBJECT. THIS INFORMATION RE-SIDES IN ANOTHER BRANCH.

END, I typed. Then I logged on again. We went through the routine, I asked it to speak Standard, gave Eln's name and ID number, and tried three of the passwords Ran sug-gested. None of them worked. I tried the whole thing again with three more passwords. Nothing. I did it all again, still no result. Within half an hour I had gone through Ran's entire list of forty-eight passwords. Many of them were gen-uine Cormallon codes—Eln had apparently wiped them all when Ran was disowned.

I logged on again, and thought about it. I typed, KYLLA

-INCORRECT. PLEASE GIVE ME A SPECIFIC CODE.

I typed, THEO.

-INCORRECT. CODE "THEO" IS NOT A SORCERY-TRANSFER SUBJECT. THIS INFORMA-TION RESIDES IN ANOTHER BRANCH.

-WHICH BRANCH?

-PERSONAL RECORDS.

It was very tempting, but I was pressed for time. SUB-JECT IS SORCERY-TRANSFER, I typed.

-VERY WELL. YOU HAVE ONE REMAINING TRY FOR CORRECT CODE.

This session, anyway. But I was running out of guesses. I thought of the shopkeeper in the jewelry store on Marsh Street. Kylla had told me his name, what was it? While I was trying to remember I decided to do one more code and log off and on again.

I typed, MARSH.

-VERY WELL.

I was about to type END, when I froze.

-VERY WELL? AM I IN SUBJECT SORCERY-TRANSFER?

-YOU ARE IN SUBJECT SORCERY-TRANSFER.

-THANK YOU.

-YOU'RE WELCOME. DO YOU WISH TO CONTINUE WORKING ON THE TIME/INTENSITY GRAPH?

-NO THANK YOU. I WANT TO COPY ALL INFORMATION ON THIS SUBJECT TO PORTABLE MEDIUM.

-WHICH MEDIUM? PLEASE NOTE THAT YOUR PRINTER DOES NOT POSSESS STANDARD CHARACTERS.

-PELLET.

-PLEASE NOTE THAT PELLET GENERATOR HAS NOT BEEN USED SINCE ITS INSTALLATION 53 YEARS AGO. WITHOUT MORE CURRENT TESTING, IT IS POSSIBLE THERE WILL BE DIFFICULTY IN GENERATION OR DISRUPTION OF DATA.

-GO AHEAD ANYWAY.

-VERY WELL.

I looked at the pellet generator beside the terminal, a small glass case with a spindle inside. Real glass, not plastic; that's Cormallon style—it could just as easily have been cut crystal. Sometimes this family got on my nerves.

While I watched the spindle started to turn. It revolved faster and faster, accumulating soft gray material at its base. The gray material grew. When it was about a centimeter wide and three centimeters high, the spindle stopped. I waited another moment for the pellet to harden, then I opened the glass and took it out. I placed it in one of the pellet-holes inside my data-case.

I typed, THANK YOU, I'VE GOT IT.

-DO YOU WISH MATERIAL ON RELATED SUBJECTS ALSO?

-WHAT RELATED SUBJECTS? I asked.

-SORCERY, THEORETICAL
SORCERY, HISTORY
SORCERY, PRACTICAL
SORCERY, CORMALLON
SORC—

I hit the "cut" button. -NO THANK YOU. Then I got a bright idea. I typed, ACCESS BY SUBJECT.

-VERY WELL.

-HOUSEHOLD SECURITY.

-THREE SPECIFIC CODES ARE NECESSARY TO ACCESS INFORMATION. YOU HAVE TWO MINUTES TO ENTER THE FIRST. IF THIS CODE IS INCORRECTLY ENTERED, OR THE TWO MINUTE MARK IS REACHED, THE HOUSEHOLD ALARMS WILL GO OFF. TIME BEGINS NOW.

Great gods of scholars! I leaped out of the chair. Then I stopped, leaned over, and typed END.

-THIS DEFENSE PROGRAM CANNOT BE INTERRUPTED.

I started to sweat.

I ran down the main stairs, skidded to a stop in the passageway and wondered if I should make for the front door; it might not open easily and would start the alarms that much sooner. I wasted half a second thinking about it and then, for no really good reason, kept running through the kitchen and down the cellar stairs. But the emergency exit just wasn't there. I pounded on the closet wall in desperation, and as I did the alarms began to sound. I took the cellar steps upward, two at a time, and headed for the front door. Then I skidded to a stop again—there were people starting down the main stairs. I reversed direction and headed back toward the kitchen. I would have to use the back entrance, although it would mean yet more alarms going off, and then a long sprint around the east wing of the house to get to the front and try to reach the aircar before everybody else did; a hopeless task, but this was no time to think about it. I hit the kitchen running flat out. As I rounded the table, the door to the other passage opened.

It was Kylla. She was wearing a nightrobe and holding a pistol. She stared at me.

Under the circumstances, I didn't know what to say. I opened my mouth, paused, and she said, "Come on."

"What?" I said.

"Follow me," she ordered, with intensity in her voice, and turned away. Having no other alternatives, I did.

She took me down the hall to a door I'd never paid much attention to; it led up some stairs to a garage. There were two aircars there, both four-seaters. She said, "Get in that one. The other one needs repairs." Then she hit a switch and opened the roof doors. "C27 activates it," she yelled to me through the car window. I punched it in and watched the board light up. Then I took off.

There was no time to ask questions, no time to say thanks, no time to look back and wave. I had my hands full just maneuvering.

This model was different from the ones I'd been taught on. The altitude control was foot-operated; what could the manufacturers have been thinking of? I kept dipping groundward as I flew. And while I tried to make sense of the controls I kept thinking, what if they've done something to the barrier? I increased speed with one hand and adjusted the altitude yet again. And where were those damned hills I was supposed to steer by? And why did I have to get stuck in a clumsy four-seater obviously designed by the Marquis de Sade Research and Development Corporation? And where *were* those hills?

I crashed through the barrier. It felt like that, but all that really happened was the familiar tingle as I passed harmlessly through. Just in time—let them do what they wanted to it, now. I scanned right and left, looking for any landmarks; and as I did I must have lost control of the altitude. Suddenly I was a lot lower than I thought I was, and a hillside was rushing up to meet me.

In rapid, useless succession, I jerked up the altitude, I veered sharply left, I saw that neither of these were going to be enough to help; I froze for perhaps one very lengthy millisecond; and I felt a burning sensation in my chest. Then I hit the brakes.

Maybe it would be obvious to people who know what

they're doing that the brakes were the first thing I should have gone for. But ever since I'd tripped the Cormallon alarms I'd been operating on a single looped program that said, GET OUT, GET OUT, GET OUT. *Stopping* had, momentarily, seemed like a foreign concept.

It worked. I still came down rough, there was no avoiding it. My teeth jarred in my head. I pulled off the safety web (the de Sade people had gotten one emergency measure right) and rolled my neck tentatively. Everything still seemed to be there, albeit in somewhat bruised condition. At this moment, though, it was perhaps more important that the car be all right. I switched on the control-check and thought, as I waited for the green light, well, it's lucky that in a crisis like this you held together long enough to hit the brakes. Pat on the back for you, Theodora, and we'll overlook the fact you lost control of the thing to begin with. But the pain in my chest continued, and I opened my tunic to see what was wrong.

I was still wearing the Old Man's bluestone pendant. It felt warm. But the back of the silk cover had burnt through, where it touched my chest, and the patch of skin underneath it was blistered, as though from a bad sunburn. I wondered if Annurian knew anything about driving an air-car; maybe I didn't deserve as much credit for hitting the brakes as I thought. I didn't want to speculate about it now, there were too many things to deal with in my immediate future; but I also didn't want the pendant in physical contact, so I pulled it off and stored it in the data-case.

The control-check came up green. I thought I could make out the hills in question farther over to my left, which would make the rendezvous just a few kilometers east. As I was looking out the window, I saw something move in the bushes, like a person's head ducking. At once I snapped my attention to the spot, although it really wasn't fair, I thought; I'd been through enough just now. Nothing else happened, but I was sure that I'd seen it, it hadn't been nerves. I got out of the car, pistol in hand.

"Come out," I yelled.

Nothing. Another bush rattled.

"You'd better come out, or I'll start shooting at random."

Slowly a man's form straightened up from the bushes.

He walked out. He was the thinnest person I'd seen in a long time, and his clothes were obviously makeshift. His hair was gray, but he didn't look more than forty-five. "Who are you?" I said.

"Arno Serren, noble lady," he said. "Please don't hurt me."

His accent was very thick, and I didn't recognize it.

"What are you doing here?" I asked. "And you'd better talk quickly."

"I'm from Tammas District," he answered.

"So?"

"Tammas? Have you heard of it, noble lady? Things are bad there."

So they were, I'd forgotten. There'd been some kind of trouble in Tammas District and Imperial troops had been called in. It had nothing to do with me, I'd never given it much thought; nor had anybody else I'd known.

"You've come a long way, sir Serren." Out of the frying pan, into the fire.

He shifted feet nervously. "I have a long way to go, noble lady, I didn't mean to interrupt anything you might be doing—or to trespass—or to do anything to annoy you. I'd better be on my way."

"Where?"

"Uh, I was going to the Northwest Sector, noble lady."

Oh, gods, what an innocent. To leave Tammas District and go to the Northwest Sector. I couldn't shoot him, I just couldn't. "Sir Serren, I'm going to do you a favor."

"Oh? "The idea didn't seem to make him happy.

"You wouldn't last a week in the Northwest Sector. And I can't leave you hanging around here to answer questions. So, I tell you what—I'll take you with me."

"You don't have to do that, noble lady. It's too great an honor, believe me. I'll just be going—"

"Get in the car."

"Really, noble lady—"

"Get in, now. I'm in a hurry." I gestured with the pistol. He began moving, very slowly, toward the car door. As he touched it, I heard a squeal from the bushes, and a short, brown human figure raced out and joined him. It was a woman. She was similarly dressed, and clearly very upset.

They started talking very quickly, too quickly for me to follow their accents.

"This is my wife, Heida," said Arno Serren.

"Honored by this meeting," I said. "Get in the car, fast."

And so we all took off. It had been a very eventful six minutes.

Three minutes later I touched down at the correct spot. I got out of the car and Ran grabbed me by the shoulders. "We saw the car go down," he said. He looked sick. "Are you all right?"

"Just shaken."

He let out his breath, the same way I'd done when I found the Net link room empty.

I said, "We have to hurry, I tripped the alarms."

He cursed. I said, "It's not that bad, Kylla said the other aircar needed repairs—they'll have to use ground vehicles or horses, it will take longer."

"Kylla?" he asked. "Never mind, you can tell me later."

Meanwhile Arno Serren and Heida were getting out of the car, very uncertainly. They had the look of people who try to stay in the background, wherever they find themselves. Ran's eyes widened.

"Who are these people?" he said.

I told him. He said, "You brought strangers with you at a time like this?"

"You said no witnesses."

"I didn't mean for you to bring them along!"

I said, "I'm not going without them, Ran."

He stood there, breathing hard for a second. Then he said, "Karlas. Tyl. Get over here."

Karlas got on one side of me and Tyl on the other. Karlas' hand touched my elbow, preparatory, I suppose, to picking me up and throwing me in the other aircar.

Ran said, "Get those two back in the car. Tyl, you can drive them to the city. Karlas, you ride with us."

Karlas looked confused. He went over to help Tyl get my two new responsibilities into the stolen vehicle.

Ran called, "Tyl, be sure and ditch the car somewhere far from our house. And don't lose track of our guests."

"Yes, sir," said Tyl. He held out a hand to help Heida Serren enter the car.

"Well," said Ran, "shall we go?"

I climbed in, followed by Karlas. Ran handled the controls. When we were a good twenty kilometers away, he said, quietly, "Kylla helped you get out?"

"Yes."

"Well," he said.

We were all silent for a few minutes. Then Ran said, "What went wrong?"

I told him about the closet door that wasn't there, and about setting off the household security alarm program.

He frowned. "I just don't believe it. How could you have done anything so stu—so risky, Theodora? You're usually so careful. Weren't you thinking? Didn't you realize that if there were anything in the household security program you should know, I would have told you? Of course it's tighter than the general security program, it was set up separately, as part of the package, when Grandfather got the Net links put in. I've been in it a hundred times. Theodora—"

"Look, I know I screwed up, but really, Ran. You fill me up with Ducort and anarine, and then ask me why I do something stupid?"

He bit his lip. Karlas said, "It doesn't affect intelligence."

"Much," I reminded him.

Ran looked over at him. Karlas said, defensively, "She's just a little tiny barbarian. Maybe her system didn't have the capacity to handle it."

A while later Ran said, "Still, bringing those two refugees along was not perhaps our wisest move. I respect your sentiment, Theodora, but we really ought to get rid of them."

I said, "Oh, give it a chance. Isn't it a Cormallon tradition to take in the cream of the ones heading up the Northwest Sector route?"

He considered that. After a bit he stared to smile. He probably missed all the servants he left behind at Cormallon, I thought. Karlas and Tyl were all right, but they didn't wait on him hand and foot. And I suppose he also missed the idea of *household.* He wanted one, even if it had a leaky roof and the noise from the bar next door never stopped.

He said, finally, "I wonder if either one of them can cook."

I grinned. "We can always ask."

Chapter 18

When we got back, I went straight upstairs and fell on my bed. Ran had to sit up waiting for Tyl and our two refugees to reach home, so he could redraw the circle of protection. I slept through their arrival and through the subsequent reshuffling of bedrooms. Most houses in the capital have plenty of rooms, but five sleeping chambers was our present limit; Ran had no intention of sharing his room or letting me share mine, and as a married couple the Serrens seemed entitled to their own. So Halet was routed out of bed and asked to move in with Tyl. When I got up, late in the morning, I found Halet rolling fitfully on some cushions in the parlor, red-eyed and irritable; apparently Tyl snored.

Ran at least was happy. He was up ahead of me, as were the Serrens, and Heida was setting a huge plate of hermit's eggs, smoked saffish, and half a pellfruit in front of him. Arno was still working at the stove. They must have been up hours ago and at the dawn market.

I sat down beside Ran. "Impressive," I said.

He said, "It tastes good, too."

And just last night he'd been implying a quick shooting would be in the best interests of all. Yet once they were in the household they were members like anyone else, and here he was sitting smugly over this breakfast as though he were personally responsible for it.

"Hermit's eggs for me, too?" I asked.

"Ask your sycophants," said Ran, through a mouthful of saffish.

"They're not my sycophants," I said.

Heida hurried over with a cup of tah. "Noble lady," she said, setting it in front of me. "We'll have yours ready in just a moment. We have spices, too, if you want salt or pepper."

"Heida, I'm not a noble lady, hasn't anyone told you?"

She looked flustered. Ran smiled around a forkful of egg.

"I'm sorry, noble lady. I didn't mean to be impolite."

I had the feeling that "Theodora" would be a long time coming from this woman, and that even if I succeeded, I'd be the only one in the house she called by name. I gave up the attempt to foist my outworld principles on her. "How about 'my lady'? We're house members now, you know."

She smiled in relief. "Yes, my lady. We have sliced red peppers, if you would like them?"

She went off to help Arno and I said to Ran, "It reminds me of the first time you told me to call you 'sir.' "

"Undisciplined little tymon, weren't you?" he replied.

I ignored that and took a sip of tah. "I take it you'll be analyzing the pellet data today."

"Of course."

"Do you want me to stick around? I did some analysis on Athena."

He shook his head. "Go to the Square, as usual. We'll look guilty if we break our patterns too obviously."

"Does it matter? Eln's going to have a pretty good idea it was one of us."

"The council won't, and there's no need to get their attention."

I didn't want to bring it up but felt it had to be said. "They've acted without proof before."

"Not without manufactured proof, and that sort of thing takes time."

"And you don't have a Net link code."

"I'll be using Halet's."

Well, there was nothing more to be said. I sipped my tah.

Apparently he was dead serious about keeping to pattern because he showed up in the Square in late afternoon. He dropped by my tinaje tent before going to set up among the games players. "How's it going?" I asked, when I'd sent off my latest customer.

"Huh," he said, sitting down for a minute. "A lot of numericals, a lot of charts. It's going to take a while."

"We do have the right data, though, don't we?"

He looked tired. "I dearly hope so."

"I can help, if you need it."

"It's not just the analysis; it's what it means. We've got a fine graph, for instance, and I can tell you the formula that describes the curve on it, but what it's doing here I have no idea. I thought from the points on the vertical axis that it was some kind of lunar cycle; but it isn't, quite." He ran a hand through his hair. "Eln's had years to study this, I'm just beginning."

Someone rustled the tent wall; a customer, asking admittance. "Damn," I said.

He rose. "I have to go anyway. I'll see you tonight."

That night was spent going through printouts. We sat on the floor of the parlor staring at one sheet after another. None of it meant anything to me; I could see why Ran hadn't leaped at my offer of assistance. This was heavy going.

Some time after midnight, Ran put down a roll of charts, leaned back against his pillow, and closed his eyes. "No," he said.

"Get some sleep," I said. "You'll do better when you're not so tired."

"Look who's talking. It was just last night you were crash-landing a car outside the Cormallon barrier. A very expensive car, I might add."

"Would you want me to crash a cheap one? Get some sleep."

He smiled, very distantly, eyes still closed. I left him there and went upstairs.

Someone was shaking my arm. "Wake up. Come on, Theodora, wake up."

"What? What?" I opened my eyes. Ran was standing over me, and a dim light was coming through the window slit. "What time is it?"

"Almost sunrise. Listen, I've got it."

"What?" I said again. He went over to my basin, poured water onto the sponge and brought it back to my bed-mat. He started wiping my face with it. "Hey!" I said. "Hey, that's cold."

He threw the sponge back onto the washtable. It hit the towel with a spongy splat, like a wet snowball. "Listen," he said. "The graphs. They're time-intensity graphs."

"So?"

"Intensity of sorcery," he said impatiently. "On a time axis, because it changes over time—waxes and wanes, just like the moon."

"I don't see why."

"It's not his, you see. He doesn't get it in one lump sum—he has to draw on it continuously, and some times he can draw more than others. So he has to time his plans to fit with how much he can draw on, do you see?"

"I guess. Sort of."

He smiled. "Which gives us the obvious corollary. We time our plans to fit how much he can draw on, too."

I sat up in bed, beginning to get the idea.

Ran and Karlas started disappearing for long periods of time. This did not surprise me. I continued my time in Trade Square, keeping up the pretense of normality over the next several days. Ran told me, over dinner, that the graphs showed the worst low point of the next two months coming—for Eln—in two days' time.

"What does that mean for us?" I asked. "You said he might have a mirror-spell, didn't you? What can you do?"

"For that matter," he said, "what can he do to me? He's taking sorcery from Stepan—what if I aimed my own mirror-spell at Stepan? I've had years of experience in laying boobytraps; I've been in the field and Eln hasn't. He'd be an idiot to do anything directly."

I said, "Why don't I feel like applauding? You're both invulnerable, is that what you're saying? And yet somehow I think you have something in mind."

"All right," he said. "It's nothing you have to worry about. You're not involved in this one."

I put down my fork. "What *is* this one?"

He said, uncomfortably, "I've been meaning to say—you know, Theodora, that I didn't tell you about the Cormallon ground defenses for a reason. If you'd spent days worrying about them ahead of time, you would have been working against yourself in terms of the feedback circuit."

"Yes, I understood that. What's the point?"

"I just wanted to be sure you knew."

Was this in the nature of a last will and testament? I

hoped I was just being nervous. "Tell me what's going on," I said.

"Look," he said, "we've been struck close to home before. It took months for Vale to dig me out from under. And when it happened, you lost control of the cards first. In terms of magic, we're linked. I don't want to open up any doors right now that we may not want open."

I leaned back. "I'm a security risk, is that it?"

"I knew you'd say that. You're not listening. Eln's the best theorist on Ivory in this generation—he's doing things people aren't supposed to be able to do. His point of attack might be the cards. It's nothing personal."

I looked down at my empty dinner plate. "He hasn't tried anything before," I said.

"He's never been under this much pressure before."

I was silent. He said, "It's dangerous. Particularly with this new facility you have with the cards. I don't know what you're tapping into, but it worries me. You can't control it, and we don't have time to study it."

"All right," I said.

"You understand, I'm not being arbitrary—"

"Yes, all right."

He studied me. He said, "We've got more Ducort in the kitchen. Would you like some?"

"No, thank you."

"Well—Halet's got us a second loan from the bankers, and we might not have much longer to spend it if things don't work out. Would you like to go to the Lantern Gardens?"

"No, thank you. It's late." I rose from my place.

"The show will only just be starting."

Tyl had come in halfway through the meal, and gulped down his food in his usual silence. Now he looked up and said, "Won't you, my lady? I've never been to the Lantern Gardens. I'd like to come along."

So two nights before whatever was going to happen was going to happen, I went out to the Lantern Gardens, escorted by Ran and Tyl. I painted on all the cosmetics Kylla had given me, and not just to make it a grand occasion. I was also hoping the manager wouldn't remember me from the last time I was there.

* * *

I was in the Square as usual the next day when Eln came to see me. Stepan was absent this time. He came alone on his floater, maneuvering carefully through the market crowds. It was a fine sunny day, not like the last visit when he had the place to himself.

I was between customers. "Hello, Eln," I said.

"Beautiful day, Theo, and I'm happy to see you're no worse for wear."

"Worse for what?" I said. Was he going to accuse me of the Cormallon break-in?

"For the two and a half Pink Ringers you downed at the Lantern Gardens last night."

"Oh. Barely felt them, I assure you."

"I believe it. And you struck me as such an abstemious girl when you first appeared at Cormallon. For a little outlander, you're developing quite a capacity. Have you been gene-tested for alcoholism? Something to bear in mind if you're going to go on this way."

I squinted up at him from where I sat. "Yes, it is a beautiful, sunny day," I said.

"Sorry about the excess sunlight," he said. "Can't stand it, myself. If you'd let me into your tent here, we could both be in the shade."

The rope I'd tied to the pole might just be high enough today to accommodate him. "Come on in," I said, crawling backward.

He managed to maneuver inside by holding the floater about a centimeter off the ground. "Snug, but serviceable," he said. "I suppose you'll be glad when you don't have to squat under a makeshift canvas anymore."

"Oh?"

"The *Queen Emily*. She takes off at the end of the week."

"Oh, yes."

He cocked a head in my direction. "I don't detect that scholarly enthusiasm, Theo. Is there something I should know?"

"Eln . . ." I said. "How's Grandmother?"

He looked serious. "I don't think she has long. She hasn't let me into her room in months." He paused, then said, "I grew up with the idea of Grandmother. She's like a mountain or a rock, you don't imagine anything will happen to it in your lifetime. Now it's like she's gone already. You know, I used to go to her room every night after dinner—even when I didn't show up for dinner—and talk her down so she wouldn't be mad at me."

"Mad at you for what?"

He smiled. "For whatever I'd done."

"I'm sorry," I said. "I don't know much about families. Or death. I don't know what to say."

He said suddenly, "You're not leaving, are you? On the *Emily*, I mean."

"Maybe I haven't made up my mind. Give me a couple of days, and you'll see for yourself."

He nodded. "You're not leaving. I thought you might not."

There was a tug on the front of the tent just then, and I called, "Busy! Come back later!"

He glanced briefly at the tent opening and said, "You do tinaje for everybody else, but not for me." It was the very echo of what Ran had once said to me, and I tensed. Was he trying to let me know that he had our house bugged? But he seemed to mean it just as he said, could it be a coincidence? "Why not, Theo? I've got some extra time, and riding in the same position every day is hell on my back."

I thought, you ask why not? Because I'm withdrawing from you, and I don't want to do anything to bring us any closer. I'm not going down with you. I may be like you, but I know when to let go.

I sat back on my heels, and he sighed. He looked around the tent, and his gaze rested on my notebook. "May I?" he said.

He leafed through it. "A varied collection," he said. And we spent the next hour talking about my notebook stories. He was probably the only person on Ivory who could have talked to me about my work the way an Athenan would. We agreed that there had been very little drift in the oral storytelling lines over the centuries, and after we compared the northern and southern thematic differences, I said suddenly, "Were you responsible for the aircar fire? Did you know I was inside?"

"Yes," he said, and his voice was unhappy but unashamed. His eyes met mine easily.

"Yes to both questions?" I asked. Never willing to let well enough alone.

He said, "Are you going to send this collection to the University Press on Athena?"

"Yes."

"Then let me tell you a story, too. It would be nice to think of something I've said being read by other people, even if they are barbarians."

I said, "If you make up the story yourself, I couldn't honestly include it. The book is supposed to be folktales."

He smiled. "This is an old one." So he told me a story, short but neat, and I wrote it down as he talked. And I wondered, which is Eln, the one sitting beside me now or the one who tried to kill us? I tried to imagine Ran on a murder attempt one week and teaching his victim sa'ret the next. Imagination failed utterly. He was too straightforward emotionally; the idea of being a friend and an enemy at the same time was beyond him. (And that, I realized suddenly, was how Eln had gotten so far so quickly. Ran had iron rules. He couldn't let himself distrust his brother, not till his face was rubbed in the evidence.)

When he was finished I said, "I've heard this story before; there's a version from Earth. Several versions, actually. But it's got Ivory written all over it."

"I'll take your word for that. You'll keep it, then?"

"I'll keep it." And I got the point of the story, too, which was not to ask questions you don't want answers to. So I shelved matters of guilt and responsibility for the time being.

He said, "I must be going. I'm sorry about this, Theo, but as they say, it's one of those things that happen because we are in this world. I won't be so rude as to say it's for your own good, although, as a matter of fact, it is." He was maneuvering the floater out as he spoke. I followed him outside.

"What are you talking—" I stopped short. Four uniformed Imperial officers were standing outside the tent. "*Damn* it."

"Thank you for waiting," said Eln courteously to the officer in charge. "Please take this for your trouble—" he handed a small bag to the man "—and convey my thanks to your captain. I'll send him my regards as soon as I can."

"Our pleasure," said the officer. He turned to me. "Please come with us, gracious lady."

I looked at Eln. "It's all right," he said, "it's nothing lethal. Best just to accompany these good men, Theo."

For some reason I believed him. And the officer had thrown in that "gracious"—he'd been told to be polite, and why waste that on a soon-to-be corpse?

"Be seeing you, then," I said to Eln.

"I'm afraid not," he replied, "but don't forget those notes I left in your ship's cabin link." And to top it off, he waved as they led me away.

I thought we'd be going to jail, but instead I found myself being taken up the steps of the Athenan Embassy. "Hey!" I said. The officers ignored me. I was led through those well-lit corridors decorated with tasteful Athenan minimalism I'd learned to know so well, back when I first became stranded. The ambassador's secretary, a young man with an unattractive blond mustache, told the officers that the ambassador would be happy to see us; which was more than anybody had ever told *me.*

We entered the ambassador's office. He stood up to greet us, smiling for the benefit of the Imperials. It was the same man I'd dealt with in my first year on Ivory, whom I'd last seen in the Lantern Gardens under unusual circumstances; silver-haired and distinguished, everything an ambassador should be. He said, "Won't you gentlemen have a seat?"

My captors eyed the straight-backed Athenan chairs warily; "No thank you," said the officer in charge. "We won't take up your time, gracious sir. Can you identify this woman with us?"

"I can," said the ambassador.

"Theodora of Pyrene?" asked the officer.

"Yes," said the ambassador.

"A distressed Athenan citizen, without a work permit?"

"That's correct," said the ambassador.

"You pig," I said.

"Thank you," said the officer. "Any objections to deportation?"

"Wait a minute—"

"None," said the ambassador.

I said, "You officious pig. You were too regulation to send out my loan request to Athena, and now you've got your hand out under the table like anybody else."

"Will that be all, officers?" he said.

"You sure you want me back on Athena?" I asked him. "The Board of Ethics might not like what I've got to say."

He looked slightly pale, but said, "Well, then, Sirs, thank you for consulting me. My secretary will show you out."

One of the officers took my arm. "You kanz!" I was losing my temper, I really hated this man. Eln might kill me, but he'd do it for a good reason. This one was just careless and nasty. "Kanz," I said again. Another officer took my other arm, and they started to pull me away. "Pig! Ethical moron!" I found my vocabulary running backward chronologically as my fury mounted. By the time we reached the door I was throwing in Pyrene epithets. "Anti-social! Enemy of unity!"

They pulled me out.

So this was the *Queen Emily*. Of course I hadn't planned on staying in the brig, but at least it was clean and well-appointed. There was even a Net link here, although its security protection was rather stringent. I could read a few novels and get into the ship's itinerary, but that was about all. Eln had said something about notes, but maybe they were time-contingent; or maybe they were confined to the terminal in the cabin I should have had.

I sat down in the cushioned chair by the link—a soft, adjustable, Tellys chair, that conformed to my back; it was lovely, and made you wonder what the first-class cabins were like—and I considered my situation. My personal effects, including "jewelry" (the Old Man's stone) and "one deck playing cards" (guess what) were in the purser's safe, somewhere on the administration deck. I had a receipt for them. Meanwhile, what was happening to Ran while I was in here? Eln wouldn't have had me picked up now for no reason—improvisation was not his style at all. I ought to have run the cards for Ran, whatever he'd said; maybe I could have seen this coming.

So here I was, on a first-class liner, bound for Athena,

and I wasn't even paying for it. This was where I'd been aiming for over three long years. This was the culmination of all that planning and working and constant attention to money.

This was what they called irony.

Chapter 19

I spent the night on a bed that was higher up from the floor than I was used to, so that I banged my knee painfully when I rolled out in the morning. Then I took a shower in the wash stall that appeared when the wall button was pushed. Then more sitting around.

It worried me. Take-off wasn't until tomorrow; Eln had gotten me out of the way ahead of time—why? I wished for the thousandth time that I had my cards.

In late afternoon the door opened. Two men came in, in Ivoran robes, holding pistols in a way that suggested they were very ready to use them. At once I thought two things: one, that Eln wasn't taking any chances, and two, that I shouldn't have threatened the ambassador yesterday. Scared amateurs can do anything.

"Theodora of Pyrene?" asked one man. He was tall and bearded, older than the other.

"Why do you want to know?" I said.

"I'm Hedron, this is Pory—"

Pory interrupted. "She looks like just another fuzzy-brained foreigner to me," he said. "How do we know this is the one?"

"Kylla sent us," said Hedron to me.

"Prove it," I said, as I backed up toward the Net link.

He smiled. "This is the one," he said to his companion. He turned back to me. "Too long, too well I know the starry conclave of the midnight sky; too well the splendors of the firmament—"

"All right, all right." For a second there I'd thought he'd lost his mind. "Why are you here?"

"We're to take you off the ship," he said.

"Then what?"

Pory said, "Then we give you some money and a message, and let you go. Can we get moving?"

"Well?" said Hedron.

"Right," I said, and picked up my empty wallet-pack and followed him out of the room.

The detention section was automated, and I was the only guest there; so we didn't even see any ship's personnel until we were two decks up and heading for the exit locks. The people we passed ignored us, assuming I suppose that we were new passengers for the Ivory-Athena leg, and had a right to be wherever we were. But before we got to the exit, I pulled on Hedron's robe. "Wait a minute," I said.

"What's the matter?"

"I left some things in the purser's safe. One thing in particular, that I need."

Pory said, "We're not supposed to look after your personal possessions. We're just supposed to get you off the ship."

"And we ought to hurry," added Hedron.

"If Kylla had known about this, she would have had you stop for it. It's important."

They looked at each other.

"It's important," I repeated. "In fact, she probably wouldn't want me at all, without this."

Hedron said, "The administration deck isn't too far. All right."

Pory looked unhappy. I said, "One other thing. Can I ask a favor?"

"What now?" said Pory.

"I've got a reputation to think of on Athena. If there are people around the purser's office, and there probably will be—could one of you hold a pistol on me, as if I were your prisoner? I'd appreciate it."

They muttered, but agreed. Lucky thing, too; I didn't like the way the purser looked at me when Hedron asked him to open the safe. He didn't look any happier when Hedron took off his shirt, tied him up with it, and locked him in.

We lost no time in getting off the ship after that. We marched quickly through the port, off into the city, and didn't slow down till we reached the maze of alleyways behind the Lavender Palace. "All right," said Hedron. Pory stopped, opened his wallet, and brought out a small bag of tabals. I accepted it.

"What about this message?" I said.

Hedron said, "Pory, go over to the jeweler's shop there, and see what's good in the window." Pory left, not without giving me a sulky glance. When he was out of earshot, Hedron said, "You're not to go back to your house. You're to use the money here, buy whatever weapons you think necessary, rent a solo-driving cart, and leave the city by way of the Ostin road. About two hours' ride there's a stand of tasselnut trees on a hill to your left. You'll be met there."

"Met by whom?"

"I don't know; but Kylla said to say, by just who you think. I hope that's clear to you."

"I hope so, too. Thanks for all your help."

He bowed. "Honored by this meeting. Next time you're going to be rescued, try to keep all your possessions in one place."

The sensible thing to do was to go to the wagoner's first; no point buying weapons without a place to stash them. The wagoner was small, pot-bellied, and earnest—he was very earnest about renting me a four-team cart with driver, at only (he said) half the going rate.

I said, "Just a solo, please."

"A solo, gracious lady—believe me, no one in the capital will respect you if you drive a solo. A driver, now, and a fashionable looking team—"

"Friend, I'm no tymon just off the ship. I know what I want. How about that blue cart with the canvas cover? Is it available?"

"A wheel was being fixed," he said.

"So is it fixed?" I asked, jingling my coins.

"Of course, gracious lady, it's in perfect condition. But you'll need at least a paired team—"

"I want one animal, modified for strength, with a drive implant. Of course, if it's not available . . . "

"Not available! We have every drive animal on the market in this establishment. See for yourself." He led me over to the pens, and we quickly settled on a modified six-legger.

I liked this one; it didn't have horns, and regarded me with a look of uninterest which was reassuring. The wagoner handed me the control box. "Ten tabals a day, and it comes to you fresh fed."

"Thanks. I've never driven one of these before. Which button does what?"

"I beg your pardon, gracious lady? You're not saying you want to take my best cart and you don't know how to drive it?" He looked horrified.

"Oh, come on, sir. It's all straightforward, isn't it? The animal's trained and implanted? Really—I've piloted *air-cars*, sir, I can certainly handle a wagon." And crashed aircars, too, but there was no need to bring that up at this time.

So at last I was driving the wagon, rather tentatively, through the city streets. My six-legger was rather large, but the wagoner had sworn up and down it was herbivorous, and besides, implanted animals have never bothered me deeply; they're practically machines anyway. There was an arms shop on the northwest wall, by the exit to the Ostin road. I picked up a couple of short swords, four rifles, four knives, four pistols, and four hotpencils and energizers. Then I thought about it and picked up a pistol and holster for myself. Call me paranoid, but my short stay in the *Queen Emily*'s brig had gotten me thinking about where I was going in life and how the plans of mortals come to naught, and a lot of other things that the philosophical tomes of the university had proffered; hypothetically, I'd thought at the time.

I drove out past the remains of the old city wall, into the meadows just outside the capital. The sun was still high, in spite of the hour, and the ground I rode over smelled sweet. It was nearly summer. I was on the Ostin road, heading west—this was the easy part, just follow the road until I came to the stand of trees on the hill. Unless I passed it when it became dark; unless I wasn't ready at the right time, because I was driving too fast or too slow to know when I was "two hours" out; unless there was no one waiting for me there—or worst of all, the wrong people were.

It was past twilight when I reached the hill. I stopped the cart and waited. There were no villages nearby, and the last town had been an hour ago; no farmhouses, no inns.

It was deserted. The evening air blew against the back of my neck.

After a few minutes a figure detached itself from the grove of tasselnuts. I jumped off the cart and drew my pistol as it walked down the slope toward me. "Hello, tymon," said Ran's voice. "A bit late, but good to see—" He saw the pistol and hesitated. "Were you planning on shooting me?"

"I didn't know it was you, idiot." I dropped the pistol back in its holster, ran up the slope and threw my arms around him. Maybe the stay in the brig had had more of an effect on me than I'd realized, but a good long kiss seemed the logical thing to do.

"Well," he said, looking rather silly as an expression of embarrassed pleasure suffused his face. "Well," he repeated. After a minute he said, "I suppose we'd better get going; we are on a time limit."

"Oh, are we?"

He helped me up into the seat and climbed in behind. He turned to survey the back of the cart, now full end-to-end with newly purchased weaponry. He started to smile.

"I got your message," I said.

"So I see."

"Well, I didn't know what you might need," I said defensively.

"Did I say something ungracious?" Still, he looked suspiciously near amusement.

"Are we meeting Karlas and Tyl?"

"No, they're taking care of other concerns." He picked up the wagon control box. "You know, when I told Kylla to have you rent a solo, I really wasn't sure you could drive one of these."

"This is my first time, actually."

He'd been holding out the box for me to take, and now his hand froze. "Your first time?"

"Yes, but I must say I think I'm every bit as good with it as I am with an aircar."

"I see." He returned the box to his lap. I hid a grin; this made us even for his superiority over the excess weapons.

We continued northwest along the Ostin Road. "How far are we going?" I asked.

"A few hours' ride. There should be enough moonlight

tonight to get by. We don't want to miss the turnoff, though; I'll tell you when to start looking for it. Then it's a quarter hour through the trees, and up the Na'telleth Road. Tevachin Monastery is on top of a hill, it shouldn't be difficult to find."

I turned to look at him. "Why are we going to a monastery? Are you withdrawing from the world?"

He laughed. "You say that with such irony. I must be a lot farther from na-telleth-rin than I thought. All right, as you've noted, I'm not joining up; I'm going to avail myself of the monastery's services. They're famous as a meeting place; they provide supervision, security, even arbitration if it's requested. Their reputation is spotless—they see that the rules for a meeting aren't broken by anybody. They're completely disinterested, totally incorruptible, and open to anyone who'll pay their fee."

"Very professional," I said, after a moment. "You're meeting Eln there, aren't you?"

"Does it bother you?"

I shook my head. "It's about time. This situation can't go on forever." I was glad he was willing to attempt negotiation, though surprised Eln had offered it. Or had he? "Whose idea was this?"

"That's the odd thing. I'd been thinking about it for weeks, but only settled on firm plans a few days ago. Before I could make any arrangements, one of the Tevechin monks came to me in the market with Eln's preliminary offer." He frowned. "Our dates coincided. I don't like that. He should be at his weakest point now; why risk coming out? But he *is* at his weakest point," he added with quiet intensity, as if he were talking to himself. "I know he is. I'm sure of the analysis."

"Numbers don't lie."

"No. Unless the data was faked—no, that's too far-fetched."

"Anyway," I said, "I'm glad you and Kylla are on speaking terms again."

"So am I." He stretched his legs out on the foot-rim, and smiled happily. "I suppose she decided that the time for this pretense of neutrality was over."

I raised an eyebrow. "*Pretense* of neutrality?"

"There's no such thing as neutrality, Theodora," he said calmly. "There's indifference, and there's choice."

We came upon Tevachin Monastery at midnight. Pools of rust-colored granite blocks showed under the torches set in the walls. Despite the hour, people were crossing the yard by the main door, leading horses to stable, carrying waterjugs, and seemingly intent on every kind of errand. Trade Square was deserted at this time of night—if these people were leaving the world behind, they certainly seemed to have brought a lot of it with them.

A boy in a brown tunic with no outer robe ran down the front steps toward us. He paused breathlessly, by the wagon, putting one hand on the driver's steps. "Ran, declared-to-be-Cormallon?"

Ran said, "Yes."

"And this is your witness?"

"Yes," he said again.

"Honored-by-this-meeting," he said quickly. "Please come with me, gracious sir and lady. You're expected inside."

We dismounted and started to follow him up the steps. "Your wagon will be taken care of," he said.

Ran said, "Do you know if the one I'm meeting has arrived yet?"

"He's not expected till morning," said the boy. "They say he's been delayed by some problem. Or rather, that's the gossip, gracious sir. No one tells me anything official; you'd be better off asking the abbot."

Ran smiled. "I'm sure your gossip's right. He's probably dealing with a major problem right at this moment."

The boy looked at him. As we were in the hallway then, I said, "These portraits along the walls, are they members of your order?"

"Past abbots and teachers, gracious lady." He led us down another corridor. Interesting order; half of them looked like schoolmasters, and half of them looked like horsethieves. I stopped to peer at one unshaven countenance who had particularly shifty eyes. "If you could move along, gracious lady," said the boy.

"Sorry," I said, and followed. I wouldn't have bought a used wagon-beast from that man. Or a used virgin either.

"Here we are," he said.

The sign over the old wooden door read: "If the fool would persist in his folly, he would become wise." The boy pushed it open and stood aside.

"That sounds familiar," I said to Ran, frowning. We entered the room.

The abbot was a tall, heavyset man, more physically suited to be a wrestler than a spiritual leader. Maybe he *had* been a wrestler before he declared na, telleth. He bowed to Ran and held out a hand to me.

"The outworlder! Athenans shake hands, do they not?" And he enveloped mine in a hurricane-force, but somehow friendly, crush. "I trust I performed it correctly," he said as he peered at me hopefully from beneath bristly red-brown eyebrows.

"Oh, perfectly," I assured him, glancing at my flushed knuckles. Perhaps one day he'd be introduced to the Athenan ambassador; let that gentleman get his share of what I got.

Ran said, "I understand the person I'm meeting isn't due till morning."

The abbot sighed. "So much for secrets in this House. Still, sir, you may be assured that whoever mentioned this to you would not have brought it up if you were not one of the principals. It's only among ourselves that we can't seem to keep effective security."

"Quite all right," said Ran.

"Believe me, private matters never leave Tevachin."

"Your reputation assures it," said Ran politely.

The abbot motioned us to some red silk cushions. "Well, it is true your man is delayed. We expect him before sunrise, though—I hope this doesn't disturb your schedule unduly."

"It's within my parameters," said Ran. "I can adapt."

"Good, good. And we have beds ready for you if you wish them; food, baths, meditation rooms—whatever is your preference. Or, Brother Camery could take you on a tour of the monastery. He's quite used to dealing with those who are still tied to the wheel—he's the Master of Novices. Does a lot of negotiating with the families; he doesn't mind the company of the unenlightened, I assure you."

"That's very kind of you to say," said Ran. "But first, do I take it that the sunrise meeting seems to be firm?"

"Circumstances would support such a view. Two of our monks are accompanying your man at this very moment; and he's given his bond to appear during this day." An Ivoran day is from sunrise to sunrise; so the latest Eln could show up was in about six hours. "What can I say?" added the abbot. "It's as firm as anything is in this life."

"In that case," said Ran, "I would like a meditation room. My witness might want to see the tour, though."

I looked at him in surprise. He said, "Unless you'd rather have a bed, Theodora. But you seem pretty awake."

I turned back to the abbot. "The tour," I said, "Thank you very much."

Brother Camery was an apple-cheeked old gentlemen with wings of thick white hair that went back on each side of his head, leaving a rosy baldness on top that matched his chubby pink face. He was talkative, charming, and sharp-eyed, with that "retiree look" I was coming to associate with many of the monks. "Happy to oblige," he said, when I apologized for the lateness of the hour. "I often don't sleep until dawn in any case. Many of my duties are night duties."

"Oh?" I said. What do novices do at night, polish the breakfast silverware?

"Here we are," he said. He shook out a large ring of keys. "We can see the kitchens first, or the dining hall, or the gardens, or the library—"

"Is that a library with books?"

"What other kind would there be? Or we could see the Arena of Magic, or the Hall of Delights, or the Initiation Wing. Most outsiders," he lowered his voice confidentially, "wish to see the Hall of Delights."

I said warily, "Maybe we could work up to it."

"Then perhaps the Arena?"

"As you say," I said, and we started down the red-tiled corridor. "I understand the meeting I'm to witness won't take place till morning."

"So I hear," he agreed. "Dawn and sunset are the traditional times for a meeting. I'm to be one of the outside observers myself; quite looking forward to it."

We were passing more portraits. There was a wide doorway with another sign above. I didn't know all the words on this one. "What does that say?" I asked Brother Camery.

"The Road of Excess leads to the Palace of Wisdom," replied the master of novices. "It's the entrance to the Hall of Delights." He chuckled. "Given the hour, probably half my novices are in there right now, gathering wisdom." He leaned over and put his ear to the door. I joined him, unable to resist.

There was either an orgy or a torture session going on inside. From the occasional punctuating giggles, I decided it was an orgy; unless the torturers were both sadistic, and from the tone of their voices, about fourteen years old. "I thought you left the world behind when you came here."

He laughed. "There is more than one way to purge desire. It's a disease we're all born with, and here we inoculate against it. 'You never know what is enough until you know what is more than enough.' "

"Do all your novices spend time here?"

"Most do. For some, this is not the way. But the majority of people have a great deal of foolishness to root out. 'He who desires but acts not, breeds pestilence.' "

I looked at Brother Camery with some impatience. These sayings were beginning to get on my nerves; and they were very familiar, somehow. The brother smiled back at me benignly; it was hard to imagine him as a pimp, but I suppose he saw his duty and he did it.

On the way to the Arena, I said, "The furnishings here are very impressive. I didn't expect a monastery to be so well-appointed."

He shook his head. "The taxes," he said mournfully. "You have no idea. But we do the best we can. As the inductor of novices, young lady, I can say with some pride that my services bring in a fair sum each year."

"How so?" We were going down stairs, and more stairs. It was making me jumpy, being this isolated with a stranger. I tried to determine if there was reason for my discomfort or if I'd just picked up the natural paranoia any Ivoran feels in unusual circumstances.

"The novice fee," explained Brother Camery. "We generally charge fifty percent of the individual's net worth at the time of application. He can dispose of the other fifty percent in whatever way he wishes."

By now we must be a good twenty meters underground; way too far to yell for help. I said, "I didn't know the families allowed individual property, in that sense of the word. I thought everything was held communally." The whole point behind Eln's mudslinging against his brother was that Ran had separated his money out from theirs, a clear sign that he no longer identified his interests with the family's.

"Most families practice communal financing," agreed the Novice Master. "But one can always ask for his share and resign."

"Share?" It was the first I'd heard of it. "I didn't think a family membership could be converted to money."

"Everything can be converted to money," said the Novice Master.

It was probably the closest this planet came to a universal religious statement.

He continued, "Often the applicant will put the other fifty percent back into the family treasury, as a goodwill gesture, although there's no rule that they have to. So the families usually come out with a profit of sorts, and they think well of the monasteries and don't make a fuss when people come to us."

The corridor was blocked here by two immense wooden doors. They were bright crimson, with the sorcery symbol painted half on each, and an iron bar drawn across. Brother Camery reached for the bar. As he touched it, sparks flew and the sound of electrical sizzling came and went. He drew back his hand sharply, grasping it hard with the other.

"Oh, dear," he said.

"Are you all right?" I asked. The hand that had touched the bar was turning an unpleasant shade of pink.

"Yes, thank you. Nothing to be concerned about. I should have thought—but the meeting isn't scheduled until sunrise. I hoped we might enter the outer rings. I suppose they put the protections up when they thought it might be used at midnight, and when your party was late they just left them up." He raised his voice toward the door. "May we enter?"

The answer was an ominous rumbling, like a stormy sea. It swelled until it filled the corridor, then faded away.

"Not promising," he said. "Well, I must apologize for having brought you this way for nothing. Still," he brightened. "You'll see it all at dawn, won't you? And at its best, which few visitors do. I've only seen it used twice, and I've been here for fifteen years. Of course, I'm often away gathering up my novices when duels are taking place."

"When what?" I froze.

"When duels are scheduled to take place. My duties involve a great deal of travel—"

"What duels? What do you mean by duels? And what do they have to do with me?"

He seemed at a loss. "You're to be a witness, aren't you, at the sunrise meeting?" I must have given him a look as blank as his own, for he went on, "I understood—unless I was mistaken—that there was to be proper duel magical, to settle an internal Cormallon matter. We were to provide the arena, the outside observers, and the arbiter."

I continued to stare.

He said, "I'm sure—yes, I *am* sure—that I'm not mistaken. Certainly there's a duel scheduled. We have everything set up and ready. And I must say, they could not have chosen a better House. No rule-breaking here; not in five hundred years. And we handle everything, so there's nothing for the principals to worry about but their performance. We open the rings to magic, we seal off the arena, we have clean-up crews, even provide burial with our own services, should the victor not want the responsibility." He paused. "Always providing there's something left to bury. Are you all right, child? You look terribly pale."

I said, "I have to go."

He said, "Of course. This way, my dear."

Chapter 20

By the time I'd climbed the third flight of stairs I was dead-angry. I left the Novice Master far behind, clanking his keys, as I stalked down the main hall. I saw the boy who'd first shown us in, and stopped him. "My companion is supposed to be in one of the meditation rooms. Do you know where he is?"

He was startled by my tone. "Uh, yes, I can show you—"

"Then show me." I was grinding my teeth.

He led me down the hall to a room in another wing. One of the younger monks was sitting on a stool just outside, and rose to stand between me and the door.

"Excuse me," he said politely. "This is a meditation room."

"I know," I said, and aimed for the door again. He moved to block. I stamped my sandal down on his bare foot and reached for the knob.

His arms clamped around my shoulders, pinning me against his chest. "Excuse me," he said in the same courteous tone. "Would you be Theodora of Pyrene?"

"Yes," I said, tentatively. I stopped struggling, partly because I felt guilty about his foot, which would be black and blue by dawn, but mostly because it wasn't working.

"I have a message for you." He turned around, taking me with him, and we both faced out into the hall. Then he released me.

"Oh?" I said.

"Your companion asked if you would mind leaving him undisturbed until dawn."

"I mind," I said.

"He said, if you have any interest in keeping him alive, you would please respect his wishes."

Damn damn damn. "Were those his exact words?"

"Virtually. He did not say 'please.' "

"All right." I turned away, then looked back briefly. "Sorry about your foot," I said, not really with graciousness.

The monk returned my gaze. "What foot?" he asked.

I walked away followed by the boy, who had stayed to watch the entire encounter with frank interest. I was glad somebody around this place beside myself wasn't na' telleth.

"Where are you going?" he asked. It was a good question.

I said, "Are there any other meditation rooms free?"

"Dozens," he said. "It's a big place."

"So I've heard. Could you take me to one?"

"Of course." He took the lead. "How did you like the arena?"

"I haven't seen it yet, but I gather it's just a matter of time."

"Oh. I thought Camery took you there."

"It was locked."

He seemed disappointed. "I was hoping you could tell me about it, I've never been in there. I don't think old Camery's been there twice since he lost his name."

"His name is Camery, isn't it?" I asked.

The boy looked up at me with that "we-have-to-excuse-the-tymon" look I'd seen so often. "Camery is an old word that means 'counselor.' It's the traditional reference-name for the Master of Novices. Other brothers have other nicknames; they shift around a lot. But nobody keeps his birth name, gracious lady. It would confine his behavior."

"Confine it to what?" I said.

"To what he expected of himself." He looked confused, more by my needing to question it than by the topic. "Here we are, gracious lady. Meditation rooms can be locked from the inside, if you want to."

"Thank you. Listen, could you, or could somebody else, come by before dawn and get me? I don't want to lose track of the time."

He grinned. "No fear of that, the bells will toll half an hour before the duel. It's a big event here, you know."

"Oh," I said. He bowed and sauntered off down the corridor. I went inside.

* * *

The room was small and bare, with a gray woven rug and a pile of pillows. There was no window. An iron lamp hung from the center of the ceiling, flickering.

Maybe I was making a major mistake. Maybe this was not the time to ignore Ran's advice and leave the road of caution. But I was at a loss, I needed answers, and there was one place I'd been taught to expect them.

I pulled out the pack of cards.

Sitting there on a faded blue pillow, under the lamp, I held the cards in my left hand until the warmth of my body heat penetrated the deck. I was not going to snatch. I was going to creep up on them gently, bearing my destination in mind every step of the way. Above all, I was not going to think about how many hours remained until dawn.

It had never taken me so long to begin a reading before. Finally I drew the center card and turned it face up on the rough gray rug. The illustration was the Evening Star. Four-pointed, hanging low on a dusky horizon of shadowed hills, and watched by two figures facing away, toward the star, too indistinct to identify even as male or female.

The star drew me up to it like dew from the grass. I was hurtling through the twilight, the sky around me growing blacker and blacker. The star was many-pointed now, with arms stretching in all directions, touching the earth and the heavens in a blaze of incandesence. Energy surged up the arms to the center, where I was pinned like a butterfly in helpless joy. It was beautiful and frightening.

Back in Tevachin Monastery, the small and worried part of me that watched came to a decision and broke physical contact with the card. Abruptly there came a sensation like a blow to the back of the head, and all of me was sitting on the pillow in the meditation room, unsettled and a bit sick, wits scattered in all directions. Along with the blow to the head came an afterimage: Eln imprisoned in the center of the star. His arms and legs were the star's arms, pinned down somehow and yet reaching in all directions. It was as if he were a starfish—or a spider—even as I'd thought it the image shifted to a luminescent web, and I was kicked out of heaven and back to Tevachin.

Gods. That was one to give you the shakes; I'd never

felt anything like *that* before. And did I have any idea what it meant? Not a clue.

This is doing no good, said one part of my brain to the rest; best put these cards away and let Ran handle things whatever way he wants. Doubtless that was the part of my brain responsible for my sanity—I noticed that my left hand, still holding the rest of the pack, was trembling. I made an effort to stop it, to no visible effect.

How many hours left till dawn? I drew out another card before I could change my mind.

But I was no longer relaxed. Too much information, I thought vaguely, on too many levels. I realized suddenly that accessing what I would call the "symbolic" level of the cards was like reading a line of poetry. There was a lot being communicated—and it was subject to interpretation.

Enough of this, I thought, snapping shut like a clamshell. I'm not one of these na' telleths; give me plain language. And finally I brought myself to look at the card.

It was the Prisoner card, I'd drawn it before. The man in chains melted into a man in ropes even as I watched; it was Stepan. Another man, about the same age and wearing a cheap brown overtunic, walked behind Stepan's chair. He pulled on the ropes as though testing their strength, then nodded and said something to someone outside the frame. I bent over closer, trying to get a better look.

The man in the brown overtunic was Tyl, and it didn't take sorcery to know the person he was speaking to was Karlas. I sat up straight and considered the matter. So Ran had Stepan tucked away somewhere; that wasn't surprising when one thought about it. He would have done that, if he didn't kill him.

Then this was his method of preparing for the duel; to separate Eln from his magic source. In the meditation room Ran could take care of the spiritual side of preparation, but he was not one to overlook the practical.

I drew a third card and laid it right of center. The Traveler, with her rucksack and her staff, striding through a forest in red fisherman's trousers. That brought back memories. Was this supposed to be me? I didn't want it to be; the thought of involvement made me nervous. Then the clothing changed to an embroidered robe, and the staff disappeared, and the figure was mounted—and it was Eln.

Mounted, but he and his floater were both inside an aircar, and a pretty luxurious one it was. Traveling fast. The night sky flashed by behind his image. The seats on either side of him were occupied by two brawny men in monk's robes. I watched for several minutes and could see the sky lighten to pearl and Eln's features coming into relief. He was talking to the monks, no doubt trying as host (since I assumed the car was his) to amuse his escorts. The last thing I saw was the jumbled stone mountain of Tevachin Monastery growing in the window beyond.

Almost here, then, or would be by sunrise. What kind of preparations had *he* made? You would think the cards would be more forthcoming.

I packed the deck away in its case and left the room. The corridor was deserted. There was a long, narrow window at one end, and a few stars were visible through the bars. It was still full night, then; maybe what I'd seen in the final card was the future. Unless it was the past . . . but it had been on the right side of the center . . . no, you could drive yourself crazy second-guessing the deck. Keep your first impression, it's usually the right one.

I found my way back to Ran's room. The monk I'd argued with earlier still sat on guard outside, in the same position I'd left him; I decided not to stop.

Eventually I found the main hallway and the entrance. It was not a comfortable place to wait: no benches, no cushions, just a stone floor. Thinking it over, it occurred to me that this was not a place where people stood heavily on custom, nor indeed where they cared much one way or another what a tymon might do. So I sat down in the middle of the hall, facing the entranceway, and waited.

At least the floor was clean.

There was no way of judging the time from where I sat. Hours seemed to pass. A few of the lamps had begun to sputter, and I'd had a lot of time to think, when the main doors opened and Eln came in with his two escorts.

Typically, he was still talking as he entered, his head half-turned to face one of the monks; then his gaze moved over me and he fell silent.

"Theo," he said a second later. "What are you doing here? If you'll forgive my triteness in asking," he asked.

"They tell me I'm a witness," I said.

"Ah," he said, and nodded. "I might have known, sacred custom and all. Wish I had time to talk with you, sweetheart, but I'm running late. You wouldn't believe the problems I've been having . . . maybe you would. Still, we'll laugh about this someday, if we're drunk enough. Maybe we can get together in the Lantern Gardens some night and give it a try." He seemed ready to go on his way.

I said, "This is *stupid*, Eln."

"I agree completely. Was there anything else? I really am late—"

"Then *why* are you going through with it?"

He sighed. "When something has to be done, it has to be done, Theo; that's the only universal law there is. I'm as weary of all this as anybody, believe me." And he did look very tired at that moment, not just in body but in mind. "I want it to be over. It's worth going through all this, to be able to say that in a few hours it will be done. Settled. Behind me." He started to move down the hall, then stopped and smiled wryly. "Say, Theo, shouldn't you be lifting off around now?" I blushed. He said, "Nobody ever stays where I put them." He moved on a little farther.

I yelled, "Damn it, Eln, go home!"

He turned back for the last time. From the look on his face you'd think I'd said something funny. "When I remember all the times I said the same thing to you. Listen, Theo, I lied when I saw you in Trade Square. The deal's still open. When this is over, I'll get you another ticket, if you want one." He left.

It was so unfair. I wanted so much to hate him wholeheartedly. The gods knew I ought to hate him, after what he'd done. Why was it so easy to forget what he'd done, and what he'd tried to do? Not to mention what he would *still* do if he could . . . Eln and his sister were very much alike in some ways, I saw suddenly; they were both the sort of people who got away with a lot. I couldn't see Ran doing the things Eln had done and still being loved, still being the favorite. What must it have been like growing up in that family? Why, I couldn't even total up the treacheries Eln had committed, against his brother, against me, against Ran's first card-reader, against (for all I knew) Stepan.

There was a jeweler on Marsh Street who still wanted to know where he was.

So why was it so easy to forget all this? Because he was charming? Did that give him the right to hurt people? Or was it because he hurt so much himself? Sometimes I couldn't look at him without cringing.

I hadn't stood when Eln came in. I still sat in the shadow of the open door, feeling helpless. Tears were starting down my face. I needed an hour or two of mental collapse, but the patch of light on the floor beside me was gray with the threat of sunrise.

I got up and walked very quickly toward Ran's room, wiping my face. As I did so, the bells began to toll.

The monk on watch was gone, and I felt a stab of panic. What if Ran was gone, too? I pushed open the door.

Ran stood there, dressing with the help of two monks. They looked up briefly as I entered. One monk handed him a crimson-and-gold belt, with gold tassels, and he clasped it over his tunic. "Do you think the white outer robe?" he asked them. He looked at me. "What do you think, Theodora?"

My face must have been a puckered and reddened mess—it always was from the least bit of crying—but Ran was studiously careful to avoid comment. I said, "What the hell do you think you're doing?"

One of the monks got up from where he knelt around the back of Ran's robe and started toward me. Ran said, "No." It was only one syllable, but I could feel the enforced calmness in it. "I'll take care of it. Theodora, I can see you're upset about this, but we did discuss it on the way here—"

"I didn't know this was what you meant! I'm a tymon, I don't know everything about your stupid culture!"

"I'm sorry if I was unclear—"

"And now that I know, I'm telling you it's *stupid*."

Ran said to the monks, "Would you do me the courtesy of waiting outside? I'm almost done anyway."

One of them said, "The procession is supposed to start in ten minutes."

"I know," said Ran. "I'll be ready."

They left, ignoring me. I said, "Ran—"

He cut me off. "Listen, because I don't have a lot of time. It's too late to do anything now. Understand? The contract's been signed. We're both under monastery enforcement. It's past time to back out. With that in mind, do you think it's a good idea to push me into an argument when I've spend the last six hours calming myself down for the duel? I have to be totally in control of myself to get out of here alive, and *I am not at my best under pressure.* If you want to kill me, getting me upset right now would be a good way to do it."

I lowered my voice, and forced myself to speak as if I were commenting on the weather. "I really would prefer that you didn't do this. I don't know anything about contracts, but there must be some way of getting out of it. What's the penalty for noncompliance? Confiscation of goods? We've gone without before—"

"The penalty is death," he said, in an equally disinterested tone of voice.

It was the strangest argument I have ever had. It was the one I most wanted to win, and the one I tried hardest not to care about when I had it.

"You can't think of any way out? Tell me the truth," I said, not as if I really wanted to know.

"Face it, Theodora. It's settled. It will happen. "He was pulling on the white outer robe as he spoke. "See if the back is even?" he said.

I checked. "It looks fine."

"Was there anything else you needed to say?" he asked.

For the life of me, I couldn't think of anything beyond grabbing him by the sides of the robe and shouting "Stop this, you idiot." But that didn't seem to be wise, under the circumstances. "Nothing," I said.

He opened the door, and held it for me to go first.

The procession started from the main hall. Eln wore dark blue silk, and a white outer robe much like Ran's. Maybe it was his, and maybe the monks spared no expense when other people picked up the fees. Probably cheaper in the long run to have each duelist already decked out in a decent burial robe. Someone handed me a candle.

I followed directly behind Ran. Someone from Cormallon must have met Eln here; a young man in gray, vaguely familiar, walked behind the floater. He couldn't have shown up this late; he must have been here the whole time Ran and I were. Apparently the monks could keep news about outsiders to themselves after all.

We filed down the halls to the back of the monastery. There seemed to be more than the usual number of monks hanging about in doorways, watching us pass. We did not turn to the stairways, as I expected, but continued out of the building and into a covered tunnel of gray stone that led downward into the hill. By this time there were about twenty of us in the procession; I recognized the abbot and Brother Camery. A half dozen of us on line were women, but I was the only one who looked to be under the age of ninety. The ramp spiraled downward interminably.

At last we came up against double doors with the sorcery symbol half on each, twins to the ones Camery had shown me last night. The man at the front of the line stopped, reached into a velvet bag, removed a red cap of three cylindrical sections, and placed it gravely on his head. "The Protocol Master," he announced. The doors creaked open.

As each person entered the Protocol Master would say, "Eln Cormallon, principal. "His witness, Jermyn Cormallon." "The Master of Novices." "Duelmaster and Arbiter." "Ran, declared-to-be Cormallon." He put out his hand to stop me.

"Disarm, please," he said, in a more conversational tone.

Ran looked back. "She's not wearing anything," he said. "She never wears anything."

I pulled open my outer robe to show the holster underneath.

Ran sighed. "Once they start," he muttered.

"I was nervous," I said. I pulled off the holster and pistol and handed them to the Protocol Master. "What about my knife?" I asked, before anyone else could bring it up.

"You call that fruit-cutter a knife?" asked one of the witnessing monks after me on line. Monks left the rules of courtesy behind when they dropped their names, and were rude or polite according to whim. They could get away with it because nobody took na' telleths seriously.

"We're only interested in energy weapons," said the Protocol Master more kindly, seeing my discomfort. "They might disrupt the force-patterns inside. That would be most dangerous."

"Oh," I said, not understanding. He let me pass through the doors.

I was totally bewildered. We'd gone *down,* hadn't we? So what were we doing outside, on what appeared to be a hillside? We were standing in what seemed to be some sort of amphitheater, on the edge of the center arena, and around the sides steps rose up to three or four times the height of an Ivoran. Beyond that, I could only see sky.

The monks filed out into the amphitheater and lit torches around the inner wall. It was still dark down in the arena. I looked around and saw the other monks had gone up into the seats, and as I peered up at them they seemed to become fuzzy and indistinct. I turned slowly around, frowning at the seats.

"As observers, they are not allowed to intrude on the event." The voice startled me. It was the Duelmaster-Arbiter, standing beside me. He was a tall man in silver, with an old, old, face. He reminded me of the Old Man of Kado Island, and I liked him, perhaps unreasonably.

He said, "Do the principals have anything to say to each other? This will be their last chance to do so. No record will be made, either by writing or on tape, of any words spoken now."

Eln was about to make his way to the other side of the arena. He halted and turned, an expression of polite interest on his face. Ran stopped also. He said, "I have nothing to add."

"Nor I," said Eln.

"I trust you're in good health," said Ran.

"Adequate. I trust you're the same."

"Yes." He turned. "Duelmaster-Arbiter, I think we've said all there is to say."

"Apparently," he agreed. The Duelmaster motioned them to move to their places.

I followed Ran. For all their surface coolness, there was a great deal of emotion in that moment, emotion of the sort I have never liked, mixed emotion. Hatred beneath good manners is an Ivoran specialty, but here there was something both familiar and repellent to me; it was as though they were too close to each other to breathe and extreme feelings were the only kind left to them. I wondered if such strong and confused emotion was rare, or if I had simply never been close enough to another person to be aware that they were capable of it. I wondered if I were capable of it. I wondered if it would be a good or bad thing if I were. And I wondered fleetingly and for no logical reason what my guardian-mother on Pyrene had thought when I left without looking back. It was the first time that any thought of leaving Pyrene which was not tinged with relief had ever crossed my mind.

I turned with some haste to the Duelmaster-Arbiter. "Where do I go?" I asked him. "What should I be doing?"

"Stay here on the side, under the pillars. Be ready to help your man if he needs it. Watch everything."

"That's all?"

"That's a great deal." He looked down at me. "You're an outlander. Has anyone explained the event to you?"

"No, Duelmaster, they haven't."

"Well, it begins when I declare it begun. There are rounds of combat followed by periods of rest; a round lasts about five minutes."

"Five minutes doesn't seem very long." I said.

"When two sorcerers are trying to kill each other, five minutes can contain eternity. I've never seen a duel that lasted beyond fifteen."

I didn't like the bald way he put it. But what I really didn't like was the bald fact of what was happening.

"I must go out now and read the contract," he said. "There's a bench, if you want to sit."

"Thank you, I'll stand."

He moved out into the center of the arena. Ran came over to stand beside me; across the ring I saw Eln and his witness waiting, too. The Duelmaster-Arbiter called, "Attention, principals and witnesses. The contract has been signed and agreed to this day, under the enforcement of Tevachin. All mirror-spells have been stripped. No vengeance is contemplated against anyone for anything which may take place today. Let all witness."

Ran sat down on the bench. I didn't know how he could. The Duelmaster said, "Tevachin attests to the fact that papers have been left with responsible Cormallon parties, absolving Ran Cormallon of any infractions and passing inheritance back to him; these papers to be opened at noon unless word saying otherwise reaches the main estate. Tevachin attests to the fact that arrangements have been made to release one Stepan Cormallon, and to terminate the employment of all other persons, unless word saying otherwise reaches the capital. Let all witness."

He lifted an hourglass, turned it gently up and down again. The sand, if it was sand, glittered like gold dust. "This is the measure of one round," he said. "When the sand is falling, all rules of the duel apply, and will be enforced by Tevachin. Between, before, and after the rounds you may do as you like—once the first round is over, you are free to leave, if you like, and not come back. But once a round begins, you are bound to stay in the arena until the end. Am I clear?"

I saw Eln nod, across the way. Ran stood up. "Clear," he said.

"Ran—" I said, and bit it off. He walked down into the dueling pit. Eln came in from the other side. The Duelmaster came up and stood beside me, briefly touching my hand.

The arena was a granite hollow, a grainy gray-white surface that sloped to center. The floor was dingy with ancient dirt. "The sun," whispered the Duelmaster to me, and I looked over my shoulder to see the brightness in the east. The top rows of the other side of the amphitheater were exposed in the light, showing three old nuns swathed in robes against the morning chill. "Now," said the Duelmaster, and because his voice was so low I thought he was still talking to me. There was a muted rumbling of distant thunder that seemed to come from all directions. It fused and intensified until it came to sit underneath the arena. I thought, "earthquake." I wanted to run, but no one else seemed disturbed. I glanced up toward the three nuns, but the top row was dark again; I turned hurriedly to look behind, and the sun was gone. There were no clouds, it was just gone!

It hit me then at last, far too late. All the figures, all the calculations, all the driving engine of rational thought that made the outrunners of the theme; I'd forgotten that what we were dealing with was *magic*. As electric power lived in the massive force of water breaking through a dam, as it lived in lightning, the force retains its essence. Ivorans had come to terms with magic, they let it serve them and give them comforts, a wolf-creature tamed to a dog. They took the idea of passion and made legal marriage out of it, and so were able to make daily use of it. And I could see now that they were right to do so; I would rather room with a dog than a wolf. But the dog still had its teeth, and beneath the marriage sheets the bodies and hearts were unchanged.

They were still in the arena, like standing stones, in their white silk robes. Then Eln moved somehow—I couldn't see it, but there was a flash of midnight blue from his tunic in the midst of all that white and gray—and he rose into the air; and all at once there was an eagle there, a huge thing only a few wing-beats from the bottom of the pit. And not quite an eagle, for the claws were enormous. I was too startled for a second to look at Ran, and when I turned back to him I saw a blood-red dragon, at least ten meters from top to tail, its narrow head stretched into the air. The jaws opened and a stream of fire jetted out, scorching the eagle. It backed up hurriedly, the feathers on one side turning a grayish black.

"Oh, gods," I said weakly. I heard the Duelmaster's voice, as though from very far away, saying, "Yes, mythical creatures are always best for a beginning. Use them while you have the strength, that's the strategy."

I must have groaned. He said, "Are you all right, little outworlder?"

"How can this be happening?" I asked.

He said proudly, "Tevachin has the greatest dueling arena in all the world. It has been used for nothing but magic for the last fifteen hundred years, and all the thoughts of generations of monks and nuns have gone to building its power. I'd like to see a transmutation of such size and speed as that eagle was be tried in any other arena! And I don't care how good the sorcerer is."

The eagle was circling the dragon, looking for an opening. Another approach, another stream of flame. "Eagles aren't mythical," I said dully.

"I beg your pardon?" asked the Duelmaster.

I grasped his robes and tugged. "Is any of this actually happening?" I begged.

"You should really enroll in the morning novitiate's class

on the nature of reality," he said. "However, I know what you mean, and the simple answer is no, it is not. Like all simple answers that is a lie; but it's the best I can do for you, child."

"What happens," I said, "if the eagle kills the dragon?"

He seemed faintly surprised. "Why, I don't know, outworlder. Are you asking me to speculate on the change in linear events that occurs when one person dies? As someone who appears to be acquainted with both the dueling parties, you should know better than I."

The last stream of fire hadn't gone as far as the others, and the eagle hadn't seemed to have minded it as much. Now it stooped for a run at the dragon's side. The dragon swiveled its neck around, but too slow and too late; a rip ran through its hide, tail to throat. Blood started to drip, starting at the tail. The blood was black.

The eagle made another run, still avoiding the head. This time it didn't pull back at the final moment, and the force of the collision knocked the dragon half over. Another slash of the talons. A futile stream of fire, way off target; the dragon was immobilized. The eagle began to slash at the underbelly, pulling out the guts onto the floor of the pit.

And suddenly the dragon was gone. On the other side of the pit stood, of all things to find on this planet, a grizzly bear. It stood three meters tall, brown, a perfect copy of what I'd seen in the Zoo of Past Species on Athena.

It growled. The eagle beat its wings, just once, and seemed to compress itself into a ball; when it opened out again, it was a lion in mid-spring, heading for the bear. It was hard to follow this phase of the combat; for a moment I wasn't even entirely sure who was what. But the golden blur was Eln, and the snarling mass of fur was Ran. They rolled down the side of the pit, brown and gold, and streaks of red.

"I thought the dragon was dying," I said to the Duelmaster.

"Each one can change as often as he likes—that's generally whenever he's losing. The opponent must transmute to follow. Until, of course, the loser has no strength left to change. Then he must stay to face the consequences."

The bear's fur was matted, but I couldn't tell whose blood it was. It tried to swipe at the lion, but they were too close; still, there were strips of red on the lion's back. As I peered closer, trying to see what was happening, the lion fastened its teeth on the bear's throat and shook it. The bear's head moved back and forth, its paws waved feebly—and it escaped in a flash of silver. An arc of shining metal, like a spit seed, and a fish was flying through the air. The floor of the pit was covered now in a foggy sort of water.

I let out my breath. I hadn't realized I was holding it.

The fish was less than a meter long. It hit the water beautifully and came up in a leap a moment later. I looked around the pit. Where was the damned lion? The fish leapt and swam its way through the foggy carpet, searching. Then something broke the surface. A moist, reptilian worm, rising higher—and higher—and higher. A sea serpent, gods, and it was enormous; as big as the eagle had been. Wouldn't he ever run out of energy? The tongue flicked out, the worm head turned from side to side. It slid beneath the mists again. The fish made another leap, and the serpent broke through the water as it did. It grasped the fish in the curve of its own body and started to squeeze.

Change again, dammit, change to anything! It looked useless even as I thought it; who would change to a defenseless thing like a fish unless his power was so low his choices were few? The serpent squeezed harder. I couldn't even see the fish, suffocating in the wet wormy flesh.

"Time," said the Duelmaster. I'd forgotten he was there. The word "time" echoed off the walls, and the misty water rolled back. The fish was dropped, gasping, in the center of the pit. The serpent melted and shrank and became Eln once again, on his floater, in the immaculate silk robes.

"Why isn't Ran transforming?" I said to the Duelmaster.

"I don't know," he said, and as he said it I was running down into the pit. What I would have done, I don't know; the fish began to waver and stretch into a robed figure before I reached the arena floor. He was still gasping, though, and his robes were marred from lying in the dirt. He grabbed my arms and tried to rise. We stumbled out of the pit, up to the first ring, where he quietly collapsed on the floor. I looked over at the Duelmaster to see if he could help; the man had seated himself on the bench and taken out a book!

"Ran? Are you all right?"

He nodded, choking.

"Do you want me to do anything?"

"Wait," he got out at last. A minute later he said, "I'll be all right."

"Do you want water?"

He got out a strangled laugh. "I've had enough *water—*"

I sat down next to him on the granite. "How long have you got?" I asked.

He shrugged. "Maybe five minutes. I don't know. It's at the Duelmaster's discretion."

"Let's hope he's got a good book."

He seemed to be pulling himself together. I said, "Ran, this doesn't make sense. You've got Stepan away from him—don't give me that look, it's obvious—so where is he getting his magic from? He's made three transmutations, and he hasn't lost any power at all!"

"It doesn't matter."

"Kanz it doesn't matter. Shit it doesn't matter. You can't go back there, he'll kill you."

"I need to get Cormallon back."

"I'm talking about your *death,* you idiot."

"It has to be done."

"You monomaniac, you won't get anything if you go back. Did you see the size of that sea serpent? Maybe it was hard to tell when you were being suffocated—"

He looked up at me. "Theodora, listen. If anything happens to me, go to the Abbot. He's got a letter for you, I wrote it in the meditation room. There are some things in it that might help you get to Athena, if you still want to."

"The hell with that! Everybody wants to help me. Help yourselves!"

I wasn't getting through. That was all there was to say; I wasn't getting through. I'd never had an all-consuming passion in my life, I was always the reasonable one, and I could give out all the logic and rationalism in the world and I had to face that *nobody was going to stop what they were doing.* Somebody was going to die here, within the next few minutes, and it was beginning to look more and more clear who that was.

The Duelmaster looked idly at us, playing with his bookmark. I got up and walked over to him. "Finish your chapter," I said.

He turned to me a face with the merest hint of amusement. "Very well," he said. He opened his book again and dismissed me from his attention.

I stepped away from the Duelmaster, to go back to Ran, and I caught sight of Eln across the way, beside his witness, untouched, unconcerned, as though he were the center of the universe.

He *was*. Eln in the heart of the star, energy traveling up the arms—all at once I understood.

I went to Ran, squatting down beside him on the cold granite. "Listen." I said urgently. "I know what it is now. He has more than one source."

"What are you talking about?"

"As soon as he drains one, he moves onto the next one. You've cut him off from Stepan, but he's got others—he can just keep going while you get weaker and weaker. Today may be the low point in his draw from Stepan, but he could be anywhere in the cycle with the rest."

He frowned. "How do you know there's more than one source?"

"I *know*. Anyway, what else can it be? His third transmutation was just as powerful as his first—that's because you were fighting three different sorcerers in there, Ran. And who knows how many more he's drawing off?" He looked thoughtful, and I pressed it. "You can't go back in—he might have a dozen more to fall back on."

He considered the matter. "It can't be a dozen. He'd never find a dozen people to agree to give up their magic, even temporarily. With luck he might find four besides Stepan . . . which would mean there's only one left. I can handle four."

"And if there are five?"

His face was stubborn.

I got up. "Fine," I said, and started toward the arena floor. Eln was at the opposite edge, looking interested.

"Will you come back here?" came Ran's voice, annoyed. "That won't do any good." I kept going. "Whose side are you on, anyway?"

I knew he was saying it to irritate me into returning, but it *was* irritating just the same.

Across the arena Eln was waiting with a quizzical smile. "Theo, sweetheart, you're supposed to be on the opposite side; ceremonially speaking, of course."

"You're winning," I said.

He laughed. "Does that mean you're changing sides?"

I shook my head. "You and Ran come from another universe; ethically speaking, of course."

"Well, then? Sorry, do you want a seat?" He motioned to the bench nearby.

"No. Tell me, how many have you got?"

He didn't ask how many what. "Been at the cards again, haven't you? Have you mentioned this to Ran?"

"Naturally."

"Naturally," he agreed.

"So how many?"

"If I tell you, will you tell Ran?"

"Yes."

He grinned that morning sunrise grin. "Really, Theo, I think under the circumstances you can hardly blame me for declining to answer."

His witness had been hanging around the fringes of our conversation. Now he moved in uneasily. "Eln, you shouldn't be breaking your concentration. Send her back."

Eln didn't look at him. "Thank you, Jermyn. I thought you were going to behave yourself if I let you come along?"

The young man dipped his head, embarrassed, and walked away.

"Overenthusiastic," said Eln, "but a good heart."

"Not like the rest of us, then. Why are you here? You've got what you wanted, why don't you go home and enjoy it?"

"I don't have everything I wanted," he said simply.

No, not with Ran still around as a thorn in his side. What should I say? Go home and try to ignore your brother? Maybe if you don't kill him he won't kill you? Was there one chance in a thousand that I could talk either of them into stopping?

No. All my life, when I found myself in a situation I hated, I withdrew. Light years, if necessary. Was that wrong? If the Cormallons had spent some time learning the art of withdrawal, none of us would be in this position.

So withdraw, then. Leave Eln, leave the whole arena—

you know what's going to happen, you don't have to witness it as well. "Good-bye," I said, and turned.

"See you," he said, unrepentantly.

I was a few steps away. I looked back at him, I don't know why—to try to imprint his image in my memory, maybe; I had no intention of seeing him again, and it would no longer be possible to see Ran.

His clothes hadn't even gotten mussed in the first round; blue silk suited him, his hair was light for an Ivoran. Rare in every way, I had to admit—physically, mentally, emotionally. I still wanted to protect him if I could. A crazy feeling—he wasn't the one who needed protection.

But there was still that disarming sense of tenderness. Damn it and damn this stupid planet, too, because I didn't see any way out of this that would leave any of us whole. I glanced back at Ran, who was sitting on the wide ledge at the other side of the arena, watching, breathing deep with visible intakes of breath, preparing everything he had for the next round. Which wouldn't be enough. Why couldn't Eln have left things as they were? Why couldn't he follow custom and confine murder to strangers? In that instant I wanted to stop him—to kill him if necessary—to see that he couldn't hurt anybody ever again. I felt the stone around my neck pulsing warmly with my heartbeat. Ran was going to be dead as soon as the Duelmaster put down his book, and I didn't have any idea what I could do about it.

But Annurian of Kado Island knew very well. "Eln," I said, and I took my hand from the pack strapped to my side and tossed him a round, black object. He caught it neatly. It was the onyx cat. Fresh from my bare hands, the scent of it all on its stony skin: the tenderness and the understanding and the gratitude, the hatred and the wish to end all this. An emotional confusion more than equal to his own. He looked up from the cat, his dark eyes widened in surprise. "Theo, sweetheart—" he said. "I can't—" And he looked down at his chest, at the knife handle suspended there, and I looked down, too, at my empty fingers and the empty sheath under my robe. "Theo," he said again. The bluestone pendant was a fire against my skin. I ignored it.

What had I been thinking? For a wild second I tried to convince myself that I hadn't done this, that I wasn't responsible, although I could hear my thoughts still echoing: the mechanical choice of target, Vale's remembered voice telling me the location of the heart, tracking the nipple line, at the fifth intercostal space. The abdominal aorta would be easier, but the head of the floater masked it. The carotid artery, then, I seemed to hear the Old Man's voice: but I rejected it. Cut throats were the way cattle were killed.

I knew Eln's upper body intimately, from all the days of sa'ret practice in the garden. Now a red spot was spreading over the blue silk, just above his left nipple. Beads of sweat appeared on his forehead. His face was drained of color. His eyes met mine in disbelief. He lost consciousness as I watched, his body sagging down awkwardly off the floater, the straps on his legs holding him to the seat.

Ran pulled me out of the arena. The Duelmaster was talking, making some kind of announcement. "The Cormallon matter has been settled privately," I remember him saying; "Thank you for your time and attention."

Ran grabbed hold of my upper arms, his hands like ice through the robe. "Are you all right?"

I pulled away. "Of course I'm all right." It occurred to me that he might yell at me, that he might think I'd usurped his male prerogative to slaughter, or something like that; but I'd underestimated him. He was of a practical mind. Eln was dead and Cormallon was legally his; the details were not relevant.

"Come on," he said, "I'll get you out of here. Can you walk?"

"Of course I can walk." It wasn't clear even to me quite why I was so angry at him. I strode past him, up the ramp and out of the arena. I walked all the way up the tunnel, into the monastery, through the halls, and out the front doors. Once there I didn't know where to go next.

I paced in the yard, from the trees to the front steps and from the steps to the trees. After some amount of time had passed, Ran came out. He said to me, "I've arranged to borrow an aircar from the abbot. You can rest at Cormallon. By the time we get there, they'll have read Eln's documents. They may not be sure, but they'll let us in."

"I don't need to rest. "And I didn't; my system was throbbing with energy.

"Come along anyway." He took me by the hand. "I know *I* do."

It was a long ride to Cormallon. Ran said once, "That was an amazing throw. I didn't know you had it in you."

I grunted. With help, apparently I did. I fingered the stone around my neck. I suddenly wondered what would happen to Eln's stone. It was a pretty good guess that it wouldn't be laid in honor in the library at Cormallon. Swept up with his clothes, by the monks, to be burned or sold? What about his witness? Would he take care of it? I hadn't looked back at either of them when I left the arena. How convenient things were on Ivory, when you paid the proper people; we would never have to think about these details again.

We rode for an hour or so. After a while I said, "You'd better land this thing, I'm going to be sick."

We landed on the dirt hills near Amshiline. I was ill, on and off, for the next couple of hours. Somewhere in between the waves of nausea I got this crazy idea: That I had to go and talk to Grandmother. She saw herself as the moving spirit of Cormallon, and I guess the rest of the house did, too; there was nobody else who could give me absolution. Maybe she wasn't supposed to see visitors, but Kylla would find a way, I knew, if I let her see how important it was. Not that there was much chance of forgiveness in that quarter, really. Eln was always her favorite.

Ran rolled up his outer robe and placed it on the dirt under my head. I wanted to tell him he didn't have to help me. I wanted to say that I was as na' telleth as anybody, that I wasn't upset, that what made me sick was the decision; that I was contaminated by the act of choice. Luckily I was too weak to say any of those things. He got a canteen from the car, poured water over a cloth and wiped my forehead. He held me when I was heaving sick and said things like, "There, now, get it all out, you'll be all right." And all the while he had a pinched, abstracted look on his face, as though he wasn't even there.

* * *

It was afternoon. Ran called ahead and found that Eln's documents had been read, and that several hours ago Grandmother had sent a letter with them to the Cormallon council giving Ran her full support. I thought resentfully that if she had given Ran her support a lot sooner, maybe we could have avoided this past day. We rode in silence through the gray, rain-filled clouds of early summer. Below, on the hills ranging toward Cormallon, was a line of fires. I looked down and my mind flashed to the bowl of fire I'd seen in the cards, the torch Kylla took from Eln. I looked at Ran's face, drawn now and white as my own.

"What are they?" I asked.

"They're funeral fires," he answered.

"For Eln? How could they know?"

"They don't," he said shortly.

We landed in the front compound, and the goldbands who came out to bow Ran inside all wore silver; the color of change, the color of mourning.

They were Grandmother's funeral fires.

Chapter 21

No absolution, no higher judge.

I am a person who makes lists. This was something to add to the list of things I'd noticed changing as I got older. I'd noticed that making a fool of myself no longer seemed to be the soul-rending experience it once had been; that when I was badly treated by others, I understood when to make a fuss and when not; and now, I saw the third item: the knowledge that there was no court but the one in my head, and its judgments were all life sentences. I suppose I'll find other things to add as I go along . . . but the first two bits on the list had been a comfort to me; I saw now it would not all be that way.

I didn't go to the ceremonies, not the family ceremonies that went on for a week (and to which I would not have been invited in any case) or the House ceremony that took place two days after we arrived. I stayed in my room, mostly. Nobody expected any duties from me, and Ran and Kylla were busy. It was several days before people started to notice me beyond polite inquiries as to my health and my room.

I wasn't eating at that time. I want to be clear about this; I wasn't trying to commit suicide, or anything so dramatic—it was simply that the sight of food made me feel ill. I drank water, milk, and tah in great quantities, but although from time to time I could feel hunger stirring in my belly, as soon as I looked at a bowl of soup or a cake, I had to turn away. I was perfectly aware that human beings can last for many days without food and that the time would come when my hunger would be great enough to overcome the revulsion. However, I was beginning to alarm the household, which made me feel badly.

I accompanied Kylla down to the kitchen one evening in

an effort to set her mind at rest. She said that Herel had made me a light casserole of egg, cheese, and bacon, and although the very thought of it made my stomach turn over, I agreed to go with her and give it a try.

"Here she is," said Herel, pulling out the bench for me to sit. "It's warming in the oven. Just you wait a minute." I hated being treated like a patient, but they'd gone to a lot of trouble. I sat down beside Kylla and Herel brought the dish from the oven with great ceremony and set it before us. Then she called, "Tagra! I asked you to bring the plates." And Tagra stepped out of the pantry doorway and carried two plates to the table. She planked them down with just enough force that one couldn't, quite, call it rude. I looked into the scarred face for a moment and met eyes just as wounded.

I hope my own eyes didn't have that trapped look. Gods, when was the last time I'd used a mirror?

She raised one eyebrow, beautifully ironic, just the way Eln used to. "Was there something else?"

"No, thank you," I said, and she left the kitchen. I picked up a fork. "I didn't expect she would still be here," I told Kylla.

She was cutting a wedge off the casserole, with difficulty. Without looking up, she said, "Where else would she go? This is her home." She got the slice onto my plate. "There we go," she said with satisfaction, handing it to me. She licked a finger and said, "Beautiful work, Herel. Go ahead and start, Theo, don't wait for me."

I put down the fork again. I said, "I'm sorry, Ky."

It had been two weeks, and I was walking through the back garden, smelling the aroma from the kitchen, thinking that maybe the human race hadn't gone so wrong after all when it decided to get energy from food. Maybe I should try it. Ran joined me there just as I was sitting down under the sa'ret equipment.

"I was thinking about having all this pulled down," he said, motioning to the bars and the platforms. "But then I thought you might want to use it for arm-work when you go back to doing The River. What do you want me to do?"

"Leave it up," I said. The sun was high, and the shadows of the bars made cross-patterns on his face and robe.

"All right," he said.

After a while I said, "It's a nice day for summer. Not too hot."

"No," he agreed.

Herel's voice filtered through the trees, calling someone. A moment later a goldband came by, carrying a tray. He was familiar, but I couldn't remember his name. He inclined his head to Ran and said, "Call for you on the Net."

Ran signed. "Probably more expressions of sympathy. I'll be back in a little while, Theodora." He pulled himself up and brushed off his robe.

The goldband put down the tray on the ground beside me. "Excuse me," he said, "but Herel sends these to you."

There were three small pastry-cakes. Ran lingered for a moment looking down on them. "I'd steal one, but they were obviously cooked for you." And so they were; there was a thick coating of dark icing on each one. Everyone "knows" that barbarians like lots of sugar. Herel was going to destroy me with her polite attentions—not a day went by but she fired up her oven to make me something, and how could I get rid of it nicely? I couldn't even crumble up her offerings and hide them in my room or stuff them in the trash; one of the goldbands on cleaning duty would be bound to notice and tell her. There are no secrets in a house with servants.

The goldband who'd brought out the tray said, "She said to leave it here for you."

"And not to take no for an answer, I'll bet," said Ran. He grinned. "Don't worry, Theodora, there are lots of boulders to hide it under. Just wait till we're out of sight."

I hoped he wasn't adding telepathy to his other talents. They left, and I lay down under the bars and let the sun warm my face.

The cakes were fresh and smelled delightful. After a few minutes I sat up and said, "well," to myself. I picked one up. Try as one will to be sick, I thought, health gets the better of us all. I took a bite.

And I was shocked when Ran jumped down beside me and knocked the cake out of my hand.

"Spit it out," he said.

"What?" I said through a mouthful of icing.

"Spit it *out*," he said, and even as he started to repeat it I spat out the mess onto the dirt.

"Did you swallow any?"

"No," I said. "Who—"

"Tagra." He sat back on the ground and ran a hand over his forehead. "I thanked Herel for the cakes and she said she hadn't made any. Jad said that he'd gotten his orders relayed by Tagra. I checked her room; all her things are gone." He was breathing hard.

The goldband—Jad—came running up. "Medical?" he asked. Ran shook his head. Jad said, "I sent someone to ask at the stables. Tagra took a horse about an hour ago—that would be just after she spoke to me and asked me to take the cakes out of the oven for Herel. She must be a good fifth of the way across Cormallon territory now . . . if she's heading northwest."

"And of course she is," said Ran.

"The aircar's in good shape. There's a lot of cover in that direction, but we're used to spotting people heading for the Sector. We can hunt her down, sir."

Ran closed his eyes. He took my left hand in his. After a moment he said, "No. Let her go." He opened his eyes and looked at me. I nodded.

Jad said, "As you say."

It was three weeks after Tevachin that I happened to wander into the Cormallon library. I'd been taking regular meals, to Herel's great relief, and to my own, in a way; breakfast, lunch, and supper at least provided some structure to my rather rootless days. I'd been avoiding the library, perhaps because it was where I first met Eln. But it began to look like a potential refuge now, where I could get a measure of personal relief in the sometimes bloody-minded, joyfully conscience-free memories of past Cormallons. Nobody in the household mentioned Eln's name—not *once*—and it was getting on my nerves.

It was easy to see the new addition to the room. There were bouquets of flowers all around it, vases standing on the floor and tucked with difficulty into the shelf. There were flowers that I'd never seen before, sent in from other parts of the continent, expensive fire-lilies from hot-houses in the capital, and in one vase there was even hearthwhistle from the meadows around Cormallon. And only one lonely bluestone pendant on the shelf. I picked it up.

And had one of the major shocks of my life. I heard my name.

I had the presence of mind to keep hold of the pendant as I found a cushion and sat down.

"Theodora, cherie," I heard, in what was not quite a voice, but had the tones of Grandmother running all through it. "Theodora, I am repeating this over and over again in the hope that you can hear me. You are the only one who will receive this; if my grandson picks up the stone, he will hear something quite different. I would like to ask your forgiveness."

What?

"When my first grandson was born, his father had his cards read. The cards said that Eln would cause great trouble in our House one day. The configuration was certain; I know, I was the card-reader. I couldn't lie about a reading, but I put my foot down when his father talked about sending Eln away to be raised. Send the child out of our control, where we couldn't see what he was doing? My son was always an idiot. One would think he had never heard of old stories.

"But I couldn't let Eln be killed, either. It put us all in danger, but I could not allow it. He was my first grandson, and he was a beautiful child. After all, we did not know how this trouble would come; perhaps not by Eln's choice, perhaps not his fault. This was an excuse, I know. What difference did it make to the safety of our House whether it was his fault or not?

"He was always a delightful boy, I loved to talk with him. Doubly precious, when I thought of the trouble I'd gone to to keep him alive.

"But I had to watch him, just the same. I knew when he made up his mind to regain his place in the family; I knew when he decided to kill his brother. He was going to wait until I was out of the way and then he was going to bring murder to our House. And by the time I was dead, he might be strong enough to succeed—I couldn't wait for that to happen. I began to exaggerate the effects of my illness; not much of an exaggeration, I knew I was dying. With Kylla's help I began to shut myself out of the day-to-day affairs of Cormallon. I retired to my rooms. And I *held onto life*.

"As I hoped, Eln felt safe enough to begin taking over in earnest. It was dangerous for you and for Ran, but the danger would have come anyway, and this way I could keep an eye on things. Kylla kept me informed of everything that went on in the household. I did what I could; it was through my intervention that you were not killed in the aircar fire—Ran was not quick enough in his shielding—and it was I who had Kylla arrange for you to be taken off the *Queen Emily*.

"I know today that it is over, my duty is performed, finally I can let go. Finally.

"I beg that you will not judge me too harshly. You will think, perhaps, that I have interfered in your life. But something had to be done, there was a choice to be made. I loved Eln best, but I could not allow him to retake Cormallon, nor kill his brother for that end. This is Ivory, Theodora, we cannot trust our courts and police as Athenans can; those institutions exist here mainly to collect taxes. Families must make their own justice, and the tragedy of it is that the prisoners we judge are the people we love.

"Well, there is something I can do for you. If you truly want to return to Athena, I do not think Ran will stop you. Keep the onyx cat, if you like, it has performed its service for me in keeping me informed of my grandsons' minds. More importantly, from your point of view: I have removed the curse from Ran's cards, so you are free. Although, you know . . . there is no need to tell him that, little one."

The message faded with a brief visual image of Grandmother's bedroom, the table with the star-maps, and the awareness that Kylla was coming in with a tray.

I sat and thought about things for a long time.

After a while I picked up the pendant again. The message was fainter this time, tinged with other thoughts, other memories. A tah plantation to the south, plants with huge leaves, as big as I was. Faces with labels attached like a faint perfume: father, mother, husband. Eln as a child. Ran, too . . . the label was "young brat," but it was affectionate, and I was glad of that. If there was a message for Ran,

I couldn't read it. Finally I returned the pendant to the library shelf.

Things were coming together that had never made sense before. I was beginning to see that Grandmother's plans had gone way beyond controlling possible harm from Eln. That damned onyx cat . . . no wonder Ran had drawn away in Braece. He grew up in this house, he knew Grandmother for the unrepentant manipulator she was. He knew she wouldn't have given the onyx cat to anyone if she didn't expect it to stay in the family.

This needed thinking about.

I left the library and headed for the back garden. In the downstairs corridor I met Ran, coming the other way. I put up a hand, and he stopped.

I said, "Have you been in the library since Grandmother died?"

He knew very well what I was asking. "No," he said, with the slightest touch of embarrassment. As a dutiful grandson he should have been, but I could sympathize with a wish to avoid this particular mark of respect.

"I think you should go up there."

He said, "You've never given me a hard time about family custom before."

"I think she left a message for you," I said.

He paused. I said, "I don't know the retentive quality of bluestone. If you wait too long, could it get lost in the stream of life memories?"

He said slowly, "That's possible."

"Well," I said, "It's up to you. I'm going out to the garden."

I left him standing by the stairway.

An hour later he joined me by the mirelis vine, one of my favorite spots in the back garden. I couldn't tell if he'd been to the library or not.

It was a tall mirelis, in summer bloom. I sat with my back against a rock, and Ran lay down on the grass. It was a companionable sort of silence, but I made no assumptions from that.

Mirelis flowers have a sweet center, so I'd heard. Ran pulled down a blossom, opened the petals, and pulled out the tiny silver bulb inside. He offered it to me. "Have one?"

"Thank you, no. I'm already addicted to tah."

"This isn't addictive."

"Not technically. It's a euphoric, though, isn't it?"

"Coward," said Ran, as he popped it into his mouth. He put his head down on the grass again. After a while he said, "I've been wondering, Theodora. The funeral's just over, I know, and there's still a half-year mourning period . . . but these things take time, and I was wondering if we should start making arrangements now."

"Arrangements for what?" I toyed with the idea of trying a mirelis anyway.

"For the wedding. Kylla's been asking me, too, and we ought to set a date."

I sat up with a bounce. "I beg your pardon?"

He turned his head. He looked perfectly serious. "I understand wanting to put if off, I've felt the same way. All the fuss and the relatives and the arguments over details—it's like holding two jobs at once, and we shouldn't postpone reopening the sorcery practice, either. But we have to get it over with eventually."

I continued to start. "Did I miss something here?" I asked. "When did we get engaged?"

He blinked. "I thought you expected it. Everybody else expects it. You're my card-reader, you have to come into the family sooner or later . . . and I assumed that we . . . uh, that is to say, we . . . get along . . . you're a little old to adopt, Theodora. I'm not bringing you in as my daughter, that's definite."

"Well, I should hope not!"

"Well," he said, "there you are." And he smiled. "A barbarian in the family is just what we need. Speaking personally." He pulled himself up on one elbow. We were dangerously within kissing distance, I thought, but then I considered all the time we'd spent harmlessly together on the road from the south, and decided he wouldn't take advantage of that.

He did. About ten minutes later—or maybe it was fifteen—I became aware a goldband was standing over us.

It was Jad. He appeared totally unconcerned and unembarrassed. "Sir," he said, "Supper's ready."

Ran rolled over, sighed, and said, "Whatever happened to discretion?"

"Herel told me not to come back without you. She made two dishes just for you tonight."

"You're more afraid of offending Herel than you are me?"

"Yes, sir," said Jad calmly.

Ran nodded. "We're coming." He stood up and offered me a hand. I took it.

That must have been quite a message Grandmother left him. On the way back to the house I decided to spend the next morning on the Net, looking up ships' itineraries.

Chapter 22

Certainly Ran was taking a great deal for granted. I wondered if he'd come upon any of the "young brat" imagery yet.

I hadn't eaten much at supper (to the minor alarm of Herel, who feared I might be backsliding) and woke in the middle of the night ravenous. I made my way down to the kitchen, where I found the lights on and Kylla, sweaty and blood-spattered, standing at the sideboard in her trousers plucking a groundhermit. Two naked hermits were piled on the trestle next to her, their heads beside them. Her bow was propped against the wall.

She looked up. "Theo!" she said happily. "Just in time. I didn't dare wake Herel. Grab a bird, start plucking, and maybe we'll be out of here by dawn."

"Uh, I just came down for a glass of water."

She laughed. "I only wanted to scare you. This is the last one. But if you want to be helpful, you could wash those two and wrap them up and put them in the icer."

So I did. When she finished the last groundhermit, she handed it to me and said, "Be right back." She vanished while I cleaned it and put it away, then reappeared in her nightgown. She'd found time to splash water on her face and arms. "Oh, sweetheart," she said, "what a night. I love it like this, two moons out and stars all over the place." She threw herself down on the bench. "It must be the wild romance of the night that kept you awake."

"Hunger," I said. "I skipped most of supper."

"You know, I see why you and Ran get along."

"You said that to me once before," I said. "Listen, Kylla, about this getting-along stuff—"

"What about it? You mean you've already heard? I wanted to be the one to tell you."

"Tell me what?"

She gave me a satisfied smile. "Lysander Shikron's been officially accepted by the family as my fiancé. Ran gave his blessing and argued the council around. The Cormallons and the Shikrons are as of this moment on speaking terms."

"Kylla!" We hugged. Then we talked about the wedding plans, about Lysander Shikron's physical characteristics, and about the general quality of life. Kylla still had not told her promised husband that she smoked a pipe and liked to sit with her feet up. ("We'll work up to that," she said.)

"We'll have to be careful not to get married the same day," she said. "Bad luck for two weddings in one family."

I frowned. "Ky—" I said.

"Hasn't he brought it up yet? Heavens, try to get a man to set a date for a social function. I'll have to have a talk with him—"

"That's not the point, Ky."

"What *is* the point?" She seemed genuinely puzzled. "Is there something wrong? Theo, darling, whatever it is, we'll carry it out with the trash and never mention it again. You're not already married, are you?"

"No!"

"Well, that's all right, then." She smiled. "Although if your husband were on Athena, we could just pretend he didn't exist. Change your name, pay off the necessary officials, or hire someone to make him behave. Not to really worry . . . I'm thirsty. Would you like some tah? It's my own blend, half green tea and half Ducort tah, mixed."

"Yes, thanks."

She came back in a minute with two wine bowls and two tah cups. The wine bowls were very old, with painted scenes on the inner rim. "The tah's boiling," she said, "but I had a better idea." She poured wine for us both. "Ducort tah and Ducort wine," she said, "two things that make life worth living. Anyway, that's what Eln always used to s—"

She stopped.

"Go ahead," I said.

"I'm sorry, Theo."

"Kylla, what nobody here seems to understand is that I *want* to talk about it. You people—this planet—when you don't want to deal with something you ignore it, pretend it doesn't exist. That's not the way I am. I need to understand things as they really are. Or were."

"You'll never make na' telleth that way."

"Maybe not."

She leaned over. "All right. Nobody's here. Let's talk."

Four hours later the sun was rising. Across the room, on Herel's huge range, sat a pot with the remains of old noodles stuck to the bottom. There were dirty plates all over the table. Kylla leaned back against the wall and patted her belly. "I think I might be sick," she said.

"Me, too."

"You know, I don't think you're supposed to put oil with noodles when you boil them."

"They did taste a little funny. But the sauce helped."

She nodded. "I don't know if I can make it upstairs."

"I don't know if I can move," I said. But I helped her up and we headed for the door. "Anyway," I said, "If I do end up trying to run the estate, you'll be around to tell me what to do."

"Don't count on it," she said sadly. "I'll have my hands full with Shikron."

"A cheery thought," I said.

She grinned. "Try not to let it influence you."

According to the Net, no ships were due to lift for Athena for at least three months. Two freighters would be going in late summer, and a few weeks later two passenger liners were scheduled to go. I wiped my question from the Net just in case Ran decided to check up on me; Grandmother might think he would go along with this, but I wasn't going to take any chances. I would relax and enjoy a vacation until the departure date.

Well, not quite a vacation, for two reasons. The first was a bound volume I finally held in my hands, with a Standard title: *A Branch of the Common Tree: Riddles, Proverbs, and Folk Tales of Ivory.* Collected and Translated by Theodora of Pyrene. It wasn't my original notebook, of course; that had been in Ivoran, in a combination of real characters and my phonetic renderings. I had the Net print out the final version and a shop in the capital bound it for me.

I wanted to dedicate it to Eln, but Ran might find out

and he would never, never understand. I thought about dedicating it to Vale, or Irsa, or even Seth, who'd told me most of the stories. But that didn't feel right either, and anyway none of them would care.

Nor did I know what would happen to it when it reached Athena—maybe the Board wouldn't like it. Maybe it violated some pet theory of somebody's; it was possible. But the hell with all that; it wasn't important enough to worry over.

Important enough . . . I opened to the dedication page and wrote, in characters, "Ishin na' telleth."

Now the only problem was whether to send it in storage or deliver it personally.

Meanwhile, there were other calls on my time. Ran had won his fight, and there were people to be paid off. I know these details because he began to instruct me in the household accounts (the very heart of the mystery) and seemed to feel that tracking the rewards for our allies would be a pleasant introduction.

"You want me to do accounts?" I said, with wariness.

"It's money," he said, laughing. "How dull can it be?" ("It's numbers," said Kylla to me later, "and it's boring.") Two people in every branch could access the Cormallon treasury directly; here it was Ran and Kylla. " 'For a peaceful life,' " quoted Ran, " 'let the women worry about the money.' After the wedding, I'll transfer my access to your name."

I grunted noncommittally.

He said, "Kylla can show you how to set up my expense account. I like to draw an allowance every week or so. Not a good idea to carry around too much coin, you know."

"Very true," I said. And he went away and let me play with the cash flow.

Karlas, Tyl, and other involved members of their ex-family were in receipt of Cormallon House and family shares. They were setting up an import company to deliver things up from the south to the capital; what they were delivering, I did not ask.

The Serrens made a quick speech about their eternal gratitude to the House of Cormallon; then they asked for their shares, resigned, and opened up a cookshop (on-premises dining, with tables and benches) in one end of a building on the north side of Trade Square. It was a good location; not only would they pick up the spillover from the market crowds, but a lot of tourists made their way along the north side of the Square to get from the port to the Lavender Palace. Heida and Arno asked if I would drop in from time to time during the first few weeks, and let them know what dishes foreign barbarians preferred; although they did not phrase the invitation in exactly those terms. I decided they had what it took to make it in the Square.

We never heard about Tagra. I assumed that she was in the Northwest Sector by then. Ran thought that she was probably dead, but Tagra never struck me as the sort of person who let go of things easily, and I wished her the best, within reason. It hadn't been much of a murder attempt, anyway, more of a game of chance. She left it in my hands—if I still felt too miserable to eat, I would live. If not, there would be one barbarian and one goldband less in Cormallon.

So the weeks passed. We entertained Lysander Shikron regularly, and when he wasn't in Cormallon I was often invited to the capital to dine with his family. Ran asked me along to all the places he was asked to, and it seemed easier to accept. I would have dearly liked, however, some advice from someone I could trust.

I returned to the library often those days; there was something comforting in touching the rhythm of Grandmother's mind. Unfortunately it was becoming more clear with each visit that to her dying moment she regarded Ran as the same boy who refused to behave on initiation day. She thought he needed spurring to perform his duty. And to her dying moment he resented it.

"You spend a lot of time in there," he said one day, as I came out of the library.

"Trying to understand things," I said.

"Try asking me," he said.

How could I let that go by? We went out to the courtyard. A light drizzle was falling in the pool.

Ran said, "There's a banquet in the capital six days from

now. A dozen officials and a delegation of Cormallons from the Serenth Peninsula. I hope you'll attend."

He'd been like that the past few months, thoughtful and considerate. Either that was the way one was with a future wife, or he still wasn't entirely sure that I wouldn't skip out.

But if there was any uncertainty in his mind, he wasn't showing it. I said, "Ran, tell me, when I first gave you my onyx cat, you thought it was some kind of trick of Grandmother's, didn't you."

He paused and looked uncomfortable. "I'm sorry about that. It's just that . . . you seemed fond of me, apparently. So I assumed that—look, Theodora, you're not going to ever mention this again, are you?"

"Not if you answer now."

"I assumed," he said, "that Grandmother had put an attraction spell on the cat. And that was why you—I mean to say, you were only going along with the spell. Look, is this funny?"

"Sorry," I said, trying to stifle the laughter. "You mean all those symptoms I memorized, like increased heart rate and all that—you thought I'd fallen for a spell?"

He didn't answer. I said, "Ran, I'm afraid I have to set you straight. I was experiencing those symptoms within about three minutes after you sat down by my pitch in Trade Square."

For once he looked surprised. Maybe Kylla's right about men.

This is the story Eln told to me that day in the market before my arrest.

> There was once a rich merchant who married a wife who was, many said, too young for him. One day he returned unexpectedly from a business trip and found his housekeeper waiting for him at the door. She said, "For some time now my lady's behavior with men has given me cause for alarm. Today I took two trusted servants and entered her bedchamber without warning, in an attempt to discover the truth of the matter. It took several minutes to break the door. When we entered we found the mistress sitting on the great wooden chest in which she keeps her linens. She will

not allow any of us to open this chest, even though we told her it would be best to establish her innocence before your return." The merchant thanked the housekeeper for her efforts, and went, most unhappily, to see his wife. He said, "My dear, I think perhaps I should unlock this chest of linens." She replied, "Do so, if you have no intention of trusting your wife and the mother of your children." And she threw him her keys and stalked away. The merchant thought for a while, then called his servants. He had the chest carried outside and buried, unopened, in the garden; and no one ever brought up the matter again.

It was a story I'd heard in three similar versions before, when I'd studied on Athena; one was from a place called France. Maybe Eln had even heard it from his Grandmother. But it struck me that it was the tale most redolent of Ivoran thinking that I had ever heard.

I didn't know if I wanted to be *that* trusted.

The banquet with the Serenth Peninsula delegates was in late summer. I went as Ran's guest. Our seating arrangements changed every three courses, and between the third and seventh course I enjoyed a delightful conversation with a dog-breeder from the Marble Cliffs on the north side of the peninsula. We didn't find out we were both Cormallons until our last course together. I finally woke up to my obligations and turned briefly to the woman on my left, whom I'd been ignoring, and introduced myself.

She looked at me strangely, which made me look at her strangely, and I realized that I knew her. I said, "You were with the Athenan party I met in Teshin Village . . . ?"

"Yes. We're due to leave on the *Queen Gretchen* in a week."

"I'm sorry, I've forgotten your name."

"Annamarie."

"Yes. I'm sorry I didn't recognize you—you look older in Ivoran clothes."

She said finally, "Your name is really Theodora?"

"Yes, I'm afraid things were rather complicated in Teshin—"

"Theodora of Pyrene."

I laughed nervously. "I don't owe you money, do I?"

She said, "But Theodora, haven't you been to the embassy?"

"Many times. What about it?"

"The *fund,* hasn't anyone told you?"

I said, "No."

So she told me. Since I left Athena, the Board of Student Affairs (prompted by my companions of the trip out, now suffering unexpiated guilt) had instituted a fund in my name. It revolved with the other theater and dance funds, and over the last few years they'd collected three hundred thousand dollars. At the going rate of exchange—

"That's over half the price of a ticket," I said.

"Yes, that's the point." said Annamarie, smiling broadly. "We brought the bank draft with us and deposited it at the Athenan Bank here in the capital. We told the ambassador all about it, didn't he tell you?"

That filthy kanz. With the tabals in gold I had with my own banker, this put me over the top. And with no charity from any Cormallon.

"Let me get this straight," I said. "All I do is establish my identity at the bank, and they give me three hundred thousand dollars?"

She said, "Yes." And she added, "They've got your finger and retina prints."

I grinned back at her. Just then the sixth course ended, and we all had to get up and change seats. "Well, thank you very much," I said.

She looked puzzled. "Don't you want to stay and talk?"

"It wouldn't be polite." Besides, I had some thinking to do. The nice dog-breeder on my right tugged at my robe.

He said, "Will I be seeing you again?"

"I don't know," I said honestly.

And then I had to sit beside one of the Imperial officials, who smiled and said, "You're engaged to young Cormallon, aren't you?"

"Yes," I said, to cut it short.

"A tinaje artist, too, I hear."

Oh, damn, was he trying to prove how thorough his background checks were? Just what did he want? Was I about to be offered a bribe on some Cormallon business?

He leaned closer. "Maybe you could do me a favor."

"Oh?" I leaned farther away.

He looked embarrassed. "I have this problem with my lower back. . . . "

Well, what are we to do with all these facts? They float in and out of consciousness, seemingly unconnected, just when I most need a pattern.

Do you know that I think about Ran all the time, even when I'm doing other things? I can say that because I'm going to erase this section from the record when I'm done. I've heard about this sort of obsession though (the archaic term is *infatuation*), and they say it passes. I hope to the gods that it's true, because it can become very wearing.

As for Ran, who takes me for granted in a way that is a great compliment, who is willing to ally himself to me for life although he knows *nothing* of my genetic background, who assumes I'm far more competent than I think I am . . . he's not infatuated, in the sense of the word I implied above. The Ivoran word for that kind of mind/body obsession would translate as "crazy." I've run the cards, and I know him. His erotic adventures have been varied, to say the least, but his emotional life always comes up surprisingly barren. He's never loved anyone in his previously too-easy life . . . too easy before he met me, that is to say.

But I think it was in the plans Grandmother had for him. I think maybe she held herself responsible for his problems. I think she had some kind of lifetime design involved, and we've only gotten to the tip of the iceberg.

Or am I falling into paranoia? What do we do with these facts?

They all seem to think this marriage makes sense. But what Ran doesn't seem to realize—or Kylla, or Grandmother—is that the water has become too tainted to drink.

I've been badly shaken, not only by the idea that I'd killed someone but by the dawning realization that I was not the same country scholar who'd left Athena. All this time I'd thought I was compromising, when what I was doing was *changing*.

Be honest. We're not talking about tolerant views on bribery. We're talking about killing a human being. A consciousness that's not there any more, and that was the point of the exercise. There's no use confiding in Ran about this;

he's Ivoran born and bred, he knows that there's always something gnawing away at your vitals, no matter how happy things look; unless you're a true na' telleth. It was an act performed, to him; a thing done. To Grandmother it was a necessary thing. To Ran it was a reasonable thing. But at bedrock, at my core, I find I still have the soul of an Athenan, and the question I must ask myself is this: Was it a good thing, or a bad thing?

And the answer is *yes.*

All right. I understand now, I admit I will be forever detached from whatever culture I live in—very like Eln. I've lived on Ivory now for over half the time I lived on Athena, and how can I change that fact? And I'm not going back to Pyrene, no matter how confused I become. There is no "home," there will never be a home in the way other people take one for granted.

Two roads, then. Ran can be difficult when his desires conflict with mine, but of course it's taboo to kill a member of the family without good reason, so I won't have to walk on eggshells around him. And my position is quite a strong one, thanks to Grandmother. I wonder if she saw something like this coming when she placed her curse—doing something in a fit of temper has come to seem less and less like the old woman.

But is that a happy ending? What sort of children, if any, could we have? And how dangerous would it be for me? Or given the statistics on male life expectancies in the Great Houses, what happens when Ran dies young, leaving me this little kingdom I am not qualified to run?

On the other hand . . . I have the money. I have the expertise, given my tutoring in Ran's tricky ways, to get aboard the *Queen Gretchen,* now due in port, without leaving a trail. But if I do return to Athena, it won't be as a scholar. Too much has happened for that ever to be more than a hobby. It hurts to acknowledge it, but university life has come to seem, well, boring.

Athena must have spies on Tellys and Ivory, though I don't know how I know that. Surely there are job opportunities for someone who can talk like an Athenan scholar and bribe like an Ivoran aristocrat, and who speaks several languages (albeit some of them dead) with colloquial accents.

It doesn't sound unpleasant. My classics teacher used to say that the ancients believed you could tell if prophetic dreams were true or false only if you knew how they came to you; false dreams came through the Gate of Ivory and true dreams came through the Gate of Horn. Trust me to get it backward. Still, maybe it was a fitting reversal, for an ex-scholar. The trouble with telling true dreams is you never really know, not for twenty years or so, if you were right.

But whatever happens, there's too much history here.

I boarded the *Gretchen* five days ago, an hour before take-off, under an assumed name. I'm in my cabin now, on a first-class deck, dictating this to my terminal. You don't know how dry your throat can get in five days; there were hours at a stretch when I had to give up and use the keyboard.

I left a note for Ran, telling him where to pick up the cards and the onyx cat. I told him that Grandmother had lifted the curse. I said I would miss him. And I apologized for not attending Kylla's wedding.

Many weeks ago I sent to Tevachin to see if the monks retained any of Eln's effects, particularly the bluestone ring he used to wear on his left hand. They still had it—it had looked valuable—and they were willing to send it to me for a nominal handling fee. It arrived in a small wooden box, lined with velvet. I made sure it was there, then closed and locked the box. I had no intention of touching this one. Perhaps I'm oversensitive, but dealing with Annurian's mental reflexes seems more than enough for one lifetime. I wrote out a letter to the jeweler on Marsh Street who'd been Eln's companion, and sent the letter and the box to him by messenger. I'm sorry to say that I didn't remember the jeweler's name. I didn't want to send a letter telling the death of someone close to a person whose name I'd forgotten. But he needed to know, and I had no right to censor the information.

The messenger came back saying that the store was closed and the jeweler had moved, no one knew where. So now I have a carved wooden box, four centimeters by six centimeters, which I have no plans to ever open. What else could I do? I could hardly send it to Cormallon and ask them to place it in the library.

I think Eln would have liked to go off-planet. I hope someday I find a place for him.

The cabin I've drawn is pretty sumptuous, but I haven't brought much to it in the way of personal objects. The wardrobes and drawers are empty. I didn't take any Ivoran clothes when I left, just a couple of tunics and trousers to wear aboard ship. Beyond that, I have in my possession one cut-rate dagger; a stone pendant belonging to a rebel, killer, and ex-prime minister; and a ring from a person whose mental problems I will not begin to try to define. Just some mementos from friends. Souvenirs from a trip that lasted a little longer than I planned. That is the attitude to take, I think.

I finally went to the dining room tonight. It was the first time I'd been out of my cabin since I watched the world of Ivory fall away from us in the lounge monitor. Table 53A, my assigned dinner seat. It was a very small table, since I'd not signed up as part of a party when I boarded.

Ran was sitting there, inspecting the menu. I don't know if anyone reading this is surprised; I found that I was not surprised. I was not expecting him, but I was not surprised.

He looked up as I took my seat. "Do barbarians really eat snake?" he asked.

"Some do. I understand it's a delicacy on Tellys."

"Amazing." He reached into a pocket, brought out a pack of cards and placed them on the tablecloth. "You left some things behind recently. One should be more careful."

How had he gotten my message out of the Net beforetime? And even harder, how had he gotten the cards away from Irsa? I'd told her to hold onto them until after the ship left.

"Ran, you could read them yourself."

"Not as well as you." He said, "Do you realize I've been sitting here alone for five days? I was beginning to think you'd keeled over and died in that cabin of yours."

"I'll bet you didn't expect to see me in first class." I said, assuming he knew perfectly well how much I'd had stashed away here and there.

He said seriously, "Theodora, I always expect to see you in first class."

"Well, the feeling is mutual, but can you afford to be away from home for this length of time? Do you know how long this voyage is, one-way?"

"Forty-one point six standard days," said Ran, who may or may not have had an hour to prepare for it, but who would not dream of setting one foot on board without knowing these things.

"You think you've got thirty-six days left to change my mind." I stated.

"Me?" He smiled. "I'm going to Athena to register as a student. They take all ages, I understand. I've always said to Kylla that our House should open its doors, scan new horizons . . . "

"So you're going to let yourself be taught by barbarians? You're going to live in student housing and share space with superstitious people who won't know what a sorcerer is? They'll confiscate your pistol when you land, and anything else you've got on you, by the way." I didn't believe it for a second.

He had picked up the fourth formal vegetable fork by his plate, and was regarding it with amused contempt. The ways of the barbarian, I could see him thinking. No, I didn't believe that story and I wasn't meant to.

Still, it was an interesting image. Would he really go through with it if I didn't agree to come back? Just how stubborn was he?

Student housing . . .

"What's so amusing?"

"Nothing important. I was just wondering, Ran, have you tried any magic yet? Does it work in space?"

He gave a slight smile. "That's the sort of information, tymon, that I really wouldn't feel comfortable sharing with someone who wasn't of my House."

Point one for his side. He said it very courteously, too. And when he was finished speaking, he lifted up my right hand from the table and kissed the inside of my palm.

Thirty-six days. I wouldn't want to make any bets on who would be holding the deck of cards when I finally made it back to Athena.

TWO-BIT HEROES

Chapter 1

In Tuvin Province they serve you chocolate in the morning. It comes in little round cups with flat bottoms and no handles, and people drink it, by and large, outside their homes—in the markets, in sidewalk stalls, on the narrow balconies of the whitewashed houses. It's a warm and sunny place, being north, and all those chocolate drinkers sit there in the mornings with their hats on. Taking in the illusory peace of Ivory's fresh new day. Before they all rush out to swindle and cheat the competition.

That's a generalization, of course, and an unfair one. Particularly coming from me, and considering all I saw and did in that province. Looking back now, it's amazing the amount of trouble I got into there, and have always seemed to get into on Ivory in general. It never happened to me anyplace else. It seems to be what my teachers on Athena would call "an interactive effect." But I acquired a taste for morning chocolate in Tuvin Province, and a taste for Trouble, too. Although I wouldn't expect anyone else to understand about the latter, except for one or two of the Cormallons.

But by all means, let us be chronological. I had just passed my twenty-fifth standard birthday. I had returned to Ivory for the second time in my life. And I was standing alone in the hills of Cormallon, a long hike from the main house, picking cherries for that night's dessert.

It was a cool day for early summer, but being a barbarian I wore a sun hat anyway. Just then I'd taken it off—a round straw thing that came to a peak in the middle—and was filling it with black-red cherries. The morning sky was a long, glorious blue dome and the wind was gentle, and somewhere around the forty-fourth cherry I was deciding how pain between the shoulder blades could come between one's intellectual appreciation of the day and the actual joy of it, when I heard the distant whirr of an aircar.

If you know me, you'll know there was no horse nearby to be frightened of it. I was only mildly curious myself, being safe behind the Cormallon barrier. I held my heavy straw hat in both hands and waited, and a few minutes later a car I'd never seen before landed on the hilltop.

Kylla came out. She was dressed conservatively (for Kylla) in a shimmering blue and gold robe, with long gold hoops in her ears and her mass of black hair pulled back by a blue and gold thong. No gold swirl on her cheeks; she must have been in a hurry. She jogged down the hill and grabbed me and spun me around.

"Theo, Theo, Theo," she said happily.

Really, it had only been four days since we'd seen each other.

"Lysander gave me an extra hundred in gold for shopping," she said.

So that explained it.

"And now you can come with me," she added. "Ran said you were going to town today anyway."

"When did you talk to Ran?" I asked.

"Half an hour ago, on the Net from the capital. He said you had to go in today to talk to some hateful man from the Athenan embassy. Darling, they're not giving you trouble over your citizenship, are they?"

"No, nothing like that. Just a routine visit. —How did you get the hundred in gold?" I asked, knowing that would divert her.

She smiled widely. "Every time he looks at Shez his heart just melts into a puddle." Shez was her baby girl Scheherazade, currently at the stage where she could stand up if she held onto something.

"Where is the little monarch? Didn't you bring her with you?"

"She's up at the house, Theo dear, waiting for her aunt to come back and change. So give me a cherry, and get into the car."

I gave her a handful, which is the world's usual response to Kylla, and got in.

* * *

On the way to the house she said, "Theo, you have to tell me when the wedding is. How can I prepare if I don't know?"

"Must you always ask this, Ky? You'll be the first to find out, I promise."

All right, I was having a few second thoughts. That's not the same as cold feet. I was young and in love and wondering about the wisdom of settling down for life with a man who, by the standards of his own government, was running a criminal organization. And that was only one of the lesser problems you dealt with when you dealt with Ran.

All this certainty on the part of others was getting irritating. Gifts had already been coming into Cormallon on the strength of rumor alone. (Just four days ago I'd been speaking with Kylla on the Net and opening some boxes. Something red and speckled crawled out of one box and started walking across the floor. It was insectoid. I gasped and dropped another box on it. Kylla, on the screen, had seen me vanish and kept saying "Theo? Theo?" I checked for a corpse—found one, to my relief—and came back to the Net. "I didn't know what it was," I explained, "so I killed it." Kylla could find no fault with my logic but said, "What will we tell Third Cousin Graza?" It seems that in some parts of the world this type of rare insect is used, still living, as a sort of brooch. "Yecch," I said, and Kylla had to agree with that, too, but the problem of what to put in the thank-you note remained. "You'll have to get married now," she pointed out. "We can't return it." Not to mention the difficulty presented by the shards of glass that were all that remained of whatever had been in the box from Great Aunt Evelina that I'd dropped with such lethal effect. "Thank you for whatever it was," dictated Kylla with a wicked grin. "It was useful from the moment we received it.")

All this attention to a wedding I was still not entirely sure was going to take place was getting on my nerves.

"Well, what stage are you at?" asked Kylla, never one to leave anything alone she took an interest in. "Have you exchanged marriage-cakes yet? There was a full-moon-and-a-half last week."

Leave it to Kylla the Relentless. "I'm not supposed to tell you that," I said.

"Nonsense. It's a modern world, Theodora. —Heavens, you should know that. You're an outlander. And don't be put off by those stories about not making the cake if you're menstruating. Just lie and say you aren't. It's hard enough going four consecutive months without that, too."

There is, in case you have not noticed, no stopping our Kylla. Certainly she had had no difficulty in marrying the husband of her choice, in spite of the fact that the Shikrons and the Cormallons had been enemies for the last three centuries. Today they were allies. And so far as I knew, her husband *still* didn't know that she smoked a pipe. Perhaps someday when she was a respected postmenopausal grandmother she would reveal to him that she liked to sit with her legs up. I wouldn't count on the pipe part coming out even after her death.

But you know, in spite of Kylla's inability to take a straight line when a curved one was available, I think Lysander understood in the main what he was getting when he married her. Nor have I heard any complaints.

My own potential wedding was another matter entirely.

"Where does all this pressure come from?" I asked. "Neither Ran nor I have said a word about marriage to anybody, I swear, and we've got three thousand tabals worth of gifts up at the house."

"How many have you sent back?" she asked swiftly.

Good point. "All right, we haven't gone out of our way to deny it."

She snorted and banked the car; we were coming in toward the main house. Below us the pavilions and garden were spread out in early summer flowers. "When the first of Cormallon disappears from the planet to go after a young lady—leaving House affairs in the hands of two barely adequate cousins—it may be assumed that his intentions are serious. When he returns again *with* said young lady, it may be assumed he was successful." She was silent for a moment as she curved in to land; Ky took risks, but she was actually a magnificent flyer. We touched ground like thistle, and she powered down. "So unless you've got a more plausible story for me to spread—"

"What about my being here to finish my doctoral research?"

She snorted again. No Ivoran took a story like that seriously, which was a pity, because it only showed how far off Athenan Outer Security was when they thought it was believable. I did try to straighten them out—well, you'll hear more about that later.

"Look," I said, pointing to the great entranceway as we got out. The door that would open only for a Cormallon was standing wide, and Herel the cook was on the top step supporting Shez, who stood very shakily. She wore a crimson robe with black borders and her big dark eyes were shining. "Mama," she called. She kicked out one leg and would have gone over if Herel hadn't been holding both her arms. "Mama" and two or three other words were about all Shez said that anyone could translate, although she talked a lot.

We went up the steps to greet them, and Herel gave Shez to her mother, and I gave Herel my hatful of cherries.

Five hours later Kylla dropped me off in front of the Athenan embassy. I went up the steps under the white statue of Pallas Athene, armored and with an owl on her breastplate. Her face was clear and expressionless in a mode that was meant to suggest rationalism but always reminded me of insipidity. This is not meant as some symbolic comment on Athenan society; it's just a statue.

I knew the front lobby very well by now—indeed, I'd known it on a more continuous basis during my first, involuntary containment on Ivory. I walked over the floor's eight-sectored wheel of colored marble, each sector representing one of the great branches of knowledge, and showed my pass to the duty guard.

He compared it to a list. "Room 805," he said. At least in the Athenan embassy there was never any surprise at my height and coloring. I took the stairs—a little exercise being welcome after my long flight in with Kylla from Cormallon—and knocked on a door at the end of a quiet corridor.

This is going to be hard to explain to anyone who is not as socially detached as I am. I have no great loyalty to Pyrene, the place where I was born and escaped from. I have no great loyalty to Athena. I have no great loyalty to Ivory, either, although when my marriage to Ran became official my citizenship would be Ivoran. Still I suppose, if pinned down, the place whose ideals were closest to my own was Athena. As far as I am concerned, any society that glorifies the scientific method is worthy of respect, regardless of its parochial views in other matters.

Nevertheless, the rules and procedures of Athena often seemed incredibly childish to me.

What I did from time to time, therefore, was to visit this certain gentleman whose name had been given to me back at the university, and tell him what was going on on Ivory. For a long time I told myself that I wasn't a spy. Eventually I realized that this was pretty much what spies did. They related moderately uninteresting facts, most of which were not classified.

I wasn't even completely honest with the Athenans, because they had no idea that Ran was well aware of my trips to the embassy and what they entailed. He was mildly interested, but no more. Like most of his countrymen he had no conception of what Athena or Pyrene thinks of as "patriotism." In terms of identity, Ivorans feel a sense of natural superiority over outworlders; but they have no particular attachment to the government in the capital, which they consider an endurable nuisance, put there to collect taxes and make their lives difficult. Some of the higher ranges of the aristocracy, the ones eligible for the throne, saw things differently; but they were an exception. I hadn't felt equal to trying to make this understood to the Athenan officials—I suspected they would look at it as a security breach. As though Ran ever gave anyone information that wasn't wrung from him at virtual gunpoint—well, all married people have qualities that irritate their partners.

You see, it was this outworld understanding of Ivory that I was working to improve. I didn't know any great military secrets—I'm by no means sure that there were any to know—but I was in a unique position to make Ivoran thought processes more clear to Athenan ones. There was a lot the two worlds could have done, if only they weren't always stumbling and offending each other. Studying magic was only the beginning.

Not that it wasn't an uphill job.

* * *

I pushed open the door of 805 and found a small room with a desk, three chairs, and two men—neither of whom I knew.

"I beg your pardon," I said. "I must have the wrong place."

"Who are you looking for?" asked the one behind the desk. He was relatively young, dark-haired, and well-dressed in the current Athenan mode I'd left behind a few months ago. The other man had a gray beard and slightly more conservative clothes; although he sat in a visitor's chair his posture was relaxed, even a touch lordly. I had the sense at once that his rank was superior to the other man's.

The question gave me pause. The person I reported to was the officer of Athenan Outer Security. I wasn't at all sure he wanted to have somebody wandering the halls looking for him under that title. As for his listed official title, I didn't know what it was. His first name was Samuel; possibly not that helpful, but the best I could do.

"Is Samuel around here?" I asked.

They glanced at each other. "Samuel's been recalled," said the man at the desk. "May I ask your name?"

Well, it was no great secret. "Theodora of Pyrene."

"Then you're in the right place," he said. "Come in."

I came in, not very happily, and took the third seat. The man at the desk smiled. "I'm Thomas Cashin. I'll be taking Samuel's place here."

"I hope he's well?" I asked.

"Illness in the family," said Thomas Cashin. Every single person who leaves the embassy before his time does so because of illness in the family.

"I see," I said.

Thomas Cashin opened a folder and, looking down at it, said, "I've been bringing myself up to date on your career. You've gotten around a bit, haven't you? Left Pyrene at first opportunity, changed citizenship to Athenan, left Athena at first opportunity . . ."

"That was an accident. You must have that in your records. And my citizenship's still Athenan."

"For the moment, yes. Tell me, does your husband have any idea you report back to another government?"

"No," I lied firmly. If I couldn't explain that one to Samuel, I wasn't even going to attempt it with this one. As for my in-between state, partway from engaged to married, it was even more complicated and none of his business.

"He doesn't ask you where you go when you come here?"

"I'm a free individual. I go where I want. He doesn't check on me."

"And yet you stated, in an interview dated 8.923 standard, that women on Ivory are not given equal opportunity with men. You stated then that you considered Ivory 'primitive' in this regard." His head dipped over the folder at the appropriate spots; "8.923," and "primitive." Nothing like getting your facts straight while missing the main point.

"That's true," I said, "but it's not the whole story. Women in the lower classes scramble for a living right with the men, out of necessity. At the higher levels they're usually kept out of any profession that requires public access. After all, in a society where murder is a game, the producers of the next generation have to be kept out of the line of fire. And when the families tend to be businesses, that's a hard business decision."

I used the same tone I used to use in class discussions. It goes over better with my fellow Athenans, who look contemptuous when you raise your voice.

"But your husband is of the nobility—"

"Gentry, maybe," I corrected. "Or high bourgeois. We're not one of the Six Families. His grandmother was noble," I added helpfully.

"*Whatever* he is, he's not 'scrambling for a living,' as you put it—"

"Oh, he's not?"

"—and yet you say you wander around freely."

"My case is different."

"Yes," he said, and now the slightest tinge of contempt edged into his voice. "The cards." His head dipped over the folder again.

I decided to wait until he asked a question before I responded. I was tempted to get up and leave, but why disrupt my plans because of one thick-headed official?

The cards used to be a big secret, but now that I'm not the only one who can use them it's just another chapter of history.

He said with stronger contempt, "Tarot cards," and I

controlled the reflex to correct him. "You assisted your husband in his family business by reading Tarot cards."

I still waited. We were getting close to the sore point.

"Sorcery," he said. "*Magic.* Apparently you want the Athenan government, the most rational, reasonable body of people in the universe,"—arguable—"to believe in this con game put forth by the citizens of Ivory, that they can work magic."

Not all of them, I thought, but still didn't correct him.

"Well?" he said.

"Well what?"

"What do you have to say?"

"I'm sorry, did you have a question?"

He closed the folder with a slam. "I have a question. You're damned right I have a question. How can you expect to sell us this mass of nonsense without a shred of evidence to support—"

"There's evidence. There's plenty of evidence. What we don't have is a theory."

"Oh? I thought you presented this story of alien gene-tampering—" He reopened the folder and started flipping through papers, not finding what he was looking for.

"That was just the favorite theory of a friend of mine. Nobody really knows. *I* don't know, all right?" This particular line of questioning rubbed me a little raw, for reasons that went beyond lack of courtesy.

I was irritated, if the truth be known, not only by his obtuseness (his *barbarian* obtuseness, my reflexes kept saying) but by my own personal neurosis. The fact was that the magic of Ivory had been a thorn in my side ever since I'd learned it was real. Oh, it didn't bother the Cormallons—as far as Ran was concerned, you did this and this and you got electricity; you did that and that and you got magic; what was the fuss about? But it went against my entire understanding of the universe. Of course, the more the years went by, the more I had to admit my understanding of the universe was probably pretty flawed. But it had served me well in other times and places, and besides, the scientific method (and I will stick by this ship no matter how it rocks) has been the greatest step in human freedom and clear-thinking ever made. That results can be replicated by experimentation has made all the difference between truth and a good colorful myth. —I like myths, mind you, but they should know their place.

And then came Ran. I could deal with his disruption of my personal code (stealing is always wrong, sex is essentially boring) but none of that bothered me as much as his casual use of magic. The most irritating thing is that eventually—and I have to believe this—the magic of Ivory will be incorporated into the "scientific" view of the universe as we know it on Athena. It will probably take a battery of scientists and several cooperative sorcerers both on- and off-planet to determine under what conditions this thing we call magic works. But it will happen eventually.

The hardest part will be the cooperative sorcerer. Knowing Ivory as I do, I will be long dead by the time this happens. You see why I'm annoyed? *Other people will know the answer.* I just happen to be living at the wrong time. Oh, yes, I'm grateful that I got free of charge things past philosophers would've given years off their lives to know; I understand the composition of the stars. But it's not fair!

Could I make any of this clear to the successor to the post of officer of Outer Security? No.

I did try.

"Look—people don't always understand the forces they use. In fact, it's the *usual* pattern to use things that work before you know how they work. Maybe in another generation or two we'll know, but we don't now and we'll just have to live with it. That's what reality is about. Do you believe that only the things you personally understand can exist? Do you think if it doesn't have the seal of approval of the University council that it has to be imaginary?"

And on and on. Not a dent, I swear to you.

He was pretty condescending about it, too. I will spare you the details of the three solid hours I spent in room 805.

The thing that annoyed me most about him was that he registered his disbelief in his voice every time he found an inconsistency. Since life is made up of inconsistencies, that was most of the time. Take this business of the status of women on Ivory, which we returned to not once but twice—I tried to make him see that people confound their roles all the time; that doesn't mean the roles aren't there. Kanz, he was living here now, why didn't he just go out and talk to people? Cashin probably went through his entire day without ever speaking to the natives on a personal basis. Surrounded himself with Athenans wherever he went—the old ambassador had been like that.

"Take Queen Elizabeth the First," I said. It was early evening by then, and I wished the room had windows. Kylla must be getting impatient. The gray-haired man, who hadn't said a word, was close to dozing. He came a bit awake then, looking puzzled.

"Queen Elizabeth the First?" asked Cashin.

"Queen of an island nation on Earth at a time when female submission to the male was considered as handed down by God—who was a man. But she wasn't only head of state, she was a very popular head of state. Did I make *her* up?"

Cashin cleared his throat uncomfortably. Clearly it had crossed his mind that I *had.*

"To return to the issue at hand," he said (kanz, he was the one who kept changing the subject), "isn't it a bit convenient that this Ran Cormallon chose you to assist in his business? How can you be sure that he wasn't sent by the Imperial Secret Service to get close to a foreign national?"

The thought of Ran, Kylla, or any other Cormallon letting themselves be maneuvered by the Imperial Secret Service was laughable. The Secret Service wouldn't have a chance. However, my face wasn't getting warm because of that, or because Cashin had apparently taken a course in how to insult one's allies. It was because Ran had initially offered me a job out of typical Ivoran expediency—I had no family network and could be conveniently murdered later on if I didn't work out.

Every family has its quirks, though, and I saw no reason to share them with Thomas Cashin.

"It's getting late," I said. "I'll be expected home for dinner—"

"Hit a soft spot, have we?" said this annoying man. "What if the whole relationship were a setup? These locals convince you that they're sorcerers, that you're some kind of magician—"

"I have no magical talent, sir. Nor do most people on Ivory. Even here it's comparatively rare—"

"Then what about this whole fabrication of your being hired to read cards?"

I bit my lip. This had all been gone into with Samuel, and a few other people, but saying it to Cashin. . . .

"Well?"

"It was a special circumstance," I said finally. "I used a cursed deck of playing cards."

He closed the folder again with a final and triumphant snap. "I think it's pretty clear, Theodora of Pyrene. You're a constitutional troublemaker. An attention-seeker. A misfit in your birthplace, you try to make up for it by stirring things up everywhere you go. Well, a professional therapist is doubtless called for—I note you did see a few of them while on Athena—but it is hardly the province of this embassy to handle that for you."

I felt my face turning red again. Nobody likes to hear personal insults, but if this kanz knew how carefully I went through life trying *not* to be noticed—

I stood up. "Good-bye, officer," I said, hoping my voice sounded steady. "Please let me know when someone takes over your job who can actually perform it." I was at the door when the gray-bearded man finally spoke.

"Wait." I looked at him.

"Please wait," he said. He glanced at Cashin. "Thomas, I'll see you in the conference room in ten minutes."

Cashin hesitated. The older man said, "That will be all for now."

Cashin got up and left his own office. Gray Beard gestured me back to the seat. "Please?" he said.

I sat down. "I don't think we've been introduced."

"Merril Zarmovi. Sorry I didn't mention it earlier." He was absolutely cool and comfortable in his manner. It was no problem for him to say "please" and "sorry" and probably no problem for him to say anything else he ever had to say. I should have been delighted after the session with Thomas Personality-Plus Cashin, but instead I found myself thinking: This man is dangerous.

"You must excuse Thomas," he said. "He learned interrogation, not interviewing. It's the way they teach them nowadays. Just a fad, I'm sure; it will pass in a few years."

That *had* crossed my mind; after all, the man had been so consistently argumentative. "So this is just some psych game you fellows like to play?" That was even more insulting in its way—there were things I was seriously trying to accomplish, and if I wanted to improvise I'd join an acting troupe.

"Well, not entirely. Thomas was sincere, it was his manners I must apologize for. However, his views are not those of Athenan Outer Security."

"What does that mean?"

"It means that we'd like you to continue to drop by, Theodora of Pyrene. Please don't concern yourself as to how much we believe and how much we don't believe. That's not the sort of thing a person can spend time worrying over in this life. Just come by and talk. We'll serve you coffee if you like; you must miss it on this planet."

I considered it. "I doubt if Officer Cashin wants to have coffee and cookies with me."

He smiled. "No." He took out a thin gold rectangle with embossed lettering and handed it to me. "This is my card. Ask for me directly when you come; I'm the Undersecretary for Extraplanetary Affairs."

I took it. "Did you know Carl Spitav?"

"The old ambassador? I wouldn't have accepted a posting here if he were still around. He was a bit of an ass."

I smiled and pocketed the card. "Well, I guess there's no harm in visiting."

"No harm in the world," said the undersecretary, and he held open the door to show me out.

Kylla had a few words to say when she came by to pick me up.

"You missed an entire afternoon of shopping," she said.

"You can show me everything you bought back at the house," I said. "Do you and Shez want to stay with us or at the Shikron place? Is Lysander in the capital with you?"

"Thanks, sweetheart, I was counting on your asking. I told them to deliver my parcels to Ran's security station at your house. No, Lysander's back at the main estate—it drives him out of his mind when I take him shopping. I think that's why he gave me the extra hundred in gold, really—he told me to take a week off and get it out of my system."

"I don't understand why you're not running the finances, Kylla. I thought that was customary in Ivoran houses."

"The Shikrons are ass-backward that way. But I didn't put up a fuss when they told me—you know how boring it is to keep the House books, Theo."

"I know that, all right."

"And this way I spend more money than I ever spent when I had to be *responsible.* —Even you would loosen up and throw some cash around, darling, if Ran were giving you an allowance instead of the other way around."

"That may be so," I admitted, for I felt the weight of being trusted with Cormallon's finances.

"You better give him a temporary increase, though," she added, as our aircar neared the roof of the Cormallon house in the capital. "He'll need it to get ready for the wedding party—"

"Kylla, *please*—"

"Here we are," she said, making a perfect landing in the empty cistern. We climbed out, our voices echoing on the walls, and took the steps to the roof entrance.

"It's been a long day for me," I said, and it had been. A long hike in the early morning, a ride into the capital, and a long interrogation at the embassy. "Could we just have a quiet evening?"

Her eyes went wide. "Of course, Theo." She patted my hand reassuringly. "You know we only want to please you."

Chapter 2

There was a message from Ran on the Net for me. His voice came on, deep and casual, as usual. "Theodora, I've got a possible client. I'll bring him to the house for you to meet at the third hour. Don't do surveillance on this one—I told him I'd give him dinner and introduce him to my wife. I'm taking it slow here, so we won't bring up business until I signal you, all right? Treat it as a social-occasion with a House ally. . . . For the moment."

He signed off there. I called to Kylla, who was in the next room, "Did you hear that, Ky?"

"I heard it."

"That's kind of unusual, isn't it? Ran doesn't socialize with clients."

"Most of them are scum," said Kylla.

"Well, yes. But a lot of them are socially respectable. And anyway, introducing your wife to one . . . that's pretty radical, isn't it? If I have to meet them, I'm usually introduced as an assistant in the business."

"Theo," she called, "I swore I wouldn't bother you again, but is Ran saying you're his wife to make a respectable impression on this client, or, well, how far along are you on the ritual?"

"Oh, look," I said. "There's another message." I hit the accept.

"Greetings to the gracious lady Theodora of Pyrene. This is Vathcar Timoris, liaison to the Pyrenese trade delegation. Octavia of Pyrene has expressed an interest in meeting you during her stay on-planet. It is not our wish to intrude on the privacy of any member of the House of Cormallon, but if this is agreeable to you, please contact my office via return message. Thank you for your consideration."

I stood there, completely disoriented. Octavia? Here on Ivory?

A moment later I realized Kylla was standing in front of me. "Theo? What's the matter? I called and you didn't hear me."

I focused on her face, its lines bent with concern. "Kylla!" I grinned. "I think I have a friend in town."

You have to have bounced around from one place to another as much as I have to appreciate the feeling that sentence gave me.

"Someone from the university on Athena?" she asked.

"From Pyrene." I found one of the chairs that Ran had had made especially for me, and sank into it. It was a thousand times more comfortable than the usual Ivoran standard of scattered pillows on the floor.

"Pyrene? You've never talked about Pyrene much, you know. I always had the impression that you didn't *have* any friends there." She paused. "I didn't mean that the way it sounded."

"No, it's okay, I didn't have much in the way of friends. I mean, from my earliest memories, the rest of the crèche seemed to go one way, and I went another. But Octavia—"

Octavia was a tall, blonde, plain-faced girl who liked games (which I hated) and sang in the chorus (I couldn't carry a note) and was in many ways just another member of our crèche-group. But she had a soul of deviltry and wicked eyes, and— "Kylla, if you'd ever seen her swinging on the bathroom doors while imitating an ape, you'd never have forgotten it either." Octavia and I had been inseparable for about six years; I remember that when she was assigned to a different study-class than I was, people actually came up to me and offered their sympathy. It was Octavia who joined me in putting wads of wet paper in the crèche study machine on that glorious night before graduation.

Then she'd gone to another city to follow her assigned track of career internship, and I'd eventually gotten the scholarship to Athena.

"Great gods of scholars," I said. "Octavia. Oh, Ky, I've got to call her."

She was smiling. "Well, call away, sweetheart; it's nice to see you enthusiastic. You're always so damned controlled."

I was already on the Net. The liaison's office was closed, but there was a standing order to put me through to the inn where the Pyrenese delegation was staying. A few minutes later I heard:

"Octavia of Pyrene here, machinery export specialist. May I help you?"

"Tavia? It's Teddy. I just got your message!"

"Oh, hello, Teddy. I heard you were on Ivory." Her voice was calm.

"Tavia, I can't get you on-screen. Don't you have your visuals open?"

There was a pause. "I didn't think they used visuals here."

"Well, not as a rule, but there's no law against it. No reason *we* can't."

My screen shimmered and I saw Octavia, a decade older but still nine-tenths the same, still more than recognizable. I felt myself grinning.

"Tav, you look wonderful."

She blinked at the screen. "You've changed, Teddy. You look completely different."

Well, I'd lost some weight, and the Ivoran clothes can be a little flashy if you're not accustomed to them. She didn't say it as though it were a compliment, though.

"Well, the years have been eventful. I heard you got married."

"Yes. Two kids."

"Are they with you?" I asked, and then shut up. My reflexes were all screwed up from the time on Athena and Ivory; of course they weren't with her. They'd be in a crèche. I said quickly. "We must get together. How long will you be on-planet?"

"Six local months in the capital, and six in the provinces. I just arrived last week."

"I can't get over it! Talk about luck, I never thought I'd see you again. What about dinner tomorrow? We can go to the Lantern Gardens and drink tah and wine until they throw us out."

She smiled, a little amused at my enthusiasm. "Tomorrow's fine. Can I bring someone from the delegation?"

"Well, if you want." I'd been hoping for a chance to talk

about old times, and new ones too, I guess. Still, Kylla might want to come, and I didn't want her to feel left out.

"I might bring someone myself. I'll see you at the third hour."

"Off, then, Teddy."

"Off, Tavia."

I cut the connection. I'd ask Ran as a matter of form when he showed up, but I doubted he had any interest in meeting someone from my past. Ran's view of the world was what you might call Ran-o-centric; in spite of having stayed on Athena, I don't think he really believed that I'd *had* a past before I met him.

Maybe it was a reaction to all that self-sacrifice they'd tried to instill on Pyrene, but I found his blatant ego refreshing.

Kylla said, "Hadn't you better change, if you want to be the respectable wife by the time Ran brings this person home?"

I looked down at the robe and wide trousers I'd hiked in this morning, sat in for the trip, and sweated into during my interrogation this afternoon. "Oops."

Kylla grabbed my elbow and steered me toward the closet. "I'll help you get ready, and then I suppose I'd better get going myself. You know how nervous these clients can be; I don't guess he'll want a Shikron hanging around while he explains his illegal activities."

Ky's instincts for clothing and cosmetics are impeccable. I washed up quickly and put on everything she laid out for me, and then ran down to the door while still hooking a gold hoop in one ear.

Ran was showing his guest in. I darted a look out to the street before the door closed and saw a closed carriage pulled by two implanted driving beasts. Closed carriages are unusual in summer, when rain was rare. So this client preferred discretion, did he?

"My wife and House associate," said Ran, as he pulled off his blue outer robe. "And my sister," he added, gesturing to Kylla. "May I present Tarkal Vellorin?"

The client bowed. He was in late middle age, balding, strong and stocky-looking—he looked like a man whose life was just at the point where he was most in control of it. His bow was graceful, and while his head was down Kylla met my eyes and made a face, and I knew that she recognized him and his name wasn't Tarkal Vellorin.

"My sister's of the family of Shikron these days," said Ran. He smiled. "I didn't expect to see you here, Ky. Where's the most beautiful girl in all Shikron?" he asked, looking around for Shez.

"Right here," said Kylla, as she gave him a peck on the cheek.

"No, the *other* most beautiful girl."

"Ah. She's at the house with her nurse right now—" meaning the house the Shikrons kept in the capital, a big place by the canal, "—and that's where I should be going, too. I'm in town for a week of shopping, so you'll see plenty of me yet, brother. 'Bye, Theo." And I got a peck, too.

" 'Bye, Kylla."

As she left I caught Tarkal Whoever Vellorin glancing in my direction. I smiled impassively. His thoughts were plain: Why had the first of Cormallon married a barbarian? I dress in the most irreproachable Ivoran clothes, but nothing can hide the fact that I tend to be the shortest and lightest skinned person in any room, and that my hair, instead of being black, is a red-brown color that always takes them by surprise. Ran and Kylla were both perfect Ivoran products: Tall, dark-eyed, vibrantly beautiful. Standing next to them, I tended to wonder what I was doing there myself.

Fortunately Ran's tastes were exotic. One might even say perverse.

Not that I'm complaining.

"I've ordered supper from the Golden Oven," Ran said then. "I thought we might eat on the balcony over the courtyard. How does that sound?"

"Excellent," I said, and took our client's outer robe like a dutiful wife, pretending not to notice the dagger in his belt, nor the more bulky lump by his lower leg. Actually I was fairly drooling by that time, as I hadn't had time for lunch.

He must have called in his order early; the Net signaled someone at the door before we could show our guest upstairs. "We'll need a fork for the messenger," said Ran, making a quick detour through our tiny kitchen before joining me at the door. We opened it to find a boy in the livery of The Golden Oven, with a carton in his arms. A wagon out on the street was full of similar cartons; another boy stood guard over it.

"Come in," said Ran.

Tarkel Whomever was watching us, as was only normal. Ran took the buckets from the messenger's box and set them on the low table nearest the door. They both began methodically opening the containers, and delightful smells filled the room. Ran handed the fork to the messenger, who took a small bit from each bucket, put them on a plate, and ate them. Most messengers get all their meals this way; they tend to be healthy and well-fed, and only a small percentage come up unlucky.

Ran was peering into the food speculatively. He pointed at a container of diced groundhermit and chicory; there was a piece there slightly darker than the others. "Try that one," he said, and the messenger dutifully ate it.

While we gave the boy a few minutes to see if he would fall down dead, I moved in to spoon the food onto our good plates. As I bent over the sweetcakes I whispered to Ran, "Gentleman's wearing more than a knife." My eyes went to our client, and I tapped my lower left leg against the table.

Ran nodded. So that our guest wouldn't think we were plotting, I called over, "Would you like brown rice or white?"

"Brown, please, lady Theodora."

He was certainly polite.

By the time I'd finished laying out the meal, Ran had thanked the messenger and given him a tip. I motioned toward the street and Ran gave him an extra coin. "For the boy on the wagon," he said.

"Thank you, gracious sir." He ducked his head and ran out.

We picked up what we could and Ran said, "This way, noble sir—"

Noble sir? Still, he might just be extra-polite.

"We'll have to come back for the rest," I said.

"Allow me," said our client, and he lifted one of the plates and followed us upstairs to the balcony.

In Ivoran houses the courtyards are off the street, protected. Our house in the capital had only a tiny interior space with a dry fountain and two lonely coyu trees. Still, they were showing their leaves now, and the cobbles around the center were in good condition. And the grass around that was lush and cool in the late evening breeze.

There's no taboo about discussing business over a meal, but our client didn't seem forthcoming; so we talked about horses (Ran's contribution), tinaje healing (mine), and even skirted the monotonous topic of Ivory's balance of trade with Tellys.

"I suppose the barbarians are not fond of Tellys either," he said, near the end of supper. He'd emptied three of our painted winebowls.

Ran raised an eyebrow.

"No, I suppose they're not," I said. There are four habitable planets in this sector, and I'd habited three of them. Tellys was not popular with any of the others, but if you ask me it was sour grapes. Anyway, they couldn't hold on to their technological lead forever, and if they wanted to charge us all through the nose meanwhile, Ivory could hardly pretend that moneymaking went against their own way of life.

Our client put down his last sweetcake finally and brushed crumbs from his hands. "An excellent meal, sir and lady, and only what I would expect from your distinguished house."

"Thank you," I said, and Ran nodded his head politely.

"Now, sir Cormallon, I wonder if I might have a word with you in private, on a matter of business?"

Ran had been half-reclining on a pillow with a cover of purple silk thrown over it. Now he sat up. He said, "Theodora is my assistant, noble sir. She's a complete professional."

"That may be so," said the noble sir, "and I mean no offense. But when you hear my story you'll see that it's rather sensitive."

Ran considered, then nodded. "Theodora, wait downstairs. I'll call you when we're finished."

I rose at once, bowed to Tarkel Possibly Vellorin, and left the room. The egalitarians back on Athena would've had a fit, but Ran outranked me and in front of a client like this one it was important to maintain the illusion, at least, of discipline. His opinion of our abilities would depend in part on how well he thought Ran had control of his House.

Anyway, I went straight to the downstairs study and turned on the monitor.

" . . . several weeks ago. We didn't take it seriously at first, but our House has been going through a lot of changes lately, and when we'd had time to think it over it didn't seem a bad idea. My daughter says the boy is pretty enough, if that matters, and the Atvalids have always been good, solid members of the Empire."

Ran refilled Tarkel's bowl. "Why consult me then, noble sir? You favor the marriage, and the alliance seems sound. What services can you want from a sorcerer in this instance?"

Our client looked down at the wine, troubled. "This is in strictest confidence, my friend." He had just moved on to a term that was still formal, but more intimate than "gracious sir." Apparently we were getting to the good stuff. "The Atvalids are quite beneath us socially, however sound they may be. You might wonder why we even consider the alliance, when we could link with almost any family on Ivory."

Ran said nothing, but looked open.

Tarkal pursed his lips. "The fact of the matter is that our family does not enjoy quite the favor of the Emperor at this time, may he have long life. I don't want to go into the details, but we would prefer not to irritate him with an . . . ill-considered . . . match."

I noted that our visitor appeared uncomfortable, and I didn't blame him. Politics can be lethal on Ivory, and politics, business, and marriage were all part of the same piece as far as the nobility was concerned.

"Ill-considered?" prompted Ran.

"I have had reports lately from Tuvin Province, reports of the boy's father. From what I hear he may soon be as unlucky in the Emperor's regard as we are, in which case. . . ."

"Yes," said Ran. "That would be unfortunate."

"I need more information," said Tarkal. "There is still time to call off the deal—that is, the wedding—without a scandal. But we must know where we stand."

"No doubt you've sent spies into Tuvin," said Ran.

"We have. And they've come back with a lot of rumor, that's all. I'm not saying that rumor can't be as damaging as fact, but right now I very much need to know what the facts are. They say he's gotten involved with some unsavory elements in local politics—" here Tarkal lowered his voice, "—and he *is* the Governor, you know."

I smiled. Being the governor of an Ivoran province would put you well above ninety percent of the population; but still far below the Six Families.

"They even say he's been making a fool of himself over some of the Northwest Sector outlaws. Really, can't he just hang them when he can, pay ransom when he needs to, and leave them alone? My people tell me he sees himself as the savior of the local farmers and ranchers."

Ran made a sympathetic noise.

Tarkal bent closer. "Your own estate, my friend, is very near the Sector; though on the southwest side rather than the east. No doubt you've had to deal with scoundrels fleeing through your lands."

"Well, from time to time," said Ran. The Cormallon method of dealing with the "scoundrels" is to recruit them; but since that was a prison offense, it would hardly be wise to mention it.

"Go to Tuvin," said Tarkal the noble sir. "I would be most beholden to you if you would. Find out what you can to keep my unlucky House from embarrassing itself further. Really, sir, we would be terribly grateful." He brought out a bag and laid it on the table; the bag jingled. He placed a rolled piece of paper over it, probably a money order.

Ran put his hand on the bag, but more as though he would push it back to Tarkal. "I don't see why you need a sorcerer for this, my friend. Why not do it the old-fashioned way, with informers?"

"Because," he said, "I've heard that sorcerers have tricks that can lead them to finding out things they need to know. Is that true?"

"Possibly," said Ran.

"Sending a few spies into Tuvin to ask questions about the family of the girl engaged to one's son is understandable. Having done this—having been seen to do it—well, to take the time now to set up informers within Tuvin would be perceived as . . . rude."

"Whereas one or two sorcerers are a lot less noticeable."

"You drill right to the center, my friend."

"Thank you." Ran drummed his fingers on the table. "Saving the reputation of a distinguished House like yours would seem to call for a high compensation."

"You haven't looked at the money order yet," said Tarkal, leaning back.

Ran unrolled it and read it. The expression on his face didn't change. He put the paper back on the table.

"How long would I have?" he asked.

Tarkal sat up again. "You must understand in full what it is we require. First, yes, a complete report on the provincial governor. But we could go to any sorcerer if simple information was all we needed, true? I want your expertise as a House leader, one who's spent time in the capital—I want you to include in your report not only the obvious, but what you think we should know. I mean that in the broadest possible sense. And I want your recommendation at the end, as to whether you believe an alliance with this family will be a good idea. I'm not saying we would follow such a recommendation, but we want it. You see why we come to you? We're contracting for not only the data, but your analysis of the data."

This was unadulterated flattery, but it was based on truth, and Ran knew it.

"How long?" he said again.

"The earliest possible date for the wedding is next spring. We would need to settle firmly with the Atvalids well before then—before winter at the latest. We can argue over the monetary arrangements, of course, but probably the Feast of Enlightenment is the latest we could keep them waiting."

The Feast of Enlightenment is in early fall. That gave us several months for this project—longer than some assignments, shorter than others. I was glad the Ivoran year was as lengthy as it was.

Ran drummed some more. "I'd want a contingency fee if the matter wasn't settled to your satisfaction. Considering the time I'd have to devote to it, and that I'd have to be away from my practice in the capital."

"Of course," said Tarkal, smooth as sugar icing now that he saw things going his way. "This amount here is for you to keep in any case. The rest will be paid on receipt of the information."

For a moment Ran really did look startled. That money order must have listed a massive figure. I couldn't help grinning, but I hoped for his own self-respect he didn't realize how badly his facade had cracked.

The crack only showed for a moment, though. Then he was showing Tarkal down the stairs. I hurriedly shut off the monitor, and before they left I heard him say, "I'll leave for Tuvin tomorrow, and give you a preliminary report from there. Nothing indiscreet. I'll hold onto the main things until we meet again."

"I look forward to it, sir Cormallon."

"My pleasure, noble sir Sakri."

Sakri? Great gods, the Sakris owned half the planet. I heard the door close and Ran came into the study.

"Did you get all that?" he asked.

I nodded. "Sakri, huh? I guess the concealed weapons are understandable. He's probably used to a platoon of bodyguards."

He took one of the few chairs in the house, and the only one with wheels, and twirled in it unhappily.

I could tell you what he was thinking, and as a matter of fact I will: Ran wanted to bring more money into the House of Cormallon because he'd neglected his practice for the last Ivoran year. He'd spent that time on another world in our sector trying to convince an unreasonable barbarian—me—to be reasonable. That meant almost no revenue was coming into the House treasury from the capital. Oh, Cormallon was in no danger of bankruptcy; the other branches were all sending in their regular shares. But he, personally, wanted to bring things at least up to normal. He'd once been accused of stealing from the treasury and I think the whole topic would always be a sensitive one with him.

On the other hand— "The money annoys you, doesn't it?" I asked.

He looked even more annoyed. "I don't know what you mean."

"An amount that big. It kind of gives you the feeling you don't have any option but to take it, and you don't like not having options."

"You haven't even seen the amount."

I was quiet. I wasn't going to tell him that his jaw had practically dropped to the floor on the monitor.

He moved about forty-five degrees in the chair, and swung back again slowly. I said, "I wish you hadn't told him we'd leave tomorrow. I had an appointment for dinner with an old friend."

His eyes gradually focused on me. "What old friend?"

"Octavia of Pyrene. She's here with the trade delegation."

"Oh. Pyrene." He dismissed it. I told you he didn't have a lot of interest in my past. Then he said, "You want to run the cards on this?"

"It's a little late, isn't it? You've already accepted."

"All right, don't run them," he said. And he got up and went upstairs.

I pictured my partner and quarter-husband as he'd just looked, sitting in his "thinking chair," considering his latest sorcerous commission. With his berry-and-white robe pulled back, his dark eyes weighing the pros and cons, his feet tapping with suppressed energy. Brought up in the paranoid splendor of Ivory's upper classes, Ran found it difficult to share his thoughts even with his allies.

What was I doing on this planet, with a people so long divorced from the main river of humanity that they might be literally another species? "When I look at Ran, sometimes I see an alien," I once confessed to Kylla.

"All married people feel that way," she responded, casually flicking soot from the gold silk collar that hung in folds around her shoulders.

Two weeks ago, on the night of the moon-and-a-half, we'd baked cakes of sugar and flour and vanilla and cinnamon, and given them to each other in a room facing the raising moons. When we ate the cakes, it meant that we were one-quarter married. Then we'd made love for the rest of the night, though it wasn't required for the ceremony.

Four consecutive months make a marriage. Witnesses aren't even necessary, though it's good to have them if you ever plan on going through the confusing system of Ivoran divorce. When people talk about attending weddings on Ivory they mean the wedding celebration, which is after the fact and pretty much a good excuse to gather together a large group and cut loose.

Four months make a marriage. And two people. Maybe love wasn't enough, or maybe I did have cold feet. Anyway, there was still time to pull out.

Chapter 3

"He didn't ask us to kill or sabotage anybody," I pointed out.

"Yes, a refreshing change."

Ran likes to go fast. I can stand it in an aircar, but we were on the ground, heading north on the Tuvin Road. There are sand swamps for about two hours of the journey between Avernith and the beginning of the Iron Hills—I kept trying to blank out this mental picture of the car zooming off the road into the swamp, leaving nothing behind but a burp.

Aircars aren't a great lot of use in the part of Tuvin we were going, or in the Northwest Sector in general, as the winds over the High Plateau are treacherous and highly variable. Anyway, I bit my tongue until we reached the section that runs by the river, a green and pleasant stretch of land, and I said, "If you don't like the project when we get to Shaskala, you can always return the money and call it off."

This was my way of saying I could run the cards for us when we got there. I was beginning to regret not having done so back in the capital—though Ran could always have run them himself now, since the deck was no longer cursed.

"I'm going through with it," said Ran, not looking at me.

This was his way of saying he was going through with it.

Fine. After a minute he said, "I think Grandmother left the deck bonded to you when she removed the curse. You're better at running them than anybody else."

Implying that it was my duty to read them, then, not his. I let that one lie as well, and watched the scenery for a while.

Those of you who have been following my little adventures may be wondering just what I was doing back on Ivory, anyway. I wondered myself, a lot.

When I took the outbound liner away, I had every intention of never coming back. But fate, as always, had a few more custard pies up its sleeve. I suppose that considering how badly my life had derailed from my well-laid plans before, I should not have been surprised.

Custard pie number one was Ran showing up on the ship. But I was strong, I was firm . . . actually I was in a continual state of confusion, but I did manage to get off the ship when we grounded. I figured Ran was gambling on my taking the round trip back with him—he was first of Cormallon, he couldn't afford to be away from home for long periods.

Ran got off at Athena with me. Pie number two. I heard him ask the customs official if he could arrange a student visa from this end. I'd been through a lot by then, and went out to the transport tube in a daze. It would've been more courteous to have stopped and given Ran my address, but somehow I had no doubt he would find me.

Listen carefully—the next sound you hear is the collective release of an artillery of pies. Strange things happened to me on Athena. Oh, I knew returning would bring some discomfort, that I'd made necessary adjustments to life on Ivory; I just hadn't counted on a sense of disorientation that persisted for months. The very day I got back I took a cab to my cluster to get some sleep, and I remember walking in the door and staring at the floors. The floors, for heaven's sake. They looked different. "Were they always this way?" I asked a clustermate, who brought in my bag. He looked at me blankly.

"The floors," I said.

"Of course." The floors were long, polished wooden planks; of course they were the same, the whole house would've had to have been ripped open to change them. But—

"How would they be different?" he asked.

"I don't know."

The buildings were plain and boring; the money was strange; the clothing was comfortable, but the fashionable designs were aesthetically unpleasant. People stood farther away when they spoke to me than I was accustomed to, and they touched a lot less. Once I had found this distance granted a dignified and comfortable sense of reserve; now it seemed stiff and priggish. But more than that, I found that I didn't have a lot to say to anybody.

No one could join me, or even showed much interest in, what I had gone through on Ivory. No one except the professional therapists, and I stopped looking for help there soon enough. They like to think they're objective—though they'd never be so presumptuous as to say so aloud—but they're as culturally bound as everyone else on Athena. How could they not be? When I would mention some trivial incident of bribery or smuggling (normal life by the rules of Ivory) I could sense that they wanted to lead me gently to the realization that I'd let myself get sucked into "wrong" behavior. Again, they never said so, but you'd have to be a fool not to feel the pressure. Like those literature teachers who skillfully guide the class discussion until it reaches the thematic consensus the teacher wanted in the first place. (Lesson plan 101, discussion of poem "Two Roads to Everige": How would poet feel if other road were taken instead? Assist in free exchange of ideas until class agrees "the same way.")

The only person on this whole damned planet who knew how I felt was Ran. He took the temporary student visa that outplanet scholars took, and was placed in a cluster in the same city I was in. He turned in his weapons and didn't say a word; he wore Athenan clothing and ate Athenan food and except for the occasional flash of controlled contempt in his black eyes he made no resistance at all to the barbarians.

I opened my eyes from a nap and saw the High Plateau filling the window. It had been visible for hours as a distant landmark, but now the top was too far above us to see—instead I had a clearer view of the rocky cliff that faced us. Somewhere along the way the road we were on would join with the Winding Road that led, after a long and (please gods) careful drive, to the city of Shaskala, halfway up.

We were still traveling at a furious rate. We overtook a wagon being pulled by a bored-looking freight beast, with a farmer just as bored sitting on top. Ran gave them no opportunity to move to one side. Without slackening in the slightest, he zoomed around the wagon and back to his favored spot in the road. The driver glared at us from his position and waved a whip toward our car.

Ran looked over, saw I was awake, and said, "Sorry."

"I had no idea a single money order would make you this eager."

"Theodora. Will you look at the sun? I wanted to get us to Shaskala before nightfall, but we're not going to make it. I don't think we'll get in before midnight."

"What of it? We'll sleep late."

"We'll have to drive up the Winding Road in the dark, tymon."

My gaze went to that sheer cliff and its inhuman height. "Don't they have lights on that road?"

"No."

I cleared my throat. "Ah," I said.

I found myself tracking how long it took the sun to reach the top of the plateau. It was difficult to fall back asleep.

When I said Ran put up no resistance to the barbarians, I meant it—he performed all the duties of a temporary Athenan citizen. He honored all the rules and customs, outwardly. But as the drudgery of the academic year progressed I started to hear rumors about certain outlandish events that seemed to gather around Ran's vicinity. And I wasn't the only one who suspected him of being a disruptive force. Why, the dean of students actually asked me to—but that's not what I'm telling you about right now. My point is that Ran did everything he was supposed to do by his visa—a contract is a contract—and made it nearly impossible for anyone to expel him. I was amazed, in fact, at how tractable he was. This unnatural docility was brought home to me forcibly about half a year after our arrival.

Ran was putting in his six weeks of compulsory labor, and I was on my way back from a long trip to Varengist Point (where he was cleaning out recycling tubes that couldn't be cleared automatically—I came out to visit him, sure he would say that this was the final straw. But he didn't) and I had a wait between connections. I sat up in the terminal for five hours until the dawn bullet for my cluster was due to leave.

There was one other passenger waiting with me, a plain-looking, stocky, rather severe woman about thirty years my senior, her brown hair pulled back in a bun. After an hour without speaking she took out a flask of whiskey and offered me a drink. I accepted. Then I sat down on the hard bench beside her, trying to examine her without being obvious. She wore the circle-and-arrow pin of a full scholar; for her to carry a flask of alcohol was eccentric, and to offer it to a stranger was brave. We're rather puritanical on Athena.

But I soon learned her reputation was beyond being harmed by this friendly gesture. I won't give her name here, it wouldn't be fair; but she was one of the greats of my field, close to a legend for the younger generation. She told me that she'd read my collection of Ivoran folktales and been impressed by it. (For all I know she may have been courteous enough to say something similar to every young scholar she met. Nevertheless, it was good to hear. She had some pleasant things to add about my Standard translation, which I will not bore you with here, but which I'll admit I've never forgotten.)

We emptied the flask between us. And in the course of the next four hours she pinned me down, question after question, until not only had I revealed much of my research methods, but an enormous amount about Ran and me.

"Do you think I'm crazy for believing in sorcery?" I asked.

"I wouldn't presume to say so, dear," she replied, tilting back the flask for the last drops. Her view of reality was more flexible than mine—I don't think she really cared about the verifiability of sorcery from a scientific point of view. She was more interested in whether I was going back with Ran. I sidestepped that particular question as far as I was able.

Finally, as the sun appeared over the Voltaire Dome Irrigation Fields, and we stood in the wind by the bullet, she reached out for my sleeve and pulled me closer. A bullet conductor was walking by, and she lowered her voice.

"Honey," she said, "you're a top-drawer scholar. I can say that because I'm one myself, and I can tell you how important, and unimportant, it is." She watched until the conductor was out of earshot, the morning wind whipping her coat back. Her face was flushed from the whiskey.

"They've misled you, though, sweetheart, and I'm going to tell you the truth. Doctorates are a dime a dozen, Theodora, but a good sexual partner is hard to find. If he makes your toes curl—" she used a more earthy expression here, "—then it's probably as good as it's going to get, and better than most people ever have."

I was shocked at this coming from a conservative scholar, and one of her age. We were taught to put our work before anything. I said, "Surely you can't recommend marriage based on sexual attraction alone."

"What do you mean, 'alone'? Didn't you tell me the man is cleaning out sewers for you right now? What more do you want? If you're waiting for a revelation from the gods—" The bullet's windows and doors shuttered open, signaling readiness for boarding. She kissed me hastily on the cheek. " 'Bye, honey. When you're not sure what to do, think about me. I'm living alone in two rooms over the cultural museum. Oh, I'm not crying, I've got a good life. But if I'd known what I know now, I'd've done a lot of things differently." She clicked off in her sensible bootheels for the express capsule, and I entered the third-class student compartment. I never saw the woman again.

"Hang on, tymon," said Ran, as he made the first hairpin turn onto the Winding Road. His visual attention was wholly on the road, but he smiled and said, "If you want to close your eyes, or move to the emergency door, I won't take it as an insult."

"Why would I do that?" I asked, keeping my gaze staunchly from the drop that fell away on my right.

He scared me by withdrawing a hand from the controls long enough to pat mine. "We'll go together, anyway, and Kylla will give us a hell of a funeral."

"Will they let her do that now that she's a Shikron?"

"I'd like to see them try and stop her."

After a minute he said, "It's not that bad. The cliff wall is reflective. I think we can go on."

"You were planning on turning the car around on this little road if we couldn't?"

He seemed surprised. "I had no idea you were so nervous about this, tymon. After all the aircars you've crashed in your time—"

"One! Only one."

His smile widened. I said, "Close shaves don't count."

Have you ever heard some of the old legends of Earth? There was a people who lived in the ice and snow, on the edge of subsistence, and sometimes they would hunt for seals under the ice. A hunter would find a hole in the ice, and lie down with spear at the ready and wait until a seal came up for air. The hunter had to be inhumanly patient; he couldn't move or make a sound for hours, for fear of warning away the seal. And maybe one would never come up.

Ran didn't make a single complaint about Athena. He listened to mine, though. After a while it began to seem petty of me to keep him waiting around when he'd much rather be on Ivory—never mind that I hadn't asked him to come. I was well aware of that, but it began to seem petty anyway.

So, you may think, Ran waited until my guard was down and then suggested that we book passage for Ivory. No, he was better than that. I had to finally suggest it myself.

I won't say that the woman with the rooms over the cultural museum didn't enter my mind. Mostly, though, I felt like a damned seal.

And since I couldn't think of anything to do about it, I found myself on the *Queen Julia* with a one-way ticket.

When I spoke of my memories of Tuvin Province a while earlier I spoke, as most visitors do, of Shaskala, the only city there. Shaskala is a romantic name for an Ivoran city, but then it was settled mostly by Andulsines who came over the equator from the north, bringing their silly but delightful habit of drinking chocolate in the morning. They were either coming up or going down the Winding Road from the High Plateau (who knows which) when they decided to settle in the cleft by Don't-Look-Down Waterfall, and build there their Andulsine houses with real balconies (that looked out toward the street, as though oblivious of enemies). Some of the back balconies in the eastern quarter jut over the cliff. Children play on them as though the heights mean nothing, rolling painted balls and sticking their legs through the shaky iron railings. I don't know what shocked me more, those balconies or the ones facing the street.

They tell me Shaskala is a beautiful city from a distance. I never saw it from a distance, since it was pitch-black by the time we turned off the Winding Road into the cut that leads to the main street of town. In the silence of night I could hear the waterfall muttering loudly somewhere to our left.

"I just want to sleep," I said. Ran grunted and rubbed his eyes; he'd been peering out at the edges of the narrow road for the last few hours.

Three candles in a window marked an inn, and we stopped the car in front of it.

"Give me money," said Ran, and I counted him out some gold pieces from our purse and followed him inside.

It ran on electricity, like most of Shaskala; the candles in the window were for tradition. The entrance hall was a bright and welcoming yellow. Sometimes I think I like electricity better than the power packs that light the houses of the wealthy back in the capital; I know it's carcinogenic, but it's a different kind of light, very human-made. Power packs mimic sunlight too well. You never know if it's day or night.

Ran hit the carved attention-stick against the block on the front desk and a minute later a clerk came out, looking sleepy.

"I hope you have a room available," said Ran, putting a coin down on the counter.

The clerk was young, short, and sandy-haired, unusual for an Ivoran; he ran a hand through his hair, shook his head as though to clear it, and focused on us. Then he stopped dead in his tracks and stared.

I looked down at my robes; nothing wrong as far as I could tell. And he was staring at Ran, too, and Ran looked tired but normal. Now the clerk turned back to me, as though refreshing his memory.

"Gracious sir?" said Ran.

The gaze swung dumbly to my quarter-husband. Really, I suppose there can't be many travelers coming off the Winding Road in the middle of the night, but wasn't this a bit much?

"A room for the night, and possibly longer," said Ran. "And we have a car outside."

"You have a car?" asked the clerk. His voice was young and uncertain.

"Why shouldn't we have a car?"

The clerk swallowed. "No reason. Would you care to sign . . . uh, to sign in?"

"Can we do it tomorrow?" asked Ran.

"Uh, certainly. Of course. If the gracious, I mean the noble sir would come this way. . . . "

He started off toward the stairs and Ran followed. I picked up the carved attention-stick and examined it. It was brightly colored, and sculpted to resemble a caricature—of somebody real, I would bet. The figure was male and middle-aged and wore the mixed colors of a certain brand of hero from the Ivoran traveling theaters, a hero as much a butt of the gods as a force for good, and a bulbous nose seemed to be the main feature of the face. Putting someone on an attention-stick is not exactly an act of respect, when you think about what people do with that stick all day. The nose looked a lot more battered than it must have been when it was new.

"Are you coming?" Ran's voice called.

I put the stick back and went up to bed.

An hour later I rolled off the mattress, quietly, so as not to disturb my bedmate. I was too overtired to sleep.

"Where are you going?" asked Ran. His voice was wide awake.

I was about to tell him I was going to pee, if he was so damned interested, but on impulse I decided to tell him the truth.

"I feel like running the cards."

He sat up. "I'll come with you."

He padded after me into the sitting room. We had a two-room suite, thanks to Ran's standards and Tarkal's budget. I sat down cross-legged on the thick, multicolored carpet, and brought out the deck.

Ran sat opposite and was silent. He never pushed at this stage.

I started dealing out the cards. The first was a handsome young man in blue and crimson, carrying a sword: The

Hero. I watched the card and waited till it changed, the handsome features melting into an older and uglier face with a bulbous nose . . . perhaps I was generating that from the figure on the attention-stick downstairs? I frowned at the card and the visage changed again, this time to a man with gray in his hair and the face of an accountant. Or anyway, to do that group justice, the face one expects of an accountant. I could see more of his body now; he was sitting on an embroidered cushion, looking thoughtfully at a piece of paper.

I looked up and met Ran's eyes. "Nothing meaningful as yet."

I set out the second card. "The Wheel," I said. "A change of fortune."

"We just had a change of fortune with Tarkal's purse."

"Umm." Maybe. Nothing specific from this card, so I drew another.

The Fall, or The Height: A lone figure, too far away to tell its gender, standing on a precipice. Just the thing for Shaskala, I thought sourly, and as I watched the figure became Ran. He was wearing the clothes he'd worn today, but they were somehow more faded, or dirtier, or maybe it was the light; it was nighttime and his robes were blown back by the wind. He was going to fall, I knew it—

I pushed away the card. "Nothing meaningful."

"What was it?"

"Stay away from heights." I let out a shaky breath.

He waited, then said, "Are you going to do another?"

"Not tonight. Gods, I'm tired all of a sudden."

Ran started gathering the cards for me. He stood up and went to the cushion where I'd tossed my belt and wallet earlier, and bent over to retrieve them to replace the deck. I don't think I've mentioned it, but he was naked as the day he was born. I was wearing an underrobe. Unlike me, Ran was totally unself-conscious about being nude.

It was a pity, I thought, as I watched him, that Ivoran clothing showed so little of the body's outline. I'd loved it when he wore Athenan shirts and tight pants.

"What are you smiling about?" he asked.

"I was remembering that black outfit you wore when you took me to the party on Athena."

"Oh?" He smiled. "I seem to remember getting a very positive reaction to those clothes."

"Certainly from me."

He helped me to my feet and kissed me. He was showing a rather positive reaction himself, I noticed. We headed back to the other room, and Ran convinced me that I wasn't as tired as I'd thought. It was a question he was unusually good at debating.

I woke early the next morning and couldn't get back to sleep, so I got up quietly and padded out to the sitting room. Its two windows faced east, and broad bands of sunlight cut across the Andulsine carpet. I went to look out, and found myself looking down—and down—and down. I stepped back. Our inn was on the very edge of the cliffside. Maybe we even overhung, and had boards of wood propped against our underside to keep the whole inn from tumbling down to oblivion.

I would rather not know. I pulled my gaze resolutely from the window and did some preliminary sa'ret stretches.

There was a knock on the door. "Who is it?" I asked, keeping my tone low so as not to wake Ran.

"Chambermaid, gracious lady," said a girl's voice.

It was a little early in the game for anybody here to want to kill us, so I let her in; and I was rewarded for my trust with my first cup of hot Tuvin chocolate. The chambermaid was about seventeen, with curly dark hair, and she carried two cups on a lacquer tray.

"My husband's asleep," I said.

She lowered her voice to match mine. "Will you be wanting a fresh cup for him later?" she asked.

"Please. And, tell me, would it be possible for someone here to run out and get us some breakfast? We're both rather tired this morning."

"Of course, gracious lady," she said, and held out her hand for the money. Ivorans are very obliging people, and never hold you to house rules if you're willing to pay extra. "If you like, this one can go to the stalls down the street and bring you back some fruit." (Pay no attention to the excessive honorifics; they mean little on Ivory, where they'll call you "gracious sir" while slitting open your purse. Or your throat.)

"Thanks, I'd like that. And a slice of fresh bread, too." I gave her some coin and went to wash at the basin in the washroom.

A short time later she returned with the fruit and bread on a plate, and another cup of chocolate. She inquired very courteously which I wanted her to taste, but I told her not to bother. I gave her more money—always correct behavior I'd learned—and she bowed and went away.

I saved some of the fruit for Ran and put the plate down several feet from the window. I like a view on a nice morning, but this particular one was a bit overwhelming for my taste. This way I could glance at it from time to time as I ate, whenever I felt up to the experience. I sat sipping the cup of chocolate and let it drain down into my toes. It was, after all, a beautiful day; I had a new city to play tourist in; nobody was trying to kill us; and I was one-quarter married and in a mood to be pleased by that fact.

I heard bare feet behind me.

" 'Ware heights," said Ran, as he padded in. His hair was wet.

"That was meant for you, not me."

"How do you know?"

That was a good question; how *did* I know? There was no real reason I couldn't have been standing just outside the frame of the picture I'd read last night, ready to take a good long fall. I had a feeling, that was all, which could be from the cards or could be wholly self-manufactured. I shrugged. "Maybe I'm wrong. There's fruit on the sideboard for you, and chocolate. I put the saucer over the cup to keep it warm."

He went to collect them. "We'll need tah," he said, for we were both addicted.

"They serve it later in the morning up here. About an hour or so before lunch. I asked the girl."

Now, that had worried me badly for a moment, when I first saw the chocolate. What if they didn't have tah in this city? I'd have brought a supply if I'd thought we would be cut off. But fortunately the citizens here were firmly addicted. The tah price in Shaskala, I learned later, is set by municipal law.

Ran ate and drank thoughtfully. Then he put down his cup of chocolate—half drunk, the man had no appreciation—and said, "Theodora, have you given any thought as to how we should proceed on this information-gathering spree?"

Something in the way he said it made me cautious. "Only the merest, vaguest outline," I said.

"And how are you feeling this morning? Hardy and healthy?"

I looked at him. "You want something."

He grinned that Cormallon grin, a variety of smile that should be treated as a controlled substance. "I have an idea," he said.

Chapter 4

Ran's ideas always partake of a form of logic, however warped; the safety of following them, however, is something I will not speak for. Twenty minutes of arguing later found me lying on the sideboard, arms outspread, candles at each point, like the human sacrifice in some ancient folk thriller.

"Your sorcery usually isn't so dramatic," I said.

"Drama helps you to concentrate. It's a well-known fact. You can hear a pin drop during a good theater performance, and why? Complete concentration by the audience."

"Let's skip the candles, then. I'm afraid I'll knock one over and burn down the house. I promise to concentrate without them."

"Shush," said Ran. "We have to have props for this. The equations I got off the Net all use props. I can't change that variable now, I don't have Net access in this town." His voice was reasonable but distant, his focus elsewhere. He was rifling through a collection of notes he'd printed out back in the capital and taken along. "Not this one, not this one . . . ah. Here we are. We can use this with minor modifications. It's meant for an inanimate object, but there's no reason we can't attach it to a human being."

"Oh, really?" I said.

"You should be thinking of your definition. Are you thinking of your definition?"

I muttered and tried to think about it. After a minute I turned my head and saw him with a pencil in his mouth, frowning at a piece of paper. "It's no use, Ran, what I'm really thinking is these candles feel pretty warm so close to my body, and what would happen if I kicked one—"

"All right, all right." He got up and moved them away.

"Here." He took the dregs of our breakfast and scattered some pieces of pellfruit at my head and my feet. "Better substitution anyway; a living object to assist in placing a spell on a living object."

"I don't see why you can't place this spell on something like a piece of jewelry, anyway."

"Tymon, we've been through that. We want a spell that will let us identify by touch the people who are most likely to give us information. If I went around touching everybody with my ring until we stumbled on the right informant, it would make people nervous. They're sure to think I'm poisoning them or laying a curse, or at best out of my mind."

I turned over, knocking down some pellfruit, and lay on my stomach. In the morning sunlight I could see that the carpet beneath us showed an elaborate series of scenes from the life of Annurian the Rebel. I opened my mouth to point it out to Ran, since we had both known Annurian, but then I closed it again. He already thought I wasn't concentrating on business. I said, "Well, why not put this spell on yourself? I don't see why you have to drag me around touching people."

"My dear sweetheart and quarter-wife. If I went about shaking hands with everybody in Shaskala, they would lock me up. But from a barbarian, they'll accept it. Now turn back over and *concentrate on your definition.*"

My definition. "Want to hear it?"

"Please."

"We want to identify anyone willing to speak to us about the governor and not tell anyone they spoke to us."

From the corner of my eye I saw him shake his head. "Not good."

"What's wrong with it?"

"Anybody in town might be willing to speak to us. But not all those people will have relevant information."

"Kanz," I said. "All right, wait, let me think."

When it comes to sorcery, you have to formulate very carefully what you're trying to do. Magic, at its very best and most tame, as every good sorcerer wants it, is also at its most dumb. It does what you tell it. It does exactly what you tell it. And it does only what you tell it. I understand a lot of people have died accidental deaths down through the years because of this.

"How about this? We don't need positive information,

since the Governor's PR will be broadcasting that anyway; so we require someone with negative information who is willing to share it."

"Closer."

"What do you mean, *closer?*"

"What if they have some juicy negative information they're not willing to share at this point, but we can talk them into it? We don't want to confine our subject pool too strongly."

Wizards had never gone on like this about their subject pools in any non-Ivoran books I'd ever read. I got up on one elbow. "You know, this isn't my idea of a honeymoon, Ran."

I'd used the Standard word. He was taking out one of his little packets of colored dust and holding it up to the light. "What's a honeymoon?"

I told him.

"Ah. A *seravan.* . . . We don't follow that custom here with principal wives."

Principal wives, eh? "Ran, you don't ever plan on taking on any official concubines someday, do you?"

"Of course not, sweetheart," he said, not meeting my eyes. "The thought never entered my head." Ran knew he was dealing with a Pyrenese-Athenan prude, and was scrupulous about not offending my sensibilities. Openly.

"Because on Pyrene we were strictly monogamous."

"So I understand."

"And back on Athena, a group marriage means multiple husbands as well as wives. Just a warning."

"You want to lie down and run the spell, Theodora?"

I lay back down and waited. Ran said after a moment, "What about your definition?"

"Cast it, Ran, and don't press your luck."

It was late morning, leaning toward noon, when we got outside. Oh, by the way, I was primed to meet anybody who had negative information and *negative feelings* about the Governor. Negative feelings would give us a lever to work with, and somebody like that would be less likely to report us if we tried to buy him off.

So this was Shaskala, white-roofed and pure under the heavy blanket of sunlight. We were halfway up the plateau, but the air didn't feel any different; it was still hot, for one thing. "You know much about this place, tymon?" asked Ran, ready to fill in his barbarian partner.

"I've heard stories about it."

As a hitchhiker planet, Ivory was settled slowly and haphazardly, and the far corners of the world bred oddities of custom. Thanks be to the gods, they'd stuck mostly to one language, but even there the dialect differences were extreme. Shaskala was stranger than most places for several reasons. First, it was near the Andulsine border, and mixed northern and southern ways of life. Next, for reasons that would take a separate volume to explain, the Shaskala elders had made an aborted attempt to go into the business of manufacturing items from Tellys. This happened about twelve years back, but the effects are still being felt. And last, it was the traditional trading place and dumping ground for those who dealt with the Northwest Sector.

Tuvin Province overlaps the Sector by a six-day march. There are no paved roads. Certainly, much of what comes into Shaskala for trade is respectable stuff: Meat from the herds of Northwest ranchers, grain from the wheat that grows on the high plateau. The banks of the river below the city are lined with mills and slaughterhouses. But what Shaskala is famous for in song and story is stolen goods.

Refugees from all over the southern continent have headed like lemmings for the Northwest Sector since the btime of the first Emperor, and any number of them have stopped in Shaskala, changed their names, and settled. Meanwhile, their brothers, sisters, and cousins have raided and thieved their way across the plateau, then come to the city to trade.

We made our way through the Shaskala streets. A bell began to strike, deep, tolling strokes; four of them. I looked around and spotted a clock tower in the cliff face to the west. A glimpse of midnight blue and gold caught my eye next, and I pulled Ran's arm. "Look at that carpet!" The city was full of Andulsine rugs and tapestries. Ran let me drag him over to the piles of carpet under a striped awning, where a man in a checkered robe had just turned away.

"Sir!" I called. "Gracious sir! Would you care to discuss the artistic merits of the blue-and-gold Voba pattern by the pole?"

He turned back, and I saw a small white cup in his hand.

"This one cannot speak with you now, I'm afraid." He lifted the cup.

"It would only take a moment, gracious sir."

He raised an eyebrow. "Don't you see that it's time for tah right now? The gracious lady had better come back later." He turned and disappeared through a door in the wall at the back of the shop.

He'd used the direct form of "you"—his way of telling the barbarian to straighten up. I made a face at Ran, and he shrugged.

We went back to the street, where the crowds had thinned. The balconies of the buildings on both sides were now full of people in patterned Shaskala robes, drinking from small white cups. Pots of tah steamed on little metal warmers beside them. A small collection of tables in the gutter to our left now had tah cups out on them, and the servers there seemed to be the only people working in the city . . . no, strike that; I saw that one of the waiters was leaning against a wall, sipping idly.

"We'd better wait a bit before we go to City Hall," said Ran. "Something tells me all the officials will be sitting around taking their tah fix."

"We haven't had ours yet today," I pointed out.

"True. Sir, may we?" he called to the waiter, then held out a chair for me.

We sat and took tah cups from the communal pot. While I sipped I glanced around, then touched Ran's arm.

"Look." I pointed to a torn poster on the wall nearby.

"REWARD for STERETH TAR'KRIM and ANY AND ALL members of his band. 2,000 tabals in gold for any information leading to capture. Report to the Governor's office, City Hall."

"What kind of name is that?" I asked. " 'Grain-Thief,' 'Rice-Thief'?"

"One of the Northwest Sector outlaws. One of the governor's problems, maybe. We'll see."

"I guess we will." I sipped the tah and looked at my hand. My body didn't look any different now that a spell was on it. Sometimes I expected a glowing halo, or a troop of flying dragons, or some other explosive results.

Sometimes I got them.

* * *

"Honored by this meeting," I said to the Keeper of the City Records, extending my hand.

The Keeper of the City Records looked down at my hand as though wondering what to do with it. "The honor is mine," he said, and we finally shook.

A courteous gentleman. When our hands touched, I was alert for any feelings or perceptions that might arise from Ran's spell. Nothing.

I glanced at Ran and signaled with my eyes that this one wouldn't work out.

Ran sat back and smiled at the official.

"You said you had some courtesies you wished to observe?" said the Keeper.

"Yes," said Ran, "our group is associated with the House of Rivis. We'd like to set up a new branch in Shaskala, and of course before we purchased the land we thought it only polite to inquire into any formalities."

"Ah, if only all travelers were so considerate," said the Keeper. He smiled at me. "In terms of my department, our needs are small . . . perhaps three hundred tabals to accelerate the paperwork, and another two to handle any negative findings that might arise during the title search."

"The gracious sir is generosity itself."

The Keeper made a modest disclaiming motion with his hands.

"But I wonder if we might intrude further," said Ran.

"Please," said the Keeper, "let me know how I might serve you."

"We're strangers to your most excellent city. Could you be our guide in the confusions of municipal order? I would hate for us to pass over anyone else who needed . . . formalities observed."

"Sir, your wishes are so reasonable, it is a delight to grant them." The Keeper pulled out a piece of paper from his desk and began writing. "The first person you should see is the Director of Utilities. This is an estimate, mind you, but I doubt if he will ask for more than one hundred fifty. Then you'll want to speak to the Tax Assessor . . . that, I fear, will be more costly. . . . "

We met and promised bribes to over a dozen officials in the Shaskala City Hall. We were a popular twosome.

Over half of them extended invitations to dinner, which we put off. Whatever their wishes were for possible alliance with our imaginary group, none of them harbored any meaningful ill-will against the Governor. "What's wrong with these people?" I asked Ran as we got back to our room and I flopped down on the cushions. "What's happened to politics when jealousy, spite, and hurt feelings are no longer part of the game?"

"It's a good spell. I refuse to believe there's a problem with the spell."

I considered the matter, staring at the ceiling. "Maybe we're targeting the wrong group."

"How do you figure that?"

"The folks at City Hall are old, entrenched politicos. They have their bribes set down to half a tabal. They know the good and the bad, they aren't shocked by anything . . . I don't think they really care one way or another who the governor is, or what his policies are, as long as they don't impact on their daily business."

"So whom do you want to target?"

"What about the women?"

"What?"

"The women. What if we accept some of these dinner invitations and get introduced to the women at home. I'll bet they know the inside gossip on everyone worth knowing in Shaskala, and they've probably got opinions on it, too."

"Good point. I don't know how much they'd be keyed into local politics, though."

"How much did your grandmother know? And she never even left Cormallon. And Kylla recognized your client."

"She did?" His voice was startled. "When did she tell you that?"

"She didn't have to tell me."

He pulled off his outer robe and stepped over to the breeze from the window. Blue sky and clouds showed beyond, and the first touches of twilight. "All right, tymon, we'll try it your way."

"Good." I rolled over on my belly. "And what about getting some evening tah around here, anyway?"

He came over to join me. "Shops close early in this town, sweetheart. We'll have to get a few bags tomorrow morning and brew it ourselves."

"Yeah? You know how to make your own?"

He was pulling off my sandals. "Of course."

"Come on. A day never went by in your life that someone else didn't provide for you."

He removed my gray outer robe, folded it neatly, and dropped it on a cushion in the corner. "Where do you get these ideas about me?" he asked.

Ran was already gone by the time I got up. He left a note—in Ivoran, my reading skills had improved—saying he'd gone to buy a supply of tah. I washed and dressed, wondering what was keeping the chambermaid.

There was a knock on the door. "Gracious lady, it's me," she called. Her voice sounded different, as though she were upset. I opened the door.

She looked right and left in the hallway and said, "Gracious lady, you'd better leave this establishment quickly. Your husband has just been arrested, and I think there's a warrant out for you, too."

I stared. What could we possibly have done? Sorcery is illegal, of course, but nobody cares and, besides, who would know?

"There must be some mistake," I said.

"No doubt," she said politely, "but you'd best take what you can grab hold of swiftly and come with me. There's a side exit to a stableyard, and I can put you in the loft till dark."

None of it made any sense, but in case it was true I decided to be discreet. I pulled on my moneybelt and took an extra overcloak and hat and followed her warily down the back stairway.

At the entrance to the stableyard she said, "You'd better put on the hat, you're too conspicuous without it."

I held her back. "See here, what am I supposed to do at dark?"

Her large, brown eyes met mine. "I have a suitor in the police. He can get word to your friends if you'll tell me how."

"My friends? What friends?"

She took my hand. "The yard's empty now! Quick!"

We ran to the stable. Two drivebeasts went on placidly

munching, ignoring our entrance. She gestured to a ladder. "Come up with me," I said, "we need to talk."

She followed me up. There was a window where I could see across the yard to the inn; a face appeared in a window on our floor, and I drew back. The chambermaid scrambled over to sit beside me in the hay.

I asked, "You've no word on why he was arrested?"

"Not officially . . . but we all assumed it was the obvious reason."

We? "What obvious reason?"

"Gracious lady." She smiled. "Everyone knew, soon as you checked in, that you were Cantry and he was Stereth Tar'krim. Who else travels with a barbarian wife? And arriving in the middle of the night, and not signing any names—please, we're not stupid. Not that anyone would have dreamed of giving you away."

Stereth Tar'krim. The wanted poster I'd seen on the wall by the tah vendor's came back to me. The leader of one of the Northwest Sector outlaw bands, with an extraordinary amount of money on his head.

My eyes narrowed. "Wouldn't have dreamed of giving us away? With a reward like that?"

She smiled, immune to my suspicion. "I'm sure Stereth Tar'krim's people can pay a friend more handsomely than the Governor's agents can. And not expect to get half of it back in taxes, either."

Reasonable. "He's not Stereth Tar'krim," I said, "and I'm not this Cantry."

"Gracious lady—" she began, shaking her head.

"But we *are* wealthy, and we like making new friends. No harm in that, is there?"

"None at all," she agreed, gazing demurely downward. "You could make two new friends today, if you wished." I looked interested, and she said, "My fiancé, Hilo. He's a lieutenant in the Shaskala police, and he has duty in the detention cells this season. He has to bring messages there two or three times a night, for the guard officer on duty."

I still had some antipathy toward Imperials, based mostly I suppose on my experiences with them during my first stay on Ivory. But local cops seemed to me to be neither more nor less corrupt and special-influence seeking than the rest of the planet's organizations. I was willing to give Hilo the benefit of the doubt.

"He would know where my husband is being kept?"

"More. He could get a message to him . . . and if he can be of small service in getting him out . . . if my lady has any ideas . . . he would be happy to place himself at your disposal."

"You two talked about this before you came to get me."

She smiled again, as far as she would acknowledge it. "It's so difficult, gracious lady, waiting and waiting to get married. We're not even quarter-wed, because my father says Hilo has to have a furnished house before anything else. You have no idea, all the little things that have to be bought—towels and silverware and rugs—"

"Yes, yes, I got the point earlier."

"Hilo's an orphan, and has no family home to take me to."

I sighed and brought out my moneybelt. "No man is an orphan," I said, "who has good friends."

She practically clapped her hands at the sight of the gold. "My lady is only a barbarian on the outside," she said. "Inside, she has the heart of a true and civilized Ivoran."

Heaven forbid.

Hilo came to see me about an hour later. I spent that time remembering in despair how we'd paraded from one City Hall office to the next all through the day, displaying ourselves to every major official in the city. Stereth Tar'krim and his barbarian companion. It was a wonder we hadn't been arrested a lot earlier.

Hilo was more plainspoken than his fiancée. He was a tall, good-looking dark-haired man in the blue-gray uniform of a municipal cop, and he wasted no time in getting to the point, albeit in a friendly way.

"He's on a floor by himself," said the lieutenant. "The Governor's overjoyed, and doesn't want to take any chances on losing him. There are three men on duty outside."

"You understand, as I told your fiancée, that he's not Stereth Tar'krim."

"I understand your words." said Hilo agreeably, without committing himself as to any belief in their truth. "I might wonder why you don't both call witnesses in your behalf."

"We don't have any witnesses in this city. And anyway . . . look, Hilo, to be frank—we're not Northwest Sector outlaws, but we're not using our real names either. It's a complicated story."

"I see. Well, it's all one to me, my lady, to be equally frank. If you want my help, you've only to speak."

I considered. Ran, being a true child of Ivory, is against revealing any information until it is torn from him by violence. However, there are times when it has to be done. I hesitated, then said, "Excuse me, Hilo, but aren't you taking a chance by opposing the Governor's wishes in this?"

"I have no great love for the Governor," said Hilo simply. "Most of the department feels the same. He's a crazy man, my lady, he's trying to reform the city government. He's published rules about bribery and extortion, which wouldn't be so bad, but he's actually trying to enforce them. Now I ask you, how can a young man ever expect to marry and raise a family on the salary of a city policeman without accepting gifts from time to time? Is it reasonable, gracious lady? I put the case to you."

"Uh, it does seem to be asking a lot. I'm afraid I don't know much about municipal salaries. . . ."

"Take my word for it, the man is out of his senses. If the department were made up only of people who expected to live on their pay, it would be empty."

"I see. Well, I suppose you could move to another city—"

"Shaskala is my home, gracious lady. I just hate to see what this kanz is doing to it."

I hid a smile. It had only just occurred to me, this late in the conversation, that my Athenan teachers would have seen the ethics of the matter quite differently. I put out my hand. "A barbarian custom," I explained, "to seal our bargain."

We shook on it. There was no sorcerous glow, no explosion, no doves and balloons in the air. But quite suddenly I *knew*. Bless honest Hilo's heart, he was every bit as corrupt as he claimed. My smile returned, and this time I made no attempt to hide it.

"My husband is a sorcerer," I said, committing myself, and finally my uniformed friend looked surprised. And wondering how they would all take it, I added, "I have sort of a plan."

Chapter 5

Stereth Tar'krim and his barbarian companion, eh? I'd met a few semi-legendary figures on Ivory but I really hadn't planned on stepping into any storybooks myself. When the first moon was high over the city to our east, I was waiting in Damask Lane with a slaughterhouse meatwagon and two drivebeasts. The wagon stank.

Have I mentioned that before coming to Ivory I'd only eaten artificial meats? No matter. I held onto the reins and wondered if the streetsingers would make up a new song about the daring escape of Stereth Tar'krim. I hoped that they would. Better than they should make up one about the double execution of the outlaw and the friend who tried to break him out of jail.

"Theodora?" said a low voice nearby. Only one person in the city would call me that. It was a sickle moon, and I peered through the darkness at the alley's mouth, still trying to make out some sort of figure when a hand touched my arm.

I must have jumped a foot. Only the conflicting fear of notice kept me from yelping wildly. "Are you all right?" said Ran's voice.

I put my hand over my heart. It felt as though there were a pigeon trapped in there. "Fine, just fine," I hissed, resenting the question. I saw his outline dimly now; he was still wearing the good clothes he'd gone out with that morning, and looked none the worse for wear. Break the man out of prison, and he was in better shape than I was.

Hilo appeared on the other side of me. "You look surprised, my lady," he said. "Didn't you think it would work?"

Truthfully, I hadn't. I'd never planned a jailbreak before. I'd participated in them, but that's not the same thing.

"No problem at all, really," said Hilo, grinning. "I brought him his dinner, and the coins I'd taken from the guards were under the plate. I just said, 'Tymon sends you this, and I'll be back in an hour.' Didn't say a word to me, you know, I wondered if he'd heard."

Adrenaline made Hilo talkative. It does that to a lot of people. The first time I'd been in a similar situation I'd practically pulled Ran's clothes off afterward. Hilo went on, "So I come in an hour later, and all three of them are stretched out at their posts, dead to the world. I took the keys, and here we are."

By giving Ran things that belonged to the duty guards, Hilo had made them vulnerable to sorcery from a distance. I said, "The only iffy part was whether you could win the coins away from them."

Hilo smiled smugly. "That was never in doubt, gracious lady."

Ran had climbed in beside me in the wagon seat. "What now?"

"Down the Winding Road," said Hilo. "It'll look like any wagon on its way to the slaughterhouse distribution centers below. That's where they pack the meat in ice, or dry and salt it. Anyone asks, you say you're from a small butcher shop in town, looking to get a few coins from some excess carcasses."

Ran turned to me. "Have you paid this fine gentleman?"

"Partially," I said. "I believe we could do better for him."

He bowed to Hilo. "My House will be in touch."

"I have every faith in you," said Hilo. He threw us a salute as our wagon drew out of the lane and we headed toward the Winding Road.

The city was dark and silent. It was early in the night for a meatwagon to travel, but not unheard of. "I hate to lose another car," said Ran, referring to the one we would have to leave behind.

I turned to look at him in the dim moonlight. "Be glad you're alive."

He said, "Isn't that an employee lesson carved on the doors of the cheaper brothels?"

"Really? I'm surprised you know so much about the cheaper brothels."

I heard his low chuckle and felt him put one arm around me. "All right. Thank you very much, Theodora. I won't say I wasn't worried."

Long ago, the Shaskalans planted a grove of sutu trees at the edge of town. They whispered in the night breeze as we approached, their feathery tops swaying. The air should have been full of their heavy spice, but the stench of our cargo blocked it.

I pulled sharply on the reins. "What's that?"

I pointed down the incline of the road, half-hidden by the grove, where a necklace of small fires hung in the night. Ran leaned forward and put a hand on mine.

"They're too big for torches," he said.

I peered through the swaying trees. "Oil drums," I said finally.

"A roadblock."

"For us? How could they get ahead of us like that? They shouldn't even have missed you till morning, and even if somebody came in and saw, how could they move so quickly?"

"Who knows? But nobody matching my description with a barbarian friend sitting beside him is going to get through there tonight." He'd taken the reins and was turning the wagon around.

"Wait a minute here—where are we going?"

"I don't know. I don't know." He looked no more pleased than I did. "But you remember that road, Theodora, how narrow it is. There's no way we can get past without being seen."

So we clopped back into Shaskala. The sickle moon was high now. I looked at the faces of the buildings as we passed under the balconies. The whole city felt like a prison to me, one we couldn't get out of.

Halfway down the main street I said, "Keep going."

He turned tome. "What?"

"Keep going. Don't stop. We can't stay in this town anymore, and if we can't go down we'll have to go up."

Ran's face was blank, as it always became when his thoughts were especially turbulent. "But there's nothing up there but the High Plateau, and the Northwest Sector."

"Then we'll have to go to the Northwest Sector."

He continued to look at me. Then he turned back to the

reins, and the wagon rumbled on through the Shaskalan streets, and out to the outlaw road.

It was windy farther up the plateau, and the road became more narrow. We wouldn't have made it in a groundcar. But the night was clear and the drivebeast had been bred for this kind of climb.

I said, "You're all right, aren't you?"

"Sure, why wouldn't I be all right?"

"You're holding your right arm."

He shifted in the wagon seat. "I slept on it."

I thought about what we were riding into, and said, "I wish we had a map with us. I only have the vaguest memory of what this territory looks like. Still, one of the ranchers must have a Net connection—we can get through to Kylla or somebody in the family, and they can come and get us."

He said only, "A Net connection? In the Northwest Sector?"

Well, he was being a cheerful companion. "You sure you're all right?"

"Theodora, trust me, I'm fine." He took his hand away from his right arm. "Under the circumstances, a little worry is normal."

"Umm."

A few hours later we came out onto level ground: the top of the plateau. Ran shook himself to attention and said, "I think we should bear straight ahead. Most of the big ranches and farms are along the main track." He looked at me. "Are you getting tired, tymon? I can take over. I didn't mean to leave you on your own, I guess I was preoccupied."

"That's all right. Agonizing over our future has kept me pretty busy."

He took the reins and the drivebox. "I don't suppose we have anything in the way of supplies, or anything to build a fire with?"

"Nobody anticipated this part of the trip. We've got a ton of dead animal flesh, though. Hope you like it raw."

He nodded glumly at this information. "You know, the laws of magic say that some people are like lightning rods. I don't know what it is about you, tymon, but whenever you come to this world I end up cut off from my family, traveling under an assumed name, and without any money."

"Are you trying to lay responsibility for this at my door?"

"No, no. Heavens, no."

Grotesque shapes loomed on either side of us in the darkness, the wind-twisted trees of the plateau. They seemed to crawl sideways on the ground, their branches frozen in spasm; some of them had managed to sprout and retain a few leaves, though, and they rustled as we passed.

Ran said, "I guess we should be thankful it's a clear night. I always heard the skies were misty up here."

"For a clear night you can't see very far. Do you think we should hole up till daylight?"

And a voice, not Ran's, said: "I wouldn't think so. Not with the distance we have to cover."

A speedy getaway is simply not an option with a freighthauler. I hit the STOP on the drivebox and reached for my weapons. Ran had already dived back over the seat, and I remembered that he was still unarmed.

"Please!" said the voice, reprovingly, and a large shape lumbered from the tree-shadows. It was a man seated on some kind of modified riding animal. The man was normal-sized but the mount, its white fur pale in the moonlight, came up past the wagon seat and could easily have carried two or three. "Let's not be unfriendly," said the man. His voice was a pleasant baritone, and what I could see of his face showed him to be relatively young, and not at all bad to look at.

"Since you're at our mercy anyway," said a new voice. I spun around and saw another man, shorter and stockier than the first, his hair shaved close to his head, standing at attention on the back of the wagon. His pistol was pointing directly at Ran.

Two more figures appeared on the roadside, both armed. "Kanz," I heard Ran mutter. He stood up.

"Can I help you gentlemen with something?" He looked around and said, "Gentlemen and lady, I mean."

That made me check again. It was dark, but one of the people standing on the side was either a woman or a crossdresser.

Moonlight was directly on the face of the mounted man, and he grinned. "Des Helani, honored by this meeting. May

I present Mora Sobien Ti—" the woman inclined her head, "—and Lex na'Valory, and Grateth Tar'briek standing behind you with the pistol. As you can tell from his name, Grateth was in the army and he knows how to shoot, so a word to the wise."

"I was in the army, too," said Lex na'Valory sullenly. He was a large man, solidly built, with short, wiry black hair.

"I didn't mean to imply you weren't," said Des Helani.

"And at least I had an honorable discharge," the man went on.

"He also lives up to his name," said Ran, and Lex na'Valory glared at him. "Road-names," Ran continued speculatively. "I take it that you're outlaws."

"And you're taking it well, too," said Des Helani. He dismounted and approached the wagon. "May I ask you both to get down?"

I held onto the grip and put one foot in the stirrup-step. A hand was on my arm; supporting me, and then Des Helani stepped away. Ran jumped down beside me, looking suspicious. This close, and with the moon on his face, I could see that the outlaw's eyes were cat-green, unusual but not unheard of for an Ivoran. His hair was brown, not black, and a lighter brown than usual. He saw me looking at him and he stepped forward and put a hand around each of my upper arms.

"Hey," said Ran. The stocky bandit with the pistol moved toward him.

But Des Helani merely swung me around so that I was facing the moon, now low in the west. "So it's true," he said happily, "suddenly the world is full of lovely barbarian women." And he bent and kissed my hand.

Ran looked disgusted. The moon was on his face, too, and I could see his lip curl. It's true, our bandit's manner was clichéd, but it was a conscious clichéd that he invited us to join him in. His tone so clearly said, "Please overlook my excesses, and play this game with me. I'm having too much fun to stop."

His energy was contagious, and I found myself smiling. I don't doubt that if I'd had a handkerchief to drop he would have bowed as he picked it up. In the constant dance of male and female, this was clearly a partner who always let you know where he was stepping next.

Mora Sobien Ti put a hand on the reins of our drivebeast, her brown skin bleached by the dim light. "If none of you minds," she said in a cool voice, "we do have a long way to go. And it'll be dawn in twenty minutes."

"Right," said Des Helani, suddenly all business. "The barbarian can ride with me, she's too small to be any problem for my mount. Lex and Mora, you can share the other mount, and Grateth can watch over our other new friend as he drives the cart."

So there was another of those tall animals tethered nearby. I said, "You really want me to climb all the way up there on that thing?" It came out more hollowly than I'd intended. The outlaw laughed. "It's modified, sweetheart, it wouldn't know how to be aggressive if it wanted to. And if you hold onto me tight enough, you won't fall off."

I had to climb up onto the wagon seat before I could maneuver onto the beast. Ran helped me. He said, "I think I should mention that we don't have any money. And I have doubts about anyone wanting to pay ransom for us."

"Ransom? The thought never entered our minds." Des Helani saw to it that I was settled and added, "You're the sorcerers who were staying in Shaskala. We've got work for you."

He touched his heels to the mount's side and we moved off. I turned briefly and saw Ran standing on the wagon, his face studiously blank.

So as it turned out, Hilo was on everybody's payroll. Not only were we paying him and this outlaw band as well, the City of Shaskala was still giving him his regular salary. It may not have been unrelated after all, that a roadblock had forced us in a direction most people avoided. And I really didn't think the chambermaid back at the inn would have anything to worry about when it came to buying those sheets and towels and things that are so important for a young couple just starting out in the world.

The sun comes up quickly on the plateau. I didn't know it then, but this was one of the rarest things there: a clear morning. I turned once and saw a sunrise of incredible beauty; turned again a few minutes later and it was over, the sky a simple shade of gray. There were fewer trees along the track. On all sides of us an ocean of short coarse grass fanned away into eternity. There were plants here and there in it that I'd never seen before, and purple and white flowers with spiky leaves. Not that the ocean was entirely flat; there were hills and valleys all the way around us, and we forded three streams before noon.

We stopped at the third and everyone filled their canteens. Des ("Call me Des, dear heart, you have my friendship already") let me drink out of his and then filled it again. Far in the distance I saw a farmhouse nestled in one of the little valleys. "Why didn't we stop before?" I asked. "Your canteen was empty."

"Hasn't anyone told you about the Northwest Sector?" Des splashed water on his face. "Three out of four water sources here are poisonous."

"Oh." I exchanged a glance with Ran, who'd pulled off his outer robe and shirt and was taking the opportunity to do a quick wash. Getting out of this territory was looking more and more difficult.

Ran gave a slight shrug and dried himself with his shirt. I said to Des, "How can you tell which are poisonous?"

"By asking someone who knows," said Des. He held the reins to his mount and motioned to me. "Up you go, sweetheart." He hauled me over; he was stronger than he looked.

"Des, are you the Stereth Tar'krim everybody is looking for?"

Lex na'Valory gave him a leg up and he climbed on in front of me. "Certainly not," he said. "We're just good friends."

Daylight showed Des Helani to be in his early thirties, with a long and easy grace that sat well on a mount. Lex na'Valory and Grateth Tar'briek looked about the same age, or perhaps Grateth was a little younger. Lex's face bore a constant expression of discontent. Grateth was stocky, even-tempered, competent, and never far from his weapons. He carried at least two knives that I could see and I noticed that whatever he was doing, Ran seemed to be in his line of sight. Both of them wore the army in their posture, but somehow what seemed like discipline in the way Grateth held himelf became resentment when you watched Lex na'Valory. Mora Sobien Ti was older, with streaks of gray in her black hair. Her outer robe was short, more like a jacket, and her inner robe was cut like a riding skirt. I'd never seen a riding skirt on this planet. They all bore the air of people who were used to the life they lived; who washed and drank when they could and paid no attention when they couldn't.

As for me, I ached from riding and dreamed of stretching out in one of the professional baths back in the capital.

"You barbarians are such fragile creatures," marveled Des Helani when we stopped for a brief rest, and he saw me trying to contort my body into some position that would give it relief. "Cantry is the same way."

"Cantry?"

"You'll meet her. Another barbarian, you could be sisters."

We went on and the afternoon grew mistier and mistier. "This is more like it," said Des. Our mount picked its way along the trail and I heard the wagon behind us.

"You prefer this weather?"

"All outlaws prefer this weather, darling. You'll get to like it, too."

That did not strike me as encouragingly as he'd meant it to.

In late afternoon we came to the edge of a low valley, a wide, shallow saucer of land in the middle of nowhere. Two twisted plateau trees marked the start of a trampled pathway that led down through the long grass. Our wagon followed Des Helani's mount into the mist, and after a few minutes I said, "There's a building." I was still riding behind Des and I felt him take a deep breath.

"That's ours, darling," he said. "That's our home. A little wet on rainy nights, but serviceable."

Stone walls broke through the mist. As we drew nearer I could see the whole thing: An ancient wall of gray stone with taller, equally ruined buildings within. An old monastery? A fort? Physically, it would be hard to tell the difference between the two, at least on this world.

Des slid off his mount and helped me down. He said, "Mora, we'd better salvage what we can of the meat. Some of it smells a bit high."

"I'll take it to the cookhouse," she said, and stood by the wagon, her arms folded, waiting for Ran to get down.

Ran climbed down slowly. Mora took the drivebox from him and led our cart and beasts away.

He came over and stood beside me. "Well?" he said to Des Helani.

"Please," said Des. "Guests first." And he motioned us toward the entrance. Grateth and Lex na'Valory fell in behind us.

We entered what I later found was the main building of the fort. It had a large public hall and ten smaller rooms, five on each side. About half of them were lacking their fair share of the roof. A fire burned on the floor at one end of the hall, and at the other was a collection of mats, cushions, boulders, and a truly excellent large table of gleaming darkwood, with any number of candles on it. It was dark and smoky in the hall. And at the end we were headed for, it was crowded.

A good dozen outlaws were stretched out at their ease on the cushions. I couldn't take them all in then; there were men and women, young and middle-aged, dressed colorfully and drably, busy and idle. Most of them wore trousers, like the fishermen and outdoor-working provincials I'd seen in the past; but beside that, many wore jackets or short outer robes of intricate, patterned colors that reminded me of Andulsine carpets. These people certainly weren't trying to blend into the scenery—crimson and gold, midnight blue, swirls of deep purple—a treasure of color moved in the darkness, flicked into prominence here and there by the store of candles.

And as for the jewelry, my sister-in-law Kylla would have been considered downright conservative.

Des Helani's stride lengthened, and he stood straighter. "I was magnificent!" he called. "Shall I tell you how magnificent I was?"

"Can we stop you?" said a voice.

"Tell us, Des!" said a woman, laughing. "Tell us how magnificent you were."

"I was glorious," he said, and by then we'd reached the center of the group. A young man with a face beautiful even by the standards of Ivory sat there on a boulder, polishing an old short sword. "But first, introductions," Des continued. He passed by the young man and stood in front of another, older man holding a sheaf of papers. This one was in his thirties and had the look of a scholar—or an accountant—with mild dark eyes and prematurely graying hair. He was wearing spectacles.

"Allow me to present the most sought-after prison-guest in the Northwest Sector," said Des, declaiming the words like an actor. "Stereth Tar'krim. Stereth—" suddenly his voice dropped into normality, "—these are the ones from the message."

Stereth Tar'krim blinked up at us from his cushion. He put down his papers, stood, and adjusted his spectacles as he frankly looked over Ran and me.

For your sake, imaginary reader, I will pause here and tell you what spectacles are. Picture a small circle of glass bordered by a rim of gold wire. Then picture a matching circle of glass, connected to the first by more wire. Now imagine someone *looking through* these circles of glass—each circle being directly in front of an eye, you see. Of course, they're not floating there in air before this person's face—they're held up by a bridge over the top of the nose, and anchored by extensions of the wire that reach back and over the tops of the ears.

You'll probably be wondering about the purpose of all this. It's not an adornment—anyway, not generally. It's an aid in vision. You see, the glasses are not just normal glass; they're actually lenses that compensate for eyesight problems. You can see versions of them in pictures of people from history. If you're wondering why Stereth Tar'krim didn't simply have his eyes fixed or replaced, you've failed to grasp the point that first as an Ivoran and then as an outlaw, he was in no position to have that done. Even if he knew about the option.

Anyway, the contraption may sound unstable, but it really does sit on your face without any difficulty—except, as now, when Stereth had to push it back up the bridge of his nose.

Excuse me for interrupting my history at such a dramatic meeting, but it was something you needed to know.

Now—as I said, Stereth pushed back his spectacles, peered at us, and said, "Honored by this meeting. Des, we got your relay. I see you took the initiative."

"You said I was in charge."

"I know. You were. You did a fine job."

"I was magnificent! . . . Wasn't I?'

"You did the right thing, and I'm glad you didn't wait to consult me. We might have lost them."

Des grinned and relaxed. Ran glanced at me and we exchanged careful looks at how wanted we apparently were.

"I hope you weren't alarmed at being invited here," Stereth said to us. "I hope Des made you as comfortable as possible."

"He was charming," I said.

"He always is," said Stereth. "And now, if I may ask, which of you is the sorcerer?"

I said nothing, and Ran stood there looking unhappy. Finally he said, "Gracious sir—"

Stereth Tar'krim interrupted him. "The rules here are different. You can call me Stereth to my face, and what you call me otherwise doesn't matter."

"Stereth," said Ran. "May I ask what makes you think that either of us is a sorcerer?"

Stereth smiled, a very mild smile. "We keep trained messenger-birds here. Later, when you have leisure, you might go and visit the coop over by the west wall. We share these birds with friends of ours who are too far away to visit."

"With a Shaskalan cop named Hilo?" I asked.

Stereth said, "It's good to have friends. A bird from Shaskala returned to one of our stations, near where Des' group was operating. He took it upon himself to arrange this meeting."

From the cushion where he'd deposited himself, Des looked up. "I was magnificent."

Stereth gave in gracefully. "Yes, Des, you were magnificent."

"He wasn't that good," said Lex na'Valory.

"We can use a sorcerer," said Stereth. "We need every edge we can get, just to survive. We can pay well."

"With stolen goods and tabals," put in Ran.

"Is a professional sorcerer in any position to make moral judgments? How many people have you ruined or killed? Is sorcery not still illegal in the empire, or have I missed something?" Stereth's voice was gentle, toneless, and made me shiver.

"People accept what I do as part of life," said Ran, making no more vain pretense as to which of us was the one they wanted. "It's technically illegal, yes, but nobody cares. But you're—"

"An acknowledged outlaw? Liable to hang? Very likely. That's not a moral inferiority, though, it's just the reality of my greater relative risk." He said it reasonably, like one business person speaking to another about the ups and downs of the market.

"I was going to say, you're a bandit. You rob innocent travelers and raid people's homes."

Stereth took no offense. He smiled, touched the shoulder of the unnaturally handsome boy with the sword, and took over his seat on the boulder. "I hate to get into these morality contests. Won't you sit down?" He indicated the pillows and cushions scattered on the hall floor.

"Thank you, I prefer to stand."

Generally making someone look up at you is considered a psychological advantage. Stereth just looked relaxed. If anything, it made Ran seem like some schoolboy or employee called into the main office for a reprimand.

Stereth said, "Since your options have pretty much dwindled, why don't we talk about your salary?"

"I'm not working for you."

"I can start you with a retainer of two thousand tabals—"

"That's very kind of—"

"And both your lives." A silence descended upon us all. I heard someone in the group crack a nut. "Perhaps your wife should have some input into this," said Stereth.

I opened my mouth and Ran said, "She's not my wife."

Des Helani sat up straight, and Stereth's face showed very faint surprise. "Oh? Des—"

"That's not what I heard from Shaskala," said Des.

Ran said, "It makes life easier in inns and in our job if we just say that we're married. But she's my assistant—and a recent assistant at that. We only started working together a few weeks ago."

It's hard to keep people as hostages for one another when they barely know each other. But how believable this would be—

Des called, "Is that true, darling? If I'd know you were free, I'd've let you ride closer to me."

I met his look squarely and said, "If we'd ridden any closer, I'd be pregnant."

This brought whoops from Des' friends. Stereth turned to me and allowed a genuine smile to form, lifting his iron control by about ten percent—just enough to let pure, shared enjoyment show—and I realized this was another one who could turn on the charm. He said, "You're not as quiet as you look."

"I don't think you are either," I said slowly.

Our smiles held. Then Stereth pushed up his glasses again and turned back to my non-husband.

"So you're saying any threats I might make to your friend would be pointless."

"Ishin na' telleth," said Ran. "It's all one to me. A business decision—you should understand that."

"Oh, I do. —Cantry, put that jar down and join us." He was looking up and I followed his gaze to see a narrow balcony running the length of the hall. A young woman was carrying a large clay jar, about a third as large as she was tall, and now she set it on a place on the balcony with a lot of other jars. She had short, curly fair hair and was slightly built—the other barbarian. She wiped her forehead with one arm and called down to Stereth, "I'm not finished yet."

"You are for now," said Stereth. "We have guests. Des can finish for you later."

"Thanks," said Des. "It's not my turn to carry water till tomorrow."

"Claim the credit," said Stereth. "Tell her it was your idea."

Cantry had disappeared from the balcony, and a few seconds later she reappeared in an archway across the room. She walked over to stand by Stereth.

He said, "My wife, Cantry. —These two people say they aren't married, beloved. What do you think? Do they look married to you?"

Cantry slid one arm around his waist and evaluated us. Her eyes were light brown, her face was clear and childlike. This was the barbarian I'd been mistaken for in Shaskala, whom Des said might be my sister? She was my height, but that was about it. Her hair was blond, for heaven's sake.

All barbarians look alike to these people. Cantry said finally, "They feel married to me."

"Me, too. But people get that look just from being together, they say. You start to resemble your pet lizard after a few months."

Stereth was clearly enjoying playing with us. He couldn't have any proof, though. Ran said, "I'm not going to work for you, and neither of us would bring in much ransom. You may as well let us go."

"Let you go! —Des, did you tell these good people they would be held against their will? Forgive me. You can leave any time. Any time you feel up to traveling alone across the Sector. We've confiscated your wagon, but you can still go on foot. Try not to eat or drink anything, and if you meet anybody on the way, just say you're innocent travelers, and I'm sure they'll let you past."

Not to mention that directions had gotten a little confused in the mist on the way here.

Ran was silent, and Stereth said, "You see what I mean about options." He motioned to Cantry, who brought over a bottle of wine and some bowls. Stereth poured, drank some to show it was clean, and handed us each a bowl. "Still." He smiled. "The sun is sinking, the night is young, and I'm sure we have much to discuss. We don't ask each other our birth-names, here, but if you want to volunteer them it's all right. Otherwise, we'll just have to say 'hey, guest' until we come up with nicknames for you both."

"I already have a nickname," I said. The wine was red and incredibly strong. "Gods, don't you water this stuff? —Tymon, that's my nickname."

" 'Tymon.' And this doesn't offend you?"

"Not if it's said with respect and affection."

"I shall endeavor to meet your requirements. And your, um, business associate . . . ?"

Ran looked up from the bowl. "Call me Sokol," he said.

Sokol is a word frequently seen in Ivoran literature. I used it myself a great deal when I collected folktales all through the south. It means "anonymous."

Stereth gazed at him as a man will who has suffered a thing too long to take offence at further indignities. "Sokol," he repeated. He sighed. "I can see," he said, "that this will take some time."

Chapter 6

The Ivoran word for rice, krim, is also the generic term for grain, and covers wheat, corn, oats, rye, and barley as well. But you see the importance they place on rice in their culture.

Rice doesn't grow anywhere on the High Plateau, and it didn't grow much in Tammas District, where Stereth Tar'krim grew up—he was Davor Metonid then. There was an aborted revolution in Tammas District: Burned fields, food shortages, and an influx of unsympathetic soldiers from the Emperor's special forces. None of this had much to do with Davor Metonid, except that his wife and child were hungry and his job at the Imperial Records office went up in flames (literally) when the district capital was burned. He stole two loaves of bread from a black marketeer who was under the protection of the Imperial Guard Captain and after being hung from a pole for an afternoon he was cut down (quite without malice) and sent to the district prison. His nearsightedness would not allow him a berth in the army, where most convicted felons ended up.

His wife and child died, whether from sickness or starvation is hard to say. One may have advanced the other. In any case, Davor Metonid now had only himself to worry about, and a two-year stint in Tammas District Prison.

I don't pretend to know what was going through his head at that point. However, somewhere along the line, with fourteen Ivoran months still to serve, Davor Metonid engineered a group escape. He took four men with him. They killed six guards on the way out—nothing like burning your bridges, apparently. Hanging is the penalty for attempted escape from an Imperial prison. Killing a guard is considered worse. Once out, he suggested they make for the Northwest Sector, a good month away on foot. They disagreed. They all had friends at home, they said, who would hide them while they figured out what to do. Davor made no attempt to argue; he said that he had no friends himself, wished them luck, and left them. They were all captured and crucified within the next few days. Davor came to the Northwest Sector, to the High Plateau, and began his career.

It started with two loaves of bread back in Tammas District. And that's why he was called Stereth Tar'krim. Rice thief.

Being in an outlaw fort in the Northwest Sector is a little like being in the army. You meet a lot of people from a lot of different places, and learn any number of personal histories. And somehow none of the personal histories, however different from your own, weighs as much as the fact as you are all stuck in the same present situation.

I woke up on the women's side of the sleeping quarters. If Ran hadn't come up with that story about our just being business associates, we could've slept together in one of the little rooms off the hall and it would have been comforting.

I sidled up to Ran while we were waiting on line to get access to the waterjars for our morning wash, and mentioned that fact to him.

"It was a good idea. Anyway, I didn't have a lot of time to think." Ran shivered in the early morning cold. His chest was bare. "Somehow I never anticipated standing in a ruin in the Northwest Sector, being offered a retainer by a killer with glasses."

"Pardon," said a voice nearby, and the gorgeous youngster who'd been cleaning his short sword last night walked past Ran, this time carrying one of the tall waterjars.

Ran turned to watch him. "Did you catch his accent?" he asked me.

"What accent? He didn't have one."

"That's what I mean. If he wasn't born out of the Six Families, he was damned close to it. He talks the way you and I do, Theodora."

People have claimed before that I've picked up Ran's high-toned accent. I have to take it with a grain of salt, because I've never been entirely clear that Ran had one. The boy came back past us empty-handed, on his way to get another jar. He paused and bowed to us both.

"I'm making up the water schedule," he said courteously, "and if you have any preferences, I would be happy to incorporate them."

"Preferences?" I asked.

"As to which days you would rather be on water-carrying duty. The well is out back. This bunch seems to require a great deal of washing, not to mention drinking."

Ran blinked. "Water-carrying? Me?"

The boy regarded him.

Ran said, "I thought I was a guest."

The boy said, "A long-term guest. You might say we're all long-term guests."

"I've never carried water in my life. Don't you have people to do that?"

"There are no servants here, Sokol. You'll find that we're all equals before the law, all liable to equal execution. I carry water twice a month, and they call *me* Sembet Triol."

Sembet Triol—nobly born. That put him one up on Ran. The Cormallons weren't one of the Six Families, they were one of a dozen or so that claimed to be the "seventh."

"You have a preference, Tymon?" he asked me.

"Any day is fine."

"Sokol? It means getting up before everyone else."

"Any day is equally vile."

"Very good, then. Glad to have you with us," he finished, bowing yet again, and then he went off to fetch more water.

When I got to the front of one of the lines, a woman who said her name was Carabinstereth, with an extraordinary heart-shaped face and slanted blue eyes, upended a jar over my head. She did it with enthusiasm and grinned when I yelped. "Cleanliness is one of the Eight Virtues of Private Life," she pronounced, mischief in those alien eyes. Her hair was cut like a round cap on her head—shorter than I'd ever seen a woman wear it on this planet.

"Discretion is one of the others," I said, when I could talk again.

She clapped me on the shoulder. "A scholar," she said happily. "We're going to get along fine, Tymon." She wiped my face and handed me the towel. "Run along and don't miss breakfast."

I used to really be a scholar, you know. No, dammit, I still was one, in spite of not quite making the doctoral requirements. Wasn't my *Riddles, Proverbs, and Folktales of Ivory* being suggested for the Cross-Cultural Myths and Legends program?

Thoughts like this popped up from time to time like armed guerrillas in my path. Here on the High Plateau they seemed particularly alien and foolish. And pathetic.

Breakfast was outside in the damp grass, where a great slab of meat was roasting over an open cookfire. I thought I recognized the carcass from our wagonload. People were standing about talking, sitting on rocks or on one of the low, crumbling walls of gray stone that went all over the grounds. I spotted Ran eating alone and sat next to him.

"Maybe if we told these folk our House name they would offer us for ransom," I said.

He shook his head, his mouth full of breakfast meat. A minute later he said, "I don't want the Cormallon treasury losing any more money because of me. And think what it would do to my reputation."

"Still, living out our lives in the Northwest Sector has very little appeal for me."

"It's more serious than that. We were mistaken for Stereth Tar'krim and Cantry back in Shaskala. If I call attention to us now—well, I don't want the Cormallon name associated with treasonous activity in the Northwest Sector."

"Maybe we could turn this band in. You'd be a hero then, wouldn't you?"

"I don't want our name even to be in the same sentence as treason in people's minds. You don't know how nervous the Prime Minister can get. Entire Houses have been destroyed before this."

I looked around at the outlaws chatting over breakfast. "Do they consider this treason? I thought it was simple robbery and murder."

"When it comes to the Northwest Sector, there's a very fine line in people's minds. Armies have come out of here before. Annurian started quite a fine little revolt before he was captured."

"Well, and he went on to have a good career, didn't he?"

Ran dropped his bone on the ground. "Annurian was bought off with an army post because he was too successful. Nobody anticipated he'd go on to become Prime Minister."

An argument broke out near the fire between Lex na'Valory

and a tall woman in violet trousers. Ran continued, "And I suppose his ex-comrades were less than pleased when he began arresting them. No, the whole issue is one we're well out of."

"Except that we're not."

"Not yet."

I ripped into a small leg bone, thinking that there was a time when that sort of thing had really disgusted me. I said, "When is Cormallon going to find us? Before Stereth gives up on us, I hope." Ran pursed his lips. I said, "What? Won't they be looking? Don't tell me the First of Cormallon can disappear and nobody will notice."

He said, "We might have gone anywhere from Shaskala. Even assuming we'd be traced to Shaskala to begin with—we did use assumed names there. The last time anybody from Cormallon heard from us we were in the capital."

"But they knew where we were going!"

He looked sour. "What did you tell them?"

"I told Herel not to expect us back for several weeks, and to have Spet handle the household accounts. And I told Kylla we were going away on a project . . . and a honeymoon."

"I told Jad to take care of local matters and consult my cousins in Mira-Stoden if anything difficult came up. I did give him a number to leave messages at in Shaskala—but Jad is good about these things. Shows proper initiative. Short of an armed revolt, I don't think he'd disturb me." Ran brightened. "There's a full family council meeting, all branch heads required, on the fourth of Dumare. If I don't show up for that, it'll definitely draw attention." Then his face fell again. "But that's double-edged. If I don't show up, the representatives will start to wonder about my reliability. Particularly in view of my jaunt to Athena. Not to mention the . . . trouble . . . I was in before."

"But when they see it wasn't your fault, that you were kidnapped—"

"Careless, then, as well as unreliable."

We pondered this in gloomy silence.

"Dumare is three months away," I pointed out.

"And we definitely have to escape by then."

"You don't think it can be *sooner?*"

I must have sounded ready to strike out over the hills

there and then, for he crooked a smile. "I'm only telling you what it can't be later than."

I pictured us out on the plateau, in the rain and wind, with a troop of bandits on our heels. And no sense of direction, no knowledge of safe streams or safe people, no money, leagues from anywhere . . . and with some angry police waiting at the end of the Shaskala Road. Assuming we could even *find* the Shaskala Road.

Carabinstereth appeared. She tossed her bone toward the fire in a perfect arc and said, "It's a beautiful day, isn't it?"

The dawn mist had mostly dissipated and the afternoon mist had not yet closed in. It was still fairly cloudy, though, and I'd become used to clear skies and straw sunhats on this planet. I said, "I can't wait to see what your bad weather is like."

She grinned. "Sokol, I had the honor of dousing your companion this morning in the wash line. If you'll both come with me now, I'll have the honor of showing you our mounts so they can get used to you. Stereth says you're to join us tonight."

Ran's eyes were wary. "Join you in what?"

I don't know if you—my imaginary average Standard reader of this—can tell, but if these don't sound like normal Ivoran names, it's because they're not. They're "road names," identifiers that all Sector outlaws pick up along the way. Using birth-names is considered bad manners, and sometimes grounds for being killed. Partly this is blind tradition, and partly it's due to the fact that the Imperial cops are not above threatening people's families when they feel it's appropriate. If Ran didn't want his real name coming to anybody's attention, you can imagine how people felt who had more to hide.

Here then are the outlaws I came to meet over the next few days—the names of the cantry tar 'meth, or "companions of the road."

The "Companions of the Road"

Stereth Tar'krim—grain thief or stealer of rice
Cantry—sidekick or companion
Des Helani—cheater at cards

Mora Sobien Ti—late-night woman (Prostitution is not a crime on Ivory, though—I found out later she'd been arrested on murder charges, but still don't know the story.)
Carabinstereth—hell on wheels (won't even try to translate this)
Grateth Tar'briek—escaped four times (from the army, now under death sentence)—literally, "four times of captivity"
Komo—bad breath
Lex na'Valory—bad temper (literally "without balance of humors")
Juvindeth—stubborn (literally, "one with no voice who insists on singing")
Lazarin—too clever for his own good
Paravit-Col—more lucky than smart (nickname from Ivoran traveling theaters, usually given to third son in plays)
Sembet Triol—nobly born
Clintris na'Fli—"too tight-assed to dance"—perhaps the worst of any of these nicknames. This was not used to Clintris' face. In the second person she was called "Natavrin," or "record-writer." She did have the neatest handwriting of any of the companions.

And last and least:
Sokol—anonymous
Tymon—foreign barbarian without manners

I suppose Cantry's name was the most generic, but it was also the most mysterious. She'd appeared with Stereth soon after he came to the Sector, and since they were always together, and nobody knew who she was—*Cantry*.

I'd wondered about translating these road-names into Standard in writing this—calling Stereth Tar'krim "Rice Thief" or Cantry "Sidekick"—but I'm afraid that would give you a more colorful idea of things than what really existed. Some of them may have had an anecdotal basis, but these were mostly just used as names, like Linda or Edward back home.

I did notice that there weren't any nicknames like "Killer"—nothing about murder. But then, Lex and Komo and Grateth had apparently killed any number of people in their combined fifty years of service, and I suppose it wasn't really worth mentioning as far as they were concerned. Besides, Ivory tends to treat crimes against property more seriously than murder.

As it turned out, what Stereth had in mind for us was a cattle raid. Cattle raids are the bread-and-butter of outlawry, or so they explained it to me. The company had robbed any number of homes, towns, and travelers, but they weren't wealthy because money is only good in how far you can spend it. People who sold to outlaws inflated their prices hundreds of times. Somewhere someone was getting rich, but it wasn't in Stereth Tar'krim's company.

Ran's two-thousand tabal retainer would not have done him a lot of good—not on the plateau, anyway. Cattle, however, would bring an adequate price at one of the temporary market towns set up all through the Sector; and what you didn't sell you could eat.

It was all very practical, they explained to us, as they helped us up on those huge mounts and we rode out into the mist and moonlight. Lex na'Valory rode behind me, and the mount behind Ran carried Grateth Tar'briek. Ran turned to look at me just before his mount disappeared behind the two twisted trees at the head of the outlaw's valley. *They're trying to get us too involved to get out,* the look said.

They're doing a good job of it, too, my look replied.

Smell, and confusion, and trampled grass; mostly smell. Sector cattle are mods, like our drivebeast and like Stereth Tar'krim's mounts; designed for life on the plateau, able to live on the short, moist grasses; and docile, with every trait of aggression removed. Ready to be led, literally, to the slaughter.

Actually, the relationship to the mods I'd used as drivebeasts in the past went farther than I'd thought. We reached the edge of an isolated ranch where twenty or thirty head of cattle appeared and disappeared in the mist, impossible to count. Now and then I could see the lights of a house, very far away in the distance. I sat on my mount, uncomfortable and uncertain of what to do, as the other outlaws moved forward into the herd. Deep, unhappy lowing came all around us. Lex na'Valory rode closer to me. In his hand was a length of rope whose other end was around my mount's neck. I supposed I should be grateful it wasn't around my own. When his head was near mine he yelled, "You're going to switch!"

"I'm going to what?"

He jerked his chin toward the herd. "We'll spot one of the leaders, and you'll ride it out."

The hell I would. "Why not kill me back at the fort?"

He looked disgusted. "They won't hurt you, they don't know how. You get on, you grab the horns—we've done it before. If it's one of the dominant bulls, they'll follow him out."

"You think I'm going to steer those horns like a groundcar? You're out of your—"

"We've done that, too. But you don't need to. When you're settled, I'll hand you this."

He held out a small drivebox in one hand.

Now I was really worried. Stereth had saddled me with an escort who was mad. "They're not implanted," I said, trying to state the obvious as forcefully as possible.

He nodded impatiently. "They were designed by the same company as your drivebeast. Most implants are only amplifiers. If you're on top of the animal, this works as well. I'm telling you, we've done it!"

I looked at the drivebox. It was very tiny for its type, able to be palmed in one hand, or even part of one hand. Simple directionals, and stop and go.

I looked back at Lex distrustfully. Of course, you could never tell what these Tellys imports were like; maybe the company *had* marketed all its mods on the same general design.

Three steermods came out of the mists toward us. Carabinstereth was beside them on a mount. "Take the lead one, Tymon!" she called. Far behind her, in the distance, the mists parted and I saw the lights of the ranchhouse snap off. My eyes must have widened because she turned and looked. "And hurry!" she yelled. She dug in her heels and moved out past us.

Maybe the people in the ranchhouse were just going to bed.

Still, there was probably a price on everyone's head here, and no harm in hurrying.

Lex maneuvered close to me, and when he judged we were in sync with the lead steermod he lifted me out of my saddle and held me on his own mount. This was unexpected, and my involuntary kicking made my mount gallop ahead, apparently what he'd had in mind. Then he pulled in closer and dumped me on the steermod. "Grab the horns!" he yelled.

I flailed for them and just got hold, after winning a long scrape down my forearm from one tip. "Are you ready for the box?"

"No!"

I held on for dear life. The beast moved like an earthquake. I wailed, "If I let go my knees for a second, I'll fall off!"

"I know!"

"If I fall off, I'll get trampled!"

"So be careful!" He kept holding out the box, and eventually I reached out one hand and grabbed it.

I was up around the mod's shoulders, one hand on one horn, my bare legs wrapped compulsively around him and my robe flying behind. I maneuvered the tiny drivebox up into the top of my palm and first joint of my fingers so I could at least partly get hold of the other horn. I could reach the buttons, barely, and tested the directionals.

They worked! If I'd had the attention to spare, I would have let myself be more relieved than I was. I did waste a second glaring at Lex. Who cared how docile these cattle were if I got killed under their feet?

"Come on," he said.

Hadn't there been some ancient Earth queen who'd ridden home from a cattle raid on a bull or a pig or some other legendary animal? This alien raid was an hour's wild ride, under the mists and the moons, through sudden clear pockets of small valley, to the two bent trees that marked home territory. Eight head of cattle were on my heels the whole way. We did all the outlaw tricks, riding through the poison streams and leaving clues that pointed in other directions.

It may sound romantic, but some things are best experienced secondhand. My legs were crying with pain in the first five minutes, but I didn't dare loosen my grip. My back joined in the general torture shortly thereafter. And of course, it's never pleasant to think you might die at any second. I paid no attention at all to those clever outlaw tricks; I just longed, wished, dreamed that I could be back at that damp fort, the site of my kidnapping.

At last we were there. I slid off into someone's arms—Lex na'Valory's, as it turned out—and my knees buckled as I tried to stand.

Ran reached my side at once. "I got in before you," he said.

"What were you doing?"

"I was on another dominant mod." He supported me halfway to the main hall of the fort, until I felt I could take a few steps on my own. "I brought in twelve head of cattle. How many did you bring in?"

"The hell with you, then," I said, and continued inside under my own power.

Stereth smiled an evil smile when I entered. He was pulling off his boots and his jewelry, dropping a long gold chain onto a crimson cloth beside his mat—Stereth liked to sleep in the main hall, though he and Cantry would disappear now and again for privacy. "Out courting tonight, Tymon? Did you have an interesting time?"

"You could have warned me about how I was getting home."

"I thought you and your sweetheart might enjoy a surprise."

"We barely know each other, Stereth."

"Yes, so he's said."

Cantry came out of one of the smaller rooms, stretching. She wore a mint green robe and bare feet. Apparently she'd been asleep.

I said, somewhat testily, "You missed an active night, Cantry." Subtext to Stereth: Do you play favorites with your lovers when it comes to handing out the unpleasant tasks?

Stereth got it at once. He said mildly, "My wife usually rides the chief steermod home. It takes a lot out of her, I thought she deserved one raid off."

Cantry herself was quiet, as usual. He said, "She's a tiny barbarian, like you. Suited to the job."

"You had Sokol ride one, too, and he's not a tiny barbarian."

He smiled again. "I thought it might help loosen him up. How about it, Tymon, do you think he'll start to be reasonable? —But I forgot. You hardly know him. How could you possibly judge."

I was going to start grinding my teeth if I stayed here much longer. "I'm going to bed," I stated, and walked, or rather staggered, toward the jumble of mats on the women's side.

"Good night," said Cantry.

"Pleasant dreams, cattle-thief," said Stereth. He didn't say it mockingly. He said it affectionately.

If I dreamed, I don't remember it.

Chapter 7

A hand on my shoulder woke me around dawn. For a second I was completely disoriented, not even knowing what planet I was on, or which I *should* be on. Then memory flooded back in a wave of relief—there was the crumbling stone wall, the pile of blankets; this was where I'd been kidnapped to.

There was still order in the universe. My life since childhood had been defined by being in places where I had no intention of staying.

Ran was bending over me, a finger on his lips. I looked around the hall; everyone else seemed to be asleep. I'd bedded down a little away from the other women, probably a reflection of my psychological state, so I ought to be able to move without catching anyone's notice. The room was still dark. The fire was making that start-and-flicker that meant it was dying. I got up very quietly, leaving my sandals, and followed Ran out.

The valley was cold and dark, and the grass was damp against my feet. I noted that Ran was not carrying his pack, just a blanket rolled under one arm. I said, "You're not thinking of running away, I hope."

"A feasible opening has not yet arisen." I knew that tone of voice, and he had a pleased look on his face for someone who was admitting a lack of control over the situation.

"Then why are we out here?" He dropped the blanket and put his arms around me.

"Because we haven't had one minute of privacy for what seems like years."

Good heavens.

"Are you sure this is a good ide—"

Ran kicked the blanket open.

* * *

A while later I said, "Weren't we taking a chance?"

Ran said smugly, "Nobody's visible to the night lookout until they get at least a hundred meters from the main building. I checked."

"Not very efficient."

"It wouldn't be, in a prison, but the place was built for defense. You've got dirt on your cheek. Hold still."

He rubbed it off with his thumb. I said, "And after the hundred meters, the whole band would be after us. We'd have to leave without alerting the lookout."

"I know."

I waited for further comment, and when it didn't come I said, "There's not a lot of point in being kidnapped with a sorcerer unless he can use magic to get you away."

He sighed. "I have been thinking about it, Theodora. First, there's the lookout—"

"A seeded illusion. Non-grounded to our persons, aimed at just one target. Those don't take massive preparation."

"I'm glad to see your studies continue. All right, I've considered it, and there are risks . . . but if we know who'll be on duty on a particular night, it'll up the percentages in our favor."

"So—"

"Well, where do we go after we leave this valley? I hope you have some idea, because I don't."

I was afraid he'd say that. "I was hoping you had some trick I hadn't gotten to in the texts yet."

"I'm sorry, but you've had the full survey course. The rest is just detail."

How depressing. I spoke from my scholarly past: "We need to gather more data."

He checked them off on his fingers. "Nearest towns, roads, friendly and unfriendly areas. Or rather, this being the Northwest Sector, *neutral* and unfriendly areas. Maybe we can get to a farm and pay off one of the people there to travel to Shaskala and call for help."

"Huh. Let's hope they're willing to work on credit. Stereth's got all our cash."

"And he's a lot nearer. Easier to turn us over to him, if he's looking. And from what I hear, these Sector farmers stay pretty close to home. If there's a drivebeast, he's probably needed on the farm. So would everybody else in the family be, too. But at the moment, it's the only thing I can think of."

And we didn't even know where the good water was. But we were both aware of that, so I didn't say it. I turned my head and saw Ran looking thoughtfully past his toes at the beaten grass path that led to the lip of the valley. Gloomy though our conversation was, it was comforting to have him there. I hated to have us break up and deal with the outlaws on our own. "I suppose we'd better get back inside," I said, not very forcefully.

"It's barely dawn, you know. They won't start rattling the waterjars for another couple of hours."

I turned on my side and rested my head on one elbow. "Tell me about when you were young," I said, since he almost never talked about it. And I suppose I didn't want to think about the Northwest Sector for a while. "Tell me what it was like growing up in Cormallon."

Ran stirred underneath the blue outer robe he'd put over us. "You really want to hear about that?"

"You never talk about it."

"I didn't think you were interested."

We were lying in a niche between the side of the fort and the stone gutter that ran around the inside of the old defense wall. The valley was becoming gray in the distance, the hills visible. I felt guilty suddenly, because I'd always thought it was Ran who wasn't interested in that kind of thing.

I said at random, "Did you know this used to be a monastery of fighting monks?"

"Yes. The Torasticans. They're extinct now."

"Why are they extinct?"

"Monks shouldn't fight in obvious ways."

Whatever that meant. Sometimes Ivory felt as close and familiar to me as my first private bedroom; and then I would run up against these alien bricks.

He said, "This is the rectory wall we're lying against."

"Tell me about when you were young," I said.

"Well, for one thing, there were more people in Cormallon then. My parents were still alive and my mother's sisters were always coming to stay with us. I had a thousand aunts."

"You did? Where are your aunts now?"

He thought about it. "They stopped coming when my mother died. I could still visit some of them, I suppose."

I snuggled closer. "Tell me about your thousand aunts."

So he did. One story brought up ten others, and the valley turned greener. It was a clear morning, as the plateau went. We still had plenty of time before the others would be up. I listened to golden childhood days, days blessedly ignored by all the grownups but for a few of the servants. He told me about the afternoon in the midst of the spring rains, when the goldband Evina had stripped the covers off all the tables and cushions and bedding and hung them outside, because there was a story that spring rain was especially pure.

"She wasn't supposed to do it," he said. "But Kylla and I were thrilled. We wandered the halls all day, looking at this new country. Cormallon seemed totally different, all the rules suspended. We made noise everywhere and ignored the aunts who told us to stop because—after all—everything had changed. And the rain kept hitting the roof like an army of arrows."

He stopped suddenly and said, "I didn't mean to make it sound like an oasis of sanity. There were plenty of bad spots, even in Cormallon."

"I don't believe there are any islands of sanity for children. Each generation warps the next into something like those trees over there."

Ran looked at the pair of grotesques on the valley's horizon. "They're beautiful trees."

"They're not happy trees, though."

"No, they're not happy trees." A gust of wind made a violent dance around the corner of the rectory, and Ran pulled his cloak more tightly over me. "Considering the few things I've heard you drop about your childhood, I'm amazed you turned out as relatively normal as you have."

I looked at him with some surprise. I didn't remember mentioning anything at all about my childhood, certainly nothing significant, and in any case it never crossed my mind that he would remember it if I had. Ran's concerns were circumscribed by Cormallon, or so I had always believed.

I pulled the robe up around my neck. "Tell me more about your aunts."

"Umm. Did I ever tell you about the time my Aunt Segunda went to Veerey in disguise and fell in love with a jabith player? Well, she claimed she fell in love—" fell into madness, is the literal Ivoran term, "—but it turned out she just wanted to learn to play the jabith. You see, my father went crazy whenever there was music in the house—"

So far, all Ran's stories of his eccentric aunts and cousins tracked back to his father in the end. I wondered if he was aware of this, or if it was a pure coincidence. I'd seen a picture of Ran's father in a room in Cormallon: A stocky man with a white-gray beard, standing with a stiff grace beside one of the Cormallon horses. He wore an old-fashioned lace inset on his inner robe. The dark eyes looked out with formal reserve, giving nothing away.

It occurred to me suddenly that Ran never gave anything away either. This was a little alarming, but after all there was no need to read too much into it, Ivory being the place it was. How would Ran look with a beard? Facial hair was a rarity here, the Cormallons must be a throwback.

I realized with a start that Ran was still talking. ". . . the konoberry tree along the walkway in the courtyard. You've seen that tree, Theodora, remember it? Near the pool? Those dark purple berries would fall down onto the pavement and then they'd be ground under the heels of everyone passing by. Every year the walkway would be covered with purple stains—they'd fade little by little with every passing rain, and usually the last of them would be gone by Anniversary Day. My Aunt Sella was obsessed by it; she wanted the walk kept clean for some reason, I guess it offended her sense of order. She'd always be stooping down picking them up—I can still see her, she was a skinny little woman with a green outer robe, with her hair coming out from its pins—and she'd pick them up one by one and put them into a little bag and give them to the cook. Konoberries are poisonous, you know."

"So the cook had to throw them out."

"No, the cook had to boil them down and put the essence into the poison vials we keep in the basement preserve room. Stacks and stacks of konoberry poison we had, and whoever uses it?"

"Poor cook," I said, snuggling closer under his arm. "Was that Herel?"

"No, Herel came the next autumn. This was a regular cook we hired from the capital. We found Herel while she was running off to the Sector for strangling her landlord, didn't I ever mention that?"

"Great Paradox, no."

"I could have sworn. Anyway, one year my father caught Aunt Sella's obsession and said that this summer, by heaven, we would not have a purple walkway. We all had to tiptoe around the clumps of berries and we were forever sweeping them off into the flowerbed—surreptitiously, of course, as my father didn't believe in Cormallons handling brooms."

"Your father sounds a little unpleasant."

Ran seemed surprised. "Does he?"

"Every context you've ever mentioned him in was disagreeable."

"He was . . . difficult to live with. It's true we were all more comfortable when he was away, which was most of the time, come to think of it. Although, he was a very friendly man when he was drunk. That's why we loved holidays."

The earnest way he said it made me start laughing. He said, "What? Come on, tymon, what's so . . . " Not getting an answer, he rolled over on top of me and tried to change the subject.

A voice said, "Well, well. Talk about overactive!" We pulled apart hastily and sat up. Clintris na'Fli stood about three feet away, her hands on her hips, her usual look of faint condescension in her eyes. "Keep this up and you'll get my vote for Couple of the Sector."

You haven't really experienced all the ups and downs life has to offer until you've been caught in the act by Clintris na'Fli. Her solid body was planted there as though she were ready for attack, and now she folded her arms like an unhappy schoolteacher. Our local bluestocking raised her head and called, "Well?"

Gods of scholars protect us. Stereth was at the end of the rectory wall, and the others from the band were emerging from the fort, looking sleepy but highly interested.

Ran jumped up, taking the outer robe with him, and I quickly adjusted my clothing. *Go on, Ran. Explain this.*

"Ah . . . Stereth. I didn't know you took this interest in your band's private quirks."

"It's a small place," said Stereth, who was clearly starting to enjoy himself again at our expense. "We gossip." Damn, he wasn't even bothering to hide his smile. "No personal relationship, Sokol? Barely know each other, Tymon?"

The company gathered around us in a circle. I'd wondered occasionally what it was like to be the focus of attention of a whole group of people . . . now I knew. It makes you think about throwing up. Not that they appeared liable to violence; on the contrary, they were far too amused.

"It's the first time we've done anything like this," said Ran, although it would probably have come across better if he weren't fastening up his robe while he said it. "It must have been the stress of being kidnapped. We're really just casual lovers."

"Ha!" said Clintris. "I listened to you talking about an aunt. Casual lovers don't spend time discussing their relatives."

Ran's temper started to show. He said, annoyed, "How would you know what casual lovers do?"

Clintris' brown face went a shade darker, and somebody snickered. She lunged forward, slapped Ran in the face, and turned and walked very quickly out of the circle.

Ran's hand had gone up with automatic swiftness when she slapped him, but it hung there, frozen. He dropped it slowly. Then he turned to Stereth and said, "I'm sorry. I didn't mean that as a reflection on her sexuality—just her spontaneity."

Stereth rested one booted foot on the side of the stone gutter. "I'll try to broach the subject with her delicately, should the opportunity arise." He gestured toward the low wall. "Care to sit?"

Ran spoke warily. "Are we going to be here long?"

Stereth just kept his hand out in the direction of the wall, and Ran sat. Cantry came around the corner of the rectory then, holding her green robe with one hand and something else in the other. She handed Stereth his spectacles. The bandit leader breathed on the glasses, rubbed them on the arm of his jacket, and placed them on the bridge of his nose. "Now," he said, in his precise voice, "this is what we're going to do."

"I'm not—" said Ran.

"You'll have your chance to talk in a minute. Since neither of you seems willing to approach the pool of truth even at gunpoint, we'll skip the issue. Fine—you don't know each other."

A voice said, "Does this mean I can court the barbarian?"

"Shut up, Des." His glance didn't even waver. "Now we're going to come at this problem from the opposite angle. Tymon."

I looked away from Ran, startled. "What?"

"I'd like you to do a job for us."

"I'm not a sorcerer."

"You don't need to be. We've got twenty head of cattle in the outbuilding. If we keep ten to slaughter as needed, that leaves ten to dispose of. I want you to take them to Kynogin Market Town and sell them for us."

"You want me to sell stolen cattle? I wouldn't know how to go about it."

"Carabinstereth will fill you in. She did it last time."

I thought about all the reasons why this was a bad idea, and the pause lengthened. Apparently he was going to keep us all standing here until I gave the right answer. I said, "I wouldn't know how to control ten head of cattle to get them anywhere—"

"Carabinstereth will fill you in."

I didn't know whom to sell them to, or for how much, or whom not to approach, or what to say . . . I knew the reply to those objections, too. "Will somebody come with me to help?"

"No. You'll be alone." I opened my mouth and Stereth added, "Sokol will stay here."

Ah. Stereth's little way of letting us know that he understood the situation—that I'd have to come back if he kept Ran.

Still, that wasn't to say he would kill Ran if I tried to leave the Sector. He wanted a sorcerer, after all, and maybe I could get to a Net link and call for help. . . . I looked at Stereth, standing there calmly. How many people had he killed already in his career? Then I looked at Ran, and plain as anything I told him telepathically, "Come on. Let's just admit it and get it over with."

Ran's eyes were stubborn. I sighed and said, "So. Carabinstereth will fill me in."

Later, when we were walking in to the wash line, Ran said, "Have you run the cards?"

"How could I? The only privacy I've had since we got here was just now. And we were occupied."

"Do it. Do it as soon as you can. And then come straight to me."

Half an hour beyond that, while I was toweling down, I went to Ran and said, "What happened to the cook before Herel?"

He looked blank. "I beg your pardon."

"You said you took Herel on as cook the next autumn. What happened to the first cook?"

"You do get caught up in side issues, tymon."

"I just like to know how the story comes out."

Ran is willing to humor lunatics as long as they're in the family. He said, "The first cook died. She opened a jar of konoberry poison instead of a jar of blackberry jam. They look just the same, you know. And organization is especially important when it comes to poison."

"I suppose it was a lesson to everyone in keeping labels straight."

"It was. The most annoying thing from my father's point of view—aside from having to find a new cook—was that we now knew that somewhere in the rows and rows of konoberry poison jars there was one that was actually blackberry jam. It made you think twice about using any of them."

Possibly there was a moral in there somewhere. I said, "So what did you do?"

"Do? We didn't do anything. I suppose they're all still down there in the basement, unless Herel threw them out."

Carabinstereth, it will not surprise you to learn, filled me in. She also accompanied me as far as the main road to Kynogin Market Town. We walked side by side through the cold, rough plateau grass, the strap of one lead in my hand, the other, to another mod, in hers. Eight more steers plodded docilely behind us.

Her blue eyes were inlaid in her pure Ivoran face like mosaic chips, alien to the rest of her features. They sparkled with mischievous energy. "You don't look too downcast, Tymon. I guess your lover must be good in bed, for a man."

"I, uh, we barely know each oth—"

"I know that, my dear barbarian, you've made it very clear. Are you married? What's your real name?"

It's not the custom to ask anyone in the Sector what their real name is, but I should have known from Carabinstereth's hair and clothing, not to mention her outlaw eyes, that she paid little attention to rules.

"What's *your* real name?" I returned.

She stopped and bowed with a dramatic expanse of arm, nearly causing a three-steer pile-up. "Lesrenic Beredar Chaniz, honored by this meeting. I used to be a captain in the Imperial Honor Guard."

I stared. "I didn't know they let women in the Imperial Honor Guard."

"Oh, they prefer it, Tymon, when it comes to escorting the young and innocent daughters of the Six Families. Guard and escort oftentimes become quite close, you know, and as far as the families are concerned, a bit of female intimacy is all to the good—preparation for life, you might say. Whereas a trip over the mattress with a strapping male guard would be a nasty thing. You see the subtle difference."

"Yes," I said. "They don't have good contraception on this planet."

"Got it in one, light-eyes."

"But your manners—" I stopped. *Are so provincial*, I'd been about to say. Country was written all over them.

"Yes?"

"Nothing." I felt my face turn warm. "Did they really expect you to bodyguard all alone? Without any backup?"

"What backup would you mean, Tymon? Not old-fashioned muscular *male* backup? Really, I would have expected a more forward-looking attitude from an outworlder—"

I had the feeling she was laughing at me, but I also had

the feeling I may have offended her. "I'm sorry, Carabin, I don't know much about that sort of thing."

"Never mind, light-eyes. Five years of dirty tricks in the Provincial Women's Auxiliary, and you'd never feel the need for *backup* again, trust me. That's where I used to—ah. Here we are." She stopped and pointed down the long gray slope to a dirt track that curved away through the mist and sunlight. "It'll take you straight to Kaytown. When you reach the track, I advise you to turn around and look at this hill. Fix it in your mind so you'll know where to leave the road on your way back." She patted her steermod companionably, slipped the lead up into its collar, and said, "You are coming back, aren't you, Tymon?"

"So far as I know," I agreed.

"Because Stereth can be a bit overly severe at times. I like him, but the truth is the truth."

"I'll make every effort to be back by dark."

She handed me a waterbag and said, "Best of luck. I'll stake out the hill after sunset, in case you get lost."

So the blue-eyed outlaw troublemaker went one way, and the barbarian using the assumed name went the other. I felt very funny walking down the slope, and I realized with some surprise that this was the first time I'd been left totally on my own since Athena.

Ninety minutes later I reached a grove of those objects that on the plateau pass for trees; I stopped and tied the leads of the two collared mods to some branches. "Keep this to yourselves, fellows," I said, and I knelt down and took my deck of cards from the pouch around my waist.

The grass was cool and not as wet as I'd feared. I shuffled the cards and thought about our present situation. Then I drew out the first, Ran's identity card.

A picture of one of the branches of the Silver River, far to the southwest. A dam holding back the natural force of the water, creating an artificial lake. Spear Dam: I'd heard of it before. Trees on either side, very pastoral. I touched it with my finger.

The dam groaned. The water pounded against it, the lake rose, and rain fell from the sky in sheets, worse than the spring outpours. The great blocks of stone moved slightly from the enormous pressure. So far no great devastation had struck, but it was only a matter of time.

I sat back and watched the picture become stationary again, the sky return to painted blue with fluffy cotton clouds. I'd never come up with an identity card like that before. In fact, I'd never turned up that particular card at all. Ran must be under a greater strain than I'd thought—unless this card was the future. The deck did not always pay attention to tenses.

I could always comfort myself by interpreting Spear Dam as simply representative of Ran's stubborn nature. It's not that he was always as immovable as those giant stone blocks, but there were five or six topics in the universe that it was pointless to argue with him on, and his family honor was one of them.

Let's see what else we had. . . . I put down a second card.

The Hunter. A man in brown holding two bloody groundhermits by the neck, gazing out past the borders of the card as though in search of further prey.

Stereth, looking younger and more conservatively dressed in a leaf-colored robe and boots, was moving through the darkness of a southern town. The trees lining the streets were lush and green, not the orphan children of the plateau; you could almost smell their fragrance, the rich scent of Ivory summer. The sky was clear and full of stars.

He moved quickly from one shadow to another. At the city wall he was joined by two other shades. One of them limped; both carried bulges that suggested they were armed. Stereth pointed to the top of the wall and then to his left, and they all moved off that way. Was this his escape from Tammas? It was always a strange sensation, viewing the past . . . from what I'd heard, the men with him were doomed.

Suddenly the colors changed: Stereth was older. He wore the purple jacket with gold thread that I'd already seen. He was standing in a white stone room—not the fort—and Ran walked into the frame of the card. They were arguing. Stereth had hold of Ran's arm.

I bent over, as though that could let me hear better, moved my finger and lost the window. The card turned back into the Hunter with his catch.

And what did that mean? That scene had to be the future, and Ran was definitely alive—although Stereth was not pleased—which meant either that I would make it back from Kynogin, or Stereth wouldn't kill Ran anyway.

This didn't really help me, I decided. I turned up a third card.

The damned cliff again. Beware of heights. Disgusted, I scooped up all three cards and replaced them in my pack. I untied the leads and brought my stolen cattle out again to the track. "Come on, friends," I told them. "You know as much as I do." The docile followers lined up right behind their misled leaders, all trudging to the butcher together. Misled was the right word, I decided. And we all went off to Kynogin Market Town.

Chapter 8

In the Sector, even the most permanent of market towns are temporary. Kynogin was the dowager of these, being all of fifteen years old, at the juncture of three main roads, and with structures of actual wood and stone.

I saw it first from the hillside—a carpet of colored roofs and tents, ropes of lanterns, and tall decorated pillars signifying two clean wells. It was just as much a patchwork maze once you got down into it. Aside from the three roads that cut through, there were no streets to speak of; just clusters of tents and small buildings that sat where their owners had decided, on the spur of some moment ten years back, to put them.

Cattle were a normal, even boring, sight in a market town. I passed a farmboy with three mods for sale, and notices on the walls about auctions to come. Stereth's contact was supposed to be in the blue-roofed cabin at the edge of town, where a small tacked paper said, "Ocel Formix, dealer and auctioneer." I hit the flat of my hand against the door.

A plump man wearing the beaded cap of a na' telleth organization poked his head out. "May I be of service, gracious visitor?" Then he peered down at me and said, "Cantry!"

Let me repeat: Cantry and I look nothing alike.

He frowned. "You're not Cantry."

Now he seemed wary. I said, "Ocel Formix?"

"He's away at the auction in Dace."

Oh, splendid. How is it that plans always work out this way? No one had told me what to do if Formix wasn't there.

I said, "I have ten steermods here." A bare statement of fact couldn't get me into too much trouble.

"Yes, so I see." Apparently he was going to confine himself to pure observation also.

I sighed. "How much?"

"Uh, do you have statements of ownership?"

I was tired, I had had a bad week, and I refused to bring these damned animals back with me again. So I looked him in the eye and said, "Cantry has the statements of ownership. She must have forgotten to give them to me."

He licked his lips nervously. I waited. Then he said, "Well, I suppose I could give you twenty tabals apiece. As long as this Cantry can get the statements to me in the next few days."

"Terrific. Let's do that."

So he counted out two hundred tabals, and I re-counted them, because anybody who belongs to a na' telleth organization is a little funny in the head to begin with. Then he said, "Will you be staying for the Governor's speech?"

"I hadn't planned on . . . what speech? Is there a Net link in this town?"

A Net link! I could call Kylla. If anybody could get us out of this mess discreetly, it was Ran's remarkable sister.

The dealer chuckled. "A Net link on the plateau? Who would ever spend the money?"

"But you said the Govemor—"

"The Governor is here. Surely you didn't miss the platform they set up at the crossroads for his speech."

I was glad I'd gone no farther into town. The Governor had never actually seen me; still, I'm a great believer in keeping a low profile. "I'm not sure I can stay, gracious sir," I said, throwing in the honorific a little belatedly. There was no point in forgetting our manners just because we both seemed to be criminals.

"Ah, that may be so . . . gracious lady." He appeared a little hesitant to award the title to a barbarian. "But I think you'll find the Governor's speech of interest, if I might recommend it."

"I'll see if I can fit it into my schedule," I said, and we both bowed. Then I left, still not entirely sure I'd done the right thing.

I came out of the dealer's house facing the rust-colored stone wall of the building opposite, and stopped short.

A poster of Ran's face hung there. Not even a sketch,

but a full 2-D repro, and I could see the top of the robe he was wearing when he was arrested in Shaskala.

"Great gods of scholars and fools, protect and preserve us." I said it out loud, and stepped toward the poster. The words STERETH TAR'KRIM were big enough to see from here. Also the amount, ten thousand tabals.

"It's sort of ironic, isn't it?" asked a voice by my ear.

I started and saw Des Helani standing there in a somewhat less flashy tunic than was his usual wont. He smiled his slow, dry smile and said, "Considering how hard he's trying to disassociate himself from our little group."

"This isn't funny, Des."

"I didn't say it was funny. I said ironic."

I looked him up and down and said, "Aren't you ruining this little loyalty test by your presence?"

"Oh, piffle—" said Des.

Piffle?

"Everyone knows you're in love with that sorcerer boy. Although all things considered, you might prefer a man." He leered in a friendly way. Des was probably all of three years older than Ran.

"Does Stereth know you're here?"

"What our glorious leader does not know need not concern him. Tell me, Tymon-of-mine, as long as we're alone . . . have you ever attended the races in the capital?"

And here I'd thought he was working up to a sexual proposition. "Which ones? —Not that I've attended any."

"The flyer races, of course, in Goldenweed Fields. Half the city goes there, sweetheart. Are you telling me you're not a follower of the Silver Stripe or the Jade Bar?"

The Stripe and the Bar are the two sets of flyer teams. He was right about half the city going there, especially when the rainy season was past, but I'd always felt that I'd lost enough money in my time.

"Gambling doesn't appeal to me, Des."

"What a waste. So I take it your friend Sokol doesn't go either? You spend your time together instead, tripping through fields of flowers, enjoying the fruits of innocent love?"

"We spend our time working, mostly." This was the truth. "You have a point here, Des?"

"I was wondering—in an abstact way, I mean—about the effect of sorcery on a flyer race."

I stiffened. "The people in the capital are dead serious about their flyer races. They live and die for them."

"So I assume, from the amount of cash that changes hands."

"Great gods. I have no idea what the penalty for fixing a race is, but I would bet—"

"Decapitation, after being given to the flyer pilots. The decapitation is merely a formality at that point."

"Gods. And you bring this up like it's a trip to market—"

"Trips to market are dangerous, too, Tymon. That's why I'm here."

"I can see why you're here. And you can forget it. Ran has no intention of—"

"Ran?"

Kanz. Kanz. Kanz. Born idiot, got stupider as you got older. At least I hadn't said any last names.

"See here, Cheater-at-Cards," I said, scrambling his road name to bring out the meaning, "do you want to be friends or enemies?"

"Friends," he said at once. "I never want to be enemies."

"Then I think a little understanding, from one friend to another, would be in order here. All right?"

He smiled. "You only have to ask, Tymon. And I'm sure I can count on you to be understanding, too—"

"Pay him no mind, whatever he says," called a new voice. I turned and saw Sembet Triol walking toward us, holding a stripped sapling branch as though it were a weapon of noble antiquity. In his case, that meant he held it comfortably and tapped it against the wall of the dealer's house. He wore a dark blue-green hood and must have left his sword at home.

"Did the whole crew come?" I asked Des.

"I asked Sembet to keep me company," he answered reasonably. "I don't like to travel alone." Des didn't like to do anything alone; he got nervous without an audience.

"Boys—" I began. This is the outlaw version of "noble companions" and can be used to both men and women. "Have you heard anything about the provincial governor being here today?"

They looked at each other. Sembet pulled his hood down low. "No," he said.

"When I was walking toward the winehouse I noticed the center of town was pretty busy," said Des.

"The dealer told me there's a platform up at the crossroads, and there's to be a speech. He thought I should hear it."

Sembet asked, "Did he say why?"

"No."

Des said slowly, "I think we ought to go."

Sembet's eyes widened. "Isn't it enough that we took off without telling Stereth? You want to parade around in a crowd of potential informers, not to mention any number of provincial guardsmen? With a *barbarian* in tow? —No offense, Tymon."

Des said, "I've seen two or three barbarians here already. This part of the Sector is full of them, because of that deal Shaskala tried to make with Tellys way back when. Where do you think Cantry came from?"

"Cantry's description is in half the guard offices across the Sector!"

I said, "Then why the hell do people always think I'm her? We don't look anything alike."

They stared at me. "Is that a joke?" asked Des. "You could be twins."

"She has blonde hair!" I yelled.

"So she does," agreed Des, "but—" He stopped and looked at Sembet. "She does, doesn't she." He frowned.

And I suddenly realized neither of them had taken this into account before. It wasn't that they didn't know. But they were both Ivoran born and bred, and ninety-nine percent of the people they'd ever met had dark hair and dark eyes. Whatever that gestalt of visual cues may be that lets you look at a face and remember who a person is, *coloring* had never entered into it for them. They hadn't meant to belittle my sense of identity. They'd just been trained differently.

And I'd been trained differently, brought up in a heterogenous society. Pyrenese who didn't think nature had made them flashy enough would dye their hair and skin. It hadn't occurred to me that anybody else would use a different system to identify people.

My anger had left by the back door while I was working this out. "Sorry to be so touchy," I said.

"It's all right," said Des kindly.

"When the rains fall, the groundmarks vanish," agreed Sembet. "But I still don't believe attending the speech is a good idea."

Des said, "You can give her your hood."

Sembet's hand went to his hood as though he were protecting himself. "I wore it today for a reason," he said.

"A crowd of small-time provincials," said Des. "Come on. Whoever knew you before, they're not likely to be in this bunch."

Sembet looked at him. Des was treading very near the line here. Still, there was no point in pretending that he wasn't nobly born; he couldn't hide it any more than I could hide that I was a barbarian. He began untying his hood. "The *Governor* might recognize me," he muttered.

"We'll stay near the back of the crowd." Des took the hood from Sembet and arranged it over my head. "Allow me." He tied it just right, not too tight or too loose, and then gave the whole thing a slight tilt to the left. "Green is your color, Tymon."

"Don't I get a vote in any of this?" I inquired.

Des grinned. "Come on, friend, be a sport. You wouldn't let two of your best companions-of-the-road go off on an adventure by themselves."

"Be a sport," agreed Sembet. "Why should Des talk one person into doing something stupid when he can talk two?"

What an invitation. I said, "Des, Stereth should keep you behind bars when he doesn't need you." Des smiled, because he knew that meant I was coming with them. I pulled the hood farther around my face.

It took a while for the crowd to gather sufficiently. We were near the back, as Des promised, up against a records office just off the crossroads. "We should be in the road, where we can retreat if we have to," I said.

"Women," said Des. "You take them out, you give them clothing accessories, they're never satisfied."

This was addressed to Sembet, who was not amused by it. He was constantly scanning the crowd and a permanent frown seemed to have settled over his features. I said, "Is this really dangerous for you? Do you want to leave?"

"No," he said abstractedly. "As long as I pay attention, I think it'll be . . . Kanz." His eyes widened.

"What?"

Three men in official regalia were mounting the platform. Two of them wore the high blue felt hats of Imperial Favor, and one had the white silk sash of "honored public guest" tied around his outer robe. His hair was platinum-colored, tied in a very un-Ivoran ponytail, and his skin was fair.

"See," said Des, "no need to worry. There's even a barbarian on the speakers' platform."

Sembet continued to stare. At last he said, apparently to himself, "Why? Why come here now? I refuse to believe . . ."

"Who are they?" I asked, tugging on his sleeve.

"What? Governor Atvalid, of course, just as you said." He paused and looked confused. "And his son Vere."

"Well, what's wrong with that?"

Four men in dress-gold militia uniforms took their places at the four corners of the platform. Two of them raised slim horns that should have been gold as well, but were a dull bronze under the cloudy sky.

Sembet said, "Vere wearing the blue hat? And why isn't he at school? He was two years behind me, and I wasn't finished myself when—" He stopped, suddenly aware he was discussing his personal life. Just then the horns sounded, beautiful and clear in the cool air, more like the heralds of an evening of music than a call for attention.

So this was Vere Atvalid, the Governor's oldest son; engaged to the daughter of one of the Six Families and making them nervous thereby. And Nor Atvalid, the target of the investigation we'd been asked to run a short while ago in another lifetime. I stared openly at them.

Of course, Nor was responsible for putting Ran's face up all over the Sector, so he got no marks from me. Other than that, I had to admit he had a good, strong look about him, an air of honesty and competence. He looked as though he could do government paperwork and put his shoulder to the wheel of a stuck wagon with equal willingness, and equal success. Probably all a front, I told myself. For one thing, nobody gets to be a full provincial governor without kissing bottoms all the way up to the prime minister. Some people can get away with minimizing that aspect of Ivoran officialdom more than others, but even so. . . . Actually, he looked very familiar. Something about that bulbous nose, and those lines around the mouth. . . .

Good heavens. I'd seen him caricatured on an attention-stick only a few days ago in Shaskala. A stick that was pounded against a hard wood block several times a day in the best inn of the city, just in the nature of things.

Governor Atvalid was not a popular man. Hilo hadn't liked him either, now that I recalled. And yet he looked so honest and reliable.

As for Vere, he was . . . average. Tall and well-featured, but so are most Ivorans; black-haired, ditto; he did seem very young, though. Not necessarily in himself, just too young to be standing on a platform beside older men, with all this pomp and circumstance. The hat did not favor him.

"Is he a friend of yours?" I asked Sembet. He didn't answer.

Governor Atvalid stepped forward, touched the band at his throat, and his voice boomed out over the crowd. "Friends," he began, "and fellow subjects of our most glorious Emperor. I am happy to find Kynogin Market Town as busy and prosperous as when I left it last. May it endure as long as any city in the Empire!" There was some polite applause and foot-stamping at that. "The graciousness of your reception honors me. . . ."

I'll skip over that part. Floweriness and flattery are normal modes on Ivory, and in speeches they can go on and on. Somewhere in all the sugar and honey, Atvalid managed to convey that he and his entourage were making a circuit of all the major towns in the Tuvin part of the Sector (of which Kynogin was the jewel and cornerstone) in order to speak personally with the farmers, ranchers, and traders (who in Kynogin were the backbone of the entire Sector) so that he could present them with the principal gift of his House.

"Kanz," Sembet muttered when we heard that.

I flicked a glance at him and then turned back to the Governor, who was leading forward the barbarian. The platinum-haired guest, that is. The Governor said, "But first, allow me the happiness of making you acquainted with one who will be our ally, both yours and mine, in prosperity. Gracious sir Hippolitus, Pyrenese Trade Representative to the Northwest Sector."

To the Northwest Sector?

My jaw was hanging open. This made no sense. How could Pyrene be sending out representatives to minor areas of planets? And assuming Atvalid got the title wrong, or adapted it deliberately to please his audience—what the hell was a Pyrene trade rep doing out here in the back-end of nowhere? And what was he doing on a platform being introduced to the locals? And why—

Atvalid was going on. I made an effort to cut short a mental picture of Hippolitus leading a string of steermods into a cargo ship. That would be the most expensive meal anyone on Pyrene ever ate.

"I never asked you," said Des, "are you Pyrenese?"

"Shut up," I said.

"My friends," intoned the Governor, "Gracious sir Hippolitus, as representative of the Pyrene Minerals and Resources Board, would like to speak to you."

Hippolitus smiled. "I hope that I, too, may address you as 'my friends.' "

He spoke with a flat, affectless accent, the kind that comes from an implant, the same kind I used to have. If he left Ivory within the year, his memory of the language would start to fade.

My usual inclination is not to call attention to myself, but I wondered if he knew my friend Octavia, also a trade delegate. If I could get a message to her, and she could get a message to Kylla. . . .

"Carium," he was saying. "It is our hope to set up carium extraction pits, developed in partnership with you, the local citizens. We will be in sore need of people to fill the jobs that will have to be done, and I can promise a share in the profits to anyone who joins up."

Sembet said to Des, "Have you ever heard of carium deposits in the plateau?"

"No," said Des. "But then, I can't say I ever paid much attention."

The Governor took back control of the platform, after prolonged applause for Hippolitus. No doubt the word "profit" had done it. "But my friends," he said, "before this new era of prosperity begins, we must stamp out the ways of the past, the customs that shackle us to poverty and spiritual darkness."

Des, Sembet, and I looked at each other. Spiritual darkness?

"In other words, my friends, we must put a stop to the outlaw bands that prey on innocent citizens and bleed our province dry. Gracious sir Hippolitus has assured me that as soon as we can guarantee the safety of his people, the carium project will begin. I hope you agree with me that that day should be soon!"

A mixed response to this. Some enthusiastic supporters, I noted uneasily, and others holding back. There were plenty of people in the Sector who made a second living by fencing outlaw booty.

"In line with this," said Atvalid, "a bounty of one thousand tabals will be placed automatically on the head of any outlaw, whether specifically known to us or not. More importantly—" he paused for a sip of water from a glass that suddenly appeared in an underling's hand, "—I hereby make the capture of Stereth Tar'krim our first priority. And I promise a free pardon for any outlaw who performs his citizen's duty by turning in this thief and murderer to the Emperor's justice."

As of one mind, Des, Sembet, and I began edging backward through the crowd.

"To demonstrate the seriousness of my commitment," Atvalid went on, "I have named my own son, Vere Atvalid, as District Steward, with the express purpose of dealing with the outlaw bands. The success or failure of this noble enterprise will be on the Atvalid House alone. The results of success, naturally, we will all share in, as will our Pyrenese friends; the results of failure, the displeasure of the Emperor—" had there been a slight pause there? "—will be on my House only."

"The man is suicidal," I heard Sembet mutter, as we neared the corner of a winehouse. "And to drag *Vere* into this—"

"Heralds!" ordered the Governor, and a giant poster was unrolled down the front of the platform.

It was a new color poster of Ran, his head about six meters high.

"Great Collective Spirit of all Mankind," I breathed. It

was an oath from my childhood that I had forgotten entirely till that moment.

"Tymon, come *on*," said Sembet, pulling at me.

The crowd was thinning here. I walked quickly after them, keeping my head down.

Chapter 9

I was in a mood to walk. I was in a mood to walk for several hours, in fact, without company to distract me, but unfortunately Des and Sembet had brought a wagon that they'd left behind at the dealer's.

Out on the lonesome road, the fairy-tale mist coming down yet again, they began to converse worriedly.

"Stereth will have a fit," said Des.

"He won't have a fit, that's the awful thing," said Sembet. "He'll take it absolutely coldly. And then tomorrow he'll have some new plan we'll all have to follow."

"That's what I mean by a fit," said Des.

I sat in the back of the wagon. "Will he be worried about somebody in the band turning him in?"

"Nobody will turn him in," said Des shortly, without looking around. "Nobody's that crazy. Stereth would kill them."

"If he's in the Governor's jail, I don't see how he can kill anybody."

Sembet shook his head. "He'd find a way." He spoke as one who dismisses an obvious truth, the better to concentrate on those things that really needed attention. "You know what this is going to do to our contacts?"

"I don't want to think about it," said Des.

"You see," said Sembet to me, "the *band's* all right. It's our town contacts we have to worry about."

"A thousand for each of us," said Des gloomily. "Every time we say hello."

"Our payments are never going to match that."

"What's wrong with Atvalid, anyhow? He's going to bankrupt his *trelid* treasury."

"Des!" said Sembet. "There's a lady present."

Des looked at him in disbelief from the security of his lower social class. "Harmless alliteration," he said.

"It's all right, Sembet," I told him. "I've heard worse in the capital marketplace every day before breakfast."

"The world is going to chaos when women can wander through the market before breakfast. I don't know what your family was thinking of. Do you want to ride up front, Tymon? The seat's probably more comfortable."

"If it's all right with Des."

Des grunted. I squeezed in between them and tapped his shoulder. "Are you mad at me?" He made another dissatisfied sound, but did not elucidate. "What's the matter?" I asked.

If he weren't a grown man, I would call it a pout. "You told me to shut up. Back at the crossroads."

I blinked; had I? "I'm sorry, Des," I said, patting him on the arm. "I was so involved with the speech. It must have just come out without my thinking."

He perked up. "That's all right, Tymon. You were distracted."

"Why don't you tell me about your racing scheme," I suggested, and he launched into it without further encouragement. Des is one of those people who blossoms under constant positive reinforcement. I don't mind that, actually; I prefer treating people well to treating them badly. There are enough confused individuals in the universe who don't seem to respect you unless you cut them up from time to time.

He told a good story, too. He *would* start to inch his arm around my waist now and again, but I removed it in a nice way. I never had a brother, but there was something brotherly about Des, for all his virility; now that I knew him I was about as attracted to him as I would be to a large, friendly dog. I didn't say that, though.

"Cut the nonsense," said Sembet from the back the third time Des tried to get physical. "Tymon's spoken for, anyway."

I let it pass. Unsuccessful deceit is just depressing.

We pulled onto the fort's grounds and I could see Ran standing at the end of the rectory wall. "Hey, Sokol!" Des yelled, grinning. "Did you know how popular you—"

I put my hand over his mouth. "If you don't mind," I said, "I'd like to break it to him gently."

He considered, then shrugged. "I wouldn't do this for anyone else."

"Yeah, Des, you tell that to all the barbarians. Thanks." I poked him on the arm and jumped down.

Ran was walking warily toward us. "What? What is it?"

My eyes went to the hillside and he turned to meet me there.

When I was sure we were out of earshot I said, "New problems." I told him about Atvalid's speech and the growing notoriety of his own facial features. He took it more calmly than I'd expected.

"If they're cracking down on the bands, that's all to the good. There'll be fewer outlaws between us and the edge of the Sector when we leave, and these people will be too busy with problems of their own to follow us."

"Ran, your face is all over Kynogin Market Town, and I'll bet it's in every major market town in the district. You're famous. You're the star outlaw of the Northwest Sector. You're the House of Atvalid's number-one priority. Maybe I haven't been expressing myself clearly—"

He got that faint look of smugness that meant he wasn't quite ready to share what he was thinking. "Tymon—"

"Wipe that look off your face, Ran. You can't take two steps in public without everybody rushing off to claim Stereth Tar'krim's reward. You'd better have a *reason* for being cheerful—"

"I do," he said. "It's eleven days till we'll be half-married."

Just when I was ready to yell at him.

He went on, "If we weren't in full view of the fort, I'd kiss you." He said it as though his mind were on that subject even now.

"Why do you do this?" I asked, hearing my voice go low. "Do you like to drive me crazy?"

"I checked in the cookhouse, behind the main building. They've got flour and sugar for the cakes."

"Do you think this is quite the time, when we're being held prisoner by a band of outlaws and you're wanted by everybody in the Sector?"

"Why postpone it? We'll only have to do the whole four

months again later. And you might come up with some tymon-reason why not. You might need to run off to Athena for three academic credits or something."

"I'm trying to talk to you about matters relevant to our survival." It was good to know the stuff for the marriage-cakes was there, though. "Did you check the vanilla? . . . Never mind. You're changing the subject. Three academic credits, my maiden aunt—you're planning something and you're in that I'm-keeping-it-to-myself mood. Keep up with that attitude, Ran, and you can forget the damned marriage-cakes."

"They've got vanilla."

"What about eggs?"

"Iffy. Some days yes, some days no."

A voice called from the main building. "Sokol! Tymon! Come in for the meeting!"

I recognized the voice as my guide of the morning. As we started down the hill, I said, "Carabinstereth says you must be good in bed."

"Really? And I haven't even demonstrated for her yet."

Ran had a streak of cool humor, but he rarely gave into it in front of anybody. It was just another of the things he usually kept to himself. I said, "Gods, you're cocky today. What are you planning?"

He smiled. At the doorway to the fort I stopped and said in a low voice, "I forgot. I ran the cards on the way to town."

"And?"

"Not much. You live for a while longer. Nothing about me."

"Well," he said, "what information you have is nice to know."

We stepped inside, and in a normal tone of voice I said, "Yes. Thank heaven I'm not the sort of person who keeps things to herself."

I'd thought the meeting would be a discussion of the news from Kynogin Market Town. This was not outlaw style. Instead I found people settling the details of tonight's party: Wine and bredesmoke pipes were brought out, and lots were drawn for lookout duty. Stereth did not approve of everybody getting drunk at the same time, apparently, and this rule was iron.

Carabinstereth handed me a stack of priceless painted winebowls. I laid them out beside a pile of battered wooden spoons and some cracked stewplates. "I don't get it," I said to her. "Can't the party be postponed, given the state of emergency?"

"It's the emergency that brought on the party, Tymon. This is the way we decide things. More efficient than a provinicial city council."

I looked at the growing pile of winebottles, bredesmoke bags, and general unidentified drugs. "Whoever's still on their feet at the end of the evening gets to vote?"

She laughed. "What a delightful thought. This sort of thing is too important to vote over—though I'd be interested in seeing the results of that kind of poll, Tymon. Zero votes, if I know my brothers and sisters."

"Then why the blow-out? A final kick of the heels before we all get arrested?"

"Keep your voice down when you say things like that. There are those who'd be mad at you for bringing bad luck."

Grateth Tar'briek joined us and gave me a quiet smile. "Though I wouldn't be one of them, little Tymon." His strong soldier's hands pulled the corks of three winebottles in succession, and he began pouring into the bowls.

"Supper's not ready," said Carabinstereth.

"So much the better," he replied. He ran a hand through his cropped hair, took a few swallows of wine, and said, "Ah." He pushed one of the bowls toward me.

"Thank you, but if you knew my pathetic tolerance you'd ask me to wait for supper."

"As you wish. But this is the way we settle problems, Tymon. Everyone who can, gets drunk. We talk about the problem . . . if we feel like it. Maybe we talk about the best vintage of Ducort red, or our past sexual histories—"

Carabinstereth made an exaggerated yawn.

"—or anything else we feel like. Sometimes very late at night a couple of people will start talking about how long it's been since they've seen their families, and we have to throw them out. We just talk. And then we all pass out."

Carabinstereth grinned. "And then, in the morning—"

"—when we're all feeling like kanz that's been left out in the sun—"

"—and we really don't even want to *know*—"

"—Stereth will get us together and say he's got an answer."

I looked at them both. "You're not joking with me?"

"It never fails," said Grateth Tar'briek.

"He's a genius," explained Carabinstereth.

"I see," I said a little blankly. Then I considered my two informants and said, "You both get along extraordinarily well."

"Old army grunts," said Carabinstereth fondly, linking her arm through Grateth's.

I said, "Lex na'Valory's from the army, too, and nobody seems to like him."

"Nobody ever liked Lex," said Grateth. "Not even his old outfit, from what Komo says."

"Not even his mother, from what Komo says."

"I believe Komo," said Grateth earnestly. Carabinstereth laughed, and he raised his winebowl to her lips and tilted some into her mouth. Clearly they were very, very old friends.

Suddenly I imagined what would happen if Ran and I got away, and Stereth's troop was captured by the provincial militia. I'd heard of flashbacks, but this was flash forward: A picture sharp as noonday sun on the capital streets, of Carabinstereth with the rope around her neck; then the pull, the changing color of her face, the uselessly kicking heels. Grateth watching, next on line.

I put my hands on the makeshift table. "What's the matter, Tymon?" I heard her say. "You look like a ghost. Grateth, help her to sit down."

I felt his arms around my waist guiding me over to the cushions. I let him help me down. Carabinstereth was at my side a minute later with a new bowl. "Water's in this one," she said. "You've had a long day, sweetheart. Somebody should have said what a fine job you did with the cattle. Drink up, now."

I drank. It was good water, from the well outside. On Ivory when you bring up well water you make a sign to propitiate the ghost of the well. That's not some kind of nature spirit, they don't believe in that sort of thing; it's the ghost of the person who will one day foul the well by committing suicide there, or being murdered. It's a future ghost, and the propitiation is to keep it farther in the future.

Besides, any ghost born of suicide or murder would be dangerously far from na' telleth, the proper spiritual state of not-caring. As I was myself.

Besides the people on guard duty, Ran was the only person who did not get drunk that night. Clintris na'Fli took a guard post voluntarily; she enjoyed disapproving of her fellows far more than she would have enjoyed drinking with them. Grateth and Komo played flute and tigis-drum. Halfway through the night, Cantry got up and began a slow dance with Paravit-Col while Stereth watched. Paravit-Col was the youngest in the band, and his movements were awkward but enthusiastic. The dance got pretty close in places. I was sitting in a corner trying to be an impartial observer, or as much as I can be on unmixed wine, and I was just a little bit shocked. This was not the custom anyplace I'd been outside the Sector. I kept glancing at Stereth, but he didn't seem anything but mildly interested—although I was beginning to realize that with Stereth it was hard to tell.

The flutesong and drumming finished and Cantry pushed herself back from Paravit-Col, sweating and bright-eyed. She'd already had several bowls of wine. I saw Stereth raise his own empty bowl and Cantry walked over, hooked up a bottle from the table as she passed, and poured him some more. She hadn't even been looking in his direction when he gestured. Then she gave him a kiss as strong as the unmixed stuff we were drinking, bending down to do it as though it were a continuation of the dance.

This was a relationship I was not going to figure out. Not that I was in any position to pass judgment.

When Cantry's head went up, Stereth said, "Tymon."

I was startled. "What?"

"Come here and sit next to me."

I went warily. He patted the pile of brocade cushions beside him. He said, "How many bowls have you had?"

"One."

"Have another." He handed me the bowl Cantry had just brought over.

"Uh, thank you." I took a sip.

My eyes found Ran across the room, sitting with his arms across his knees on his bedding. He was watching us.

Stereth said, "What did you think of the speech today? I've heard from Des and Sembet."

I wondered how much he'd heard from Des. If Des had reported on Ran's first name, Stereth would already be working on finding out his last. I said, "The Governor seems pretty serious about this."

"It's been festering for a while," he said. "What about the new Steward?"

"He looked young and uncomfortable."

Stereth gave a distant smile. At the other end of the hall the fire crackled. The air was full of bredesmoke, making it hard to think. He said, "Your Sokol isn't the most friendly and outgoing of men."

My gaze went to Ran, and on its return I looked with some fondness to where Des lay sprawled on his back contemplating the roof. Apparently he was still conscious, just noncommunicative. He'd already brawled with three male outlaws, propositioned every female member of the band he'd run into, including Cantry, and defended Clintris na'Fli to his disbelieving friends, saying that she would be quite attractive if she'd only take her hair down from that net and wear some decent clothes. One of the men he'd punched earlier stepped carefully around his outflung arm. "He's no Des Helani," I agreed. "But I think he'll stay the course longer than Des would."

"If I may be forgiven the question, what is it you see in him, anyway?" A heavy cloud of bredesmoke lazed by, and Stereth coughed. Behind the spectacles his eyes were red.

I smiled. "Well, he's considerate, when it occurs to him to be . . . are you all right, there, gracious sir?" He was coughing again. "You've already gone through a whole pipebag. Maybe you've reached saturation point."

"Go on," he choked out.

"He's a true partner. When times get hard, he doesn't whine or blame it all on somebody else. He takes me for granted."

"You consider this a positive trait?"

"He takes for granted that I'll be as competent and as loyal as he is. He's got a nicely honed sense of irony, though you have to watch for it. And he never forgets an obligation."

"Ah." Stereth picked up a discarded pipe, drew in the smoke meditatively, and this time he didn't cough. Then he said, "That's it? That's everything?"

"Well, not quite." I hoped my pale barbarian skin wasn't flushing, though it probably was. "What does Cantry see in you?"

His lips quirked. "I don't have to guess, I've been told. Cantry fell in love with me the moment I bashed my head on the underside of a table in the county records office in Shaskala."

A few hundred questions came to mind, such as what were you doing under a table in the county records office? But what I asked was, "You mean you were injured and she felt sorry for you?"

"No, no. I was hiding from a contingent of Shaskalan cops, and when they'd left the room I miscalculated and put my head up—and *bam*. Just a little bump due to my own clumsiness. Cantry was watching, I felt like an idiot. She told me later that her heart left her body and flew straight to me at that moment."

"Because you bumped your head."

"Apparently. She said she'd liked me before, but this was the thing that pushed her over the edge."

He held out his pipe and I took it. "Relationships are strange things."

"You have the right of it there."

"One of the old storytellers—the lady Murasaki—says there are those moments, moments that aren't visible to other people, when 'a person whom you at all times admire suddenly seems ten times more beautiful than they were before.' "

"Of course. You haven't felt that? —Just breathe in the smoke and hold it in your lungs. Don't work at it."

I exploded in a series of coughs. "No, I've never—never felt—damn—" There didn't seem to be any oxygen left in my body. Stereth took the pipe away.

"Never mind," he said kindly, and I didn't know if he was referring to my failure with bredesmoke or my emotional life. "Some other time you'll have more luck." He slipped the pipe into a pocket. "Was the Governor's son wearing the blue hat when you saw him?"

I blinked, disoriented. My own eyes must be turning red by now. "Yes."

"Then he's already entered officially into his post. Surprising we haven't felt the repercussions before this."

"Maybe you have. Maybe the provincial militia are lining up outside even now."

He smiled. "That much I would have heard about."

Ran had stretched out on his pallet and was pretending to sleep. He still faced in our direction.

Stereth said, "So let me have the tymon's opinion on how we should proceed."

I was surprised. "I don't know anything about the Sector. Only the folk stories."

"The story of Annurian and the Purple Band? Annurian and the Dragon Rumor? It's good to know at least one person escaped his sentence, even if he's a legend."

"He used to say those stories were exaggerated."

There was silence, and I looked up from my empty winebowl and realized that I hadn't meant to say that.

"You know Annurian?"

It's not that it's a secret, but there's no point in bringing it up. I still wear Annurian's bluestone pendant. On the whole I'd rather not discuss it, if you don't mind.

"I knew him in retirement. He's dead now."

"He talked to you about the Sector."

"A little. I had questions about what I'd heard. I always need to know how stories come out."

I was surprised that Stereth believed me, and impressed. It wasn't a claim you would necessarily believe, based on the facts, and given Stereth's position he must be used to lies in all forms. This thief and murderer must have an extraordinary degree of sensitivity to know who was telling him the truth.

He was quiet. After a moment he said softly, "So, then, did he tell you how the stories came out?"

"Some. The ones I asked him about."

"I can tell you how this one will come out." I looked at him. His face was blank behind the glasses. "We're the most successful band in the Sector. We've stolen more cattle, more tabals, more transportable wealth than . . . anyone now living. But we're not working toward a goal, a pardon, some kind of imagined prosperity. We're postponing death. No one here will see their families again."

The wine was making me feel sick. Stereth's voice was low and none of the others heard him; there was laughter and singing in the room. I felt as though I were trapped in some bubble of silence with a condemned man. With a condemned prophet. It was too heavy to bear, but following this path of logic would lead to Ran lending his talents to the band, our only exit closed.

I said, "Other people have escaped the Sector. It happens every now and then."

"It's happened three times, not counting Annurian."

Students of history are rare on Ivory. His voice went on, inexorably clear. "Three revolutions have started in the Sector. They all started with outlaw bands who grew into small armies. After they took everything they could take on the plateau, they marched on Shaskala and on the towns in Tuvin Province, and started down the coast. Three times in nine hundred years."

Down the coast means toward the capital. In each case the Emperor panicked, or did the expedient thing, depending on your point of view. On Ivory, revolutions never topple governments and institute democracies; when they become a threat they're bought off by the Imperial Government. Nobody ever celebrates the date some army liberated its first city . . . because the armies have always turned around happily and gone home as soon as the money and favors were heaped on them. And nobody has ever started a revolt yet on this planet that was based on an actual conception of the rights of humanity; it was always their particular rights that held their attention.

Venn the Pirate was the last before Annurian, and he was six hundred years ago. He was more immediately successful than Annurian, too. He didn't bother negotiating for his men and stepped right into a ministership.

I laughed. "Maybe Ivory has the right idea. Anywhere else there'd be fighting in the streets and general massacres. You know you've won on this planet when the Emperor sends the Prime Minister to ask what it is you want."

"I don't think he's on the way to ask us, Tymon."

"But it can be done. Annurian got a pardon and the prime ministership, in the end."

"Annurian was a martial sort of man. A general. I'm no Annurian."

"Battle isn't the only means of waging war. I mean, there's politics. Public opinion. The point is really to annoy the Emperor anyway, not kill people. Look at the Water-Margin Heroes. The smugglers of Tarlton."

"I've never heard—"

"And of course, Robin Hood."

"Robin Hood?"

"Talk about a public relations triumph. He robbed all the time, and people loved him. He didn't even have to pay them to help. They wanted to because he was a hero. And even if it didn't happen just the way the stories tell, the fact that the legend has had such a hold on people's minds—"

"Wait, wait." He poured me more wine. "Start at the beginning."

I looked down at the bowl. "I shouldn't. Everybody here has more body mass than I do."

"Never mind about that. I want to hear about Robin Hood."

I took another sip. "Oh, you like folk stories, too?"

"I can't hear enough of them," he said, in a tone of absolute seriousness.

But my mind went back to the alcohol. "You're doing so much better than I am. Although you did give your last bowl to me. How much wine have you had?"

"None."

I considered that. "But you went through a bag of bredesmoke."

"Other than making my eyes red, bredesmoke has no effect on me. It's some kind of biochemical eccentricity."

"Wait a minute. You're the only one at the party who isn't drunk." I said it accusingly.

"Sokol isn't drunk."

"No," I said slowly. "That's true. And do you know what? Sometimes I think you and Sokol are alike. I'm not sure how you're alike, but I don't think . . . I don't think it's in a good way."

"Robin Hood."

"What?"

"You started to tell me about Robin Hood."

"Oh, yes. Well, it starts in a beautiful greenwood called Sherwood Forest, where it never seems to get wet or snowy . . . which considering the geographical location, I consider most improbable." And I told him about Robin Hood. I'd done three papers on Robin Hood back on Athena, and I had him down cold, regardless of how much wine I'd put away.

I don't remember passing out. In justification, I must say that I think the bredesmoke clogging the air had something to do with it. And I slept the sleep of the stoned and the innocent, having no idea what Stereth would do with this harmless little story.

This is what happens when an outlaw kidnaps a scholar of myths and legends.

Chapter 10

They did try to wake me at some point in (I think) the morning; but I resisted, and after some distant discussion I was permitted to enjoy unconsciousness for a few hours more. When I finally got up, I found the fort busy, without the aimless conversation and cardplaying that were the usual custom between robberies. I stopped Carabinstereth, who was hauling a large sheet of glass with colored lines on it, and said, "What's going on?"

"Can't talk now, Tymon," she said. "Got to get this up."

Ran was nowhere to be seen. I washed and wandered outside to see if there was any food to be had. The day was gray and cloudy, with pockets of mist hiding the trail that led to the hilltop. As I stepped outside, a wagon drew up from the mist, with Clintris na'Fli in the driver's seat. It was an open wagon, a canvas cloth covering a mass of objects in the back; Clintris dropped to the ground with a thud, nearly skidding on the wet grass. She saw me and followed my glance to the wagon. "Where's Stereth?"

"I don't know. I just got up."

A raised eyebrow expressed her opinion of my lack of discipline. I said, "You were on guard duty. You didn't drink as much as I did."

"If I had, I could handle it better than a tymon."

Clintris didn't say the word with respect and affection.

She went on, "Call Stereth and tell him I'm back."

"Find him yourself, *Clintris*."

Her face darkened. I might be the only person who'd ever called her by her nickname to her face, but she'd heard it before. I don't know what would have happened next, but fortunately Stereth appeared at the door. "Good," he said, putting on his glasses. "And right on time. Did you get everything?"

"Nearly. There weren't enough hammers."

He was pulling the dropcloth off the back of the wagon. There were bags and bags of some unidentified material, about the size of large sacks of flour. There were shovels, picks, hammers, and other hardware; a militia light-rifle; and . . . was that a *bathtub?*

It was. A huge metal country bathtub, big enough for three people. Five, if they knew each other well.

Behind me, Des' voice called happily. "Just what we need!"

Stereth turned. "No doubt you mean the shovels and hammers."

Des made a face and dismissed these references to physical labor with a wave of his hand. "We can *heat* the water that goes in here!"

"Enjoy it while we have it," said Stereth. He was counting the bags.

Ran appeared at the doorway, looking a little pale. Stereth glanced up from the bags and met his eyes. Ran turned and went back inside.

I followed him in, hearing footsteps just behind mine. I touched Ran's arm, realizing only when he whirled around that Stereth was right on top of me. Ran said, "Now that you're acquiring all these things, you won't need any assistance."

It had the rhythm of a conversation only lately interrupted. I stepped out of the line of fire and watched them both.

"All the more," said Stereth. "Now that the wheels are turning, your contribution will be even more valuable. Now it won't be wasted on some two-bit thievery."

"Am I supposed to feel flattered that my talents will be used on something more seriously harmful?"

"Yes, you should. You'll be making history. Look around you; nobody here wants to be your enemy. We know that powerful and complex sorceries require preparation. We'll provide you with any material you need. We don't have Net access here, but I think we can fill any other order you make."

Ran's temper was rising. "Do you know the penalties for using sorcery as a weapon? For using it in any manner deemed treasonous by the Emperor?"

"Decapitation. What of it?"

"Decapitation for the entire family! Not just the guilty party!"

"But nobody knows your family, Sokol." Stereth smiled. "So you have nothing to worry about, do you?"

Ran didn't answer. Stereth said, "Unless you think we'll figure out who you are. But we'd never share the name of a member of the band with anyone, not even if we were all standing on the collective scaffold."

"No?"

"No. Not if they were a member in good standing."

Ran's eyes narrowed. "Has it occurred to you that I could agree to your terms and then sabotage your project? Only a fool would try to blackmail a sorcerer."

"When you come up with something that hasn't occurred to me, I'll let you know." His voice was like an icepick. Des had joined us; now he put his hand on Stereth's arm.

Stereth let out a breath and spoke calmly. "Well, the day is young. You can join the others working on the roof, for now."

Des said, "I beg your pardon? The roof?"

"There are thirty bags of quick-set in the wagon outside. Let's see if we can do something about these leaks, shall we?"

Des spoke hesitantly. "You mean, climb up on the roof and do things to it?"

"*Repair* it, Des. Times are changing. We need to be able to do other things besides steal." After a moment Stereth added, "Not that I have anything against stealing."

Des said, "Couldn't we kidnap a carpenter?"

Stereth patted him on the shoulder, walked over to the fire, and clapped his hands. "Everybody! Friends, we need to talk."

Des whispered to me, "Means *we* need to listen." His hands disappeared into his jacket and he sauntered over toward the fire.

I looked at Ran. "You know what this is about?"

"I'm not sure," he said. We joined the group at the fire.

Grateth, Lex, Komo, Carabinstereth—the ex-soldiers were standing in a knot with that easy physical confidence I was learning to associate with them. Carabinstereth's foot rested on somebody's pack. Clintris na'Fli was by the doorway, standing awkwardly, as she always did. I suddenly recalled a voice saying, "You don't live enough in your body." Advice I'd gotten a few years ago, on my first trip to Ivory; I think I've gotten past that point now, but although Clintris was older than me, her mind and body were clearly not even on speaking terms.

Cantry, Paravit-Col, Mora Sobien Ti. Juvindeth and Lazarin, from last night's guard-duty. Des and Sembet Triol, on the other side of the fire. Everybody I'd met so far was here.

Stereth said, "Don't worry, this will only take a few minutes, then Komo and Paravit-Col can go back to look-out. You need to know that I'm making some changes."

Some uneasy looks in his audience. He grinned. "*Voluntary* changes. Anybody who doesn't like them is free to leave; and this time, I'll even provide transport to Tarniss Cord's group up at Deathwell. No bitching about being tossed out on your own."

Now the looks were more wary; what could possibly be coming? He said, "First, consider what we have here. We're a bunch of small-time outlaws, living from run to run. Oh, sure, we're the best around; but what does that mean? As sure as I'm standing here, each of us is going to end up with a neck snapped by the Imperial collar; that's assuming we don't die during a run."

Somebody muttered, "Gods, Stereth." Several people turned away. This was not the kind of talk his audience wanted to hear, and the logical way he was presenting it was clearly only horrifying them more.

He asked, "Has anyone here ever met an old outlaw? I haven't." He waited a minute then said, in a more gentle voice. "I'm not waiting for that to happen. I've made other plans. You can come along with me, or not; it's entirely up to you."

I wondered if that was how he presented his case to the men he'd escaped with from Tammas District Prison.

Des said, "What plans?"

Stereth took off his glasses, polished them, and replaced them. It took at least thirty seconds. Nobody moved a muscle.

Stereth said, "I'm not going to go into detail now, particularly since I don't know who's staying. But what I propose to do is to follow in the footsteps of Annurian. I'm going to annoy the powers-that-be until they offer me a pardon—me, and anybody who's with me." He smiled. "I'm going to start a little bit of a revolution."

A dozen people started to talk at once.

"—only a handful of us!"

"We're no army!"

"—no weapons, no training—"

Stereth waited, then raised a hand. They quieted and he said, "I wouldn't even try this if I didn't have a plan. You'll have to take my word for that; have I been wrong so far?"

Silence. Stereth said, "But what I'm going to be doing will be more dangerous than any run we've ever been on. That's why I'm giving you a chance to back out now. —That doesn't include you, Sokol. You stay."

Grateth spoke up. "If they declare us a rebellion, they'll *torture* us before execution."

Des always supported Stereth publicly, but I saw him nodding, a horrified look on his face. Apparently Grateth was speaking for Des' innermost soul with that point.

"You can leave if you choose," said Stereth. "But anybody who stays is in for the long run—all the way to a free pardon. Or the scaffold. Whichever way it goes." He paused, then said, "Speaking for myself, I have no intention of dying. At any time."

Carabinstereth laughed. She said, "I'm in."

"You don't have to decide immediately," he said.

"Kanz, why not? You're not an altruist, Stereth; you wouldn't be doing this if you didn't have the odds already figured. I'll hitch up to *your* wagon, sweetheart, and let you find that pardon for us both. Gods know, the ride will be interesting."

"I'm in, too." It was Sembet Triol. "She's right. What have we got to lose?"

They all started to declare in. I decided it was a tribute to Stereth in a way; they must have a very high opinion of his abilities. Either that, or they weren't sure he meant it about transporting any backers-out to another group. Komo was one of the last to commit himself. He stepped forward, and with a roar of bad breath he cried, "Let's do it! What can they inflict on us that we don't already face?"

Des was standing next to me by then. "Intense physical pain," I heard him mutter.

Stereth turned and said, "Des? You're the last. Are you in?"

"You know me, Stereth."

"Yes. I do." His lips quirked. "All right . . . brothers and sisters. From this moment on, we have a mission."

I hadn't been asked to declare myself. This was a relief in one way—I'd been worrying about it, but Stereth evidently recognized that if Ran was going to hold back it would be a good idea not to push me—yet at the same time it meant we were staying more in the category of "hostages." More in the expendable category, that is to say.

"This does not reassure me somehow," I said to Ran later, as twilight rolled down the side of the valley. "But maybe it's a good sign. They'll be too busy to care about us."

"Are you joking? It's a hundred times more dangerous for us to be here now, if *he's* serious." No need to ask who *he* was.

"How do you mean?" I asked, with more than a trace of edginess. How much worse could things be, after all? And did I really want to know?

"If anybody finds out that two Cormallons were here, involved in out-and-out sedition—"

"Oh, the damned Cormallons! The family, the family, the family! The Cormallons can look out for themselves, they have for a thousand years! What about *us?* We're the ones in danger!"

Ran looked at me, surprised. "The Cormallons *are us*," he said.

I had a feeling I'd horrified him deeply. But I was sick of all this care and tenderness expended on his House—I wanted some of it expended on me. Or, at the very least, on us. When we died of foul-water poisoning on the plateau, I suspected that the Cormallons would not be in the forefront of my mind.

He said, "We'll have to leave at once."

"What do you mean, at once?"

"You know the route to Kynogin now—"

"That's all I know! Aside from the fact that your face is

plastered across every market town in the Sector. What were you planning, cosmetic surgery?"

"A planted illusion—"

"A planted illusion has to be cast individually for each recipient. As soon as we meet more than two other people, you won't be able to hold it. Do you think I've forgotten what you taught me?"

He kicked a stone out of his way with more force than necessary. "I know it's dangerous, but we have no alternative. Look, tymon, we have to separate ourselves from these people! Great bumbling gods, a deliberate rebellion against the Emperor? The more distance between us and them, the better!"

"I thought we'd agreed that we needed more information before we could try an escape. Nothing's happened to change that, and something may have happened to get us to stay longer."

"For what possible reason would we stay?"

"Well, what if Stereth gets his pardon? Then we'd be free without any trouble."

He repeated, dangerously, *"What if Stereth gets his pardon—"* The words came out with a kind of rumbling rhythm, like some sort of force building up to something very loud and messy.

Just then a voice called, "Tymon! Sokol! Mora'd like you to give her a hand, Tymon, and Carabin's wanting you in the stables, Sokol." It was Sembet Triol, walking out into the twilit valley like an illustration from a story, the ambient light glowing from his face.

I looked at Ran's face and saw the portcullis come down. How did he do that so quickly? Ran was rarely angry, and never in front of outsiders. A cold politeness was the most they ever saw. I touched his arm and said, "We'll talk about this later."

He started to follow Sembet back to the stables. "There's nothing to talk about," he said to me.

Politely.

Eight days passed. Ran, Des, and Sembet stripped to the waist and sweated up on the roof, even in the cool air of the plateau. Toiling side by side with someone of even higher birth than he was seemed to silence Ran on the subject of appropriate employment. Mora Sobien Ti and Paravit-Col knocked apart some of the stone from the fort outbuildings and carried it to the roof for them to use in the repair work. After the main roof was secure, they went on to do the cookhouse and the stable.

Our "discussion" concerning methods of escape was not continued. For the time being we both avoided the topic, sticking to day-to-day essentials of life in the monastery-fort.

I was helping Mora one morning, carrying some of the stone we'd cannibalized from an unidentified shed, when I looked up toward the cookhouse roof. The sun had come out for an hour, the way it does in the Sector, without any warning; the constant breeze was ruffling the long grass. Des, the tallest of the three, was bending over the crest of the roof, scooping sealant from a bucket. Sembet was kneeling there with a trowel, evening it out around the stones. Ran stood on the edge of the roof where a pulley had been rigged to take up the stones we were bringing. I sent up the new pile and he hauled it in, waved, and carried it to Sembet.

They were all young, competent, and absolutely alive; and I found myself thinking that it was almost worth being kidnapped by a bunch of outlaws to enjoy the sight of three men I liked with their shirts off. Then I chastised myself at once. Frivolous thoughts like that were not going to get us anywhere. Nevertheless, I turned to Mora and heard myself saying, "It's good to be alive, isn't it?"

She looked up roofward, grinned, and trudged off to get some more stones.

"We should have saved the main roof for last," said Des that afternoon. "Now that we're practically professional builders, we could've done a better job."

"You think you've got the hang of it?" asked Stereth. He was stretched out, his head in Cantry's lap, for all the world like a respectable and worriless citizen on his day off.

Des said, "Sembet and I can mix the quick-set in about five seconds a bucket, and set it for any damn hardening time we want. And he's an artist with the trowel—in two years, I don't think you'll be able to spot where we did the repairs."

"What about Sokol?"

"Sokol's not bad either," said Sembet Triol from where he sat, exhausted, by the doorway. "And he knows it, although I don't think he'd admit it."

"He'd make a good *apprentice*," said Des wickedly.

Tired though he was, Sembet was polishing his ceremonial sword again. He said, "Are we going to be hiring ourselves out as a troupe of itinerant house-builders?"

"No, Stereth, no," said Des, in honest warning. "I couldn't do this for a living. You're a friend of the heart, but that would be asking too much."

"Des, believe me, I will never ask more from you than you can perform."

"You're always telling me I can do anything."

"And you always agree."

Granted that these were dangerous people, I was going to miss them when they were all executed. The odds against Stereth's getting a pardon for any of them were wildly remote.

Stereth sat up, kissed Cantry's hand, and said, "Des, come and join me for a while. I want to draw you some pictures."

He'd done this with several members of the band already. I watched as Des went and stood over a large pane of glass which Stereth drew colored lines on in washable marker. He dropped the sheet of glass over what looked like a map.

Then Ran entered the fort, heading straight for the waterjars to clean the sweat and sealant off his hands. He paused near Des and Stereth and watched them quietly for a moment before continuing on his way.

I joined him. "Know what's going on?" I asked in a low voice, nodding toward the pair.

"Not a clue."

"Didn't Stereth give you some idea when he was pressuring you to join up?"

"He spoke in generalities." Ran wiped his neck with a washcloth. He glanced over at the bathtub, where Paravit-Col and Mora were splashing happily. Ran didn't bathe with strangers.

"Why were you late? Des and Sembet have been in for an hour."

"Clintris na'Fli made a pest of herself until I agreed to work on the roof of the coop."

This was cause for surprise in more than one direction. Ran performing voluntary manual labor for a member of the band? Not to mention the fact that he didn't even like Clintris. My surprise must have showed, because he smiled. "No point in the birds being miserable. They hate wet."

"I didn't know it was Clintris who took care of the messenger-birds."

"She likes them better than people, I think." He threw the washcloth down and strode over to his pallet.

He stretched out and I sat next to him. I hesitated, then said, "Know what three days from now is?"

"The moon-and-a-half," he said. Bless his heart. "I've been thinking about it. I don't know how we're going to cook the cakes, or get any privacy either."

"Maybe we should postpone it."

He sat up. "No, no, no. Put that right out of your mind, tymon."

Everybody has plans, and nobody wants to let me off the hook. Not Stereth, not Ran, not Kylla when it suited her, not the Athenan embassy officer. Some of these people are quite fond of me, but they all have no hesitation about disposing of my life. In fact, the closer they are, the more willing they are to do it.

We sat there and I watched the two bathers in the tub. Paravit-Col was young, everyone's kid brother, with a charming lack of confidence and a taste in clothing that was even more flashy than the band's usual. Mora Sobien Ti was one of the oldest there, maybe in her fifties by standard reckoning; gray-haired, but with a good face and figure. They might have come from almost any part of Ivory, from any family, from opposite ends of the continent and social structure. You couldn't tell by their accents. They'd been in the Sector too long and their language had followed the evolution to "road speech." But they sprawled in the hot water with the ease of old family members, violating more than one Ivory taboo. I supposed that, eventually, being cantry tar'meth broke down a lot of barriers.

Ran sat stiffly on the pallet. I could feel the warmth of his body, and also the tension. Whatever being cantry tar'meth did, I could tell he wasn't going to let it happen to him.

"Wake up, Tymon," said Stereth's voice. "We're going on an adventure."

I opened my eyes to see his boots near my hand. "It's the middle of the night," I said.

"No better time."

People were starting to move about softly, pulling on their clothes, splashing water on their faces. Des, Lex, and Carabinstereth—the three people who'd been invited up to the glass sheet the longest—were already dressed. Stereth nodded to Lex and he went out, no doubt to open the stables.

"I don't want to go on another cattle raid." My voice sounded like a three-year-old refusing to eat her porridge, but just the same I meant it.

"Fine, Tymon," said Stereth, humoring me.

"I mean it!"

"We're not going on a cattle raid. Satisfied? Now get up."

Even Ran was pulling on a short outer robe, but I sat there. "If we're not going on a cattle raid, where are we going?"

"Wherever we're going," said Des, "you'll be the only one not dressed for it."

"The hell with you," I said, without anger, and began feeling around for my socks.

"You're mean when you wake up," said Des.

A short time later, booted, jacketed, and semi-aware, we were lined up by Stereth for inspection. He shook his head. "What a group. You know, I didn't get these gray hairs back in Tammas District.'

"So you've told us," said Mora.

"It's true. It wasn't until I met you lot that I learned what worrying is. Being Stereth Tar'krim's taken years off my life."

Mora made a rude noise. Although I didn't analyze it at the time, standing there with the band I felt a sense of closeness, the sort of thing Ivorans tell you you're supposed to feel with a family. I didn't know this either, but that kind of warmth was common among outlaws just before a run. We were all aware that something dangerous was coming, but I wasn't frightened. Well, I was somewhat frightened, but it wasn't anything I couldn't handle; my situation seemed humorous rather than desperate. People laugh a lot more before a run, and I didn't know that either.

"Everybody breathe," said Stereth, and there was laughter. I was surprised to realize I *hadn't* been breathing.

"And don't get too excited," he went on, "because this isn't the main event. It's only a rehearsal."

Gods, I was almost disappointed. What was wrong with me, anyway?

He said, "It's time to fill you in on what we're going to be doing. In ten minutes we're going to ride north to where the Mid-Plateau Road leads into the Shaskala Road. At some future time, two groundcars are going to come down that road from the west. Each car will be carrying anywhere from seven hundred to eight hundred thousand tabals." Seeing the looks of shock on his listeners, he said, "It's the quarterly tax money from the northern farms and ranches."

"Gods, Stereth, are we going to steal that?" The surprise on Paravit-Col's face made him seem about twelve years old.

"Yes."

"But a *groundcar*—we can't attack a groundcar. We've only got mounts and wagons—and knives—"

Stereth smiled coolly. "And the cars will be armored, too."

"Gods!"

Des spoke up. "Stereth's got this all planned out. It'll work. Would I be going if I didn't think it would work?"

Stereth said, "You all declared yourselves in. I told you it would be more dangerous than the usual run."

Lazarin said, "But groundcars—"

"I anticipate zero casualties from this," said Stereth, in his accountant's tone. "If I'm wrong, if anybody gets hurt, I'll re-open my offer of safe passage to the Deathwell band. Nobody has to go along with it who isn't comfortable." They glanced at each other. "But if I'm right, and we're successful—I don't want to ever hear any opposition from anyone again. We're going to be busy, and I don't have time to spend fighting my own people."

They began to nod. "All right," said Paravit-Col.

"I want your road-oaths on this," said Stereth.

There was silence. Then Carabinstereth said, "You have mine."

"And mine," said Komo.

The other ex-soldiers followed suit, and then the rest of the band.

Nobody asked for mine. I was relieved. My feelings were also hurt.

Outside, the mounts were waiting in the gathering mist. A wagon was ready as well; Clintris climbed to the driver's seat. I heard Grateth's voice say, "What about prisoners? There'll be two men in each car, that's militia procedure."

Stereth's voice came back: "If one or two are quick enough to surrender, we'll hold them for ransom. Otherwise, it's too dangerous. We'll kill them as swiftly as possible."

I dropped hold of my mount's lead and it stepped back, startled. Somehow I'd only been anticipating danger to myself.

No, I thought. No. I can't take any more responsibility like that. I just can't.

I was halfway back to the fort when Des caught up to me. "Sweetheart, what's the matter?"

"I can't go."

Some of the others were joining us. Carabinstereth and Mora, Lex and Lazarin appeared out of the mist. I could just make out Stereth behind them. Ran was nowhere to be seen, and I found myself hoping he hadn't chosen this minute to try an escape, because it would really be just too much for me to deal with right now. Of course, Ran would never have ridden off and left me there, but I was too keyed up to be thinking properly.

"I can't go," I said again. "I'm sorry."

"What's the problem?" asked Des.

"I'm an Athenan scholar," I declared, reverting to the only classification from my past that I'd ever consciously chosen. "I don't kidnap people for money, and I don't kill them."

Nobody told me I was being an idiot. They all just looked at me, and several of them turned to go about their business. As he was attaching a knife sheath to his belt, Des clapped me on the shoulder. "Everybody has these minutes, Tymon. But don't live in the past. It won't get you very far." And he went back to his mount, as though the matter were ended.

Ran was here by now. Stereth waved to the others and they went away, but he stayed. Stereth came over to me and said, "Have you ever killed anyone?"

I suppose I could have lied, but I nodded.

"A stranger? Or someone you knew?"

"A friend."

Ran glanced at me, but said nothing. Stereth grinned and rested one gloved hand heavily on my shoulder. "You were born to the Sector," he said. He pulled me back toward the riders. "Come on, I'll help you up."

And then I was riding numbly out into the damp night mist.

It rained twice on the way there, which seemed odd to me for the time of year; but then, the plateau is an odd place. Southward, in Cormallon, we would be coming on high summer. Blue flowers called herox came out around now, and the fields would be full of them. Or so I'd been told. I'd never seen Cormallon at that particular time; I'd planned to see it this year. In the capital, Trade Square would be slowing down during the noon hours, and anybody who could create some kind of shade with cloth and sticks and the sides of carts would be doing it. And Shaskala would only be saved from complete incineration by its altitude.

But on the top of the plateau, protected by layers of cloud, we could still wear jackets most of the day. A lot of the others managed to get sunburned anyway; Des had, working on the roof. Deceitfully, though, it still felt cool, and the constant wind blew through us all, and the rain fell. Twice.

I didn't want to be here any more. I didn't want to be at Cormallon, either. I wanted to be by myself somewhere, in a little house with a comfortable outlander-style chair on a porch, and no commitments for as far ahead as I could see. Not on Athena; the gods knew not on Pyrene. Was there anyplace I *did* want to be?

"Right here," called Stereth, pulling us all up short.

There was a grove of twisted trees on a hillside, dense bushes all around; practically a jungle, for the plateau. I slid down carefully and tied my mount at a tree trunk. I don't dislike large animals, but they make me nervous. I prefer the predictability of mods to native creatures—it's a pity humans don't come in the modified variety. And thank the gods I wasn't required to deal with horses, the old-fashioned kind that Ran's family liked. I would have disgraced myself long since.

The mist was lifting somewhat. Stereth's glance went around the band in a quick circuit; everyone accounted for. I didn't doubt he'd know at once if we came up short. Then he took us to the hilltop under the two moons and gestured, as though offering the kingdoms of the world.

What we saw was a dingy little road, suitable for sturdy groundcars if they weren't too large. Probably the most traffic it ever saw was the occasional mount or wagon, or a half-dozen steermods being led to market. For someone with my background, it was hard to accept the huge peopleless expanses of space on this world. "Rehearsal time," said Stereth. "The cars will be coming from that direction. Tymon, Komo, and Cantry will be here with me in this grove. Most of the rest of you will be in that stand of trees on the far hill—Carabinstereth will be in charge. Walk over there, get used to what you can see and where you'll be. Des, you'll supervise the road crew. Pick whomever you want to help. If Lex has a suggestion to make, you'd better listen to him. Your life will be in his hands."

Des spoke in a businesslike manner, far from his usual fooling around. "Grateth, Komo, Sembet, Sokol—give me a hand. Get shovels from the wagon." I turned to look at the wagon, now fully visible in the clearing air. Good heavens, was that the bathtub loaded on back?

It was. Des' crew gathered their shovels and he led them down to the road. They started to dig.

Several hours later the following things had been accomplished: People had been moved back and forth all over the hills and the road; Lex na'Valory had had three major arguments with Des and any number of minor ones; and a large hole about one meter deep had been dug across the middle of the road. There were also a dozen individual and collective briefings that I hadn't been included in.

A blanket supported by skinny branches was stretched over the hole and dirt and pebbles were layered on top of it. A side hole had also been dug out from the north wall of the pit, more or less grave size. It wasn't level with the bottom, but about two hand-widths above it. There was a separate access from above. Des, I saw, took a keen interest in everything relating to this pit. He even laid himself out in the side grave for a moment.

I didn't know what was going on in the grove across the road. The wagon and its contents had disappeared, and a gulley that led down the hillside had been widened. Sembet walked up and down this gulley a few dozen times before disappearing back into the trees.

Lex na'Valory had been given custody of the single light-rifle. I questioned the wisdom of that, but I questioned it silently, to myself. I was always polite to Lex—you never knew what would set him off.

Stereth saw me watching the most temperamental member of the band as he walked from one spot to another on the hill across the way, and he must have read my expression. "Lex is the best marksman in the Sector," he said.

"Lex?" I'd never thought about his past. I'd rather imagined him springing full-grown and borderline psychotic from the army stockade.

"You're a worrier, aren't you?" said Stereth kindly. "Lex will do his part. Relax."

I would have been a lot more relaxed honeymooning in Shaskala while on a routine case, and whom did we have to blame for that? I didn't say it, though. After all, Stereth had been trying to reassure me.

We broke at dawn for breakfast: Bread, cold meat, and beans from last night's supper, washed down with clean water from the canteens. Afterward, Des said, "Are we finished? Have we practiced everything?"

"We've practiced everything," agreed Stereth.

"Does this mean we can go home and sleep now?" I inquired.

"This means we should all go and position ourselves," said Stereth. "The cars will be coming through in about an hour."

The urge to sleep vanished totally. Stereth certainly knew what to say to get the adrenaline pumping.

I said, "I thought this was a rehearsal."

"We've rehearsed," he said. "Now we need an audience."

Des grinned, and I looked at him resentfully. Under pressure his physical cowardice seemed to disappear. Not mine, frankly. I try not to make a pest of myself about it, but I may as well be honest in these pages.

Cantry joined Stereth and me on our hilltop, and the others vanished into the grove across the way—except for Des, who lowered himself into the grave.

"What is he doing?" I asked Stereth.

Sembet came down the gulley and was now obligingly pouring more dirt over the access to Des' hole. He stamped on the dirt when he was through. Now the only way out for Des was through the main pit.

I said, "Stereth?"

"He'll be all right."

So we sat there and waited. Cantry was her usual silent self. For all I know she may have been a chatterbox when alone with Stereth, but she said nothing while I was there. As I found out later, she must have had a lot on her mind then.

Three-quarters of an hour later I heard the sound of the groundcars. Stereth took Cantry's hand. He said, "Ready?"

I glanced over at them. He wasn't addressing me. Cantry's eyes were shut and she was pale even for a fellow barbarian.

"Stereth—" she said.

"You can do it." He moved behind her and put his hands on her shoulders, as though he could physically transmit his own certainty.

Another minute. I could see the cars now: Dull metallic gray, with the gold insignia of the provincial militia.

Stereth spoke in his usual cool voice. "They're half a mile away, at the bend in the road. Gray with gold markings."

Cantry's face was clenched like a fist. The cars came closer. I didn't understand how the pit could help; the first car might go in, but the second would just stop and two men with light-rifles would get out. And that was only if the pit had any effect at all—a sturdy groundcar designed for this terrain would probably just climb up on its own.

Then the other car would circle the hole and they'd continue on their way, leaving us behind like a pack of fools . . . please the gods. At least nobody would fire on us then.

I'd heard Stereth tell Des earlier that no one had ever attacked a tax shipment before. He'd said it as though it were to our advantage, but I took it as evidence of good sense on the part of the rest of the world.

"Almost," said Stereth. "Almost . . . *now*. Now."

I saw the lead car swerve abruptly, half up onto the grass. Then the driver brought it back to the center of the road—*beyond* the pit. So much for Stereth's strategy, whatever it was.

"Good," said Stereth. "Perfect, sweetheart, you were perfect."

Cantry's eyes opened and she took a deep, shuddering breath. Stereth kissed her cheek without taking his attention from the road.

The second car, seeing no obstacle, continued down the center. When it hit the pit it dropped suddenly, as though a lift had miraculously appeared in the earth. Simultaneously, I saw that the color of the gulley on the other hill had changed from brown to gray.

"What the hell—" I said.

"Quick-set," explained Stereth, not looking at me either. His eyes were bright behind the spectacles.

Mixed and released from the giant bathtub, I realized, finally making the connection. My mind clicked on a bright image of the outlaws straining as they tipped it over at the head of the gulley. It would be timed to harden within seconds, no doubt . . . if they did it correctly.

The car in the pit roared and butted against the side. Quick-set now covered the bottom of the hole. The lead car, seeing what was happening, had stopped and was backing up. The car in the pit tried to exit a second time, but didn't have quite enough momentum. It moved farther back for a third try.

The doors on the lead car opened and a man in the gold vest of a part-time militia officer got out. He began walking toward the pit. Probably he intended to offer a tow if the other car couldn't get out on its own. Nobody had ever tried to attack a tax shipment before; he must have thought this was just some huge pothole left by the recent rains in a road that was poorly placed between two hills.

His chest exploded. I jumped. *Lex*, I realized. On the other hill, with our sole light-rifle. A warning shot hit the open door of the car at almost the same instant.

The door slammed shut and the first car began to leave the scene. Grateth told me later that the drivers are responsible for what money they carry; this one was speeding off to cover his ass and protect his life at the same time. His superiors would be angry at a militia officer being killed, but they wouldn't blame the other driver for that. They'd only blame him for losing the money.

The car in the pit had stopped moving. So this was why Stereth had arranged whatever he'd arranged to let the first car past: His opposition was now halved. So was the money, but no doubt he'd taken all that into account in his businesslike way.

But where did this get anybody? What could we do to that elephant-hide vehicle anyway? Stand around outside it like the beseigers of an ancient city, with our pitiful knives and light-rifle, waiting for the occupants to get hungry? All the drivers had to do was stay inside and wait for help.

"Fifteen seconds," said Stereth under his breath.

Grateth also told me that the one overwhelming paranoid fear everyone who drives an armored vehicle has is of fire. Of being trapped in that thick metal tomb while burning to an agonized crisp. It's an understandable fear, since every armored driver who died within a car has died of extreme heat—it's about the only thing that will get through the skin. The car survives, but the people don't; the doors fuse shut.

Des waited a full fifteen seconds in his grave. Then, hoping very strongly that the quick-set had indeed hardened, he rolled out into it. The wheels of the groundcar were firmly stuck, but there was enough room to crawl under the carriage to the two bottom sensors. Bits of quick-set clung to him as he wriggled through. He kept flicking them off. At the left and right front corners of the undercarriage were two red lights, both glowing in operational mode. Des pulled out the hotpencil I'd seen him take on back at the fort, screwed the bottom, and watched as the top turned white with heat. He took a match out in his other hand

and activated it. Then he reached as far apart as he could with those lanky arms of his and held the pencil to one sensor and the match to the other.

I couldn't see any of this at the time, but it must have shown up on the board as though the underside of the car were on fire. What I did see were the doors of the car slide open and two men with rifles jump out and run. They took off in opposite directions. The one on our side of the road must have had a second of enlightenment, abruptly grasping his situation; he threw his rifle as far away as he could and fell to his knees, hands behind his head, screaming something unintelligible. The other man kept running.

They were both killed nearly simultaneously by Lex na'Valory, the best marksman in the Sector.

Euphoria and repulsion make for a sickening mix. I was the only one suffering from it, though. Everybody else was on top of the world.

Except Ran, and not for moral reasons—or anyway, not for morality of the kind I'd been taught. Once the attack was over he came straight down from the grove, marched up our hill, and grabbed hold of Stereth with both arms. "She's a witch," he said, meaning Cantry. She still looked shocked by what she'd done.

"Is she?" said Stereth.

"There was a steermod in the road. I saw it. It was an illusion, targeted to the people in the car."

"Is that why it swerved?" asked Carabinstereth, following her problem child up the hill. She'd been in charge of Ran, as part of her group, and didn't want to see him do anything stupid now. "Go, Cantry!"

"I don't know what a witch is," said Stereth. "Take your hands off me."

Ran put down his hands. "A native talent. One of the old women who live in the hills and con people out of their money with a few minor tricks."

"Well," said Stereth, "she's not old."

"She's a barbarian! How can she have any talent?"

"Are you accusing her of something, or not?"

Ran was silent for a moment, having so many complaints to file he was clearly unsure where to begin. "If she has talent," he said finally, "she should apply to one of the

Houses that handle that sort of thing. But she shouldn't be free-lancing, she shouldn't be out in the Sector causing trouble, and she shouldn't be doing things that I'll get blamed for when people figure them out! —And she shouldn't have any talent, anyway! She's a barbarian!"

This was touching on Family and House honor, and as I've said, Ran made no compromises where they were concerned.

Below us, on the road, three corpses sprawled messily. I wanted to leave.

"She's doing the job you refused," pointed out Stereth. "Do you expect to retain a monopoly on sorcery when you won't even perform?"

I said, "Do we have to debate this now?"

They turned and looked at me, both surprised. Des' voice, behind me, said, "She's right, Stereth. We've got a whole mess of money down there. Shouldn't we get it loaded?"

Des was filthy and bits of quick-set clung to his clothing. He was glowing with energy, though, and unable to stand still long enough for a discussion. I know the effect. If we didn't give him something to do quickly, he would probably throw one of the women down on the ground and start to get passionate.

Stereth must have seen it, too. "All right, Des, let's start loading. Sokol can finish criticizing me later."

The bathtub and the mired car were left behind. The wagon was stacked with boxes of gold tabals. The mounts were watered.

When we left, Ran helped me up on my mount. I never did master the ability to climb on by myself. He must have been involved in the quick-set mixing; bits of it clung to his cloak as well. "Are you all right?" I asked him.

He shook his head. Then he went to his own mount and climbed on. I dug in with my heels a little and caught up to Stereth, just ahead. "Why did I even have to come?" I asked, still seeing in my mind the scene we were leaving behind. "You didn't give me a job. I could have stayed at the fort."

He seemed faintly surprised. "I thought you would want to come, Tymon. You're the one who told me Robin Hood used to steal from tax collectors."

For a moment I was disoriented. I'd completely forgotten mentioning it to him.

What in the gods' name had I said? "I was drunk," I protested.

"You tell good stories when you're drunk," said Stereth, in a friendly way.

Ran met my eyes. I put my head down and followed the rest of the band over the hills.

Chapter 11

If you want to know the truth, I believed then (and still do) that Ran's so-called moral objections to helping Stereth were less based on morality as I had learned it than on pride and status. It was not as though my quarter-husband's hands were free of blood.

Even granting the circumstantial nature of morality—that something which is acknowledged wrong, like killing, becomes right when it takes place in war or in the defense of a child—Ran was Ivoran-born, and should have no difficulty in jettisoning his qualms when the chips were down. "Enemies" are another category here, and dealing with them is a matter of what one can get away with. And surely the members of the provincial militia were rapidly becoming our enemies. There were posters of Ran all over the market towns to prove the point.

There were two things that held him back, and I don't know which was stronger: First, that he was a Cormallon, and these were Northwest Sector outlaws, one step below servants on the social scale; and second, when everything smashed up it would be essential to keep the Cormallon name completely uninvolved. A whiff of sorcery, and who knew what the prosecutors might pick up on?

And here was Cantry, blowing in sorcery on a high wind. That, and Ran's posters, and I knew why he was looking as sick as he did on the ride home. It surely wasn't because he was picturing the remains of the three tax collection guards back on the Mid-Plateau Road.

I applied some pressure with my lower leg and my mount obediently moved in closer to Ran's.

"There is a positive view to all this," I said.

He looked over toward me with the face of one who has given up on positive views.

I said, "If Cantry's a developing sorcerer, Stereth won't need to hang on so tightly to you and me."

"She's not a developing sorcerer. You can't be a developing sorcerer any more than a savage can be a developing engineer. A little native ability means nothing without years of training."

"She did pretty well on the road."

"A two-second illusion. She probably wasn't even sure herself she could do it. Theo— Tymon, can't you see the difference between that and fireballing a ship, making the blood-temperature of an army rise to 200 degrees . . . giving temporary hemophilia to the front line of an enemy battalion? How can you even begin to do any of those things unless you know what you're doing?"

"Gods, Ran, war here must be horrible."

"I wouldn't know. We haven't had one in a long time."

That was true . . . centuries, wasn't it? Back when the invisible dome was first placed over Cormallon. And I didn't know when the last Pyrenese war had been.

"What about defensive things?" I asked. "If you won't help Stereth by giving him a weapon, what about putting a force-field around the fort, like the Cormallon barrier?"

Ran glanced back and forth, checking for the proximity of the other riders.

I said, "I wouldn't have said it if anyone could hear."

"I know that. There's no harm in checking. First of all, the Cormallon barrier took generations of work to get to its final strength. And what good would it do the band to put a shield over the fort?"

"If we're attacked—"

"They can wait till the food runs out and pick us off as we come out. It isn't a self-sufficient little nation, like Cormallon is. The end result is the same: Death for everyone. And for that you suggest I advertise a sorcery similar to my family's most well-known defense?"

Ran doesn't need sorcery; he can use logic as a weapon. "Excuse me while I check for cuts," I said. "I was only trying to cheer you up."

"Don't try. Let me sulk luxuriously in the blackness of the situation."

It began raining again.

* * *

They had the fire started by the time I got inside the fort. I borrowed somebody's outer robe and pulled off my wet things and tried to make myself, if not comfortable, less miserable.

Stereth was handing out shares—small shares, apparently.

"We need a larger treasury," he was saying. "We're expanding. We need capital."

"Expanding into what?" asked Paravit-Col bewilderedly. "We're not a business. We're *outlaws*."

Stereth regarded him with friendly interest. The expression, and his glasses, made him seem like a large, intelligent rabbit. "Didn't you swear not to give me a hard time before you rode out last night? I hope we have no word-breakers here. We all know the penalty for forswearing an oath given on a road-name."

Paravit-Col backpedaled quickly. "I was only expressing an interest," he said.

I didn't know the penalty. I didn't ask, though. I thought it best not to be seen to inquire into the subject too closely.

Lex na'Valory said, "I was to get a bonus."

"You got one," said Stereth, "for good planning and excellent shooting. Then you got a cut, for not following orders. They canceled out."

Carabinstereth grinned as she took her own bonus.

"You can't match my shooting," said Lex.

"I can't match your ego either," Stereth replied. "I told you to accept a surrender where it was practical. Your pay cut will help make up for the ransom we could have gotten from the guard you killed."

Lex muttered, but took his share and went to the fire to count it. He only put up with that sort of talk from Stereth; everyone else had to tiptoe around him.

"I didn't know the militia paid ransom for its members," said Ran coolly.

Stereth said, "His family would have paid. Here, Sokol, take your share; I hear you mixed the quick-set perfectly. Lucky for our Des."

Ran stepped up to the box where Stereth was counting out tabals and looked down at the pile of gold. Stereth smiled and said, "You did earn it, and not by sorcery. Why hesitate?"

"No reason at all," said Ran, and he pulled off the mud-splattered silk scarf from around his neck, opened it, and held it out for Stereth to drop the coins into.

I could read Ran's mind on this one, and no doubt so could the rest of the room, for Stereth said, "Besides, it'll get you farther when you decide to escape."

"Good point," agreed Ran.

He tied up the scarf and glanced over toward me. "Doesn't Tymon get a share?" Two bags of gold went farther than one.

"Our Tymon was there as an observer," said Stereth, "and observers don't get paid."

I'm glad he saw me that way. I prefer to go through life as a neutral. I hate to make decisions.

"And now," said Stereth, "we start spending our money. Des—"

"I'm going to sleep! . . . Aren't I?" said Des.

"When you feel entirely equal to it, Des, sometime within the next day and a half, I want you to put on your best clothes and ride over to the Hock-Tyan Farm. Grateth and Komo will go with you."

Des, who had been lying against some cushions in a half-doze, snapped up straight. "Are you crazy? We've stolen four mounts from them in the last two months alone. We'll be *shot*."

"They might hang you," said Lex.

"It's doubtful they'll do either," said Stereth. "It wouldn't be in their interests. —Oh, and I think you should take Tymon." He smiled. "It'll be educational for her."

"You were the one who told him about Robin Hood," reminded Ran, when he kissed me good-bye. It did not escape our notice that Stereth was still sending us out separately.

It was a first in the band's history, no doubt: Four of us wearing clean clothes at the same time. I followed along behind Des, ahead of Grateth and Komo, wearing an outer robe borrowed from Juvindeth that was swirled in red and white patterns, Shaskala-fashion. The others wore outlaw-style jackets, but not their gaudiest. "Leave the jewelry behind," Stereth had said, and Des made a face but complied.

I'd wondered about Stereth's wisdom in giving Des such

a major role in the tax-collection robbery, but upon hearing the details I decided that they'd probably needed to go with the tallest person with the farthest reach—to get to the undercarriage sensors. Des was clever and charming, no doubt about it; but he'd never struck me as overly responsible. Yet here we were, on the opening salvo of Stereth's grand campaign, with Des leading the way.

I was beginning to get a vague idea of direction on the Plateau. We were going north and west, which should mean that we'd cross the Shaskala Road some time; though not near the Mid-Plateau connection, I assumed. There were likely to be patrols around that spot by now. I pictured the three bodies again, and shivered.

"You cold, Tymon?" called Des. He'd peered around to check on me, not having any high regard for my abilities to steer my mount. "Want my jacket?"

Really, there was no defense against Des. He was probably the only person in the band who would have pulled off his jacket and tossed it to me; Ran would have offered, but he would have felt compelled to comment on my lack of forethought in dressing, first.

"No, thanks, I'm all right."

"You shivered," he pointed out.

"I was thinking back to the militia guards."

He looked at me blankly, not getting it. I said, "If I get colder, I'll let you know."

"All right." He turned back ahead.

Grateth and Komo followed silently behind. We topped a hill and suddenly a vista opened: Hills, fields, and pockets of mist, going on forever. Brown patches on a distant green backdrop that must be steermods. And no people anywhere but us four.

It was beautiful enough to hurt, but it was part of the package that came with danger and loss of freedom. I never thought I'd be nostalgic for the burning summer of the capital, the noise and glare, the jostle in the marketplace.

We came to some stone fences, unusual for farms in this part of the world, with rows of green stalks on the other side. Generally the farmers just sprayed a pheromone around their boundaries that steermods have been bred to recognize as "out of their territory." The pheromone has to be periodically reapplied, but then, as any farmer can tell you, fences have to be periodically rebuilt. And the pheremone is cheaper and easier.

Des said, "The Hock-Tyan Farm's been in the sâme family for generations. Can you imagine generations of people willingly choosing to live in the Northwest Sector?"

"It's a very beautiful place," I said.

"It's pretty. But it's *dead*, Tymon, there are no people here."

"Except outlaws," said Grateth, drawing up. "And would you want to meet us?"

"Humans have always chosen to live in funny places," I said. "Besides, they have other farmers and ranchers for company."

Des peered eloquently north, south, east, and west at the lonely expanse.

I said, "All right, so they have to travel a little to visit them. Maybe they like the quiet."

Des made a gesture of repellence at the idea of anybody liking quiet.

"It's not all that private," said Grateth. "Look."

Far down the rows of stalks, somebody moved.

Grateth said, "If he gets to the house before we do, they'll kill us as we approach."

"Go," said Des.

Grateth's mount went flying, and Komo's followed. They were over the crumbling wall in a second, and trampling down the stalks while the farmer fled.

I bit my lip to keep from being a pest. I hate to see anybody that scared. I don't even like to startle the birds that feed on marketplace garbage when I walk by—I make wide detours so I don't have to see their wings beat an alarmed mass take-off and their chests pound—

Grateth and Komo brought him down in the dirt within minutes. I watched as they dismounted and hauled him to his feet, and let out my breath. It would be easier for the fellow from this point on; anything is better than terror. Maybe it's because I'm a coward myself that I can empathize so well with fear.

They brought him back to us with his hands tied behind. He was young, maybe sixteen, with a torn shirt and the trousers of a provincial worker. He wore a wide-brimmed green felt hat, too—his family understood the effects of sunburn on the Plateau better than expatriate outlaws did.

Des said, "Hello, friend. Honored by this meeting. Are you of the Hock-Tyan family?"

The boy glared up at him from beneath the crooked brim of his hat. One eye squinted as though Des were framed by sunlight; but he wasn't. A squint like that is the lower-class way of saying "I don't choose to trust you."

Des laughed. "Ishin na' telleth. You're welcome to *my* name, though—Des Helani, gracious sir. And the lovely lady beside me is Tymon. And Grateth Tar'briek and Komo had the honor of meeting you just before me."

The boy glanced briefly at the two men on either side of him, apparently not surprised at hearing road-names. Then he folded his arms and stared back at Des, waiting.

Des said, "Help him up, you two. He can sit in front of me when we ride in."

The boy's eyes widened. Grateth and Komo boosted him up on Des' mount. Once on top his head turned right and left, confused by this new perspective on his world. He made an effort and twisted back to look at Des.

"What are you doing?"

"Visiting," said Des. "Being neighborly. A little late, but that's better than not at all."

The boy said, "My uncle Tades will kill you. For stealing our mounts." When there was no immediate answer, he pursued it: "What'll you do about that?"

I wondered myself. We followed the stone wall until we reached a gate, and Komo opened the lock for us, making the ancient metal hinges scream. A dirt path led far ahead, cutting through the tall stalks until it disappeared around a corner somewhere near the vanishing point.

We rode down the path, spiky green leaves rustling in long, oceanic waves around us. It was eerie. Komo spoke at last, in a loud whisper—it had to be loud to be heard over the crop—"Should I ride out first?"

"No," said Des, "we want them to see the boy."

Something in his diction reminded me a little of Stereth, but I decided it was imagination. The mobile green curtain around us encouraged bizarre ideas. You wondered what you would ride into when the stalks ended.

"I'm not a boy," said our hostage, several minutes of green silence later.

"Sorry," muttered Des. The breeze ruffled the pale fur on his mount. The animals at least were immune to the general spookiness; nervousness was bred out of them.

And then a curve, and between one footfall and the next we were out of the alien country and in a clearing on a shallow hillside, near a stone house with two chimneys and a covered well. Laundry flapped in the wind. Normality.

A pistol shot singed the ground in front of Des' mount. It took a few steps backward.

"It's all right, baby, it's all right," he said. His grip tightened on the boy. "Hello!" he called. "I've come with a message for the Hock-Tyans."

Silence, the stalks and the wind. He called, "I'm not here to cause any trouble. I have good news, news to the advantage of your House."

"What news does a cantry tar'meth have? Let the boy down and say it." The voice was older and male.

"Tades Hock-Tyan? I'd rather speak face-to-face, gracious sir." He kept hold of the boy, who had started to wriggle. "I mean no harm, sir, I'm just sort of nervous."

A man appeared from a corner of the house. He was stocky, short for an Ivoran and with a fine, fuzzy beard. Funny-looking by the standards of his people, but the expression on his face would have cut short any laughter. "Your road-friends are nervous, too," he said, "or they wouldn't be holding weapons."

I realized for the first time that Komo had a knife and Grateth a pistol. Des said, "Put them away." They did so. I admired their discipline, and hoped Des wasn't crazy.

The man said, "You come holding our boy and riding one of our mounts. Is this polite?"

Stereth had specifically asked that the mounts we took not be ones stolen from this farm, but Des showed no annoyance at the slip-up. He slid down at once. "Do you want it back? It's yours. Or would you prefer compensation?"

The boy, left to himself, slid down the other side and ran into the house.

We all regarded each other. The man said at last, "Tades Hock-Tyan, honored by this meeting."

"Des Helani, likewise. This is Grateth Tar'briek, Komo, and the lady is Tymon."

"Honored, gracious sir," I added, feeling there was no need to waste my capital accent if it would impress anybody.

He inclined his head. "You said you had a message."

"And a gift," said Des. He unbuckled a pack from his mount's gear and held it out to the farmer. "You can open it, or I can open it. Whichever you prefer."

"You open it."

Des reached into the pack and removed two bags. He hefted them and let their jingle be heard; and said, "Eight hundred gold tabals."

He extended the first bag toward the farmer, who made no move to take it. He stared at us. Des placed the bags in the dirt by his feet and moved back to stand with his companions.

"What are you doing?" asked the farmer, at last.

Grateth and Komo were in the dark as well. Something came over me, and before Des could reply I spoke with the certainty of inspiration: "It's from the quarterly tax shipment," I said. The farmer turned to me. "It's your share."

"It's my *what?*" he said.

Des smiled and whispered, "Very good, Tymon."

Tades Hock-Tyan blinked and stared down at the bags. He still made no move to pick them up. Then he looked up at us and said, "Would you care to come inside for some tah?"

"They say that when your tax money is gone, it's like a funeral. You're never going to see it again, no matter what anybody says." Tades Hock-Tyan poured us new bowls of wine to go with the new cups of tah.

There had been no need for Des to point out the justice of our mutual position on taxes. It is the deeply held belief of all people on Ivory that the government exists for the sole purpose of extorting money from them. Nor are they far from the mark.

Komo reached for another seed-cake, stuffed it in his mouth, belched, and said, "Excellent cake, my friend. My compliments to your wife."

There was a moment of silence at this faux pas. Tades was part of the outer life of the Hock-Tyans, like the facade of an Ivoran building; the inner life, the women and children, were only shared with trusted associates. Komo should not have even hinted at their existence. He'd spent all his life with his army mates and outlaw bands, and was oblivious to the glance that passed among the other four of us.

Des leapt in to cover the gap. "If I might bring up the subject of business prematurely," he began—we'd only been there twenty minutes—"I'd like to discuss that matter of advantage to your House."

The farmer smiled, his fringe of beard making him look like some woodland nature spirit. "The tax money and the return of our mount are of advantage already."

"But we'd like to be of further service, if you'll permit."

"So?" He took a long draught of the impossibly strong Sector wine. "Say on, then, and I listen with a favorable ear."

Des leaned over. "Our leader regrets the troubles that cantry tar'meth such as ourselves have caused you over the years. He's sent us to offer apologies and recompense."

Our host's eyebrows raised. "Kind of him," he said noncommittally, "and you've done so."

"He'd like us to go further, though. Now that we're convinced of the error of our ways."

"I listen."

"He'd like to make a treaty between our band and your House."

Tades Hock-Tyan began to laugh. "A treaty? Like what the Emperor has with Tellys?"

"Why not?" asked Des. "Who rules the Sector, the Emperor or you and me? Why can't we make treaties if we want to? What's the empire done for you lately?"

Hock-Tyan set down his cup of tah and said seriously, "What has it ever done in the Sector since the beginning of time?"

"Exactly," said Des. "Except take your money. But we're remedying that."

Our host stroked the fine hair of his chin. Then he said, "No. I say this meaning no offense. I won't have our House involved in treasonous activity, and that's what they'll call it when they find their pockets empty."

He and Ran must have gone to the same school. Des said, "We're not suggesting that you support us openly. If anyone asks if you've heard from us, deny it. *We* will. Keep your money in a secure place. As time goes by, we may be able to add to it."

"What would you want of me, then?"

"Your friendship. We promise, no more mounts stolen, no more fields trampled. You just . . . keep us in mind. Don't join the militia if it asks for volunteers to hunt us down. Tell us if you hear anything of interest. Is that too much to ask?"

"You're asking to be a House ally, and I don't even know you. Our allies go back ten generations."

"It's a new age," said Des.

Hock-Tyan sat there silently, thinking. Then he said, "What's the name of your leader?"

At that moment a small whirlwind burst in from the lit doorway that led toward the kitchen: A boy of about five, plump and messy-haired, with fiery dark eyes. He wore a torn red jacket, and must have just come in from outside. He snapped a carved wooden pistol from his belt, pointed it at Grateth and yelled, "Zip!" Grateth blinked mildly. The boy shot Komo, too, but he was too busy swallowing more wine to react. Then the child shot Des. "Zip!"

Des took it in the chest, tottered, reached for the side of the table, groped, fell sideways over the cushion, and gave out an alarming death rattle. Then he lay there in total stillness. Des was a ham.

The child was both shocked and thrilled. He walked over to Des' corpse and poked it experimentally with the snout of his pistol. Des' shoulder moved with the pressure and then fell back when the pistol was taken away. "I *killed* him," the boy announced, with great pride. He looked over at Hock-Tyan, his eyes brighter than ever. Then, with a child's instinctive understanding of the parallel roads of fantasy and reality, he slapped Des softly on the arm to get his attention. "Who are you?"

Des opened his eyes. "Who are *you?*"

"Bedis Jer Hock-Tyan."

"If I get up, will you kill me again?"

"Maybe."

Tades Hock-Tyan spoke up. "Leave our guest alone, Bedis, you've troubled him enough. Take off your jacket in the house. And go in the kitchen." The boy moved away from Des disappointedly. Tades watched him go with a thoughtful look. He said, "And tell your mother and sister to come in and say hello."

Des sat up. "You honor me," he began.

"I know I do, but I think you deserve it. Let's not speak of it further."

Treaty or no treaty, it was going to be socially impossible for Stereth's band to steal from this farm again. I was glad. They seemed to be good people, even if they did try to kill us first.

A minute later a fat gray-haired woman entered, followed by a teen-aged girl with a silk bow in her hair. The nephew—our ex-hostage—peered around from the edge of the door. "Welcome, sir Helani," said the wife, who had clearly been listening behind the door. I would have done the same.

We all rose and exchanged bows. The girl with the silk bow smiled at Des. I could understand it—he was the picture of a storybook hero—but hoped he wouldn't rise to the bait. We were just starting to get along with these people.

"You were telling us your leader's name," said the girl. I pictured the whole family pressed up against the door.

Des turned to Tades and said, "Our leader is Stereth Tar'krim."

The girl clapped her hands. The farmwife cried, "I knew it! What did I tell you, Tades, our mounts were stolen by Stereth Tar'krim himself." She turned to Des. "He's a fine-looking man, sir Helani. I've seen the pictures."

Everybody on the blasted plateau must have seen the pictures. I felt my heart sink.

"He's young," said Tades, "for so successful an outlaw leader."

"He's a genius," said Des simply, only saying what I knew he believed of Stereth.

Tades bit his lip. "A treaty with cantry tar'meth is a big step. I don't know what my ancestors would say."

"I know a face," said the wife, "I'm never wrong. And

when I looked at the poster of Stereth Tar'krim I said, 'That man has eyes you can trust.' This is someone who understands debt and obligation, Tades. He'll honor a contract."

"*Please,* father," said the girl, whose motivations were so clearly suspect her mother bundled her out of the room before she could ruin the situation.

Tades drew himself up and bowed. "If you'll stay to dinner, sirs and lady—if you have room for it—I'll consider the matter, and give you my answer with the sweet after-meal wine."

The woman's face broke into a victory smile.

It was full dark on the plateau when we left the farm. The unmixed wine of the Northwest Sector was bringing me to a whole new understanding of my lack of capacity. Back in the capital, I'd thought I'd been doing rather well.

The Hock-Tyans had signed up as allies. I think Stereth's reputation had had as much to do with it as Des' hand with women and children. It's true that the people of Ivory are ruthlessly practical, and money often seems to be their chief love; but anyone who thinks they are not moonstruck romantics as well has never seen them at the theater. They cheer on the heroes, laugh at the fools, hiss the villains, and cry openly at parted lovers—in short, they are as easily manipulated as seven-year-olds, and the price of a ticket is the only thing I've never heard them grudge. They love a good story; a good story has a hero; and heroes fall into a lot of categories on Ivory. Stereth was on his way to writing his own story, and there were doubtless many who felt a bit part in it was worth risking their lives.

When you've been a collector of myths and legends as long as I have, you become aware of the distinction between glamour and reality. I would as soon be back at Cormallon, picking cherries for dessert. Still, I understood the pull for Stereth's followers and was not so presumptuous as to try and stop them.

"Comfortable, Tymon?" Des inquired. I was sitting on the bow of his saddle, where Hock-Tyan's nephew had sat on the way in. Tades had suggested we take their mount back again, but I don't think he expected anyone to agree.

As the small barbarian of the group, it was clear who was going to have to share.

Past the mysteries of the crop— "What is this stuff, Des?" "No idea, Tymon, I'm a city boy myself. I don't think it's wheat. Maybe it's rice." Grateth's voice rumbled behind us: "Are you crazy? It's nothing like rice." Komo's voice, thick with drink: "It's wine."—and I still don't know. Even I've heard that wine comes from grapes, but Komo made a good case for some sort of local variant distilled from these plants. We were still arguing about it leagues later, at the Mid-Plateau Road.

And far down the road in the blackness, there came a shout. It was just any shout to me, but Grateth said, "Militia."

"Kanz," said Komo. "What're they doing at this end of the road?"

"Break up and ride," said Grateth, and Des said, "Go!"

I'd thought the night of the cattle raid had been a wild ride. I dug into the soft neck fur of Des' mount, clamped my legs like a vise, and held on. We scrabbled straight up and over the first available hill. All I could hear was the wind and the muffed sound of hooves in the dirt. Ten minutes later Des brought us to a stop and said, "Shh."

We listened. Nothing but night and the edge of a moon on the horizon: We might have been alone in the world. Then, far away, a soft pounding.

"Kanz," he said in my ear. "They're following *us*."

With all affection to Grateth and Komo, I, too, would have preferred it differently. We flew down the other side of the hill and headed . . . south, I think, though I was losing track.

"Here." Des slowed us down.

"Why are we *stopping?*"

"Get down." He slid off and helped me dismount. I lost my footing and nearly went head over heels down an incline that appeared out of nowhere. Des kept hold of my hand and jerked me back to my feet.

The mount picked its way down the slope behind us, calm as ever. Bless his engineers. At the bottom of the ravine we stepped into a shallow run of water.

"It's too dark to see a thing," said Des. "We'll wait down here for them to pass."

The water was cold. "Is this stream poisonous?"

"Yes."

"Will it hurt us to stand in it?"

"I don't know. I never tried it before."

"Kanz."

We both shut up then and waited.

Two hours later we rode into the grounds of the fort. Grateth and Komo were already back, and people were waiting for us. Ran was prominent among them.

Des dismounted and swung me down. He grinned at Ran and said, "She's safe and sound. No problem at all, in fact—" as he opened his arms to include the others,"—you people worry too much."

Ran gave him one of his unreadable looks: I left Des to enjoy his boasting and took Ran to one side. We went around the corner, out of the wind and out of earshot. "You're smiling," he said to me.

"Am I? We were nearly caught by the provincial militia. They were six meters away from us at one point, I could hear their gear jingle."

"Then why are you so happy? Your eyes are shining."

"I don't know," I said, and pushing him a little farther against the wall I started to pull off his outer robe.

"And what are you doing?"

"I don't know that either." Having gotten rid of the outer robe, I unbuttoned the top of his tunic.

"Heavens," he said, and his voice had lost its moodiness, "you're usually not this aggressive."

"No?"

"I'd forgotten the effect adrenaline has on you."

The clothes pile was growing. "Shut up," I said, and although Ran outranked me in House hierarchy he did not appear offended.

In fact, the next morning he ran a hand through his hair and said, "If only we could reproduce that chemically."

I was rinsing my mouth with a dipper of water from one of the jars. "I thought you preferred being the aggressor."

"A little change never hurts. A person doesn't like it to be always their idea, it makes you wonder.'

"You know I'm generally inhibited."

"Oh, I know. In all sorts of ways."

I looked at him. "What does that mean?" I'd once had a similar diagnosis from an itinerant monk. That had irritated me, too.

"Nothing," he said, like one who's opened a door he meant to pass by. He got up, came around behind me, and kissed me on the neck. "You've come a long way for a barbarian."

"No, wait a minute, for once I'd like to know just what people mean when they tell me—"

"Did you know tonight's the moon-and-a-half?"

My thoughts transferred at once to the more immediate highway. "Are you sure?"

"The second of our four nights. We'll be half-wed, my tymon, if nothing goes wrong."

Getting married by degrees isn't as frightening as doing it all at once. I'm not sure I could have handled it the other way. Aloud, I said, "And I don't know if we're going to manage the cakes."

"You mean you don't know *how* we're going to manage the cakes. It's a question of strategy, not of choice."

"You know, you and Stereth really do have a lot in common."

He gave me a hurt look and said, "There's a larder in the cookhouse. Steal from it when you get the chance."

Which leads logically to that awful moment in the afternoon when I found myself on trial. Ran came running into the cookhouse when he heard about it, along with half a dozen of the band.

Juvindeth and Clintris had me standing against the wall, both their knives out, looking very unfriendly. Carabinstereth came in just behind Ran, still puffing, and gasped out, "What happened?"

Juvindeth's eyes narrowed in my direction, but before she could speak Clintris said, "She was stealing from the stores. She's running out on us."

Juvindeth added, "And you know she'd never make it out of the Sector without turning us in."

Carabinstereth looked at me reproachfully. I was beginning to grasp how Ran must have felt that time he was accused of stealing from the family treasury. I said, "I just wanted some food. Is that a capital crime?"

I immediately wished I hadn't phrased it that way.

Juvindeth said, "Where's Stereth?"

Lex na'Valory answered her. "He's gone with Grateth and Des on an errand."

"What of it?" asked Clintris. "Why wait?"

"Good point," agreed Lex.

Why did I have to draw *this* group? Clintris and Lex would've been at home in the arena, thumbing-down every passing gladiator. I said, "I want to see Stereth."

"I don't give a pile of kanz what you want," began Lex, but Ran interrupted.

"When did you get put in charge? This isn't your decision."

Carabinstereth jumped in before Lex could have one of his fits. "It's true, it's her right. We'll wait for Stereth."

You have appealed to Stereth. Unto Stereth . . . But why should he look any more kindly on the situation? This was a postponement, not a commutation.

Lex muttered, "Sokol's her damned boyfriend. If she's dead, he won't have anybody to put it to. Why should we listen to him?"

"He probably put her up to it," said Juvindeth.

"Yeah, would she be cutting out alone? Turn out his pockets, too." Lex saw the look on Ran's face and broke into a wide grin.

Enough. I yelled, "All right! I was stealing from the damned stores. Gods, haven't I put up with enough? Do we have to drag my personal life into this?"

Their faces turned to me, taken aback by the outburst. I'm not given to outbursts generally, and I've found that when I do succumb they seem to have twice the effect. I could see them wondering, What does she have to be angry at *us* for?

"Tonight's the moon-and-a-half! Sokol and I were going to be half-married! First you kidnap us, and then when we try to have the ceremony anyway you threaten to kill me! This was supposed to be our *honeymoon!*"

Ran must have agreed it was a little late to deny it. He didn't say anything. There was total silence among the group, and then Carabinstereth asked in a small voice, "What was she stealing?"

Juvindeth said uncertainly, "Eggs. And flour."

"Flour?" Carabinstereth glared at her. "Are you out of your mind? What would she be doing with flour on the road? She might as well bring along mud!"

Juvindeth looked down at the floor, humiliated.

"What a group!" Carabinstereth cast a general hard look around at everyone. "May the gods witness what I put up with. I see where Stereth gets his gray hairs."

Lex began, "I don't see how I was supposed to know—"

"Shut up," said Carabinstereth. "Go back to the main hall and get some cloaks and pillows. Clintris, fire up the oven. Juvie, you're going to come with me over to Barine Hill. —Lex, what are you waiting for? Unless you want Stereth to hear every stupid thing that went on here today—"

Lex vanished. She turned to me. "Please overlook this unfortunate incident. Would you mind waiting in the main hall? I'll be with you shortly."

I'd had no idea Carabinstereth could call up a courtly accent like that. It must be from her bodyguard days. Ran seemed even more eager to leave than I was; he took hold of my sleeve and drew me out into the dull plateau sunlight.

I glanced back at the stone dome of the cookhouse. The clanging sound of the ancient oven starting up came from within. I found I was weaker than I'd thought, and took hold of Ran's arm.

"You know, I wasn't sure I was going to get out of that room."

"I kept looking at the cleavers," he confessed. "I'm not sure I'll ever feel the same way about kitchens again."

"We're really in serious trouble here, aren't we? I don't mean today. I mean, being with the band."

He put an arm around my shoulders. "Come on, tymon. It's the moon-and-a-half. Even if we can't do the ritual."

We stayed in the main hall, lying on the cushions like invalids, while Lex gathered things up around us and muttered to himself.

* * *

A hand on my shoulder woke me from a light doze. It was Carabinstereth. I sat up and looked around at the dim hall; it must be dark outside already.

"Come on, Tymon, into your things." She held out a colored robe and I got into it sleepily. Outlaws were always sharing clothing; you took what was clean and didn't make a fuss.

"It's silk," I said in surprise, when I felt it on my skin.

"Cobatree silk," she said. "Best in the world. Better than that stuff that comes out of worms."

She was leading me across the hall to the door. "What's going on?" I asked. "Where's R— . . . Sokol?"

"He's just excellent, little barbarian. Shake the sleep out of your head. Rub those funny-looking eyes."

"You're a fine one to talk about eyes." Her own jeweled irises glowed in the dark like a satisfied cat's.

We crossed the rough grass, cold against my feet. "You didn't give me time to put on my boots."

"We're not going far." We came to one of the monastery's smaller buildings and she kicked the doorstep with the edge of her boot. The door was opened by Mora Sobien Ti.

"Did she finally wake up?" asked Mora, the edges of her mouth curved in a gentle smile.

"This slug?" inquired Carabinstereth. "I poured icewater on her."

Mora drew me in, kissed me, and went out the door. They closed it behind them. I turned and saw a single stone room, a half-missing ceiling open to moonlight, and a wealth of cushions, cloaks, and silken bolts of color. A small oil lamp was set in one wall. Bits of crumbled green were scattered on the floor, releasing an earthy scent: Night-gathered herbs from Barine Hill. An old wooden shutter, carefully cleaned, had been set in the middle of the room as a tray, and two round cakes were on it. The symbol for "tymon" was painted on the wood by one cake, and the symbol for "anonymous" was by the other.

"They said they were careful to make them from the ingredients each of us stole."

A bundle of shadows by the far wall moved, and Ran stood up. He spread his hands to indicate the pirate paradise around us. "Well," he said, "this is a little embarrassing."

I think I've already mentioned the sudden veers into sentiment true Ivorans will make. There is nothing more typical than their practical bloodthirstiness of this afternoon and their advancement of love's cause tonight. Ran told me, with a trace of discomfort, how Lex and Carabinstereth had supervised his washing and choice of clothing, and how Lex had doused him in perfume.

"It's an awful brand," he said, "but I couldn't tell them no. They were absolutely fixed on it."

"I like the smell."

He shook his head. "Barbaric taste. But what can we expect?"

We snuggled down onto a pile of cloaks. "Like nesting waterbirds," I said. Moonlight poured over the room.

"Um. I only hope it doesn't rain."

Late the next morning Ran and I walked over the grounds toward the main building. I still needed some sandals or boots; the grass was cold. Not the crew, though—Grateth passed us on a silver-furred mount, heading toward the track that led out of the valley, and he ducked his head in salute, smiling shyly. There was friendly chatter from a group clearing up the remains of the breakfast fire. Some of them waved to us.

Clintris and Mora smiled as they went by, and Clintris called, "We've saved you breakfast."

"We didn't want to interrupt you," said Mora. "Tah and fried bread, in the cookhouse, whenever you want it."

They went on. Ran was quiet, even unhappy-looking this morning.

"They're embarrassed about yesterday," I said, with some surprise. "They *like* us."

"Wonderful," he said, seeming, if anything, more depressed than ever.

"Take a walk with me," Ran said, about an hour later.

I'd been taking a nap in the dimness of the main building. I got up, puzzled, and followed him out to the grounds, past the spot where Clintris na'Fli had drawn such spectacular attention to us. I assumed he wanted to speak to me privately, but when we crossed the wall and kept going, a good sixty meters past the stones, I stopped abruptly. Ran still hadn't spoken. I said, "What are you doing? The lookout will have them all after us! I'd rather not have to defend myself again, you know—yesterday was bad enough."

He pulled me on. "Lazarin's the lookout today, and with Stereth away he decided to join Des in a card game on the roof. Neither of them are paying more than occasional attention to the view."

I snatched my arm away. "Are you crazy? This is supposed to be it? Our great escape, in broad daylight? Where's your waterbag—"

He was forced to stop. "Stereth will be back this afternoon, we won't get another chance. We'll have to do what we can for water in Kynogin—"

"Where everybody will recognize you as Stereth Tar'krim!"

I swiveled my head back as I argued; the fort was lazy today, without Stereth to push it along—people were indoors napping, playing games, doing a lick or two of work in desultory fashion. Ran was right, there would probably never be less attention paid to us than now. But what difference did that make, if we couldn't get off the Plateau?

He said, "I'll stay hidden in Kynogin while you bargain for transport."

"Hidden where? Bargain with what? Did you pack up your gold tabals on the way out of the fort?"

"We don't have a choice! So *come on*."

He made the mistake of reaching for my arm again, and I stepped back. "Why are you so determined to clear out today? Why don't we have a choice? Ran, *what have you done?*"

"What have I done? What have *you* done!"

We faced each other. "Want to tell me what you mean by that?"

He waited stubbornly, not answering, then looked back toward the fort. Time was not on his side. He said, "Theodora, you're losing your edge."

"What the hell does that mean! When did I become a piece of cutlery?"

"This is what I'm talking about. You're not seeing these people in the proper light at all any more. Stereth sends you riding off with Des on missions, and you come back lit up like the fountains on the Imperial grounds. You're *enjoying yourself,* Theodora."

It might have made a better argument if we didn't each have to keep whipping our heads around to make sure we weren't being watched. "I eat cold, greasy animal-corpse meat for breakfast, I sleep on a blanket on hard stone, there isn't anything to read for kilometers, and you tell me I'm enjoying myself. Well, I'm glad you let me know. Next time tell me sooner!"

"You like these adrenaline rushes, Theodora, I've noticed that before."

"Look who's criticizing! The man who patented the adrenaline rush and introduced it to the masses! I didn't know what physical danger was till I met you—" I was starting to sputter, so I took a deep breath. "Anyway, this has nothing to do with choosing a logical time to escape."

He bit his lip. "It does if I'm losing my partner."

"What?"

"You *like* these people."

I stared at him. "You say it like an accusation."

"What else?" His eyes looked back at me with hopelessness and rare anger. "You're not an outworlder anymore, you're a Cormallon!"

"Look, if you tell me what I am one more time—"

Suddenly he put his hand on my arm, in an entirely different way than before. I glanced around quickly. Carabinstereth was walking toward us, through the damp grass.

We waited till she reached us. She looked from my face to Ran's, then said, "This is why I never got married." She scuffed a boot in the dirt, and without any blame in her tone whatsoever, she said, "In the heat of battle you probably didn't notice, but you've come a little far from the wall. People are edgy with Stereth away, so I wonder if—as a favor to me—you'd come back in closer."

"Battle" was a strong word. Or maybe it wasn't. We accompanied her in, past the crumbling stone wall, an uncomfortable silence among the three of us. I'm not one of those people who enjoy a full-blown argument. I hate them. I felt as though I'd eaten too much and then done too many push-ups. As though I'd been squeezed dry. As though I had to move slowly and carefully, or something awful would happen, to my body or my life.

"And what did I miss?" asked Stereth the next day, as he handed his mount over to Lex.

"Uhh . . . " said Lex, looking toward Carabinstereth.

"Nothing of interest," she said. "How was your errand?"

"Let me tell you," he began, and they walked together into the main fort.

Lex shrugged in the direction of Ran and me, and took the mount away.

Stereth's errand had taken him and his two most valuable lieutenants to almost every farm and ranch in the surrounding area. Between Stereth's reputation, Des' charm, and Grateth's solid, competent presence—not to mention the gold Stereth freely handed out—the success of his treaty project was complete. Or nearly complete, anyway; the Pemhostil Ranch, the largest of all, refused to even talk with them.

Stereth wasn't put out. "Good," he said simply. "We're parasites. We need to live off *somebody*."

That night he added, "But we're going to be busy in future. We'd better stock up now—cattle, mounts, whatever we need. And it'll be a good object lesson for the other respectable citizens; they'll be glad they signed with us."

"You want to raid Pemhostil," said Carabinstereth.

"Tonight," he agreed.

Pemhostil covered a wide range of territory—enough so that outbuildings were scattered here and there, housing employees paid to protect the stock. Cormallon covered twice as much ground, but it was so safe there that a similar outbuilding had been designated for Kylla to use as a retreat, when she wanted to be alone. Lacking the Cormallon barrier, the Pemhostils provided their people with weapons, and sent them out in numbers.

By now, however, Stereth's band had left off any vestiges of democracy, or even anarchy, that it might have pretended to. If Stereth thought it was a good idea to invade Pemhostil, they were willing to oblige.

A night of nerves, hard riding, and confusion; shouted

orders under the full and half-moons. Stereth had everyone turned out, knived, booted, with dark jackets to make us harder to see—we were going to survive for a long time on what we took from this raid, he said. Fires were set in Pemhostil, to draw out the people and to drive the steer-mods where we wanted them to go. I've forgotten many of the details of those chaotic few hours, but I remember being aware at one point of Ran on a gray and black-furred mount, just over my left shoulder. Cattle swirled in a torrent around us. I pointed back to where the nearest outbuilding stood on a hill, its windows lit with yellow lights, its open doorway a square of yellow-against the blackness.

"What happened to the people that lived here?" I yelled.

"What do you think happened to them?" Ran called back, annoyed with me, himself, and the world. He turned the mount around with difficulty and spurred it toward the knot of companions on the burning horizon.

What did I think happened to them? I echoed. The ranch was alive with the lowing of cattle and the crackle of fire. This was Ivory, not Sherwood Forest.

Chapter 12

I know. I was the one who told him about Robin Hood.

The Pemhostils were maddened, naturally, but they got no sympathy from their neighbors, which was perhaps one of the points Stereth wanted to make. There was always the danger that one of our new allies would prefer the exorbitant profit of turning in Stereth Tar'krim to being a silent partner of his band; but as Des pointed out, they would have to locate him first, and then balance the promise of more money to come from the band's Sector activity versus the amount of the bounty—and the certainty of outlaw retribution.

Having signed most of the immediate threats into our cause, Stereth turned to the serious business of getting other outlaw bands to cooperate. He issued a tah invitation to Dramonta Sol ("Blood Mountain"), the leader of the largest group in the Sector. Dramonta's band operated on the Deathwell plain to the northeast, two days' ride by mount; he was known for keeping his ransoms and killing his hostages. When I heard about Dramonta, in fact, I was glad that Des had kidnapped us.

It was all very civilized. We'd been sweeping out the hall and laying the table for hours. Napkins and tah cups were at hand, sparkling clean, and Lex and Komo were discreetly placed at corners with a view of the yard, holding a rifle and pistol respectively. Finally, ten mounts rode onto the fort grounds, led by a dried-up little man with an intense expression and a young woman in a black jacket, her hair pinned up like a lady of the capital.

"Marainis Cho," Des told me, nodding toward the woman. *Never-Too-Late*. "I wouldn't mind making her close acquaintance. Dramonta's a pig, though."

"Why?" I watched as the pair dismounted and returned

Stereth's bows. No pretense here that the official posters of Ran were anything but a joke; outlaws knew too much about each other.

"He chooses a new second-in-command every couple of years. Picks the best-looking female in the band and disposes of the last one."

"Gods!" Marainis Cho undid the top button of her jacket, showing a gold choker necklace. She followed Stereth and Dramonta inside, her eyes down. "Does she know what's in store? Or do you mean something harmless by 'disposes'?"

"Harmless? With Dramonta involved? Hell, Tymon, I don't know if she knows. It's a sin, though. Look at the way she walks. You can see light between her legs. Know what that means, when a woman—"

"Spare me the male folklore, Des. I can't believe Dramonta gets away with that in his own band! We wouldn't stand for it here."

Six of the riders Dramonta had brought along were milling in the yard, talking with Grateth, Mora, and Paravit-Col. The other two riders had gone inside.

"Makes for bad feelings in the band," agreed Des. "People give Marainis a hard time about it, from what I hear."

"They give *her* a hard time—" I shut my mouth, took a breath, and said, "Carabinstereth's right. It's an insanity gene, tied to the Y chromosome."

"You can't expect them to be glad when somebody sleeps her way to second-in-command—"

"I'm going inside now. Clintris could use help with the serving." I turned and started for the main building.

"Come on, Tymon, I didn't say *I* felt that way—I'm only quoting what other people say—Tymon!"

I went in through the main hall, past the fire, and up to the low table Stereth had had installed two days ago. He glanced at me as I came in; the place was almost empty. I stayed anyway. I was nosy.

I joined Clintris in the back, where she was struggling to carry the kettle and a plate of cakes. "Take it," she said at once, holding out the kettle. I took it, and she straightened out the good robe she'd put on for the occasion. "Good. Tah's already in the strainer. The warmer's been charged. Just pour the water in, and for heaven's sake don't spill any."

Clintris was not fond of me, but then she was not fond of anyone, and when she needed help she didn't debate over where it came from. I carried the kettle to the table, removed the painted ceramic top from the pot, and released the aroma of black tah into the room. I poured slowly, the way I'd seen other people do it, and then I put the kettle on the stone floor and stood against the wall, as though waiting to be of further service.

Stereth glanced my way again, but didn't ask me to leave. From a quirk in the corner of his mouth I suspected I was amusing him. Good.

Clintris returned to the cookhouse for more pastries. Dramonta took a sip of his tah cup, but left the cake he'd been given untouched on his plate. No wonder he was such a dried-up little man, I thought. Probably his only pleasure came from killing his hostages and lovers.

"Kind of you to invite us," he said, pursing his lips austerely as he replaced the tah cup. He had a capital accent, and an upper-class one to boot.

"Gracious of you to come," said Stereth. "Marainis, I hope the cake meets with your approval. Please don't be polite if it doesn't; there'll be more coming at any moment."

I wondered if that were a swipe at Dramonta. He really should have taken a bite; to show he didn't think it was poisoned. Marainis spoke in a husky voice, "Thank you, it's delightful. I haven't had berry dressing since I was a child."

"Umm, and it's a very nice headquarters you have here," added Dramonta, in an effort at courtesy I had not expected of him. From the things I'd heard, I suppose I'd started to picture him as drooling and throwing cutlery.

"Thanks, but it's nothing compared to your own organization, I understand—"

And they tossed flowers at each other until my feet started to hurt. It's the way of Ivory. Finally Stereth allowed himself to be coaxed into detailing his ambition of winning a collective pardon from the Emperor. He didn't mention Robin Hood. I didn't think this would be a good audience for that, myself. He discussed the history (the folklore, really) of outlaw pardons, while Dramonta shifted in his seat, and finished, "If we can be enough of an irritant long enough, without getting caught, they'll offer us a buy-off."

"Enough of an irritant and they'll send in the provincial militia—or worse, Imperial troops."

"Well, I did say 'without getting caught.' "

Dramonta put down his tah. "You're young. It's to be expected that you run off half-cocked, getting yourself into trouble before looking—"

"May I ask the flaw in my plan?"

"We're not an army." Dramonta handed his cup to Marainis, seemingly forgetting that he wasn't at home. She glanced down at the cup in her hand, raised an eyebrow, and set it on the table. "There are simply not enough of us to *be* an irritant, from the Imperial point of view. And only the Emperor has the authority to buy off acknowledged outlaws. Not the Governor. Who will be the one you really irritate."

Stereth smiled. "Enjoying your tah?"

"Yes, thank you."

"It's black tah, from one of the Ordalake plantations."

"It's very nice," said Dramonta, a little impatiently.

"Did you know that all the tah from the plantations around the western lakes comes across the Northwest Sector? That's about ninety percent of the black tah used on this continent."

"Well, that's fascinating."

"And since it comes across the Sector, they can't use airtrucks. It all moves on the ground."

"Thank you, I'm aware of the tah shipments. I've robbed enough of them in my life."

"Of their money. Not their tah."

Dramonta frowned. "What would I do with a hundred sacks of tah? We take a sack occasionally, for personal consumption—"

"Of course."

"But I fail to see who would profit from stockpiling tah sacks to rot in the Sector. And in this climate? It'd start to go bad in a few weeks."

Marainis, who'd been listening bright-eyed, turned to him. She opened her mouth as though to explain something, then shut it again and picked up her tah cup. She regarded Stereth from over the rim.

Stereth said, "Imagine what would happen along the coast—and in the capital—if the tah shipments stopped coming through the Sector. There are a few green tah plantations in the south, and I assume the red would still come from overseas, but that would never be sufficient to meet the demand. And by far the tah used most is black."

Dramonta was silent. I couldn't tell what he was thinking.

Stereth went on. "Maybe the Palace and the noble Houses would arrange to get hold of what little tah there would be available—which of course would only add to the friction."

"What friction?" Dramonta burst out finally. "They can drink chocolate in the morning! Or tea."

Stereth seemed disappointed in him. "Have you tried going without tah for a few days? Have you been through withdrawal symptoms?"

"No, but what of it? It won't kill them."

"No." Stereth grinned. "It will only irritate the hell out of them."

It didn't work. Dramonta wasn't going to play, and after another cup or two of tah to satisfy honor, he and Marainis mounted up and took their team home. Several of our band looked depressed, but Stereth put a hand on Des' shoulder and said, loud enough to be heard, "Never mind. He's only one man. The others will be interested."

And as it turned out, he was right.

By the red quarter-moon, High Summer Night, there were three other bands bedding down with us in the fort. Ran was appalled at the numbers he had to share space with. He didn't even get a break in the water-carrying, because now three times as many jars had to be hauled. I knew all this from observation, because we hadn't spoken to any great degree since our argument on the day after our half-wedding night.

I considered the even tenor of the scholarly life that I had once anticipated. Then I considered the ideal that had replaced it, of working with Ran in the capital and at Cormallon. As I walked beside him into the hall one morning, while he grunted under the weight of a waterjar, I said, "I suppose normal life will start sometime in the future."

"Huh. Since meeting you, I've forgotten what a normal life is."

This was an old joke. "You're not going to descend to blaming me again—"

"It's a luckspell. Somebody's saddled us with seven years of bad luck. Five more to go—think you're up to it?"

He set the waterjar down in the washing line, straightened, and pushed a fist into the small of his back. I said, "You'd know if there were a luckspell on you."

"Very cleverly applied, tymon—they put it on you, and now it's spilling over onto me."

At least he was still talking to me, even after I'd appalled all his notions of House honor. And I will say this for Ran: If he'd really believed there was an ill-luck spell on me, he would have stuck with me for the five years. And he wouldn't have expected any special praise for it, either, he would expect me to take it for granted. This sort of knowledge made him a lot easier to live with when he became difficult.

I was about to make some sort of comment when I saw Carabinstereth climbing up onto the sideboard table. "What in the world is she doing?"

"Everybody!" yelled Carabinstereth. "Could I have your attention? Everybody—I mean, brothers and sisters, ho, listen!"

Stereth had started the "brothers and sisters" form of address. People weren't sure of names, what with all the strangers coming and going now, but he wanted to engender a feeling of intimacy; an idea that we were all one band. Anyway, I assume that's what he wanted. His reputation was growing by leaps and bounds, though, and one band or not, the newcomers seemed to put Stereth's original group on a pedestal. ("Did you really rob a tax shipment?" asked one man curiously, to me—with a look in his eyes as though I were a pirate queen. I teetered between feeling uncomfortable and a temptation to swagger.)

"Brothers and sisters? Thank you." Carabinstereth stood precariously near the tah service. She grinned her outlaw grin. "I have some announcements. —Hi, Paravit, just put the jar down and come and join us. First, in an effort to improve the efficiency and safety of every member of this band, physical training will begin this afternoon in the hall. By physical training I do not refer to calisthenics, sa'ret, spot-dancing, body building, or some other . . . recreational activity. I refer to methods of disabling, maiming, and killing people, with and without weapons. Don't worry if you don't consider yourself in good physical shape." She grinned again, looking at our faces. "You won't need to be for the tricks I'm going to teach you. I'll be taking the women shortly after lunch—don't eat too much, sisters—and Komo will take the men tomorrow morning. Every female not on duty will report to the hall—"

There was a babble of disagreeing voices. Carabinstereth raised a hand. "Ladies! I know that none of you will want to pass by an educational opportunity like this. Gentlemen, you will *not* be in the hall while my class is going on; you will report to the hall after wash-up tomorrow morning. Any man seen here after class begins will be used as a demonstration model." She paused, then said more seriously, "Come on, boys and girls, it's not optional. It's the word according to Stereth, so make the best of it. Or argue with him, not with me."

She got down from the sideboard and was immediately surrounded by people all talking to her at once. I turned to Ran. "What do you make of that?"

He was thoughtful. "When it comes to conducting robberies, outlaws have never placed a high premium on physical training. I suppose it would be useful. Or do you think he's anticipating a pitched battle?"

That was a frightening thought. "We'd be crushed."

"He must know that. Of course, it would depend on the aims of the other side. If they wanted to take prisoners, to make a good show on the execution block—political mileage, you know—and they came in close enough for some real hand-to-hand . . . then we might keep them occupied. Long enough for Stereth to escape, anyway."

"Ugh. I don't even want to think about it. I'll be over the hills and down the hermit-hole long before the first charge—and you'd better be with me, half-husband."

"No fear."

We went back to finish washing up. I said, "I suppose I should go find a hermit-hole this afternoon, too. No point in my showing up for training."

"Why not?"

I was surprised. "Look at my size! I'm a barbarian. I'm smaller than most women I meet, let alone most men. Come on, now—whatever Carabinstereth's 'tricks' are, don't tell me some big fellow couldn't knock me out with one hand. And if he's got a knife or a pistol—I mean, physical facts are physical facts. I *avoid* trouble, Ran, that's how I survive. Fortunately, most people don't take me seriously."

He smiled and kissed my forehead. "I take you seriously, half-wife."

Ran will *do* things like that just when you're trying to make a point. Talk about knocking the weapons out of your hands. Clearly he didn't need to bother with training, either.

"I mean, people who could hurt me. Remember when I first learned who Annurian was? He would have killed me if he thought I was a threat."

"So, and if you were this hypothetical giant armed male, would you have been a threat to him?"

"No. I couldn't have turned him in, he was a friend."

"Maybe that's why he knew you weren't a threat. Go on, tymon, take the class. Learn a few dirty tricks. I won't worry as much about you when we're not together."

I frowned up at him. "You never told me you worried."

"What would have been the point? But now that you can alleviate the worry . . . keep me from getting gray hairs like Stereth . . . "

"All right, all right. You win. I'll change into those provincial trousers you hate and go to class."

He smiled and hugged me in one of his rare public displays of affection. Like most Ivoran men I'd met, Ran was a poor loser but generous in victory. With women it seemed usually the opposite. Maybe it depends on which you've had more experience with.

One man was in the class after all—Lex, Carabinstereth's partner, decked out in shin protectors and a padded helmet. After they ran a half dozen or so attack demonstrations and went over the twists and kicks with us, Carabinstereth announced, "And now you will all line up, and Lex will attack you."

We all looked at each other. Lex was psychotic.

"Children," said Carabin, with reproachful affection. "We won't do anything you haven't seen today. This afternoon only, Lex will hold back. Take advantage of the situation. Tymon, you go first. Lex will jump you from behind."

"Me?"

"Somebody has to go first."

"I don't remember anything we did." I didn't, either. I had a vague memory of snap-kicking a cushion that Lex had held . . . and then there was something about the arms, wasn't there? Really, I had no idea.

Her lips twitched. "No one ever does. Walk out to the middle of the mat, Tymon. Don't turn around, you'll know when he reaches you."

I walked out slowly. Everybody in the hall, all twenty-eight women, were watching me. My heart was jackhammering in a sick and wild rhythm and my brain seemed to be nonfunctional.

I was grabbed from behind. I turned into the grab, bringing my elbow around as I went, smashing into Lex's padded helmet. Then I kneed him in the groin (a lot of Carabinstereth's lessons centered on this area, and Lex was careful to have padding there as well), and when he doubled over I smashed the other knee into his skull. The whole thing took about a second and a half, and then I was staring at Lex on the mat.

"My gods," I said. "It worked."

"All right, Tymon," called Carabinstereth. "Move off the mat now, so you don't make Lex nervous. While you're both on the mat, you're enemies."

I walked over to the side and watched Lex pull himself up slowly, with a grunt. He moved unsteadily toward Carabinstereth and whispered to her. She bit her lips, and I couldn't tell if she were upset or laughing. Then Lex returned to the head of the mat.

Carabin said, "Sisters, Lex has decided that since this is your first lesson, he'll go slowly with this particular attack drill. Everyone can, uh, take it easy. . . . All right, next—Selene—take the mat . . ."

Several days later:

Carabinstereth clouted Berwin on the ear, though not

hard. "You're *thinking*," she said, as though it were a dirty word. "Stop it this instant."

It was Carabinstereth's professed ambition to get us to stop thinking. "This is conditioning," she announced to us all, early in the game; "you know how scared you are on the mat? Good! We want you to be scared! By the time you get out of here your reaction to a spurt of adrenaline will be to go into a drill."

Heavens, was that really the way Carabin lived her life? I made a mental note never to irritate her. But our instructor really had nothing to worry about in terms of the nervous line of women waiting by the mat, for as soon as we got into live drills, thinking was no longer an option. The watchfulness for an opening and the reaction to it when it came was about all there was space for in one's head. When an attack came this way, we did this. When it came another way, we did that. Often you couldn't remember what had happened when it was over.

Sometimes there were bits and pieces. I remember one drill near the beginning, when my opponent had just been doubled over with pain into the perfect position for a head-crack. But I blanked out on my training; stood there for an eternal portion of a second, reflecting that the only blow I could think of could only be administered from a ground position, and here we were on our feet. What in heaven's name was I supposed to do?

A minute later he was on the ground and I'd returned to the practice line, and Juvindeth, just ahead of me, said, "Good *work*, Tymon!" and a woman I didn't know shook her head happily and said, "Wonderful!" And you know what? To this day I have no idea what I did.

Apparently this was a common phenomenon. There were other common points, too, points that took me by surprise because they went far beyond physical combat.

There are things you learn in this life as you get older, if you will forgive my saying something so obvious. But many of those things you'll have been warned about in advance—you would think all of them, wouldn't you? And yet some come out of nowhere and yank you off your feet, and there you are, ass-down on the ground with a look as shocked as if you were the first human in all of history to face this particular blow. I had never suspected, for instance, when I was younger, that my state of mind could be so at the mercy of certain outside things. I had had no idea that something like "being in love" could change my entire point of view, making a spring of ridiculous satisfaction that lay just under the surface of everything I did. It was a totally nonsituational happiness, or situational only in that it related to proximity to Ran. Kidnappings and other such things were irrelevant to it. I'd been an Athenan rationalist and scholar; I'd felt pride in work that was well done, the pleasure of learning, of completing things I'd set out to finish. But this was something scarier, something clear outside of myself; I might as well be injected with a happiness drug.

I will tell you now that I was not pleased with it, or as not-pleased as I was capable of being while humming every morning and smiling at odd moments. But at least I learned that I was not alone in this mental vulnerability, it was part of the way we humans were wired. I labeled it an exception to normal life, and put it aside. Now under Carabinstereth's tutelage I learned new exceptions (and how many exceptions could there be, I worried, as my mental lists grew).

For one thing, there was the rollercoaster I went through at drill. Dread, dread, dread, as I waited in line, mixed with some anticipation. Then the fight itself began, and the fear was gone; there was no room for anything but an intense concentration. Then Lex or Grateth would be down and I would return to my place, feeling emotion start to seep back—in this case a blind euphoria that lasted for hours, sometimes for days. In talking with the other women afterward I found they were going through exactly the same cycle. It had never crossed my mind that humans were so predictable, that we could be turned on and off so easily. The very concept was anti-Athenan. And it bothered me a great deal.

But there was more. At supper on the third day we were waiting in line by the cookhouse for some stew when two men from another band walked past the line and went straight to the bowl. They didn't necessarily mean anything by it; there were only three of us on line, and we were behind the rope that marked off the serving table so they may not have seen us. Line jumping happened every now and then because when the supper rush was over there was no line at all, and people got used to just walking by and taking what they wanted. When it did happen everybody waiting would look at each other, wondering if they should give up and rush for whatever was left in the bowl.

Without thinking I called, "Friends, the line's over here. If you're wanting supper." They turned, looked confused, then dissatisfied, then joined the line. When I reached the bowl, the server that night said, "I'm glad you did that, sister. I hate it when they jump the line." But as I ate I found myself thinking, why in the world did you do that? You've never done it before, you always let them past.

Understand, I spent my childhood on Pyrene, where I learned early never to volunteer, never to complain about unfair rules, and never to call attention to myself. These attributes, developed into fine talent, have stood me in good stead in my life. It's thanks to them that I could move from one culture to another and particularly that I blended in as well as I did on Ivory, where my physical characteristics were so different.

So what in heaven's name had come over me now?

I talked with the other women before the next session and many of them had done similar things. The aggression level in our class was clearly rising. One of them had picked a verbal fight with someone who'd tried to criticize her choice of tah. One had given an ultimatum to her lover about where they were living when Stereth got us pardons. I was shocked. Somehow I'd associated aggressive behavior with "the silly things men do." Clearly I'd been kidding myself—here we were, as vulnerable as anybody to it. This was frightening; were we all going to end up as Carabinstereths?

I put the question to the other women and we looked at each other in horror. We liked Carabinstereth, but being her was another question entirely. Good god, when would you ever *rest?*

It was Carabinstereth who set us straight. "It'll wear off, my friends," she said, when several women told her, wide-eyed, what they'd done. She laughed. "It doesn't last very long, really it doesn't."

She was right. The pendulum swung back, although it didn't stop in exactly the same space it was in when we began. It still troubles me. What else will I learn that can change me even if I don't want to be changed?

Chapter 13

"Children," called Carabinstereth. "Mora tells us that she held back in this drill because she thought Lex's eye protectors might not be strong enough. This is not your concern! Kindly bear in mind that when he's on that mat, Lex is not our beloved instructor, he is an enemy. Our aim is to push those eyeballs right back into his squidgy little brain! If permanent damage and death occur, then joy be to us all. Anyone I catch holding back—"

I was halfway down the line that afternoon. Juvindeth, standing just behind me, pulled off a boot and shook it. A pebble dropped. She said to me, "So, you and Sokol have another wife."

"I beg your pardon?"

"Your senior wife. She must be upset about not knowing where you are."

"We don't have a senior wife."

Now it was Juvindeth who looked confused. "That day in the cookhouse, when you said it was your honeymoon—"

Oh. The custom that was not followed here with principal wives. I said, "Well, I'm a foreigner, and since I'm going to be the only wife he ever has, I wanted a honeymoon."

"Oh, I'm sorry. He doesn't look that poor. I guess the sorcery business has its ups and downs."

"Poor?"

"Not to be able to afford another wife. It'll be lonely, just the two of you." She put a hand on my wrist in comfort. "You should move in with his family, if he has any. They'll be some company for you, anyway."

The Ivoran view of things was sometimes disconcerting. I said, "I don't think you quite—"

"Our time's up for today," called Carabinstereth. "You're all doing excellent work. Now gather 'round, because there are a few things I need to tell you. —Don't worry, Sel, we'll start with you first tomorrow." She gave Selene a wicked look. "Now, I'm going to warn you about something. You've all got friends or lovers in the band, and you all talk a lot. That's fine as far as it goes—but you'll be better off not bringing up your training around the men, even if you've done something you're particularly proud of and want to share it. This is because—and I'm telling you, it's going to happen—some of them are going to want to fool around with you. They'll say, 'Show me what you've learned, sweetie,' or they'll creep up behind you, or some damn thing." She took a swallow from the waterjug. "Now, I'm not going to say that isn't from some deep-seated male urge to sabotage any woman who might be a threat, because it probably is."

Nicely done, Carabinstereth. You know how to win friends and influence people. I looked toward Lex, whose face showed no expression. Our instructor continued.

"But to be honest, that's not all it is. For one thing, they'll think it's cute as the dickens that you're learning this stuff, and they won't believe for a second you could hurt them. And well, for another—it's the way they deal with each other, too. Horseplay. You know how they throw fake punches at each other for the hell of it."

Nods from the other women, although I could not imagine Ran throwing fake punches at anybody.

"Well, we're not teaching you horseplay. We're teaching you to maim and kill. And we're teaching you not to think about it. So what happens when some guy tries to have fun with you? Either you hold back, which ruins your conditioning, or you damage him."

"So what do we do?" asked Mora.

"Try to avoid the situation," said Carabinstereth. "But if you can't, it's more important that you maintain your training. Don't ever stop and think, friends, or you'll answer to me. Strike, that's all."

We all looked at each other. Maim or kill one of our guys?

"I know," said Carabinstereth. "But *don't think.* Anyway," she added, "men who've been through serious training themselves—deserters and whatnot—usually won't give you trouble. They understand how it works, you can talk to them. It's the green apples you have to worry about, and they're less valuable as fighters."

We didn't have to wait long. That very night Paravit-Col crept up behind Juvindeth while she was doing the dishes and grabbed her. She whirled, smashing her elbow bone into his face, and managed to stop herself before she followed up with a knee to the groin. "Oh, Parry," she cried. "I'm so sorry."

Paravit-Col had his hands over his face. Blood was spurting freely from his nose, which we later learned was broken. He hadn't taken more than two steps back, however, before Komo clouted him on the ear.

"Good for her," said Komo, who'd been eating a pellfruit nearby. "I warned you not to do that."

I was glad Komo wasn't *our* instructor.

Later, I wasn't sure. Carabinstereth had no criticism about not following up with the groin blow—there had been time enough after the initial reaction to register the data that it was an idiot ally instead of an enemy. But she made Juvindeth run three drills in a row with multiple attackers, as punishment for having told Paravit-Col she was sorry.

Tarniss Cord, also known as the Only Outlaw Who Uses His Birthname, had a headquarters over a day's ride north of us, and west of Dramonta's territory. Tarniss Cord had started out in Dramonta's company and eventually paid a fee to be allowed to set up on his own. Rumor had it that he still paid tribute to his old leader for the right to continue as an independent.

"Why do I have to go?" I asked Stereth. "Who am I? I'm not anybody."

"You're company for Des," he replied. "Besides, Cord has a soft spot for barbarian women, and I'm not sending Cantry."

Ran was out at that moment with a crew in the cookhouse, trying to clean it up from the major singeing it had taken when the ancient oven backed up at dinner the previous night. I wished he were there. It was reassuring to at least look at each other's helpless expressions as we were carted off on another mission for Stereth.

Des walked over and joined us. "Hey, Tymon, I hear we're running off together."

"We'll see," I said noncommittally.

Stereth smiled. "All right, children—as our Carabin would say—I'm about to tell you everything I know about Tarniss Cord's group, and what I want you to say to him."

Des sat down and crossed his legs, looking attentive. I sighed and leaned against the wall. He began, "There are thirty-two people in Cord's band. He has three lieutenants; their names are Ishal, Cabrico, and Daramin . . ."

Half an hour later I passed Mora Sobien Ti in the courtyard on the way to the mounts. I said, "Will you tell Sokol I've been sent off for a couple of days? I don't think it's anything dangerous." Probably. So far as I knew.

She said, "Of course, Tymon. Road-luck to you, and to Des, too, I guess. Are you going with her, Des?"

He paused near the mounting block. "Sure. Tymon and I are running off to start a new life in the territories."

She smiled. "Then road-luck to you, too, Des. Bring me back a present."

Des grinned, bent over and put one arm around Mora's back. He kissed her good-bye. I've never forgotten that picture: Des was young and tall and brimming with confidence; Mora was graying and marked by a life of endurance. For a moment there they both looked like gods, or anyway something other than human, something that transcended; something that would last. Then Des let go. He took the halter of his mount from Lex and swung into the seat. "I'll see what I can find for you," he promised Mora.

For a quarter of a second I had one of my flashes of the way all this had to end; Des and Mora's bodies thrown down from the execution block like offal.

Des pointed his mount toward the two blasted trees at the entrance to the valley. He twisted his neck around. "You coming, Tymon?"

"Right behind you, Des."

Ran emerged from the cookhouse, wiping soot and sweat from his face. He looked toward me and stopped dead.

"Ask Stereth," I called helplessly, and followed Des away.

From the look on my half-husband's face, this was going to be very difficult to explain.

* * *

There's an old Imperial fort on the Plateau called Deathwell. It's a real fort, not a monastery like Stereth's hideout; a big, sprawling place, not used for the last eight or nine centuries because it was said to be a seat of bad magic and ill luck. Too many executions had taken place there, too many treacherous blows had been struck—within the ranks of the military hierarchy and without—and too many of them had left a bad sorcerous smell behind. It was a place to be avoided by any sensible person.

Tarniss Cord was a rulebreaker. Deathwell was his headquarters. I saw it first from the top of a hill, the clouds heavy above us and the cool plateau wind ruffling the fur of my mount.

"Gods, it's enormous," I said to Des.

It loomed over that part of the land like a giant black fist.

"The Imperials don't do things by halves," he said.

"This isn't my idea of a hideout. Surely everybody for leagues around must know about this place."

"They don't think anybody would be crazy enough to live there," he said, signaling his mount to go down the hill toward the trail that led up to the fort. "And if it does cross anybody's mind, they keep it to themselves. Nobody wants to have to go there in person to see."

"But Stereth thought it would be good if *we* went."

He grinned. "Cheer up, Tymon. If we die at Deathwell, we'll die like heroes in a play."

I lagged behind. "How dangerous is this, anyway?"

"I'm joking, Tymon, I'm joking. We have diplomatic immunity. Come on, you wouldn't let your companion-of-the-road go on alone, would you?" For Des, this was the unrefusable question. Someday I should use it on him, I thought as I caught up to him and we started up the hill.

At closer quarters I could see the disrepair; the lost stones sitting by themselves in the grass near the wall, the place where a diverted stream had dried up long ago without Imperial engineers to maintain it. There were characters cut into the stone of the wall, graffiti left by soldiers who'd been dust for centuries. "An early death to Captain Nayle," said one. "I want to go home," said another, simply. A five-line poem was scratched at what was eye-level for me on my mount; somebody must have stood on something to do it. Not all the characters were still legible. "The breezes are warm in the capital. The [?] of my first [?] home are sweet. But my soul longs for the scouring wind of autumn and the evenings of cold rain."

We were near the main gate. A voice floated down from somewhere above us: "All right, my friends, you can wait there." We halted. Des didn't move, so I didn't either.

The voice called, "Are you the messengers?"

"We are!" yelled back Des. We searched the top of the wall, but there was no sign of life.

"Then you can give me your names."

"Des Helani and Tymon. And the acceptance was relayed by Ishal of your band."

There was silence again. We waited, and five minutes later the massive gate swung open. I looked up as we rode inside. The clouds above us were heavy and filled with the promise of cold rain.

"We've been watching you for twenty minutes," said Daramin cheerfully. Her long black braid bounced against her fanny as she preceded us into the heart of the fort, and I could see Des trying to tear his gaze away from it. "You're not fast riders, are you?"

He cleared his throat. "Uh, no. That is, we like to be careful."

"Us, too," she said.

Twisting passageways and unexpected sets of stairs went on for quite a while, and we didn't see another soul. I was beginning to consider that Tarniss Cord's thirty-odd people could live here pretty successfully even if the occasional riding party did come by and look through the fort. They seemed to disappear very well when they wanted to.

A stone fish blew a plume of water into a font at the entrance to one stairway, and Des paused to wipe his face. "Don't drink that water," said Daramin sharply.

He looked up, puzzled.

"Our supply's been fouled," she explained. "That's what Cord's working on."

We passed three other fonts as we descended the staircases, all beneath each other vertically, all presumably useless. There were no windows now, not even tiny ones. Daramin took a torch from the wall. "We have a generator," she explained, "but they never bothered to lay wire down here. I guess they didn't come down too often."

We were deep inside the hill that Deathwell was built on by now. Perhaps this was where they buried the bodies of strangers who came bothering them. I glanced at Des. He walked with such confidence; thoughts like this never crossed his mind. And in any case, his attention still seemed focused on Daramin's braid as it bounced hypnotically from one buttock to the other. I wondered again about Stereth's wisdom in sending Des as an emissary.

We came out at last into a great pillared cellar. Rows of kegs covered the far wall and racks for weapons—some even with weapons in them—were stacked against another. A dozen lamps swung from the ceiling. In the corner the stones of the flooring had been broken up and a pit dug; picks and shovels were scattered nearby and some kind of pulley system rigged above the hole. A man stood there straddling the entrance. He took up a bucket and dumped a load of earth onto a growing pile near the kegs. His shirt was off, his brown skin was sweating, and he looked like a prizefighter. His hair was longer than any Ivoran male's I'd seen. He wore it in a ponytail that was plastered now to his back. He returned to the pit and called down: "How does it look?"

The reply was muffled.

Daramin brought us over, bowed, and said, "Tarniss Cord . . . our visitors from Stereth Tar'krim."

"Honored by this meeting," said Des formally. I bowed.

The Only Outlaw Who Used His Birthname wiped his brow. "I, too, am honored." He glanced down at the pit again, then back at us. In a less formal tone he said, "I don't suppose either of you is an engineer."

"I'm afraid not," said Des.

Cord said, "The dowser told us this was the best spot to try. And really, we ought to be able to go down at any point here and hit the same water supply. So we're just digging down, shoring up the hole, and hoping for the best. I suppose if we're going about it wrong we'll find out soon enough."

"Ah," said Des.

I said, "From what Daramin told us, I thought your

supply was fouled. Why do you want to dig another way into it?"

Daramin and Tarniss Cord looked at each other. A taboo topic? Cord said, "Daramin, why don't you go check on Ishal's inventory? I don't want any more arguing over shares." His lieutenant nodded, smiled at us, and left.

Cord said to me, "It's not something we dwell on here. We took some hostages from a lumber convoy recently, and three nights ago one of them committed suicide. He threw himself down our well. The body's still jammed halfway between the second and third stories, we're working on getting it out. But we can't use that accessway any more."

"I take it you took steps to propitiate the well," said Des.

"Naturally. But the way things are, we'll need a new one dug. It's our first priority at the moment." He smiled. "But I can talk to you as I work. Care to take a bucket?"

Des unhitched a heavy bucket of earth from the pulley. Then he handed it to me.

Shortly we all smelled as bad as Tarniss Cord did. He promised us real baths before we returned to Stereth. "Rows of tubs," he said. "For the soldiers, you know. We won't be able to get the water level as high as you'd like, though. We're hauling it all in by the wagonload until this crisis is over."

We talked as we moved dirt. If Tarniss Cord had a soft spot for barbarian women, you couldn't prove it by me. He certainly seemed more than willing to let me share in the labor, and if he did any flirting it must have gone over my head. On the other hand, Des surprised me. He remembered every detail Stereth had briefed us on, and used it all. He was reasonable, he was persuasive, and in fact he reminded me a lot of Stereth while he was talking.

But Cord held back. "Dramonta hasn't agreed to join you," he said.

"Dramonta is wrong. But you don't need to follow him down the wrong path."

"Easy for you to say, my friend. Have you heard I pay a tribute to Dramonta?"

"The whole Sector has heard," said Des coolly. "They say your nickname ought to be The Only Outlaw Who Still Pays Taxes."

That hit home, I saw. Cord practically flinched. It wasn't like Des to make a dig like that, but it was like Stereth.

Cord said, "I've heard of your band's reputation. Who hasn't? But I have a life to live, and people I'm responsible for right here. I don't want to make any more enemies than I've got, and if a share of booty will appease Dramonta he can have it."

"A pardon would reduce your number of enemies considerably," Des pointed out.

"Pardons don't help dead people. Look, we all know the Emperor could crush us to pulp if he cared to make the effort. And spend the money. So why give him a reason?"

"Look, uh, gracious sir. What we all know is that when it comes to money the Emperor is so tight he squeaks when he walks. He doesn't *want* to send an army here. Pardons are cheap. —And as for friends, as opposed to enemies? Stereth has a lot more friends than you do right now. And that's not accidental. They believe he can succeed. *I* believe he can succeed. What have you heard about the tah blockade?"

He was puzzled. "The what?"

Des explained. Finally Tarniss Cord said, "It may be possible. But I'm a cautious bastard, that's why I'm here and in charge. I tell you what, gracious sir. If Stereth can take every tah shipment between now and the beginning of Fire Moon, I'll accept his offer. He'll need a long reach, though, my friend. And plenty of luck. Tell him Deathwell will be watching."

"And if he has reach and luck? Will you give a road-oath?"

Cord laughed. "You won't leave without an assurance, will you?"

"No, sir."

"You ask a great deal of a stranger, you know. If Dramonta finds out even this much of our conversation, he'll kill me."

"I'm not asking you to swear with your hand over your heart," said Des coolly. "Someplace lower down would do better for me."

Cord's smile vanished. "If you think I don't have what it takes to run a band of outlaws, you're mistaken. Whatever direction I choose to take them in."

Having gotten his effect, it was time for Des to step back and be conciliatory. "I don't question the courage of anyone who would willingly live in Deathwell. I'm just asking you to shine a little of it in my direction."

"I've said that I'll accept if he can begin the blockade. I swear it on my life as a cantry tar'meth and on the lives of every man I'm responsible for." He spat. It just missed the pit. "Satisfied?"

"Yes. Thank you, sir." Des took hold of my arm. "Come along, Tymon, let's see if we can find one of those baths. Unless you'd like us to continue helping, sir?"

"Get along, both of you. And remember, I'll be watching."

We stayed that night at Deathwell, through a thunderstorm that howled like a three-year-old, with no pause for the nerves of its listeners. Daramin took care of us; I never saw any others of the band the whole time I was there. Tarniss Cord really was cautious.

Sometime toward morning, when the blackness had changed to gray through the windowslit and the after-storm hours held an unnatural stillness, I heard a skittering sound in my room. I was sleeping on a cot in one of the tiny officer's rooms on the fourth story; Des was next door, and Daramin was somewhere within shouting distance on the floor. The generator was off for the night and there were no candles, but the lightening sky brought the objects in my room into dim relief.

Something moved over by the bureau. I sat bolt upright. Behind the bar of soap I'd brought from the fort, behind the hairbrush—

Kanz. It was a frangi.

Pyrene is responsible for the frangis. They are indigenous to that planet and we (I say "we" as a native-born) have to take the blame for carelessly transporting the vermin around to our neighbors.

Fortunately, they're only slightly poisonous to most people. However, that was not why I froze. I don't know whether it's their blindness, or the silence when they move on some surfaces or the rustle when they move on others. Or the way their radar causes them to dart at you unexpectedly. Or their repulsive, repellent, gods-cursed, sickening appearance, or the way they rub their—never mind. But they scare the beejeebers out of me.

If I could make it out the door before it got anywhere near me . . . it skittered toward the edge of the bureau, and suddenly I was standing outside the room. I slammed the door and looked around the corridor, sweating. Daramin was around somewhere, but I wanted to avoid letting Tarniss Cord's group know what a coward Stereth had sent them. I walked over to Des' door and pounded on it.

"Wha, what—" Des is difficult to wake up. I went inside and closed the door behind me, just in case the frangi got out of my room.

"It's me, Des."

"Tymon . . . I'm sleeping."

"Des, there's a frangi in my room."

He peered dimly up at me from the bed. "What?"

"There's a frangi in my room!"

He continued to stare at me disorientedly. "Yeah?"

Didn't he realize this was a crisis? "If you can't do something about it, I'll have to stay here for the night."

"Ty, I'm always happy to share a bed with you, but . . . you say there's a frangi in your room."

"You've grasped it, Des."

He ran a hand over his face, sighed, and stood up. "All right, come show me where it is."

"It was on the bureau last time I saw," I said, making no move to follow him.

"Double and triple kanz," he said, and left. He was gone for several minutes.

Finally he returned. "All taken care of," he said. "It's dead."

"You swear?" Sometimes Des was a little loose with the truth when it came to his personal exploits.

"I swear on my continued hope of existence. On my road-name. On my mother's sainted head—"

"Where's the body?"

He lowered himself into the bed. "You don't want to know. Good night, Tymon."

I started for the door. He called, "Tymon—" and I turned.

"Uh . . . sweetheart, I'm sorry if I was a little difficult. I'm . . . not good at killing."

For Des to admit there was anything he wasn't good at was uncharacteristic, and generous. I said, "That's all right. I appreciate your understanding of my little quirks."

"Well, we all have them." He settled into the bed.

The next morning had the momentary clarity on the Plateau that follows a particularly vicious bout of weather. You could see for leagues. "Not a good day to travel," said Des. "Unless you're a respectable citizen."

We were riding through a section even more desolate than usual, with only the wind-twisted trees for company. The sky was incredibly beautiful. Not far from here, I knew, was a homemade gibbet on a hill that we had passed on the way to Deathwell. It was the sort of place where disgruntled farmers and ranchers took outlaws they'd captured, when they didn't feel like traveling to the authorities. No doubt it was less popular now that the Governor's reward was in effect. A skeleton still swung from it, though. ("Tev! Good to see you!" Des had called as we passed it. "How are you doing these days?" Des' sense of humor sometimes left something to be desired.)

Remembering his handling of Tarniss Cord, though, I had to admit I had done our Des an injustice. He was more letter-perfect than I ever could have been. And he hadn't rushed off afterward into the gathering rain-clouds, either, but waited out the night like a sensible boy. He knew quite well what he could do and what he couldn't, regardless of his boasting.

I told him of my admiration. This was the sort of topic he never minded hearing about. "It was nothing, Tymon," he said casually. "It was just important that Cord take us seriously, so I keyed in a little personality change."

"Gods in assembly, Des, you should be in the theater!"

"I was. Three years in the Sotar Touring Company. Didn't I ever mention it? I was Copalis in *Death of an Emperor.* 'This night, my friends, this night when the lighted boats of Anemee will never reach their slips on the lake of noble souls; this night—' " In typical Des fashion he'd veered not into Copalis, but Petev, the character who'd killed him and had the better lines. It's one of the most famous soliloquies in all of Ivoran literature, the speech Lord Petev practices to himself on the tower by the Imperial Palace the night the dynasty went through a name change. Des declaimed it to the vast emptiness around us, charging his voice with a rolling melodrama suitable to the infinity of grass and sky.

I let him finish, then took my hands from my mount long enough to clap.

"Thank you," he said. "Tarniss Cord is nothing compared to a provincial audience. And besides, I had plenty of practice for yesterday—by now, I can do Stereth better than Stereth can do Stereth. I can do him so that everybody recognizes him."

"They recognize him now."

"No, I mean really recognize." He touched his hand to the bridge of his nose as though adjusting a pair of glasses. "I hope, Tymon, you're not going to make a fuss about a simple request." The voice was an echo of Stereth's, and the words were from his briefing for the trip to Deathwell.

The cool jade eyes turned to me, and I marveled at their precision. You could almost see a beam of white light marking the track of his attention. I said, "All right, you've made your point."

He ignored me. "Because one recalcitrant in the band is enough. Our goal is going to take a full commitment from every person here—"

He went on, doing a play-by-play, only slightly improvised variation on Stereth's speech. It was more shocking to hear it from Des, though. There was a quality in it that I'd never fully realized before. It was like looking at a portrait and becoming aware of a facial feature whose prominence one had never grasped in the original. Stereth's manner was softened physically by the spectacles and behaviorally by his closeness to the band; but this quality was there in him. It was the thing that made us careful around him, even when we didn't consciously recognize why—and Des had located this chip of ice and pried it out.

It was still three kilometers to the gibbet, and the ride was spooky enough. I snapped, "For the gods' sake, Des, break character or I'll go out of my mind!"

He must have known from my voice that I was serious. His head tipped forward and he raised one hand. What in the world? Oh. Removing imaginary glasses.

"Sorry," said Des' regular voice.

We rode in silence for a minute. Then I said, "Do you ever do Stereth *for* Stereth?"

"Ha, ha," he answered briefly.

"And what in heaven's name are you doing in the Northwest Sector?"

"Ah, well, Tymon, when I left the troupe I got into a bit of trouble in Mira-Stoden. A friend of mine had an idea for making money quickly, but it didn't work out."

"But you're so good, why didn't you stick with it?"

He knew at once I meant "stick with acting," yet seemed surprised by the question. "There's no money in it, Tymon," he said reasonably.

I absorbed that. "Of course. My mistake, Des."

About five minutes later he said, "You get to meet a lot of women, though."

A guard whom we didn't know stopped us at the entrance to Stereth's valley. "Des Helani," said Des, in response to his challenge. "And who the hell are you?"

"I'm the lookout," said the guard. He was practically a boy, younger than Paravit-Col by several years. Then he said, "Des Helani! And Tymon? You two are from the original band, aren't you?"

Des softened under the influence of the obvious hero-worship in the boy's voice. "Yeah, we are. I hope the original band is still here."

"Oh, yes, sir! Things haven't changed that much."

We'd only been gone a couple of days, but things seemed different enough to me. More new bands had come in, and though I found out later that Stereth had mixed them and sent over half out again under the leadership of Komo and Sembet Triol, there were a good two dozen people in the yard as we entered. Mostly women. I found out why as we walked through the hall; it was afternoon, and the men's practice class was going on. That was a bit unreal, too—it was not a mirror image of our own by any means. Many of the moves were the same and many of the moves were different, but what was most different were the epithets Lex and Grateth yelled at the recruits. "Kanz! Worm! Boneless sloth! What do you think you're *doing!* You're *thinking* again, aren't you, you shell-less turtle, you tax-collector's asshole!" I walked on, startled, and mentioned it to Carabinstereth at the next practice session. She just nodded. "The men get torn down, and the women get built up. Don't ask me why, it's just that it seems to work."

Stereth took our reports on the Deathwell trip. Des said, "Things have been happening here, too, haven't they?"

"We've been busy. I heard there was a tah shipment from Ordralake coming on the Shaskala Road so I decided to have Komo intercept it. We're not taking hostages right now, though—we don't have space for them."

Des said, "I'm glad you decided to make a move, or we might've lost Tarniss Cord before you even knew he was available." Stereth had merely nodded, unsurprised, when Des reported that part of our conversation in Deathwell.

"It seemed a good time." He turned his attention to me. "Well, Tymon, what was your impression of Cord?"

I said, "Stereth, when you say you're not taking hostages, does that mean you confiscate their weapons and let them go?"

"No. What did you think of Cord?"

"I think he's a cautious man, like he says he is. I think he's honest . . . as honest as you can be and still run a bunch of cantry tar'meth."

He smiled briefly. "Speaking of weapons, we now have six light-rifles. I'm issuing one to each group that goes out. Not everyone who joins us now can stay here; we can't turn the place into an army camp. So we're training, processing, and releasing them into newly formed guerrilla bands. If you want to go out with one, Tymon, let me know. Obviously I'm not going to send Sokol away, but since you two seem to be having trouble—"

I was startled. "What do you mean, having trouble?"

"Maybe not trouble. A strained relationship."

"Who says our relationship is strained?"

"Perhaps I misunderstood. It was an impression I got from my conversation with him on the day you left for Deathwell. I apologize for my misconception. Des, could you go through the roster with me over here—"

I was dismissed. Of course I went straight to Ran. He was just out of practice class, walking toward the waterjars to cool down.

"Ran, Stereth thinks our relationship is strained."

"Stereth's views are of no concern to me."

Uh-oh. That was not a good answer. "Does that mean it's not strained?"

He stopped, wet a rag in the water, and wiped his neck. "It may be pulled a little thin, Theodora. I wouldn't say it's strained. But it's not exactly robust, either, when I don't even know where you've been for the last few days."

"Stereth didn't tell you? I went to Deathwell with Des Helani to meet their leader."

"Really? Did you have a nice trip?"

I was getting a little annoyed myself. "Tolerable. Look, you seem to be forgetting we're not here voluntarily. I can't choose where I go and what I do."

"No." He was silent. "Were you successful? Did the Deathwell leader agree to come in on this craziness of Stereth's?"

"Conditionally. Des got him to swear a road-oath. It was great to watch, I had no idea he was that good at protecting Stereth's interests. I mean, you know I think the world of Des, but—"

"I know."

Suddenly a lot of things became clear. I put a hand on his wrist to halt his washing. "Des is one of the sweetest people I've ever met. And his entertainment value is priceless. But I'm about as attracted to him as I am to that furry thing with the teeth that he rides."

He said, "I didn't ask, did I?" and he bent over to clean his face. But the edge was gone from his voice.

One hurdle surmounted and several dozen more to go. I sat out on the broken wall that evening by myself, and thought gloomy thoughts. He'd probably walk out of the fort tonight if I agreed to go along with it—a suicide walk, as far I was concerned, and I'd always considered him a model of enlightened self-interest. Ran and I had never had such major differences over strategy as we'd had this summer in the Northwest Sector. And a close analysis could not help but reveal that the difference in strategy were based on deeper differences as to what was important and what was not.

I had to accept the fact that being kidnapped by outlaws was not having a good effect on our engagement.

* * *

Ten days later was graduation day for my practice group. Just to up the ante, Carabinstereth was allowing the men in to watch, and any of the new women who were interested. If we made it to the end of class, we wouldn't be novices anymore. Standing between each of us and the end of class were Lex, Komo, and Grateth, who would be attacking us with hands, feet, knives, clubs, and pistols. And anything else that entered their perverted heads in the course of the event. Needless to say, every student was a wreck for at least a full day ahead of time.

I'd told Ran not to come. I was afraid of messing up and looking like a fool in front of him. For some reason he had a high opinion of my abilities, and I didn't want to destroy it. He told me he was on water-duty anyway, and would be busy hauling jars all morning.

I waited on the line that day, watching the blunted knives being laid out on the floor, feeling sorry for myself. *I didn't ask to be here.* The knives, by the way, though blunted, could still do serious harm if we weren't careful. The clubs were regular clubs. And the pistols were supposed to be discharged, but one never knew when an extra store was being held. *If Ran really cared, he'd have shown up anyway.* Oh, terrific. Now you'd like him to read your mind. *No, but I'd like him here . . . in case I don't screw up. But if I do screw up, I want him far away.*

The lead woman on line was called out on the mat, and the fun began. It went with sickening quickness. Our attackers were quick, clean, and dedicated to their work, but our class was trained to meet them anywhere they were taken. Then, about halfway through, all the rules went out the window. They started pulling people out of line at random, changing single attacks to multiples, throwing in moves we'd never seen. Mora was beside me in line; she turned and whispered, eyes wide. "It isn't *safe* here anymore." We looked at each other, both well aware that that was the conditioning message for tonight.

Well, if they wanted us to be able to operate in a state of fear they were doing a good job of provoking it.

And then Carabinstereth was gesturing to me. "Your turn, Tymon."

And I was out in the middle, alone. Then something was around my throat, and I stomped on someone's feet and turned and saw a knife in Lex's hand, and grabbed his wrist—and more things happened, and suddenly I was getting up and Lex was down on the mat. Something was dangling from my neck and I pulled it down dumbly and looked at it: A rope. Lex had tried for a garrotte first.

It was the only time anyone had tried that move, but that hardly accounted for the applause. I walked slowly toward Carabinstereth and the end of the line.

"Nice work on that other knife," she said.

I said, "What other knife?" and she pointed and grinned.

As it turned out, Lex had had a second knife. I hadn't realized it at the time, I'd just hit his other wrist as I came around and didn't even see it go skidding off across the floor. My friends on the sidelines had been horrified when they saw it first come out, but since I'd never seen it myself I felt as if I were accepting their acclaim under false pretenses. I probably would have been much more scared watching the scene than living it.

"I ought to kill you, Carabin," I said, knowing full well I should be very angry with her. Lex and Komo were as careful as they could be, but I *might* have gotten seriously hurt.

The grin was unimpaired, however, because Carabinstereth knew perfectly that I couldn't be angry at this point. I was just getting hit by the euphoria that washes over you after a win.

She bowed and waved me back in line, where two women hugged me. Lennisa was on my left in a brown leather vest; she was from the latest band we'd taken on. "Your fighting was so exciting," said Lennisa. "Even the fellow carrying the waterjars put them down and started yelling 'Go, Tymon, go!' "

Startled, my gaze snapped to the balcony. But it was empty.

Chapter 14

While I was being conditioned in the many ways and means of killing and disabling, Stereth was busy. Not a tah shipment on the plateau escaped the watchful eyes of our band or the network of allies surveying every eastern and southern road. The system of messenger birds was expanded and Des was sent from one market town to another, from one outlaw rendezvous to the next, spreading charm and good fellowship and arranging for supplies.

Sembet Triol handled the messages, and acted as courier when needed. One afternoon I saw him striding hurriedly across the grounds from the coop to the main hall, with an air of urgency impossible to mistake. I followed him.

He went straight to Stereth, pulling off the blue cap he wore on the roof where the coops were set up, and began talking before he was halfway down the hall. "You know that shipment you told me to keep an eye on? The Ordralake being brought west for air freight?"

Stereth put down the paper he was holding and stood up. "Yes."

"They got it through the Waste and hauled it down to the low country all right. Then they were going to load it onto an airtruck at Jessul and fly the long way around the plateau to get it to the capital."

"Well?"

"The airtruck blew up as soon as it took off."

Stereth was silent. Then he said, "Was the tah on board at the time?"

Sembet Triol nodded. "Eighty thousand tabals worth. They were trying to make up for the regular shipments that didn't get through. It was a superfreighter."

Stereth looked up suddenly and met my eyes. "What are you doing here?"

I said, "I didn't know you had friends as far away as Jessul."

He bit his lip. "No."

"How many people were on board?" I asked.

He shrugged. Sembet answered, "Three."

"Don't pin this one on me," said Stereth. He picked up the paper he'd been reading. "Thanks, Sembet."

"What does that mean?" I asked.

Stereth ignored me. I turned on my heel and left the hall. "Don't take it personally," said Sembet, out in the filtered light of a cloudy afternoon.

It had been six weeks since the last tah had gone south. By now every canister and jar in every village and town would be turned upside down and packets that were years old would be ripped open and rationed out. I knew what the results of this would be from having gone through withdrawal myself. Soon the citizens of Shaskala and points south would get headachy, and some would have stomach cramps. Then they'd become short-tempered. The day would seem longer and harder to get through, they would feel less alert. The headaches would get worse . . . and then they'd get better. Going off tah was easier than going off a lot of drugs. Nobody ever died from it, but it was annoying as hell. And then there was the habit of ritual that surrounded tah . . . for Shaskala, what would happen at the midmorning hour, when the merchants would all slow down and look involuntarily for the tah bowl to be brought forth? As for those farther south, breakfast for most of the population meant tah and not much else.

I really started to wonder when the next truckload of tah they tried to ship by air to the capital had a mechanical problem and dumped six hundred tons of cargo into Lake Kasheral.

"I suppose they could boil the lake," Sembet said to me, a few days later. We were talking in the coop loft when one of Stereth's feathered messengers flew in. Clintris deftly detached the paper and handed it to Sembet, who read it and laughed. You can fit a lot of message onto a little paper on Ivory, where one character equals a word, sometimes even a phrase.

"What is it?"

Sembeth said, "We'll have to send a reply messenger to Vergis Market Town. Des wants to be reminded why he's stopping there."

I started to laugh. "Tell him never to change."

Sembet, who was already scrawling a reply to go out with the rider, wrote at the bottom, "Tymon says don't ever change."

A voice spoke from the entrance to the coop. "And that should be no problem. Stereth says that Des takes direction well." Ran stood framed in the neverending cloudy twilight. "Can I talk to you for a minute, Tymon?"

That was not his happy tone of voice. As I followed him outside, past the main building to the stone wall, I noticed for the first time that he'd lost some weight since Shaskala. The grounds were more crowded these days, and I didn't even know half the people around us. We had to speak in low voices.

"Theodora, how can you be doing this?"

"Doing what? What have I done?"

He hitched himself up to the top of the wall and sat there. "The way you joke with Sembet. The way you talk to the women in your class, even to Stereth—you fit in here like a glass of water poured into the Silver River. What do you think's going to happen to these people when the government catches them?"

"Well, I know the odds aren't good, but with a little luck Stereth will get us—"

" 'Them.' 'Them,' not *us*. You've got a problem, Theodora—maybe you're a little too close to see it. You're just too adaptable."

"Look, I may not be a real cantry tar'meth, but I like the company. And they've been good to us, they treat us the same way they treat themselves."

"May I remind you that these people kidnapped us? We are not in their debt. How they can casually assume we owe them any loyalty—"

I glanced at him in disbelief. "Are you serious? You shanghaied *me* when I first came to this world, and then expected me to be a loyal Cormallon member."

"One situation has nothing to do with the other! I hired you honorably—"

"Without exactly spelling out the job requirements."

He put up his arms. "Let's not dredge up minor details from the past."

Suddenly all our circling struck me as funny, and I started to chuckle. He was taken aback. I suppressed the laughter, took his hand, and said, "I hope you don't ever change, either." On impulse, I kissed him on the cheek. "Your ego is a great comfort to me."

There were a few whistles and catcalls from witnesses to the kiss. Actual physical affection was usually reserved for the shadows here in outlaw country. The more people showed up in the bands, the more the couples would disappear into the back rooms and stablelofts. "Yeah, yeah," I called back. "Don't you have some work to do?"

"Tymon!" came Sembet's voice. "Can you give me a hand with this?"

I ignored the call. Ran said, "Why do you do these things?" But he said it, shaking his head, the way a farmer will talk about the weather: Familiar, and not likely to be changed by any human agency.

I said, "You know, before this summer, I used to only yell at you when you kept things to yourself. You've been good about that, anyway."

"Thank you. I suppose in a little place like this it's harder to collect secrets anyway."

"Or keep them once you have them."

"That, too."

Sembet's voice sounded again. "Tymon! Where are you, anyway?"

"I'd better go," I told Ran.

He sighed. "Go."

"You're not still upset?"

"As is my habit, I have resigned myself to the fact your attitude will never improve."

"Good enough," I said, and left.

I should have seen then that things were coming to a head. Ran was betraying more edginess than he generally allowed anyone to see, the fort was reaching bursting point in terms of population, militia sweeps had increased on the roads. And on the sixteenth of Kace, Fire Moon came, and Tarniss Cord issued an invitation to a joint council feast to Dramonta Sol and Stereth Tar'krim.

Stereth left the monastery fort under the command of Komo and Mora Sobien Ti, and brought most of the original band with him to Deathwell. Eight of the most promising candidates from the new bands formed a guard of honor.

We rode up the hill to Deathwell two days before the feast. Stereth halted his mount by the poem on the wall near the gate. He sat there for a long time. I was near Cantry, and I heard him turn and say to her, "Do you ever think that your best friend died before you were born?"

There was something hollow in his voice that went beyond his usual flat tones, and Cantry's reply in turn held a trace of nerves. "You're under a lot of stress, Stereth. You're feeling pressure, that's all."

He hesitated beside the poem. Cantry said, "Come in with us, love, everybody's waiting."

His mount moved on, and we all passed under the gates: I hoped that Tarniss Cord meant us well.

As a courtesy to Tarniss Cord, Carabinstereth agreed to teach one or two practice sessions for the women of Deathwell while we were there. The rest of us were assigned duties preparing for the feast—not only food, but decorations to impress Dramonta Sol and his band. Cord was the nominal host, but he was more of an arbiter, bringing two potential allies together. Our band, as the supplicants, had to put up the wine and meat for Dramonta. "We have to make everything nice before he gets here," said Des to me, as he hammered garlands into the wood molding around the arches in the great dining hall. "We have a word for this where I come from, Tymon. We call it *brownnosing.*"

I handed him some nails. "We have a similar term on Athena."

He grunted and motioned to a pile of garlands on the floor. "Why don't you help out a companion of the road," —Des' way of getting what he wanted— "and put some of those up along the arches by the other rooms?"

So I found myself stringing garlands around the entrance to Carabinstereth's practice session. The women were already lined up for their first routine. I saw the white, strained faces verging on nausea, and thought, heavens, it's just another drill. Don't take it so hard. But I remembered how nervous I'd been in their place.

Clintris came over to where I stood on a table. "But you can't work out here," she said. "It'll distract the students."

I said, "Are you joking? They wouldn't notice a marching band at this particular moment. Have you forgotten what it's like on that line?"

A faint smile appeared on her face. "You have a point." She picked up a garland. "Do you need any help?"

Oceans would part, and fish would dance on dry land. "Uh, well, thank you. I just need to finish this section here—"

"No trouble," she said, and she climbed up beside me. As she stretched for the nail at the far end, and I held the garland and looked uncomfortably toward my feet, she said, "I've been wanting to apologize for giving you such a hard time when you first appeared. I don't know what I expected from a barbarian, but you've been very . . . normal, Tymon."

"Oh. Well, thank you."

"Not at all," she said, and deftly hooked the rest of the string. "There. Any other places we need to cover?"

"The front entrance."

"Fine." She stopped and came up with an armful of white and yellow flowers. Her face was buried to the chin. "Coming, Tymon?"

That night, Stereth took me aside. He motioned for me to follow him out past the officers' cells to an aisle bordering a parapet on Deathwell's northern side. Slit windows let in blackness and stars. I saw a lookout pass along the outside of one of those windows. We waited till he'd gone, and Stereth said, "This time you won't be an observer."

My stomach turned over. I waited.

He said, "You're going to be seated next to Tarniss Cord at the feast. One of his lieutenants will be on the other side. Des will be on your right."

I was still silent. He said, "Nothing to say yet?"

"Fine, I can draw a map of the table. Thanks for bringing me up to speed—"

"Jumpy little tymon, aren't you? Here, this is for you."

He put a knife into my palm. It felt slippery. "Stereth, I think you have me confused with somebody else."

"Calm down, little one. You don't even know what I'm asking yet. All I want you to do is keep an eye on our host and make sure he behaves normally. Which I'm sure he will do. I've spoken with Cord at length and I'm impressed with his reliability."

"If you're so impressed, why do I have to keep an eye on him?"

"No harm in being careful, Tymon."

"And why at the feast? Do you have other people watching him the rest of the time?" When he didn't answer, I said, "And why don't you have Lex or Grateth do this?"

I was still holding the knife. Stereth lifted it from my palm and slipped it, sheathed, into the pocket of my outer-robe. "First," he said, "because I told you Cord has a soft spot for barbarian women. He'll like being seated next to you, and won't think anything of it. Everybody knows barbarians are as innocent as newborn puppies. Second, Lex and Grateth have the army in their bones, everyone who looks at them knows it. If I asked Cord to sit between them, it would make him nervous." I just stood there, and finally he said, with a trace of impatience, "Come on, Tymon, surely Carabinstereth has shown you how to kill with a knife."

"She has." *And anyway, I've done it.*

"The chances of your being called on to do anything are exceedingly remote. Otherwise I wouldn't ask it of you. This is soft work, for a soft outlander. That's all it is."

I was silent. Stereth said, gently, "If you can't behave like an Ivoran, maybe you should have stayed home."

I turned and went back along the passage and down the steps to the hall below, feeling the shape of the knife against my thigh through the cotton of the inside pocket.

Ran, of course, felt that Stereth's request was perfectly understandable. He had no great liking for Stereth, but arming me, he said, was "simple self-defense." "Anyway," said Ran, "if he thinks nothing will happen, then most likely nothing *will* happen. He seems pretty good at this sort of thing."

Cheery. All very cheery.

* * *

By the evening of the banquet I was in a bad state of nerves. Dramonta and his entourage had ridden in that afternoon. Dramonta accepted the overly courteous solicitude of Cord and Stereth as his due, and dispatched Marainis Cho to assist with the preparations—or more likely, to keep an eye out for poison and relevant gossip. It was to be a traditional feast, totally communal, so gossip was all she was likely to get.

The tables were covered with stolen Andulsine silk. Ran was on a ladder, putting up the last of Des' cursed garlands. Stereth's people rushed in and out, laying the dishes and putting more flowers from Deathwell plain in the center of the tables. Cord was making Dramonta comfortable in the commander's suite. I thought Stereth was with them, but he appeared suddenly in the archway at the dining hall entrance.

I was laying silverware on the table, or trying to. Somewhere around the third dish I found that my hand was shaking. A minute later I heard Stereth's voice saying, "Sit down, Tymon. The bench by the wall."

I found it and sat. Stereth seated himself beside me and took my hand. "You can handle this. It's easy. All you have to do is not be afraid."

"Oh, that does sound easy."

"It is. Look at me. I was nobody back when I was afraid. Now I'm Stereth Tar'krim."

"Don't be afraid of several thousand militia? Don't be afraid of the Atvalids?"

"Don't be afraid of dying. Of hurting other people. Of hurting yourself. Of pain. Of the dark."

"Of anything."

"Of anything. When you're not afraid, nothing can hurt you."

Stereth's hand held mine with all the physical certainty of a falling boulder. His voice matched. I thought: That's all right for you; they took your family away from you, you didn't have anybody left to keep you human. Then I said, "What about Cantry? What if she dies today, or tomorrow? What if we lose and she ends up on a scaffold in some market town?"

Cantry was setting the table with stacks of bowls. She

wiped her brow with one arm and bent to straighten the shimmering tablecloth. Stereth turned and watched her, his face unreadable. "If it happens, it happens," he said.

Gods.

He gave me back my hand and stood up. "Will you need help with the silverware?"

"No."

"Good." He went off to supervise the decorating.

Ran left his hammer at the top of the ladder and came over to me. "You'll be all right, Theodora. You're a Cormallon, you can do anything you have to." He kissed me and went back to work.

My friends and allies, concerned for my welfare. Eager to share their alien views of life.

I didn't think they would work for me. I would have to stumble through this the best I could and hope to scrape some method or meaning from it later.

Cantry had somehow gotten missids, the little fishes from the southern rivers, brought in still fresh for the banquet. You almost never saw fish on the Plateau; it was always steermod beef—fried, ground, grilled, broiled. Cut up in chunks in soup and stew. In thin strips with eggs for breakfast. Across the table I saw Dramonta cast a pleased look on his dish of missids.

Tarniss Cord said to me, from the fringed and embroidered cushion by my left, "Your band has outdone itself."

"They're a resourceful bunch," I said.

Cantry was supervising the service. She stopped by my cup and poured tah from a four-legged, blue-and-white porcelain tah pot. She gave me a reassuring smile before she passed on to Des.

Jacik sat on Des' right. He was a tall, very dark-skinned man, whom rumor had was Dramonta's food taster. I could hear him and Des talking about the latest news of flyer races in the capital. Des said something low, and they both laughed. Across the table, I noted that Dramonta didn't take any particular item from the communal bowls until Jacik had consumed it first.

Ran was seated further down the row on my side; I couldn't see him. I was very aware of the knife inside my robe.

"Were you born on Ivory?" asked Tarniss Cord. "If I don't trespass on your privacy."

"No. I was born a long way away from here."

"You've adapted excellently. Your accent is perfect."

"Thank you."

"Our well actually worked out, by the way. That's Deathwell water in the tah."

"Oh, really."

It was hard to concentrate on the conversation. I let it peter out naturally and he turned to his friend on his other side. Meanwhile Des, free of responsibility, chatted to the food-taster on his right with his usual ease.

Somewhere around the fourth course, I saw Jacik looking restlessly around the table. Des, alert, said, "What is it?"

"The wine bottle. I'm dry, and the little white-haired barbarian seems to have vanished."

Des put out his hand to block Jacik from rising. "Don't move, I'll get it. You're our guest."

He retrieved the bottle from the other end of the table and poured for Jacik.

Jacik sipped the unmixed wine and said, "You're a sporting gentleman, Des."

"Least I could do for a fellow player. Here's to the Jade Bar."

They drank to the Jade Bar racers. A little while later, Jacik's winebowl slipped from his hands and fell to the table. "I'm sorry," he said. "It's not cracked, is it?"

Des examined the bowl and sopped up the red dregs that had spilled over onto the table. "Nah, it's fine. They can take a lot of hard living, these bowls."

"Like us," said Jacik, and Des laughed. He poured more wine. Jacik picked up the bowl again and raised it to his lips, then watched in blank puzzlement as it slipped from his fingers again. This time the spilled wine ran onto his robe.

Des interrupted. "You fellows from the Deathwell plain aren't used to the pure spirits, are you? You can't just tilt it back like you're drinking the mixed kind and expect nothing to happen."

"Look, I'm not some kid. I've been drinking this stuff for . . ." He looked suddenly unhappy. "I don't feel too well."

"Sit back, take a few breaths. Want me to help you with your collar?"

"No, I . . ." He tried to stand. "Kanz—" His eyes went across the table to Dramonta Sol's.

Dramonta put his palms on the tabletop. He tried to push himself to his feet. He fell back again. He reached inside his jacket; when his hand came out I saw the glint of a small pistol.

I blinked. A dagger had sprouted from his neck. I looked down the table; most of the guests were unaware that anything had happened yet. Des was doing something underneath the tablecloth, and Jacik's mouth was gulping open and closed like a fish. His head slumped. Des pushed out a hand to keep him upright, and I saw it was red.

Somebody screamed. Other people were yelling, and still other people were telling them to be quiet. Dramonta's six lieutenants were sprawling on the table. Of our own band, Lazarin, sitting beside Stereth, was also dead. Dramonta's aim had probably been off. Finally I turned to Tarniss Cord. His eyes were fixed and intense, his fist was clenched around a fork, he was breathing hard; but he wasn't moving.

Thank the gods. I'd forgotten about him entirely.

Stereth's voice came tersely from the other end of the table. "Cord, you'd better send somebody out to make sure Marainis Cho doesn't come in."

"Right," said Tarniss Cord. He tapped the man to his left on his shoulder and stood up. They both left the room.

I started to get up myself, but my legs wouldn't support me. I thought vaguely: It could be poison, but it feels like nerves. I was aware of Des getting up, moving away somewhere, then coming back and standing behind me. "Little tymon, you're shaking like a leaf in a high wind."

"Speak for yourself, Des."

Des held out a hand and observed it as it trembled. "Yeah." He swung down onto the pillow beside me. "Considering how excitable I get normally, you may have to pull me down from the walls soon. I feel like my heart is about to jump right out of my chest and do calisthenics on the table." His feet, I noticed, were tapping to a staccato rhythm of their own. For all his brawling, Des was not naturally violent in any final sense. He was a card-cheat, a liar, a boaster, and a heavy drinker; but when it came to cold applied violence it went against all his instincts, and the effort involved showed in his body.

I said to him, "It was poison, wasn't it? Where was it? We shared everything, didn't we?"

"The tah pot. It's a special pot, the kind the nobility uses—pours from a second compartment when you touch it right. They use it for their games. Sembet told us about it."

"Nobody warned me."

"Sweetheart, only the people involved knew. Although you were kind of involved. You knew your own role." He took a deep breath and added, "It was konoberry juice. Sembet recommended it. He said hardly anybody uses it anymore. That's because it doesn't kill at once, it paralyzes the legs first and then the hands . . . that's why I couldn't let Jacik try to get up—" Des was on a talking jag.

I said, "Konoberry juice is purple."

"Not when you take the skin off the fruit and distill it, it isn't. It's clear."

Stereth was walking down the center aisle. "I want this place cleaned up, now. I don't want any of the other bands seeing what happened, it'll affect their judgment." Stereth's voice was the same one he used for assigning water duty; no trembling there that I could see.

Des looked up wearily. "They'll know—"

"Knowing and seeing are two different things. Help Tymon with Dramonta's body. Sokol, start washing down the floor. We don't want the blood to set."

Ran rose to his feet and started for the waterjugs, an expression of revulsion on his face. Stereth caught it. He put out his hand and took hold of Ran's arm as he passed. Ran waited.

"If you'd given us the benefit of your sorcery, this day would have been less bloody." For the first time a hint of intensity had crept into Stereth's voice.

I had a strong, disorienting sense of deja vu, then realized why: This was the scene I'd witnessed in the cards. Only now I could hear it as well as see it.

Stereth still had hold of Ran's arm. He said, "Satisfied?"

"This has nothing to do with me."

"No? Dabbler . . . dilettante . . . here on the Plateau for a holiday. I gave you a chance to help us avoid this."

"This?" Ran glanced around the dining hall, at the bloody silken cushions, at the overturned winebowls and scattered fruit, and a look of contempt came over his face. "This would have happened in any case. You were set on killing these people. If I'd helped, it would only have been . . . neater."

"Lazarin might still be alive."

Ran made no reply to that unanswerable sentence. They glared at each other, frozen, Stereth's hand still clamped around Ran's arm. I could feel the tension from where I sat. Just then Lex appeared at the other end of the hall. As he strode forward he called, "Stereth?"

"What?" Stereth didn't move a muscle.

"Cord's outside. What do you want me to do to him?"

"With him, Lex. *With* him, not to him. I seem to be having trouble getting you to understand that we're allies."

"Well, how long do you think we'll be allies?"

"Until one of us decides that we aren't." Stereth let go of Ran's arm. He turned to face Lex.

"You didn't say what you want me to do *with* him."

"Ask him what he wants."

"He wants to see you."

"Then send him in."

Lex turned and started walking back down the hall. Then he said, "Oh! What about Marainis Cho?"

"I'll need to see her, too, when we're ready. She speaks for Dramonta's band now."

"She's outside right this minute. She knows what happened."

"Well?"

Ran spoke. "No doubt the lady is reluctant to come in."

Lex's glance went to Ran, then back to Stereth. He said, "She said to tell you she thinks an alliance would be a fine idea. She wants to be sure you understand that before we go any further."

The corner of Stereth's mouth turned up. "Tell her I understand," he said. "And that we would be honored by her presence. And that I hope she'll come in."

Lex went back outside. Ran said, "I have things to do." He walked away from Stereth and went to help drag the bodies off the cushions. Stereth watched him.

I'd thought that I'd forgotten that run of the cards, finding the deck's visions, as they could sometimes be, less than helpful in our personal lives. But I must have been more aware of that card than I'd realized, because now I felt its lack. Life in the Sector had been easier than it should have been for me. I'd believed that Ran, at least, was safe. But he was no longer protected by the future, he was as vulnerable as everybody else, and a glance around the killing floor was enough to see that that was very vulnerable indeed. And seeing the look on Stereth's face, I knew it was even worse than that.

Chapter 15

I was awakened two nights later at the monastery fort by a hand over my mouth. I realized almost at once it was Ran.

I sat up, looked at him kneeling in the shadows by my pallet, and realized as well that this was serious. He stood. I followed him to the door, knowing that any sprawled bodies I stepped over—if they had any awareness of me at all—would assume I was heading for the privy. Or if they saw two figures, they'd assume we were looking for privacy; it happened often enough.

Outside the door, Fire Moon cast a ruddy tinge on the landscape. I'd only been asleep a couple of hours; the second moon was still below the horizon. It was quiet. I could hear some of the mounts moving about in their stalls.

Ran's hand emerged into a sliver of moonlight, then vanished again, as he rubbed his head tiredly. "There isn't time for us to talk," he said. "I have some things I need to do. Give me twenty minutes and meet me by the trees at the entrance to the valley."

"What is it? This is it, isn't it? Do you think Stereth's going to—"

"Twenty minutes. I'll explain everything."

I glanced up toward the roof and said, "If I get that far from the fort, the lookouts will spot me."

"No, they won't." He said it with finality.

There is a tone people get in their voices when they are very serious. Once, when I was six, my crèchemates and I were on holiday at Gold Sands, on Pyrene, and there was a coromine leak at a plant next door. One of our supervisors came to the edge of the pool where I was swimming, put out her hand, and said, "Theodora, come out." It was customary for us kids to wait until the grownups' thirtieth or fortieth call until we left the pool. And the supervisor didn't yell or seem upset; but I went straight to the pool-steps and climbed out and took her hand, and we headed upwind for Medical.

I said to Ran, "Twenty minutes." As easy as that.

And he disappeared, satisfied, into the shadows.

I sat near the door, listening to the mounts, the wind in the grass, and the fullness of silence on the Plateau. I was looking oft in the direction of the twisted trees. It was time, there was no denying that; it was plain in Stereth's eyes that Ran's deferment was at an end. Maps and waterbags notwithstanding, the deadline was upon us. After a while I got up and peered into the dimness of the main hall: Clusters of sleeping bodies in the worn and dirty clothes of Sector outlaws, their flashy colors and jewelry invisible under the cover of night. If this was really our bid for freedom, I could approve it intellectually, but for a second I was close to tears. They looked so vulnerable lying there.

Then I turned around and started walking up the track toward the trees.

I was not alone when I got there. A Plateau farmer, late-middle-aged, wearing a navy jacket and cap, sat smoking a pipe. His back was against one of the trees. I knew his jacket was navy because I could see it in the light of the cinders from his pipe. He smiled a smile of pleased innocence when he saw me.

"Honored by this meeting," he said in a rusty voice. He blew some smoke out slowly and patted the grass beside him. "Care to join me, gracious lady?"

"Thanks, I'm waiting for someone." Had Ran arranged for transportation with this man? "Uh, is there a reason why you're here? Not that I mean to criticize."

"I always get restless at Fire Moon. Sometimes I go nightherb gathering."

"This isn't a very wise place to gather herbs, gracious sir."

He smiled, this time slyly. "How can you say that, my lady? I see three types of jevetleaf within a few steps of where we sit."

I bit my lips, wondering how to warn him off. What the hell was he doing here, anyway? There wasn't a farm in miles.

"I appreciate your concern, though, Theodora," he added.

I met his eyes. Amusement, pleasure in success, delight in his own ability . . . I wouldn't mistake that ego anywhere. "Ran," I said, with certainty. His lips started to turn up, and I punched him in the arm.

"Hey! What's that for?"

"For being a royal pain."

"That's not fair, Theodora. I had to know the illusion worked, and I couldn't very well ask one of the outlaws, could I? It was a necessary test."

I considered punching him again. "Sherlock Holmes used to give the same excuse to Doctor Watson, and I always thought he deserved a good thrashing for it, too."

He rubbed his upper arm and said, "I have no idea what you're talking about. I never heard of a sorcerer named Sherlock in my life." He gave me an aggrieved look. "We've got a long way to go tonight, and since we'd never get away with taking mounts from the stable, we'll have to travel on foot. Do you think you're up to it?"

"You ask me now? Would you like to share with me where we'll be going?"

"Kynogin. You know the way, and it's the closest place for us to get some transport. It's also the first place Stereth would have us looked for, but we won't get away fast enough by walking."

"Glad you've got this worked out. What about the passersby in Kynogin? How are you going to maintain an illusion in several dozen minds at once?"

His farmer's features were proud. "It's not a planted illusion, Tymon, it's projected—attached to me personally. It'll hold for anybody who looks at me. Remember that assignment we had a couple of years back for the Gold Coin House, attaching illusions to the bed-performers?"

"Wait a minute. It can't be done." I did remember the commission from the Gold Coin house, and it had taken weeks of Net work, calculations, measurements—we'd brought in extra staff—"I don't believe that even you could hold all those calculations in your head."

"Theodora, darling, how do you think sorcerers worked before the Net was brought in? I used paper. Stolen from Stereth's supply, chucked in several holes in the wall as I went along. Lucky nobody used those particular rocks when we were mending the roof."

"I haven't seen you scribbling on any papers."

"The suspicion in your tone is ill-deserved, sweetheart. I had to do a lot of the initial calculating in my head, and transferred it to writing whenever the opportunity arose."

He *had* been looking rather abstracted. And he'd spent a lot of evenings sitting around the fire like a silent lump, but I'd thought he was meditating. I mean, with Ran, how can you tell?

Still, it was an amazing achievement. A projected illusion—sometimes called a grounded illusion—is grounded in actuality, with any number of measurements taken of the person's body, and the differences between those measurements and that of the completed product figured down to the last decimal point. You have to short-cut a lot with formulae, of course, or you'd be measuring forever, but even those take incredible time and attention. It's a thousand times harder than a planted illusion, because the work is all done by the sorcerer. With the planted kind, the work is done by the viewer, who fills in the blanks.

There was no reason he should lie about it, but it was just so unexpected. Not to mention bordering on superhuman. I said warily, "How did you do the measuring?"

"Stereth has a tape he uses to work out map distances. I borrowed it and cut a long piece of paper and marked it to scale. Then I just had to compensate for the unit/centimeter differences. Simple."

Simple. Any minute now he would tell me he'd also taught the mounts to talk in his spare time and got directions to Shaskala from them.

I felt like an idiot. A *lonely* idiot. How could he do this to me?

"You didn't think to mention you were working on this?"

"Well, what would be the point? You're still a novice, you couldn't help that much with the calcs, and you had a higher profile with the band. If you'd kept going off somewhere to scribble figures, you'd've been missed—"

"That's not the point!"

Something in my voice must have made an impression on him. "Uh, well, I . . ."

The full enormity of the task was still sinking in. "Great gods, it must have taken you weeks. And without a Net terminal!"

"Months," he said smugly. "I could only work on it a few minutes at a time. It was hell trying to hold it together mentally."

"You must have started almost as soon as we got here."

"Well, of course—hey, stop it! That arm's still sore! What's the matter with you tonight?"

"You've been working on this for months *and you didn't tell me?* Why do you always have to be this way? What is this terminal, paranoid, keep-it-to-yourself silence—"

I was standing there ranting when I saw that Ran (an appalled look on his face) had gone to his knees, and from that supplicant's position he took my hands and spoke. "Theodora, my dearest love and, uh, most trusted companion. *Please* yell at me later. I will try to improve my habits. But I feel compelled to point out that we need to be as far away as possible by dawn."

Of course, we both knew he was squirming out of it, but it's still very difficult to yell at somebody who's on his knees calling you his dearest love and most trusted companion. "Oh, get up. Your pants must be a mess from all this wet grass."

He got up, cautiously. "So we're going to Kynogin?"

"Well, apparently. You're the first in Cormallon, you outrank me. I'm just here to follow orders."

"Right," he said, rubbing his arm, "of course. You're not going to hit me again, are you?"

"Probably not tonight."

It was still night when we reached the market town. Sabba-moon was halfway up the sky, and Jekka was low. Most of the tents and cabins were quiet, but noise came from the larger stone and wood building in the center of town.

"The wineshops here never really close," said Ran. "There'll be food, shelter, and with any luck, information."

We entered a warm, yellow-lit room with a stone hearth and a crackling fire. I looked at Ran and we both grinned. It had been a long walk. There were benches and tables, as well as a surprisingly ornate bar, but the place was two-thirds empty.

We headed for the bar. There was a very old, very tiny woman in blue trousers leaning against it, with an enormous mug of ale in front of her. The bartender stood at the other end, wiping clean some winebowls. He wore a white apron with bloodstains on it; being a Sector establishment, there was probably an abattoir in the back. He glanced our way.

"A jug of Fortune Red, if you've got it," said Ran.

I murmured, "I'm impressed. I didn't think you'd ever heard of anything but Ducort vintages."

Ran smiled at the bartender as he approached, ignoring my remark. A jug and two earthenware bowls were put in front of us, the seal broken and the stopper removed.

Suddenly the very old woman down the bar spoke. "To what do I attribute my longevity," she said.

"I beg your pardon?" said Ran.

"Ask me," she said, "to what I attribute my longevity."

Ran blinked. I said, "Gracious lady, to what do you attribute your longevity?"

"A mug of ale every day at noon, and another every evening. Nothing like it to keep the system functioning. And never, never, never drinking jugged red wine." She met my eyes suddenly. "You wouldn't believe the things they put in the vats to get it that color."

I saw Ran peering down at his bowl.

I said, "A lot of people drink it."

"A lot of people die like rats," she announced, tilting back her mug. She wiped her lips with her spotted hands. "Ask me how old I am."

"I really don't think," began Ran.

"Ask me how old I am!"

"How old are you?" he asked.

"Ninety-eight," she said firmly. She added, "I haven't had my own teeth in three decades."

Clearly this was more information than Ran needed to know, but I was fascinated. When somebody like this says "ninety-eight," they mean in Ivoran years, which made it even more impressive. In fact, considering the lack of high-level medical care in the provinces, it was a downright statistical anomaly. I said, "Are the rest of your family so long-lived?"

"My father died at fifty. Wouldn't drink the ale. My mother refused to pass on, though—still sitting round the table when she was a hundred. Like somebody who won't take a hint that the party's over."

"Really. Did you—"

Ran took hold of my elbow. "Theodora, is this the time?"

I said, "Gracious lady, I don't suppose you'd know the best way of getting some transportation. We'd prefer a groundcar, but we'll take mounts if that's all that's available."

She snorted. "Won't find neither one, I'll save you the trouble of looking. People who have 'em want to keep 'em."

"We can pay—"

"Not enough to take a person's livelihood away. Where are you from, anyway?"

When I hesitated she added, "Why not take a job with a convoy to get where you're going? From your accent, I'd say you're meaning to aim south. Convoys through here all the time, heading for Shaskala mostly. Ask Grandin."

She nodded toward the bartender. He looked up, hearing his name.

Ran said, "You'd know about convoys?"

"If you'd read the notices on the walls you'd know about them, too," said Grandin. I followed his glance to the poster over one of the tables; it seemed to be a hiring notice. "Convoy-master's upstairs," he said. "I know he's a few people short. If you line up with the others in the morning, he'll probably take you on."

Ran looked wary. "It's not a tah convoy, is it?"

"Wine, stranger—Fortune Red, from above Ordralake. Just your speed. Although you're a little old for them, uncle, they like workers who can move heavy crates. And your friend's a little small."

"Old?" came the disbelieving protest from the ale-woman. "He's fresh as a new-minted coin, a sweetrose still budding. If I were a century younger, I'd wed him myself. By the Wheel, Grandin, you don't only serve the most over-priced drinks on the Plateau, you're blind as a ground-hermit's chick."

"Wheel of illusion yourself, grandmother," muttered the bartender, as he turned away.

She muttered right back, addressing her empty mug. "I haven't deceived myself since I was twenty-two and married my second cousin. I ought to know a good-looking youngster when I see one. And his face is all over town, even if I can't read what it says."

The bartender, who'd only caught about half of that, yelled from the other end, "Anyone not yet on his funeral pyre looks young to you!"

Ran interrupted. I saw that he was wiping his palms on the side of his trousers. "Could we take a room for the night, and have you call us when the convoy-master rises?"

The old woman made a nasty-funny face, like a schoolgirl, and walked out of the winehouse.

"This isn't the city, uncle, we've only got about three rooms up there altogether, and two of them are occupied. You'll have to take mine."

Ran said, "We'll take what we can get. My niece here is tired."

"Your niece looks about as much like you as I look like my left boot. But if you want to pay for a room, who am I to complain? Just leave the furniture intact." He felt around under the bar, and I heard a jingle of keys. "You want to bring any food or drink up?"

"Our thanks, but we just want to sleep for a couple of hours."

He led us up the stairs. There was a clatter on the landing above, and a young man appeared. His legs were bare and he looked chilly, with only a long white dress shirt with a stiff collar, and a belt and holster he was buckling as he spoke. "What goes on here, Grandin? The Steward just sent me out to get hold of you. Who the hell is that crone in the street outside? She just threw a stone at our window, and when we looked out she pulled back her lips and waggled her tongue."

"I'm very sorry, sir."

"One of your many relatives? I'll tell you right now, it's not the kind of thing the Atvalids are used to. The Steward was taken aback, to say the least."

The bartender had gone all cold and formal. "I regret that my establishment is the best that Kynogin can offer—"

"I know, I know. It wasn't my idea to come, Grandin. I'd as soon be in bed in Shaskala, on a finer mattress than it will ever be your privilege to know, from what I've seen of your offerings tonight."

"I would have thought you'd prefer to be encamped with your regiment over the hill, noble sir."

"That isn't funny, Grandin." He finished working his belt buckle and sighed. "Well, I suppose the excitement's over. Just try to keep the less sane elements out of the way, could you?" He peered down the steps at Ran and me in a polite, nearsighted way. It was rather dark on the stairway. "Not more of your relatives."

"Guests for the night, sir, like your own party."

"Oh? Well, no offense meant, gracious sir and lady. —She won't come back and throw more rocks, will she, Grandin?"

"It's unlikely, sir."

"Uh-huh. Well, I'll see you in the morning." He bowed to us and started unbuckling the belt all over again as he walked away. His gold militia officer's collar was crooked.

Now we knew who was in the third room.

Ran had had two shocks one after the other. It was bad enough that an old provincial woman in shabby trousers could see right through his projected illusion, but now we were lying on a cot just a wall's thickness away from Vere Atvalid, Steward of the Province, the man whose professional aim was the destruction of Stereth Tar'krim.

We talked in whispers. "I can't believe this had to happen to us," I said. "I've only been to Kynogin twice in my life, and each time I run into the Atvalids."

"It's not that strange. This is the biggest market town in the Sector, and this building is the most likely place to put up the Steward." It was an odd sensation, lying there in the arms of my middle-aged farmer, my cheek against his scratchy wool jacket.

"Maybe I really am bad luck for you, Ran."

"No," he said distantly, "luck doesn't work that way. I'm a sorcerer and I know." He kissed my forehead, his mind elsewhere. I wondered for a moment what it was like to have a father. "And if it did, it wouldn't matter."

"You're not even thinking about the Steward."

"No. I'm thinking about the old woman."

I can't say I got any rest. Cloudy dawn light crept into the room an hour or so later. Ran was asleep, damn him. I shook him gently. His eyes opened and met mine, and it was one of those moments when you feel closer to another soul than you ever expected to be. I said, uncomfortably, "We want to get hold of this convoy-master early."

"Yes." He got up and pulled the door handle very quietly. He was still wearing his boots. I'd taken mine off to avoid dirtying the innkeeper's bedsheets; but months of servitude in the wilderness or not, I don't think the idea ever entered Ran's head. If it had, he would have removed them as well. You see, it wasn't that he was inconsiderate.

The hall was empty. Blessed, blue-ribbon snoring came from the room next door. We padded downstairs to find a barroom that was dingy and used-looking under the burden of daylight. Grandin was still awake. He ignored us. A tired drunk lay against a table, the sole patron present. Ran turned to me. "You may as well get a little more sleep. I'll wait down here for the convoy-master and sign us both up as soon as he comes down."

"I'm not tired. Well, yes, I'm tired, but I don't think I could sleep."

"Then lay and rest. Who knows when you'll next get the chance." His voice was cynical, depressed, the voice of a man who was not expecting a happy ending. The voice, in fact, of a man without any expectations at all. I didn't know how much of that came from an evaluation of our plight and how much from the surroundings.

"You'll wake me, if I fall asleep."

"I'll wake you. Relax, Theodora, look around you. You won't miss anything."

So I went back to our room and stripped off my boots again.

Suddenly the room was lighter; I must have fallen asleep after all. Ran wasn't back yet. My head was fuzzy and it took me a moment to become aware of the sounds out in the hall. The people next door were coming out—that must have been what woke me.

I saw my ghost in a small pane of window-glass across

the room: Small-looking, washed out, face puffy from sleep; a half-familiar, half-alien reflection. Just right for a half-familiar, half-alien planet. Such a lot of trouble it is to be an organic consciousness—you have to feed your body and dole out hours of unconsciousness to it and cater to its tiredness and crankiness, all to support the few seconds of friendship and courage and beauty that can be pulled from the fabric of horror known as daily life. Really, I should just sit here and dive into some meditative pool of inertia—

Footsteps quickened in the hallway. I ran my fingers through my hair and jabbed my feet into the boots and got myself to the door. I pulled out a scarf and tied it around my head to hide my barbarian hair.

"But Guardian sir, I had no idea you knew the woman," came the voice of the young officer from last night. It was clear whom he was addressing. The Steward is the "Guardian of the Province"; if he'd been nobly born, it would have been "lord Guardian," instead.

"I met her once," returned a young, sour voice. "That doesn't mean I want her tossing stones against my window all night. I didn't want her irritated, though, either—she's clearly unstable."

"She's a crazy old lady, is what she is, with all respect—do you want me to bring down the waterbags now, sir, or should we wait? I don't trust that landlord to do a proper job."

There was a sound of belongings being moved. The door was shut and there was a jangle of keys. The innkeeper hadn't offered *us* any keys. I supposed we were lucky not to have been put in the back with the slabs of meat and the kegs of plateau beer—

"No good ever comes of hiring civilians, sir. Especially not crazy provincial civilians who say they're past a century old—" The voice grunted and shifted some bags. Evidently these two were on familiar terms, in spite of their differences of rank. But then, the Atvalid boy was new to his position, wasn't he? Probably new to public life entirely, from what Sembet Triol let drop.

"She's a kyrif," said the Steward peevishly, "from a family of kyrifs. What do you expect, normalcy?"

I froze.

He went on, "If she says she'll strip the place at two

hours after dawn . . . well, we'll have to hope she'll strip it between sun-up and mid-afternoon. What more can we do?"

"We could send some more bands out to the farms."

"To do what, take tah with them? We've hit every farm between here and Shaskala, and half the western ones, too. Face it, they *like* Stereth Tar'krim. They don't like us."

The voices faded as they went down the stairs. "I guess we'll have time for breakfast, anyway," I heard the officer say. I stepped out into the hall, closed my door and leaned against it. Kyrifs?

Back when I was collecting Ivoran legends for that doctorate I never quite got, I heard about kyrifs. The story ends:

"Face west and fading sun. Close your eyes. Strip away the people from the hills and the roads. When the world is empty, strip away the buildings, the farms, the wells, the domestic animals. When they are gone, strip away the groundhermits, the hawks, the nighthunters, the insects, all life but the sound of your own heart. When you know the world is empty but for the sound of the wind running over the grass, open your eyes."

The farmboy, who was the first kyrif, followed the advice of the dragon. When he opened his eyes, he saw the farm, the hills, and the village beyond, as busy as ever; but there was no sorcery left anywhere. Thus did he strike back at his enemy, the sorcerer, who was now defenseless against his victims.

There was no sorcery in the world until that kyrif died.

When I first heard the story, I thought, *they probably killed him young.* There were a lot of people around who depended on magic, and Ivoran tales are full of revenge at a high price. Did kyrifs really exist? The Steward thought so. Still, history is rife with people in high office who fell for superstition. But then, the Steward and his officer were both so matter-of-fact about it, and that jaded take-it-for-granted attitude was the hallmark of real Ivoran sorcery.

She was going to "strip the place" at two hours after

dawn. Ran had been right, Cantry's illusion in the crossroads had come back to haunt him: The powers-that-be knew that a sorcerer was involved. Did the Steward imagine that the market towns were full of bandits, coming and going freely under a cloud of illusion? How far had his paranoia gone? Not fair to the Atvalids, I suppose; it was a reasonable assumption that people with prices on their heads would make use of illusory identities if they could. But we weren't the great force in the villages that they seemed to think. Hell, we only came in by ones and twos, just long enough to trade and leave. In fact—

In fact, the only false identity down there right now was Ran.

I hit the stairs.

Below it was a peaceful sight: A few people at the tables downing some fine-looking eggs and foul-looking chocolate; an immense decorated tah pot on the bar; Ran in his farmer guise, standing with a knot of hopefuls by the far wall, where a notice said to wait for the convoy-master . . . and eight militiamen, eight—I counted—standing about looking awkward, attending on the pleasure of their superiors. The Steward and his personal officer took seats at a table and ordered breakfast. Ran threw me a helpless glance and stayed where he was.

Should I go and join him? What was happening? Was anything happening?

The danger of acting warred with the danger of not acting. I wouldn't attract special notice with this scarf round my head, but I was still clearly a barbarian to anybody who cared to look closely. Maybe I shouldn't call attention to Ran by going over and whispering to him, badly though I wanted his technical expertise.

The old woman from last night walked in. She spotted the Steward at his table, spooning a bowl of lumpy meal, and sauntered over with the walk of a promiscuous eighteen-year-old. "Well-met, Sonny," she said as she straddled the bench and lowered herself down to join him. The Steward winced very slightly.

Was she really a kyrif? But even if kyrifs existed, would anyone be so foolish as to ask one to remove sorcery from the world? Or even from one place, if they could somehow confine the request? According to legend, the magic went away forever when a kyrif sucked it out.

The Steward's officer was having beer with his eggs and porridge. He didn't look up from his plate as he said, "Honored by a personal meeting, granny. I've only seen you by moonlight, throwing rocks."

"It must have been someone else, youngster. I'm too old to throw rocks. Ask me how old I am."

Oh, lord. The Steward said, "Venerable lady, forgive my presumption, but time presses. Will you join us for our meal? Or would you prefer to make good your claim immediately?" The man had a baby face, and he ate soggy meal for breakfast, but he knew how to talk. He and Ran and Sembet Triol could make a threesome on the Imperial bowling grounds.

"I've already started, love," she said.

The Steward looked alarmed. "I wanted to talk with you first. It's really not my intention to drain the sorcery permanently from this area. My family has enough enemies of the usual kind without creating several thousand new ones from our own citizens—"

Atvalid Junior wasn't even pausing for breath. Granny put a bony hand on his arm. "Relax, love, for one thing, there's not enough sorcery out here in the Sector for anybody to miss."

"That's not the—"

"And as I told you, I'll only be stripping a small area—this bar as the center point, and a radius of a couple of kilometers. Nearly to the end of Kynogin, but not quite."

"I did want to discuss it with you first—"

"And it's not like it's permanent, sonny, it'll come back in a few hours. I've done it before. All I've got to do is funnel the magic down into an object. It'll leak back out to its proper place soon enough, don't you worry your head."

The Steward pushed away his foul breakfast bowl, giving it a queasy look I'd have understood even without his current pressures. "You really guarantee you can confine the process."

"We've been doing it for years, my dove; there've always been kyrifs in this part of the Sector."

The Atvalids were taking a hell of a chance. So far the old woman hadn't impressed anybody with her mental acuity. The Governor's family was tying itself up with the outlaw question like a bunch of obsessives. Well, I'd heard enough to know what was going on; was there time to get Ran out of the neighborhood?

"Tod?" asked the Steward, looking at his aide.

"We've got twenty men stationed around town," the officer answered obligingly. "That's in addition to the ones in here. It's unlikely that outlaws would be present here in numbers to give us any trouble. I'm by no means convinced there are any here at all, sir."

"Then we'll go on to the next market town, and take the venerable lady with us." The Steward spoke firmly.

The convoy-master had appeared across the room, and was listening to appeals from the knot of men waiting for employment. He was very fair about it, taking them one by one. Ran was third on line.

If he could just settle the job and get sent out—

"How long will it take?" asked the Steward.

"Who knows?" said Granny.

The Steward played with his empty chocolate cup. "An object," he said meditatively. "What object did you set to hold the magic? A talisman? A knife, a jewel, a dog, a pet, a person?"

"Well," she drawled, "I wouldn't drink the beer."

Officer Tod set down his mug abruptly. "What happens if you drink the beer?" he demanded.

"Unpredictable," she said.

"Do I swell up and die?"

"Unpredictable," she repeated. "Could be good, could be bad. Or big or little. Can't tell." She peered at him with interest. "*Feel* any different?"

The officer looked at the Atvalid. "If I turn into a large brown field mouse—"

"I'll retire you on half-pay. It would only be temporary, anyway, wouldn't it, venerable lady?"

"Maybe." She stuck out a tongue and touched her nose. "I had a beer myself before I came in, and I seem to be all right."

Tod looked queasy. He couldn't stop himself from looking over his chest, legs, arms. His eyes widened. "Guardian sir, *I'm glowing!*" He held out his right arm to the Steward, as though expecting the authority of his office to put an immediate end to this nonsense.

The arm was illuminated with a pinkish light that deepened to lavender, then dark purple. I turned to Ran. He was starting to glow, too. Very faintly, not yet noticeable. The old woman looked at Tod's arm and whistled. "Lot of heavy sorcery in the neighborhood, sirs. Must be more tricky outlaws about than I'd believed, to tell you true. Hope your men are ready for them."

"Sir!" said Tod.

His Steward looked helpless, and I felt the same way. I took six steps away from where I was standing, made some noise, and approached the table like a woman with a mission. "Guardian sir, I claim the sanctuary of your office."

"What?" He glanced at me for a moment, then looked distractedly back to Officer Tod, whose face had turned violet. "What? I'm sorry, not now—"

"Guardian sir, on the word of your family! I need your protection!"

"What?" he said again, though I had more of his attention now.

I pulled off my scarf and let my unwashed-in-two-days red-brown hair show. He blinked. "I've trusted the word of the Atvalids on my safety and my reward, sir. My life is in your hands."

He started to pull himself together, raised an arm and gestured one of the militiamen over toward us. "Sergeant, watch over this woman until I have time—"

That would never do. "Guardian sir, there is no time! My name is Cantry—"

The militiaman, who'd been reaching for my arm, paused. Atvalid's face turned fully toward me for the first time. I went on quickly, "And I'm here to denounce Stereth Tar'krim!" The Steward hesitated. I pressed, "He's in this building right now—there, Guardian sir!"

And I pointed at Ran.

Chapter 16

The Kynogin Bank and Exchange is the best-built structure in that market town, aside from the wineshop; it actually has a basement dug under it, and a foundation of stone. The walls are stone, too, and the basement is divided into several rooms: The money room, the guardroom, the special storage room . . . probably one or two more that I never saw. What I did see I remember very well. I spent one of the longest days of my life at the Kynogin Bank and Exchange.

Yes, I made quite a sensation at the wineshop. It upset me to see the look on Ran's face, but I plunged ahead ruthlessly. Of course, he realized almost immediately that something was happening, but I had no way of telling him *what.*

"I swear by all bright things," I said, "that he's Stereth Tar'krim. Look at him! He's glowing. His illusion is wearing off!"

The Steward bit his lip. "He could be an innocent man suffering a side-effect from drinking this cursed beer." But he didn't say it with conviction. I was a barbarian; I could so plausibly be Cantry.

I said, "You'll see his true face in a minute, Guardian sir. You'll see I'm telling you the truth."

The Steward looked at Ran, standing there with every false appearance of calm. He said, "Who are you, sir? Give us your name, your farm and family."

Ran was a Cormallon. He did not contradict anything I'd said. From his point of view, we were House-mates, family, and half-wed; that meant he would take advantage of me in all sorts of ways without even thinking to ask permission; it also meant he would turn over the fragile ship of his life and safety to me and hope for the best. And the waves on this ocean did not look good.

"Answer me, sir, if you've nothing to hide," said the Steward.

Ran was silent. A second later his farmer's cap disappeared. His hair became thicker, his neck less square, and his eyes somehow emerged into prominence, no longer hidden by folds of wrinkles from a farmer's lifetime of squinting at the plateau sun. There wasn't a sound in the bar. They could have been watching a scene from a play.

"Stereth Tar'krim," breathed someone. It was one of the civilians.

Ran looked down at his hands, the hands of a young man who had only a passing acquaintance with manual labor. He wiped his palms against the side of his trousers and glanced at me.

"I told you," I said to nobody in particular, and sat down at the Steward's table before I collapsed.

He was flanked by militiamen within seconds. Within minutes, the gossip had magically spread through to the nearest passersby, and the bar was filling up with a crowd of farmers, fences, and ranch agents. The militia officers had to keep yelling at newcomers to quit blocking the door.

Poor Officer Tod. He was sitting on a bench, half-delirious, and a farmer's cap kept winking in and out above his head. Nobody wanted to touch him.

As for the Steward, his attention was on me and Ran. Atvalid kept trying to speak to me, but the noise from the crowd made it hard to hear. "Come on," he yelled finally to an officer. "We'll take them out."

"Out where, sir?" the officer yelled back, looking helpless.

Atvalid paused. "The bank," he said. "They've got to have some security there."

"What about him?" The officer gestured to Tod.

"Oh. Put him to bed upstairs. Have somebody stay with him."

A voice said, "You'd best get him out of the area, if you want him to revert." Atvalid looked around, and so did I. It was the old woman kyrith who'd gotten us all into this; we'd forgotten about her.

The Steward looked as though he'd like to say something

to her, if he weren't so distracted. He took hold of me by one arm and called back to the officer, "Take him over the hill and leave him with the regiment. If that's not far enough away, take him farther. Don't bring more than one soldier with you; I want them here." And he pulled me toward the door. Ran was being nudged that way, too, by a man with a rifle.

There was a lot of crowd to get through. "Is she really Cantry?" somebody said, through a thick Sector accent.

" 'Course she is. Who else would she be?"

"It's true. All those tymons look alike."

"Are you gon' pay her?"

"Yeah, are you going to give her the reward, sir Guardian."

The Steward hesitated. "If he's Stereth Tar'krim, she'll get the reward."

A man snorted. "Who else would he be? Who else have we been staring at on the sides of walls all summer?"

The Steward said, "We'll pay her. Now make way."

We were standing on the threshold, half in daylight, and I could see the imposing form of the Kynogin Bank and Exchange across the way. It was easy to imagine going in there and never coming out. Staying in character, I called, "Check on me, friends! I've earned the reward, make sure they pay up! See if the House of Atvalid honors its promises, or if I get permanently lost in the vaults across the way."

The Steward's grip on me tightened. "I said we would pay! You'll see her go free, with every tabal we promised." He added, in a hiss, "And may any bandit who's taken a dislike to you be waiting on the way out of town." I'd annoyed him by what I'd implied about his family.

"Nothing personal," I muttered, and I was bundled across the way and up the two steps to the bank. Some wit had painted in red on the gray stone of the side: Interest Kills.

I gave a pretty good story, I think. I'd seen enough of Stereth and Cantry to be able to give operational details of Sector outlawry. They wanted a location, of course, for all they'd advertised about pardons and rewards. I mentioned a couple of places on the Deathwell Plain, far enough from Tarniss Cord's territory to be safe; we moved around, I said, Stereth felt it was safer.

Looking back, I'm amazed that it didn't occur to me to declare our identities, or even just my identity as an Athenan citizen. I could prove I'd been off-planet during Cantry's early career. But it never crossed my mind, not even to be discarded.

Why did I turn him in, they asked. The money, I said, and besides, we'd had a lover's quarrel.

Money and vengeance, always acceptable. They let me alone for a while and concentrated on their captured outlaw leader in the other room. I got to keep my possessions, although they searched me for weapons; after all, I wasn't technically under arrest. They even took me upstairs at one point and gave me a bagful of money, while a couple of Kynogin witnesses stood by and they took a picture for the record.

But they didn't release me. I was in the special storage room, surrounded by boxes. To my left was the fortified door that led to the money room, where Ran was being held; to my right, the fortified door that led to the guardroom, and beyond that, to the stairs. I didn't know what they were doing to Ran. I couldn't go into his part of the basement and I couldn't go outside. I couldn't do anything except pace. I'd hated talking to them, but now I wished the Steward and his friends would come back and question me some more. I badly needed something to do.

Hours went by. *Hours.*

Finally the Steward came back. Young Vere Atvalid, his eyes tired but determined, holding the blue felt hat of Imperial Favor crumpled unnoticed in his hands. If I weren't at his mercy I might have felt sorry for him; he didn't look like a man who'd just made his greatest success and saved the honor of his House. He looked exhausted. And young.

Shift the perspective a little. Who was the hero and who the villain? The would-be Robin Hood, who commanded what was after all a band of criminals, who'd expanded his power in ruthless gangster fashion, who was, let's be clear, destroying the livelihood of a lot of innocent tah-growers west of the Plateau? Or the Atvalids, under all that pressure, who tried so hard to do right.

Just at that moment I didn't care how hard they tried. With Stereth, I could have made a deal.

Vere Atvalid sat down at the table they'd put in the

storage room and regarded me. "We know he's Stereth Tar'krim," he said.

I waited.

He said, "We checked him against the record from his arrest in Shaskala. The types match."

He seemed to want me to speak, so I said, "I'm surprised you could do that so quickly."

"I carry a Net link," he said.

How exceptionally efficient of you. I was tired myself, and fresh out of conversation.

"Do you want to talk to him?" he asked.

I looked up in surprise.

"We don't mind," he said. "I'll be happy to arrange it. This may be your last time to see him alone, before we transport him to Shaskala for public execution. I thought you might have things to say to each other."

"Thank you," I said warily.

"Not at all. It's dark, you'll want to be going, we'd best do it now if you're ready."

Dark? The whole day must have gone by. No wonder we were all so exhausted. *You'll want to be going.* That sounded hopeful.

But of course he would have some way of eavesdropping. My mind was grinding away in panic. If there was no guard left with us, the method would be mechanical, which was difficult to manage in the Sector. And yet I could hardly walk in saying, "By the way, Stereth, the Steward has a Net link somewhere. He's bound to have us bugged."

But Ran was so paranoid about strangers, no doubt the thought had occurred to him.

"Ready?" said the Steward. He stood up.

I nodded and followed him to the left door.

Ran won the town prize for looking exhausted, but he didn't seem otherwise harmed. My heart quieted down a little bit. Vere Atvalid bowed and left, closing the door behind him.

The money room was just the way it sounded: Full of money. Bags, boxes, cartons, steel drawers, all packed with tabals and bakras. A few of the penny kembits were lying around, too, but mainly they meant business in here. The steel drawers were locked with the kind of seal that can only be broken once, and on each seal was a character with a certain amount in words, and a numeral underneath. Probably anybody coming in here was searched within an inch of his life when he came out. Not that the stuff was going anywhere; the only way out was the one I'd just come in.

Ran was sitting on a bench behind a table. It was a gambling table borrowed from the wineshop, stained with red. Of course, he had other things on his mind, but I hoped being surrounded by all this money wasn't getting on his nerves. He looked up at me, not giving away anything. "You had something to say?" he inquired.

In character. He was no Des Helani, but I could hear Stereth's even tones somewhere in that sentence. Ran was playing the hand he was dealt. I felt relief and pride.

"I didn't have any choice," I said, speaking for Cantry and Theodora both.

He grunted. I said, "They paid me already." *Maybe I have a chance of getting out of here and getting help.*

"I doubt if you'll be going anywhere until after the execution."

Kanz. Was it all for nothing? "Maybe you can trade something." Like Stereth's hiding place, although that was a sickening thought. But once the others were picked up, Stereth's identity would come out eventually.

He met my eyes. "I can't think of anything." *I don't even want Cormallon in the same sentence as treason in people's minds.*

Gods. Maybe we should have been yelling at each other, it might have been more believable; but I couldn't see Stereth losing control under any circumstances. Or maybe I was wrong, maybe Cantry was the one person he *would* yell at.

No, I couldn't see even Cantry getting past that wall. Although who knows what happens when two people are alone in the dark?

"I meant to ask," said Ran. "Would you have full-quarter married me?"

My thoughts did a sharp veer. You're sitting here working out your own execution, and you want to talk about our wedding?

He added simply, "I've had a lot of time to think. I just thought I would ask."

Heaven only knew what the eavesdroppers thought. I said, "Very probably."

"Well. Good, then." He smiled a little shakily and took my hand.

The door swung open. Vere Atvalid, no doubt disgusted with the way the conversation was tending. He said, "Thank you, Cantry. You can go wait in the other room now." Not even an unadorned "my lady." He could bow over a kyrith crone in shabby trousers, but clearly he put outlaws in another category entirely. The Atvalids had their standards, the prigs. I hoped his damned wedding never came off.

I stood up. Ran said, "Sweetheart, step away from the table."

I've said before, there's a tone people use when they're serious. I was thoroughly confused, but I stepped away.

Vere Atvalid put a hand to his neck. He seemed to be having trouble breathing. Ran said, "Close the door."

He meant me, though he was staring at Atvalid. I shut it. The Steward was turning pale. He started to cough.

Have you ever seen anyone choking? Two seconds ago they were concerned about a thousand minor details, they had strong opinions on the proper design of a shirt collar and the fact that they hate vegetables. Two seconds later, and you can see in their eyes that they don't care an iota any more: It's all narrowed down to one concern only. An invasion of dragons from the Annurian legend could be taking place, and the survival of the human race could be in doubt, but the outcome's all one to them. It's not just the fact that death has its own perspective—it's the surprise that comes with certain forms of it. People have died willingly for a cause, but here they've had no warning, no chance to prepare. The body states its own case unopposed: It wants to live, and the hell with everything else.

Vere Atvalid dug his fist into his own abdomen, but of course there was nothing lodged for him to force out. He kept feeling his throat frantically, searching for an obstruction he *knew* was there.

Ran held his eyes. Atvalid bent over the table and pounded a fist against it, once. *Do* something!

Ran leaned over slowly. The soft blue felt hat of Imperial Favor had been jammed into Atvalid's belt. The edge of it was visible past his outer robe. Ran licked his upper lip thoughfully, his fingers reaching for the blue folds. Then he hesitated. "I can't take it," he said. "You have to give it to me."

Atvalid's fist hit the table again.

"Can you hear me?" said Ran, frustrated, but enunciating each word clearly and loudly, as though agony had a volume of its own that he needed to be heard over. "You have to give it to me."

Atvalid's fingers scrabbled at the belt. He took hold of both ends of the hat at once and couldn't get it loose; then he pulled it out and flung it at Ran.

It hit Ran's chest. Vere Atvalid crumpled to the floor and lay there, not moving.

I walked around the side of the table and knelt where I could see his face. He was breathing again.

I looked over at Ran. "What did you do? And what good does it do us? There are half a dozen guards in the room outside, and another dozen upstairs. Are you going to choke them all?" Apparently the kyrith had been right; the leaching of sorcery was only temporary. But I didn't see how it could help us now.

He stared down at the blue hat in his hands. He was pretty washed-out himself, but there was a triumphant look in his eyes. He fell to his knees beside me, glanced at Atvalid, and dismissed him. "He's alive." Ran took a deep breath. "I needed his symbolic permission, or I wouldn't be able to do this so quickly."

"Do what? People will be in here in a minute—"

"If they were listening, they'd be in here now. I'm not saying we're not being recorded, but *he* was the only one listening. —Watch what you say, just in case."

"He'll be thrilled with us when he wakes up. The odds on letting me go just took a nosedive."

"They were pitiful to begin with." He spoke quickly. "Take off his outer robe."

I started to pull it off, questioning as I went. "Look, I know you like to keep things to yourself, but this is definitely the moment to speak up—"

"We do the logical thing, The— uh, sweetheart. One person came in here. One person will leave. Him."

I stopped, the robe half off. "Another projected illusion? It's not possible. It would take weeks to set up."

"A planted illusion, using him as the focal point of attention. By the laws of magic, attention is energy; he has the accumulated perceptions of everyone who's looked at him recently, and he's given permission for it to be tapped. You'll wear this hat—"

Despite a couple of years of study, I could only follow Ran's technical jargon so far. One thing was clear, though. "*I'll* wear the hat?"

"Only one of us can leave. You're the logical choice."

Usually I reserve my arguments until present crises are over, but we lost three or four minutes here batting it back and forth. Ran wasted some initial time by taking the position that he was the First of Cormallon and he was ordering me to go; this had its usual effect, and he dropped it pretty quickly. I told him that he was the native here, and I had more faith in his ability to accomplish something once he escaped than I did in my own. He pointed out that the farmer illusion was no longer safe and with his face he wouldn't get ten steps outside the bank.

"If illusion won't work for you, I don't see how it'll work for me."

He said, "Give me your cards."

I handed him the pouch and went on arguing. "You could be out of here by now, and off looking for a Net link. The Steward has one."

He spread the cards in a swirl on the table, evidently searching for a particular one. "If I'm executed," he said in a voice that suggested his mind was on something else, "any evidence as to family will die with me. No one will care enough to pursue it." He pulled out a card from the deck. "Here we are."

Ran is a born egotist, except when it comes to his duty. "What about me?" I said finally, in a forlorn kind of way. "What am I supposed to do alone in the Northwest Sector?"

He looked mildly surprised. "We can't both go. Here—see this card?"

It was the rope and plank bridge over Thunder Chasm. A farmer was leading a cart and oxmod over it, a risky proposition at best. I pulled back mentally, to keep it from being more than a card.

" 'Careful Endeavor.' What of it?"

"We don't have it anymore." He tore the card in two. "The picture also represents a link between two geographical locations. We're linked, too, through being tied to this deck of cards. If we'd gone through a Cormallon marriage celebration, we would've exchanged bluestones for a while, but we'll use what we've got just the same."

I blinked. He was leaving me far behind. If he'd started to recite " 'Twas Brillig and the Slithy Toves," I couldn't have been as unenlightened.

I almost said, "Ran," but remembered in time not to use his name. He looked up from the deck and said, "Time, my tymon. We don't have any. Take the card."

I took the half he held out to me and replaced the deck mechanically in my pouch.

"Ignis fatuous," he said, "an illusion lodged in the mind of the beholder. Like romantic love." (An Ivoran speaks.) "Those who have seen Vere Atvalid most recently, or those who are on daily terms with him, will retain a strong impression of his appearance; and that appearance is what they'll see. The guards in the room by the stairs have seen him most recently. They won't stop you."

He was putting the other card inside his robe, by his bluestone pendant.

I said, "I don't look anything like Vere Atvalid."

"It's a planted illusion, not a projected one. You don't change."

"Thank you, I know the difference. I also know that only a sorcerer can place an illusion like that, and only if he's on the spot. It has to be placed on each person, one by one. So it looks like you're the logical candidate to escape, after all—"

I'll be with you every step of the way.

He hadn't said it out loud. I stared at him. "The deck," he said. "We've both used those cards so many times, we've both worried over them so much . . . they're your equivalent of a bluestone, Theo—sweetheart. If you died tomorrow, we could reconstruct your memory traces from that deck."

I had a sudden and somehow suffocating vision of my pack of cards in the library-morgue at Cormallon, among

Ran's dead ancestors, pulled out now and again for a walk through my memory.

"Attention is energy," he said again, repeating one of the hundred and ten laws of magic. "Your attention to the cards, other people's attention to Vere Atvalid—the psychic traces remain, for a while at least. I'll be able to see through your eyes and do what needs to be done. So we'd better cut it short, tymon, and get you out into the world while we can."

"And you'll be with me . . . every step of the way."

"Until you get too far out of range. We should be all right while you're in the bank, though."

I hesitated.

Ran said, "Our friend isn't going to stay unconscious forever. You've been shilly-shallying for nearly ten minutes."

"I have not been shilly-shallying!" I said, rather loudly, trying to cover up some of the confusion I felt. In all my visions of Stereth's band coming to a bad end, I'd never really imagined Ran at the end of a rope or the downside of a chopping block.

"Glad to hear it." Unlike mine, Ran's voice sounded utterly normal. "So, you think we would finally have made it to the wedding party at the end, do you?"

Well, there were a lot of smart-aleck remarks I could have made to this non sequitur, but under the pressure of the moment I condensed them. "Yes."

". . . Just checking." Ran came over, kissed me very briefly, and pointed me to the door. His hands on my arms were ice-cold, even through the sleeves of my light jacket.

I went through the door. I stepped out into the special storage room. I started to walk away. Behind me I heard Ran shut the door and twirl the lock.

It seemed to be happening, didn't it? Every step I was taking was making this reality more true.

I stepped into the guardroom. About six young men in uniform looked over to me as I did so; I made sure my glance took them all in. Now was the time for me to be arrested, if it was going to happen.

One of them stood up from the chair where he'd been drinking tah. "Sir, do you want me to stay with the prisoner?"

I shook my head, realizing sickly that Ran and I hadn't discussed voice. When I opened my mouth would they hear

Vere Atvalid, or an upset female barbarian? I continued hurriedly to the stairs.

Nicely done, tymon. Ran's thought startled me.

Ran? I sent back. There was no reply.

I got to the first landing and paused for breath. They'd dug their vaults deep, the paranoid kanz. My hand on the railing was cold and slippery.

Don't . . . won't be long now. Part of the sentence was missing. Static in magic, I thought, with no humor whatsoever. I was getting farther away.

There were footsteps on the landing above. A door closed. The feet started down the stairway.

Go back. And face six guards without an explanation? Not to mention laryngitis.

It would look better if I were ascending the stairs normally. No—the farther up I got, the more fragile was the connection with Ran's sorcery. I backed down a few steps and started up to the first landing again.

A set of deep red robes embroidered with gold thread came into view. Feet in boots, like everyone on the Plateau, but these were soft, thin yellow leather, with suede flaps. A fashion boot, not anything I'd like to take out into a Plateau night. A belt embossed with traceries of situ leaves. An overrobe of white, clean even in this climate. And a face—

"Vere, my boy!" said a voice I'd heard before, but never this happy.

The voice of the provincial governor. Nor Atvalid.

I froze. Surely Vere's father would not be deceived for long. He barreled down the stairs and threw his arms around me, somehow not noticing that I was a lot shorter and softer than his strapping offspring.

He was an affectionate father. My breasts were pressing against his rib cage. No, he didn't notice.

"I'm so proud of you!" he cried. "Forgive me for coming myself. It's not to check up on you, you know that, my dear boy. But I couldn't stay away. I swear I tried, for a full quarter of an hour I tried, but I had to come at once. You've made it all worthwhile, Vere. My very best hopes, everything I've worked for—I'm babbling, aren't I? It's a good thing nobody from the Shaskalan council is here. Well, aren't you going to say something?"

He waited. I did, too, for a handful of seconds that seemed to stretch for several hours, while my thoughts banged around hopelessly in my brain like a bird trying to escape a room.

"It's good to see you, Father," I said finally.

I tried to steel myself for whatever came.

"So you do forgive me?" he asked.

"Certainly. Uh, there's nothing to forgive."

The arms around my back again, crushing my chest. He was soaring high with joy. "Now, I know you sent for an armored car," said Nor Atvalid, "and instead you got an aging administrator. But I have an explanation, and I'd like you to listen to it before telling me it's a bad idea."

I was afraid he'd suggest we talk upstairs, but he was too excited to think of anything but saying what he'd come to say.

"This Stereth Tar'krim," he said. "He's grown too popular with the uneducated. He appeals to the same idiots who go to provincial theater and think pole pirates really exist."

Didn't pole pirates exist? That was a blow.

"We need to show them that he's *not* a success, he's a criminal. A failed criminal—that's the important thing, the failure. That's what we have to get into people's minds."

"Umm," I said, trying to sound thoughtful.

"So I've ordered a cage to be constructed here in Kynogin. A sort of prison-wagon. We can carry him back over the roads to Shaskala and let the people line up and see our captive inside. Then we can execute him publicly back in the city. I don't think we should make it a municipal holiday, do you? That would be attaching too much importance to him. And. yet we want a good crowd, you know. What do you think?"

Apparently Atvalid Senior moved quickly for somebody who'd said he was leaving things up to his son.

"Uh, won't displaying him on the Shaskala Road be dangerous? It might lure in his followers."

I was hoping to keep Ran in Kynogin for a while. Particularly if they wanted to execute him in Shaskala.

"So much the better if it does," said the Governor, with the first trace of coolness I'd seen today. "I'll welcome getting a score for the price of one. Cutthroats and scum, standing in the way of all our best interests."

Even the people whose job it was to capture Stereth Tar'krim didn't usually talk about him that way. In the Sector, where life was hard, people had sympathy for the difficult choices of others.

"Years of effort," Nor Atvalid went on. "Working for the governorship. Trying to prepare the people for a less corrupt system. Constant struggle—I know I neglected you, Vere—and always more work, always people getting in the way. Refusing to understand that I was trying to help *them*, trying to make up . . ."

The man was obsessed with this. He went on for a good five minutes on the theme of being misunderstood. If they would only all pull together and cooperate with him! But no, they followed after a passing outlaw with a good line of talk and no interest in improving things—

Trapped in a stairwell with a madman—and the real Vere Atvalid could be coming around even now. For the first time in my life I felt a hint of the panic of claustrophobia.

I put a hand on his arm. "Father, perhaps you'd like to go down and talk to the guards. They can fill you in on things. I'm a bit tired—"

He turned a keen gaze on me, making me even more nervous. Gods, he had to keep looking *down* to address me, didn't he even notice that?

"Son," he said, "I appreciate your leaving the university to complete this mission. I know your friends must have advised you to distance yourself from my little obsessions, didn't they? You don't need to answer, I wouldn't expect any differently from the world as it is. But it means a lot to me, Vere. Your grandfather would have had something to say about it, too."

"Oh . . . yes, I'm sure he would."

"Sit down for a minute, Vere."

"What?"

"Sit down. Here on the steps. I want to talk to you seriously for a minute."

Let me out of here, powers of earth and heaven! Gods of fools and scholars, all I want is to see sunlight again and deal with the troubles I have, which are more than sufficient to my needs.

I sat down.

"Son, I never talked much to you about Tammas District. You were just a boy when we were in residence there, and the troubles hadn't really started, and when they did I thought it best to send you off to your cousins. That may have been a mistake. Not that I would want you to suffer, or be in any danger, but I think like most youngsters you probably have no conception of what things were like there."

I'd heard about the troubles in Tammas District, even met a few refugees in my time; it was all pretty remote, though. And things were supposed to have settled down, anyway, except for the unemployment and the militia units always being there. There were plenty of places to go on Ivory before I ever needed to see a godforsaken place like that.

Tammas District. Wasn't that where Stereth was from?

"Grandfather Torin had only been in office a month when things started to go wrong. Poor management of the man before him, he said, and I believe him. Your grandfather's an honorable man in his way. You know that, don't you?"

I made a sound in my throat that could be taken for assent.

"Of course. You've never had much of a chance to talk to your grandfather, and I've always regretted that. He really doesn't have the energy, Vere, I'm sure you realize it's not that he doesn't care. He can barely get out of bed, after all. No one in our family has ever disgraced the Blue Hat, son, don't forget that. Generations of administrators, and no one ever had to give it back to the Emperor. Not even Granddad. —Not that there's any reason he should have. Had to give it back, I mean."

Nor Atvalid rested his arm on my shoulders. It was amazing that this man, vulnerable as he sounded now, could be the same one who put on the show on the platform in the center of town, the day I came in to sell stolen cattle.

"You see what I'm saying, son?"

"Oh, yes." I didn't have a clue, but I tried to sound enthusiastic in a detached kind of way. That may not make much sense, but if you've ever tried to discourage a harmless idiot at the All-Athenan University Mixer from trying to pick you up, you'll know the kind of tone I mean.

He took a deep breath, and let it out happily. "I've tried to ensure that Tuvin Province was different. And it was harder here, harder from the beginning, with so much territory in the Northwest Sector. —But all that's in the past. This is a turning point, and you're responsible. When the officials turn out to see Stereth Tar'krim's execution, they'll know I mean business. Son, have you reconsidered your decision?"

He said it as though it were an obvious question. "Uh . . . which decision do you mean?"

He laughed. "You've got Granddad's sense of humor. But don't tease me, Vere, tell me the truth—now that you've succeeded so brilliantly, do you begin to see the possibilities in a government career?"

"Oh! Yes, I do see the possibilities."

The grip on my shoulders tightened for a moment. When he spoke again, his voice was choked with emotion. "That's all I ask. For the moment." He stood up, not turning away his face the way an Athenan would whose eyes were swimming with tears. "Will you come down with me and show me the prisoner yourself?"

"Well, if you don't mind, Father, I'm really tired. Exhausted. I was just on my way up to get a few hours' sleep. You don't mind, do you?" I sounded as pathetic as I could.

"No, no, I should have realized. Forgive me. Go on, and take my blessing with you."

"Thank you." I took the next step, but a hand on my sleeve held me back.

"Son? I love you."

I hesitated, long enough to see he felt the hurt of it, then said, "I love you, too, Father." Well, didn't I feel like pond scum.

He kissed me on the forehead, still completely unaware that he could never have done that if his real son was standing one step above him. Then he turned and went down the stairs. I ran as fast and as silently as I could, up to the sunlight and open air.

Chapter 17

The sunlight was in my mind. I was disappointed to see that it was dark in the bank when I got upstairs, and lights were on, shining dimly on the rough stone counters and polished floor. I only remembered then what the Steward had said, and for some reason the thought that I'd have to wait any longer for good honest sunlight absolutely devastated me. I really don't know why, but I still remember that I was crushed. I felt like crying.

I'd stopped to wrap my scarf around my head before exiting the stairwell. Even so, I don't know what the handful of people in the bank may have seen as I scurried for the front door—the Steward of the province, or another knockaround denizen of the Sector in dirty clothing. The light of two moons poured in on the threshold. I got out, ducked behind the nearest passing wagon and walked along with it to the gray shadow of a grain-agent's tent, then took the back ways out of town. I might have been pleased at my success in evading notice, if my mind weren't on Ran.

Now where? I knew the direction Shaskala lay in, vaguely; probably a wheeled cage with the notorious Stereth Tar'krim inside would pass me on the road if I started walking that way. All right, so forget that idea. Somewhere far to the west was the route to the lowlands and the Ordralake districts. Also too far. I doubted if anybody had brought in a shipment of Net equipment while I was being detained, so the parameters of the problem remained as hopeless looking as ever, didn't they?

I realized that while I was considering the matter my feet were taking me on the route to the monastery fort. Perhaps my feet had a point. My own thought about Stereth came back to me: *At least with him I could make a deal.*

Back to the outlaws? That called forth a sour grin, despite the trouble I was in; the gods did like to play their little jokes on Theodora, I'd noticed it before. Ran would have a fit, or would he? Perhaps he expected me to go this way. I trusted he didn't expect me to leave him in Kynogin and call for my own rescue from some future Net link, long after the execution. A stupid lapse on his part, if he did.

Gods! Why hadn't I gone back to the money room with Nor Atvalid? Two of us would have come in, two of us could have gone out! What an idiot I was!

Still, that scenario was by no means certain. It would have been asking the superhuman for Ran to plant two sets of simultaneous illusions in every passerby. And Vere might have been stirring by then, and taking out both Atvalids was asking a lot. More likely we would have both been trapped.

Yet it hadn't even occurred to me. Kanz!

I passed the small grove where I'd once paused to read the cards, leaving a bunch of stolen steermods to wait. I hoped Stereth would be reasonable.

Stereth is always reasonable by his lights, but they are not the same lights that other people use. As I walked I replayed my talk with Ran and my prolonged journey up the stairs of the Kynogin bank endlessly. The scene in the money room was still on my mind. I wasn't sure why it bothered me, but it did. It's not that Ran was a sissy; he was normally pretty direct about getting what he wanted. But there'd been something in his eyes when he was looking at Atvalid's blue hat that I didn't like at all. I'm not at all sure he hadn't enjoyed that contest, vicious though it was. And I don't know if he would have attacked the problem in the way he did, if the scene would have had the flavor I seemed to perceive in it, if he hadn't been trying so hard to be what Stereth would have been.

A spooky thought. And one that I think we will leave behind us. The never-ending Plateau sky stretched over me to the edges of the world, and the grass was tough and hunter-green in the moonlight. It would have been a good night to be alive if I didn't know all the things that I knew.

I reached the fort by dawn. I walked down the path through the valley, thinking that the place had an empty feel about it. Nobody challenged me, nobody stopped me.

I kept walking, but warily; things were different here, somehow. I was almost to the entrance of the main hall when a voice hailed me: "Tymon!"

I turned and saw Grateth appear magically from the turf. He wore his usual gray-green jacket that he was never without, and his eyes moved to take in the whole valley.

"Where is everyone?" I asked, as he approached.

"I dunno what you're surprised about," he said, in his rhythmic Sector accent. "You and Sokol slip out like ghosts, you can't expect us all to wait about to see what follows. No offense, Tymon. I see you've come back alone."

"Yes. I've lost Sokol. I need to talk to our leader about that."

"Umm. No doubt you'll get the chance. But when I said alone, I meant without any militia. That's why we all cleared out, darlin'. Stereth sent me to keep watch and warn off any of the new bands reporting in."

I looked into his calm, jaded, born-for-the-military face. "I'm working at not being insulted, Grateth."

The face was transformed by a grin. "And a fine job you're doing." He pointed west, toward nothing I could see. "My mount's over that way, Tymon; come along, I'll take you to the others."

I followed him through the dirt and damp grass and came suddenly on a brown and black mount placidly munching behind one of the outbuildings. Grateth got on first, then pulled me up behind him. I put my arms around his waist, in the way I'd learned to do ages ago, when Des Helani had kidnapped us.

As we moved out, I put my face for a moment in the back of Grateth's soft, faintly smelly jacket. My voice came out muffled. "It's good to see you again, cantry tar'meth."

"And you, barbarian."

"Where are we going?"

"North. Stereth and the others are camped near Deathwell Fortress."

I pulled my head back. "Grateth! I was held for a while by the Steward, and I told him the band stayed on Deathwell Plain!"

"Did you?" said his voice, calm as ever. "Well, never mind, little Tymon. It's a big place, and we'll hope for the best."

* * *

He brought me to a hollow in the Plateau hills several hours north. There was no old monastery this time, not even a barn; just some lean-tos scattered around as a concession to the local weather. Deathwell Fortress loomed now and then through the mists, a distant and ominous shadow. I could see why people were nervous about the place.

It was a fairly large camp, and I saw people from Tarniss Cord's bunch carrying wood and practicing fighting in the mud along with the old band. Of course, I thought; Stereth would have told Cord to clear the fortress as well. I hope they don't all blame me for having to move out into the elements like this.

"Tymon!" yelled a pleased voice. A tall, green-eyed outlaw stood up from the group at the fire.

"Des!" I called back. I took one arm off Grateth's waist and waved from the back of the mount.

Then, "Tymon," he repeated, more sadly. He shook his head.

"Damn it, Des, don't you start with me. I've had a very bad couple of days."

My tone seemed to reassure him. "It hasn't been all chocolate and dancing girls here, you know," he said, but it was more the sort of thing he always said to me. "Stereth's unhappy," he added, in warning.

"I need to talk to him."

Grateth had halted the mount. Now he signaled for me to slide down, and Des helped me off. "Try to keep her out of trouble," Grateth told him, "while I go see what he has to say."

I said, "I want to come with you."

"Ho, ho," said Des, putting his arms around my waist and turning me so I faced the campfire. "You don't want to go in there now, Tymon. Let Des entertain you while our brother goes and smooths the way. Make sure he has no weapons nearby, Grateth. And no breakable objects."

Des was kidding, but he wasn't kidding. I decided that maybe they knew best. "All right," I agreed. "But I need to talk to him soon, Grateth. It's urgent."

"Right." Grateth touched the side of his hand to his head, as though to a superior officer, bowed and rode on.

"Real soon!" I called after him.

"What a troublemaker," said Des. "Why don't you sit down with me? Although—actually—you look kind of tired. If you want to take a nap, we can wrap you up and stow you in the back of my lean-to."

I'd missed the greater part of two nights' sleep. I did feel incredibly tired, but not sleepy at all, as though I'd been drinking tah straight through the day. "I can't. I'll need to talk to Stereth."

"One-track Tymon. I'll wake you up when he's ready to see you, but I'm telling you it won't be for a while. He's got all the section leaders in his tent, and I don't think he'll want to shoot the breeze with you until they're finished."

"Why, what's going on?"

Des was leading me over to his pile of gear, stacked by a couple of poles and a leather roof. He pushed the gear out of the way and rifled through some old, stained blankets. "I think he's arranging a simultaneous strike on a militia unit. Anyway, that's the rumor. We're all hoping it's false. —Here we are, sweetheart; nice and cozy."

He patted a mound of blankets. I found myself yawning.

"And I can't hang about too long, anyway," he went on. "There's a tah shipment coming through in a couple of hours, and I'm taking out a group to confiscate it."

"Confiscate?" I yawned.

"In the name of the people." He grinned.

"You should be in politics, Des."

"Not me, sweetheart." He helped tuck me in, then stood up to leave. I thought of something, reached out and grabbed his ankle.

"If you're going out on a run, who's going to wake me when Stereth's ready?"

He let out a dramatic sigh. "When Stereth wants to see you, you don't have to worry about who'll wake you. But I'll tell Sembet to be on the watch, all right?"

"Don't forget."

He sighed again and walked away.

It seemed to take forever to fall asleep, but I must have done it, because I kept waking and seeing the roof of the lean-to, and remembering one or another of a series of vivid dreams. I don't recall them all now, but I know in one I was in Shaskala trying to get to the execution block with an Imperial pardon before it was too late, and obstacles kept coming up to delay me. Then I woke and saw the lean-to and thought, "Only a dream." In my relief I fell right back asleep and found myself in Shaskala again, still with the pardon in my hand. It was the scheduled time for execution and I was frantic—but I thought, there was a reason, a moment ago, why you thought there was. a solution to this. What was it? I looked at the streets, the crowds, the time—it was hopeless. What could I have been thinking?

In another, I was trapped in the Athenan embassy with Nor Atvalid. I kept claiming I was an Athenan citizen, and he kept claiming I was his son.

Sembet Triol woke me up in the middle of that one. I saw his face, his carefully maintained jacket and outer robe, the short sword he was entitled by birth to carry; and the world reoriented itself. "Gods, Sembet." I took his hand in relief, and let him help me sit up.

"Are you all right?"

"I think so." I sat and tried to pull my thoughts together. "How long was I asleep?"

"I don't know. But Des only told me to watch you about an hour ago."

"Has he gone out?" Sembet nodded: "What about Stereth?"

"He's asked for you to come see him in about ten minutes. He's saying his good-byes now to the section leaders. You don't look in good shape, Tymon."

"It was such a real dream. Nor Atvalid was there—" I paused, remembering that Sembet probably knew a lot more about that family than I did. And thinking, too, that there was something in the back of my mind trying to find its way out. "Sembet, did you know the Atvalids used to live in Tammas District?"

He nodded. "Of course. Old Torin Atvalid was provincial governor for years and years."

The famous troubles of Tammas District. "I had the impression the people in Tammas got picked pretty clean."

"Yes, both before and after things went sour. The provincial government was thoroughly corrupt—"

I gave him a look at that.

He protested, "Everyone expects officials to take a percentage, but there's such a thing as going too far. There's no point in destroying the economy of people you intend living off of, is there? The rebels really had no choice, they had to fight back."

"And that's when the Emperor sent in troops?"

"He had no choice either. The Empire can hardly tolerate armed revolt, Tymon. The universe would be in chaos otherwise." There was a nobly born Ivoran speaking. As they say here at scenes of blood and destruction, it was just one of those things that happen because we are in this world.

"What about Torin Atvalid? Did he get any blame for it?"

"Well, not officially. His policies certainly tipped the balance, if you ask me. And the Atvalids came away from Tammas with an exceptionally heavy House treasury."

I considered all this in the light of my chat in the Kynogin stairwell. "I think Nor Atvalid is trying to make up for things by reforming the Tuvin provincial government."

"It would not surprise me." He shook his head. "The curse of the Atvalids: They always go too far." He tapped me on the arm. "Ready to go? I wouldn't keep him waiting . . . under the circumstances, I mean."

Stereth's tent was the largest in camp, but still not all that roomy. I recognized some of the pillows and rugs that had softened the hard stone floor of the monastery fort, and a set of chipped malachite bowls. Green and black, crimson and gold; a fitting den for an outlaw chieftain.

As ever, it was Stereth himself who did not fit the bill. Des could have pulled off the role with style, and his voice would have been heard in the back rows. Stereth simply looked up from his sheaf of papers, nodded for Sembet Triol to leave, and regarded me from his careful accountant's eyes.

Knowing my manners, I waited. After a moment he said, "Grateth seems to feel that executing you would be inappropriate."

Ice, pure ice. Des and Sembet spoke with awe of Stereth's occasional flashes of temper, but if it was true I'd never seen it. Just this arctic plain, with here and there a hint of irony or fellowship. No fellowship today, though. That market was shut down.

"That's good to hear," I said quietly.

"Don't relax. I don't take orders from Grateth."

He was silent again, still measuring me, so I didn't speak either. I knew my place by the rules of Ivory; I was the supplicant in this encounter, returning to claim a relationship I'd previously spurned. Etiquette required a low profile on my part.

Cantry came in from outside then, spared me a quick glance that gave nothing away, and placed a bredesmoke pipe and bag in front of Stereth. She took the malachite bowls and set a stack of three of them within reach, along with a bottle of wine.

Three bowls. One would have meant Stereth was drinking alone, that I wasn't being offered hospitality and should begin making my will; two would have meant that I was being given guest-rights and might have implied a commitment. But three could just mean that Cantry picked up some bowls in a hurry and didn't count them. Since accidents don't happen around Stereth, what it actually meant was that he was being as annoyingly careful as ever. Considerate of my feelings, though—one bowl would have been more than I could have handled just then.

He packed some bredesmoke into the pipe and took a puff. "All right, Tymon, talk. Tell me what you've been doing while we've been slogging up here from our nice dry home."

So I told him everything that had happened since Ran woke me up two nights ago and suggested we escape. I thought he might hurry me along through some parts, once he had the gist of the story, but he seemed interested in it all. I managed to reconstruct most of the conversation with the Governor. Since Stereth refused to either cut me short or tell me what he wanted to hear more of, I even included what the Governor was wearing when he came down the stairs. Stereth just puffed and listened.

It wasn't a large tent, and soon it was full of bredesmoke. My eyes, no doubt red already, began to water.

When I'd finished he said conversationally, "So, did you have some purpose in coming back to us, or do you just seek to renew old ties?"

I said—and there was just a touch of accusation in my voice—"Sokol is in jail because they think he's you. He's going to be executed because they think he's you."

"Well, and that's no disadvantage to the band, is it? It should take some of the pressure off us."

"Since when do you want the pressure off? I thought you wanted to be an irritant. Besides, all these farmers and ranchers you've allied with made their agreements with Stereth Tar'krim. Once the legend's gone, will they still cooperate?"

He smiled. "Des did much of the wooing. No doubt he can continue."

"It's not as good. You know that. This has been a public relations gimmick as much as anything else, and it's bad for public relations to kill a legend." He let out a smoke ring. I added, "I'm sure the Emperor will be reassured to hear you're dead. He won't have to buy you off." Two smoke rings. Three. Damn the man. "Besides, the pressure from the militia will be on again, the second they realize the tah blockade is still going. Unless you plan on letting that die, too."

My head started to ache. Secondhand bredesmoke usually wouldn't make me high so quickly, but I was dangerously low on sleep.

He said, "I take it you'd like me to get your half-husband out of custody. A risky undertaking at best, Tymon."

"Not for somebody who robs tax shipments from armored cars." I hadn't meant it to come out quite so baldly, but the sentence seemed to go straight from my brain to my lips.

Stereth smiled. Then he said, seriously, "If I took this business on, and retrieved our sorcerer from the enemy, I would expect him to be more cooperative in future."

"He will be," I said. I couldn't commit Ran without making a Cormallon promise, but I didn't need to; the obligation to Stereth would drive him crazy until he discharged it.

Stereth picked up a malachite bowl and set it between us, then put another beside it. "Care for some wine, Tymon?"

"Thank you." He poured for us both. I raised the bowl and took a sip, then replaced it. Any more and I'd be sprawled on the gold and crimson rug.

"One more thing," said Stereth. "Just as a matter of curiosity, and a favor to a friend, I was wondering if you would tell me Sokol's birth name."

I was actually shocked at this coming from him. Outlaws

don't ask their birthnames, I knew the look on my face was saying.

Sue me, replied the look on his own.

"Just a favor," he repeated.

Manners required that I not refuse a favor, just as they required that I take a sip from the winebowl and sit there inhaling bredesmoke, when we both knew damned well he was getting me stoned deliberately. But he was crossing over boundaries now, and I had to make a decision.

Under the circumstances, I would have liked to postpone it until I was awake and sober.

"And please don't insult me with some pseudonym," he went on pleasantly. "I always know when I'm being lied to."

That might be a magnificent bluff, but I'd been impressed in the past with Stereth's ability to tell truth from bullshit.

All right. At the moment, Ran's life was the first priority. We would deal with the rest later.

"Ran Cormallon," I said.

"Hmm. That's what I'd heard."

Was that also a magnificent bluff? I would never know.

He said, "I suppose I should let you continue your nap. Sembet said you were resting."

It was a dismissal, so I started to get to my feet. Unsuccessfully.

"I can't stand up," I said.

Stereth turned toward the tent entrance and called, "Sembet!" A few second later Sembet Triol entered and took my left arm. Stereth took my right. They lifted me up and helped me to the entrance.

Just before he turned me over to his nobly born henchman, Stereth said, "Tell me, Tymon, what's your own birthname? That can hardly be a state secret."

"Don't be so annoying, Stereth," I said acidly. "That can't possibly be of any interest to you."

I felt a faint shaking in Sembet, as though he was laughing.

"She's not entirely sober," Stereth explained.

"Oh," said Sembet noncommittally. He was still vibraing gently, but apparently didn't trust himself to speak any further.

"Oh, get her to bed." Stereth let us both go and went back inside the tent.

I had quite a sleep that day, because I woke up many hours later—back in the monastery fort, on a pile of jackets and robes in the main hall. They told me later that they'd tried to wake me, and ended up loading me on a wagon with the provisions. I suppose it's a sign of Stereth's trust in me, or in his ability to really tell truth from falsehood, but he moved his base back to our old haunt. "Easier to hit Kynogin from here," pointed out Carabinstereth as she helped me wash when I awoke. My muscles were sore, from the bouncing in the wagon or from stress, and I felt thoroughly wrung out.

I may have had as many nightmares as before, but this time I couldn't remember any. It felt as though I'd just climbed out of a pit.

Carabinstereth went off to do other things, and Sembet Triol came in with a jar of water. Things suddenly came together in my mind, and I spoke as though we'd just broken off our conversation minutes ago.

I tapped him urgently on the shoulder as he bent to set the jar down. When he straightened up I cried, "Torin Atvalid was Governor of Tammas District! Nor Atvalid's *father* was the person who imprisoned Stereth!"

"Yes," said Sembet, "I thought you knew."

But I was driving somewhere, and wouldn't get off the road. "Look, it was Torin Atvalid's policies that were responsible for the rebellion in Tammas. He gouged everybody—even Ivorans couldn't stand for it—and *our* Governor Atvalid—" I heard Sembet's voice in my mind, from the ride home from Kynogin that day: "Nor Atvalid never could stand his father. Whatever his father did, he'd do the opposite."

I went on more slowly, "Nor figured that the way to avoid the kind of suffering they had in his father's province was to come down hard on the other side."

"The Atvalids never did learn moderation."

"But don't you see! Sembet—Torin Atvalid *created* Rice Thief!"

"Well," he said, "it's nothing to get excited about."

There's an expression they use on Ivory: It won't make

dinner come any sooner. That was the consensus of the company on this topic. I even tackled Carabinstereth on it; surely her energetic nature would generate a little excitement over this. She was folding towels when I found her. She did look up briefly. "Oh, yes, Tymon. I think I'd heard that from someone."

Theodora rides in, a day late and a penny short. Whenever I have one of my profound insights I find out later that somebody had it first in the fifth century oldstyle and it's been a cliché ever since. That sort of thing happens to me a lot. Back on Pyrene, whenever I found a piece of classical music that I liked I was usually told later that it was a big favorite centuries ago of the Poliker Secret Police, and they often played it when they were torturing people. Believe me, news like that can affect your self-esteem in all sorts of ways. That wonderful sense of joy and discovery of the new never seems to make it through untarnished.

You're probably wondering what was happening to Ran while all this was going on. That was certainly in the front of my own mind at the time. Stereth told me shortly after I woke up that first day at the fort that Ran was still in Kynogin and still alive, and that a cage was under construction outside the winehouse.

I wanted to question him further about his plans, but he brushed me off. "I'm working on it, Tymon. Don't be importunate. Isn't there enough here to keep you occupied?"

Certainly there was. I don't think I've mentioned it before, but Des had returned from his tah raid with thirteen hostages. Thirteen. Stereth was furious.

"We can ransom them," said Des pleadingly, aware he was in trouble.

We knew Stereth was furious because he was spitting out his words with a precision even sharper than usual. "Why did you bring them to me, Des? Did you think I might benefit from meeting each one personally? What did you think I could do with them here?" "Here" was the monastery fort, by the way. Des and his crew had shepherded the prisoners (blindfolded) all the way down from the north. This spoke volumes of how careful he could be when he chose; also how far he would go to avoid unpleasantness.

Killing was hard for Des, and much as he admired Stereth, he would sidestep the hard jobs if he could.

The prisoners were still blindfolded, standing uncomfortably around listening to the debate. Ten men and three women, most of them pretty strong-looking, as caravan workers had to be. One of them was a little older and better dressed; probably the caravan-master, or the owner's agent.

Stereth was going on. "And did you think I could spare people to stand guard on this bunch? Or were you assuming we'd just leave them blindfolded, and I could take each one by the hand and lead them to the privy personally?"

Des looked extremely uncomfortable. It was the first time since I was there that I'd seen Stereth light into him publicly.

The more prosperous-looking one stepped forward. His dark hair was shot with gray and there were small diamond studs in his ears. I was standing near enough to see sweat on his forehead, above the red rag of blindfold. The perspiration had activated his perfume; I could smell a cloyingly sweet scent mixed with the stink of fear.

"Has this unworthy one the honor of addressing the great Stereth Tar'krim?"

Stereth made a disgusted face. I suppose at the moment he didn't want to hear from his liabilities.

The man's head was turned to a spot between Stereth and Des. There was a very slight tremor in his voice when he spoke, but he showed more control than I'd expected. "If you would excuse this one's presumption, gracious sirs, I would like to inform you that my wife will pay well for my safe return."

Stereth gave up pretending that the man was a stick of wood, and deigned to address him. "It speaks well for your marriage, gracious sir, but we don't have time to send any messages. We're rather busy right now."

"Great outlaw," said the man, as he switched to the still respectful but less groveling vah-form of first person, "I would be happy to give you an address in Shaskala where she might be reached, and if it would please you, to pledge my word and my family's honor not to escape."

Des threw Stereth a begging look. Stereth's rather contemptuous glance circled the room and lit on me. "What's your opinion, Tymon?"

"Me?" I was surprised at being consulted. I spoke honestly, doubting it would have any effect on his decision anyway. "I have sympathy for his wife."

The man had cocked an ear my way at the sound of my voice. He was no fool, and knew enough not to fill the next few seconds of silence with more promises. After a moment Stereth said, "You bargain for your own life. I assume that means you have no objection to our ridding ourselves of the burden of your fellow workers? One prisoner is much easier for us to detain."

The man didn't hesitate. "As agent for the Keldemir Tah Company, I can promise to pay their ransoms as well. And if for any reason the company will not pay, I will make it up from my own pocket."

Several of the band in the hall then exchanged looks. If true, he must be extraordinarily wealthy. And they liked the way he'd spoken up for his companions. These folk weren't cantry tar'meth, but they had some style.

Stereth saw the way opinion was going. He addressed his outlaws: "If we do this, *you're* the ones who'll be pulling extra shifts. Des, you'll be responsible. I want their pledges *and* I want two guards on them at all times. You can fix up one of the outbuildings for them."

He dismissed the matter. The band had kept hostages before, though usually not this many.

So Des drafted some helpers and took them out. I heard part of his "hostage orientation lecture" afterward, in which he explained that if anyone tried to leave, etiquette demanded that the prisoner be shot and the legs of everyone else be broken. He did a good job of putting the fear of heaven into them, and of course they'd been pretty cowed to begin with; none of them gave us much trouble.

They were a lot of work, though. Feeding them and carrying their wash water and cleaning out the hastily-rigged privy in the corner of their building.

It gave my arms and legs something to do while I was worrying about Ran.

Paravit-Col brought in some flyers a few days later. Notices had been posted in the market towns and at the hilltop gibbets that the notorious Stereth Tar'krim, now brought low by the forces of justice, would be transported via the Shaskala Road on the twenty-eighth of Kace. It assured any food and drink vendors who might care to set up on the road that day that they would not be asked for licenses by the passing militia.

It gave us two weeks to do the impossible. I had respect for Stereth, but knew I was asking a lot. I went to him again to ask if he'd made any arrangements, and again he brushed me off. "I'll let you know, Tymon. If you're restless, go help Mora with the waterjugs."

Sometimes Stereth reminded me of the sort of parent who discourages a child from bothering them by always bringing up chores.

I said, "Where's Des? I haven't seen him in days. Is he involved in this, or is he in some other kind of trouble?"

"Waterjugs, Tymon."

"Well, is he dead or alive?"

Stereth went on his way. I did help Mora with the waterjugs, though, and worked out double-shifts with Carabin's classes, and became quite the floor-cleaner and blanket-shaker. They were good about putting up with me. I was pretty near the edge those days.

The twenty-eighth of Kace dawned in a gray mist, with a fine coating of drizzle falling on the hills. I rose early and stood by the doorway, looking up the path toward the pair of twisted trees on the skyline. Stereth and Cantry were still sound asleep beneath a single fur blanket. My eyes ached. I wasn't really uncomfortable with my lack of sleep, though, because I'd forgotten what a full night's rest was like. I wondered what the twenty-eighth of Kace looked like from the basement in Kynogin, and I wished Stereth would wake up and light the fuse on the day's events. If nightfall came without bringing off this mission I strongly doubted there would be another chance, and the waiting was growing intolerable.

I wandered over to the waterjars and prepared to make a rude amount of noise, then paused. I can't say it was any feeling of consideration that held me back; it simply occurred to me that Stereth might not function at his peak today if I woke him. As for me, I was as close to my peak as I was going to come until the whole matter was over, so I went for a walk.

I walked for an hour. Even in a drizzle the hills were piercingly beautiful. In fact it was the last peaceful day I would see on the Plateau; and what peace there was, was certainly not in me. When I returned I found Stereth and the group awake and dressed, and Clintris na'Fli leading a line of mounts from the stable.

"There you are," said Stereth, irritably. "You might take your mount, Tymon, this whole expedition was your idea. We'll be breakfasting on the road, so don't give me that famished look." (Any look I gave him was strictly blank.) "All right—are we all ready, boys and girls? Good. We're going to bail Tymon's husband out of jail."

And this is what the Athenan scholar and the dangerous outlaws went off to attempt.

Chapter 18

A cold, drizzly ride with the smell of wet fur from my mount never being far from my nostrils. Stereth parked us on some hills overlooking the Shaskala road, but nowhere near where I'd anticipated. I'd been thinking he would lead us to one of the more empty stretches of country—the gods knew there were enough to choose from—but we were not a kilometer out of Drear Market Town. Vendors were all over the road already.

By then it was late morning, and though we'd eaten on the road we were all hungry again. Stereth sent most of the group away, not bothering to tell me where. Finally I said, "How about some food?"—thinking he'd bring out the dried strips of beef now. He smiled and tossed me a coin.

"Go try one of the vendors, Tymon. My treat."

I looked down the hill at the bakers and sweets-sellers, the stands for smoked beef coated in lemon and honey sauce, the knots of people from Drear moving about. It had stopped drizzling, and the spectators were rolling in from the farms and ranches. "You're joking."

"Not I. Your job is down on the road anyhow."

"Oh? Has this unworthy one the honor of addressing the great Stereth Tar'krim?"

"No need to be testy about it. There was just no point in discussing it with you earlier."

"And my job is . . . ?"

He told me. I said, "I fail to see how this advances our goal."

"Did you rejoin our band just to give me a hard time? Do your part like everybody else, Tymon. People here are risking their lives on your behalf."

Put that way, I felt in no position to argue. I tied a scarf around my head and went down to the festivities.

Two hours later I was sitting on the damp ground at the side of the road with the remains of a stew pie at my feet. Grateth, I saw, was nearby, wearing the clothes of a ranch-hand, letting the spotted mount he'd brought nibble at the long grass on the hillside. He patted it from time to time, fanned himself with his cap, and gave no sign that he knew who I was.

A family was on my other side, farmer-types; five children, one of them a toddler, all with country accents. They ate an enormous amount, then argued as to whether the Governor was to be disliked or admired for capturing Stereth Tar'krim. The father and mother were cautious ones, but the kids were all for Rice Thief.

"Wait till he comes by, your Rice Thief," said the father at last. "We'll see who's the clever one then. Let this be a lesson to you! Any one of you turns out outlaw, he'll get the back of my hand before ever the gibbet sees 'em. Stick to your chores, and none of this dreaming."

"But he's a *hero,*" said one of the older boys. "I never said I'd be a hero."

The mother folded their striped picnic cloth and dropped it in a basket. "Whatever he is, he'll not die in bed, and that's all we need remember."

One of the boys turned to another. "What do you think it's like, being hung?"

"You think they'll hang 'im? I heard they were going to chop 'im."

"Bet hanging's worse."

"Bet chopping is."

Well, I was so glad I'd picked this spot. Grateth was brushing his mount's coat idly, oblivious to the debate. I couldn't see anyone else belonging to Stereth.

I closed my eyes and tried to relax. Some time later I heard one of the boys say, "They're coming!"

I stood up and looked down the road. Nothing. But the kids still looked excited, so I took a few steps up the side of the hill.

Very far in the distance, movement. I stationed myself on the hillside and undid the fastenings on the respectable white outer robe I was wearing. My hands were sweating. I really didn't see how we were going to succeed; if only Stereth, like Ran, would choose to be a bit more forthcoming. Both of them could use a good Athenan therapy group.

Now there was a frightening thought. My brain seemed to slow down at that point, tracking in the same circles while I waited, forever, for the procession to reach us.

The Governor and the Steward were in front, preceded only by six militia officers in gold dress uniform. Then about thirty more soldiers, then—yes. A large cage, ornamental gold leaf around top and bottom (Ivorans did nothing by halves), with huge trundly wheels whose top thirds disappeared into humps in the floor. The Governor was bringing his man in in style. A band of red characters ran around the top of the cage, below the gold leaf: "So are all enemies of our beloved Emperor brought low."

Behind the cage, an endless parade of militia. Oh, Stereth. I hope you know what you're doing, I hope the gods will protect me as they protect all scholars without wit enough to come in out of the rain. The cage trundled closer and I saw Ran sitting in the middle, on the bare wood floorboards, his knees drawn up, his arms around his legs. As though maximizing the distance between himself and the crowds. It must have been a long journey from Kynogin.

Two officers rode to the left and right of the cage. Two people in civilian dress accompanied them: A man and a woman in city robes and decorated boots. Sorcerers, I'd bet my life; the Atvalids protecting their cargo. Damn! If only I'd pressed Stereth. Of course after my escape from Kynogin bank, they would assume the sorcerer in Stereth's company was Cantry. They were more right than they knew. Cantry would be dead if she tried her illusion-in-the-road trick here; these people were professionals.

There were shouts just down the road: A fight broke out at the beer stand. Governor Atvalid, with a disgusted look on his face, motioned for a couple of officers to go over and put a stop to it. One of the men fighting took a swing at an officer and ended up on his backside in the dirt. The Governor's mount—bred for show, evidently, danced out a few steps, and her rider began, "Citizens! If you please—" I was trying to get a better view of Ran. He didn't appear to be moving much; he wasn't even looking around. Drugged? I took a step down the hillside to get a closer look.

A yell pierced the air. Even having been warned of this much, I nearly jumped out of my boots. I turned involuntarily to the hill to my right, and stared at the five people cresting it as though I'd never seen them before.

Cantry was at the lead. She wore no hat, letting her blonde hair loose, and her jacket and trousers were the flashiest of all the bandit clothing I'd seen. There was a gold chain with a huge roc sapphire at her throat. Usually Cantry was a plain, silent shadow, but today she was an outlaw princess, and the soldiers stared at her. The four men flanking her were Lex, Komo, Paravit-Col, and Sembet Triol. Paravit-Col alone looked nervous, but even he wore his new quilted jacket of emerald green.

"Release Stereth Tar'krim!" she cried, before anyone had a chance to recover.

The Steward was the first to make an effort to deal with the situation. "Disarm yourselves and surrender, madam." Unimpressed with the show of outlaw legend, he used a form of address that was barely polite. He looked younger and grimmer than I'd seen him before, and wore a traditional high officer's dress cap of shining silver cast with battle carvings around the sides. Very nice. I'd carried his blue hat of Imperial Favor out of the bank with me accidentally and didn't notice it till I was halfway to the fort. I'd have dropped it on the floor for him if I'd remembered.

I heard murmurs of "Cantry, she's Cantry" from the crowd. I pulled off my scarf and outer robe, showing my barbarian coloring. Beneath the robe I wore the jacket Stereth had given me. I pushed a gold circlet up on my forehead. "The hell she is!" I yelled as forcefully as I could. The soldiers stared from one of us to the other, paralyzed, like the audience at a provincial theater.

"How many of them are there?" I heard somebody say.

The Steward, a man who did not react well to confusion, pulled out a pistol.

Oops. He looked toward Cantry, then leveled it at me.

A flash of green smoke, and the rumble of an explosion, shook the ground near the beer stand. More green smoke poured from somewhere to the rear of the militia column.

Somebody grabbed me from behind and, reacting like anybody trained by Carabinstereth, I nearly kneed him in the groin before I remembered it was Grateth. He pulled me up onto his mount and we rode through the green fog. I could just make out Cantry and her group riding like hell in five different directions. They'd never gotten any closer to Ran than that, and I felt sick. I twisted my head round as we crested the hill, and in the clearing smoke I saw the patch of ground in the center of the militia column, the ornate cage with its beautifully calligraphic warning.

It was empty.

I rode on, hopeful, scared, and confused, away from the distant shouting over the hill. There were more trees around this area than most parts of the Plateau, no doubt one of the factors in Stereth's choice, and we zigzagged among them.

"Hey!" I called to Grateth. "You're heading back to Drear!"

"I know!" he shouted in an impatient tone, so I let him go. Obviously I was a spear-carrier in this drama. We slowed to a walk before Grateth took us into the market town. "They'll be all over the hills looking for us," he said quietly. "Safer here. The cattle agent's one of our fences."

The cattle agent was prudently not home, but we were received by a familiar figure. "Des!" I shouted, and threw myself into his arms.

"It went pretty well, didn't it?" he said, grinning.

"Did it? Is he all right? Where have you been for two weeks? Will one of you tell me what's going on?"

Des wore his smug look, the one that said he couldn't fail to please his audience with this bit. "I've been helping Sokol, darling. The vanishing act was my idea."

"Where is he? How did you do it?"

"Well, it's a long story. He's fine, really. We just have to collect him."

I punched him, not hard, in the shoulder, and said, "Tell me what happened!"

"If I tell you, you won't be impressed."

"Des, how can I not be impressed? Sokol disappeared from a cage in full view of a troop of militia! Tell me how you did it!"

"People are always disappointed when they learn how tricks are done. Trust me. I had to assist the magician who opened for us when I was with the Sotar Touring Company, and I know what I'm saying. —Not that I told anybody how the tricks worked, I mean. I'm very discreet, Tymon."

I was puzzled. "A magician? So you did use sorcery?"

He frowned back. "Magicians don't use sorcery, sweetheart. Otherwise why would people come to see them? Any sorcerer can make an illusion so that somebody looks like they've been cut in half, but it takes a clever man to do it without magic. Why, I always had to read an affidavit before each performance, guaranteeing that no sorcery was involved in any—"

"Damn it! Just tell me how you did it!"

He saw I was serious, and shrugged. "Trap door in the cage. I've been a carpenter's apprentice the last two weeks."

I was disappointed. "Is that all?"

"I told you you'd be disappointed. I shouldn't have said anything."

"But it's so *obvious*—" I paused. "It's too obvious. And didn't they see him when he came out? And didn't they check the cage when it was made?"

"Don't teach your grandmother to suck eggs, my barbarian. Grateth, aren't some of the others supposed to be here by now?"

Grateth had been pacing. Now he nodded and said, "I'm going to look around. Stay here, and don't argue too loudly."

He left. Des sat down and stretched out his long legs. "Tymon, people see what they expect to see in this life. They ordered a cage, and they got a cage."

"And nobody saw him climb out?"

"Ah. Well, there we come to a specific point. He didn't really climb out, actually. He's, uh, still in the cage."

"The cage was empty! I saw it!"

"And didn't I just tell you not to trust what you see? Your half-husband is even now in a crawlspace under the floor, by one of the wheels. That's why the bottom of the cage looks so secure from beneath—it is, there's no exit. Paravit-Col and Komo had to go back and cut him out.

—Hope they're doing it soon. Not a lot of air in that section."

I sat down myself. "You said he was all right."

"I'm sure he is. Everybody knew what they had to do."

"Gods." I was silent for a moment, then said, "Won't there still be guards around the cage?"

"Around an empty cage? Every soldier in the troop will be out scouring the hills for Stereth Tar'krim, or the Governor'll have apoplexy. Or he might have it anyway."

"But won't they figure it out, come back and check—"

"You didn't figure it out till I told you." He ran an exhausted hand through his hair. "That's what the fighting at the beer stand and the bit with you and Cantry was for—give 'em a show, don't give 'em time to think. They're too busy to think now, too. Eventually, yeah, maybe in two or three days they'll come back and check. By then the cage will be kindling, and we'll have another legend of the great Stereth Tar'krim, who disappeared on the Shaskala Road."

We sat there, both wrung out. Then I said, "Des, you ever thought of going in for directing instead of acting?"

He laughed. "Don't give me all the credit, Tymon. This was Stereth's show. I was just a consultant."

"Your idea, though. Thank you."

He kissed my cheek. "I'll take the thanks, but I really don't deserve that either. I didn't bring up the idea seriously. I was drunk one night, and was asked my opinion—"

"The old Stereth Tar'krim Get-Your-Followers-Stoned-and-See-What-They-Have-To-Say Trick."

"Well, if it works—"

Grateth came in again. "Lex is here. We're missing Komo, Sokol, and Paravit-Col. Everybody else had other meeting places."

Lex entered a few seconds later—followed by Stereth. We all practically snapped to attention.

Stereth's eyes were bright behind the glasses. He brushed road dust off his jacket and said, "I came to tell you not to wait for Komo. He and Sokol had to take another route home. —He's out and safe, Tymon. He just has to make it back to the monastery. I haven't seen Paravit-Col."

"I did." It was Lex. "Two soldiers had him. He was off his mount. They were walking him southwest, toward Kynogin."

"How long ago?" snapped out Stereth.

"Ten minutes."

"Take Grateth and show him. Deal with the soldiers before they multiply."

"Deal with them?" That from Lex, who was worse than Des when it came to avoiding any trouble.

"There are only two. Follow them and kill them." He turned to me. "You go with them, Tymon. All this was at your request."

We found tracks where Lex showed us. There were no militia within sight; I don't know if we were just lucky or if they'd mostly fanned out by now into territory farther from town. We had a good chance of overtaking the soldiers, apparently, because Lex said the marks still showed they were walking their captive behind their own mounts.

After a couple of minutes I saw Lex and Grateth exchange looks. I said, "What?"

Grateth pointed to the ground. There were no bootmarks here, just traces of two mounts. And those traces were none too clear—as though some ultra-careful servant had followed with a broom, sweeping them up.

"I don't get it," I said.

"Got tired of walking him," growled Lex.

"Then what are they doing with him?"

Neither of them answered. We followed the tracks through some brambles and down a damp hillside, where I could finally see the slight gulley Paravit-Col had left as he was dragged through the grass.

The soldiers had gone on a merry ride. Their trail circled and doubled back, zigzagged through the prickly Sector trees and bushes, and headed back toward town.

Five kilometers outside Drear, we spotted Paravit-Col's new green jacket on the opposite bank of a stream. Coming nearer, we saw the brown of his riding trousers, and his dark curly hair. Grateth reached him first, and turned him over as I dismounted.

He had no face.

Ran was waiting back at the monastery. We took hold of each other for a while in sheer relief, then pulled away to see Stereth waiting. I reported in about Paravit-Col.

"I'll tell Mora," he said. "What about you, Sokol?"

"I also regret his death," said Ran formally. He was thinner and tired-looking, which I guess was only to be expected.

"Well you should," said Stereth. "but I was speaking of your future with the band. Your half-wife gave me reason to believe you would be more cooperative at our next meeting."

We were alone in one corner of the main hall; people were still dribbling back from the great rescue. So far Paravit-Col was the only reported casualty.

Ran turned to me, his face unreadable. "Did you give a House promise?"

"No."

His gaze returned to Stereth. "Then I'm under no obligation to honor any personal promise she may have made."

"She made no promise. I had the impression she spoke more from a knowledge of your character. She did tell me once that you never forget an obligation."

I'd mentioned it in passing, months ago. Did the man store up every damn thing he heard like nuts for the winter?

"I'm not aware of any obligation," Ran said.

Stereth let that falsehood lie there in silence, growing. Then he said, "I see you got my message about the trapdoor."

Ran's lips twisted. "Thank you," he said briefly, as though the words hurt. A second later he burst out, "Whatever you did was for your own reasons—"

"It always is."

"I never made any agreements with you or anybody here—"

"No, we all realize that."

Ran looked more and more frustrated. Stereth smiled. "We'll talk later. You should both get some sleep. The afternoon still stretches before us; no doubt we'll find some way of entertaining ourselves. And you certainly don't need to concern yourself, Ran; no Cormallon promises were exchanged."

Ran turned slowly and looked at me. I felt my face get hot.

"I'll leave you to your rest, then, shall I?" Stereth patted me on the shoulder in comradely fashion and left us.

"It was a complicated situation," I told Ran.

"The one thing I didn't want anyone here to know—"

"They were going to execute you!"

Well, our voices were raised for a good quarter of an hour. If anybody didn't know his name before, they heard it then. Eventually Ran remembered that it was beneath his dignity to yell, and slipped into the icy formality he reserved for those times when he was particularly angry. I hated it when he did that.

There was no question of a nap by the time we were through, and I stamped out to find something physical to do. Most of the bands were back by then, and as I tramped angrily through the stables and up to the coop and down to the hostage privy it started to penetrate that the atmosphere in the fort had changed. There was a grim seriousness everywhere. None of the fooling around or congratulating or friendly insults that followed a successful run. Paravit-Col, the youngest of the original band and always popular, was dead—but cruel as this may sound, that wasn't enough to explain the change. Death comes as no great shock to Sector outlaws.

"Stereth thinks we're nearing a crisis," Des said to me, when I cornered him in the hostages' outbuilding, carrying in extra blankets. He seemed to feel the prisoners were his personal pets.

"He didn't say anything to me."

Des shrugged, and I had to admit that Stereth never revealed much to me if he could avoid it. I suppose it was only sensible.

"Cantry told him," said Des.

This was a new one on me. Presentiment, if that's what we were talking about, was a rare ability. Even with the cards, I— The cards. How long since I'd run them? I ought to get them out now and see what they had for me.

Just then Mora appeared at the door. "There you are, Tymon. Come along, we're having a session in the main hall. Carabinstereth sent me to find you." Her voice was businesslike, her eyes clear. I couldn't tell if she'd heard about Paravit-Col yet, or not. They'd been lovers ever since the day Clintris na'Fli brought in the giant country bathtub.

The thought seemed to take away any naturalness I possessed, and I found that I had no idea what words to say to her. I nodded finally, and she said, "Ten minutes, Tymon." She closed the door.

I turned to Des. "Does she know?"

"She knows." That grim seriousness was even in Des' voice—Des, who'd always seemed to feel that when life started to go wrong he could just pull aside the scriptwriter for a private talk.

The mood was everywhere. For Carabinstereth to announce a double practice session was unusual enough, and I found when I got to the main hall that the class attitude was quiet and tense, not the usual slightly hysterical humor that prevailed at these times.

Some of the protective face helmets had been lost in the move from Deathwell, so Carabinstereth simply announced we would do without. Lex, of course, had his own specially padded helmet still intact; you could always count on Lex to look out for number one.

I stood on the sidelines waiting during the third hour of class. Periwinkle, the chubby girl next to me, handed me the waterjug. We were always thirsty during lessons—I remember our lips were usually dry, too, for some reason, and the women were forever smearing creams on them. Anyway, I took a swig, trying to ignore the dread I always felt waiting for my turn. I was second from the top of the line.

Juvindeth was on the mat. Juvie was stubborn as her road-name, but not that difficult to get along with, and she was as short as you can get without being a barbarian. She did a few well-aimed kicks at Lex, our instructor-target that day. Bad luck for Juvie: She was forced into a complicated maneuver near the edge of the mat, slipped, and went over. This is not usually a problem, as we were taught to continue fighting from the ground, and indeed, women usually have the advantage of men in that kind of fight.

Unless of course the man gets her in a pin, as Lex did now. He fell on top of her, holding down her arms and legs. I remembered Carabinstereth's warnings: Let a man land one good blow on your head or face, and you're done for. And Juvindeth had no protective helmet.

Lex released one wrist to administer the blow. Quick as a cat, Juvie went for his eyes with her one free hand. Lex's head went back, but he got hold of her wrist again. This time he pulled her left arm over by her right and laid part of his weight on top of them. She was now open to have her jaw or skull broken, and there was nothing she could do about it.

Carabinstereth was supervising, of course, but she made no move to interfere. She and Lex had always assured us that they would never hold back, and a fight would only be over when it was over. But for the gods' sake, they weren't going to let Juvindeth be beaten to a pulp for the sake of some stupid rule! Why didn't Carabin purse her lips and let out that damned whistle that marked the end of a drill? This was crazy!

Lex raised his arm. Suddenly—and I must say that I'd made no decision to do so—I was running for the mat. My foot connected beautifully with Lex's padded helmet. It felt like kicking an overripe melon. Lex toppled over, and all three of us were down. Juvie rolled out immediately and positioned herself for some follow-up blows to Lex's head. I'd hit the floor like a ton of bricks and the wind was knocked out of me; I watched as Juvie smashed into Lex's face mask twice, and saw the helmet roll off across the mat. She seemed unaware or unconcerned about this; she had her heel above Lex's face, about to administer the coup de grace, when Carabinstereth's whistle froze her in place.

Juvie blinked and slowly lowered her foot. She went to her knees. Carabin bent over Lex, who seemed dazed. She helped him up and over to a pile of pillows at the side of the hall. By the time she returned I was starting to get my breath back, and was sitting up on the mat, gasping.

"Well!" she said in a voice that sounded, of all things, pleased.

I looked up at her accusingly.

She smiled. Addressing the line of women she said, "Our Tymon seems to have broken custom and jumped into somebody else's fight. I think we might give her a round of applause."

And they all started clapping and stamping. I felt my face get hot for the second time that day.

"Let's hear it for Juvindeth, too!" called Carabin.

Redoubled enthusiasm from the line. But she wasn't getting off that easily. When the clapping died down I said, still sitting there, "Juvindeth could have been hurt badly. Maybe even killed."

Her eyes danced. "We knew that if something like this happened, one of the people nearest in line would run in. It was bravely done, Tymon."

She was holding out a hand to help me up. I was still resentful, but I took it and got to my feet. "It wasn't brave," I said honestly, "it just happened."

She grinned.

"How could you be sure it would happen?" I pursued. "How could you know it if I didn't know it?"

She kissed me. "Get back in line, Tymon, you haven't had your turn yet."

Gods! But I felt I had to say: "Carabin—I don't know that I would be able to do something like this in a real battle."

"Of course you would do it, sweetheart; you couldn't help it. You're *trained.*"

How many other things will change me when I don't want to be changed? Waiting in line again, in a dream of exhaustion, I heard someone ask, "Why are we going through this? The militia could walk in any time they want, and we just don't have the firepower to stop them."

It was a question that was always on everybody's mind, but one we never asked. The mood really was different that day.

Carabinstereth's voice was cool and ironic. "Well, if we never have the chance to fight, you've still had good practice. But if the Steward wants to bring a string of us in for public display, he'll hold back that firepower. And then, children, you have to choose—you can go quietly and face torture and death; or you can fight back, and face *probable* torture and death."

"I guess you're going to fight," said someone.

"I always fight," said Carabin, "but that's who I am. Of course," she added thoughtfully, "that's who you are now, too."

Chapter 19

I slept for four solid hours after class, and woke up to darkness and lit candles in the hall.

People were finishing up the day's chores, playing cards, resting. Cantry was sweeping the stone floor down through the middle of the room. There was a figure in shadow, sitting alone off by a pile of tattered scarlet cushions that flickered into rhythmic brilliance from the light of a nearby candelabra: Mora Sobien Ti. The streaks of light gray in her hair were unmistakable.

There was something I needed to do. I took a candle and went up the newly repaired spiral stone staircase to the roof of the hall. A parapet enclosed the edge; unless I stood on my barbarian tiptoes, all I could see were the stars overhead.

I sat down on the cold stone, put the candle about an arm's length in front of me, and took the pack of cards out of the pouch that hung from my belt.

Card one: In this configuration, Significator. By rights this should be Ran, as this pack had been dedicated to him at birth, but what I saw was The Burning Tower. Ran was no burning tower, even metaphorically—I stay away from people like that, they scare me. If I'd seen The Prisoner card, I would not have been surprised, but this made no sense. I looked down at the picture, so beautifully rendered: Thundercloud, lethal lightning bolt, and the screaming face in the window, wreathed by flames. I closed my eyes. I didn't *want* to see into this picture any further.

Card two, pulled out swiftly and snapped down. The Wheel of Luck. On Ivory, this card is rendered as a torture device, with pitch and sharpened nails at the bottom of the wheel. Where were these cards coming from tonight? I grabbed a third before I could have time to think. I took a breath. My eyes were closed, and I was in no hurry to open them. There was something wrong with me too, tonight—with the atmosphere in the monastery fort, with the cards, with all of us. *Do your job*, I told myself, and opened my eyes.

The Hunter, Stereth's card. Well, and nothing wrong with that, was there? I forced myself to watch it until it changed.

The man in brown and green holding two dead ground-hermits came to life; his face was cruel, and the birds in his hands were moving in feeble terror. As I watched, he wrung their necks. Then, his clothing changed to a yellow and crimson robe with fashionable boots, and he turned and looked out of the card as though he could see me sitting there on the roof, under the distant stars. Looked out at me with a hatred so hard I was physically afraid. Nor Atvalid, Governor of Tuvin Province, was The Hunter tonight, not Stereth Tar'krim.

I turned over the card and sat back. Three cards of death and destruction, as though the pack had no time to fool with Significators and configurations. No time for anything but an immediate warning. I'd never seen hatred like that on anyone's face; people had done some awful things to me in the past, but out of indifference or spite or small-mindedness—not this heavy weight of personal obsession.

I gathered up the cards, shivering. *It's a cold night, Theodora.* Yes, and maybe colder before it was over. I got to my feet and started down the staircase at a run.

Where was Ran?—That huddle in the blankets by the fire. Good, he was safe. I looked around for Stereth and found him sitting knee-to-knee with Cantry while they fed each other little bits of stew. They were the ones who ought to be on a damned honeymoon.

Hey! Wasn't tonight three-quarter night? I dismissed that thought at once—nothing pleasant was going to happen now, maybe nothing pleasant would happen to any of us ever again. I marched up to Stereth and blurted, "We have to talk."

He saw at once that I was upset. He wiped his fingers on a rag and told Cantry. "See if you can dig out some more wine." Then he motioned for me to sit.

"Stereth, something's happening. I think—I think the militia are going to attack us tonight. Any time now, maybe any second."

He studied me. "Cantry's reported some negative feelings as well. Is this barbarian premonition, or is it some kind of women's thing?"

"I'm serious!"

His voice was reasonable. "On what evidence are you serious?"

Well, they were no longer a secret. I took out my deck of cards and slapped it down on the floor beside our cushions. "I help Ran—Sokol—with professional projects. Sorcerers use cards as a guidepost to keep themselves out of trouble. This deck is Ran's personal mapping device."

"And yet you read them? You're not a sorcerer."

"It's a long story. Take my word for it. I ran these cards five minutes ago, and all they can talk about is violence and death. I have every confidence in you, Stereth, but I think we ought to get out of here."

He accepted the data—as data—and considered. "If I were the Steward, I would be home asleep now. They had a long day today, and there'll be more problems tomorrow. Why keep the troops going on double shifts? It's not like there's a deadline to capture us."

"Asleep!" Usually he was more perceptive than that. "That family won't sleep a full night till they've seen us die personally. The Governor *hates* you—and me—and I guess Cantry. The others he just despises normally."

He seemed genuinely puzzled. "Why?"

"*Why?* Stereth, I don't think you have any idea of the effect you have on people. I wish Des were here, he could explain it to you." I took a deep breath. "Look at how you've turned our lives upside-down. You knock people over and leave casual bootprints on their necks as you step by on your way—never mind. This isn't why I'm here. We have to run for it, I'm trying to get through to you."

"Tymon—"

He looked past me, toward the door. Des was coming in from outside. I called, "Des! Come here and explain—" I stopped short.

Des was staggering. He held his left arm and rested for a moment against the door. Then he continued, dazed, through the hall. He knelt down by Stereth and looked at him, bewildered.

"The kid with the yellow headband—" he began. "The kid with the yellow—" He stopped. He frowned. I leaned forward to say something to him, but Stereth motioned me back. Des began again. "The kid from Deathwell was helping me feed the tah people." Des never called them hostages. "We started outside with the empty dishes, and this light hit him."

That seemed to be the end of the story, so Stereth asked, "Where is he now?"

"He's dead," said Des. "The light hit him."

We all glanced involuntarily toward the door. "Don't go out there," I said at once.

The card game in the corner had stopped. People were looking at us.

I saw that the cloth on Des' arm was torn away, and the flesh underneath it was blistered and red, as though it were sunburned. Cantry appeared from nowhere, holding a basin of cool water, and she knelt down and helped Des out of his jacket, and placed his forearm gently in the water.

"Des, your arm—" I said.

He glanced down at it, uninterested. "That's the side the kid was on, the kid with the yellow—"

There was a wailing sound that filled the world, getting louder and louder. Suddenly the hall was flooded with a sunlit brightness that never happened on the Plateau. The full shabby dustiness of the place was palpable, with the blank faces of its inhabitants hanging there as though on some ancient, dead tapestry.

Then dimness again. Whole, blessed dimness, with nothing broken and nobody hurt.

Nor Atvalid's invitation to surrender could not have been plainer if he'd walked up and tapped on the door.

As the minutes stretched into a quarter hour, then a half hour, then the sort of eternity you find in a hospital waiting room, it became clearer that Atvalid was holding off till sunrise—for the convenience and safety of his troops, and to give us a chance to break apart mentally. There was an occasional scream from outside, marking somebody from one of the outbuildings or stable who'd tried unsuccessfully to run to the main hall. I could understand their wanting company. "I'd tell them to sit where they are," muttered Stereth, "if there were some *way* I could tell them."

Des looked up at us. The shock was wearing off. "I hope the tah folks know to stay inside," he said.

This was met with silence. Nobody had much altruism to spare in concern for the tah caravan hostages. The Governor's warning shot had awakened Ran, who was sitting beside me, holding my arm. "The hell with this," said Stereth suddenly. He stood up and crossed the room. "Lex, pick up your cards and deal. We'll have a hand of Thistle, that always helps me think. Cantry, get out the good stuff. We've had some fine times here, all of us, and if this is our last night I refuse to give them the satisfaction of cowering through it."

I can't say this was greeted with enthusiasm, but a case of wine did seem to ease the tense silence we'd been in before. Gradually card games started up again, and bredesmoke conversations, and I think, in the back of people's minds, there was a vague and undefined hope that somehow Stereth would *do something* that would get us all out of this. No one crossed the line and expressed it, however, for that let the door open to the cold knowledge that there wasn't much he could do. When I thought back on the remarkable things he'd accomplished in the past I could see that most of what he had done was by misdirection: An illusion in the road to make a car swerve; a flame by a sensor to convince someone their vehicle was on fire; a disappearing outlaw leader who wasn't even an outlaw leader to begin with. Now an obsessively hating and powerful official stood outside, with a militia regiment and heavy weaponry. Short of trying to convince him he had the wrong address, I failed to see what misdirection could be applied here.

I had half a bottle of Sector wine myself. Carabinstereth was comforting Mora, Lex and some people from the new bands were playing Thistle, and I was trying to figure out which of us might still be outside. Ran didn't join in the wine or the game; he sat by me and frowned. Stereth came over to join us.

"Kanz outside has Tellys weapons. His troops probably

don't even know how to use them. What the hell is he thinking?"

Ran finally spoke up. "He wants to win."

"He's cleaning out a troop of outlaws, not conquering a city. There aren't more than thirty of us here tonight—forty-three if you count Des' tah friends."

I said, "Maybe they'll go easy on us for not killing the prisoners."

They both looked at me. I said, "I'm just mentioning the possibility."

"We could *threaten* to kill the prisoners," said Ran.

"If we could get to them," pointed out Stereth, "and if they even knew we *had* prisoners."

The employees of the Keldemir Tah Company were probably the only people who were going to get out of this trouble alive.

"You think it was Paravit-Col told them where we were?" asked Ran.

Stereth shrugged. "The more surprising thing is how quickly they dropped everything and hauled out the heavy artillery. Don't these people have anything else to do with their time?"

I gave a short laugh. "Stereth, you made his son look like a fool. You ruined his capture of a famous outlaw leader. Besides—look, I guess Des reported to you a long time ago that the district Steward is Torin Atvalid's grandson."

"Of course he did. Though I'd already heard."

"It must have made you feel good to score off an Atvalid."

"It didn't make me feel bad." He pulled off his spectacles and began wiping them with his handkerchief. The moisture in this climate was always clouding them up, one problem I guessed he wouldn't be worrying about in the future. "Do you have a point here, Tymon?"

"They know you, too, they feel responsible for the chaos you've caused. Look, doesn't knowing about Nor Atvalid and his son, and their problems, doesn't that make them more real to you? Nor's reaction is to hate—but doesn't knowing people make you less want to hurt them?"

He replaced his glasses and looked at me straight-on. I always felt a little nervous when he did that, and I remembered that icepick feeling I got from Des when he did his Stereth impression. "Tymon, you seem to have a personal problem, if you don't mind my saying so. These people are enemies. They're not there for you to identify with just because you know their stories."

People and their stories. I said nothing. He went on, "You're a little too adaptable, that's all. Something to guard against. You're not really barbaric in other ways, so . . . I don't see what's amusing about this, Tymon. Outworlder standards of humor must be very odd." He got to his feet, a trifle offended, and went to join the card players.

I turned to Ran, who'd been silently taking in this last part. "You're not the only one who thinks I'm too adaptable."

"And I also don't see the humor in it."

"Come on, don't you perceive a pattern here? I'm fine as long as I'm going along with what you want. It's only when I take the enemy's point of view that I'm 'too adaptable.' "

We were leaning against a pile of stolen Andulsine rugs. "Theodora," he said very gently, "if you went around taking the enemy's point of view, he wouldn't be the enemy anymore."

"This is my point, Ran."

He muttered something that sounded like "outworlders."

I said, "It's ironic. The Governor hates us like poison, yet until the Kynogin Bank we never even met him. And he's the one we were sent to check up on!"

"I met him," said Ran.

"What?"

"I met him. In the Shaskala jail. He was crazy even then, he had two of the guards hold me down while a third one twisted my arm." Ran's voice was calm, reminiscing.

"You never told me this!"

"Well, there wasn't much point, and you had other things on your mind. And I know how you get, Tymon."

"How I *get*—"

He added hastily, "And I thought I'd wait till we were both out of trouble, and could plan out a nice revenge together."

Typical Ivoran motivation. "That was a sweet thought,

but didn't we agree you would start filling me in on things?"

"I'm telling you now," he pointed out.

Well, that did it. "Ten thousand provincial troops outside, we're all going to die, and you're telling me now. Great Paradox! Do you have to treat every single thing that happens to you like a state secret? Do we need to keep a torturer on retainer to get the day's news out of you when you come home? I should be privileged you chose to mention it at all!"

"Theodora, sweetheart, you're not taking this the way—"

"I'm not taking it at all! What the hell could I have been thinking? I could be peacefully doing research on Athena—*library* research. No translations, no interviews—let me tell you, primary sources are overrated!—"

I would like to point out here that the entire situation of that night was not conducive to rational appraisal. Let's cut out about ten minutes:

"—and I can only thank the gods that, if we live through this, we'll have missed three-quarter night."

"What?" I'd gotten his attention.

"Tonight's three-quarter night, my friend, and it looks like the wedding is off."

He blinked. He seemed to take this information in slowly. He groped around for words: "Uh, we could exchange tokens instead of cakes. It's all symbolic anyway. We could consider them *spiritual* cakes."

"We could consider ourselves as unmarried."

Making a major mistake, he said, "Dying unmarried would be a disgrace to my family."

Clearly he was speaking one of the first thoughts that sprang to mind. It wasn't the most flattering statement he'd ever made. I got up, not trusting myself to sit next to him with all the physical aggression Carabinstereth's classes had set to boiling, and went to watch Stereth watch the card players.

I played a few hands of Thistle, drank till my legs felt shaky, and lay down on a large cushion beside Des, Komo, and several of the newer people. I started to feel better, or as better as anyone could feel under the circumstances. The night was far advanced by then.

An unnatural calm had settled over the company, I'd

wondered about Stereth handing out liquor to people who might be fighting tomorrow—one-sided though that fight might be—but perhaps he'd known what he was doing. That out-of-control, slightly manic despair that had gripped us earlier in the evening was gone. I listened as the people beside me talked about wine, sex, the army, and anything but their families. Komo told the story of how he and Paravit-Col had returned to the Shaskala Road to cut Ran out of the cage.

"Really, Komo?" asked one of the newcomers. "I thought you'd pulled the cage off somewhere else first."

"Too difficult. There was a manager in charge of drive-beasts who refused to let us touch them. So we just cut him out, then and there, right in the middle of the road."

"No soldier stopped you?"

"Hell, the soldiers were all off chasing Sokol in the hills. Plenty of vendors and Sector folk there, though. None of them tried to stop us."

"Ooh," said the boy—nearly as young as Paravit-Col—and in spite of everything before us this night, still starry-eyed over hearing a story from one of Stereth's original band.

The talk moved on to traditional bandit topics.

"They'll behead Sembet, and probably Sokol, too, with his accent."

One of the older newcomers made this contribution. Beheading is considered more dignified than hanging, and is the required method for executing nobility. Of course, none of the Six Families ever stepped forward to claim any of its wayward members found on the killing block, but it was always possible that someday they would lodge a complaint after the fact. The sentencers were generous in the matter, and gave almost every prisoner the benefit of the doubt. The most ragged and ill-spoken dreg in Stereth's army could claim noble blood and get an ax rather than a rope.

As a result, there was a fair amount of speculation among Sector outlaws as to which form of death was preferable. Those two farmer boys on the Shaskala Road were nothing to a bunch of interested bandits on a slow night. It generally went something like: "I dunno, Tibble, with the ax at least it's over quick. None of this twisting around forever while your face turns purple." "So you say, but I saw a chop in Skeldin Market Town where the executioner had to hit the woman six times before he got a clean stroke. And I swear, my friend, her mouth was still screaming afterward." "You imagined it, Tibs, it was in your head. How could she scream without lungs?" "Your own damned head, brother. My uncle Vatherin was hanged, and except for a few seconds of kicking, it was over."

This popular topic was debated again that night in the fort, while the wind gathered to a howl and the room grew smoky from hearthfire and bredesmoke. But this time Des Helani said to the man who'd brought it up: "I don't think we should talk about it in our sister's presence." And he nodded toward me.

"Why not?" asked the man.

"She won't get a choice, mush-head. She'll be hanged."

I said, "Thanks, Des." Always considerate.

I got up, restless, and paced the hall. *They'll behead Sokol, too, with his accent.* Where was Ran? He'd been over by the rug pile when I'd seen him last-when was that? Hours ago?

I looked into the smaller rooms off the back of the hall, interrupting two trysts. Well, I would have interrupted them if they'd taken any notice of me. No Ran. This was ridiculous—there weren't that many places he could be. We were confined to one building, after all.

One building. But the north edge of the roof met the roof of the shed we'd made to house the stable equipment and the stolen tah, and that met the conical edge of the roof of the cookhouse.

No, I couldn't believe it. Not our careful, prudent Ran. But even a prudent man can do stupid things on the night before he's due to hang—or get chopped—I ran up the stairs to the roof, opened the trapdoor gingerly, and crawled to the parapet wall on the north edge. I very slowly peeped my head over the side.

There was smoke coming from the roof of the cookhouse.

I put my head down again and leaned against the side of the wall, consumed by guilt. He couldn't be doing anything this stupid just because I'd said to forget about the wedding!

Yeah? said the voice in my head. What else is he doing

out there? Is he going to emerge with a carving knife and take on the militia single-handedly?

No, the man was in the cookhouse making marriage-cakes. We were all halfway to execution, and even now the smell of vanilla and cinnamon was being carried to me on the wind.

I wondered with detached interest if he'd found all the ingredients, or he'd had to make substitutions.

Finally a figure detached itself from the opening in the cookhouse roof and started toward the shed. Under the cloudy, muffled light of the moon-and-a-half I could see that Ran was wearing the red and white robes he'd worn in Shaskala; not the sort of thing I'd advise climbing rooftops in. Then I saw he'd pulled the robes up and tucked them in his belt and was scrambling bare-legged over the stone as though wading in a stream back in Cormallon. There was a pack slung on his back.

He bent, hugging the crest of the shed, and made his way toward the wall of the main building. I moved back, not wanting to startle him as he climbed over the parapet. His head appeared, then his shoulders, then one foot was on the top of the wall. The other slipped slightly and he cursed and then got it planted on top as well, though not securely. He raised himself further, straightening his legs to strengthen his balance. The wind blew out the sleeves of his outer robe like great snowy wings streaked with blood . . . and all at once the picture from the card I'd read in Shaskala came back into my head.

Beware of heights.

Without thinking, any more than I'd thought when I jumped into Juvendith's fight earlier that day, I launched myself toward the wall. I was still running when I saw Ran's right foot step on the inner edge, and the stone give way beneath it. His arms went out frantically, trying to regain his balance. He was tipping over backward when I grabbed his waist and pulled him down on top of me.

I got a nasty blow to my back when we both landed on the stone of the roof. Of course, having my slight barbarian frame there to absorb the shock made it a bit easier for Ran.

"Theodora?" He rolled off me and put his hands on my shoulders. "Theodora, are you all right?"

I couldn't talk. The wind had been knocked out of me, and not for the first time that day. There was a time on another planet, I'd like to point out, when the hardest exercise I had all day was turning pages—and that all things considered, I find that mode of life superior.

"Theodora! Answer me! Did you hit your head?"

I knew I wasn't hurt, but it would be a few seconds before I'd be able to answer him, a few seconds that he filled by continuing to call my name in a tone that suggested he was genuinely frightened. I might have been pleased, in a way, but I felt badly about scaring him. Kanz, I thought, it's not enough I have to wait on a rooftop and save the boy's life, now I have lie here helplessly with the responsibility of easing his mind!

A couple of eternal seconds later I managed a grunt. This delighted him and took some of the pressure off me. I hate responsibility of any kind.

Finally I managed to sit up and whisper.

"What?" he said.

"What . . . the hell . . . are you doing in that damned robe?"

"Oh. This. Well, to be honest, I didn't really think I'd make it there and back. And I refuse to die wearing provincial trousers."

I started to laugh, which made my back hurt. So he helped me rest against the wall and took off his outerrobe and put it behind me as a cushion, and showed every indication of wanting to be of service in the nicest possible way, and to sum it up, I could hardly continue to resent him for this stunt. Not that I considered it the wisest thing he'd ever done. Of course, arguing with him on what was probably our last night together hadn't been an admirable move on my part, either.

He opened his pack and took out two well-wrapped marriage cakes. Apparently my body had cushioned their fall, too, since they were cracked but not actually in pieces. He passed me his, and I bowed and put it in front of him. Then he bowed and placed mine in front of me.

"You know," I said, "on Athena we'd go to a Justice of

the Peace, and the whole thing would be over in twenty minutes."

He pulled a piece out of his cake, put it in his mouth, and said, "You appreciate it more if you have to make an effort."

"Is that one of the things your grandmother used to tell you?"

He swallowed. "Not in those words. But I'm sure Grandmother would agree that I did the right thing tonight."

She probably would, too. She'd been a great believer in duty, Ran's grandmother.

I finished my cake and knelt so that I could just see over the wall. The hills around the valley were rimmed with campfires. It would have looked peaceful if it weren't so disheartening.

He joined me. "So ends the story of Stereth Tar'krim."

"Not even our story."

"Well, you never know. We might come in for a mention."

Given how much Ivorans loved their legends, it might well be so. Would tales be drifting around a hundred years from now about Sokol and Tymon and Des Helani and Carabinstereth?

"You know what we've become, tymon?" asked Ran, watching the flickers on the horizon. "We're classic heroes."

He'd used the high-theater term. I sniffed. "More like two-bit heroes."

"In any case," he said, "we're heroes with half a night still to go."

We both lay back against the silk of his outerrobe and I settled in the crook of his arm. A blast of light shot across the sky, as it did occasionally all through that night: Nor Atvalid keeping us aware of our place. "I don't suppose there's anything you can do personally," I said. It was the first time I'd backed up Stereth's attempt to draft him.

His voice was noncommittal. "Let me point out that at this stage they have sorcerers traveling with them. I'm sure they've got mirror-spells on the soldiers and the weaponry. Anything I did to them would hit me."

From Ran, that wasn't necessarily a refusal. Besides, he hadn't had me studying the Red Book of Sorcery for two years for nothing. "Don't you always tell me that it's not the spell, it's the intelligence of the person placing it?"

I could almost feel him smile.

I said, "I'd stack you up against a gang of provincial sorcerers any day of the week." This was the simple truth.

He held me closer, which was comforting, and when he still didn't answer I said, "You know what'll happen if you do nothing."

Of course he knew very well. He was imagining the same sort of scenarios I was: Des and Cantry in the Imperial torture chambers, Mora and Juvindeth lying on the Shaskala Road, their skulls split open like messy fruit.

"Theodora," he said finally, lightly, "your inappropriate friendships make my life very difficult."

I said nothing. If it made him feel better to pretend the bond was all on my side, let him. An answer like that was good enough to last me through till the morning.

So that was how we spent three-quarter night: on the roof amid intermittent gunfire, with no lovemaking, just what comfort we could take from closeness and warmth under that huge, cold, late-summer sky.

Chapter 20

Have I told you about shujenifs, classic heroes? There aren't that many really famous ones in the history of Ivoran high-theater. They're the tragic protagonists, who personify a theme that they work out according to the rules of classic drama. They are introduced, they take action (or not), they praise or rail against fate in poetic language, and then generally they die. And that's the end of the play.

Two-bit heroes, on the other hand, are done in installments—you can go to a play and see #143 in the story of One-Eyed Lenn and the pole pirates. They never really end, they just dribble on and on. Nobody feels the responsibility to treat them with respect that they feel toward the great shujenifs like Oedipus and Melara—no obligation to round out their lives with the imposed structure of drama, as handed down through the ages. When two-bit heroes play, the serious climax in act four is followed by a banana-slip in the epilogue, as the players and audience feel inclined.

And if you missed installments one through 142, it doesn't matter; there'll be another bunch of minor heroes along when the next troupe of players comes through. There are too many two-bits to keep track of all their names.

As for me, I used to collect stories. Folk tales and things, that I picked up from people along the way and wrote down for posterity, or to keep myself occupied—to be honest, it was hard to tell. But when I'd finished the collection I'd begun to realize that one of my motives in making it was this longing that I have for a beginning, a middle, and an end.

Well, everybody has an end. But with shujenifs, and proper stories, the end comes at the right time and everybody learns something. Not the messy and pointless way it comes in real life.

As I lay there on the roof there was a break in the clouds and the full moon and a half streamed through, wasting their glory on two people whose stories would be over tomorrow—one of whom, I saw as I turned, was already asleep.

I must have gotten some brief sleep myself, though I wouldn't have believed it before, because when I looked at the sky next it was whitened with the beginnings of dawn. My gaze traveled down toward the door and stopped.

Stereth was standing there, fully dressed, freshly perfumed, and wearing a pistol in his belt.

I nudged Ran. He shifted, opened his eyes, and froze.

From the look on Stereth's face, you wouldn't have known that dawn and death were overtaking us all. He said calmly; "Now that you've discharged all this sexual tension, perhaps we can talk rationally."

For once he was wrong about something. Nevertheless Ran sat up easily, as though it were a late morning at home in bed, and rested an elbow on one knee. "What is it you want?" His voice sounded almost charitable.

"Not knowing what's possible, it's hard for me to say. May I sit?"

Ran indicated the stone floor beside us. Stereth sat.

"Not that I mean to press you," he began, "but I've divided our force into two groups, under the direction of Komo and Carabinstereth. They're going to take everyone outside, with their arms raised in surrender. When the Atvalids get here, Carabinstereth will give a signal and we'll fight."

I said, "What do you think that will accomplish?"

Stereth pushed up his glasses. "Most of us will be killed in the fighting, which will be better than Imperial torture, and in the confusion one or two might actually escape. Although that's doubtful."

One or two. There were over thirty people in the fort that day.

"You could threaten to burn the tah," said Ran. "The Emperor would be upset."

I said, "Nor Atvalid doesn't care what we do to the tah."

"So speaks our Tymon," said Stereth. "She claims to understand something of our Governor's state of mind. Besides, they have to get close to us to hear our threats . . . which would mean close enough to shoot us. You see why I'm interested in hearing your ideas, sir Cormallon."

That *Cormallon* was twisting the knife a bit. Come on, Ran, I thought; for once in your life, give a little.

Ran said thoughtfully, "I suppose my name will be on everyone's lips by the end of the day?"

"Certainly not. I told you, I would never betray a loyal member of the company."

He said this with a straight face, and to my surprise, Ran burst out laughing. "A man who makes such polite threats deserves all the help he can get. Don't raise your hopes, though, Stereth. They've got at least two sorcerers with them, and I'm not omnipotent."

"I never raise my hopes." That I could believe. Stereth rose to his feet, checked his pistol, and said, "Tell me what you want."

There was a noise at the door to the stairs, and Lex appeared. Stereth motioned for him to keep quiet. Ran moved to the parapet and scanned the horizon. He swallowed nervously. I saw that he was sweating. "Tell them to take off anything yellow."

"It's a trick!"

"Shut up, Lex." Stereth regarded Ran. "What do you mean by anything yellow?"

"Yellow headbands, robes, jackets, boots. Gold jewelry, too."

"They won't like that. What are they going to do with it so it doesn't get lost?"

"They can bury it in the damned ground for all I care. I don't give a kanz." He almost never used profanity, and certainly not twice in a row. His attention wasn't really on any of us, though; he was more like a man about to disarm a bomb than one working up a feat of magic. He'd been defining and shaping for hours, just in case, and now that it was all straight in his mind he had to get rid of it or he'd go crazy. So far as I know, this is not a law of magic. It's just the way Ran's work twists him up into knots. In a sense he was as obsessive as the Governor of Tuvin Province, but being less reform-minded he was more socially acceptable.

Lord, Ran must have been playing with ideas and formulae for months to have gotten this involved.

And he'd never said a word to me.

Stereth opened the door to the stairs and called, "Komo! Carabinstereth!"

A second later Carabin appeared. "Komo's downstairs setting a good example," she said. "Want me to drag him up?"

"Just pass this along. Tell your groups to take off any yellow clothing and all their gold jewelry. Tell them their lives may depend on it—Sokol's planning something big."

Carabinstereth's wide smile lit her odd blue eyes. Her searchlight grin hit Ran and me, then she turned and I heard her clomping almost cheerfully down the stairs. I don't know if you can understand this, but at that moment I felt badly about her trust in us, because I didn't know that we could justify it. Ran was certainly giving no guarantees.

Ran's troubled gaze swept the hilltops. "Tell her to get some rope, too."

"Rope?"

He swallowed again. "You'd better tie me up."

Stereth took this in. "May one ask why?"

"Because I might start to thrash around and hurt myself. And because I'll be less of a nuisance tied up." Stereth started to open his mouth and Ran cut in impatiently. "They're bound to have mirror-spells set up. I can get through the cracks—I know tricks they've never heard of." This was spoken without pride, as a statement of fact. "But anything I give them will rebound on me, too."

Stereth's logic was unhindered by concern for his sorcerer. "I take it from this that whatever effect you generate won't be lethal. I thought you were going to kill them."

"Does it matter to you, as long as you win?"

"No," said Stereth, "It doesn't matter to me. Do whatever makes you happy." He gestured to Lex. "You heard the gentleman; tie him up." And our gangster Robin Hood left the roof.

Even at a time like this, when Stereth absented himself from a place it was like an engine hum suddenly going silent.

Lex cast us both a sulky look and said, "I'll get the rope."

"Hurry." Ran's voice was tense.

"They're starting to move in," I said. Tiny men in tan uniforms were stepping leisurely out of hiding on the horizon.

"I know. Don't talk to me, Theodora."

Half a minute later Lex was back with a dirty hemp rope on his shoulder. Heaven knew what it had been used for previously. "Give me your hands," he told Ran.

He was very efficiently trussed hand and foot like a steer-mod for slaughter. That seemed bad enough, but he said, "Better tie me to the door. I might jump off the roof."

"Jump off the roof?" I repeated, loudly. "What the hell are you going to do to yourself?"

He continued speaking to Lex. "When it starts, Tymon had better be downstairs."

"Wait a minute—"

Just then Stereth reappeared. "They're ready down below, I'm going to send them out. How are you up here?"

Ran said, "About to go. But Tymon will be happier downstairs."

I said, "I want to stay with you."

He turned to me, tiredly, and said, "*I'll* be happier if you don't have to watch."

Stereth said, "Take her downstairs, Lex."

No doubt he didn't care if I stayed or not, but he wasn't going to have anything interfere with Ran's concentration. I backed toward the other end of the roof, Lex following. "Hey! No reason I can't stay till it gets bad, is there?"

Ran sighed. "All right. Back off, Lex, and could everybody shut up and ignore me?"

Stereth at once turned to the parapet. "Care to join me for the view, Tymon?"

I didn't really want to know about the view just then. But morbid curiosity got the better of me and I went over to Stereth. I glanced briefly back at Ran, who had closed his eyes and looked not like a sorcerer working a spell but a man in a fit of depression. Outside, the troops of the Tuvin militia were marching in with unmistakable confidence. "Fewer of them than I thought," I said to Stereth. There were only about a hundred.

"All that light show last night," he replied. "It was meant to rattle us."

I looked at his face. It still gave nothing away. And though I can't say I approve of Stereth's style—I see nothing wrong with occasional moderate displays of emotion, even negative ones like fear—I had to admire him for his incredible control. Myself, I was sweating ferociously and kept feeling as though I had to use the privy.

I said, "Where are the others?" Lord, my voice was embarrassing. I cleared my throat and tried again. "I thought they were coming out."

Stereth's voice was cool. "Komo and Carabinstereth? They'll be out in a second . . . there they are. I told them to wait till the militia were near enough to see clearly that they were surrendering. Good. This will give the bastards something to watch." The merest trace of viciousness was in that last sentence. Considering these soldiers were coming to torture and kill him, I suppose it was understandable.

A knot of people was forming below, hands clasped behind their heads. They kept filing out of the fort and spreading into a ragged line. I was distracted by them myself, and it took me a moment to register what was happening to the advancing militia.

They weren't advancing. The nearest of the tan uniforms were milling around uncertainly, as though faced with conflicting agendas. They were close enough to the fort for us to see faces, though not expressions—but there was one expression visible, an open mouth yelling something, and not happily. Then the yeller removed his helmet and put his hand on his head. A second later he was tearing off the jacket to his uniform, tossing it away . . . and *scratching?*

Within seconds the soldiers seemed to have forgotten us entirely, taken up with their private hells. Light-rifles were hitting the ground like summer rain. Stereth watched as though hypnotized, a look of open delight suffusing his features, the only time that I ever saw it. But I suddenly remembered what was happening and turned back to look at Ran.

His head was pushed against the stone at the side of the entrance to the stairway door. His eyes were closed. His inner robes were wet all over with sweat, and he was moaning. I left Stereth and went over to him.

"Ran?"

He was muttering under his breath. It couldn't be the

spell because whatever it was, he'd already placed it—to spectacular effect, as far as Stereth and I were concerned.

"Ran?"

". . . hold on, hold on, can't take it back, can't take it back—"

He was straining against the ropes, pushing himself against the rough stone, saying the same words over and over and over again. Then he started hitting the back of his head against the wall. I grabbed it at once, frightened, but he fought me. He got in another good crack.

"Stereth!" I yelled.

He was too involved in the intoxicating sight of the Atvalids' troops, who were, as he told me later, running for the hills at that very moment.

"Stereth!"

He turned reluctantly.

"*Help* me," I said, keeping my hands around Ran's skull. He cracked it against the wall one more time, nearly pulverizing my fingers.

Stereth was there in a second. He pulled off his jacket and wrapped it around Ran's head while I tried to hold him still. "Lex!" He yelled. "Lex, bring a blanket!"

It took a while to get Lex's attention, too. Stereth met my eyes joyfully as we held onto the thrashing human being in our arms. "Like an army of invisible fleas," he said wickedly. "Their skin'll be coming off in strips if they keep up their rate of scratching."

I protested, "It can't just be an *itch* that's doing this!"

"The grandfather of all itches, it looked like to me. All over them, and with no possible relief. You can only stand a few seconds like that, Tymon, before you go crazy—*ow!*" That last was because Ran had kicked him in the knee, whether accidentally or deliberately was impossible to tell. It made no dent at all in Stereth's glow. "I wonder how long it will last. If it takes them to the nearest poison river, that would be fine with m—*youch*. Lex! Where the hell are you?"

Lex appeared shortly and Stereth had Ran incarcerated behind a mountain of pillows, where his efforts to smash various parts of his body onto the stone were impossible to satisfy. Stereth wiped sweat from his brow as he stood up from our mutual wrestling match.

"Well! I hope he's not going to be this way permanently, Tymon. It would create all kinds of moral problems."

"I never imagined you as having moral problems, Stereth."

"I don't, and I would hate to start. Lex, stay here and watch him. When he recovers, bring him down so I can talk to him. . . . Uh, if he doesn't recover in a couple of hours, you'd better arrange for shifts."

A couple of hours? That was an unpleasant thought. I said, "I can stay here, Stereth."

"No, I want you away from him when he comes out of it. He'll feel better that way, he didn't want you to watch."

Unexpected ruthlessness and unexpected consideration. Des could claim to understand Stereth's pattern, but I wasn't about to try. I nodded, though I knew I would be brooding about Ran every minute, and followed him down the stairs.

So Ran's method of "using sorcery as a weapon" did not involve any explosions, lethal illnesses, or hailstones the size of tennis balls falling from an angry sky. I didn't know that that would save us or the Cormallons when we were brought before the bar of Imperial justice, but clearly Ran was going for any technicality he could.

He came out of his fit after about an hour and a half, refused to move anywhere and lay there in his own sweat and torn clothes for another hour. Then he refused to talk to anybody until he'd washed.

Lex was uncharacteristically thoughtful enough to whisper this news to me as soon as Ran recovered, and by the time he actually appeared in the main hall I was nearly as giddy as everybody else.

And they were giddy. Our scouts told us that there were still observers set several miles away, but at the moment nobody showed any intention of coming a step nearer. Frankly, I wasn't sure what the band was so happy about, since the essential problem remained: They knew where we were, and if we left they would follow. But it was hard not to be happy about being alive, and about having scored off the militia, up till now a source of fear; and when I'd heard from Lex that Ran was heading for the waterjars to wash up I found myself grinning as crazily as the people around me.

The wine came out again, not that anybody needed it to be drunk. A couple of people brought out some dice and tried to get up a game of Red Geese, but it was impossible to concentrate even on something as simple as that. Des had hugged me about a dozen times, and after the dozenth he suddenly looked over at Stereth and said, "Can I go see if the tah folks are all right?"

Stereth nodded. He had his feet up on a homemade rail by the hearth, and though Cantry was with him, neither of them were talking. Everyone else was on fire, but Stereth apparently had gone as far as he planned on going by letting himself enjoy today's rout. Usually I'm a pretty buttoned-down person, but in the euphoria following Ran's performance it was as though that layer of control lying on top of my mind had been cut smoothly away with a knife; I could have done anything. Des was lucky that for once it hadn't occurred to him to suggest a roll in the pillows. In fact, my mood was so alien, I was almost relieved when Ran came in, as much for the fact that he'd keep me from cutting loose like a balloon and sailing over the countryside as that I was glad he was safe.

Stereth may have asked for him, but he came to me first, which warmed me. To be honest, I nearly started crying then, which will tell you how odd I (and all of us) were feeling. I was sitting by the wall, having changed into my old robes again for no good reason. He took my hand and kissed my cheek, and I said, "You've got a bruise."

He touched his forehead. "More than one. You'll see some of the others when my robes are off."

That pressed a button. Down, girl; normalcy, try for a little normalcy. "Stereth's looking this way. He probably wants to hear about your spell. So do I."

He smiled. "As a layman, he wouldn't appreciate it the way you would."

He has a grand smile when he uses it. "So what was your limiting definition?"

"Wearing yellow, of course—because of the uniforms, and anybody too high for uniforms would have jewelry—and within a seven-kilometer radius—"

"—of the fort. I knew there had to be some geographical limit."

He shook his head. "A seven-kilometer radius of energy weapons. That way they had to leave their Tellys equipment behind."

"I'm surprised they would figure it out sufficiently to leave them."

"People who are suffering will experiment wildly to find relief. Believe me."

"Are you all right?"

He nodded. He looked exhausted, which wasn't surprising. "I'll go check in with Stereth." He frowned. "Was that his jacket I found tied around my neck?"

"It was around your head originally."

"Oh. It has blood on it now. I suppose I'd better apologize." He walked over to Stereth and sat down beside him, and they both began talking softly. The firelight played on their faces.

I looked around and saw that Des had returned—bringing his tah hostages with him. Oh, well, I thought, they probably aren't very dangerous. And they were accepting bowls of wine from him and Carabinstereth as though they had every intention of joining the band in reaching total oblivion.

The owner's agent, the black-and-gray-haired man who'd bargained for their lives, took a bowl and smiled at Carabinstereth. His diamond studs glittered in the firelight. He took a deep draught, returned the bowl to the table, and bowed and said something ultra-courteous to Carabin, for she dimpled and gave him her best bow and smile back. You had to grant the man knew how to talk to people. Then he walked past me, closer to the fire. As he passed I could tell that his perfume supply had run out.

He pulled something from the big outer pocket of his robe as he went. His hands fooled with it thoughtfully. He stopped, ran a hand over his head to smooth his hair, and then shook out what he was holding and set it on his head.

It was a blue hat of Imperial Favor. I knew, I still had one just like it. This one was crumpled, but if it wasn't genuine, it was a close copy. He raised his voice. "Excuse me! Ah, excuse me, great outlaw, Stereth Tar'krim, and my friends and captors. Could I have your attention?"

I was still staring, and by now so was everybody else. Stereth had brought his feet down from the railing. Ran looked completely disoriented.

The man smiled. "This unworthy one is Camerial Thu. I am the Prime Minister's Negotiator, the Voice of the Emperor. My word is His."

He paused, as though expecting some reaction. Nobody moved; there was only one reason why the Prime Minister's Negotiator would be here, the reason Stereth had had us working toward through the whole long summer of hope and death, thievery and treachery. And here he was, and all of our faces looked completely blank. I felt as though I'd taken a step that wasn't there. The Negotiator's practiced smile faded slightly.

"Um, I can prove my identity easily. Governor Atvalid knows me well, for one thing, as before his present failure I was a frequent visitor to his House."

Even Stereth looked incapable of moving or speaking. The Negotiator pushed his smile back up another few watts and beamed at us kindly. "You do understand, do you not?" His voice took on a ritualistic tone.

"The Emperor has sent me to ask, what it is that you want."

Chapter 21

We were "mustered out," as Grateth called it, in Shaskala.

The Negotiator went out to speak to one of the militia observers; he came back, a day and a half later, with an escort of a hundred men who accompanied us to that city.

The Atvalids were clearly in disgrace. I never saw them after that, but I heard that father, son, and grandfather were all asked to return their Blue Hats to the Emperor. No ceremony for that, they tell me; it's not like some ancient religious excommunication. A messenger in Imperial livery shows up at your door one day and asks ever so courteously for the hat, which he waits for in your anteroom like a mail carrier waiting for a reply to some engraved party invitations; then he bows when he gets it, and stuffs it into a bag and returns to court. A short little dance, but the Atvalids would probably never recover from it.

I was sorry about that in a way, but then they were alive, and most of my friends were alive, and from a barbarian point of view the outcome was perhaps the best we could have expected.

As for Stereth's crew, we all spent a long two weeks in Shaskala, readjusting to the heat of late summer off the Plateau, waiting to be processed. The temperature here was pretty much what I could expect back in the capital, Shaskala's height above sea level making up for its more northern location, and I borrowed a straw fan from one of the bailiffs in the Justice House.

Ran was quartered in a different place, but we met most days in the long room the officials of the Justice House used to process us all. Stereth wasn't there, but much of the band was. They sat, or slept, on the long wooden benches, and played endless hands of Thistle and Sleeping Dog—Des and Grateth and Lex and Juvindeth; most of the original band was there. Not all of them had been at the fort that night, some were still out with the mixed bands Stereth had created, and didn't know yet about the pardon; but it was just a matter of time. We understood that Stereth was negotiating the details with Imperial officials, and left him to do it, although Lex was heard to say more than once that it was probably all a trick and our bandit chieftain's body was most likely rotting in this damned heat already.

So much for Lex. The processing involved a lot of individual questioning, so that the officials could create new identities for us. It would be pointless, after all, to release a lot of criminals with nothing to do but return to their thievery. This was a problem for Ran and me—we didn't want new identities, we wanted our *old* identities, but we didn't want to tell anyone what they were.

I avoided any specific documentation as to my past, and assumed Ran was doing the same. The band always addressed us by our road-names, fortunately. I was lying back on a bench by the wall one day, my feet up on the bench in front of me, wondering if there were any possible way I could get a book out of this for the Athenan University Press (which will tell you I was already drifting back into my past life), when Des came over and sat beside me.

"You've been quiet lately, Tymon."

"Anticlimax effect, I guess. I'd been expecting to be dead."

"I suppose you and Sokol will be getting back to your regular careers now."

I looked at him. "Des, I hope you're not going to bring up that idea about fixing the flyer races."

"No, no. That would be stupid. Can't I just ask an old friend how she's doing?"

"Sorry." The room was quiet, lazy, and hot. The low voices of the two Imperial examiners and their current focus, Komo, buzzed in the background. There was a ceiling fan, run on electricity like the rest of upper class Shaskala, but for some reason they never turned it on. Maybe it wasn't working. "We'd like to get back to our regular careers, but I don't know if we can manage it. These people seem very keen on hearing all about our past."

"Ah. That's tough, sweetheart. But I know you two will think of something. And at least you're not dead."

I laughed. "Very true. And in that regard, I've been thinking about your old tah-friend, The Voice of the Emperor. I wonder why he decided to negotiate, instead of giving the Atvalids another chance. Eventually they would have taken us."

"Huh! Between Stereth and Sokol, we could have held them off for months." I doubted that, but perhaps the Negotiator had believed as Des did. "And the tah would have rotted, and the Emperor was probably already sick of the whole thing, or he wouldn't have sent out his Voice."

"That's true. And I suppose the Negotiator had a career to look to as well, and didn't want to spend his life in the Northwest Sector. I guess the deal was as much political as practical, like everything else on Ivory."

"No need to be so mournful about it, Tymon. It got you out of a hole, didn't it?"

"Out of one and into another—"

Just then the High Justice, a stocky man with a blue beaded cap and blue robes, took the platform in the front of the hall. Somebody yelled, "Attention for the High Justice! Attention!"

The High Justice cleared his throat. "Uh, it has become clear to officials that the rules of civilized combat have been violated by certain members of this band. Uh—" he turned to the man beside him. "How many do we have here?"

"Twenty-two this morning, gracious sir. Eight are in holding."

"By certain members of this band, probably here in this room! I'm telling you now, I have no intention of letting such a violation pass. I find it offensive, and when we identify the culprit he, or they, will find the full weight of Imperial might on them and their family."

Des and I looked at each other.

"So I'm asking right now for you all to save yourselves some trouble. Tell us which of you employed sorcery in the recent altercation with the Tuvin militia. I'm warning you, we will find out. And it will be easier on everyone if we find out now, instead of dragging the information out of you."

Thank the gods, nobody turned to look at me or Ran.

The High Justice waited. He did not look like a man

who compromised. Probably appointed by Nor Atvalid, patron saint of reformers.

After a moment he made an impatient "so be it" kind of gesture to one of the other officials, and left the platform.

Des whispered, "What are you going to do?"

There was no answer to that, so I made none.

They questioned three of us that day, taking their time. Lex was one of them, but I wasn't worried—he despised authority, except for Stereth, and was as stubborn with appointed officials as he was with anybody else. A good friend like Des would probably crack before Lex would. Somebody was bound to tell them who we were, though; statistics alone were against us.

I wondered what they would think when they got to me. They must have considered Cantry to be the sorcerer at one time, but they couldn't prove she was the one who'd sent the Atvalids' forces running for the hills—in fact, from her lack of education, she almost certainly wasn't. And they could have one, or two, or three sorcerers to contend with; there was no way of telling. They only needed to pick one, though, to satisfy the scapegoat needs of the High Justice.

So when they led us in the next morning, I was relieved to see Stereth there. He was flanked by two officials, and he still wore his bandit jacket and trousers, in spite of his dealings with the higher ranks of the Imperial hierarchy. His eyes met mine and I threw him a look with as much pleading as I could stuff into it. He ignored me and strode to the front of the hall, where the High Justice was sitting at a table, no doubt ready to give us another little speech. The High Justice had a drink on the table in front of him, a pile of cushions under his behind, and was fanning himself gently with a straw fan not unlike the one I'd borrowed. He paid no attention to Stereth for a moment; then he looked up, unimpressed.

"Yes?"

Stereth presented him with a sheaf of three or four pages, clipped together. "I have a notice from the Prime Minister advising you that the inquiry into the use of sorcery by some member or members of my band is closed."

The High Justice blinked slowly. He took the papers, also, very slowly, and spread them out on the table. He licked his lips, took a sip from his glass, and started to read. He kept us waiting for a good twenty minutes. Finally he looked up again.

Stereth was standing in the same position, as full of patience as though he'd just stepped into the room a second ago.

The High Justice said, "May I ask how you got these so quickly?"

"Got them?" repeated Stereth. "I was given them. It's hardly my place, or yours, to dictate to the Prime Minister."

The High Justice put the papers back in order, roughly, and clipped them together. He handed them back to Stereth with a sharp gesture, as though he'd have preferred them to be a dagger. "Thank you. I've been informed."

It was a dismissal. Stereth stayed, however, and took a new, folded set of papers from the inside of his tattered bandit jacket. "I also have a set of release orders for a couple of the people here. The woman known as Tymon, the man Sokol."

Ran was standing across the room; our eyes met.

The High Justice didn't look at us—he didn't know which ones we were. He squinted up at Stereth. "The processing of this group is not complete."

"Nevertheless, they're to be released today. The order is dated yesterday, to be effective at the first hour this morning. At this moment they're already free to go—technically, of course. It awaits your pronouncement."

The High Justice pushed back his low table and got up from the cushions. He faced the room and said, "The two detainees known as Sokol and Tymon are free to go." He spat out the words like unidentified wine at a nobleman's party.

Stereth smiled, bowed, and withdrew. He gestured for Ran and me to follow him, and we wasted no time in doing so. At the entrance to the hall, I turned around and looked back.

People had settled again into their places. Carabinstereth wasn't there that morning. Grateth was dozing. During the long twenty-minute reading of the Prime Minister's papers, Des had started a game of Red Geese up with one of the bailiffs. Des' head disappeared below a bench and I heard the snap of dice hitting the wall. I smiled. Nobody in the band ever played Red Geese with Des because it was a game he won with a frequency significantly higher than statistics would dictate, no matter whose dice he seemed to be using. His head came up again, but he wasn't looking my way, and I heard his voice saying, "Oh! Tough luck, my friend!" with all evidence of sincerity.

Then the door closed, and we were outside. No chance to say good-bye. It was the last time I saw them. We were standing on the dazzling white steps of the Justice House, under the blue, merciless late-summer sky, with Stereth and two guards from the court who were apparently there to see that we both left peaceably.

Ran took a few steps down, but I turned to Stereth. "I don't get it," I said. "The High Justice was so sure of himself—" I stopped. "You bribed the Prime Minister."

He grinned. "Always start at the top, Tymon. It saves time."

I said, "But how?" When he continued to look at me with that expression of mild interest I flushed and said, "I don't mean I think it would be impossible morally."

"Thank the gods for that, Tymon."

"But you can't have enough left in the kitty to bribe someone who's rich in his own right. Can you?"

"Not everyone is as interested in money as you and me," he said.

"So how? Have pity, Stereth. Tell me what you did."

"I told the gentleman that I wasn't interested in his job," he said.

That's right—I remembered. Annurian had wound up with the prime ministership in the end. And it was traditional to get your buy-off in money and power both. Stereth went on, "I told him I wasn't interested in any of the usual posts, either."

The guards seemed to want me to move on, but I wasn't budging. "What did you ask for?"

"Minister for Provincial Affairs."

"Gods, why? I didn't even know there *was* a Minister for Provincial Affairs."

"Maybe I like the way it sounds." That damned smile was still there, as though he found me amusing. In fact, Stereth looked more relaxed and more pleased with himself than I'd ever seen him.

I said, "Is this the beginning of an era?"

The smile widened. "When next we meet—if we do—you won't know me."

"Why not? —Oh. Is that an order?"

"An order, or a favor from a friend. Whatever works."

The guard beside me said, "You'll have to come along now."

Stereth said to him, " 'Gracious lady.' She's not a prisoner now. Address her properly."

"Gracious lady," agreed the guard, unwillingly. He tugged at my arm, and I took another couple of steps away.

Stereth said, "And I wouldn't worry about retribution, Tymon; your psychological assessment was on the mark. There've been several suicides in the House of Atvalid. They're taking this very hard."

He turned and went up the steps. I continued down, led by the guard, my mind going in circles. The Governor, of course. . . . I called, "Stereth! The Steward, too?" The son had been a friend of Sembet Triol's once.

But Stereth had gone inside.

Ran was waiting at the bottom. He said, "No suspicious characters on the street. They seem to be really letting us go."

"Of course, if Stereth arranged it. I guess it'll take a while longer for the rest of the band." I glanced at the guard. He waited till we'd both stepped off the bottom step of the Justice House, then turned and went back inside.

Ran said, "They probably have a groundcar we can rent at the inn we stayed in before." As we walked down the street he said, "Theodora? Do me a favor. Don't call them 'the rest of the band.' "

It felt very odd walking that street, past the sculptured facades of the Shaskalan city buildings, dropping from one life into another. I've dropped into a few different lives in my time, and it never gets any easier. The only comfort is that now I know the disorientation will eventually fade. I don't know what I'll do if someday it doesn't.

When we reached the inn they brought out an old, battered car, a poor relation to the one we'd driven up in from the capital in another season of time. One of the inn's servants, a thin young man with a slightly snobbish look, held the door open for us to inspect it.

Ran turned to me suddenly. "We don't have any money," he said.

He must have been mentally returning to his old identity as well, for his voice held the childlike bewilderment of a Cormallon caught without funds.

"Yes, we do," I assured him. "They returned my effects to me while we were in holding." I counted out a few tabals and gave them to the servant.

Ran was staring. "Where did you get that?"

"It's the bounty I got from turning you in in Kynogin."

I had thought it was a reasonable answer. Then we were looking at each other and laughing, with more than a touch of hysteria. The servant regarded us warily, no doubt wishing the inn had required a background check. Still laughing, Ran took the door from him and held it open while I got inside.

Neither of us felt like speeding back to the capital, so we drove carefully down the winding Plateau road, and toddled along like tourists through the fields and meadows beneath. Farmers, wagons, long fragrant rows of fruit trees, and a constant cough of dust behind us from the dirt road. In the afternoon we stopped one of the approaching wagons and bought some bush-apples from a boy in a dirty robe, who let us drink from his waterbag. Later I started to doze as we went along the part of the route that lines the river. More trees, and long slopes of lawn, then the wide stripe of silver water and a low orange sun. . . .

When I woke again, hours later, it was dark and we were zooming through the bogs that line the road to the north of the capital. Ran must have kicked up the speed while I was asleep. He looked tired.

"Hello," I said, stretching.

"Almost there," he said.

Thinking about it, it was a little surprising to me that Ran hadn't headed us for the main Cormallon estate; he'd been through a lot, and it was the only place he ever felt really safe. But that was hard to reach without an aircar, and meant a long trip west, around the southern edge of the Sector. We could be in the capital a lot sooner, and I for one would be happy to see familiar surroundings.

Finally we passed under the old Northern Gate, through

the streets of cheap shops near the wall, and down one of the special boulevards built in the last century or two to handle bulkier traffic. Ran drew up at our house in the residential section, halting the car near the automated security station.

We got out awkwardly, our muscles stiff from the long ride. As we neared the front door, I saw that the light on the parcel receipt was flashing.

"The receiving station's full," I said to Ran.

He grunted. Clearly he was too tired to deal with it now.

"Probably wedding presents," I said.

"They should have been sent to Cormallon," he commented with some disapproval. And we went inside.

The first time I ever saw that house, with its rich woods and tapestries, I thought it was palatial. Now I thought of it as "snug." As I entered it, I had that familiar double-vision feeling that comes from returning to a place one has been too long away from. The rooms looked homey and normal, and alien and strange.

I took a bath. I rolled up my very much used robes and threw them in a corner, and I settled into the big white tub on the second floor. Ran had most of his robes off too, and padded in and out of the bath in his bare feet, scattering mail. "This one's yours. This one's yours. This one's yours—"

Ran was under the impression that any mail he didn't want to receive belonged to me. Apparently he'd thought the better of checking the receiving station. The Cormallon sense of duty always got to him when it had any amount of time to work.

"Kanz."

"What?" I asked, luxuriating in the water. I hadn't had a bath since—heavens, I hadn't even been able to bring myself to use that tub Clintris na'Fli had brought back, last seen abandoned on the hill with a sediment of quick-set in it.

Where was Clintris now? She hadn't been one of the people in the fort that night. Pain in the neck though she was, I hoped she was all right.

"A dozen pieces of mail from our would-be client. Probably wanting to know where his reports are . . . and then wanting to cancel the assignment. I don't look forward to seeing him."

I could believe that. Of course, we knew now that the Atvalids were no family to get allied with, but so did everybody else in good society on the continent.

"I'll have to return the retainer." Ran winced.

It was the proper thing to do. Still— "Hold back an amount equal to my old salary for the summer. As your 'assistant,' I shouldn't be paid on an assignment basis. Call it operating expenses."

He smiled. "It would leave us with something," he agreed. "Let me think about it. The man obviously doesn't want to use the Net, so we'll have a while to make our reply."

Eventually I became tired of lying in a few gallons of water, and got into my nightrobe and slippers. Slippers! How delightful. I padded around with a ridiculous smile on my face.

Ran was in the bathroom with the door closed. I could hear water running in the sink. I walked down the hall to knock on the door and ask if he wanted me to order us some food.

And stopped short. There in the shadows on the high shelf where we kept little-used items, at the end of the corridor—

—was a frangi.

Sure, give me a hard time if you want to, those among you who enjoy feeling superior. But every hero is entitled to a fatal flaw, even a two-bit hero. For the Greeks it was hubris; for Othello it was jealousy; for me it's an orange squashy thing with black dots. Ugh! I don't even like writing the name.

Fortunately, Ran had seen me get hysterical over this before, and though he'd looked disbelieving, he knew it was a nondebatable, preordained matter. I would not have to give lengthy explanations or deal with sarcastic laughter while trying to keep from throwing up at the same time.

Still, no need to scream at present, was there? Not yet, anyway. "Ran? Would you mind coming out as soon as you have the chance?"

"What is it?"

"I'll show you when you come out."

There. I hadn't made a complete spectacle of myself. I could keep an eye on the abomination and yell if it moved. It was important to know where it was, because if it got away I'd be up all night worrying where the hell it was.

A minute later Ran emerged, sliding a comb into his pocket. "What's up, tymon?"

"Ran, am I hallucinating, or is that orange thing on the ledge—"

"It is." He moved between me and it. "You should have told me it was an emergency," he said kindly. He looked around, spotted a broom and grabbed it. "Wait down the stairs."

I moved with alacrity. Behind me I heard thuds and curses.

A few minutes later Ran came down and said, "All taken care of."

Ran wouldn't tell me it if it weren't true. I walked into his arms and tightened my own around his chest until I could feel his ribs pressed into mine. "I love you," I said.

He moved his hands to my shoulders. "You never said that to me before," he said wonderingly.

"I didn't?"

"No, you didn't."

I stayed held on and we didn't speak. Then I felt Ran start to chuckle.

"What are you laughing at?"

"You came through a military attack without any trouble, but a frangi—"

"One has nothing to do with the other!"

"Apparently not," he agreed.

A long time ago, when Stereth told me the story about the day he'd cracked his head on the underside of a table and Cantry had fallen in love, I'd quoted an ancient writer: "Even one whom we at all times admire will suddenly seem ten times more lovely than ever before." And he'd pitied me for not knowing what it meant.

Chapter 22

Reader, I married him.

Sorry—you'll have to let me have that line, even though I know only the scholars will get it. You must allow me these occasional references; I can't be expected to throw off years of literary servitude overnight.

It was quite a party, too. I'd hoped for a small gathering, maybe just a few of the Cormallons we couldn't do without, but we announced the successful passing of four-quarter night to Kylla one evening in the Shikrons' villa, and that was the end of that.

She took me aside. "My dear! A patched-up, two-kembit affair? Not to be thought of! We need to show the world that the House of Cormallon values its new alliance."

"Kylla, the Cormallons aren't allying with anybody but me. I have no last name."

"All the more reason to make an official splash. And besides," she said, taking me by the arm, "your name is Cormallon."

And the matter was taken firmly from my unskilled barbarian hands.

Kylla sent out the official invitations, hired the music and the security, advised me with great seriousness on my three traditional outfits for the evening, chose a menu, and sent over extra cooks from Shikron. And this was the woman who used to try to get out of doing the household accounts. When her interest was caught, Kylla's organizational abilities were formidable; she was a juggernaut on the roll, and nobody who knows her stands in her way once she's decided on how things need to be. Technically, as a Shikron, she wasn't supposed to be involved in the hosting of a Cormallon event at all. Ran kept a low profile, saying that he had urgent business in the south, which I doubted.

But it wasn't awful, really it wasn't. I didn't know the vast majority of people who came, but they all seemed to feel that if I was on their House territory it was good enough for them. There was no exchange of bluestone jewelry, as there generally is at a Cormallon wedding celebration; I refused to accept one, and told Ran to put that thought right out of his mind. His House uses bluestones, and other items, as keepsakes, since by the laws of magic whatever one carries habitually comes to retain the thoughts and memories of the person who carried it. The first thing this family does with its dead is to strip off the jewelry, particularly the bluestones, which are considered an excellent medium for preserving psychic traces.

But I found the idea of having my habits of thought interred in the Cormallons' library-morgue a suffocating one. I'm not sure how some of the things that go on in my brain would appear to an Ivoran. Besides, it looks like I'll be leaving all these memoirs around; let posterity check into *them,* if it's so interested. Ran found my attitude surprising, but it's not as though the library was a chance at immortality, after all—the people who owned the items were dead, and these were just a lot of souvenirs. As an ancient philosopher once said, "I don't want to achieve immortality through my work. I want to achieve immortality through not dying."

So we skipped that part of the tradition. Instead I smiled through introductions to flotillas of relatives, and sampled all kinds of unidentified dishes, and downed a bowl of vintage wine to satisfy the Ducort family guests, who'd grown the grapes and sent it over in massive kegs two weeks before the event. That seemed to be the sum of my responsibilities. As the First of Cormallon, Ran had to mingle, but I stuck close to Kylla and followed her lead.

I woke up late the next day, disoriented, and with a sense of relief and disappointment; I don't know why I was disappointed, I hadn't been looking forward to the party, but it had loomed large on the horizon—rather like a giant thundercloud. Now the estate was quiet. The sun was high, Ran had flown in to the capital to arrange a final transfer of funds to our ex-client, and I was sitting on a bench in the kitchen eating a biscuit. The cook and the kitchen workers were off napping between brunch and dinner, recovering from the excesses of the previous night. I sat there by a slant of light that ran over the big wooden table, turning a corner of Herel's copper pot to gold. I ate my biscuit and thought, "Well, Theodora, you've done it now."

In some ways it was still unreal. When would it be real? When we had a matched set of little Cormallons running about the place? Or maybe not even then. Maybe we'd have to wait till I was one of these old Ivoran matriarchal grandmothers, ordering everybody around and scaring the pants off them. I had to laugh at that picture: The stooped-over, wrinkled barbarian midget, stamping the butt of her cane on the floor and telling the younger generation to straighten up.

I'd met any number of gray-haired Cormallon aunts, by the way, many of them single or widowed, and all with a huge capacity for vintage wine and late-night dancing. I was done in long before they gave any indication of slowing down.

I hadn't heard much about Stereth's band during this time. I'd given a blind message-number to a few of the members while we were in processing in Shaskala, so they could let me know how they were doing. It didn't surprise me not to hear from Grateth; he was intensely shy about approaching people. During the long days in the Justice House I'd asked Des what he thought he would do now, and he told me he hadn't a clue, which I could well believe. I checked the message box (it was in our nonNet banker's custody) periodically, but there was never anything from him. And I found that, fond though I was of Des, and much as I missed him, the fact that he made no effort at all to keep in touch did not come as a shock. I knew that if I ever saw him on the street he would open his long arms and scoop me up in a joyful hug, and I'd be as welcome as ever I was. And if I asked him why he didn't contact me, he'd just look sheepish and hurt. I'd never ask him, though. I knew why he didn't contact me. It was because he was Des.

Carabinstereth, on the other hand, did leave a message. I found it one day in mid-autumn, when the wind was swirling down the streets of the capital carrying leaves from the pathetic half-dozen deciduous trees the city boasts, and I'd nearly given up expecting to find any word from anyone.

"Hello, sweetheart," said the message, prudently not using names. "I trust you and the boy are well. I've just gotten a commission to escort a nobleman's daughter to her marriage home, and then stay on with the house guard. A southern location—don't know what I'll think of the cold. Still, how much worse can it be than riding through a soaking rain on the Plateau? And if it doesn't work out, I've got an old friend running a florist's shop in the capital who says I can work there. So have no fears for me, darling, and know me always to be,

Your friend from the old days,
C."

A florist's shop? One pitied the customers already.

As for Stereth himself, there was no need of messages. He'd set up in a lavish villa in the capital, scandalizing the neighborhood by keeping his road-name.

No doubt he was doing whatever a Minister for Provincial Affairs did.

It was three months later that I finally heard the end of our Northwest Sector story.

I found a Net message waiting for me at our house in the city saying that Octavia of Pyrene, my old childhood chum, was back in the capital after her circuit round the provinces. Would I care to get in touch?

Would I! Particularly that day: Ran was off in Braece, making an appearance at a godson's initiation, and Kylla's nurse was away visiting her family for two weeks, leaving Kylla completely at the mercy of her offspring. Over the course of the long summer Shez had reached the age of communication, and she was full of questions and constant activity. I was feeling just a trifle neglected. I do like having acres of time to myself, and waking up when I choose, and taking long baths and playing loud music when I like; but that kind of thing wears thin quickly, and you start to wonder where everybody is.

Octavia: You should have seen her that night before graduation, when we stuffed the wet paper wads into the teaching machines. While we stuffed she sang a ditty of her own devising that parodied our crèche anthem, and left me helplessly limp in my chair watching her sing, stuff, and raise her eyebrows at me as though to say, *Theodora, what could possibly be the matter?*

Or during the weekend we spent in Comiss Major, where we stood on the crest of the hill and saw snow for the first time. Or the wicked improvisations she did of some of the more boring professors in second level—

Octavia had always been more socially forward than I was. She was the one who'd taught me how to order in bars, and on nights when she'd had a few she struck up conversations with strangers that turned into lengthy song-fests and long philosophical talks that ended when the sun came up. Not that we could indulge in that way too often; just during our rare holidays. But I could ride along on her coattails, too shy in those days to strike out on my own.

Anyway, I called Kylla when I got the message and told her all these things, and asked her advice on how to show Tavia the very best of the capital. "Things she might not see on her own," I said. You need say no more when you speak to Kylla—she's more than willing to plan a social event for thousands.

"Lunch at the Lantern Gardens," she said. "—Stop that, Shez! Why don't you put all the pages back together, now? There's a good girl. —And it's such a lovely day, what about a walk in the Imperial Park afterward? They have such excellent security there, and I could bring Shez and get out of the house."

"Oh," I said, not realizing that she'd meant to come along. Now that I thought of it, I had a vague memory of meaning to invite her the first time I'd tried to meet Tavia, but back then Tavia had also talked about bringing somebody else with her. I said, "Are you sure you won't be bored? We'll probably rave on and on about old times."

"Darling, if you knew what it was like being trapped here for two weeks with Shez—no! Put that down!" Kylla disappeared from the Net picture. She returned a moment later wiping her forehead. "No, Theo, I think an afternoon out is a fine idea. Hire us all a carriage for the day, and pick me up here. I'll get some rope to tie Shez's hands."

She was joking about that last thing. I think.

So I hired us a carriage and had the driver stop at the

Shikrons' first. Tavia had told me not to bother picking her up, she would meet us at the Lantern Gardens.

Kylla was dressed to kill, of course, and her daughter wore a rich green silk robe in a flowery pattern, with silver bangles on her fat little wrists. She jingled as Kylla lifted her up and in to the floor of the carriage.

"So, darling," said Kylla, when she'd gotten Shez installed on the seat facing the rear (her chosen place), "tell me more about your friend. You never talk about Pyrene, you know."

I hesitated. "I suppose I don't, much. I was sort of a misfit there, to tell you the truth. I hated it, or most of it. It's just not that interesting to talk about."

"Nothing at all good about your life until you moved to Athena?"

"Well, there was Tavia, of course. It was her and me against the world. And you know—I haven't thought of this in years—it was on Pyrene that I started studying cross-cultural myths and legends. Only I didn't think of it as studying, I thought of it as playing. They really frown on that kind of thing there, you know—no career paths encouraged that aren't of obvious practical use."

We hit a bump in the street and Shez gave a shriek. We both stared at her, concerned, but she looked delighted. "Again!" she cried. "Do again!"

"We can't do it now, sweetheart," said Kylla. "We'll try to do it again on the way home. —Not very likely," she added, muttering to me. We would be coming home from an entirely different direction if we went to the Imperial Park, and one with better paved streets.

We drew up in front of the Lantern Gardens, and as our carriage-driver wore the livery of the best agency in the city we were bowed in immediately. Tavia had a table in the corner; I saw her blonde head over the row of bronze vessels that lined the boundary rim between sections of the establishment. Before I could yield to my first impulse to grab her, hug her, and make some silly, excited sounds, the maitre d' stepped between us and offered us a better table near the stage. "Thanks, this is fine," I said. It was so odd and poignant and delightful to see Tavia's face on this older woman.

"There will be a show in an hour's time," explained the maitre d'.

"It's kind of you to offer, but—"

Kylla said, "It might be a good idea. Shez will have more room to walk around over there. We'd be right against the wall here—"

I grinned helplessly at Tavia and waved. She waved back. The conspiracy to interrupt our first meeting had its way and we were all ushered over to a table by the ring.

We sat down and I took Tavia's hand. "It feels like decades!"

"It practically is one decade," she said. She was wearing a very conservative Pyrenese suit of powder blue with a crisp white stripe down the middle. I thought, she ought to go a bit native while she's here; the silks and things are so much fun, and they'll never let her wear anything like them at home. I'll mention it later.

I introduced Kylla and Shez, and though I thought we'd dive immediately into the past we spoke in a more detached way of what Tavia had seen and done on Ivory. It felt as though there were a gap between my old friend and myself, though perhaps I was imagining it; but it made me more awkward and the chatter less easy to slip into. While we spoke, Shez wandered around the circumference of the ornamental fountain on the side of the stage. (This was not new to me. Kylla and I used hand-signals to make sure she was always in one of our lines-of-sight.) I noticed Tavia's eyes following Shez with a look of disapproval.

"How is she?" asked Kylla, digging into a broiled samwhite.

I reported, "She's on her belly on the rim, fishing for kembits."

"Why people throw coins into fountains wherever they go is beyond me," said Kylla. "Any theories, Octavia?"

"No, I'm afraid not." Tavia certainly wasn't working at this social interaction; what was wrong? But the courteously rigorous Kylla kept the conversation flowing, bless her.

"Should she be here?" asked Tavia at one point, when the talk had returned to Shez. There was still some disapproval in her tone.

Kylla started to laugh. "That's exactly what I used to think before I had Shez!" Kylla misunderstood, I thought.

Octavia was speaking as a Pyrenese, used to the crèche system, where children were never seen by adults in the ordinary course of affairs. "But her nurse is off in the provinces, I'm afraid, so we must bear the brunt."

We spoke of any number of things; Tavia said that she was being transferred from Farm Machinery to Produce Control. And things continued to feel not right. She looked with displeasure at the tah pot that was brought to our table, and refused a cup in a way I could only call curt. There was almost a hostile tone in her voice when she spoke, but again, I thought it might be my imagination; and besides, I should leave her some slack—there were bound to be awkward moments after all these years. And she probably wasn't very comfortable on Ivory.

She'll feel better in the park, I thought. It was a gloriously beautiful place. So I suggested we cut lunch short and ride to the section of the Imperial public grounds that lie along the river.

Kylla uses the bribery method of child control. "Shez!" she called to her restless-looking daughter. "Shez, want to go for another *ride in a carriage?*"

Shez trotted along at once. When we reached the park she ran in under the statue of Lin the Younger, only to be caught up at once by a Park Security man in Imperial uniform, who lifted her, laughed, swung her down again, and said, "Wait for your nurse, darling! Oh—" He broke off, seeing Kylla and our party. "Your mother, I mean. I beg your pardon, gracious lady."

Kylla gave him her patented smile and a sincere thank you. She can always make a terrific impression, I thought, with an envy so far beyond me it wasn't even bitter. In fact, here I was strolling between two people whose social skills I'd tried to learn from in my time. It made me feel just a little like a poor relation.

Even in autumn, an afternoon in the capital is the hottest time of day. "Let's get closer to the river," said Kylla. So we took the turning to the left and came out over the first of the nine green terraces of land that lead down to the water. "Shez!" she called. "Want to go on the *moving stairs?*" And Shez dropped the flowers she'd been picking and ran after us.

Escalators are considered silly devices on Ivory, and

that's why they longed to put them in the Imperial Park. Like a silver line of expensive toys they linked the grassy terraces from top to bottom. We went down and down, till we were only one level from the bottom, and could look along the path below that led upriver. Across the water was the Palace Star Tower.

Kylla took in a deep breath of west wind and sighed happily: She pointed to the Star Tower. "Makes you think of Petev's soliloquy, doesn't it?"

I laughed, remembering the last time I'd heard that recited, by Des Helani on a windy plain on the way back from Deathwell. " 'This night of nights,' " I agreed, quoting. It's impossible not to know that soliloquy, every theater troupe on the planet had their version of it, and lines from it seemed to creep in everywhere—the lowest beggar in the market could do fifteen minutes of Petev with his hands tied and standing on one foot.

I turned to Octavia. "We're talking about a scene from a famous play." I explained. "That's the tower where it really happened in history. Not the soliloquy, I mean—that's the tower where Petev really spent the night he decided to kill the Emperor. Two dynasties ago, I think."

Kylla smiled, watching Shez explore the line of blue flowers that ran along the path. "It's one of your favorites, isn't it, Theo? Why don't you do it for us—Octavia probably hasn't heard it, and it's a very dramatic story."

"Huh! You should have heard my friend Des recite. He could do it right."

"Oh, just run through a few lines. The part where he remembers visiting the Palace when he was a child—that's the middle part," she explained to Tavia, "I always get that mixed."

Well, it is arguably the most beautiful poem Ivory has produced (I'm sorry what little I'm giving you here is in translation), so I grinned, stood up straight, and said, "This night, my friends, this night when the lighted boats of Anemee will never reach their slips on the lake of noble souls—"

As I was speaking (I couldn't declaim it the way Des could, but then he'd been half-mocking himself when he did that), I saw Shez leave the blue border of flowers to investigate something new.

Now, the escalators in the Imperial Park cut through the

terraces almost geometrically. Suddenly there's a hole in the ground, and there you are. The mouth of each escalator has hard, transparent paneling around the sides to keep people from falling in, paneling that links with the transparent panels at the outer wall of each terrace. At the opposite corners from the entrance there's a gold railpost on each side, a small space, and then the panes of paneling begin.

Shez began exploring the opening between the railpost and the paneling. But then, it was a very small opening. It had to be: It would be a long drop down to the next terrace.

Kylla, I saw, was still looking across the river.

"The golden mornings of earliest youth, charmed by artifice
And birdsong in the gardens of my sister—"

I broke off. "She can't get through that, can she?"

Kylla turned, spotted Shez, and said, "ACK!" She was off like a missile, robes flying, just as Shez slipped one arm and one foot through the opening.

Kylla hauled her out, grabbed her by the shoulders and said fiercely, "Never, never, *never* play around stairs! Never!" She pulled her daughter over to us, placed her hand over her own heart and said, "Nothing like getting the adrenaline pumping."

Shez seemed to have already forgotten the incident. She was looking with wide eyes at the children's play set (designed by a series of Imperial architects) that rose like a miniature Paradise farther along the terrace. "Can I go on the tree-slide?"

Kylla looked at me and rolled her eyes. "I'd better go see she's occupied for a while. Anyway, you two should talk."

I supposed we should. My two gaudily-robed friends moved off a short way along the terrace, and I looked at the one remaining, in her powder-blue suit. "Well," I said awkwardly. The atmosphere didn't seem right for continuing the recitation. "Never mind the rest of the poem. It's incredibly beautiful, though, Tavia, you should pick up a copy." I hoped I wasn't chattering. "The very last couplet is the most wonderful thing I've ever heard—'When sand has covered all we have built, still the—' "

"Oh, stop it!"

"What?" I stared at her, taken aback. Her face was red and cross.

"Just stop it! Always showing off, just like the old days! You haven't changed a bit, Theodora."

"What?" I repeated, stupidly.

"So what if you've read a lot of old stories! Who cares? Always bringing them up, always memorizing and showing off!"

I felt myself flush. "But I didn't memorize it, it's a famous po—"

"Trying to make me feel bad because I don't know your 'famous' things! Always grabbing the spotlight!"

I felt as though I'd stepped off not a step, but a cliff, that wasn't there. My head was whirling. Had Tavia completely forgotten our past history? She was the one who was the social success! I'd only tagged along! Reality turned upside-down.

Simple grammar deserted me. Tavia took advantage of my involuntary silence to say, "You always thrust yourself forward, you know. I could see you didn't think much of my trying to make new friends, but you might have—"

I found my tongue and burst out, "But I always admired you for the way you met new people! Remember that night in Comiss Major, in the bar, when you told that skier, 'No, I love it when men get drunk and shout stupid things'?" That skier had followed her around all three days we were there. She'd been in rare form that night.

"I didn't say that. I would *never* say that."

I blinked, unable to think of an answer for this denial. "But, Tavia, we had a lot of fun together—"

"I didn't even want to go to Comiss Major! It was your idea, always *you* wanting me to do the things *you* wanted to do! Like today, this stupid park! I knew you hadn't changed, I told Hippolitus that! What the hell could Theodora know about Ivory that would be any help to anybody? But he's the damned security staff, and I'm in stupid Produce Control!"

"I don't under—"

"I didn't want to see you, you idiot! Great Unity, the ego of this woman! Why do you think I never answered your letters?"

"I thought—I thought after I moved to Athena, the censors—"

"Blow the censors! I didn't even visit when I got my first assignment, when you were still on Pyrene!"

"You said you were busy—"

"Anyone else would have gotten the message! But not Theodora the wonder child, who reads everything in the antiquities library, and drops her Pyrenese citizenship!"

I became distantly aware that Kylla, hearing voices raised, had returned and was standing there wide-eyed, holding Shez's hand.

"But—" I groped for some common ground. "Remember that night before graduation, when we stuffed wet paper in the teaching machines?"

"Your idea, not mine! I told you the guardians would be upset! And it surely didn't go on your record, did it, not on another damned planet!"

I put my hand to my face, which still seemed to be there, though it was sizzling like a griddlecake. "I thought—you never said—"

"Oh, don't tell me this comes as a surprise—you've been getting little digs in at me all day!"

"I've *what?*"

"You ordered salad at the restaurant! Don't think I don't know what that means!" And on that indignant note, she turned and flounced off.

I stood there. Kylla came over to me hesitantly. "Theo, sweetheart, are you all right?"

I nodded vaguely.

"I think we'd better get you home," she said briskly.

I followed her out of the park.

Shez was uncharacteristically silent on the ride back. Kylla thumped on the roof of the carriage, stuck her head out, and said, "We're taking the lady Theodora home first, driver. If you haven't been paid in advance, I'll do it when we reach my house."

When we reached mine, Kylla said, "Go inside and pour yourself a good stiff drink, darling. I have to go with Shez, but I'll call later."

I said, "What does it mean when you order salad?"

"Means you're hungry, I think, dear. Now go on in."

So I did, and of course started crying buckets of tears as soon as I got through the entranceway.

Several hours later Ran came in. He kissed my rather puffy face and said, "You ought to answer your Net messages. Kylla called me in Braece and said that you spent the afternoon with a second Clintris na'Fli."

I chuckled, more because it was sweet of him to try than because I felt like it, and said, "Kylla said nothing of the kind."

"Well, she would have if she knew Clintris. She did say, 'If she weren't a friend of our Theo's, I would have said from the beginning that she was the most ill-bred, ill-mannered specimen I'd ever seen. A regular tymon, Ran—and I don't mean that the way you do when you use it with Theo.' "

Dear Kylla. Ran's voice, of course, was nothing like hers, but his facial expressions were uncannily exact.

An hour of cosseting later, I'd come out of it enough to realize that I'd come out of it eventually. When he saw I'd recovered, Ran said, "Kylla speaks Standard, you know."

"I didn't know, but it doesn't surprise me."

"She recounted a lot of your conversation with this Pyrenese woman. The reference to Hippolitus was interesting. Didn't you say that was the name of the man who was running the mining project in the Northwest Sector?"

"Yes, the Governor introduced him to the crowd that day in Kynogin—you know, when I brought in the stolen cattle. It's almost certainly the same man. Pyrene is sparing in the assignment of proper names, that's why we have so many different ones."

"If he's really on their security staff, it suggests a lot of things about his presence in the Sector. That mining story was pretty thin, but it served to get people stirred up. And it put pressure on the outlaws, which they were bound to respond to. You'd almost think they were aiming for another Sector rebellion to start."

"Oh, of course, that was clear as soon as she said it." I sniffed, still not entirely free of these stupid weeping jags.

"It was?" Ran sounded startled.

"Yes, and it was probably Pyrenese agents who added those helpful little touches in sabotaging the tah shipments

Stereth couldn't reach. He always struck me as being surprised by some of that news."

"This was clear as soon as your friend spoke? And you haven't said anything to me?"

"Damn it, I was upset!" I sniffed again. Clearly the relative importance of an alien-fomented rebellion versus a rejection by a friend bore different weights in his mind. But then, it hadn't been his friend . . . or the only friend of his youth.

He sighed. "My very dear wife."

He'd been standing; now he pulled me down onto the divan beside him. "What are we going to do with this information?"

I was remembering the day Tavia had lifted her hands to catch the snow in Comiss Major; had she really resented me even then?

Ran tugged at my robe. "What are we going to do with the information? We certainly don't want to approach anyone in Imperial government with it." Nobody on Ivory deals with the Imperial government if they can help it, and they pave the way with bribes when they must. Nor would any particular official we approached necessarily be interested in these facts—they were a notoriously self-centered bunch.

I said, "I still have my contacts in Athenan Outer Security. If they thought Pyrene was getting too much power here, they might move to stop them. . . . Or they might not. I really have no idea what their aims are. And I don't feel today that I can predict what people will do."

He kissed my forehead. "Don't get paranoid, you're doing pretty well."

"I'm disillusioned with Athenan intelligence anyway. I was thinking about dropping my connection there."

"Umm. It doesn't leave us a lot of alternatives. But I can't say I'm thrilled with the idea of letting a bunch of foreign barbarians try to influence my planet." He paused. "We do know one Imperial minister. We might tell Stereth."

I took my head from his shoulder and looked at him.

He returned the look sheepishly. "Well, you know," he said, "we *were* in the original band."

*   *   *

"The minister is asleep. You'll have to return in the morning."

We were standing at the steps to Stereth's villa, having been accompanied across his enormous garden by two brawny Imperial gentlemen with pistols. The night was warm for fall, and the air was full of scent.

"Would you please inform the minister that Sokol and Tymon are here?"

The doorkeeper inspected our clothes and jewelry. ". . . Sokol," he said, as though wondering if it were a practical joke.

"And Tymon," I added.

"On urgent business that may not be delayed." This is the almost ritual line used by important people in the capital to signal to other important people that they really do have to talk.

The doorkeeper bowed; at least we knew the right thing to say. He disappeared.

The two armed guards remained. Ran said to me, "Well, he used to wake *us* up enough in the old days."

And one hoped he would not be too irritated by it. There was a long tradition on Ivory of newly respectable ministers killing old acquaintances who popped up indiscreetly from their past. But I think we both felt that Stereth was the sort who would listen before doing anything like that. Still, Ran looked thoughtful as we waited.

A good quarter of an hour passed. My mind kept replaying the day's events. I'd never be able to hear Petev's soliloquy with solemn joy again; those shining words were forever gashed and defaced by the memory of this sunlit afternoon by the river. How could I have been so wrong?

"Produce Control," I muttered.

"What?" asked Ran.

"When I ordered salad, maybe she thought I was making fun of her for being transferred to Produce Control."

"Theodora, my very dear, if you could get your mind off the lunatic you met with this afternoon and get it back to the business at hand—"

He was right, and I was probably wrong about the salad reference anyway. The gods knew I was totally off base on everything else I'd thought about Octavia.

The doorkeeper returned. "The minister will see you.

You'll have to wait his pleasure in the visitor's room. You did wake him up, you know."

The visitor's room was a large sitting room with silk cushions and many old, enormous oil paintings that showed politically correct scenes from Ivoran history. Candleholders punctuated the pictures and carved wood and stone of the walls; nevertheless, a chandelier that clearly operated off imported Athenan power packs dominated the ceiling. A square gold table was in one side of the room, surrounded by pillows, with a holder for a tah pot in the center. We were directed to the table by the doorkeeper, who then left to return to his duties.

A moment later Stereth walked in. He wore blue and red silk robes, the outer borders embroidered with gold stitchery, and red plush slippers. Nor was that the only thing that made him look odd to me; his hair was cut neatly—well, his hair was always neat, he was fastidious about his appearance—but it was cut in the fashion of the capital. Before he reached us he slipped a pair of plain spectacles from the chest pocket of his outer robe and hooked them over each ear in the old familiar gesture. I smiled.

"Tymon!" He'd caught my eye first. "And Sokol. It's good to see you safe and sound. I've ordered tah and wine, they'll be here shortly. Please, sit down."

We sat, and he went on. "You'll have to forgive Cantry, she was too sleepy to get up. She sends her regards." I'd wondered if he kept Cantry with him, and here was the answer. Although, in a moment of paranoia, I did note that we hadn't actually *seen* Cantry. He went on, "And you two? May I presume to offer congratulations . . . ?"

He phrased it in the discreet way one asks that particular question.

"Yes," said Ran, who was used to saying it by now. "We've passed four-quarter night."

"Excellent! You know, I always believed that you both made a good pair, particularly after Tymon here made such a godawful pest of herself over your incarceration."

I smiled austerely.

He went on, "Not a classic pairing, of course. Not the obvious kind of thing that a family would arrange—"

You don't know Ran's family, I thought.

"—but having seen you both operate, I must admit it works."

Even as an old married couple, we seemed to come in by the two-bit door.

Ran said, "It's courteous of you to see us."

"Well, I knew it must be important for you to make a special visit. After all, traditionally, newly bought-off outlaws tend to kill the associates who knew them when." He smiled, and I knew he was stringing us along. I relaxed.

"You're not making any great effort to distance yourself from the past," pointed out Ran. " 'Minister Tar'krim'? You're the first I've heard of to keep his road-name."

An old man with a sleepy look about him shuffled in with the tray; Stereth took it easily from him and poured us all cups of tah. Of course, technically there was no reason he couldn't poison us, but it would be impolite to refuse. Stereth said, "Yes, it seemed the best course. Those in the Imperial Government who come from the Six Families will always see me as an outlaw; but by not taking a new name, I don't come across as a social climber as well. I'd prefer not to be seen as another parvenu begging for acceptance."

"You could have taken back your old name," said Ran.

"No, I couldn't," he said shortly, and that was the end of that.

I put in, "Besides, if your name is a legend, why change it?"

He smiled again. "It does give me a certain cachet with some of the people I deal with. And the others it keeps on their toes."

We talked of the paintings on the wall for a few minutes, till we'd all finished our tah; then Stereth poured wine for us and asked, "Is there anything I can help you with?"

Ran said, "Tymon can tell it best."

So I told him what I'd heard, and hinted at what I surmised. He listened. When I was through he said, "What makes you think I would take an interest in some scheme of Pyrene's and a few bought officials?"

Ran said, "First of all, I don't believe that the new Minister for Provincial Affairs would let anything happen to the provinces until he's had a chance to rob them himself."

Stereth burst out laughing. It was a joyful laugh, not like

anything I'd ever heard from him in the Sector. "I'm sorry Cantry stayed in bed. All right, friends, no need to go further; I'll look into the matter. Good enough?"

Ran nodded. With the immediate business cleared I put down my winebowl and said, "I've been trying to find out what happened to some of the band. Do you have any idea?"

He straighted his silk robe. "Tell me who, and I'll tell you what I can."

And so he did. Grateth had turned farmer and stayed in the Northwest Sector. Des had said something about a possible job with the Capital Touring Company, but it fell through, and his present whereabouts were a mystery. "He's not been taken out and beaten for trying to fix the flyer races, though. I checked."

"What about Sembet Triol? He wasn't at the fort that night—"

"No." Stereth bit his lip. "He was pardoned, but his noble family refused to take him back."

"But an Imperial decree is supposed to wipe out the past—"

"The Sakris are an older family than the Mellevils." The Emperor's name was Mellevil. I hadn't known that Sembet Triol was a Sakri. So was our client, if you recall—though I don't suppose it would have made any difference if we'd known about the connection. The Sakris are a large family.

"Where is he, then?"

"I don't know. He left his short sword at the Justice House, took his purse of compensation, and told me he was going west. I don't know where. I suppose we'll never know."

We'll never know. Such a final phrase. There's an expression on Ivory: Penathi so mai, "the wind we hear in the branches, that we'll never see." It means, let it go. Like ishin na' telleth, it was an Ivoran motto I couldn't live up to.

Where was the structure? Where was the beginning, the middle, and the end? All these tales and myths had never fully prepared me for the fact that there are just some things we're never going to know. *What song the Sirens sang, or what name Achilles used when he hid among the women.* Where Sembet Triol had gone and what would become of him, and why magic worked for some people and not others, and exactly when Tavia had begun to hate me.

Ran was saying, "What is this purse of compensation business?"

"I arranged for five hundred tabals in gold to go to every member of the original band, or everyone who was in the fort that night."

No gold for us? I glanced at Ran, whose look replied, *Let's not press our luck.* He said to Stereth, "What about the others?"

Stereth shrugged. "They all got pardons."

"But no cash. Some of them are going to end up outlawed again."

"There were over four hundred of us at the end," said Stereth reasonably. "The government couldn't process and pay off each one individually. They never would have taken my negotiations seriously if I'd insisted on that."

"Did you push for it at all?" I asked.

He reached for a bowl of kinuts from a nearby pedestal and handed it to me. "Life is as it is. They're better off than they were before they met me, aren't they?"

This was true, but depressing nevertheless.

Stereth was gazing at Ran now. "I hope I've been helpful. Perhaps in future you can do some service for me, gracious sir Cormallon."

Ran blanched and said, "I'm always eager to perform a service for a friend." A noncommittal generalization.

"As Minister for Provincial Affairs, I'm always looking for new talent. Theodora—Tymon, I mean—is welcome as well."

Minister for Provincial Affairs. For the first time I gave that phrase some thought. The Emperor would have been happy to give him that, because it was a post nobody wanted. For one thing, it involved actual work. For another, and this was the basic point, it meant dealing with the provinces . . . which in the view of the Six Families, were one step up from dungheaps. The overwhelming majority of food shipments, tah, weapons, and military personnel came from the provinces, but you wouldn't think it to listen to the news coming out of the capital. They were a self-involved lot there, and any provincial kid worth his salt, lying awake at night listening to the Net, wanted to run off to the capital to make his fortune. Whereas if they'd just all stay home and *organize,* nothing could stop them.

Stereth was a man with provincial experience. Surely these thoughts had crossed his mind. Perhaps I was being paranoid, but it seemed to me suddenly that all the provinces needed was somebody with vision to coordinate an alliance, and Stereth seemed just the one to do it. Or get beheaded trying.

I would be interested in following his career—from afar.

Ran, I saw, was giving Stereth's offer courteous consideration. I met his eyes across the table and softly mouthed the words, "Beware of heights."

He turned a bland smile toward Stereth. "I don't want to disappoint you, but the affairs of my House take up so much time. . . ."

Stereth made a dismissive gesture. "Think no more of it! Just an idea." He reached for another pedestal, topped by a dish of candied fruit. "Have a piece?" he said.

Ran hesitated almost too lengthily, then took one.

The doors to the visiting room closed behind us, and I drank in a deep breath. "It's good to be alive, isn't it?"

I spoke in Standard, as the doorkeeper was with us.

Ran said, "He was careful to use both our names. I wonder what he'll ask in return for keeping silent about this little chapter in our lives."

We reached the vestibule, where the doors to the garden stood open. I saw the head of a security guard beyond one of them. "Please wait here a moment," said the doorkeeper in his quavering voice. "Your escort will be along shortly." And he tottered over and took a seat on the stool by the wall.

"Whatever it is," I said, "we'll worry about it then." Nothing seemed too difficult to handle at that moment, under the dappled starlight slanting over the floor, amid the heavy scent of the roses. I breathed in perfume and night wind.

"The avoidance of death sometimes has this effect," said Ran practically, as he seated himself on a bench.

I sat beside him and wondered about a culture that specializes in buying off or absorbing its enemies. It didn't always work, though, did it? Look at Petev and Copalis in *Death of an Emperor.*

"Ran, I have a question."

He sighed. "No, I don't know what the salad reference means, Theodora. *Nobody* knows. Let's just go home and get some sleep."

"I wasn't even thinking about that!"

"Oh. Sorry. What was it, then?"

(I should tell you, in case it starts driving you crazy, as it did me, that we never did figure out what the salad reference meant. Several weeks later I got up the courage to call Octavia and ask her, thinking that if she left the planet before I found out it would dog me for the rest of my life. We spoke briefly over the Net, and I still recall her wide-eyed, angry look when I asked her if it had anything to do with her transfer to Produce Control. "No it doesn't, Theodora. You *know* what it means." The impression I got from her was one of incredulous disbelief at my nerve in pretending ignorance. Then she said, "I can't believe you," and switched off. So not only don't I know, my pet theory was knocked out of the ring.

By the way, the whole episode of the Pyrenese involvement in inciting rebellion, and our going to Stereth, became known in shorthand Cormallon folklore as "the salad incident.")

But Ran's reminder got me to thinking briefly about this afternoon, and it occurred to me that I might have ruined the expedition for poor Shez, who'd had no idea what was going on. I remembered how silent she'd been, right up till the time that Kylla'd told her to say good-bye to Aunt Theod—

"My gods!"

"What?" said Ran, looking around sharply.

"I've become one of the Cormallon aunts!"

He burst out laughing. After a minute he said, "Next time send up a few flares so I can follow your thought processes."

"Here they are," said the old doorkeeper suddenly, as the two armed Imperials who'd brought us in earlier appeared in the entranceway.

"Please follow us, gracious sir and lady," said one, and

we were careful to do so circumspectly. One doesn't fool around with Imperials.

So we left Stereth's little palace and followed them over the pebbled pathways under the stars toward the gate. Fountains splashed on either side of us. And I thought of the journey back from Tuvin in the groundcar, the whole long tired trip, and how I wakened from a nap to look out on my right at the well-watered fields near the river. It was nearly twilight and the low sun made long, delicious shadows in the lush grass. A white house with wooden pillars was set in from the road. A broad expanse of lawn ran south of it, bordered on the edges by tasselnut trees that bent toward the river. And in the middle of this sea of dappled grass, standing by herself, was a little girl who whirled her arms as though directing a great and invisible orchestra. She was too intent to see us pass.

What was in her mind? Was the man who'd come out on the porch of the white house, who stared north and south as though searching for something, her father? Of course I never saw her again, and I suppose there'll be no reason ever in my life to return to the Tuvin Road. And I thought of all the hints, all the flashing gleams on the river, all the stories we'll never know the endings of.

GUILT-EDGED IVORY

Chapter 1

Assassinations are so inconvenient.

It wasn't as though there weren't plenty of other things to occupy my attention at the time. Another summer in the capital, and I was supervising a good cleaning out of the house there, wishing we could spring for importing a Tellys dustcatcher (just an idle wish—the hole it would put in the House budget would never be worth it). My tinaje healing skills were rusty, so I'd signed on to an apprenticeship with a big-name tinaje artist who had offices in the Imperial Dance Academy. And I was taking some trouble to make a clandestine appointment at a Tellys medical clinic (we'll get back to this one later).

And to top it all off, my sister-in-law Kylla was behaving very strangely.

She swept in one afternoon when we were rolling up the carpets from the second floor and taking them down to the courtyard to be beaten. There were no clients in the house, of course, since the place was a mess; and my dear husband had taken himself as far away from manual labor as he could, remembering a sudden appointment in Braece. Danger means nothing to Ran when weighed against duty, but the prospect of actual physical work sends him scuttling like a rabbit caught on a landing pad.

Kylla invaded this prosaic scene like some exotic bird of paradise, all bangles and gold facepaint. Her black hair was caught back in a velvet band rimmed with tiny metal dangles that made a sound like distant bells; her dark eyes were rimmed with midnight blue, clear as the borders of a new map. Since her marriage she'd taken full advantage of the relaxed dress code for respectably wedded women, relaxing it to the point where her grandmother probably would have had a heart attack if she'd seen her grandchild wandering around in public this way. People as gorgeous as Kylla can get away with a lot, though

"Where's Ran?" she said to me, without preamble. Her robes swished over the head of the stairs.

"Braece," I said.

She looked around at the servants carrying down the huge carpet from the upper office, the tables pushed against the walls, the clouds of dustmotes, and nodded as though she understood. The sleeves of my worst robe were tied back, and I wiped the sweat from my brow with a bare arm, aware that I looked every bit as messy as my surroundings. "The pillows are all outside," I said apologetically.

"I'll stand," she replied. There was a jingling sound behind her, and her four-year-old daughter Shez peeked around, the bracelets on her arms slipping.

"I want to sit," said Shez.

Kylla sighed, lifted her, and deposited her atop the carved blackwood table against the wall. Shez sat regally and surveyed her domain from this new height.

"What's wrong?" I said. Kylla was not usually this preoccupied, or this morose-looking.

She started to pace. "Has Lysander called here?"

"Lysander? Why would he call here? I mean, he's always welcome—" Ran and I got along well enough with Kylla's husband, but we only tended to see him when they were together. Ran was still close to his sister, but I suspected that Lysander was accepted mostly on the grounds that he'd married Kylla.

"He might have called Ran on the Net," she said.

"If he did, Ran hasn't mentioned it. What's going on?"

Just then Shez started to chant, "I want to see them beat the rugs! I want to see them beat the rugs! I want—"

Kylla said, "Please, darling, mother has a headache."

Mother has a headache? Kylla had the constitution of a workhorse, and nothing in the universe fazed her.

"Good gods, Kylla."

"Why? What did I say?" She looked distracted.

"What is it, what's the matter?"

"Why?" She was suddenly alarmed. "Do I look bad?"

"Do you look b— You are a glorious vision of sunrise, as always, but you are driving me crazy. You look worried, is what you look. Do you want to tell me what the problem is, or do you want me to harass you with calls every hour until you crack?"

She smiled suddenly and patted my hand, still encrusted with dirt. "I'm so glad you married Ran."

It was out of left field but warming, typically Kylla; not every barbarian who marries into a good Ivoran family can expect the kind of sweetness she's shown me from the beginning. You see why nobody can stay mad at her? However— "You're off the point, Kylla."

She nodded but didn't seem disposed to go any further.

"I want to see them beat the rugs! I want to see them beat the—"

I hauled Shez down from her perch, took her to the head of the stairs, and gave her to the housekeeper who'd come out from Cormallon to help us. "She wants to see them beat the rugs," I explained.

The housekeeper took her hand and led her away. I returned to Kylla. "Speak," I said.

"I thought Lysander might have called Ran for advice."

"What sort of advice?" Lord, this was like pulling nails from stone.

She took a deep breath. "The council wants him to get married again."

I blinked. "Whoa! The *Shikron family council?*" She nodded. "Wants him to divorce you?" She shook her head. "Wants him to take a junior wife?"

She burst into tears. "They, want, him . . . to take a new *senior* wife, and make me a junior!"

Good heavens. I put my arms around her, not easy considering I only come up to her shoulder. "Sweetheart, that can't be. You were married first, you'll always have seniority rights."

"Not if . . . not if she outranks me."

"How can she outrank you if you were married first?"

"They want him to marry Eliana Porath!"

The Poraths were one of the six noble families. They outranked everybody.

I said, "I thought it wasn't customary to take any extra wives until middle age. Lysander's still in his twenties."

"But the council wants the *connection*, and the Poraths want the *money*."

"Oh." Lysander's family was rolling in it, from everything I'd heard. I guessed the Poraths weren't doing so well. My mouth hardened. And for this they were going to screw up three people's lives.

I said, "They can't force Lysander to marry, can they? He's First of Shikron."

"Lysander says they can make his life a living hell. But he also says that Eliana Porath has a face like a mud pudding, which I know isn't true. I went to school with her cousin."

"Oh, come on now. I'm sure he doesn't want this marriage any more than you do. He worships the ground you walk on, Kylla, everybody knows it." This last part at least was true.

Teartracks ran through the gold swirl on her cheeks. "I'm getting old," she said. "I'm losing my looks."

For the love of— "For heaven's sake, Kylla, you're twenty-five standard. You're a year younger than me! If there's a wrinkle anyplace on your body, point it out to me. I'll give you a hundred in gold for it."

She sniffed. "I think my fanny's falling."

"My fanny fell when I was twelve. At this point we'd need a hoist to— I fail to see why that's amusing, gracious lady Kylla." She'd smiled behind the tears. "Say, Ky, why don't we see what Ran's got stored in the way of Ducort wine?"

"It's the middle of the day."

I made a rude noise with my tongue that I'd learned from a bunch of outlaws in the Northwest Sector. "Better yet—let's go to the Lantern Gardens and see what they've got on their list of new drinks. We'll stay for the matinee and watch the naked floorshow."

She laughed. "Do you know something? I've never had the nerve to actually stay for the show."

"You amaze me. Wait, I'll check on Shez." I went into the other room and looked down through the back window to the courtyard. Lines were strung from one side of the house to the other, crisscrossing among the leaves of the coyu tree. A fortune in Andulsine carpets hung in a thousand brightly colored threads. Six men and women stood there beating (carefully) and Shez stood on the cobbles beside them, whacking away with enthusiasm. "Wham!" I heard her voice float up from below. "Wham! Zam! Ham! Tam!" Her face glowed.

"She's busy," I assured Kylla, returning. "I think we can safely get away for an hour."

"She won't be a problem to anybody?"

"Oh, they'll find things for her to do. There's still the floor cleaning, and the unrolling of the clean rugs, and hauling down the tapestries. . . . " I grinned wickedly. "All that domestic stuff she probably never sees at home."

Kylla laughed. I was glad to see it. If you've never met her before, let me assure you that Kylla is a tower of strength as a rule. *I* usually go to *her* for comfort. This junior wife stuff must really have gotten to her, I thought.

But she must have been pulling herself together, because as we descended the stairs she said, "So how are things going in the offspring department for you and Ran?"

I groaned. "Gods, Kylla, you've only just stopped bugging me about the *wedding*."

"That was a full year ago. —So how is it going?"

We barged out the front door, into the summer sunlight, and I signaled for a wagon-cab.

It was midway through the evening, just edging into darkness, the trees outside blending into shadows and the heat finally lifting a notch, when Ran entered the house. He entered tentatively, glancing around the downstairs parlor.

I said, "The floors are all clean and the rugs are back in place. It's safe to come in."

He nearly jumped a foot. I put down my book, and stood up from the divan behind the shelves where I'd been reading.

"Uh, Theodora. I thought you might have gone out." Imagine a male version of Kylla, with shorter hair and without the facepaint. When I got next to him, I could smell the expensive perfume that he bought in an exclusive shop three streets away. When I got next to him, he kissed me. He put some extra effort into it, as well he might under the circumstances. Ran is no fool.

Once I could breathe normally, I said, "How was Braece?"

"Oh, much the same. Any new client appointments while I was gone?" he asked, changing the subject instantly.

Well, if I'd wanted a furniture mover I would have married one. I let it go. "As a matter of fact, there were. Two Net messages left while I was out with Kylla today."

"Kylla was here?"

"Wait, you'll like this. One of the messages was from the gracious sir Kempler Taydo. He'd like an interview tomorrow, with a, quote, 'view to possible employment of your services,' unquote."

Ran looked amused. "Taydo of the Department of Sanitation? Is this the same Taydo we were asked to assassinate three days ago?"

"The very." I put my arms around his waist."Summer silliness."

"I'll say. Three groups of vultures circling over the same piece of budget. And with the Imperial Auditor looking on, the first one to move will be the first one executed, once the dust settles."

"I swear, Ran, I don't know how anything official ever gets done on this planet." We walked back to the divan. "Are you hungry? I saved a bowl of grapes and some seed cake."

"That's very nice of you, considering I—considering how busy I was in Braece."

I started toward the larder, then turned. "What is it about this summer, anyway? This is the fourth assassination we've been offered."

"And every single one of them too hot to touch. Never mind, we'll get a good commission soon."

"That's not what I mean. Don't people come to you for anything else any more?"

"Sweetheart, people rarely ask a sorcerer to do nice things. They rarely ask trial lawyers to do nice things. They rarely ask soldiers to do nice th—"

"I know what you're saying. Hazards of the profession. But whatever happened to love potions and luck spells? Why don't we get a nice newly wed couple asking for the blessing of random chance on their first year?"

Ran lay back on the divan and put his hands behind his head. "Is it nice to confuse someone into thinking they're in love with you? As for the newly wedded couple, it's a well-known law of magic that luck can only be bunched in one place by taking it away from someplace else. Practically all sorcery is at somebody else's expense."

"Then why do it?"

He said simply, "I was brought up to do it." Then he added, "And I'm very good at it." He was, too, the top of his profession. Ran doesn't make idle statements.

I sighed and went down the hall to the larder. His voice called after me. "And it brings in money for our House."

"All right, all right."

He said something else while I was cutting the seed cake, but I missed it. I went back inside with the plate and handed him a large glass of water, which he drained at once. It's a long ride from Braece. "What did you say?"

He wiped his mouth on the sleeve of his robe. "I said, how's Kylla? I didn't know she was coming over today."

I sat down beside him. "Oh, Ran, I think you should talk to her. She's upset."

He put down the bowl of grapes. "What's the matter?"

I told him about Lysander's wedding options.

"No sister of mine—nobody from the first branch of Cormallon—is going to be anybody's junior wife."

I nodded, unsurprised. "Kylla said you would say that."

"I'm going to call Lysander right now—" He got up, took a few steps, then stopped, as rationality took over from the sting of what he would consider an insult. "No. No, I'd better find out what kind of pressure he's under, and all the details. Yelling at him won't get us anywhere."

"You want to run an investigation?"

"I hate to take the time. If they're really pressing him—I'll call him, courteously, and ask him, courteously, if he'd like to discuss the matter. How do I look? Do I look upset?"

"You look courteous."

"Good." He headed for the Net terminal in the downstairs office, and I followed. I settled myself in the stuffed chair in the corner—one of six in our house Ran had had made just for me—so that Lysander could see me when he came on. Family allies use the visual circuit as good manners, and manners required me to match them by not hiding the fact I was listening.

The call found him in the Shikron office building, I recognized the surroundings. Why was Lysander keeping such late hours?

"Hello, Ran. Hello, Theodora." He looked tired. "Can I help you with something?"

He could be forgiven the phrasing; we'd never gone out of our way to call him, individually. If it were a social occasion, we would have left a message with Kylla at their house on the canal.

"Lysander, we're sorry to disturb you, we didn't realize you were at work. Uh, Kylla came by today . . . Theodora says she was a little upset. . . ."

He nodded, like a man receiving a sentence. "It was about Eliana Porath, wasn't it?"

"Yes," said Ran in a neutral voice. "We were hoping you could tell us more about what's going on."

Lysander let out a long breath. "Do you know why I'm still at work? I'm avoiding my relatives. I've got a flag on for every Shikron caller, telling them I'm busy handling an import crisis." He opened a drawer, pulled out a half-empty bottle of wine, and set it firmly on the table beside him.

"Imported Ducort," noted Ran.

Lysander nodded.

Ran said, still neutrally, "Do you want to talk about it?"

Lysander ran a hand through his dark hair, cut in fashionable capital mode, and opened his blue embroidered outer robe, now full of wrinkles. I'd always thought of him as a nice fellow, but rather forgettable; Kylla, however, had been in love with him for years. She'd succeeded in marrying for love alone in a world where that was rare. Perhaps more impressive, I understood that she'd engineered an affair with him on Cormallon territory back when her grandmother was still alive, a feat of planning and sheer nerve that wartime generals would be lucky to match.

He said, "It's politics, of course."

"Of course."

"Kylla won't believe that. I haven't even *met* Eliana Porath. I've been negotiating with her brother Kade—"

"You've been negotiating?" Ran's voice was sharp.

"*Talking.* I should have said talking. To keep them satisfied and the council off my back. Ran, I am in kanz so deep—"

His voice cracked with stress, and he covered it with an

obviously false throat clearing. Ran said, more gently, "My brother, I'll be happy to help you any way I can, but you have to make it clear to me: You really don't want this wedding to go through? You'll pass up an alliance with a noble family?"

Lysander threw a paranoid glance around his empty office and stepped nearer to the Net. "Are you joking? If this goes through, *Kylla will torture me for the rest of my life*."

Ran and I looked at each other. There was some truth to this.

I spoke up. "Where do things stand now?" Ran was doing pretty well with this man-to-man stuff, but I wanted a practical view of what we were up against.

Lysander said distractedly, "The Poraths are giving a house party on Greenrose Eve. Supposedly it's a holiday celebration, but considering they haven't given a party in about ten years, it's got to be so that I can get a look at Eliana without anybody's honor being officially at stake. That doesn't meant they won't take it personally when I turn her down," he added in a lifeless tone.

I said, "They're pushing this ahead pretty quickly, aren't they? That's just four days away."

"I understand their treasury's practically empty. —Don't hint about that to anyone, though! I'm not supposed to know it!"

"Lysander, of course not." I allowed the tiniest note of offense to creep into my tone. He was under a lot of pressure, but there was no reason to treat me like a typical barbarian when it comes to House secrets.

"I beg your pardon. —Wait! Ran, I can get you both invitations! You can get the lay of the land. . . ."

Ran was shaking his head, looking alarmed. "Ah, I don't think that's a good idea—" He hated formal House affairs with a passion, particularly where the nobility were involved. Born into the second layer of aristocracy, he nevertheless regarded the Six Families the way everyone on Ivory did who was outside them: with a mixture of respect, distrust, and a basic knowledge that they were all out of their minds.

"No, it'll be a perfect chance for you to see what's going on!" Lysander's voice was enthusiastic. "Sorcerers have their ways of finding things out, don't they?"

"Don't believe everything you hear about sorcerers—"

"Oh, of course not! I'm so glad you called tonight. There's still time to get the invitations sent around!"

"Lysander—"

"I'd better get busy. Theo, I'll tell Kylla you're coming! She'll be thrilled!" He disconnected, rather with haste, I thought.

" 'Thrilled' is a strong word," I said, into the sudden silence of the office.

My husband and I looked at each other. Finally he said, "It looks like we're going to a party."

Chapter 2

I don't like Selians.

I don't know if you've ever been to the lovely world of Tellys, land (according to the brochures) of powdery beaches, flaming sunsets, and labor-saving devices of all kinds. Not to mention the only one of the four habitable planets in our sector, that I hadn't set foot on—which, considering the cost of interstellar travel and the fact that I'm a private citizen, is a pretty impressive score, don't you think?

I'd never paid a great deal of attention to Tellys. I'd never planned on visiting there, and my studies were in other areas—cross-cultural myth and legend mostly, at the university on Athena, a field that involved a wide scan of the past but not much of the present. Standard culture is, well, pretty much standard; oddball, out-of-the-mainstream worlds like Ivory are rare. Tellys didn't have a lot to interest me, though I did think I might one day include it in a grand tour after a long and distinguished career as an Athenan scholar.

Of course, I hadn't actually planned on coming to Ivory originally either, and look how that turned out.

Anyway, most of Tellys is a relatively normal variant of Standard society, no great surprise, but clustered up and down the spine of mountainous islands bisecting the Eternal Sea we have the Selians—the People of the Sealed Kingdom. And I don't like them.

This is a prejudice based on personal experience—rather a contradiction in terms, but I don't know how else to phrase it. I had no opinion at all on Selians until I'd met a few of then, and gods, it's amazing how consistently unpleasant each new one is. Every one of them so absolutely secure about his superior place in the scheme of the universe. I know that this just stems from their repulsive (to me) philosophical beliefs, but it gets on my nerves anyway.

You might call this inconsistent in me, since I've always been tickled by the shameless egos of Ivorans. But the Ivoran ego seems—how can I put this—*innocent* in some essential way. Their high opinion of themselves doesn't seem to require grinding down you and me for contrast.

I'm glad the Selians are still a minority on Tellys, and it always depresses me a little to hear the occasional newscast saying how they're gaining power there. But if I hadn't learned it before, my time on Ivory had taught me that compromises sometimes have to be made with people you'd rather avoid. So I took off my jewelry and cosmetics, put on my best outerrobe for courage, and slipped out of the house one afternoon while Ran was away. Then I walked the three miles to the Selian Free Medical Wing of the Tellys Institute.

Tellys has a technological lead on the rest of us, and it extends to their medicine. Some Athenans and even Ivorans have taken medical training on Tellys, but they never stay to practice there: Non-natives are forbidden from joining the Physicians Union. Away from the drugs and devices so hard to get outside Tellys, their training doesn't count for as much as it might. But the Selian Clinic was staffed by Tellys doctors with all the latest equipment, and that's why I was there that quiet afternoon, when the rest of the capital was keeping the Day of Meditation. Tonight was Greenrose Eve, and the city would be jumping; today it was dead.

I had an agenda, of course. As far as I was able to determine, nobody had yet proven that Ivorans were a genetically different species. But they'd been separate from the rest of us long enough for it to be *possible*, and the experts I'd tried in the capital had been pretty tight-lipped about it. Ran and I had been married for a full Ivoran year, and I thought it was time to check my implant—it really should have dissolved by now—and learn what risks, if any, a pregnancy would bring. This was to be my baseline exam.

Physician Technocrat/2 Sel-Hara greeted me after a short wait. He was not much taller than I was, young, with the dyed-white hair of a pure high-caste Selian, though I noted he'd adapted to local custom sufficiently to wear a jewel in one ear. It was a large, blood-red stone and he wore it like a peacock. Not many men can carry off such drama, but clearly Physician Sel-Hara was not one to suffer self-doubts. Probably the knowledge, that he was performing his two years of altruistic duty, and could soon go home secure in the fact that paradise was his, gave him a certain edge over his patients.

"Theodora of Pyrene," he said, rather neutrally, though I thought I saw a flash of passing contempt in his eyes when they moved over my Ivoran clothing. It may have been my imagination. "Far from home, are you not?"

I made a noncommittal sound.

"I've looked through the history you submitted," he said. "Over here."

I wanted to hold onto my wallet pouch—it contained certain items that as a sorcerer's partner I don't like to be away from—but he took it from me for no good reason I could ascertain and gestured me toward the examining table.

Scanners of all kinds they had in abundance, but like all doctors, Physician Sel-Hera felt that nothing could replace an eyeball inspection. For this, a Tellys-style variation of the same device used in the back hills of Ivory provinces for centuries was employed (aggressively, by Physician Sel-Hara). Unfortunately, in addition to succoring the indigent, this clinic specialized in well-paying Ivoran citizens lured in by the reputation of barbarian medicine, and the speculums were built to scale. To the scale of the average Ivoran woman, that is, not a barbarian a bit on the small side even on her home planet. After a quarter hour of effort Physician Sel-Hara dropped the third one into a sterilization bucket and said again, "We will try a smaller size."

For those of you who know what this means, I know I have your sympathy and I thank you for it. For those of you innocent of these procedures, let me sum up the experience by saying it was painful.

"There should be discomfort, but no pain," protested Sel-Hara when I suggested that perhaps he should skip to the smallest size right now. Or better yet, after I'd taken a week or so off to heal. "After the exam, I can make an appointment for you to see the Clinic Psychologist, if you wish."

Implying that I was unbalanced for even thinking such a thought. You see why I love dealing with Selians.

The more assertive among you are probably wondering why I didn't tell him off then and there. But you have to bear in mind that a young woman with her legs up in a cold draft, trying to control involuntary tears of pain, is not in a good psychological position to take the offensive. Besides, he had information I wanted.

He tossed a fourth speculum into the sterilizer. Ever since that day, I've regarded those things the way ancient criminals must have regarded thumbscrews.

"I need to know . . . " I got out, working to keep the tremor from my voice, "if . . . there's any reason . . . gods! . . . I can't have . . . a healthy child."

"You will wait for the final report," stated Discomfort-But-No-Pain Sel-Hara.

"But I mean . . . do you know of any reason . . . why an Ivoran and an outworlder . . . " I gasped and lost control of my grammar.

Sel-Hara was apparently annoyed by the fact that I was not working harder to collude with him in the unreality that he was not causing me pain. He interrupted, in the flat accents of an implanted language, "This is not the time for talking. This is the time for listening." Then he added, as an afterthought, "How can I tell in any case? You say your husband will not come in to be examined."

I really did not feel up to discussing the complications of my marriage at that moment. I thought, if only I were a follower of na' telleth philosophy, and could rise above this kind of thing, concentrate on something else. Ivoran nursery rhymes? My mind was a blank. Out of nowhere I remembered my first class on Athena, a new-made scholar fresh off the ship, and started to chant mentally from Socrates on doctors and lawyers: "Is it not disgraceful, and a great sign of want of good breeding, that a man must go abroad for his law and physic because he has none of his own at home, and put himself in the hands of other men whom he makes lords and judges over him?" A message from the past straight to me, not that I had sense enough to take its advice. It did give me heart to go on, as Sel-Hara showed every sign of covering old and tender ground again.

I must have been muttering.

"You are distracting me," said Sel-Hara, in tones of annoyance.

" 'Of all things,' " I finished—not aloud—" 'the most disgraceful.' "

He glanced thoughtfully at his instruments. "I will use the smallest," he announced, as though it were his own idea.

So I shut up and endured, figuring that questions about pregnancy were probably pointless anyway. After an exam like this, I wouldn't want anyone to touch my body for the rest of my life.

At the Selian Clinic, you take the doctor you're assigned. That's the way the Selians are.

Have I mentioned I don't like them?

Four hours later I was at the Poraths' house party. My body still felt as though someone had tried to ram an interstellar liner through it earlier that day, but I ignored it.

Ran and I had hired a carriage so we could arrive in appropriate style with Lysander and Kylla, both of whom were uncomfortably silent during the ride over. When we stopped at the gate, Lysander reached out a hand to help Kylla down and she gestured it impatiently away. Ran and I pretended not to notice.

A security guard in white and slate gray bowed, and inquired whether it was our gracious party's pleasure to have our carriage driver directed to a proper location for the evening. He spoke the words by rote, clearly not impressed in the slightest by our matched pair of fashionably designed six-legged drivebeasts, decked out in crimson and bells. Looking down the road toward the parking area, I could see why. I considered the Cormallons wealthy, and we were, but tonight we were poor relations. There was even—

"Ran, look! The seal of the Athenan embassy on that carriage!"

He looked politely where I was pointing, then turned back toward the gate.

I said, "Why are the Poraths inviting outplanet visitors?"

He shrugged, his mind obviously on other things. It had gotten my attention, though. I still retained a dual citizenship from Athena; who was here tonight? Anyone I knew? Anyone I'd heard of? If it was one of the eighth-floor people from the embassy, would they ask why I hadn't been around to report over the last year?

Ran touched my arm, and we followed the security guide through the gate in the outer wall.

The Poraths lived in the old section, north of the canal, in a huge, rambling U-shaped villa that was badly in need of repair. The gate we entered led to the middle of the U, the Poraths' garden, a place of night-blooming roses and blue pools lined with white stones; around the garden, bordering the house itself, were three low, covered porches with wooden pillars of red and green lacquer. The lacquer paint was suspiciously fresh looking. The livery of the security staff was suspiciously fresh and neat, as well, and there were at least a dozen. No doubt hired for the evening from a bonded firm here in the capital, though they were discreet enough to wear Porath House colors.

A shadow flowed out of the evening shadows on the porch wing nearest us, and something glittered jewellike in its midst. A scaled snout emerged, small, bandy legs . . . a lizard the size of a small child dragged itself to the edge of the porch. The body was dark green, but the flash from its eyes was emerald bright. A long tongue showed itself briefly, then retracted, as it tried to leave the porch and go exploring. A leash circled its neck, I was glad to see. The leash was garlanded with flowers, but seemed to be doing its job, for in its restlessness the lizard had pulled it fully taut.

"What the hell is that?" I asked.

"It's an emerald lizard," said Ran, in an uninterested voice.

"Is it Ivoran?"

"Of course. You don't see them much around here, they have to be imported from the western islands. It's been a fad of the families to have them as pets."

"What's wrong with a nice puppy?"

He smiled. "Emerald lizards are fairly tame. And they don't spray poison unless they're provoked. Supposedly."

"Poison?"

He pointed to the translucent sac in the crook behind the lizard's neck, just above the collar of the leash. "See, it's been emptied. Perfectly safe."

"I'm sure," I said. Just then a servant girl of about nine,

robed in three shades of red, her hair set with jewels, stooped to pick up an empty glass from the floor of the porch. She patted the lizard on the head as she did so, then set the glass on a tray and continued on her way. The lizard tongue went in and out, in and out, and a sound not unlike purring reached me where we were standing.

"Just the same, I don't want one in our house," I said.

"Not likely, at the price." He took my hand and turned me back toward the main party. We made our way into the throng.

The garden was clogged with guests. Grass was trampled right and left, food and drink servers maneuvered their way around the rim of the blue pools, and I saw a square of ripped silk outerrobe snagged on a thorn near the gate. Flute players were somewhere—somewhere high? I looked up and saw a treehouse filled with musicians. The Poraths were putting a lot on this roll of the dice. If their treasury was near empty tonight, they'd be in debt tomorrow.

"Ky—" I turned to address my sister-in-law and saw her standing at the garden entrance, nostrils flaring, scanning east and west like a hunting falcon with only one prey on its mind: the infamous Eliana Porath.

I said, "Do you know what she looks like?"

"No."

Neither did I, beyond the fact that Lysander had said she had a face like a mud pudding. "You know, Kylla, this wasn't her idea."

"I know that." Kylla's expression did not change. Eliana Porath was about to start a new Trojan War.

Lysander stopped and tapped Ran. "Kade," he said. "Oldest son." He was looking toward a strapping, broad-shouldered young man with hair so short he could have been in the army. His face was brown and his muscles seemed to put him out of place in this array of peacock robes. His own blue silk outerrobe was open over an undertunic of plain, respectable white that might have been a work outfit; an inappropriate touch. Kade was laughing at some joke made by one of a knot of well-dressed people around him. As I watched, he stopped one of the servers, snagged a drink, and offered it to one of the other men.

Lysander said, "As soon as he spots me, he'll be over here. He's really pushing the marriage." On cue, Kade's glance passed over the crowd and Lysander twirled toward Ran, presenting the first son of Porath with a view of his back and a finely embroidered silk panel.

"You'll have to speak with him eventually," said Kylla coldly.

"Ran, help me," he said. "It's going to be a very long evening."

Ran drew him away. "Show us some of the other players," he said kindly. Kylla and I followed.

I drew a breath to say, *You're a little hard on him, aren't you?*—then thought the better of it and let it out again. "Do you know any of these people?" I asked her.

She glanced around indifferently. "Edra Simmeroneth—I went to school with her. Some of the provincial Sakris."

We passed the Athenan ambassador. He and I looked at each other. I've never been introduced to this one, but he might well have heard of me—I'd made enough of a pest of myself to his predecessor. Most likely he was only wondering what a fellow barbarian was doing in full Ivoran dress, attending a party of one of the Six Families. Occasionally I wonder things like that myself.

"Think anyone will get killed here tonight?" I asked Kylla. The nobility play some strange games among themselves.

She got hold of a glass of something pink off a passing tray and took a sip. "It would be rude, at a party," she said.

She turned then, and the contents of the glass went over the front of a young man trying to cross between her and the edge of one of the pools. "I'm so sorry! I beg your forgiveness, gracious—uh, noble sir." With a party like this one, it was better not to take any chances with your honorifics. "My clumsiness calls for a thousand years of penance—"

Sometimes these apologies can take days. The young man—I saw now that he was no more than a boy, really, slender and light-haired for an Ivoran—bowed and raised a hand to cut her short. His mouth had quirked very slightly with irritation, more at the apology, I think, than the spill, which had only seemed to surprise him.

"It's nothing," he said.

"I'm afraid I've ruined your suit," said Kylla.

"Ishin na' telleth," he said, *I'm not about to care*. Not

with a shrug verging on rudeness, the way you hear it said every day in the streets, but a calm statement of fact. Then he bowed again, with great self-possession for one his age, I thought, and went off into the crowd.

We watched him go. "Well!" said Kylla. Then she looked around, and her eyes narrowed. "Where's Lysander?"

We'd lost Lysander and Ran.

If they were anywhere near Eliana Porath, we were in big trouble. Kylla and I wandered through the garden for an hour, cadging drinks and eavesdropping, but they were nowhere to be found. I spotted another barbarian across one of the larger pools, a fair-skinned blond woman talking animatedly to two men who had "important" written all over them. One of them had to be somebody very high up in government, because although he wasn't gauche enough to wear the Blue Hat of Imperial Favor to a social occasion, he wore a large pin on his robe in the shape of a hat, just to let us know.

They seemed to be arguing. Her hair was pulled back in a long Tellys-style braid, and underneath her open robe she wore snug-fitting Tellys pants. Although the Blue Hat held up his end of the argument, I saw that his eyes kept straying down toward those pants as though he couldn't believe what he was seeing. The woman was edging past middle-age, but with an undeniably trim figure. She looked away for a moment in pointed disgust with what someone was saying, and her eyes met mine.

She frowned, put her hand on the Blue Hat's arm, and asked him something. He turned and looked across the pool toward me. He shrugged. I heard the word "Cormallon" drift over the water.

Well, I suppose a lot of people had heard how Ran Cormallon had married a barbarian. It was nothing to get nervous about. Was it?

"Kylla, who is that woman?"

"What woman?"

Just then the flute players stopped playing and three clear horn notes split the summer evening. The guests fell silent. In the center wing of the house, the door to the porch opened and six stout security guards appeared carrying a sedan chair. of ornate black wood. Atop the chair was an old woman in a shiny robe of royal purple. She looked pudgy but small, nearly as small as I am, dwarfed by the massive chair. Grandmother Porath, no doubt. The six sedan carriers, all in matched costume, carried her easily down the two porch steps into the garden. They let the chair to the grass with perfect coordination, where it sat like a throne in the clearing. In grandmother's wake came a girl of about eighteen, in a white robe with white satin slippers, her straight dark hair falling down her back. Two white puppies followed at her heels.

I turned to see how Kylla was taking this. She was absorbed, too intent on the scene to notice me. Then I looked around the garden for Lysander's reaction, but he was still missing.

The old woman gestured impatiently and Eliana—if that's who she was—came forward at once and handed her a blackwood cane carved at the top to match the sedan chair. Grandmother glanced down once, to make sure she would miss the puppies, then stamped the cane several times for our attention. It didn't make much noise on the ground, but she certainly did have our attention.

"Dear friends," she said. "You give us joy by coming to share our Greenrose Eve. Our house has been quiet too long. We trust it may always be filled with the sounds of visitors, like you, who will ever be welcome." She spat in the direction of a flowerbush. Then she said, "As a token of our regard for you, further entertainment has been provided. Eliana!"

The girl hesitated, looking genuinely uncomfortable. I supposed all hundred people jammed into the garden were staring at her.

"Eliana!" said her grandmother again, in the voice of one who brooks no nonsense.

Eliana stepped forward. Her cheeks were pink. It wasn't cosmetic; they'd been pale before. She raised her arms straight to the sky, her white robes falling around her. She was certainly graceful, no doubt about it.

"I ask," she began.

"Louder," snapped Grandmother.

"I ask the blessing of good fortune on this gathering," she said, more loudly. "Wine for the thirsty, conversation for the wise, and entertainment for all."

Grandmother thumped her cane again. And snowflakes started to fall from the sky! It took a moment to register with the guests, who probably, like me, thought it was confetti. Until the points of cold landed on our hands and faces and disappeared, melting. There was a stunned silence and then a roll of applause that filled the garden; snow had fallen on the capital maybe twice in the winters of the past century, and now it was high summer. Obviously the Poraths had hired a sorcerer and promised him a fortune. You didn't see conspicuous display like this every day; it was the kind of thing the Six Families used to do forty or fifty years ago, before it went out of fashion.

Grandmother looked smug. Eliana had retreated to the safety of the area behind the sedan chair. The old woman peered around and called, "Jusik! My son! Where's Jusik?"

There was a ripple of activity among the people on the porch, and a few minutes later a man in his fifties rushed out, puffing, and presented himself to her. The First of Porath bowed over her hand, still out of breath.

She said, annoyed, "Where have you been?"

"Arranging the caterers, Mother."

"You've been sampling the goodies while I'm out here working?"

"I'm sorry, Mother. They had to be told where to stow the wine."

"Hmm, I'm sure they did. Never around when I need you, Jusik. I want you to tell the musicians to play some real music. "Trampling the Moons," or "Cousins Greeting," not this silliness they play today. I want to see some dancing."

Jusik Porath—shrewd businessman and tyrant to the rest of the family, or so I'd heard—looked around the garden uncertainly. "I don't think there's a lot of room for dancing, Mother."

Not unless we all shrank to the size of mushrooms. Grandmother Porath said, "You told me there would be dancing!"

Jusik's voice was lowered. "That's *tomorrow*, Mother. On the boat."

Ah. Not everyone was invited on the boat, apparently. But Lysander, of course, had gotten us aboard. If he could have arranged it, I think Lysander would have had us accompany him to the privy, he was that nervous about dealing with "the marriage thing," as he called it.

"Well, have them play something anyway." At once Jusik Porath raised his arm and made a motion in the air, and the flute players started up again. If I hadn't been standing relatively nearby, I wouldn't have heard the rest. "And Eliana, I want you to mix. Let people see you. You've got nothing to be ashamed of."

"Grandmother, I—"

"Oh, pooh, child, I know you're nervous, but you'll get over it. You can make too big a thing of modesty, you know."

"But you've always said—"

"I know what I've always said, but listen to me now. See if you can find this Lysander Shikron and walk by him a few times. You're a beautiful girl, Eliana. Mind you don't approach him, now! That'd be too easy. You must never look like you want the same thing your husband wants, girl, that's the key to success in a marriage."

Eliana mumbled, "We're not married, yet, Grandmother."

"No, and if we left it in the hands of your brother you might never be. Money's not enough to seal a wedding match, and he's a blockhead if he doesn't see it. For favorable terms, they've got to want what you've got. Where's Auntie Jace? She'll see you do it right." The old lady looked around, then jabbed her son with one elbow. "Get Auntie out here. She can go 'round with Eliana and keep her out of trouble."

Jusik bowed and spoke to one of the servants, who ran inside. I turned to see if Kylla was anywhere near critical mass, but she seemed under control. As far as I could tell.

A minute later a little, middle-aged, black-haired woman ran out. She wore a scarlet outerrobe and practically prostrated herself in the gathering snow at granny's feet. Going a touch far, I thought, but Grandmother didn't seem offended.

The woman extended her arms straight out; she was holding something. "I've brought an umbrella for you, Grandmother," she said breathlessly.

The old lady made a motion, and one of the sedan bearers took up the umbrella, opened it, and held it above Grandmother's head. It was a huge scarlet thing, and the man held it as though he were personally unaware of any snow.

Fortunately it wasn't falling very heavily; but the garden was definitely colder, and what had fallen was sticking in patches on the grass. Like Eliana, I was wearing thin satin slippers, and I wondered if the Poraths had really thought through the consequences of their excursion into climate control.

Grandmother said, "Auntie, take little Eli around to meet some of the guests, would you? I know I can count on you to see she makes the right impression."

If Auntie bowed any further, her head would be in the snow. "Your confidence honors me," she said. Then she stood straight and added, in an entirely different voice, "Come along, Eli."

"Auntie Jace, I—my feet are cold. Can I get a pair of boots first?"

"What nonsense! Your feet would look enormous in boots. Is that the way you want people to remember you? Don't forget, 'It takes the endurance of a warrior on the inside—' "

" 'To make a delicate flower on the outside.' I know. But—"

"Then come along at once." She held out her hand like a young mother on the way to the park with her five-year-old.

As they moved off into the crowd, Kylla turned to, me with a look of disgust on her face. "She's still in the charge of a nurse."

Dangerous though it might be to defend Eliana Porath, I felt obligated to say, "Ky, you know she's expected to have a chaperone."

"But a *defensive* chaperone. Not a nurse-chaperone, at her age."

I watched Auntie Jace and Eliana disappear among the guests, and saw a tall woman detach herself from the knot of people by the porch and follow them. The woman wore a robe tied back behind a pair of trousers that would have seemed provincial if they weren't embroidered silk, and there was a suspicious bulge on one side of her hips. "I think she's got one of those, too," I said to Kylla.

A voice said, "There they are!" and Lysander and Ran made their way to us.

"And where have you been?" Kylla inquired, as her husband meekly kissed her cheek.

Ran said, "We were talking to Kade first—didn't you see him catch up to us? And then we had to see the steward about the overnight arrangements. I sent back to the carriage for our cases, Theodora, and they're already stored in our room."

Kylla said, "How many of the guests are sleeping over at this house party, anyway? The house is big, but I think they'll have trouble tucking everybody away in a manner they'd be accustomed to."

There was a reason for her asking. Lysander glanced at Ran, who gave him no help, then hemmed and said, "Well, actually, just us four are actually staying for the whole night. But there'll be plenty of people on the boat ride tomorrow."

"I see," said Kylla.

"I thought there would be more houseguests," said Lysander. "But it wouldn't be polite to refuse at this point."

"I said that I see."

Ran put in, "We do have something of a problem, though." He turned to me and said, apologetically, "The Poraths keep cats."

"Oh, gods." This put an entirely new complexion on the matter. "Cats, in the plural?"

"Three," he said, with sympathy. "Scythian yellow toms. I made inquiries, and I think they're mostly confined to the kitchen and downstairs."

Kylla looked bewildered. Ran explained, "Theodora is allergic to cats." He used the Standard word "allergic," which has no Ivoran equivalent.

"I never met anyone who was allergic to cats," she said, with interest. "What do you do, go into fits?"

"Everything but," I muttered. It always turns into a big deal when I find myself required to visit people with cats. The hosts invariably offer to move the cat to another room while I'm there, proud of their sacrifice, and they look at me disapprovingly when my thanks aren't effusive enough. Moving the cat accomplishes nothing—it's the little invisible bits from the cat hair that drive me to thoughts of suicide, and they're all over the house.

"You want to go home?" asked Ran.

Kylla and Lysander looked at me, waiting. I had the feeling that both of them would kill me, for different reasons, if I said yes.

I said slowly, "It *might* possibly be manageable, if they've never been in the upstairs rooms—

"Wonderful!" Kylla beamed. "Darling—" this to Lysander—"do you know if we'll be staying next to Ran and Theo?"

"Uh, we'll be on the same floor," began Lysander. We all knew Kylla was wondering if somehow Eliana would be packaged and delivered to Lysander in the middle of the night, an unlikely event, but our Kylla was not her usual practical self.

"I think we'd better check on the cats' territory," said Ran. "The steward said they belonged to some odd person with the name Auntie Jace. Some maiden relative, I guess."

"A hired nurse," Kylla corrected flatly.

"Oh, you know her. Can you point her out?"

Kylla didn't move. "She's small, with curly hair, and wearing a scarlet robe."

Lysander said helpfully, "I'll go search for her—"

"The hell you will," said Kylla, grasping his sleeve and pulling him back. "Theo and I will locate this person. You two can go see that our things are left properly in our rooms."

I gave Ran a look that said, Trust me, it's a good idea. He touched Lysander's shoulder and said mildly, "Why don't we do that?"

Still slightly bewildered, Lysander was led away toward the house.

Kylla turned and began stalking through the party like a lioness on the prowl. She spotted Auntie Jace and cut her out of the herd with the practiced gesture of one accustomed to being noticed and obeyed. Eliana, standing miserably behind her, was ignored.

Auntie Jace took a step forward in response to Kylla's signal. "Yes?"

I jumped in, wary of how Kylla might handle this. My only current aim, after all, was to avoid a night of allergic suffering. "Your pardon, gracious lady, but we were told you own three excellent cats in the Porath household?"

". . . Yes," she answered, confused.

I smiled. "We're in the Shikron-Cormallon party. We'll be staying the night. Perhaps you've heard?" She nodded. "Forgive my weakness, gracious lady, but I'm afraid I suffer from an unusual ailment—an aversion to cats." I used the Ivoran word, which covers both allergies and emotional antipathies.

"I don't understand," she said.

"I sneeze, my nose runs, my eyes get red, I have difficulty breathing . . ."

" Ah. Yes, I've heard of it. You're the first I ever met with the sickness . . . gracious lady." She openly observed my barbarian coloring, and threw in the gracious lady as though she wasn't quite sure whether I deserved it or was trying to con her.

"I was wondering whether you could tell me if the cats tend to go in the upstairs chambers."

"I don't understand," she said again.

A long explanation followed. Finally she said, with a hint of triumph, "I can solve this easily enough, my lady. I'll just lock the cats in the kitchen for the night."

I took a deep breath. "Ah, yes, that's very kind of you—"

"They won't be happy about it, you know. " She fixed me with a severe look.

"No, yes, thank you, that's very thoughtful, but—"

"They'll probably wail all night long, they're used to the freedom of the house. They don't do any harm, you know."

"I'm sure they don't. But what I really need to know is whether they ever go in the upstairs bedrooms. . . ."

A quarter of an hour later, I gave up. I was never going to know whether they went in the upstairs bedrooms. For all I could get out of Auntie Jace, they might spend their afternoons there wenching and chasing mice through the lace bedclothes. At last I said, "Thank you, we'd better go now."

I nudged Kylla. Actually I had to nudge her twice, as I found she was staring at Eliana Porath. "We should leave, Ky."

Auntie Jace said, "Good evening to you both, then. And the cats will be in the kitchen, so everything will be just fine, won't it, gracious lady?"

"Just fine," I agreed. I pulled Kylla away.

We walked toward the porch. I kept hearing a strange

sound. Finally I said, "That isn't you gnashing your teeth, is it?"

". . . stupid idea . . ." I heard in a stream of muttering. ". . . council full of old men . . . if he thinks I'm going to stand by . . ." She stopped, looked up at the stars, took a deep breath and let it out. "So!" she turned to me brightly. "The offending cats will be locked up, and everything will be fine." She patted me on the shoulder and went off toward the porch steps.

"Oh, everything will be just perfect," I agreed. I followed her into the house.

Chapter 3

The party broke up rather earlier than it might have, probably due to soggy shoe syndrome. But don't think the Poraths' display was a failure; they'd impressed the hell out of everybody, and were more than pleased with themselves. The room we were shown to on the second floor had a glassed window facing the garden, well over my eye level. When the servant had left, I climbed up on the chest of bedclothes beneath it and screwed it open to get rid of the musty smell that pervaded the entire house, and to dissipate any residual cat allergens.

I climbed down again and said to Ran, "I am not happy."

He said, "They're doing their best. You're annoyed because Kylla's annoyed." He hung his best outerrobe on a peg by the door.

"And the room's chilly."

"You just opened the window."

"And I'm not closing it, either."

He smiled. I sighed and pulled back the quilts. If he wasn't going to fight back, it was hardly worth my being righteously indignant.

Ran got in next to me. "It's kind of nice being chilly under the covers. Reminds me of last summer, in the Northwest Sector."

"You can get nostalgic about that? At the time you didn't impress me with your cheerful outlook."

"But Theodora, we were 'courting the moon.' " This is a little bit like a honeymoon, but before the wedding party. Take my word for it, getting married on Ivory can be a complicated business. "It made being kidnapped by outlaws bearable." He kissed me. Oh, well, the hell with the cats. I helped him out of his party tunic. "What a day. I hate dealing on a social level with the Six Families."

"I can tell." His neck was like cordwood. "Let me make you more comfortable . . . "

"Why, Theodora, what a surprise."

"Oh, shush." Ran's so controlled as a rule, so damned intense when he has something to be intent about, that I like breaking him up. About twenty minutes later he said in a mellow voice, "You know, you're really getting good at this."

I looked up, shifting mood immediately. "What do you mean; I'm *getting* good? We've been married for a year. What was I like before?"

"Not again." He sighed. "That barbarian self-consciousness is your biggest enemy."

"I am *not* self-conscious." I felt myself getting red. "No more than anybody else, anyway." I turned my face into the pillow so he couldn't see my fair outlander cheeks catching fire.

A second later I felt a cool finger touch the edge of my face. "I guess I didn't say the right thing. —Theodora? Are you coming out of there?"

"No," I said, muffled, into the pillow. Not until the evidence was gone.

"You know, you shouldn't take the idea that you've improved as an insult. Whatever you were like before, I was more than happy. You barbarians take this whole subject so seriously—"

"You're digging yourself in deeper," I said, to an air pocket in the pillow.

"Ah." He fell silent. After a few seconds he said, "Do I take it we're finished for the time being?"

"Good night, Ran."

He pulled back the edge of my tunic, kissed my shoulder, and prudently turned over and settled down for the night.

Looking back, I tend to think of that day as the Evening of Snow, followed by the Night of Cats. I had good reason to look back on it later, but we'll get to that. As I lay there in the dark hour after hour, perfectly awake, it became more and more clear to me that the Porath house felines had the run of the upper bedrooms. In fact, as my nose turned into a geyser, it became clear that they spent substantial amounts of time there.

I got up in the dark and felt around in my case till I found my handkerchief. About an hour later I got up and felt around till I found Ran's handkerchief, a thing of pure dazzling linen that I hated to use for its necessary purpose. I made the mistake of rubbing my eyes, and one of them started to itch fiendishly.

Ran, of course, slept the sleep of the innocent through all this. A base part of me longed to wake him up so that he could suffer too, but I managed to ignore it. It wasn't his fault, after all. (Base Part of Theodora: "No, but he's put it out of his mind easily enough, hasn't he? It would serve this household right if you died under their roof, then maybe they would have listened to you!" Under the pressure of prolonged discomfort, I was rapidly reverting to a five-year-old mentality.)

Eventually I found myself lying there listening to the sound of my breathing—an audible, wheezing sound, like a steel whistle. My windpipe felt as though it had closed up to the size of a straw.

This wasn't working. And perhaps more seriously, I only had about a third of a handkerchief left. A dark future loomed before me.

I got out of bed, padded across the carpet, and took the Andulsine quilt off the chest by the window and a bound copy of Kesey's *Poems* from my case. I stole a look at Ran, draped over the majority of the mattress, dribbling into the silk pillow sheet. The man was dead to the world. Not that he wasn't a fine-looking corpse. I thumbed my unhappy nose at his sprawled figure, and taking my stiff, damp silk shoes, I left the room.

It was verging on dawn—still very early, as it was summer—and the house was quiet. I went downstairs, threaded my way along the halls, passed through the darkened kitchen, and emerged onto the long wooden porch that faced the garden.

There I found a new world. Past the steps of the porch, snow covered everything. The fountain, the rocks, the discreet lights of the garden, all transformed by a white, alien weight. The party might as well never have happened. The silence had a quality one never heard in the capital. Possibly I was the only one who had ever seen this sight: That new-morning-of-the-world freshness that marks a virgin snowfall, but laid over the rich, verdant, never quiet, never-ending summer of a capital formal garden. I may have been the only human, at any rate; a robber-finch sat in a wet tree bough near the porch, its yellow chest puffed for warmth, surveying the view with a look that I could only have called dazed if I'd seen it in my own species. Over on the east wing porch, the emerald lizard lay stuporous in the chill, a scarlet blanket thrown over him, the leash in a flowery pile on the floor. By now, of course, the garden should have been full of birdsong and insect hum, and the rustle of a housecat or two on the prowl.

The cats wouldn't want to go out and play today, I thought with some vindictive satisfaction. I settled down onto the chaise at the side of the porch and pulled the quilt around me. I felt better than I had all night. After about half an hour my nose stopped running, and I fell asleep to the constant throb of my right eye.

A couple of hours later, it felt like, I heard sounds. Opening my eyes from my cozy nest in the chaise, I saw three servants out in the garden, brushing snow from the paths with great straw brooms. An old, bent woman in a gray outerrobe opened the two wooden doors on the east side of the courtyard that probably led to the pantries. I heard a jingle of keys as she passed the porch. She saw that I was awake and smiled at me, a gap-toothed smile. I smiled back and went to sleep.

Something woke me again, not long after. I lay there and started to think about all the chores that had to be done before breakfast: Ran's outerrobe ought to be handed over-for pressing, he always forgot when he slept late, and I should do something to make myself look presentable—I stopped. What would I accomplish in life that was better than what I had now? Lying here under the purple and blue rectangles of the quilt, with a copy of Kesey's *Poems* by my feet and the wet branches and clear false-winter sky in front of me. The muted sounds of pots and pans came from the kitchen, letting me know that someone else was up and there would be society when I wanted it—soon enough, in fact. I looked out at a speckled black bird sitting on the railing about two feet from my face. Oh, it was good to be human, and have consciousness, and be on the receiving end of ten thousand years of my ancestors' effort, that gave me this quilt and this sheltering porch and the muted sounds that came from inside.

Yes, I felt pretty satisfied with myself as I burrowed down into the quilt. It was one of those moments that come once or twice a year, the kind that give such spiritual sustenance you can deceive yourself into thinking you can handle the rest of your existence. "While I enjoy the friendship of the seasons, I trust nothing can make my life a burden to me." That's from one of the ancients, who made a great deal about living by a pond. I spent the chief part of my life on Athena reading through the old records, and I must say they do add texture to one's adventures.

Musing sleepily on one level, while on another I enjoyed, animal-like, the warmth of the quilt and the cold of the air on my face, I became aware that one of the pairs of distant footsteps was coming closer. I opened an eye.

The redoubtable Auntie Jace. She was glaring at me in disbelief.

"Uh, hello." I straightened the blanket. Absurd to feel so guilty suddenly, as though I'd been caught stealing from my hosts. The look on her face would have been appropriate if I'd had.

"What do you think you're doing?" Suppressed outrage was in her voice. She was wearing a rainbow nightrobe that she pulled more tightly around herself, her knuckles white.

"I couldn't sleep in my room, so I came down here." What time was it, anyway? The kitchen staff was still mostly asleep, from the sound of it.

"Not sleep? In the fine room the Poraths have given you? I saw the bed linens changed only yesterday, saw it myself!"

"Yes, I'm sure—"

"And saw the room was swept out, too!"

Didn't do a very good job; though, I thought. "Yes, well, I told you I'm allergic to cats—"

"Made me lock up my dear friends; and here you are downstairs anyway! Insulting our hospitality!"

I'm not at my best when I'm half-asleep, to begin with; and social crises often throw me completely off stride. A lot of thoughts came to me: That she hadn't locked up her dear friends, because I'd seen them roaming the halls on the way down; that the open air here was more friendly to my allergies than any room inside, upstairs or down—though I couldn't see me making that clear to this tiny madwoman.

My mind was a blank. Frantically I thought, What would Ran or Kylla do?

And an answer came. I sat straight up, took the apology out of my voice, and said, "Forgive me, but is this the way to address a guest?"

She actually took a step back. I remembered that she was only a retainer here, and I was not her guest in any case. Still hearing Ran's coldest tones in my mind, I echoed, "If the Poraths have some objection to my behavior, I trust they will honor me with it. I would not want to cause them any offense after their generosity of yesterday."

My most formal capital accent: It's amazing how the words will come sometimes when you pretend you're somebody else. Auntie Jace looked shocked.

She stood there frozen, so I added, "Should I go and inquire of them if they have some complaint to lodge?"

At this she took several more steps back, then turned and went down the porch steps, off through the garden. She was wearing ankle boots under her rainbow robe. I heard her muttering as she squished through the snow: "No consideration for other people . . . barbarians making themselves at home . . . never thought I'd live to see it. . . . "

I closed my eyes again. Maybe I should have stayed upstairs. But no, I'd've been a complete wreck by morning, and they still expected me to go on that damned boat ride today. And it would have caused quite the little brouhaha if my throat had closed up completely during the night.

I fell asleep imagining the tomb marker: She Died Polite.

When I woke an hour later, A Scythian yellow tom was sitting on the edge of the chaise watching me. Lethally long-haired, champion shedders that they are, I had not perhaps picked the best house to stay overnight in. Out here in the open air, though, I felt confident enough to actually consider stroking him before common sense reasserted itself.

The house was up and stirring, so I returned to our room for a quick wash and dress, then took a plate of hard market bread and Iychan apples out to the porch again for breakfast. This morning was the boat ride on the old capital canal. As it turned out, our carriages didn't leave till almost noon, and I spent a boring few hours in the nasal safety of the garden, where the winterspell was breaking up and the ground was turning muddy. I left the social niceties to Ran, who claimed I was laid up (in my room, he allowed them to infer) with some malady of my delicate barbarian constitution. The Poraths expressed proper sympathy and promptly forgot about me, to my relief.

I wandered the length of the garden, down to the guardhouse by the gate, and back again. Two of the Scythian yellows followed me as I went, in instant and touching loyalty. This is typical of my experience with cats.

At noon, when Ran emerged to accompany me to our carriage, he observed my new followers. He shook his head. "Why do you let them rub against your ankles? This always happens, Theodora. You know that they know you're allergic."

"Yeah, but they also know I'm not going to kick them away." Increasing my speed to avoid one of the toms, I began shaking the hem of my robe, careful not to touch any gold hairs. "I thought this was a *morning* boat ride."

"Try to get the nobility out of bed before noon. Eliana was dead to the world—wouldn't even answer till an hour ago, and came out still yawning. Just as well, I guess. I wouldn't want to have to watch her and Kylla stare at each other over the marmalade. Grandmother and Jusik are the only punctual souls in the house."

We came to the gate, and one of the security guards stepped over to open it for us. He was young, with curly brown hair cut short, and he wore his uniform with a faintly uncomfortable air. "Noble sir and lady, may I ask you if the family looks ready to leave yet?"

He must have been preoccupied; no "forgive my presumption," or any of the usual superfluous layers of politeness. Ran looked at him speculatively. "They were getting their cloaks when I left. If you're to accompany them on the boat, I'd suggest you prepare to go now."

He nodded. "Thank you, sir. Thank you, my lady." His eyes met mine briefly, and I couldn't help but be struck by the fact that they were a remarkably deep, fine shade of brown. I also couldn't help noticing there were black circles in the sun-gold skin beneath them. And that both eyes had a reddish cast that usually comes from a recent abuse of drugs or alcohol. Not that there was any need to be judgmental: One of my eyes had no doubt had a similar appearance just last night, from quite a different cause. He hauled open the gate, waited till we were through, closed it, and started walking back through the garden toward the house.

"Where are Kylla and Lysander?" I asked Ran.

"They're riding with the Poraths in the family carriage."

We looked at each other. I said, "I hope Grandmother Porath has some discretion in the seating arrangements."

"You know," he said, "I rather doubt that she does."

The boat was big for a canaler. There were two levels for passengers, an enclosed one on the main deck and an upper level open to the air. The musicians, I saw, had been brought back for the day, and their ranks had swollen to include more horn and string players.

About two dozen of last night's partygoers had been asked back for the ride. I saw the blond Tellys woman, again talking animatedly, this time to a knot of three new people. She spotted me across the room as I came in and I saw her react. She made a motion to her listeners as though she were going to leave them, but one, a woman, put a hand on her arm and said something. And then the blond woman was off again, gesturing authoritatively as she spoke. She was a naturally strong talker, it seemed.

The boat loaded up and cast off into the canal. I pressed my face against the glass as we pulled out, and saw a carriage drive up madly to the pier, stop short, and discharge a red-faced man in multicolored robes who threw something down in disgust and waved his arms angrily before whirling around and getting back in his carriage. Apparently some people are too tardy even for the nobility.

I turned back to the big salon on the main deck. Here all was happiness and light. Grandmother's chair had been brought in, and when the musicians struck up, a look of serene joy came over her—you wouldn't have known it was the same woman. Kade took his sister Eliana out onto the floor and led six other couples in a pattern dance, one of the stately things I hear they do at court. They "bowed to the sun," "bowed to the moons," "laced the boot," "kissed the stranger," "circled their partners," and did any number of complicated figures before the tune was over. Lacing the boot was particularly complex. One young woman flubbed it and had to be drawn back into place by the person next to her, several beats too late.

The second the music stopped, Grandmother Porath stood up—it seemed there was no pressing constitutional reason for her to use her sedan chair—and walked to the head of the couples. "Kade!" she snapped. She held out her hand. He bowed, took it obediently, and Eliana withdrew from the dance. I noticed that her defensive chaperone, the tall skinny woman, followed her as she moved away.

And this time there was none of that slow, stately stuff. Grandmother led them in a wild country pattern dance, and if you've never seen one I can only say it's a lot like the previous dance, only about a hundred times more enthusiastic. Speed and the ability to jump are essentials.

Ran had wandered to the front of the salon to watch the jabith player, and I found I was standing next to somebody familiar. Sixteen or seventeen, light brown hair, nicely dressed . . . He was watching me, too. "Excuse me," I said. "Have we met, noble sir?" The "noble sir" prompted my memory; this was the young man Kylla had spilled a drink on last night.

"We were nearly introduced," he said, with a dry look that told me he had not forgotten. "I'm Coalis." He gave it to me in three syllables: Co-al-is.

I must have looked blank. He wasn't offended by it; apparently he expected people not to know who he was. "Kade is my brother," he explained. Apparently he did expect people to know Kade.

And he was right. "Ah," I said.

"You're the barbarian that Cormallon sorcerer married," he remarked. Usually they don't come right out and say it.

"Yes. I'm Athenan."

"Oh? What's your field of interest?"

Now, that was an unusual thing for an Ivoran to say. "Cross-cultural myths and legends. I haven't done a lot of work in it lately, though."

"No, I'm the same way. Other things interfere."

I raised an eyebrow. "What's *your* field of study, noble sir?"

"Coalis, please. It's na' telleth philosophy."

"You're—" I stopped.

"What?"

"I was going to say, you're a little young for na' telleth philosophy, aren't you? I tend to associate it with the old and jaded."

He said without emotion, "No point in not getting a head start."

I supposed not. I wondered what the Poraths thought about their second son opting out of the game. Well, he seemed like a frank sort of boy—"Are you planning on going into a monastery? Or is this just a personal study?"

"I've been accepted at Teshin. I go on the winter solstice." He took a glass from a table and sipped at it; I saw it was water. "My family wants to give me the summer to change my mind. Prediction is fruitless—" This is a na' telleth saying—"but I see nothing so far that would change it."

I've always been fascinated by this sort of conversation with strangers. Completely ignoring etiquette, I said, "I suppose they've been throwing you at nice young girls for months."

"They have. It's a pointless exercise. Sex isn't prohibited to monks, you know, only passion. And marriage."

What's wrong with passion and marriage? I decided not to say it; it seemed like the kind of answer that would take up the rest of the day.

"What do you think of this wedding thing?" "Wedding thing"—I was starting to sound like Lysander.

He understood what I meant. "Not the best idea Kade's ever had. But Grandmother's supporting it, so I guess it will happen." He might have been talking about the rain.

I was saying, "So this was Kade's idea—" when Ran approached and took both my hands. He nodded his head toward the dance floor.

I stood fast. "Coalis, this is my husband, Ran Cormallon."

"Honored by this meeting," Coalis said agreeably. "We passed at breakfast, I think."

"The honor is mine. Come on, Theodora, dance with me."

"My leg's broken."

"I know the jabith player, he used to live with one of my aunts. He's going to play 'The Other Side of the Mirror' next for us. I know you can do that one, I saw you do it at our wedding."

"The other side of the mirror" is an Ivoran term that implies the meeting of life, love, and death; that sunny mornings are followed by rainy afternoons, and that we'll all come to dust in the end. The other side of the mirror is a skull. Unless you understand that it's a wildly cheerful dance, you'll miss the point.

I said, "Coalis here is a na' telleth. He'd probably love to dance this one."

Coalis smiled austerely. Ran pulled me out onto the floor.

I found that we were standing, alarmingly, at the far right of the double row of dancers. "We're lead couple!" I said.

"I know."

The musicians looked ready to start up any moment. I hissed and pulled his sleeve to make Ran face me. "We'll have to go first, and everyone will be watching us! I don't know this dance that well!"

"Nonsense. You'll do perfectly well, you always do."

Ran's often overinflated views of my capabilities can be soothing, but there are times when reality must be injected into a situation. I turned to the woman on my left and smiled politely. "Would you mind being lead couple? My partner and I are going to the bottom."

Ran said, "Theodora—" but I ignored him, grasped his hand, and pulled him to the end of the row. "That wasn't necessary, was it?" he said, as we took up our facing positions.

Ran's ego rarely admits other viewpoints—actually, it's one of his more endearing qualities. Mind you, he'll yield to my wishes often enough, he just makes it clear that he thinks I'm crazy.

At that moment Grandmother Porath announced, from the chair she'd retired to, "We'll begin this dance from the left side! Musicians!"

The row of dancers all turned to us. I felt the blood leave my face.

"Barbarian self-consciousness," murmured Ran. "Don't panic. We can do this."

My mind had gone completely blank.

"Left-right palm touch," said Ran, as the music started up. "Then place, advance, place. And *turn*—no, to your left—"

Moments of terror followed by moments of enjoyment. I've always gotten a kick out of that backwardskipping thing during the jig, and did this time too, until I skipped right into the two people behind me. However, we all seemed to survive it.

When it was over, we all bowed and I said to Ran, "I need to go somewhere and sit down." I felt as if I'd been digging ditches for a day and a half.

"Kylla and Lysander must be on the top deck. I hear there are benches up there."

"Terrific."

We made our way across the salon to three doors behind the musicians' seats. Two of the doors had stairs going up. Ran said, "One of them's probably to the watch. —You look tired. I'll see which one goes to the upper deck." He started up one of the staircases. I leaned against the doorjamb, turning to face the salon, and found my sleeve tugged—by Grandmother Porath, who'd come by to harangue the musicians.

"I know," she said, sympathetically. "Sometimes it's so hard to know where to go."

I wasn't sure whether she meant directionally, or if it was a reference to my nearly sending four people keeling over in "The Other Side of the Mirror."

I said, "Do you mean in the dance or in life?"

She cackled. "The dance. I've *done* life."

"Theodora?" Ran's voice floated down. "This is it."

I bowed to Grandmother Porath and went up the stairs. At the top it was all sunlight and soft winds, and the buildings of the capital passing slowly on either side of the canal. About a half dozen people had come up here for the relative silence and the relaxed atmosphere; Kylla and Lysander were sitting on a bench near the railing. Ran and I joined them. A striped awning had been set up to shade this side of the boat.

"Nice," I said tentatively, wondering how things were between them.

We were passing under Kyme Bridge. Lysander said, "You can see the roof of our house if you stand in front."

"We'll probably be passing it in another ten minutes," added Kylla, calmly enough. At least they didn't seem to be throwing things.

Unfortunately, one of the Poraths chose that moment to invade the upper deck: Kade, architect of "the marriage thing," and probably the person Kylla least wanted to see, next to Eliana, emerged from the stairs. He peered around the deck, then started angrily toward the opposite rail. The security guard who'd let us out the gate that morning was leaning there weakly, looking none too well.

You could hear Kade's voice clear across the deck. "Aren't you supposed to be watching my sister?"

The guard's voice was harder to catch. " . . . fine, on the boat . . . nothing's going to happen . . . "

"That's not your job to say! Your job is to watch her!"

" . . . job is to watch everybody . . . defensive chaperone all the time . . . better protection than the Emperor . . . "

Kade glanced around at the rest of us—I must honestly say that our group had fallen silent and was eavesdropping openly—and realized he was creating a spectacle. He grabbed the guard and hauled him over behind the stairway entrance, where their voices became unintelligible.

"Oh, well," I said, with some disappointment. A minute or so later, the guard, looking rather subdued, preceded Kade down the stairs.

Kylla turned to her husband. "Even their security guard doesn't want to spend his life with Eliana Porath."

"Oh, gods, Kylla—"

Ran caught my eye and we withdrew a few feet to the railing. He said seriously, "You know, I don't see any good way out of this. The Poraths have put their House on the line so obviously, it'd be a slap in the face if Lysander tries to squeeze away."

"That's *why* they're being so open."

"Trap or not, it'll still be an insult. And you know how the Six Families are. Murder's a game to them. They do it all the time without reason, and when they *do* have a reason—" Ran's face expressed his disapproval of killing for impractical motives; it was a judgment he shared with all the commoner classes of Ivory, right down to the market square beggar.

"So what are you saying? That Kylla's going to have to grin and bear it? She won't, you know."

"I—" He broke off, looking surprised. "Did you feel that?"

"Feel what?" Something in his voice made me nervous. I put a hand on his arm for reassurance, and just then there was a kind of shimmering, a faint tremor. There'd been an earthquake in the capital about sixty years ago, but there was no reason to think we were due for another. Except that something different and uncontrollable was definitely happening—

I took a step back and looked around, but everything was all right: The buildings, the canal, the passengers still intent on their conversations. Whatever it was seemed to have stopped.

I looked at Ran. He was leaning against the rail. "We're getting closer to it," he said thickly. His face was white.

The only thing we were getting closer to was Catmeral Bridge, near Kylla and Lysander's villa. I went back to Ran. "What is it? Do you want me to get help?"

There was a commotion on the level beneath us. Somebody yelled. A voice tried to answer reassuringly, there was another yell, and running footsteps. The window just below us was open and we could hear it all. There was a woman's scream.

I looked over the side of the boat. Someone was in the canal; a blue and gold silk robe floated, bobbing and then disappearing as the wearer sank, dragging it into the gray water. A few seconds later there was the flutter of an arm, and a dark head appeared and vanished.

Splashes directly under us marked two security guards diving out the same window. The boat was slowing down. Everyone on the upper deck had joined us at the railing to stare. "Who is it?" I heard someone ask. There was no answer. The guards cut their way through the water, diving and reappearing where the head and arm had made their last appearance. They must have spent a good twenty minutes swimming back and forth to the boat and then diving again and again. I was impressed with their training: Swimming is not a widespread art on Ivory.

Kylla, Lysander, Ran, and I all watched silently, along with the rest of the boat, until the two guards returned. There was no sign of a body.

We looked at each other. Blue and gold silk: Kade.

Chapter 4

We missed most of the confusion downstairs. I was told later that that scream we'd heard was Grandmother Porath, who'd fainted immediately and had to be laid on some pillows the crew brought out. Between dealing with her and watching the security guards dive for his son, Jusik must have been in a state.

When Ran and I went downstairs, we found Eliana being clutched by the old lady, who was lying propped against a set of red cushions, looking about a hundred years old. The two security guards were standing dripping by the bar. And Jusik was in an argument with the steersman about turning this damned boat around, *now!* so they could return home at once. A typical Ivoran of the great families, nothing was more important than returning to safe, familiar territory in times of stress. I could see Eliana agreed with him. The steersman kept trying to explain that the canal wasn't wide enough here to turn in.

Finally Jusik bowed to physical law and announced to his guests that it would be another hour before they would come around to the pier again. Please make yourselves as comfortable as possible, etc.

I found myself drifting over toward the bar and thought maybe a drink wouldn't be a bad idea. I'd never even spoken to Kade, he meant nothing to me, but it was impossible to avoid the shock of his death in the faces of the people he *had* known. And in conjunction with whatever Ran and I had experienced upstairs, it threw me off balance.

The bartender had wandered away, so I poured myself a pink ringer and offered one to Ran. He shook his head. The security guard who'd argued with Kade and then dived for him in the canal sat down heavily on a bench next to the bar, creating a puddle of water beneath it. He pulled off his wet jacket and dropped it in a ball at his feet. He glanced over toward the old woman, where Eliana sat rubbing her hands, and his face was as drawn and pale as hers.

No wonder. This wasn't going to look any too good on his record. Coalis had already taken the other place on the bench; he was staring at nothing, in a state of shock. I had the rare experience of seeing a professed na' telleth completely and obviously at a loss.

I suddenly grasped that, whatever his relationship with Kade had been, the Poraths no longer had an heir and a spare. Coalis was now first son of the House. He must have realized by now that he could forget about being a monk.

It was funny, but I could empathize a lot more quickly with the destruction of a dream, selfish though that may be, than with any sorrow over Kade, whom I'd only known as an irritant. I poured a new ringer into a large glass, walked over to Coalis, and held it out.

"Medicinal purposes," I said. "It won't do any harm."

He accepted it and started drinking. Poor kid. He'd lost that self-possession that made him seem ageless last night, and looked like what he was: A boy in his late teens, who'd just taken a major blow.

I realized that the still-wet guard next to him was shivering. "I'm sorry," I said belatedly. "I can get you one, too. And they ought to have brought you some towels." Typical insular House reaction, to take care of themselves and forget everybody else.

"Thanks," he said. He wiped his nose with his arm in a distracted sort of way.

I turned to go, when a voice said to Coalis, in pure provincial argot, "Tough break, kid."

A voice I knew very well. A voice that could not possibly be here. I turned back, shocked, to see the Imperial Minister for Provincial Affairs holding out a towel to the shivering guard. "You look like you could use this." Then he smiled at me. "Hello, Theodora."

A height between medium and tall; dark hair shot with premature gray, the calm certainty in his face of a very heavy falling rock. He wasn't wearing his glasses. Stereth Tar'krim, one of the few outlaw leaders to ever successfully get out of the Northwest Sector and into the Imperial power structure . . . and the only one who kept his old name.

I became aware that my mouth was open, and I closed it. "What are you doing here? Where were you? I didn't see you with the guests before." Not the most polite, or even most coherent greeting, but it was out before I could think about it.

"I was downstairs, chatting with friends." There's a kind of phoniness, when Stereth uses words like *chatting*, that he enjoys and likes his listeners to enjoy.

Coalis looked up dully. "You two know each other?"

I might have asked the same thing. What was Stereth doing on an intimate conversational basis with the younger son of Porath? Or rather, the first son, now. I looked at him speculatively.

He said, "I suppose this means Ran's aboard, too. I should have come upstairs earlier. Where is he?"

"Right here." Ran appeared behind him, looking, I am glad to say, nowhere near as shocked as I felt.

Stereth turned happily. "Sokol." he said. Quietly, thank the gods.

Ran's eyes went wide, and he took Stereth by the arm and pulled him behind the bar. I followed. In a fierce whisper he said, "Do *not* call me Sokol."

"Your past is nothing to be ashamed of."

"I'm not ashamed, and *don't do it.*" Ran was morally entitled to give orders on this subject, as it was Stereth's fault that we'd once used aliases to begin with. "What's going on here?" Without waiting for an answer, he added, "Look, I don't want my family name pulled into some new affair of yours."

"I beg your pardon, old friend, but you'll have to tell me what you're talking about." There was a slight edge of coldness in his voice now.

"Kade Porath. He was killed by sorcery."

I said, "He was?"

"That's interesting," said Stereth. He said it thoughtfully, not with sarcasm. "I was downstairs when it happened, but from what I heard it did sound strange."

"Are you seriously telling me you had nothing to do with this? You seem to know the new heir pretty well, Stereth. And I know how you like to make alliances."

He did not appear offended. "I'm seriously telling you I had nothing to do with it. I never lie to my crew, remember."

"You don't tell them the whole story, either. And anyway, we're not in your crew anymore." He took a deep breath. Stereth was the one person who could sometimes put Ran at a loss. "We were *never* in your crew."

This was debatable. We'd spent the previous summer as involuntary guests and co-conspirators in Stereth's outlaw band. Fortunately, the Imperial prosecuters were still unaware of this. The penalty for the use of sorcery as a weapon against the Empire is decapitation for every member of the family. Technically, that would mean every Cormallon on the planet, down to the last newborn child. I didn't want to test the law to see if they'd go through with it.

I said, "So, Stereth—did you buy new eyes from the barbarians?"

"I beg your pardon?"

"You're not wearing your glasses."

"Ah." The Legend of the Northwest Sector felt vaguely around an inside robe pocket. "I left them in my other robe."

Ran was giving me this look that said, Must we speak to him socially?

I went on, "And how's your wife?"

From his seat by the wall, Coalis was watching us all with great interest.

"You know Cantry, she never changes. Ah, Theodora, Ran, I believe you've met my secretary."

I turned and got another in the series of small electric shocks I'd been receiving all day. A member of the old outlaw band I'd never expected to see again—"Clintris?" I said disbelievingly. A stocky woman, born to disapprove, her hair pulled back severely; wearing a set of robes she never could have afforded in the old days, that nevertheless managed to seem unbecoming.

Clintris . . . Ran groaned. "Oh, gods, are they all here?"

I said, "Clintris, how are you?" There was warmth in my voice; we'd actually gotten to the point where we were getting along, by the time our adventure ended. She glowered back. What had I—

Oh. I'd called her by her road name, that we never used to her face. "Tight-Ass" would be the nearest translation.

Stereth corrected us. "The lady Nossa Kombriline."

"Oh, right. Of course." I bowed to her and she inclined her head a fraction of a millimeter. Clintris was not a forgiving sort.

She turned at once to Stereth. "Sir, I've been talking to the captain." Nobody avoids talking to Clintris if she's set on reaching them. "We'll be at the pier in about forty minutes. You have an early dinner tonight with the undersecretary from the department of power, and I believe in any case we should distance ourselves from . . . the events of the day."

"In other words, you'd like me to bundle us both into a closed carriage and go straight home."

"It's my recommendation."

Clintris—that is, the lady Nossa—was in her element as a governmental secretary, though her accent was still tinged with the provinces and the scarlet outerrobe she wore looked as though it had been hastily wrapped around a tree stump with a face. I glanced down at my own clothing involuntarily; was that how I looked in Ivoran robes?

I looked up to find Stereth meeting Ran's eyes. "I'd recommend the same course to you, old friend."

Ran looked away toward the rows of liquor bottles, as though they were the most interesting objects on the boat. "We're here with some relatives. We'll have to see what they want to do."

"Oh, yes, the Shikrons. I suppose they may feel the family has some claim on them. What with the engagement, I mean."

Typical Stereth. But I suppose Coalis had told him.

Ran said, "Nobody's engaged yet." It came out more firmly, I think, than he meant it to.

Stereth raised an eyebrow. "And nobody will be, if you have your way. I see. I guess you have more reason than I do to be glad Kade had an urge to go swimming."

He smiled. Ran turned a blazing look on him, and I grasped my husband's sleeve. "Shouldn't we find Kylla and Lysander and see what they want to do?"

I could see him banking the fires. Ran does not approve of losing one's temper in public; he thinks it's common.

Stereth is one of the only people in the world who can bring him so near to it.

"If there's anything I can do," said Stereth, as Ran turned away. "And let me know if you need a ride."

Ran strode off toward the stairwell, making a sound very like a growl.

We took Kylla and Lysander home in our carriage. They were both very quiet. Ran was sitting beside Lysander, and I held Kylla's hand.

Ran nudged Lysander and spoke quietly. "Did you know the Minister for Provincial Affairs was on board?"

Lysander blinked. "Stereth Tar'krim? Was he? I didn't see him."

"Do you know of any reason the Poraths would be associating with him?"

"The notorious Rice Thief? Maybe they thought his reputation would add to the party. I don't know, it's the first I heard of it. Why? Is it important?"

Ran slid the steel shutter open an inch; we were approaching the Shikron villa. He let it down again. "What will this do to the marriage proposal?"

Lysander sighed. "I doubt if they'll let it go. On the other hand, it was Kade's idea, and he kept pushing it. It'll be easier to kill, now that he's gone."

"Easier to kill," Ran muttered, to himself. The carriage rolled to a stop and Lysander climbed out. He helped Kylla down, and slid shut the door without a word.

We rode back to our house in silence. When we reached there, I gave Ran a five-tabal coin to tip the driver and we climbed the two steps to the door.

Ran said, "Do you think Stereth had anything to do with this?"

"The gods only know," I said, tiredly. "Let's get some sleep."

Between Scythian gold cats, murder, and old blackmailing friends, it had been a long night and day. Ran said, "The parcel light's blinking on the security station."

"Fine. You handle it—gracious sir, First of Cormallon."

He just looked at me. "You'll be better," he said, "when you've had a nap."

* * *

I was better when I'd had a nap. As a matter of fact, I was better when I'd had a full night's sleep with unobstructed breathing. As a collector of tales and an Athenan scholar, I loved to read about knights and princesses and quests, and imagine myself bumming from one perilous castle to the next; but the fact is, physical exhaustion just makes me cranky. It's not very flattering, and really, I do try—I just don't get very far in graciousness until I'm fed and rested.

I woke up next morning, got some hermitmeat and rice from the larder, cracked open a pellfruit, and padded into the downstairs parlor balancing plates. Ran was sprawled on the divan, staring at the ceiling. I'd downed half the pellfruit while still in the pantry, and therefore looked kindly on him. He was, after all, my dearest friend and the light of my heart. I said, "Last night you said there was a parcel?"

He turned his head. "Already took care of it. It was just the last three copies of the Capital News. They got sent to Cormallon and Jad sent them on here."

A pile of nondescript pamphlets lay on the floor. "I see we've got today's, too. Jad must've notified them to change the address."

The Capital News is not on the Net because it is not a very respectable publication. It has an insert called the "Gossip Gazette," and various highly placed persons try from time to time to halt its publication. But it's just too damned entertaining. Ivorans love to read about stuff like that. I understood that the Emperor got a copy every morning.

I snagged one of the Newses, opened it on a pillow, sat on another pillow, and started to eat and read. I skipped over the trade articles and went straight to the insert. "Oh, kanz," I said.

Ran looked up. "What?"

"Today's date. Listen: 'What branch of the tree of six is offering its youngest blossom to a merchant house? The lovely lady E., still fresh from school, met her potential suitor at a garden party yesterday evening. We understand the gentleman in question already has one bride, but who could refuse such a rose in springtime? And here at Gossip

Gazette, we've always heard that a pair beats one of a kind."

Ran put a hand over his eyes. "They don't actually name the Poraths . . . what am I saying? Of course everyone will know it's the Poraths."

"In case they're in any doubt, there's a description of the snowfall at the party. Where do they get this information?"

"Paid off one of the guests."

I scanned the other articles for mention of Shikrons or Poraths. "You'd think the guests at a Six Families party would be too wealthy to be tempted by whatever the Gossip Gazette can pay."

"Huh. For all we know, some of them are on the staff."

I closed the sheet. "This is going to make it difficult for the Poraths to back out, isn't it?"

Ran sat up suddenly. "It may have been the Poraths who planted that item. They were already going out on a limb to commit themselves, true? Imagine the effect on poor Lysander, picking up this paper in the morning, knowing he'd never be able to argue now that Eliana wasn't publicly compromised. That's if events had gone as planned, I mean. If Kade hadn't died."

I gave him my attention. "You think that was sorcerously caused?"

"I know it. The entire field of balance changed. And anyway, common sense will tell you that a man who doesn't know how to swim won't suddenly dive off a boat. Not when he's in his right mind."

In his right mind. I thought back over what I'd studied of the field. Sorcery cannot really affect the mind directly, but it can deceive the mind through physical changes. Giving a person the physical symptoms of fear can convince him he's afraid of something; the symptoms of lust or hunger were likewise easy to stimulate. "A fire spell? Raise his body temperature, convince him he's burning up?"

"It's how I would do it," said Ran. Then he added, "If I were going to do it publicly, which I never would."

"I don't know, it seems so unlikely. Wouldn't he just call for help? I mean, diving into the canal! He *knew* he couldn't swim, odds were good he'd die anyway—"

"Sweetheart, I see you've had the good fortune never to be near a major fire disaster. People dive off twelve-story buildings with nothing but stone underneath when their rooms catch fire. There's no force more persuasive." I had been in a fire, once, but it had been a small one, and thankfully I'd lost consciousness early on. Ran continued, "Actually, using a fire spell to kill by water is really a charming conceit, sorcerously speaking."

"And which of the guests do you think did it?"

It was indeed the question. Ran considered it, as I knew he'd been considering since it happened; then he said, regretfully, "We don't have sufficient data."

"We could make wild guesses."

"So could the Gossip Gazette. Though I doubt that they will, it's too close to real news." He walked over to join me, and I gave him a slice of fruit. "I'll have to make a condolence call this morning on Jusik Porath. It's my duty as the First of Cormallon, and having had the bad luck to be on the scene when it happened, I suppose I can't get out of it."

"Do I have to go?" I was willing to foist this one off on others if I could; rather the way Ran was somehow never around on major housecleaning days. I suppose it all evened out.

He shook his head. "If you were close to Grandmother Porath or Eliana, they'd expect you to call on them; but you'd still be under no obligation."

Ran had shed his outerrobe when he came in. Now he opened his underrobe, stretched his legs out on the carpet, swallowed a piece of fruit, and sighed in pleased physicality.

"Nice legs, stranger," I said in Standard. "You new in town?"

He laughed, nearly choking on the fruit. He slid an arm around my waist and said, "A man not married to a barbarian doesn't know what he's missing." He kissed the back of my neck. "Moon of my heart," he said in Ivoran.

Just then the doorbells jangled. We froze, like two children caught playing doctor in the back garden. I said, "If we wait, they'll go away."

He pulled his underrobe together. I said, "Ignore it."

But I knew better than that. The First of Cormallon never ignores doorbells. Or Net messages, or parcel signals, or mail of any kind. There's always a chance it might be something his duty requires of him. He pulled himself to his feet and slipped on a respectable pair of embroidered house slippers.

I waited for him to come back. Several minutes passed. I heard a heavy tread of feet in the passage; two pairs of feet, by the sound of it. The slippered pair was clearly Ran's, but his footfall was silent by nature—he was warning me that company was on its way. His voice came from the passage, overly loud: "This way, if you don't mind, noble sir; my wife is within."

I jumped up and kicked the cushions out of the way and ran a hand through my hair and checked to see my robe was done up correctly. It's not always easy to go from being freewheeling Theodora of Pyrene to a respectable Cormallon matron. Was there time to grab the plates? I dived for them, heard footsteps just outside the doorway, and straightened up again. Close enough. The noble sir, whoever he was, should have sent word he was coming, and would have to deal with life as it was rather than the more courteous fiction it could be.

The divider from the passage is just a thick cotton tapestry, half open; Ran flung it the rest of the way and bowed like a proper host.

And in walked Jusik Porath. He hadn't even changed his clothes.

Chapter 5

Ran threw me a bated look and said, "Apparently the noble sir has anticipated my call, Theodora."

Jusik, who was striding into the room like an army on the march, stopped short. "Your call?"

"Of condolence," said Ran. "I was just remarking to my wife that I should go and present my family's regret at this tragedy to your House."

"Condolence call," repeated Jusik. "Yes. Of course. Might I sit down?"

Ran gestured to a tasseled cushion far from my plates, and Jusik seated himself with the air of one making a conscious effort of control. Up close he looked both tired and restless, the lines in his face more pronounced. I'd watched him at the garden party and on the boat, and—when not placating his mother—he'd struck me as a man used to getting his own way, as the First of Porath no doubt would be. He hardly seemed separable from his family, when you thought of him: Father, son, first of his House, representative of one of the six noble branches; it was what he *was*. As he probably would tell you if you were presumptuous enough to ask.

So why at this moment, as he sat on the cushion in our parlor, did I have the sense that he was here all alone? He seemed . . . so much an *individual*. So un-Ivoran.

I didn't even know the man, but suddenly I felt very sorry for him. On impulse I knelt on the carpet, met his eyes, and said, "We mean it, you know. This must be terrible for you. If there's anything we can do. . . ."

He seemed slightly taken aback. The barbarian breaks ritual again. Probably there was a set of statement and reply we were supposed to follow here, and probably Ran was supposed to do it in any case. My sincerity must have been plain, however, as he was not offended: He even broke ritual himself long enough to lean over and touch my hand, before he gave up trying to deal with the outlander, took a deep breath, and turned back to Ran.

"Well, here I am," he said.

"I beg your pardon?" said Ran.

"Here I am. Surely you expected me."

Ran and I looked at each other.

You have any idea?

Not a clue. I rolled my eyes toward Jusik briefly as though to add, What can you expect? Maybe he's unbalanced by grief.

Ran said, "Uh, perhaps the noble sir could be more explicit?"

Jusik glanced at me. "I wonder if your gracious wife should remain."

The man deserved a lot of slack, of course, but this vagueness could get just a little irritating. Ran said, "I wonder if you could give me some idea of what we're talking about."

This was treading a bit toward direct speech early in a social call; but clearly Jusik had something on his mind . . . and the truth, I may as well tell you now, is that Ran really didn't care much about Jusik, Kade, or the whole lot of Poraths wherever they may be. He had people of his own that he spent his worry on. Not that he would dream of being discourteous.

Jusik coughed. "I've been very polite, I think, gracious sir. I've come alone—no security, no retainers of any kind, check the street outside. I come here in all good faith, and I really don't think that I deserve to be passed over like this—"

"Sir!" Ran had dropped the "noble." "We realize that you've had a terrible shock. That you're under enormous strain. I hate to be crude at such a time, but let me put this as simply as I can: *I have no idea what you're talking about.*"

Jusik blinked. "Then you refuse to answer my questions."

"Sir, it is you who refuse to ask them."

I touched his sleeve to get Jusik's attention. "Noble sir,

I'm a barbarian, remember? Be as simple and clear as you can be, and tell *me* why you've come."

He was deciding whether or not to be insulted. I added, "Please?"

Ran was about to say something else. Hidden by our robes, I jabbed him in the thigh. I didn't want to distract Jusik's attention from me, or it might take hours to get him to talk sensibly. As soon as he went back to Ran, he'd expect to be understood. Not being understood by a barbarian is normal.

"Lady Theodora, I'm here on a business matter, relating to some work of your husband's. That's all."

I jabbed Ran again and smiled at Jusik. "You refer to the sorcery business?"

"Of course. The House of Cormallon is unequaled in its practice."

"The noble sir is too kind. Such compliments are no less treasures than the gold of our House." Spend a year or two on Ivory and you'll be able to toss this stuff off, too. "Now, are you saying that you want to hire my husband to perform some sorcerous assignment for your House?"

"Gracious lady . . . not exactly. Rather, I wish to consult with him on his present assignment."

"Really. His present assignment. And which assignment would that be?"

Jusik shifted uncomfortably. "Umm, the assignment of yesterday. That is . . . the assignment . . . of yesterday."

The First of Porath, known for firmness to the point of tyranny, was near to stuttering. Ran leaned over then, and I sat back on my heels. "Is the noble sir under the impression that I killed his son?"

The adjectives are flowery on Ivory, but they don't mince their verbs. Jusik Porath looked even more uncomfortable. A lifetime of training was holding him back: The Six Families, who so often practice murder as an art form, regard straight business assassination as the lowest of taste. It was sometimes unavoidable, but one never talked about it.

Jusik met Ran's eyes with dignity. "I come as is my responsibility, as the First of my House. I come to ascertain what danger we may be in. To see what it is your employer wants of us. So public an . . . incident, surely can be nothing but a warning. I should be at home, sir, seeing to my family, but I am here in fulfillment of my duty. I dared not wait. I trust that you will respect the . . . restraint . . . I have shown."

Ran was momentarily speechless. Jusik said, impatiently, "Is it war? Whom has my House offended? You could not expect me not to ask you, not when your work was done in full view of the world!"

"Sir, do you think I'd assassinate a member of your family while I was your guest?"

"Isn't that what sorcerers do?"

The gulf between the first and second tiers of aristocracy had never seemed so wide. The scary thing was that Jusik could *be* so controlled about it—he could be that way because his pain and anger weren't directed at Ran. I don't think he thought any more of Ran than he thought of a gun or a knife, or a soup ladle.

Gods! Did *Ran* ever think of himself purely in terms of functionality? I needed to give this some thought, when time presented.

Ran said, "It's not what *I* do. And it's not what Cormallon does. I don't speak for the rest of the world." Or give a damn about it, either, said his voice. "To target your son would be discourteous and stupid both. There are far more subtle ways of killing people than a long run off the side of a boat. This whole action has the stamp of the amateur on it, and amateur sorcerers are fools of the worst stripe."

That all came from the heart. Jusik listened in silence. I said, "It's true, noble sir. I handle the bookings for my husband; if he were on any assignment, I would know about it."

Jusik glanced at me. Come on, I thought, look at me: A barbarian. An idiot child. Wouldn't know how to lie. Barely can get my shoes on—

He let out his breath. "Possibly," he said.

Ran said, "Sir, believe me, the House of Cormallon would never get involved in such an obvious project. It's only a matter of time before the sorcerer's run to ground—"

"Is it?" cut in Jusik.

"How not? The sorcerer was either on the boat itself, or his spell was grounded on some person or thing on board.

There's only a finite set of possibilities, and I assume Porath will spare no effort in following each one up."

Jusik said, slowly, "I've heard that the employment of magic leaves an 'echo' that can be traced. I suppose the first step would be to hire a sorcerer of our own to do the trace. . . . "

Ran was shaking his head. "There are reasons why that probably won't work—"

"Don't tell me them." Jusik put up his hand. "I see that I need an expert for this. Would you be willing to take it up?"

Ran's eyes widened. "Sir, just a minute ago you suggested—" He stopped, glanced around the room as though the proper phrases might be somewhere under one of the dirty dishes, then started again. "Noble sir, you've just had a shock. It's not for me to suggest a course of action for your House. I entered your property on a social basis; I would prefer to keep it that way."

"I'll be very busy for the next few days," said Jusik, straightening his robe as he spoke. He sat up straighter, seeming to put on the House of Porath again with every gesture. "It would be a great favor to me personally, if you would take up this task for us."

"With all respect—"

"And it would give us an opportunity to talk over this marriage idea."

Another silence while we assimilated this.

Jusik added, "Although it would be a favor, I don't mean to suggest there would be no fee involved—"

Ran shook his head—not in negation, more as though he'd been hit by a few too many sandbags. "I'm sure your fee would be . . . would you mind if I discussed this with my wife?"

"Not at all! I have to leave in any case." He rose to his feet with that born Ivoran grace I'll never match if I live to be two hundred. "There's no need for any delay, if the proposal finds your favor. You would have the run of my house, my grounds, the boat. Simply send a message, and I'll notify everyone to give you full cooperation." He smiled at us both and bowed. Then he turned to Ran and added, "I would prefer a swift solution."

"I don't doubt it." Ran accompanied him to the door.

He was back a few seconds later. "Well?" he asked.

I said,"Ran, I've been on Ivory for several years now, and I've sat in on any number of unusual conversations. But I have to say that this was the weirdest."

He smiled, not a happy smile. "He's still more than half convinced I'm guilty. That's why he wants to hire me. So I can let my principals know that he's looking for a meeting. Or if the price is right, so I can tell him my principals' names."

"He didn't say that."

"Yes, he did."

I found myself staring at the dirty dishes. "So you'll have to turn him down."

"That would be an admission of guilt, too. Protecting my client's identity, the first duty of a good sorcerer."

"Well, you can't take him up on it, not if you don't have a client to hand over."

"And then there's Kylla and the marriage."

I sighed. "I thought this was going to be a simple social problem."

He stooped and picked up the plates. "Theodora, why do people always think I'm guilty of something? Is it my face?"

"Has this been happening all your life, or only since you met me?"

"Good point." He balanced my cup atop the pile. "I'm glad you're finally starting to take some responsibility for this constant disruption of my life."

"Huh! If we're going to start talking about disrupting people's lives—"

"I didn't force you to come back to Ivory, that was your fate."

Yeah, fate operating under a Cormallon pseudonym. I followed him into the pantry. "So what are we going to do? Want to talk to Kylla before we get any deeper in this? We'll wake her if we call now."

"Kanz, no. Kylla would grab me by the throat and tell me to do anything it takes, *now*, to get Jusik in our debt."

"You want me to run the cards? I don't know how helpful they'll be in a situation like this. I mean, they're your cards, they don't care about Kylla or Kade. I can do a regular business configuration . . . although, technically, you haven't accepted this as a business offer."

Ran stopped short. "A *business* offer. Why was Jusik so quick to assume Kade was killed for business reasons? It's the normal assumption for most of our clients, but the Six Families practice murder as an art form. Why shouldn't Kade have been the loser in one of their damned games?"

"That's easy." I took the dishes from him and set them down. "Kade was killed by a sorcerer. You were the only known sorcerer on board, and you're not a gameplayer, you're a businessman."

"*We* can't assume that, though. There may very well have been an amateur sorcerer on board." He leaned on the side-board unhappily. "This is a mess, sweetheart. Assassinations among the aristocracy are none of our business."

"So turn him down." I smiled, knowing he wouldn't.

Another sigh. "And you know what else," he said. "Now we have Stereth Tar'krim to worry about."

At that point I wasn't really worried about Stereth, because I trusted that as an old friend he would find some way of warning us off the case if he were involved. I wasn't even worried about Kylla and Lysander's marriage, because somehow in the end Kylla always gets things the way she wants them in life. Although I hated to see her unhappy meanwhile.

I was worried about an entirely different subject. That night in bed, I said to Ran, "I want to talk to you about us."

He shifted uncomfortably. Ran does not like to talk about important topics; talk implies uncertainty, and as Cormallon heir he seems to feel the path of his life should not admit uncertainty in any area. He's known since childhood what his duty was and his life should be, so why talk?

I said, "About children."

He looked unhappy. "You don't talk about children, they're something that happens."

"They're something that doesn't happen, too. There's good reason to think that Ivorans might be different genetically from the rest of standard society. Maybe even a different species. I've looked and looked, but I can't find any hard evidence anywhere—maybe somebody knows, somewhere in the Tellys medical complex, but they're not telling if they do—"

"You went to the Tellys medical complex?"

"Just for research. On the Net."

"Oh."

"Listen to me. There's always a chance that you and I won't be able to have children. Or if I do get pregnant we have no idea what'll happen. On the other hand, if you went to the Selian Clinic, we could get a good genetic scenario, with percentage probabilities—"

"No."

"They need both parents to run a scenario."

"What do you mean, both? Have you been?"

"Why would I go without you? Anyway, I've been examined plenty of times back on Athena, so nobody's getting any novel data from me."

He was silent. I got tired of listening to the dark, so I said, "Ran?"

He said, "Look. I will not turn over any informational property of Cormallon, including my body, for study."

"Come on, Ran, we're talking about an outworlder medical clinic. It's not a rival House."

He sat up, throwing back the light summer coverlet. He switched on the light. There was no anger in his face, but I had the feeling he was upset. "Times are changing. With every generation it gets worse. We only reestablished contact with standard society a hundred years ago, did you know that?" He didn't wait for an answer. "It's not going to end now. Every time a new piece of technology is imported, we change a little more. Someday our rivals will *be* on Tellys and Pyrene, not down the road and over the hill. That's what our grandson will have to worry about; I'd be a fool to make it harder for him."

"Well." I stared at him. "I never thought to hear this from you."

He smiled wryly. "Because I spend all my time focused on whatever the current sorcery assignment is? Because I only seem to worry about this fiscal year?"

"Yes."

The smile was painful. "I'm the First; it's my job to consider the future of the House. Which will not be enhanced by handing goodies to potential enemies."

I didn't try to argue that; to an Ivoran, anyone not in his family is a potential enemy. I said, "Even if the Tellys doctors could isolate a gene in your body for sorcery—if it exists, and if they care enough to try, which I doubt—what good would it do them without the genes themselves, without any practical means of expressing them?"

"Understanding something is the first step to controlling it."

"Without the rest of the steps, the first one doesn't count for much."

"I'm not going." He switched off the light.

I waited till he settled back, then said, "If I can't get pregnant, this hypothetical grandson will never exist. Have you thought about that?"

Silence. My eyes readjusted to the dark. I looked around the small bedroom, at the dressertop with its vials and bottles and containers, at the chest, at the stool in the corner. I gave him plenty of time, then I said, "If I can't get pregnant, will the Cormallon council pressure you to marry somebody else? Take a second wife, the way Lysander's being pressured?"

He said, "I would resist that most strenuously."

He sounded like a politician holding the line against taxes. And we all know how long that lasts: I said, "You should run for one of the democratic offices." Then I slapped my pillow a couple of times to plump it up, and settled down to go to sleep.

Chapter 6

I entered the Porath house again with mixed feelings. We were intruding on a private grief, yet we'd been invited. Add to that the fact that I didn't really know what we were going to do. The role of a sorcerer is generally to *cause* trouble, not to work out how the trouble came about. When Ran needed investigating done, he generally paid people to do it for him . . . but then, the investigating was usually nonsorcerous in nature. And strictly business.

I'd run the cards, to be on the safe side, as with any client assignment; they'd suggested a good chance of success and no great danger to Ran, so I'd given my stamp of approval. I hoped I wouldn't regret it.

I touched Ran's arm as we passed the lacquered pillars of the central porch. He looked at me.

"I won't be able to stay long," I said, tapping my nose. Cats.

"Twenty minutes. We'll talk to Grandmother Porath if we can, and then Coalis."

I nodded. The lizard, at least, was gone from the immediate vicinity. Maybe there was a shed or something on the property where he was kept. On the other hand, this could mean we'd come upon a heavy reptilian shape dragging itself toward us in any dark corridor.

The doors around the porch had been hung with bolts of silver cloth, and silver paper lanterns dangled from the roof. A smell of incense came from a doorway at the right wing of the house. Kade's body would be laid out there before it was burnt.

I said, "If this were Athena, someone would have to examine the corpse."

Ran nodded. "We will."

"What do you mean, we will? We're not doctors."

"What good would a doctor be?" He used the Standard word, as I had. "We know the physical cause of death. Drowning. And if there are any traces of sorcery to be found, a doctor would hardly be helpful."

"Look, I really don't think I'm up to—"

The house steward met us at the door, and we all bowed. He was a tall, gray-haired man on the verge of retirement, as stewards often seem to be—it must be a job you work up to—and he said, "The orders of the House are to lend you every assistance." He had a kind, rather quiet voice; his whole style was that of one whom it would be difficult to shock. "I hope you'll forgive my not meeting you at the gate, but things have been quite turned around today."

"Of course," said Ran. "One of the reasons I came was to offer the sympathy of my House."

"It is much appreciated. Please come in. The guard at the gate said you'd inquired whether Coalis was at home?"

"Yes," said Ran, as we exchanged looks. Neither of us had suspected the gatehouse had a Net terminal, or even that the Poraths were on the Net; they looked dirt-poor, and the subscription fees were stiff. But there was no other way our question could have reached the steward so quickly. "We'd like to speak with him, if we may. Although we'd prefer to speak to his grandmother first."

The steward led us in through the main hall, passing the arch that opened into the kitchen. "I'm afraid Grandmother's asleep at the moment, gracious sir. Actually, I wouldn't expect to see her till tomorrow at the earliest. She was, well, given medication. She hasn't taken this well."

"I see." Ran cleared his throat. "In that case, I suppose we could see Co—"

"Sir Cormallon!" The tall woman who'd shadowed Eliana Porath through the garden party and onto the canal boat strode down the flight of stairs at the corridor's end. "Your pardon—you *are* Ran Cormallon, the sorcerer?"

Ran admitted that he was. She bowed. "Leel Canarol, defensive chaperone to Eliana Porath. My lady asked me to come down and see if it was you who were our visitors. She'd like to speak with you, if you don't mind." She wore black provincial trousers, worked in silver thread, and had a quilted silk vest above them that was also silver: half-mourning clothes, out of respect to the Poraths. I noted there was still a pistol-sized bulge beneath the vest, even here in the family compound.

The steward turned to us, awaiting our reply. Well, nothing had gone as planned so far; we might as well see what Eliana wanted. I conveyed this to Ran with a shrug, and he spoke to Leel Canarol. "We are, of course, honored by the summons. We'll follow you."

As she led us upstairs, she said, "I'm afraid Grandmother won't be able to see you today in any case." As in the couple of other great houses I'd visited (and married into) I saw that even the staff called the old lady "Grandmother." I'd bet they called Jusik "Lord Porath," though.

"Yes, the steward told us." Ran did not confirm that we were here to see her, or specify any other names. I smiled to myself. If Leel Canerol—or Eliana Porath—wanted to find out anything about what we were doing here, they would have a hard time of it. Ran gripped information like a miser.

Past a hanging of fringed purple, Eliana's room was laid out in the morning sun. It faced the garden; the branches of the coyu tree near the porch brushed her window. The room was white and yellow, clean and old. An alcove for her nurse's bed, a low sleeping platform in the center for herself, with a place for her defensive chaperone built into the foot. (One room, three people; odds were that at least one of them snored. I was glad I wasn't a Six-Families girl.) The sleeping platform was draped in a thick bolt of soft gold cloth, with the mattress and a small lamp atop it.

Some printed books near the window, no doubt with topics appropriate for young ladies. Flowers near the alcove. Two wardrobes. And this was it; this was, pretty much, Eliana's life. A city girl of good family, particularly without money, would not get out very much. The necessary supervision would be too expensive, even given the limited number of places she would be allowed to go.

It occurred to me suddenly that she might well be looking forward to a marriage with anybody, to let her into the ranks of married women and their extra freedoms.

Poor kid. She stood up from the bench by the window and waited, like a well-trained child, for our greeting. She wore plain house robes of light green, no silver anywhere.

Her black hair was pulled back through a velvet band, and hung to her waist.

"Honored by this meeting," said Ran. "Please accept the sympathy of our House."

She nodded. "I hope you'll overlook my clothes. They only just realized that I have no mourning dress." Her voice, high and clear, reported it as a fact, not an assignment of blame. "Auntie Jace, do you think you could get us some tah?"

The temperamental Auntie Jace, I now saw, had been sitting mouselike in the corner; now she jumped up and scurried for the door.

I said quickly, "That won't be necessary. We can't stay long." Besides the cat factor, we were here on business. I didn't want to open up any hospitality debts with Eliana. Besides, I'd gotten as nervous as a born Ivoran about eating untested food—we'd done all right here yesterday, but then yesterday Kade had been alive, and Ran hadn't been a suspect in his death.

Ran said, "I hope you'll forgive our haste. The lady Theodora and I are pressed for time today."

She bit her lip. Then she sat again, smoothing the green robes. "Please sit down," she said, so we seated ourselves on the edge of the sleeping platform. She cleared her throat, then started again. "This is very difficult. I suppose I should just— They tell me you've agreed to investigate my brother's death. Is that true?"

It's always interesting to watch Ran field other people's questions. He said, "If that's what you've been told, I won't deny it."

"Because, you see, if it is true, I have to speak with you."

Ran waited.

Finally she said, "I'm sorry at how self-centered this sounds. But don't you see how this will affect me? A prolonged inquiry, turning over all the rocks in the family garden, just when I'm—well, practically engaged? And you're his brother-in-law! He'll hear all kinds of things!"

"Will he?" asked Ran coolly.

"Every family has its quirks, gracious sir, and I'd prefer that those of mine be left decently at rest."

"Is the lady telling me she believes I'll pass any interesting gossip I may hear along the way to Lysander Shikron?"

"Won't you?"

I would have smiled if I could have gotten away with it without being rude. If she thought Ran would commit himself either way, she'd have a long wait. In the pause that followed, she turned to me. "Gracious lady, I appeal to you. Speak to your husband for me, I have no one to take my part. Don't I have a right to a good marriage?"

Kid, if I can't get him to cooperate on more important issues, I don't think you're going to get very far. I tried to think of some temporizing remark, but Ran spared me.

"Why 'prolonged'?" he said.

"I beg your pardon?" said Eliana.

"You said 'a prolonged inquiry.' Why 'prolonged'?"

"Well, obviously, the scope would have to be pretty wide—I don't see what this has to do—"

"Why would it have to be wide?"

"There's the gameplayers, of course, and Kade's business associates, and the gods only know—"

"Kade was a player?" She and Ran were referring to the game of controlled murder, popular among the Six Families. There were complicated rules that governed it, or so I gathered, anyway; as long as I stayed out of their way, I really didn't care what they did among themselves. I should add that when I say it was popular, I don't mean they all played it. It was really only a small minority, but that makes it a lot more popular than it is in any other population, true?

She sighed. "Father didn't want him playing. He's first son, and it's not like our House has branches to spare. He said that he'd stopped, but I know he didn't."

"I see. You mentioned business associates, too."

So she had. I'd lost track of that in the tangle of other possibilities.

"Yes." That seemed to be the end of the topic as far as Eliana was concerned.

Ran said, "I was unaware that the House of Porath was involved in any form of business."

She said, with a trace of anger, "If you'd let me marry into Shikron, we'd be involved in business enough."

"But Kade was involved already."

We waited. Leel Canerol lounged in false relaxation at the other end of the sleeping platform, her short boots resting on a stool. Auntie Jace made an exasperated sound, got up, and made a show of going to the window ledge to pick up a bowl of sewing materials.

Eliana finally spoke. "It was a personal matter for him. None of the rest of the House had anything to do with it."

Leel Canerol said, "Eliana, I wouldn't advise—"

"Oh, shush, Lely. He's going to find out anyway, isn't he?"

The more sensible of her two chaperones shrugged.

Eliana said, "Kade started a moneylending association."

This is a respectable enough activity on Ivory, though perhaps a bit declassé for one of the Six Families. Ran said, ". . . Yes?"

She seemed surprised. "That's it."

Ran and I looked at each other. I said, "Where did he get the money? Was he partners with one of the marketplace banks?" I knew a little bit about the less official banking methods in the capital, due to some money troubles I'd gotten into earlier in my life.

"Oh, no, he borrowed the initial capital on the strength of his name."

"He borrowed it," said Ran slowly. "For this to turn a profit, he'd have to lend it out at a rather high rate of interest."

Leel Canerol chuckled. "He certainly did." Eliana glared at her.

Well, well. If I understood correctly, the first son and heir to Porath had been carving out a reputation as a loanshark.

"Sorry I missed knowing him," I said softly.

Eliana looked up. "Don't tell Father. Whatever you do."

Ran stood. "We'll do what we can," he said, keeping it vague. "I'm afraid we'll have to move on, now—"

"But Lysander? Are you going to tell him about this?"

"At the moment," he said, "I consider the marriage a separate issue from the matter of your brother."

She smiled. We left her to her keepers, both aware that no promises had been made.

Coalis was a very different sort of fish. We found him lying on his stomach in the tiny courtyard attached to the west wing, reading a book of poetry. He was stretched on a patch of very carefully cultivated lawn grass of soft yellow-green, facing a miniature fountain. He sat up when we came.

"Room for three," he said, speaking of the patch of grass. "Hello, Theodora. My greetings, sir Cormallon."

He wore an undertunic of silver and a silver outerrobe. Death of his hopes and dreams, possibly. "Hello, Coalis," I said in the same direct way, not waiting for Ran to speak. "My husband offers the sympathy of our House."

Coalis smiled lazily, pleased in a gentle fashion with the way we'd just run over tradition. Na' telleths were often amused by that sort of thing. "It's appreciated. I heard you were coming, you know. Heard Eliana cornered you when you got in."

"She did," said Ran. "She seemed concerned about your family's reputation."

"Well, she probably has her reasons."

"What are you reading?" I asked.

He held up the book. "Kesey's *Erotic Poems*."

"Really, I was flipping through his general collection just yesterday." Kesey had been dead about six hundred years, but his work enjoyed a certain vogue among classicists. The edition I had was a translation to modern Ivoran, but Coalis' looked like the real thing. "What do you think of them?"

He pursed his lips thoughtfully. Finally he said, "I suppose I'm not the best person to ask." He put down the volume. "Perhaps I should have gotten the illustrated version." He looked toward Ran, then back to me. "You have questions for me," he said.

"We do," agreed Ran.

I said, "Your father thinks—or thought—that we might have had something to do with Kade's death."

Ran gave me one of his unreadable looks, but it's not as though everyone else wouldn't have thought of it.

Coalis lifted a fistful of grass. "Well, he would, wouldn't he?"

"We didn't."

"And you'd like to know where else the blame might be spread?"

Ran said, "Briefly put—yes."

"Well, it's nothing to me one way or the other. I have

to deal with the fact he's no longer here; how he got that way is irrelevant."

"Not to us," said Ran.

I said, "Eliana told us he was a gameplayer."

"She said that? How odd."

"He wasn't a gameplayer?"

"When he was fourteen, fifteen. I was that way myself at that age," added Coalis, from the height of his sixteen years. "He swore off when he reached majority, and if he ever dabbled, I never heard of it."

"She also said that he lent money at high rates of interest." I could see that Ran disapproved of my method of questioning, but he kept quiet.

"Well, now, *that* I'd heard of. I suppose I'll have to take over the business for a while, or sell it to somebody—the House could use the money, and somebody's got to bring it in now that the marriage thing is drying up. —Don't tell Father, though."

Ran frowned. "Kade brought you into the business? I wouldn't think it would hold much appeal for a na' telleth."

"Oh, I didn't learn about it from Kade."

"Then who?"

"The Provincial Minister," said Coalis. "Stereth Tar'krim."

Tripping over Stereth's name always throws me—and, I suspect, Ran—a little off balance. Particularly at a time like this, when the connection seemed so remote. Ran sat back slightly, looking as though a small, impossible-to-swat insect was buzzing in his ears. He said, "Stereth Tar'krim discussed your brother's business with you?"

"Yes, he's a friend of mine. We met at a na' telleth retreat day."

Now that was a setup if I'd ever heard one. Stereth Tar'krim was about as na' telleth as . . . or was he? I remembered a fateful hour several lifetimes ago, when I'd talked about blood and death and failure with Stereth. "If it happens, it happens," he'd said, though he knew then how likely it was; a na' telleth answer if there ever was one. Stereth . . . rebel, killer, gangster . . . monk? I shook my head as though to clear it.

"Wait," I said. "How did Stereth know about Kade's moneylending?"

"He wanted to be partners with Kade," said Coalis. "He

wanted an alliance with our House, an official alliance—he asked to be listed as an acknowledged House-friend. Father couldn't know about the business, of course, but once he was gone—"

"So he was a friend of Kade's," said Ran, trying to get this straight.

"No, Kade would have nothing to do with it. Why split it, when he could keep it all?"

"And Kade told you this."

"No. Stereth told me. Kade never knew I knew anything about what he was doing."

Ran looked irritated. "You knew Stereth, you knew he wanted to ally with your House, Kade was in the way—and you didn't warn him?"

"Why would I do that?"

Before Ran became more annoyed I said, "For one thing, to avoid the situation you're in now. Heir to Porath, good-bye to the monastery."

"Oh! Kade's death. Oh, I'm sure Stereth had nothing to do with that."

After a moment of blankness, Ran and I mutually decided to leave that statement where it lay. I said, "I don't suppose you'd know where we could get a list of Kade's vict—clients?"

"I'm sorry. I'm sure he had a list somewhere, but I've no idea where it is."

Ran let out a breath and rose to his feet, extending a hand to me. "We won't interrupt you any further, then." Clearly we were going to postpone a discussion of the hopelessness of this entire situation till we were out of earshot of the family.

Coalis didn't bother to get up. He dipped his head to acknowledge our bows and smiled politely. As we left the courtyard I saw he'd opened the book again. His feet were propped on the rim of the fountain.

We made our way through the hall that led to the garden. None too soon, I'd been digging out my handkerchief rather frequently there toward the end of the conversation. I gave a good blow, tucked the white linen square into the sleeve of my robe where I could get at it again quickly, and said, "I don't like all this talk of Stereth."

"Can you believe he'd get into loansharking in the capital, now that he's a minister of the empire?"

"All too willingly. Ministers need money like everybody else."

"But he must have negotiated a big payoff from the Emperor when he quit being an outlaw."

I shrugged. "I don't know how big. And who knows what he might want the money for? Maybe he has other projects in mind."

"Great bumbling gods." We reached the main door. It would be polite to wait for the steward to let us out; but I wanted to get into the open air. "Do you see a pattern of repetition here? With Stereth, I mean?"

"I'm not sure. What do you mean?" I reminded myself not to rub my eyes or they'd become infected.

"Remember our summer with his outlaw crew? He wanted to combine forces with the Deathwell bands, but Dramonta Sol opposed it. Tarniss Cord was willing."

I nodded. "And suddenly Dramonta Sol was dead and Tarniss Cord was in charge of all the Deathwell outlaws. I know. It's not a day I'm likely to forget. But what are we supposed to do now? We don't know he's behind Kade's murder, but what if he is? I mean, he *is* sort of a friend of ours."

Ran was silent, the way he'd been with Eliana, neither confirming nor denying. I started to push against the heavy wooden door.

"Besides," I went on, "even if he weren't, I don't think I'd like to make an enemy of him."

Ran looked at me. I said, "Come on, you know it's true. If it comes down to alienating the Poraths or alienating Stereth Tar'krim—"

"Somebody mention my name?"

Stereth stood in the doorway, smiling in the midday sun.

"It's good to be remembered," he said. "I hope you were saying nice things."

Ran took a step backward that he probably wasn't even aware of, leaving me to say, "Hello, Stereth."

"Hello, Tymon." He called me by my old road name, and now that there was nobody to see, he bent and kissed me on the cheek. Then he glanced past me. "Ran. It was good to see you both yesterday." He reached behind to close the door, but I put a hand on his arm.

"Don't, please. I'd rather get some fresh air. I'm allergic to this place." I used the Ivoran word "aversion."

"Tymon, really? All the silver crepe getting you down?" His voice was not without sympathy. He was scary that way sometimes.

"Cats. I get stuffed up."

"My poor barbarian." He opened the heavy door easily, with one arm. He doesn't look that strong until you get to know him. Sunlight streamed in, with the musty smell of old wood from the porch and a faint perfumey scent from the garden.

I ducked under his arm and stepped outside, taking a long draught of uncontaminated air. Ran followed me out. Then Stereth joined us, shutting the door behind him. "I ought to wait for the house steward anyway. I hate to be rude. We can talk here."

Ran's feelings toward Stereth I can only describe as mixed, but certainly he'd always regarded Stereth's "talks" with unadulterated suspicion. He said quietly, "I suppose you're another one who wants to question us about the investigation."

"What investigation? I came to pay a condolence call."

We looked at him.

He said, "There has been a death, you know."

"Yes." Ran took a deep breath. "Jusik Porath asked us to look into it." Everyone did seem to know that fact anyway.

"Oh? Well, best of luck to you." His tone was uninterested. "Actually, I was wondering if I might speak to Tymon here alone."

There's nobody like Stereth for surprising the hell out of you. I had no idea what to say to that, and left it to Ran. He groped for a response. "I really don't see what—"

"Oh, come on, Sokol, humor me and wait under that coyu tree there. We all know she'll just stroll over to you shortly and repeat everything I've said."

Back in control, Ran said coolly, "Then why ask me to leave?"

"Because I'll feel less inhibited in my conversation. Now, please? For an old companion-of-the-road?"

The trouble with Stereth is that he's like a force of nature. He can say "please" all he wants, but you still have the feeling that if you disagree with him on something like this, a giant hand will reach out of heaven and move you over to the coyu tree anyway.

Still, he did say "please." And asked as a friend. Ran sighed and walked down the path to the tree. When he reached it, he turned and raised his hands as though to say, Well? What more do you want?

Stereth watched him with a look of affectionate familiarity. "He's not happy. He wasn't very happy in the Northwest Sector, either. I swear, Tymon, sometimes I wonder what you see in him."

"He's happy enough when you're not around, Stereth."

He chuckled. "Because you let him have things his own way, no doubt."

"Well, you would know about needing to have things your own way."

"Touché." Stereth spoke of Ran as one would of a troublesome younger brother. "But what I want to talk to you about is doing me a favor."

"Oh?"

"What a noncommittal sound after all we've been through together. What about 'Yes, Stereth, nothing you want can be too great?' "

"What did you have in mind?"

"Do you remember Keleen Van Gelder?"

I was disoriented for a moment, thinking he meant someone who'd been in the outlaw band, though it wasn't an Ivoran name. "I don't think I know the person."

"She's junior ambassador from Tellys. You saw her at the garden party and again on the boat." I frowned. He said, "A blond woman, handsome, in her forties or fifties. A bit taller than the average barbarian. She said she tried to speak to you but couldn't get your attention in the press of the crowd."

I flashed back to the woman with the blonde braid who'd stopped her conversation and stared at me. "Yes, I think I remember. I didn't know she was the Tellys ambassador."

"She wants to talk to you."

Another surprise. "Whatever for?"

"I have no idea. But I'm trying to make some Tellysian friends and I told her I'd get you to visit her."

Couldn't he tell her he'd *ask* me to visit her? Not and be Stereth, he couldn't. "Why do you want Tellysian friends?"

"I'm a friendly person. What about it, Theodora?"

"And you really don't know what she wants."

"I really don't. I'm just collecting a favor."

I considered it. An idea occurred. I said, "Listen here, companion-of-the-road. It's not customary to exchange favors within the same family, because it's assumed that all family members are working toward the same goals anyway."

"We're not in the same family."

"I'm not talking about you and me. I'll go see the junior ambassador—"

"Thank you."

"You'll owe me a favor. Hold onto it. Should you ever, in the future, be in a position where *Ran* owes you a favor, I want you to ask him to go visit the medical clinic of his wife's choosing, and take what tests she decrees."

For once I'd thrown Stereth off-stride. He repeated, "Medical clinic." Then he said, "Forgive my pointing this out, but as his wife you seem in a unique position to make this request yourself."

"I'll forgive you," I said. "Now do we have a deal?"

"We do." We clasped hands. Ran, down at the coyu tree, dug one foot in the ground impatiently.

I said, "I'll have to tell him about Van Gelder."

"I thought you would. I only wanted you alone because you'd be more likely to agree."

"No mention of our deal, though," I said warningly.

"No, I didn't think so."

I waved to Ran from the porch and he walked up the path, looking far from pleased.

Chapter 7

When the house steward had led Stereth away, Ran simply said, "If you've taken in enough lungfuls, we'd better get to the west wing."

I'd been so expecting him to launch into a cross-examination that it left me at a momentary loss, as no doubt he'd intended. Besides— "You mean the body? Now?"

"No better time. He'll be burnt by tomorrow."

Ugh. I followed him over the path to the west porch and up the step. The aroma of bitter incense was strong here, to drive away the evil spirits. (If you've never seen Ivoran death customs, I should mention that nobody on the entire planet takes these evil spirits seriously. Well, not entirely, anyway. Nobody omits the incense either. I suppose if you offered a bereaved family member a thousand tabals to dump the incense, they'd take the cash. But I don't think they'd be entirely comfortable about it.)

Silver streamers hung over the doorway. Having already been admitted to the house proper, there was no reason we couldn't step right in, but I hesitated. "Will there be people in there?" I asked.

"Possibly. Beloved family members are supposed to keep watch over the body."

And Coalis was reading a book, Eliana was working through her options, and Grandmother was sedated. "Maybe Jusik will be in there. He might not be thrilled at our monkeying around with the corpse. Especially since he's not sure you didn't kill him, anyway."

"Jusik will be too busy at a time like this," said Ran, and he pushed aside the streamers and opened the door.

The room was empty. I hoped for his sake that Kade's popularity in death didn't match that of life but I was beginning to get the impression that it did. Except for Grandmother, of course, but they'd probably only wake her up for the funeral ceremony.

There was no coffin. Instead there was a flat board, like a wooden stretcher, set atop a heavy table. It being Kade Porath, first son of his House, the wood was a dark, carved mahogany, and the shallow silver incense bowls set on the floor at each of the four corners had the look of heirlooms. Kade's body was laid out on the board, wearing a suit of robes in gray, burgundy, and snow white. His head rested on a white satin pillow. Appearances had been maintained, I saw; somebody had been in to touch up his face with cosmetics and brush his hair. There is no embalming on Ivory, except for the occasional emperor. They consider it a repulsive custom, and about what one could expect of barbarians; the one or two people I'd asked about it had made disgusted faces, looked away, and changed the subject.

So much the better for us, anyway; aside from a little rouge and face powder, Kade was much the way he'd been when they fished him out of the canal. Ran went over at once and lifted the body's head, touching his thumbs to the base of Kade's chin. I found that I'd backed up as far as the ceremonial candlesticks lined against the wall.

"Come here, Theodora, give me a hand with this."

"Right." I walked over to the table, working for some normalcy in my stride. *Theodora of Pyrene, I had no idea you were so squeamish.*

—What did you expect? How many dead people have I seen? And I never had to touch any of them.

—You're seriously disappointing me. This is disgraceful. You're just not living up to my image of you.

—Time you found out the truth, then.

I get schizoid sometimes in moments of stress. Bear with it, you'll probably see it happen again.

I ignored the sense of repulsion and put my hands where Ran indicated, turning Kade's head to one side while Ran rubbed Kade's earlobe between his fingers, as though testing a lettuce leaf.

"The doorways of the senses," said Ran softly. "This is where traces of tampering can usually be found."

I grunted. Something about the situation made conversation difficult for me. And what did he mean by "usually?" Were there forensic sorcerers on this planet who made a career of this sort of thing? There are definitely gaps in my education, but I'm never aware of what they are till I trip over them.

He ran his little finger over Kade's lips. The finger came away red.

I said, "Does that mean anything?"

"Lip rouge," he said.

He pulled the corners of Kade's eyes back and peered into each one.

"So," he said, "What did Stereth want?"

"What?"

"What did the Minister for Provincial Affairs want with you, tymon?"

"Oh. He wanted me to meet somebody. Keleen Van Gelder, the junior ambassador from Tellys."

Ran's glance flicked to my face, then returned to the corpse at hand. "Let the head down, sweetheart. Now pull up the sleeve of the outerrobe. Why does he want you to see the ambassador?"

"I'm not sure. He wants the Tellysians to like him, and Van Gelder asked to meet me. He said he'd arrange it as a courtesy."

"No, hold it all the way back. I want to see the complete arm. What about Van Gelder? Why does he want to meet you?"

"She. Keleen's a female name. And Stereth says he doesn't know."

The glance flicked upward again. "Do you believe him?"

I shrugged. "Who knows? He sounds sincere. And I can't see any harm in a simple meeting."

"You mean you already agreed?"

"Well, yes."

Ran sighed. "I knew he wanted me to stand under that tree for some reason."

I was relieved. Ran thought he'd found the secret at the heart of the conversation, which meant he wouldn't keep pressing.

He said, "Was that the whole matter?"

"Pretty much."

"Pretty much?"

"Yes, that was whole matter. You get a little touchy around Stereth, you know."

"Sorry." He held Kade's right hand with one hand of his own, and pulled Kade's thumb with the other. I know a tinaje massage-healing type move that's exactly the same, but Kade was in no shape to appreciate it. I shifted my grip on the corpse, let a handkerchief drop out of my sleeve, caught it with the same hand, blew my nose, returned the handkerchief, and grabbed Kade again.

I said, "Are we going to have to cut him open?"

"Possibly. A little bit. We may need to take some samples."

Suddenly he threw down the hand. "Ow!"

"What, what's the matter?"

"Kanz!" He reached out slowly toward the hand, and very tentatively touched the massive ring on Kade's third finger. "Yow!" He drew back again as though he'd taken an electric shock. He stepped backward from the corpse and met my eyes. "It's the ring."

"What about the ring?"

"It's cursed."

I blinked. That was interesting. I'd traveled up and down the coast for weeks once carrying a cursed deck of cards and I'd never gotten any electric shocks from it. I reached toward the ring.

"Don't touch it." Suddenly Ran's fingers were circling my wrist.

"Come on, what am I going to do; vanish in a puff of smoke? Go swimming in the fountain outside?"

His face was stubborn. "We make no assumptions till I've had a chance to study it."

He was serious. I put my hand down. Instead I bent over the table and examined the ring visually: A large blue stone set in silver, etched with vine leaves around the setting. There were more designs etched in the band, but I couldn't see them properly because Kade's fingers were in the way. Probably there were characters inside, too; it looked like some kind of family-crest sort of thing. I'd have to pull the ring off to really tell. But apparently that was a no-no.

"If we can't touch it, how do we get it off?"

He said, "Did you bring extra handkerchiefs?"

"In this House of Hell? Of course." I went through

the pouch on my belt, pulled out a clean one and gave it to him.

He grasped the ring with the handkerchief and pulled it off Kade's finger. Then he let the ring's weight settle in the center of the cloth like the contents of a small jewelry bag and tied a knot with the corners. He hefted the small package: "There. Most likely it only affects the one who wears it, but no harm in being careful." He smiled. "This is unexpected good fortune. The curse is still operational; we can trace it back to the sorcerer who placed it. Someone's been careless."

I said, slowly, "*Too* careless?"

He was silent for a moment. "One would think that a murder-curse would be constructed to discharge itself and dissipate, not stay tied to an object like any normal spell. That's how I would do it. But who can say what's 'too careless,' with all the incompetence that's loose in the world?" He added, "When I say that's how I'd do it, I mean of course if I performed the assassination as some public spectacle, which I would never do." Ran's personal curse, his sense of professional pride, required him to point this out any number of times in the course of the investigation.

I realized I was still holding Kade's arm. I laid it down. "Do we still have to cut him up?"

"What? Oh. No, we've got what we need." He slipped the tiny bundle into his pocket. "Let's see if the house steward can identify Kade's ring."

"Ran, for heaven's sake, we can't just leave."

"Why not?" He seemed genuinely puzzled.

I waved toward the table. It looked as though some necrophiliac had been having a go at the body. "The *family*, Ran. Do you want them to walk in on this?"

"Oh." He came over and helped me tidy Kade's robes.

I said, "Damn, you smeared the lip paint when you were touching his face."

"I don't know what I can do about that at this point." He wiped some of the smear with a corner of his sleeve. The lip paint was half on and half off, giving Kade a vampiric look. Appropriate to his profession, perhaps, but nothing his family would appreciate.

"Wait a sec." I opened my pouch, pulled out the tiny

brush and pot Kylla'd given me and started applying rouge to his lips.

"What in the name of all the gods are you doing?"

"I'm being polite, damn it." Kylla'd chosen the shade carefully for my barbarian coloring; it didn't go with Kade, but he'd have to live with it. So to speak. "There." I looked at the tiny pot and brush before tucking them away. "I never want to use these again."

Ran sighed. "Your constant acquisition of new skills amazes me. May we go search out the steward now?"

I glanced over the table, the body, the incense holders, the candlesticks. Everything seemed appropriate. I blew my nose a final time. "Of course."

On being summoned, the steward met us at the front door again, not fazed in the least by our reappearance. Ran untied the knot in his handkerchief and displayed the ring. "Is this familiar to you?"

The steward studied it for a second, then said, "No."

It took us both aback. Ran said, "It was on Kade's body."

"Ah. I was told he'd been found wearing a ring. The servants who took care of the matter said that his fingers were somewhat bloated at the time; we thought it best to leave the ring where it was." He paused an impeccable pause that said *Is there some problem?*

Ran said, "But you've never seen it before."

"Not to my knowledge, gracious sir."

"If this belonged to Kade, would you necessarily know?"

"If he were in the habit of wearing it, I would. I'm also familiar with the contents of his jewelry box upstairs, and this was never in it."

That was a little unsettling. Did the servants at Cormallon know what was in *my* jewelry box?

The steward went on, "I can't answer for whether he might not have kept it elsewhere, or only just bought it." Ran was retying the knot in the handkerchief, and the steward said, "Excuse me, gracious sir, but are you planning to take the ring away with you?"

"Actually, I was."

The steward coughed. "I'm afraid I'll have to ask for a receipt, sir."

"Oh. Of course." And then we all stood around for a

few minutes while paper was obtained and the steward wrote out a description: "One ring, blue cadite, silver setting, etched with vine leaves on the outer band and the words 'Daring and Prudent' on the inner.' "

It was the first I'd heard about words on the inside of the band. They sounded like a motto. A rather contradictory, motto, in fact.

Ran was handed back the handkerchief, and we thanked the steward and left the Poraths'. My allergy-pummeled body was glad to leave, but my mind had more ambiguous feelings. Having told Lord Jusik Porath that we were innocent of any involvement in the death of his son, we'd just wound up our first foray into the investigation by pocketing the main piece of evidence and taking it away with us.

Perhaps it wasn't wise, but at the time I really don't know what else we could have done.

I called ahead to the Tellysian Embassy for an appointment that afternoon. I was fairly curious, actually, perhaps more so than I was about Kade. People get murdered all the time on Ivory, but extraplanetary junior ambassadors had never gone out of their way to look me up before.

I was passed directly from a functionary to Van Gelder. "I'm so glad you called," she said. The visual circuit was open and I could see that she was in fact the woman from the party. A closer view showed her as older looking, but deserving of Stereth's "handsome," with strong, clean-cut features. She wore elegant modified Tellysian clothes, a silky one-piece suit whose pants were tailored a little on the full side, making them resemble an Ivoran robe. "I haven't had lunch yet. Have you? It's been a terrible day and I'm longing to get out of here for a bit. There's a terrace in the Imperial park where they serve some standard dishes; would you be my guest?"

It was a little like being hit by a small cyclone. "I hadn't planned on—"

"Oh, please come; if you're not hungry, you can order one of those sherbet things and a fizz."

Well, it was a good restaurant—I'd eaten there a couple of times with Kylla and Shez. And I was still curious. "All right, but I don't think I can stay very long. Couldn't you give me some idea of what you—"

"Damn! Another call. They haven't stopped all day. I'm really very sorry to be so scatterbrained over the Net. Shall we make it in forty minutes?"

I gave in. "Fine."

"Excellent, I'm looking forward to seeing you. Oh, if you need a lift after, don't worry about it—I have the use of a carriage and driver!" And she signed off.

Well. That hadn't told me a lot. And the Imperial Park was a half hour's walk from where I was, in the full midday heat. It was a good thing I'd brought along a straw hat.

Somehow I always end up carrying things. My hat, my extra handkerchiefs, my money, a deck of cards, a list of Net numbers for vehicle rentals that had been folded so many times it was approaching unreadable, any number of hairpins—I was going to have to get this mop cut pretty soon—a copy of Kesey's *Poems* that I hadn't gotten very far in reading. . . . Fortunately my robes have lots of pockets.

I was a little disappointed, actually; I'd been looking forward to seeing what the inside of the Tellysian embassy was like. The facade was pure, sculpted, classic Ivoran style, but the gods only knew what they'd done indoors. Athenans and Pryenese are minimalists; Ivorans tend to the baroque; I had no idea what Tellysians approved of. Except that their own government limited them technologically in what they could bring on-planet, they might have anything there. Solid gold drinking fountains. Grav lifts with Old Master paintings on the walls. Ask an Ivoran, and he'd tell you they could afford it, with what they squeezed out of other planets for their tech designs. But I wondered. How many things had Ivory, for example, actually bought from Tellys? Not very many that I knew about.

The Imperial Park is cool and green, as cool as you can get in the capital in the summertime, with trees, paths, fountains, statues, artificial wading streams, and a contingent of Imperial Security whose efficiency is matched only by their extraordinary politeness. A set of terraces leads down to the river, and on the final terrace, just above the water, you will find a fairly small restaurant surrounded by a flagstoned area with white tables and chairs. I highly recommend it. The chairs, considered a pointless luxury, have seats more than half a meter off the ground—something an outworlder can appreciate—with intricate backs and arms. An overhang of crisscrossed wood provides a sun shield while creating a dappled effect. Just across the river you can see the striped dome of the First Wife's Palace through the trees.

And the food's not bad, either. I was hot and tired when I got there so I immediately ordered a cherry fizz and snow sherbet. Then I waved the brim of my hat at myself until I'd gotten back into a cheerful mood. Midway between lunch and dinner, the place was empty, so I tucked one foot under my knee on the chair in a most unladylike position and watched the white birds flying among the trees across the way, trying to remember details of a legend I'd heard about how the First Wife's Palace got built. The sherbet was delicious.

"Theodora of Pyrene?"

I squinted up toward a patch of sunlight and eased my foot surreptitiously down to the flagstones. "Yes." The woman from the Net call was there, her long blond braid falling past the shoulders of her sky-blue suit.

"Keleen Van Gelder, junior ambassador from Tellys." She extended a hand, the first hand I'd shaken in a long time. I took it. "This is my colleague, Jack Lykon," she continued. The man beside her was younger, perhaps in his early thirties, brown hair thinning on top and darker brown eyes with a friendly look to them. I shook his hand, too.

"It's a lovely place, isn't it?" she asked, pulling out a chair. Jack Lykon took the third.

"Yes, I've been here before. They've got some Pyrenese beer stocked, but it costs a fortune."

Lykon said, "They do?"—looking interested. "How much is it?"

Van Gelder turned to him with a slight smile, slanting her eyes. "Imagine paying someone to carry the mug to you personally from the south coast, Jack. That's about how much it costs."

He seemed disappointed.

Van Gelder said to me, "I see you've ordered sherbet. I may myself. Where's the waiter?"

I reached over and pushed the bell in the center of the table. The lone waiter, an old fellow who covered about an inch a minute, tottered out. Van Gelder, interestingly, ordered tah with her meal. Lykon settled for beer from the Northwest Sector.

"We're the only ones here," said Lykon, looking around uncomfortably. "I wouldn't have known the place was even open."

It occurred to me suddenly that I might have been uncomfortable once myself, sitting alone on a terrace being served by a thousand-year-old waiter. All those social doubts: Should I be here? Are passersby watching me? What do the restaurant people think? But I'd been hanging around Ran too long. Wherever you were is where you were supposed to be, by definition; Cormallons are never treated below-status, except by the confused; and waiters and cooks can think what they like, as long as they provide the excellent service you are paying them to give. End of story.

Or perhaps it was just that I was getting old.

Van Gelder shrugged. "If we're alone, so much the better."

Enough of comparative social philosophy, too. I said, "The Minister for Provincial Affairs made your invitation intriguing. May I ask how you know him?"

She grinned. "A good diplomat never claims greater acquaintance than a local figure may wish to allow. You'll have to tell me what Minister Tar'krim said about our relationship, before I can confirm or deny."

So, she could be inoffensively discreet, too. I said, "Is it asking too much to inquire about why you wanted to see me?"

"Not at all, Theodora.—I hope I don't offend in calling you Theodora. I know Pyrene custom only provides one name for its people, and I understand that you're Pyrenese."

I looked down at my empty sherbet bowl. "I was born on Pyrene, but at the moment I've actually got joint Athenan/Ivoran citizenship."

"That must make you virtually unique."

"I wouldn't know. I don't have any statistics on the matter."

She seemed to be flipping through an invisible folder. "Pyrene, Athena, Ivory. Out of the four habitable planets in this sector, Tellys is the only one you've never seen. Or have you?"

"Well, it's nothing personal. You know what interstellar travel costs, ambassador, it's not something many private citizens can afford. Other people picked up my tab—well, except for one trip, and I had a little help on that—and I had to go wherever the ticket was stamped. I was on a government scholarship to Athena, you know."

"I'd heard that. I also heard that you paid your own fare from here to Athena a couple of years ago. A remarkable achievement, at your age."

I blinked and said, "I had no idea I was such a topic of conversation in embassy hallways."

She cracked a smile. "Perhaps we don't get out enough," she acknowledged.

Our waiter began his snail-like progress from the pavilion of the restaurant proper. We were speaking Standard, but none of us made any attempt to continue the conversation until he'd deposited his load of three large plates, tah cup, and beer mug, and returned inside. You wouldn't think he could carry a sheet of paper successfully, but he negotiated the load with a flawless execution. This was a man with experience in his field.

"He must have been waiting tables while our ancestors were still working to go multicellular." I'd said it aloud. Lykon broke up. I looked at him, surprised.

"I was just thinking the same thing," he said. Then he went into another fit of chuckles.

Van Gelder raised a perfectly groomed eyebrow and said to me, "Jack gets set off by things sometimes." She took a sip of pink tah. "Anyway, he takes an interest in biological references. But we'll get to that."

Would we? This would be an unusual lunch.

Chapter 8

The junior ambassador from Tellys wiped grease from her fingers. She was talking about sorcery, a subject I have more than a passing interest in. "There've been two Standard papers on Ivoran 'sorcery'—only two, in the hundred years we've been in contact. Both by eccentrics, both paid little attention to by the Athenan University Committee. The latter one was slightly more exhaustive. Written by a kinsman of mine, a Tellysian, named Branusci."

I leaned forward, already interested. Following my first stay on Ivory I'd hunted the Athenan libraries obsessively for any work on Ivoran sorcery, and found a single paper. The second, if it existed, must have been indexed under some other subject.

"It was indexed under 'Stage Magic,' " she said, veering into telepathy. "Not an appropriate category, really, but that was the approach the article took. Branusci studied eight marketplace sorcerers—not perhaps the best pool, to begin with—and decided, in the end, that any of their effects could be duplicated in some 'rational' fashion. If there was no visible and outward evidence—as in a luckspell, where the results could so easily be ascribed to random chance—then what did it prove? If there was visible evidence—say, with a visual illusion—then a holographic projector could do as well. Or any number of other methods, to achieve other effects."

"There are no holographic projectors on Ivory."

"Branusci points out they might have been smuggled in."

"You don't sound impressed with your kinsman."

She shrugged. "If a man can levitate an elephant, saying that you can do the same thing with strings and pulleys is hardly the point, is it?" She put down her tah cup. "The

Athenans like to think of themselves as rationalists, but I suspect they're just afraid of looking silly."

I'd had the same thought myself more than once.

She went on, "Otherwise, why wouldn't they put the same rigorous, thorough study into it that they put into dissecting the dozen variants of a legend?"

"Interesting you should choose that metaphor. My field of study was cross-cultural myths and legends."

She smiled austerely. "What an amazing coincidence."

I laughed.

She leaned forward. "Let's hypothesize for a moment that 'Magic is real.' Or to put it another way, the more respectable sorcerers of Ivory are tapping into something we have not previously had experience with. They've learned rules for using this . . . whatever it is . . . that seem to work for them. Whether they want to call them spells or something more acceptable to standard culture is irrelevant to our purpose, for the moment."

It was nice to hear somebody talking about Ivoran magic in the language I'd grown up in. I don't mean Standard.

She wiped her lips with the green linen napkin our ancient waiter had provided. "Even given the extraordinary lack of interest on this planet in strictly academic matters, there must be theories about magic. Where it comes from, why it can be accessed by some people and not others. . . ." She let her voice trail off.

I said, "I've heard the three most respectable theories and about twenty more oddball ones. But nobody really knows—knows in a good Athenan sense, I mean. Nobody has any evidence." This is the simple truth, and I saw no reason not to share it.

She nodded. "It doesn't surprise me. But one can hardly help zeroing in on some genetic relationship."

I was silent.

"This is speculation, of course. But I understand your present husband accompanied you to Athena a couple of years ago. He's a top-ranked sorcerer here in the capital, they tell me. One can't help wondering if he was able to continue using his abilities away from this planet. You would think that he *would* be able to, if sorcery is more linked with genetics then geography. But the whole subject is so out of the usual ken, I'd hesitate even to guess."

I was becoming uncomfortable. My Athenan past taught me to revere the free sharing of information, and on one level I would have been pleased if a serious inquiry into the messy category of magic had been taken up by the standard community. After all, they might make some breakthrough on the subject, bringing it into a neat line with the laws of the universe as I had once known them, and they might do it before my death. That bothered me, you know. That I'd gotten involved in a subculture based on a force that even the people who used it didn't understand; and that someday, people would figure it all out—too late to tell Theodora.

On the other hand, this was veering close to House secrets. Ran had indeed tried to use sorcery during his foray into culture shock on Athena, and I knew what the results were.

As a Cormallon, I did not feel at liberty to tell anyone.

I said, "Life is complicated, isn't it?"

"More so every year," she agreed. "When I was twelve, I understood the universe thoroughly."

"Me, too."

Jack Lykon spoke up suddenly. I'd nearly forgotten he was there. "Keleen," he said, "tell Theodora who I am."

She touched his hand. "Jack is a very talented genalycist."

"Is he?" I looked at him with new interest.

"He'd be just delighted, intellectually, if he could meet your husband."

"Yes, I'm beginning to understand that." I took a deep breath, knowing I ought to head them off before they made the mistake of offering a fee. "Look, it's nothing against you or Tellys. I know that someday people are going to have Ivoran sorcery down pat, quantified, boxed up in little boxes with ribbons. And good for them. They'll probably call it something other than sorcery when that day comes. But they're going to have to do it without my help." Damn, they looked so understanding. I hate it when people do that. "You seem to know a lot about sorcery, for an outworlder. But I don't know how much you know about the Houses of Ivory. They're all paranoid, all selfish, and their loyalty is only to themselves."

Van Gelder quirked a smile. I said, "I know. I'm making them sound so attractive. They do have one great virtue, though: They won't go out of their way to hurt you if you don't present an obstacle."

Van Gelder's smile had vanished. She said, "Not something that can be said of all human cultures."

I didn't pick up on it at the time, I was too busy going for my point. "What I'm trying to say here is, I'm a Cormallon. Sorcery is a Cormallon specialty, and I can't share information on our House business with anybody. It would be considered as working against our best interests—even if you offered to pay us."

She said, "A minute ago you spoke of the Houses in the third person; now you speak in the first."

"Blame it on my schizoid history. I'm not Pyrenese, and I'm not really Ivoran; all I really know I am, at this moment, is Cormallon. And if the universe takes five centuries to get around to cracking the sorcery game, then that's how long they'll have to wait."

They stared at me, and the pause lengthened. I felt myself getting red. It was probably as close to a patriotic speech as I'd ever been qualified to make. The silence became more awkward, and I groped to fill it. "Look, the bottom line is, my House will never agree to share any secrets with the Tellysian government."

They looked at each other. Van Gelder leaned back in her chair and tapped her silver spoon once against her empty sherbet bowl. She said, "But Theodora, my friend, we do not speak for the Tellysian government."

I hoped my jaw wasn't touching the floor. *"What?"*

Lykon said, "Keleen—"

She rode over him. "No, we speak neither for the Tellys Unity nor the Sealed Kingdom. We speak for a much smaller, more controllable group. Your families here make House allies, don't they? I think we'd like to be regarded in that light."

"We?"

She crossed her arms, still leaning back, and smiled. Lykon looked unhappy. "Tell me, have you heard much about the Tolla?"

I sat up, shocked. "Great gods of scholars."

She nodded. "That's right."

* * *

I'm going to have to stop here and tell you about the Tolla. If you already know about them, you can skip ahead, but I don't want to leave anybody behind.

I think you already know I don't like Selians. What you may not be aware of is that the Selians are a historically recent development, only germinating after the destruction of Gate 53 cut off our sector. Unlike Tolla propagandists, I can't tell you that they were involved in blowing up the gate, because they didn't exist at the time, but I have to admit that that's about the only obnoxious act that can't be laid at their door. As a group, I mean. As individuals they may be perfectly fine. I'm sure someday I'll meet a Selian I can like. . . . The nice ones probably stay home and don't go out in public.

Anyway. About sixty years ago the other worlds started hearing discomforting news events coming out of Tellys. The Sealed Kingdom declared independence around then and somehow got away with it—I don't know the ins and outs of Tellysian politics—and after stewing in their own self-congratulation for a while, started to become more and more militant.

(I know. This is all my own view of the matter. I can't give you somebody else's view, can I?)

Selians seek to perfect the universe until it reaches a state that matches the ideal; at that time the Perfect Kingdom will exist in reality as well as an abstraction. "The Perfect Kingdom Is At Hand" is a prime Selian credo. Understand, this has nothing to do with temples or supreme beings—on the contrary, they feel perfection is attainable with their own hot little hands. Selian houses are spotlessly clean. If Selian children don't match the physical ideal, they are dieted, exercised, and surgically altered, or else constantly humiliated for the rest of their lives.

Their definition of perfection, and their mechanism for attaining it, are based on two things: The worship of Fate (under the leadership of the Selian Central Committee), and a sense of differentiation. Differentiation means in the aggregate sense that the Selians are superior to other people. Fate means that their destiny is to one day have that superiority acknowledged. In the most peaceful way, mind you; their object is not to kill or torture. They only want to help others to understand that their ordained place is in service to the Kingdom. Once this understanding is reached, the universe will start to operate on the level it should be at.

As you may guess, any group this hierarchical is pretty rigid within its own ranks, as well. From what I understand, there are at least twenty separate levels, from the top three classes, who dye their hair silver-white to *differentiate* themselves—it would be a pity if their fellow citizens failed to recognize their natural superiority—down to the dregs at the bottom of the ladder, who are nevertheless a rung above anybody not Selian.

Women are placed just beneath the bottom rank. This is where the Tolla come in.

I must have been about thirteen, still living on Pyrene, when I saw the first news spot out of Tellys. It was a clip from a Unity talk show, with a regular Tellysian host, interviewing a Selian man. He wasn't silver-haired, so he couldn't have even been highly placed in the SK, but he was amused and contemptuous of the non-Selian interviewer. The interviewee was considered news because he'd just been acquitted of killing his wife. He'd been accused of setting her on fire because she was a bad cook. They showed a picture of her remains, a brief interview with the woman's sister—who had very little to say—and then cut back to the husband.

They cut back, and he smiled widely, showing a set of straight white teeth. It was the smile of somebody who has gotten away with something.

Since that first interview I heard the occasional stories of dowry murders, of a rise in female emigration from the Sealed Kingdom to the Tellys Unity—until there was a swift law passed forbidding women to carry identity papers themselves, or to travel when not under the supervision of an authorized male.

I know that none of this is historically new, but that's my point—this is a modern, industrialized, technologically advanced world I'm talking about. One that had seemed relatively sane before the destruction of Gate 53.

The rest of Tellys seems to consider the Kingdom a temporary aberration, and lack the ability or will to do much about it. After all, they were only about fifteen percent of the world population. And they were only preying on their own people. And in case you haven't dealt with any Selians, I ought to point out that they are not crazed lunatics who run around foaming at the mouth. Even for them, wife murderers are not on every corner, and except for the dye job, most of them look pretty normal. They have trades and families like any other society, and some of them do a lot of good. Altruism is built into their philosophical structure—kind of a noblesse oblige attitude; the upper ranks are expected to devote several years to collective good works. That's how the Selian Medical Clinic came to Ivory. It's amazing what a sincere case some of them make for their way of life.

Not that I, personally, like them. But I feel obliged to point this out.

But where slavery exists, you get abolitionists, and where the Selians exist—you get the Tolla.

They appeared one day, leaving a note famous for its brevity on the body of the gentleman interviewed by the talk show. "Shot by the Tolla." No manifesto, no explanations—for murderers, you had to like them. And then there was their choice of label, *Tolla,* "The Wrath of the Goddess." The word came from an old legend, a selection not without historical charm. They were, as much as we could tell from so far away—I was still on Pyrene at the time—a group of hitwomen. Soon they didn't bother to leave even brief notes; everyone knew who they were.

On Pyrene they were considered an interesting footnote, an eccentric example of life away from civilization. On Athena, I found, they were strongly disapproved of as a terrorist group. "One acts to change unjust laws; two wrongs don't make a right; if they weren't ashamed of what they were doing, they'd stand trial openly." Their anonymity seemed rather practical-minded to me, but I did not express this view at the time. Public opinion is a powerful force on Athena.

So now here I was, shocked—and I have to admit, a trifle delighted—to be facing someone who claimed involvement in the Tolla.

The life of a plain sorcerer's apprentice had been getting monotonous. It would be nice to talk to someone who did exciting things.

* * *

I said, glancing at Lykon, "I didn't know they let men in the Tolla."

"What a narrow way of doing things that would be," said Van Gelder. "Not that I said that either of us were in the Tolla. I speak hypothetically."

I was completely fascinated. "Your government doesn't even like the Tolla. They're always trying to capture them. Or is that an act?"

She shook her head. " 'The Tolla are a terrorist organization. We do not condone their actions.' And we're perfectly serious, Theodora—I speak now as a representative of the Tellys Unity. When a government lends itself to acts of terrorism, it loses its moral center."

She seemed to mean it. I said, "Then you're not Tolla yourself?"

"On the other hand, what a private individual may feel impelled to do should not have repercussions beyond his own conscience. One may disobey a law, and nevertheless believe that law to be necessary."

"That's not what they teach on Athena."

Her long, sunburnt fingers tapped her plate. "They can afford to be finicky on Athena. The most that happens to anyone there is getting tossed off a committee."

I'd once heard of a man who'd committed suicide after getting tossed off a committee. However, I suppose that would seem an unjustified response to someone involved in an organization whose purpose was so openly lethal.

I suddenly became aware that the sun was past the striped dome across the river, and that afternoon was practically evening. Two other tables had somehow become occupied, and I hadn't even been aware of it.

"This is fascinating," I said honestly, "but I'm not sure how it affects me or my House."

She hesitated. "From your records, I thought you might lean toward a sympathy with our cause. You're not the usual Athenan scholar. Was I only reading into it what I wanted to believe?"

"No . . . " I said slowly. "If you want the truth, I have mixed feelings about the subject. But I've seen people killed for less reason than the Tolla has. And if you were shooting somebody today, I'd step out of range of fire and go on my way."

Lykon made one of his rare remarks. "That's all we really expected."

I turned to him. "You look too gentle to be in the Tolla."

He smiled. It was a gentle smile. "It evens out," he said. "Keleen looks like a very general, doesn't she?"

I had to admit that she did. Everything about her, from her well-chosen semi-but-not-quite-Ivoran wardrobe to the knowledgeably applied cosmetics, spoke of planning. The few items that seemed to have escaped her control, like the ray of lines around her eyes, only gave weight and character to her looks. It was a good thing, really, that she had a slightly burnt complexion; otherwise one could be put off by her inhumanly precise elegance. Strength was in every bone and angle; but strength in the service of what?

Lykon, on the other hand, with his quiet, good-humored face, might as well have a sign around his neck saying "Trustworthy." If you ran into Jack Lykon while your city was falling, you'd give him your child to hold while you hammered your fists against the seal of the last departing ship. It *seemed* like the sort of face that is well-attached to the soul behind it, but until we knew this for sure I resolved to hang onto my wallet and my skepticism.

He sighed, looking at his empty mug, and said, "Do you think I could get another beer? I hesitate to ring for the waiter. . . ."

"Yes, he might not make it out till autumn." I squeezed the button on my airtight jar of cherry fizz and watched a stream pour into my glass. "If you're just thirsty, this might hold you till you get the real thing." I offered him my glass.

How much did they really understand about Ivory? Would they pass the test? He took the glass and drained it, getting a head of fizz around his mouth. Silly, but endearing, particularly in a balding terrorist. He said, in Ivoran, "My thanks."

Van Gelder seemed quietly amused. Points for their team. If Cormallon did make some kind of arrangement with them, they wouldn't disgrace us.

A sudden breeze blew up from the river, ruffling the table napkins. Here I was, naive, apolitical Theodora of Pyrene, sitting with two enemies of the Tellysian government, and I just didn't feel in any great danger. I suppose the Tolla has to recruit somehow; there must be some way, even if it's not the most reliable, of feeling out when to tell, and when not to tell. And perhaps it wasn't a great leap of faith at that—I wasn't a citizen of the Tellys Unity, I had no stake in what their world did. My very disinterest was a shield. Nor are Ivorans in the habit of mixing in governmental matters at all, if they can avoid them.

However they'd come to their conclusion, it was a correct one. I had no intention of telling any Tellysian officials about them. Even if I had, all the Tellysian officials were at the embassy, and it was more than possible Van Gelder had some system in place there for dealing with civilians who tried to bring embarrassing things to their attention.

It occurred to me that it must be useful for the Tolla, having a junior ambassador in their pocket. Maybe their influence went even further than that; I'd never been to Tellys and had no feel for their pattern of views in general, but it was no secret that the Kingdom was not well-liked there, to say the least. Quite apart from their politics, Unity citizens couldn't help but feel that the Selians had had a lot of nerve, seceding the way they did. There must be a good amount of underground support for the Tolla there—surely there was sympathy for their aims, if not their methods.

If they really were a power at home, allying with the Tolla might not be a bad idea for Cormallon. As long as it was a secret alliance. And a group like the Tolla must be pretty used to the concept of secrets.

She said, "Will you at least take the proposal to your husband? He is the First of his House, is he not?"

"Ambassador Van Gelder, I'm still at sea as to what your proposal *is.*"

"Keleen, please."

"Keleen." Always glad to address a member of a dangerous terrorist group by their first name.

"The Tolla face certain problems currently," she said, in a brisk, businesslike tone. That reference to "our cause" a minute ago was the closest she tended to come to speaking of the group in the first person; it was always third-person, always an official distance. "First, Unity nationals are searched before entering the Kingdom. And in the last planetary year, the Kingdom has begun searching people who are traveling internally from territory to territory.

Even long-range weapons that are already on Kingdom soil need transport, obviously; and then there's the matter of getting recharges to those weapons."

"I see." Nobody had ever spoken to me before on the subject of weapons running. I may have given up my opportunity for a degree on Athena, but living on Ivory is an education in itself.

"It's not like this planet; the officials are very chancy when it comes to bribery. There are always old-fashioned items like knives and clubs that can't really be controlled, but I'm sure you see at once that the proximity required for application makes capture much more likely."

"Oh, definitely. First thing I thought of."

She took me seriously. "Well, it goes without saying. So some people have been looking into the matter of weapons transport in general. The majority have been approaching this from the angle of transport; but it occurred to . . . others . . . that it might be rewarding to approach from the angle of the weapons themselves."

"You just said that knives and clubs . . . "

She smiled faintly. "Living on this world cannot help but give one a more creative attitude as to what constitutes a weapon."

" . . . Oh."

"I understand the tragedy of young Kade Porath has been traced to sorcery."

"Yeah, I'd heard that, too."

"A vivid demonstration of its capabilities, I must admit—"

I sat up straight. "What do you mean, demonstration? *Was* Kade's death some kind of demo for you people? Are you already negotiating with some other House?"

She seemed honestly surprised. "Good lord, no. When we get to the demo stage I'm sure we can find someone less visible than a first son of the nobility. What do you take us for?"

"Honestly, I have no idea what to take you for. You'll have to tell me."

Jack Lykon said, "The Tolla had nothing to do with Kade Porath. It's true. I mean, for god's sake, Theodora—that would be murder."

I let that line lie.

Van Gelder said, "My principals' only wish is to enter into a long and profitable relationship with your House. I understand the penalties for using sorcery in an organized way here—against the government, that sort of thing—can be quite severe. But let me point out, there are no such laws on Tellys. Sorcery is not even recognized there. This would seem to open up a whole new area of expansion for Cormallon, Theodora. Surely it would be your duty to communicate my offer."

"I'll think it over."

"Good plain Ivoran tabals would be placed in your House account—no nasty, suspicious foreign money, I promise. In return, a consultant relationship would be opened, regarding how best to handle the weapons problem I described earlier." She reeled it off as though from a business contract. "No actual sorcerer would have to travel to Tellys to do the executions, not unless it proves absolutely necessary. Some form of weapon that can be used by any knowledgeable person will do the trick nicely."

I raised my hands. "You've made it all very clear, ambassador." Suddenly I'd had enough of murder for the day. I found myself wishing I could lie down and sleep for twenty hours, like Kade's grandmother.

Van Gelder seemed to sense my withdrawal. "I hope I haven't offended in any way, Theodora. I was under the impression that your husband took on assassinations from time to time himself, so it hardly seemed—"

"Yes, I know. All right." I stood up. "I'll consider passing the matter on."

Jack Lykon rose at once and shook my hand. I still couldn't see him as Tolla. It would be easier to imagine him as a country veterinarian, rising to a spot of mild indignation only over the occasional mistreatment of puppies. I said, "I may want something from you, though."

"Me?" He looked surprised.

"I'll let you know," I said. Reflex almost made me bow, but I caught it in time and confined myself to a polite smile in the ambassador's direction.

She said, "I have a carriage at the Lin Entrance."

"Thank you, I'd prefer to walk. I have some thinking to do."

She inclined her head. "A very great pleasure, Theodora, whatever you decide."

Well, that's why she was an ambassador. I left the terrace, made my way to the upper level of the grounds, and took the Walk of Plum Trees down its ruler-straight course to the Kyl Entrance. From there it's about a half hour to our house.

I like to walk in the early evening, when a cool hand finally lays itself on the feverish skin of a capital summer day. Of course, by then any passing breath of air is considered cool, not to mention blessed. The shops next to the Kyl Entrance of the Imperial Park are known for their ridiculous prices; it's fun to look in the windows, guess the tag amount, then peer closer and have the shock of seeing how thoroughly your imagination has underestimated.

So, while playing this innocent game I considered the less innocent ones being proffered by these two Tellysians. What should I do? Probably I ought to disapprove of the Tolla, but the truth was that I didn't. At the same time, I had no wish to get personally involved; by nature I'm neither a martyr nor a soldier, and had my hands full just trying to lead an honorable life where I was. As for Ran—I tried to imagine Ran agreeing to share House secrets with any ally of less than five hundred years, and failed miserably.

This seemed to get us nowhere. At the same time, Jack Lykon was a genalycist, and a genalycist would be a useful person to have in my life this particular year. If only—

I passed a shop with an antique book on display; a gold-encrusted cover, opened with a key, and the words "Stories of the Third Empire" in gold and crimson letters of ancient calligraphy.

I collect stories, you know. At one time I thought it was a vocation, but lately I've come to wonder whether it's a hobby. Whatever the stories of the Third Empire were, I could probably track them down more cheaply elsewhere—

Stories. I'd collected stories from Ran's family, too. Tall stories, legends, anecdotes, recollections—not all of them believable, but all of them interesting, and none, unfortunately, released for public consumption. They were in a notebook back in my room in Cormallon, tucked under a pile of things on a table by the window. I hadn't taken them out in months; hadn't been back at Cormallon in weeks.

Damn, I couldn't remember the details, but hadn't there been one about a similar alliance? One of Ran's legions of aunts had told me, when she was passing through the estate on her way to some kind of appointment in the capital . . . her dressmaker's, that was it. Come on, Theodora, you can remember the dressmaker, what about the plot of the story?

There had been a House of brewers, on the edge of the Northwest Sector, who'd been having some kind of trouble with deliberately contaminated beer—Jack Lykon's choice of beverage must have reminded me. A pair of reps had requested a House alliance with Cormallon to track down the saboteurs, but there was some reason the alliance couldn't go through—something about offending our long-time allies, the Ducorts (though I didn't see why; the Ducorts handle wine and tah, and consider themselves above honest beer). So what had happened?

The First at that time had figured a method of weeding out any contaminated tubs, and tracing back any sorcerous damage to the beer to its source. Nonsorcerers could use the method, but only by a quick education in Cormallon techniques and the use of House materials. I couldn't recall the sorcery involved, but I remembered the political answer: Three brewery employees had been adopted into the House of Cormallon and then loaned back to their birth house to supervise the beermaking.

This was the crux: The adoption gave Cormallon House justice rights over the lives of the brewers. They'd all had spells placed on them that prevented their spilling any House secrets to outsiders. Gag spells, they're called, and they're the kind of thing that can be very dangerous, very complicated; and only done with the person's consent. The brewers accepted it out of self-interest, being well-paid for their cooperation. When the crisis was over, Cormallon released them back to their birth house—with gags intact, and if I know the Cormallons, probably some memory impairment. (The latter was never admitted. Removing memory is easy; what's hard is to be *selective*.)

So no alliance, Cormallon pockets its fee, the brewers get their reputation for good beer returned . . . I never found out what happened to the three shifted employees. Spells that fool around with memory and volition are risky things; if the three ended up committing suicide somewhere down the road, I would not be surprised.

On the other hand, the Tolla was by definition composed of high risk-taking individuals.

Given a choice between a lengthy gene search for hypothetical magic abilities and a workable weapons program, Van Gelder would go for the weapons. Pure research was not her aim. And if we could work out a trade, perhaps she would lend me Jack Lykon for a day or two . . . because research *was* my aim.

The next question would be, was Jack Lykon a high risk-taking individual?

And what in the world was I going to tell Ran?

Chapter 9

As it turned out, I had time to think about it, as Kylla and Lysander were in the parlor when I got home. They were both holding drinks, which I thought was a good idea on Ran's part, and since nobody seemed to be throwing anything at anybody, I walked right in.

Lysander was seated on the red-fringed cushion by the table. He raised his glass an inch when I entered, and nodded. "Theodora." Kylla, who was half-sitting, half-lying on the divan, now sat up straight and patted the space beside her. "Theo, sit by me. Ran's telling us about your day. It sounds wonderfully gruesome."

I loosened my outerrobe and sat down. Nobody asked me where I'd been, which made things simpler, so I took a sip of Ky's proffered drink—a Soldier's Delight, apparently; Lysander must have stopped somewhere on the way here and bought a flask to go. It was not the custom for old aristocratic families to keep the ingredients for mixed drinks in the house, and it never occurred to Ran that we might stock up. Most of the time I didn't feel the lack, but there were occasional nights when Ran was off putting in an appearance for one of the Cormallon branches and I was stuck in the capital; when the Net seemed supremely uninteresting, and I'd sung all the old Pyrenese songs I could think of in the bathroom, and I found myself wishing for a nudge to get to sleep. No point in opening up the expensive Ducort for that.

Gods, I hoped Ran wasn't going to get himself killed in his profession any time soon. The mortality rate for the upper-rank males of Ivory is relatively high, and that thought did tend to surface from time to time, presenting itself in all its bleak surfaces. I'd been alone most of my life, but I was rapidly losing the knack for it, if it wasn't gone already. It's probably like languages—you've got to keep in practice to handle it with any confidence.

"Theo?" inquired Kylla. She was holding the glass. So was I. I let go, and she said, "Something on your mind?"

"The usual mess. Ran tell you I used up your lip rouge?"

"That was the pot I gave you? Ugh! Theo, that was Cachine Cosmetics, it cost a fortune. What were you thinking?"

Good old practical Kylla. For one paranoid second I wondered if we should be sharing all this data with her and Lysander, considering they were, technically, suspects; but I stamped "unworthy" on that thought and put it back in the closet. Of course, we'd never gotten to know Lysander as well as we might. . . .

Lysander said, "You were about to show us the ring."

Ran did his handkerchief trick once again and made the silver and cadite lump appear in the center. Lysander whistled. "I never saw anything with a curse on it before. That I knew of."

Kylla, an old hand from a house of sorcerers, shrugged. Her long gold earrings tinkled gently. "It's not a thing of beauty," she said. "Kade's taste must have run to the obvious . . . I can't say I'm surprised, having met the sister."

Lysander said, quickly, "Can you use this to identify the sorcerer?"

Ran covered the ring again. "Yes and no. I've been examining it all afternoon—it seems to be safe enough as long as you don't put it on your finger—and the curse is still operational. So by the Rule of Connectivity, we ought to be able to stand wherever the sorcerer stood when he ignited the spell, and follow the spoor back to trace him."

"If only we knew where he was standing," I said.

"Yes," agreed Ran.

"I suppose you could request the use of the boat," said Lysander. "Take it out toward Catmeral Bridge, and move randomly around on the decks till—"

Kylla interrupted. "Does it have to be on the boat?"

Her husband looked puzzled, but Ran said, "No, I was going to mention that little problem. As long as he knew Kade had the ring on, the sorcerer could have been anywhere in line-of-sight—and the lounge deck had big windows, remember—to set the curse loose. That means it could have been somebody on the roof of a warehouse, or on the garden wall of one of your neighbors' houses, Ky."

Lysander groaned. "Anybody in the city, that means."

"Or on Catmeral Bridge," said Kylla.

We all looked at her. I said, "Why the bridge?"

She set her drink on the floor. "There was a man there. I noticed him because he was leaning over the rail, staring at us. It annoyed me." True, at the time Kylla had been in no mood to be stared at, or to be anything else, actually. "It was mid-afternoon, and the Catmeral isn't a covered bridge, right? And it was hot and sunny—the place was practically deserted, and the one or two people crossing over were racing their little fannies across and darting back into the shade. But not this man. He had his arms on the rail and was just leaning there, glaring down. I thought, Who does he think he's looking at, anyway? Then I thought, This one is strange."

Ran said, "Lysander, did you—"

"No, I didn't see him. It's the first I heard of it. But then, my back was to the bridge most of the time. I was facing Kylla."

Ran turned to his sister. "You didn't mention this before."

"Well, if I'd known he was going to drown a Porath, I would have paid more attention! Anyway, then there was that splash down below, and I forgot all about it. Till now."

Ran glanced at me. We'd been on deck at the same time. I said, "I wasn't facing the bridge either." He looked unhappy. I added, "That security guard was up there with us for a while. The one Kade chewed out about not covering Eliana? But I don't remember if we were near the bridge then, or not."

Ran brightened. "Even if he wasn't, he could help us physically place who was where on the boat. Security guards are always making visual sweeps. We could call the Poraths and find out what service they used, and make an appointment to see him before we take the boat out again."

Lysander said, "Could you call them tonight?"

Poor man, Kylla must really be putting the screws to him at home. He definitely wanted the murder, the wedding, and the Poraths taken care of and far away.

Ran glanced down for a second at the bunched handkerchief, then slipped it in the inner pocket of his robe and gave Lysander his full attention. "How are things going, by the way, with your own problem? Has Jusik been in touch since the boat ride?"

Kylla swung her own gaze full on him as well, waiting with that patient, without-mercy born Cormallon expression on her face. Lysander grabbed hold of his glass and downed a long swallow. "He did call," he admitted. "He suggested I might attend the funeral tomorrow. I told him I had to be out of town. He didn't insist."

"Well," said Ran after a moment, "perhaps he won't insist on the marriage, either."

"He might be all the more in need of the money, though, now that Kade's gone," I contributed. The look Lysander shot me was not a kind one.

He said, "I'm sure they all want Eliana to marry money, but there's no reason I have to be the money. I think if I struggle enough, they'll let me escape. After all, it was Kade's pet idea, and he's gone."

Conveniently. Ran's eyes met my own, and I thought, Tsk, tsk. What unbrotherly suspicion. If Lysander's surname had been Cormallon, Ran would have no doubts about his character; if he'd killed Kade, he'd report that fact to Ran so we could all deal with it more intelligently. Despite past experiences, Ran still believed Cormallons could do no wrong.

"We'd better get back," said Kylla, standing up. "I promised Shez I'd kiss her goodnight. It's bedtime now, and she'll torture her nurse till I get there." She gave me a peck on the cheek, then whispered, "How are things going? Missed any periods yet?"

"For the love of heaven, Ky!" I glanced over toward Ran and Lysander, who were continuing the conversation by themselves.

She smiled unrepentently. "You know, I never thought of you as having any nurturing instincts whatsoever. Or not till that afternoon my robe got stuck in the door at the jewelry shop and you spent the hour shaking keys over Shez's carriage to stop her wailing."

"It had to be done."

"And making noises like a ship taking off—"

"All right, Ky."

"Somehow I'd just never pictured you having such a good time with the next generation."

"I know." Kylla saw me as the kind of person who'd mix up the pram with the grocery bags and send the baby off for delivery because I was too busy thinking of which third-person form to use in a translation.

She kissed me again, then went to the low table by the wall and picked up a wrapped bouquet of flowers that I hadn't noticed before. She grabbed and swung them without respect for their delicacy, as though they were a frying pan.

"What are they?" I asked. "I've never seen them before."

She brought the bouquet over for me to inspect. "I don't know their name," she said, "but they're in season now. Lysander bought them for me on the way here."

They were a violet blue, made up of masses of perfect, tiny petals that fooled the eye into thinking they were a single entity from a distance. A rich scent rose in a cloud from the wrappings. "They're wonderful! There must be hundreds of petals. Ran, what are they called?"

"No idea," said Ran.

Kylla bent over and patted my hand with friendly patronization. "We're all glad you like them, Theo. Ran, buy this woman more gifts. If a few flowers get her this excited, she must be deprived. When's the last time you gave her jewelry?"

Ran stopped and thought. "I don't think I ever have."

"Great gods," said Lysander, revealing volumes about his own relationship. After a moment he said, "What do you do when she's mad at you?"

"If she's been angry with me, she hasn't told me. Theodora, have you been angry with me?"

I said, "Not since that time in the Sector last summer. And neither of us had any opportunity to go shopping then."

Kylla said, "Brother, rectify this matter. I speak as one with your interests at heart. Come along, Lysander."

Her husband followed her to the door. "Ran, you'll let me know—"

"I'll keep you up to date," Ran assured him.

They left. Ran said to me, "If we want to interview the security guard, we'll probably have to get to his office early tomorrow, before his shift starts. That means rising at dawn."

"Kanz, komo, and the destruction of profit." He was unsurprised at my immediate profanity; Ran knows I hate to get up early. Mentally I revised my schedule: I'd discuss the Tolla's offer with him tomorrow night—otherwise we'd be up till dawn debating it, and I'd be a wreck in the morning.

"Want to hear about my tests on the ring?" he asked.

"Tomorrow," I said.

"Want to tell me about your meeting with the Tellysian ambassador?"

"Tomorrow."

He walked over, knelt by the chaise, and put his head on my thigh. My hand went out to his hair, thick and soft. He lifted his face. "Don't tell me you're tired already. The night is young."

The night wasn't all that was young. He slid his hands up to the drawstring that held my underpants, removing them without disturbing the silk of my outerrobe, a rewarding but complicated movement that required my cooperation. For a moment the memory of what he'd said the other night flashed through my mind, about my sexual performance. Just the sort of thing a self-conscious barbarian doesn't need to remember. At once he said, "What is it?"

"Nothing. Please don't let me interrupt you."

He chuckled and completed the maneuver. When he was finished, I said, "Ghost Eve before last, you gave me a necklace of caneblood with a jade pendant."

He'd stood up as I spoke. Now he bent over. Just before his lips came down on mine he said, "I wish you'd thought of that while Kylla was in the room."

Loden Broca Mercia, security guard with the Mercia firm, was on the day shift of his current assignment. He reported into the Mercia office on the corner of Gold Street and Luster at two hours after dawn—and dawn comes early in the summer. I was not at my keenest edge of awareness, to make my point more plain.

The offices were small and bare, only to be expected, I suppose, of a place where people were mostly sent out to work in other locations. No windows, only some vents and a ceiling fan to redistribute the heat. The building was old, modified for power packs in the visitor's area but with the smell of oil lamps coming from the other rooms.

I sat on a bench, nodding, while Ran established the following facts with the Mercia branch head: That the Poraths had hired a full dozen guards, spread over two shifts, with livery modified for the occasion. Five of these guards had been on the boat when Kade went swimming. (Between five guards and Eliana's personal fighting chaperone, Loden Broca had probably been right when he'd told Kade his sister was in no great danger.)

Loden Broca, as his name implies, was of the House but not the family of Mercia—a firm of good reputation, small, but listed on the registry of fine Houses in the Golden Virtue Administration Building in the Capital Triangle. Still, what did that prove? Go into the Capital Triangle with enough coinage, and you can get anything listed anywhere. The Beggar Monopoly, the House of Helad, was top of the registry, from what I'd heard; they threw enough money at government officials that they were supporting the entire city police force. Anyway, that was the rumor. But the Mercia Guard Firm had a good reputation by word of mouth as well, and that was more to be relied upon than any official writings.

Loden Broca had joined the House of Mercia two years ago, after paying for and receiving their course of education in Mercia security techniques. He was about twenty standard years old. The average age of the guards on duty at the Poraths' had been thirty-one; the average length of service, eight years. (Ran always likes to go for the numbers. Sometimes they come in handy.) Loden Broca was apparently just starting his career. As his branch supervisor made plain, losing the first son of the family one is protecting was not a good way to begin.

"He's on probation," said Supervisor Ben Mercia, a trim, gray-haired man somewhere near his fifties. (Of House and family both, my reflexes pointed out at once; how far could you advance in this particular organization without snagging an adoption? Maybe Loden Broca should look into another line of work.) "I can assure you we're dealing with the matter appropriately, gracious sir. Every man on duty that day is undergoing a performance review. If Lord Porath wants to initiate disciplinary action—"

"That's not why we've come," said Ran.

"We've already returned our fee—our entire fee, not just that day's. But in plain fact, not every contingency can be anticipated. We offer no guarantees. If Lord Porath wants a face-price, I can only point out that first, we would never be able to pay the equivalent of a first son, and second, that this act would not make him popular with other security agencies or indeed other Houses—firms would be reluctant to sell their protection if they were to be held responsible for every . . . odd circumstance . . . that arose—"

The words were rolling out like an opened bag of marbles. Ran gave up trying to find an opening and simply overrode him. "We're not here for that purpose, sir. We only wanted to ask a few questions of you, Loden Broca, and possibly some of the other guards on duty that day. That's it. Any reference to monetary arrangements will have to be gone into with the House of Porath itself."

Ben Mercia stared at Ran suspiciously. "You said you represented the Poraths."

"Not monetarily."

The suspicious look remained. "Grant me your indulgence, gracious sir. I'll return in a moment." The supervisor turned and went into another room, closing the door behind him.

Ran sat down beside me on the bench.

"He's checking us out," I said.

"I thought you were fast asleep," he replied. "The sound of your snores was making conversation difficult."

"What lies you tell. No wonder the man doesn't trust you." I closed my eyes again, my head leaning against the old plaster wall. "Anyway, I wasn't asleep; I was just—"

"Resting your eyes, I know." Suddenly he jabbed me in the side.

I didn't respond. "Ran, I can't keep you entertained every single moment."

"No, look, open your eyes."

I did so. Loden Broca had just entered the anteroom to our left. Another man was with him, slightly older, and familiar-looking. I said quietly, "The other one—was he on duty, too?"

Ran frowned, remembering. "He directed our carriage driver the night of the garden party. And I think he was on the boat."

"Let's talk to them both, as long as we've got them."

He nodded. "The supervisor better finish his checking before they leave for their assignments."

Loden Broca had curly, wind-tousled brown hair, a jaunty step, and a quirky half-smile that he bestowed on the dispatcher as he was handed his schedule for the day. It was the sort of half-smile that suggests all this paperwork is a joke, but he'll be tolerant enough to go along with it. A few short encounters don't make a secure base to speculate, but I had the strong impression that Loden Broca was one of those men who do not like authority as it applies to themselves.

I recalled that when we were first entering the pleasure boat, Kylla had made some remarks about his being extraordinarily good looking. I watched him closely as he touched his companion on the shoulder, making a joke. He was handsome, certainly, and I remembered that his eyes were particularly fine, but her comments seemed far beyond his desserts—more appropriate to a young god than a nice-looking boy on a planet that was overrun with vibrant and beautiful people. Ran put him in the shade.

Ben Mercia's door opened. He nodded to us, then called, "Loden! Trey! Come in here!" He turned to Ran and said, "Trey Lesseret was on the Porath detail as well; I thought you might want to speak with him."

It's nice to be anticipated. "Thank you," said Ran, as though it were no more than his due, and he added, "I trust I do not keep you from your duties." It would be easier to question them away from their supervisor.

"Not at all," said Ben Mercia, sinking down on the bench by the window with what was almost a smirk. "I'm happy to stay and be of help."

"Commendable." Ran rose to exchange polite bows with the two men entering the room. I got to my feet as well and made that incline of the head appropriate in the wife of a first of Cormallon, rather than the smile and matching bow I sometimes made in the course of easier social encounters. I'm not really sure why; but I didn't feel at home in the Mercia Guard Service building, and wanted all the formal status I could get. I saw from a brief look that Ran took notice of my choice of greeting. "Loden Broca Mercia, Trey Lesseret Mercia, we've met briefly before. I'm Ran Cormallon, here on behalf of Lord Jusik Porath. This is my—" Wife? Assistant? "—colleague, Theodora Cormallon." And let them make what they will of the last name.

"Honored by this meeting," said Trey Lesseret, and Loden Broca mumbled the same after him. Lesseret had at least a half-dozen years on his friend; he looked to be brushing thirty, a little shorter and stockier than Loden Broca, who was muscled, but on the slender side. Lesseret was paler, too, and his hazel eyes squinted toward us as though we were standing in the sun instead of with our backs against the wall of a windowless room in a cheaper quarter of the capital. He put one foot up on the boot-polisher stool by the bench. "Take it you're here about Lord Porath's boy."

"Boy" was debatable, coming from him. Kade and he were probably of an age, though Lesseret looked as though he'd packed more experience into the time than the ex-first-son of Porath had.

"Yes," said Ran, "a terrible tragedy."

"Terrible," agreed Lesseret, adding briskly, "so how can I help you, gracious sir?"

"My colleague and I are trying to get a better idea of what happened. Physically, I mean, in terms of placement. Who was where. Anything anybody saw."

"I was in the lounge most of the time," Lesseret said at once. "My house-brother here was above-deck for a bit, having a smoke—" he gestured toward Loden Broca—"but I stayed by the musicians for the whole trip. Get a better view of the salon that way, you know."

I said, "So you would more or less remember where people were?"

He turned to me. "More, rather than less, gracious lady. It's the kind of thing I pay attention to."

"What about you?" Ran addressed Loden Broca. "You could do the same for the upper deck?"

The guard smiled. "You, this gracious lady, and another man and woman were the only people on the front side.

There were three others looking down the canal by the railing in back."

"Not including Kade."

His smile vanished. "No. But he only came up for a moment."

I thought Ran would ask Loden Broca now if he'd seen Kylla's mysterious stranger on Catmeral Bridge. Instead he pulled a familiar handkerchief from an inner pocket and untied the knot. "Both of you had a good view of Kade Porath," he said. "Can you tell me if he was wearing this the entire time he was on board?" He pulled out the last of the knot and extended the massive cadite ring.

Lesseret was making a shrugging gesture, but Loden Broca's expression was one of surprise, followed by blank incomprehension. His gaze went up to Ran's, a furrow cutting the golden skin of his brow.

"What are you doing with my ring?" he asked.

He got everyone's attention in the room, no doubt about that. Neither Trey Lesseret nor Ben Mercia knew what significance the ring had, but they wanted to hear more. Ben Mercia *insisted* on hearing more, to Broca's acute and obvious discomfort. Ran solved the problem by buying the guard's services for the morning for a rather inflated fee, and a quarter hour later found the three of us wandering somewhat aimlessly down Luster Street, looking in vain for a place to sit and talk. The Mercia agency, when it came down to it, was happy to put another guard in Loden's place for the day if it could get an extra fee from us, and postpone its natural curiosity (in the form of Ben Mercia) in the higher cause of House profit. Ben Mercia knew his duty.

"Your ring?" repeated Ran, as he scanned the scruffy shopfronts at this end of Luster.

"A family inheritance," said Loden Broca. "The only one I've got, really. Boldness and prudence, the Broca mottoes." He smiled that twisty grin. "My father left it to me, and enough to put a down payment on security school. Though we don't know how that'll turn out, at the moment. I'm on probation."

Ran said, carefully, "Would you have any guesses as to where we found the ring?"

"You said Kade Porath was wearing it. That wouldn't surprise me. I gave it to him."

I looked at his face as we turned the corner of Luster and Tin. He didn't seem to find anything unusual in the statement.

"Pure charity?" prompted Ran.

In this part of town people who ran small-scale, miserable businesses out of their homes sat on doorsteps, by windows, even in the gutter, trying to catch a breeze as they weaved and sharpened knives and made paper animals for the tourists over in Trade Square. There wasn't enough room here for courtyards in the back, so they took relief where they could, heedless of danger. But then, they were in more danger from each other than from any violent, gameplaying nobility, who probably wouldn't be caught dead in this neighborhood. I'd stayed in the equivalent of this sort of place when I first came to Ivory, but we'd had a bit more space—my inn had had a courtyard. That practically made me a merchant prince by comparison.

Loden's face wore a wincing, sheepish look; he seemed to be picking through a pile in search of the proper words, and not finding any. "It wasn't," he began, and stopped again. We passed a massive, elderly woman in a faded orange robe, sitting on a stool by the curb, sharpening kitchen knives on a wheel. A bolt of ragged striped cloth had been rigged for shade in the branches of the spindly tree beside her. As we passed she moved her stool back an inch, further into the shadows. "You see—" said Loden, and discarded those words, too. The old woman in orange glanced up and met my eyes; there was a crazy look there that, taken in conjunction with all these sharp objects, made me uncomfortable. I walked around to the other side of Ran.

"It's like this," said Loden. He paused one more time. I had a momentary urge to yell *spit it out, man*!—which, fortunately, I got the better of, because he finally achieved takeoff velocity. "I play cards," he said, "not, you understand, that I'm a gambler. Just as a pastime. But it happened that I lost a lot of money one night—I'd had a few drinks, you know how that is," he said, confidingly, though in fact I had no idea how it was to get drunk and gamble my savings away. It was an alien concept. But then, other people are alien to us in so many ways I try to be careful about making any quick judgments. "So I ended up owing these fellows some money. And since I didn't have any to pay them back, I borrowed some."

"Transferring your debt to someone else," I said, puzzled. "I don't see the point."

"Well, it got these guys off my back," he said reasonably.

"This new loan was at a lower rate of interest, then?" I asked.

"Not exactly. Ah, no, it wasn't. But it was only one person to worry about."

Finally outlines were emerging from the mist. I said, "Did you by any chance borrow this money from Kade Porath?"

Ran stopped. He turned to Loden and said, "Are you trying to tell us that Kade was your creditor as well as your employer?"

"Well, yes, it's not as if—"

"Was this before or after the house party? I mean, did you meet Kade through being assigned to the Poraths, and borrow the money then?"

"Uh, no, I borrowed it back at the beginning of spring. Five months ago. Kade knew I was with the Mercia agency and he chose us when he wanted to cover his sister's party. He said he may as well make sure I kept getting a salary."

We were midway down Tin Street. Ran looked irritably around for a route out of this neighborhood. "Doesn't this hook up with Grapefruit Alley somewhere?" he said, seemingly in my direction.

"You're asking me? You've spent a lot more years in this city than I have."

"But you're the one who's map crazy."

This was true. I like to know where I am, in the larger scheme of things. Since philosophy gives no final answers, I make do with maps. I'd unofficially inherited a lot of them from Ran's grandmother—an incredible woman who'd never left the estate in all the decades since she'd married into the family, but who had closets full of starcharts, geological surveys, and plans showing the waterpipes under cities I'd never heard of. The servants were still running across them occasionally in pantries and under old sets of drawers.

Grapefruit Alley leads into Trade Square eventually,

so—"It would have to be in that direction," I said, pointing crosswise over the road.

"There's a robemaker's in the way," he said, implying my contribution was less than helpful.

"That isn't my fault. I didn't build it."

Loden Broca looked from one of us to the other uncertainly.

Ran kicked a loose stone with the edge of his sandal and we continued down the street. "How much did you owe?" he said, suddenly addressing Loden again.

"About four, well, five, uh—I don't see what this has to do with anything."

"Neither do I," said my husband disarmingly. "You brought it up."

It took another few seconds for the logic of this to penetrate. Finally Loden said, unwillingly, "Five hundred and fifty tabals. But it only started out as three hundred."

"Oh." Noncommittal.

"The thing is, I'd missed a payment. And Kade kept giving me a hard time about it. He wanted something, and I don't *own* anything, except this ring, so . . . he said to give him that. So I did."

"When?"

"On the boat. You saw when he came up to get me. He was mad, because I hadn't paid him, and he saw my ring when I had my hand on the railing on the stairway."

Ran and I looked at each other. I said, "You were wearing it openly when you got on the boat?"

"I had it on my hand, if that's what you mean by openly."

"And this was a spur-of-the-moment thing?" asked Ran. "Nobody had any reason to believe you'd take the ring off? Kade never demanded it before?"

"No, it was the first time he'd mentioned it. I wore my ring all the time, you don't expect somebody to ask you for a family heirloom. But, look, I didn't think I was in any position to say no, especially with my house-brothers all over the ship. You aren't going to mention this to them, are you?"

He said it so wistfully, like a little kid. Well—more like a little kid trying to get away with something.

Still. If this was true, maybe we should give him whatever slack we could. After all, somebody was trying to murder him.

Chapter 10

Loden Broca couldn't confirm Kylla's story about the sinister watcher on Catmeral Bridge. "I went down below before we were close enough to the bridge to see," he said. "Why, do you think that might have been the sorcerer? It *was* sorcery, wasn't it? Kade didn't just have some kind of weird fit? I mean, he never struck me as entirely normal."

Ran stopped by a wide, unpaved opening between two buildings. "Grapefruit Alley," he said to me, pleased, bowing slightly as though he were presenting me with it as a gift. "It's a good half-kilometer from the robemaker's," he had to point out.

"It probably curves around behind it when you get further in," I said. (It did.)

Loden said, "Gracious sir?"

Ran turned a courteously meaningless smile on him. "Thank you so much for your help, sir. Please take the rest of the morning off, with our compliments to your supervisor."

Loden stood there a moment, looking bewildered. I felt a little sorry for him. "Do you have any enemies?" I inquired.

"Well, uh, not really . . . there are a few people who've gotten mad at me sometimes . . . ah, why do you ask?"

Ran took hold of my elbow and pulled me a couple of steps into the alley. "No reason," I said hastily. "Just wondered." Apparently we were not telling Loden Broca Mercia that he was a potential murder target. This did not seem quite right. But Ran always has his reasons for acting the way he does. I don't always agree with him, but he does have them.

"Gracious lady?" asked Loden, still with that confused expression, like a just-born puppy trying to come to terms with its suddenly colorful lifestyle. Oh, it was a shame not to at least warn him.

"Sorry, can't chat," I said, as Ran set a walking pace that took us deep into the alley and around the corner of a building with remarkable speed.

"Why aren't we telling him?" I asked, when he'd slowed down enough for me to get sufficient breath.

"We're doing this for Jusik Porath," Ran said, "whatever he may think. He gets our first report, not somebody in the Mercia agency."

"But in a situation like this—"

"A situation like what? We still have no hard evidence, only suspicions."

"But if Loden's telling the truth—"

Ran finally slowed down a little. He glanced back along the curve of the alley. "Then we'll visit him later and suggest that he take care."

I considered that as we walked. Within a few minutes we reached the beginning of the market stalls that line Grapefruit Alley all the way up to Trade Square. Every other cart was a food cart, and the smells would detour a truckload of monks on their way to the Court of Contemplation. Heavily spiced meat of every description, cut into cubes and stuck on sticks; cut into slices and added to hot rice; shredded into a dusting of protein and sprinkled over yellow and white vegetables. Raw vegetables and fruits in the cart next door, and eight sorts of flavored water in the cart beyond that. There were stationers, too, and dollmakers, and all the usual mishmosh of Ivoran businesses, but Grapefruit Alley was—contrary to all appearances—the gourmand's heart of the world. Not even the bustling cookshops around the Square itself could match these dirty-looking vendors, who'd handed down their three meters of turf from parent to child since as far back as anyone's ever heard. One of the refrigerated carts we passed was stocked full of Pyrenese beer; how the beggarly seeming gentleman behind it managed that, when the most exclusive restaurants in the city were often out, was a mystery.

A mystery. I glanced over at Ran. "What are you going to tell Jusik?"

"Nothing, maybe, for the moment. We don't know anything for certain yet."

"Maybe, but I don't feel right leaving Loden twisting in the wind while we get our thoughts together."

So we walked along in more silence, getting our thoughts together. I said, "Let's try Kylla's theory."

"The mysterious stranger on the bridge?"

I saw it had occurred to him, too. "Why not? We don't need a boat to test that one. You just need to stand where the sorcerer stood, to start a backward trace—so let's go to the south railing of Catmeral Bridge, Ran, and see what we can see."

The alley turned into a straightaway around that point, cutting diagonally across the streets in the center of town. A long way off in the distance I could see the opening into the bright sunlight of Trade Square. You could almost hear the noise from there. Ran said, thoughtfully, "We do seem to be going in the right direction for it, don't we." The section of the canal crossed by Catmeral Bridge is half a mile north of the Square.

I grinned. I had to admit that Loden Broca or no, I was curious about this thing with Kade, and hanging about on open bridges in the midday sun seemed a small price to pay, at least at that moment. Just then my gaze fell on a cart-stall piled to overflowing with blossoms of red, white, violet, blue, and burnt gold—and the violet ones were versions of the unidentified bouquet Kylla had carried so jauntily away with her last night.

The fat face of an old woman was framed beyond the heaps of flowers; her head just topped the merchandise. "Oh, Ran! Look! Could you—"

He trudged over toward the cart. "I know," he said mournfully. "The little purple ones."

He handed over a coin—I didn't even have to advance it to him—and all the way up to Catmeral Bridge I carried a huge bunch of lavender bells in my sweaty hands.

Midway over the bridge we stopped and looked southeast, down the canal. The waters were dark and still. Not many folks used the canal these days; farther up, the neighborhood watch had had to institute stiff rules about garbage dumping. That was ten (Ivoran) years ago, before my time. "The Year of the Big Stink," they called it. Kylla was just entering her teens then, staying with friends in the capital, and she told me she'd gone the whole summer drenched in perfume, like every other person who could afford it. The street vendors had all had little shelves set underneath their carts, covered with cologne bottles for passersby to purchase if they ran out of supply.

I watched a ragged boy play in the dirt near the edge, ignoring the glare of noon sun. He looked down at the water, then went back to his play—it wasn't the sort of water you felt tempted to swim in, regardless of the summer heat.

I glanced over at Ran's left hand, where the cadite ring sparkled. He'd scared me when he put it on, but he'd said shortly that (a) it was necessary and (b) he could handle it. His mood hadn't exactly been upbeat, so I didn't press my concerns.

"So far, nothing," said Ran. He said it grimly. His tone went beyond the temperature and a walk through the less glamorous parts of the capital. He hadn't been at his best since we stepped into Grapefruit Alley, in fact, so I turned to him and touched his arm to get his attention.

"What's the matter?"

He sighed, and said gently, "I suppose you mean beyond the fact that Kylla's unhappy and I've been taken for the assassin of a first son of the Six Families. And beyond the fact that Stereth Tar'krim is another possible suspect. And beyond the discomfort of this entire morning."

"Yes, beyond all that." Those were all things I had every faith he could handle.

"All right," he said, "I'm angry. I've been thinking about this ever since Loden Broca told us about his ring, and getting angrier with every step."

"Angry?" It took me completely by surprise. "What is it, what are you angry about? You've always taken this kind of thing in stride!" Whatever I meant by "this kind of thing" . . . sorcery, assassination, the general distrust of humankind.

"Whatever sorcerer did this—" He took a deep breath and let it out. "Whatever incompetent fool—" Another breath. "It wasn't enough that he acted in public; he targeted the wrong man, too. And not because it was one of those accidents that 'happen because we are in this world.' Because he was careless and stupid and didn't give the same thought to this you or I would give to planning a dinner menu—"

"But he couldn't have known Loden would lose the ring. Loden said it himself: Who would have the nerve to ask for a family heirloom?"

"What difference does it make?" His face was slightly flushed; he really was angry. "Using an object like a ring is brainless to begin with, when you're dealing with something as permanent as death. I've been training to be a sorcerer since I was eight years old, and seeing negligence like this—something I would have avoided *when* I was eight—" His fists came down on the railing, and he let the rest of the sentence go. Finally he said, "What's he doing being a sorcerer? Throwing mud on all our reputations, leading clients to distrust us. And beside that—besides that, it tramples over the field itself. The beauty of sorcery is based on symbol and function being allied, on everything having its proper aspect, on dancing the dance so carefully— Theodora, sweetheart, it's so beautiful when it's all done the way it should be done. I know you're not a practitioner, but you've studied it now; you must see that."

I saw that not agreeing at this moment would be tantamount to a divorce. And truly, I did *almost* see. I nodded.

"And this fool thought he could do it as crudely as pointing a gun at someone. Even *that* takes experience and training."

I didn't know what to say, so I took the safer route and said nothing. A moment later Ran took hold of my arm and said, hoarsely, "Let's finish the sweep of the bridge and find this kanz." We started down the midpoint of the arc.

Dancing the dance, he'd said; like "The Other Side of the Mirror," that I'd danced (granted, with several errors) on the afternoon that Kade died. Dances on Ivory are complex and never spontaneous, unless you're a trained and acknowledged artist; great sorceries, too, I supposed.

He stopped suddenly a few meters away, with the look of someone who'd been punched in the stomach. The fact that he wore the ring still bothered me; I ran over to him and grabbed one arm, in case he had a sudden desire to dive in the canal. "I've got it," he said. "Gods! I didn't think we'd get a trace this quickly. I figured he was probably just some stranger Kylla saw." He looked over at where my hands still gripped him. "What are you doing?'

I let go. "You made me nervous."

He blinked and shook his head slowly. "My dear tymon. Really."

"Be that way, then, but don't expect me to dive in after you if you end up in the canal."

He smiled. "This way." He pointed southwest, back in the direction we'd come.

We walked down the bridge, with me still watching him narrowly. No point in not being careful. For some reason my suspicious nature seemed to cheer him up, because he slipped one hand around my waist, beneath my outerrobe (so no one would notice and be scandalized), and said, "I haven't asked you to recite the hundred and ten laws of magic in a long time."

"Don't tell me we're going to have a review quiz now."

"Just a hypothetical problem, Theodora. If you were going to assassinate Kade, would you have used a ring?"

"Considering your strong views on the matter, as you've only just expressed them, I'm not likely to say yes, am I?"

"Humor me, and give me your best answer."

We were off the bridge and getting farther from the dark waters of the canal, so I put my mind to the problem. "No. I would treat it as a variant of the search hierarchy, using inside and outside traits. I would place the spell on the person himself, and tie him to it by definition."

"The definition being?"

"Well, I'd have to research who Kade was. Rings, clothing, and general appearance would be outside traits; I'd leave them for the icing on the spell. The heart I would base on inside traits, where you're less likely to go wrong. In Kade's case, I don't know—greed for money is an inside trait, and he seemed to have that, though probably half the people on the boat that day did, too—"

He interrupted. "Never mind, tymon, you've made my point. You're already ten times the sorcerer this idiot is, even just in theory. It's a pity you don't have the gift."

"I read your cards for you well enough."

"Because the virtue is in the deck. You'd be a top-rung professional if you were gifted yourself."

It was nice that he thought so, since the Cormallons lived

and died by sorcery; it was their vocation and avocation; they followed it like an art and a sporting event. But I had no desire for the gift. I got pleasure from reading the cards (for reasons too voyeuristic to do me credit), but beyond that magic held no great allure for me. Maybe I'd seen them all working too hard at it for it to keep its romance. Or maybe it was just that there were so many other horses crying to be ridden—the scholarship of folklore and storytelling, my training in tinaje, even the recordkeeping and accounting expected of me at Cormallon—for me to want to submerge myself in artistic obsession.

Still— "You think I'd approach magic with the proper flair?" I asked, pluming at the compliment.

"Well, you'd be patient and careful," he said, dwelling instead on my grayer virtues.

There you are: You can't bother my Ran with murder or sabotage, but carelessness upsets him. Ah, well, we must take our compliments where we find them in this world. We continued, following the sorcerer's trace back the exact route we'd taken, till the street we were on emptied into the noisy expanse of Trade Square. Here open tents and awnings sprouted in multicolor abundance and vendors sold rugs, pots, fruit, weapons, live fowl, themselves, challenges at gaming contests, lucky names and numbers, promises of expertise in any field wanted, tickets to the Imperial Dance Company, baths in battered old metal tubs, displays of balance and agility, feats of memory, lessons in spoken Standard, recycled car parts. . . . I'd set up daily shop here myself, back when I'd first gotten stranded on Ivory without money or work, and with no connections to supply either.

We stepped into the controlled chaos and my gaze went at once to the spot by the wall where I used to sit beside Irsa, who sold fruit from a cart. But it was the height of the day; there were too many people passing for me to see if she was there. "Irsa!" I yelled, hoping to see a face pop up from the mass of strangers. As I squinted, Ran tapped my arm and pointed to the ring. "We're getting closer," he said loudly, against the noise. I squinted at the ring instead. It didn't look any different to me than it was before.

"How can you t—" I began.

The crowd in front of us parted, and a groundcar made its way slowly through. I stopped in my tracks and stared at it. Who would be fool enough to drive a groundcar through Trade Square? Even wagon and carriage drivers took care to detour to the streets around. The unlucky car was low-slung, covered in durasteel, with no way to peer inside at the no-doubt impatient face of the driver.

Suddenly it accelerated sharply, causing the knot of people remaining to jump aside; there was cursing, and somebody gave a piercing scream, in apparent pain. I stood, rooted, for an eternal millisecond, before my fear seemed to pick me up bodily and toss me out of the way. The groundcar barreled through. I rolled on the ground, not the only person down there, and the noise of the marketplace dwindled to a distant hum backing the main sound of my beating heart. I put my hands against the ground to push myself up, and felt how shaky and weak they seemed. Hands on either side of me helped me to my feet. Long-taught reflexes reminded me that nobody in Trade Square takes hold of you unless it's to distract you from their pocketpicking, and without thinking about it I tried to shake them off.

They wouldn't shake. I looked left and right, at two men in faded robes who were pulling me away. I opened my mouth, and a length of white cloth was dropped over my head, pulled tight between my lips, and tied in back. I felt the fingers behind my head, tying it, ruffling my hair—an unpleasant feeling, even aside from the fear. So there were more than two of them. My legs were still free, and I kicked out at the men on either side, but unfortunately I was not at a good angle to do much damage. I aimed a vicious one behind me, but that unseen gentleman had prudently dropped back a pace.

We were only a few steps from a small, jury-rigged tent by the wall of a building on the edge of the square. I was hustled toward the opening. One of the few fully covered tents in the marketplace; once inside, nobody would know I was there. I could be within a few inches of Ran and he'd have no way of knowing. Assuming he wasn't going to be dumped inside next to me. I half-hoped that he would be.

It had all happened in seconds. I was pushed inside, where I stumbled in the sudden gloom. Hands shoved me down onto the ground; at least there were some cushions scattered there. I turned, awkwardly, to look up.

A knifeblade glinted in the dim light. As he dropped to one knee, one of the men pulled it from a sheath on his belt and drew back to—there was no mistaking this—get a good angle when he shoved it into my body. There had been no hesitation, no stop to rest, no attempt to talk to me. I'd been walking in the square thirty seconds ago, chatting with Ran. I was paralyzed with terror and disbelief.

The knife was drawn back to strike. The world turned a sharp, sickening corner and shrank to this few meters of space, the dirty tent, and the man with me. I wasn't thinking about Ran, or anything else. If you'd asked me my husband's name, I doubt I could have told you. I doubt I could have told you my own name.

Then the blade paused. By whatever incomprehensible rules the universe used, that had got me to this tent, the weapon hesitated. I no more expected to understand a reason for it than I expected to understand why I was there. The man turned. I followed his glance to the tent flap, where the other two were waiting outside. Except that one of them seemed to be lying on the ground, taking a nap in the sunlight. The man with the knife—the only important person here, from my point of view—twisted around, launched himself to his feet and out through the opening. I lay there, pretty much at my limit in handling simple breathing, and picked up scuffles and yells from the world outside as my ability to hear turned itself back on.

A fat, gray-haired woman with a mountainous chest appeared in the tent flap. In her hand she held a heavy brass lamp with blood and hair on one end. She peered in and grinned a wide grin that showed teeth were a minority population in her head. "Theo, love," she said. "I thought it was you."

Irsa, my old mate from the days of no money, who sold pellfruit and red pears to support her innumerable children. I mumbled something. She came farther in and knelt beside me. "Are you all right, child?"

I nodded. But logical speech felt a long way beyond me, as did getting up. She puckered her lips in sympathy. "I yelled for the protective association, and last I saw your friend was being chased over Kymul's Table of Pleasurable Devices. He won't be coming back, you know." She put a hand on my forehead, like a young mother testing for fever.

"I hope you didn't want to question the one lying out front; I don't think he'll be rising from where he is."

"Uhh. Irsa. . . ."

"He didn't hit you, did he, sweetheart?"

I shook my head. "I'm sorry . . . I don't know what's wrong with me . . . I just can't seem to. . . ."

"Had the life frightened out of you, I 'spect. We shouldn't be surprised; that groundcar nearly did the job, too; did you realize it was coming straight at you in particular? Jumping two skulls in a row is more than anybody ought to have to put up with, at least in the same five minutes. The body's not made for that sort of thing, you've got to rest up in between. Do you think you can sit? I can get you water from the bottle on my cart."

She helped me sit, and a shadow crossed the opening of the tent. Ran. Irsa turned; she knew him, and satisfied herself with a mere disapproving look. "You could keep a better eye on her, you know," she said. "You're the one who got her to leave the market, where she was safe."

His clothes were covered with dirt. "Safe," he repeated. He made a sound that could have been a laugh, but wasn't.

"Safe I said and safe I meant," said Irsa. "Nobody tried to kill her in all the time *I* knew her."

Ran knelt down, more as if he didn't have the strength to stand than as a convenience in talking to me. "You're all right," he said. He seemed to be telling me.

I nodded. "He had a knife," I said. My voice embarrassed me by suddenly coming out like a child's.

"Mine probably had one too, but they got separated from me when a couple of angry people tried to run after the groundcar. Pure luck."

Pure luck. Three minutes ago we were walking across the market like a pair of innocents.

I made out a mound of pillows in the dim light behind me; they weren't much help in trying to get to my feet. Not that it would have been so comfortable to stand up anyway. Ran and Irsa were both stooping under the low roof.

"What are you doing?" asked Ran.

"Trying to get up."

"You're the color of new paper. Stay where you are for a while. We're not late for anything."

It was a bit embarrassing how my body had just switched

off. I'd been in tight spots before—you can't really hang around professionally with the Cormallons and *not* be in tight spots—but the wall of eternity had never thudded down so forcefully in front of me. So quickly. While I was alert and conscious, and yet without any time to prepare for it.

The other side of the mirror is a skull.

I admitted, "Maybe a couple of minutes' rest isn't a bad idea."

He put his arms around my shoulders, and since there was nobody but Irsa to see me snuffle on his robe I let him do it. As a matter of fact I was quite glad about it.

After a moment, Irsa said, "Children, who's the fellow back there?"

At once I tensed. My alarm systems were apparently still quivering. But her voice had been casual, and Irsa was no fool. "What fellow?"

"Behind you there."

I stopped snuffling and turned to the mound of pillows between me and the wall. In the gray light I could just make out some sort of non-pillow shape on the far cushiony slope. Irsa got up and held open the flap of the tent a little farther.

The pillows were wet, I now realized. "The fellow's" throat had been cut.

Without speaking, Ran and I pulled the top cushions off and tossed them aside for a better view. I think we each had the same idea.

The bar of dim sunlight showed a man of middle age, completely bald, still wearing a green felt cap to protect his skin. He was pale for an Ivoran, but not sunburnt; he'd probably taken good care of himself, didn't go out much in daytime, stayed in his tent when he plied his trade. Assuming this was his tent. Well, he'd escaped sunburn. The bloody crescent under his chin was dark and already starting to cake. I couldn't swear as to what color his robes had been originally. The pillows beneath him were soaked.

Ran extended his hand toward the other side of the pile. He still wore the cadite ring. There was a bruise on the fingers on either side of the stone, probably from when he'd thrown himself away from the car. His hand stopped a few centimeters from the man's face. He turned to me.

"Our sorcerer," I said.

He nodded.

It was a pretty gruesome sight, and added to it was a fecal kind of scent I'd only just become aware of; but I found there was no more space left in me to be shocked, or even surprised. And in terms of luck it was all of a piece with a miserable day that had gone before it.

I glanced around the tent and saw a torn sign tacked to one canvas wall:

LUCKSPELLS . . . . . 5t.–15t.
LOVE FILTERS . . . 10t.–25t.
CURSES . . . . 2t.–8t.
DELIGHTFUL ILLUSIONS . . . 17t.–30t.

YOUR PAST AND FUTURE,
WONDERS OF ALL KINDS, PLEASE INQUIRE

That certainly seemed to nail down his professional identity. I guess we could have skipped the ring after all.

I said, "I think I'd rather rest someplace else," and Ran extended a hand to help me up.

I turned to Irsa. "What about the protective association? Will they report this to anybody, will they want to question us?"

"I don't see why, sweet. It's nobody's business. This fellow probably paid his dues like everybody else, but I'll tell them you two had nothing to do with it, and who cares about the rest?"

Ran said, "Thank you."

"Ah, it's nothing. The cops like to stick their noses into every silly thing, like they'll find a payoff somewhere if they keep looking—but we'll just roll the gentleman up in one of Ton's old rugs and carry him away tonight, when the market breaks up."

Ran understood at once. He said, "Theodora, do you still have your moneypouch?"

My hands went under my robe, to my belt. "Yes." I opened it and counted out tabals until Ran waved me to stop. He collected the coins and gave them to Irsa.

He said, "Please thank them for their kindness."

She smiled, displaying that lovely, half-toothless mouth

again. " 'The gratitude of a virtuous man is worth more than gold.' "

"True, but 'the excellence of friendship is a coin no emperor can mint.' "

They might have exchanged a few more anti-money aphorisms just for the heck of it, but Irsa was busy dropping the coins into a bag inside her outerrobe, counting them as she went. We waited courteously for her to finish, then we all three left that tent forever, stepping out into the brightness of a normal market day in high summer.

Irsa's first victim had been dragged away, perhaps in the name of neatness; I saw his legs protruding from behind a cart of sugar ices. Belatedly, I said, "There was a third man."

Her face creased. "Was there, child? I didn't see him. He must've dropped out before the other two went for the kill."

I nodded reasonably. I was functional, but behind it my mind was still playing back the last ten minutes over and over. The aim of today's excitement became clear. There would have been three bodies found in the tent, throats cut. I gagged involuntarily.

A skinny young man in a brown robe walked up to Irsa. He wiped sweat from his forehead. "No luck, Mother. We tracked him as far as Brindle Road, but he must have climbed atop a carriage or some such thing. He vanished."

I don't *think* this was one of Irsa's surfeit of children; I think he just called her mother out of respect and familiarity; but in the two years of our market association I'd never laid eyes on any of her family. Though she complained about them enough.

The young man's glance passed on to Ran and me. "I'm very sorry," he said, sketching a bow.

Ran bowed himself, then shrugged. "It happens. We appreciate your effort."

It must have been a wild chase; Brindle Road was well over a kilometer away. Whatever were we going to do now?

Around the three of us, Trade Square bustled with its usual enthusiasm. Nobody could say these people didn't have energy. "Six tabals?" I heard someone cry nearby. "*Six tabals?* Are you out of your mind? Don't our children play together like brothers and sisters? *Six?*"

Whoever slashed our sorcerer had gone into that tent recently. Probably it was the same knife-wielder I'd been introduced to so abruptly; he and his friends could have waited with their draining corpse till Ran and I came in sight. We could question the nearby vendors, offer a reward. . . .

Why bother? I knew the system here as well as anyone.

Five hundred people in Trade Square, and I'll bet none of them had seen a thing.

Chapter 11

As Irsa had said, the car was coming straight at us. It's hard not to take a thing like that personally. Meanwhile, tired and wrung-out as I was (and no doubt as Ran was, though he never admits to such), self-preservation gets the wheels of the mind to turning. In order to wait for someone, you have to know that they're coming; that much seemed obvious even in my state of rapidly descending IQ. Who knew we were tracking the sorcerer?

Well, practically everybody who had anything to do with the Poraths knew that we were looking into the matter. And the Poraths knew an amazing lot of people. Assuming for a moment that Loden was the real target here, why pick the boating party to aim for him? Maybe that public display was no accident. Maybe they wanted it to be seen, and a scandal to start?

Really? said that annoying schizoid voice in my head. *How much of a scandal starts from drowning a journeyman guard? Who of any importance would ever care?*

All right, but the point is that the Poraths and their hangers-on are not definitely out of the picture, regardless of who the intended victim was. Now, Ran pulled the ring off Kade's finger yesterday. Any number of people could have heard about it by now, and if they assumed the logical next step, that we could somehow trace the sorcerer by it . . . apparently a hired sorcerer, who might be willing to drop his ethics and name names—

A hired sorcerer, just doing his job. The same way Ran does his job.

—Shut up. Anyway, the point is that . . . is that . . . we don't seem to really be any closer, do we? Almost ended up on the floor of that ratty tent, soaking the rest of *that fellow's* pillows, and we still don't have the faintest idea of who's responsible.

Perhaps a holiday and a good book would be in order.

Ran agreed that any further action could wait till tomorrow. We both went home and I sat in the downstairs study with its specially imported chair—a desk chair, but a marvel of soft upholstery—and I tilted it back and put my feet on the desktop, while Ran went out to the cookshop for our dinner.

I noticed that we had messages waiting on the Net, and I exerted myself so far as to reach over and push a button.

One of them was the House secretary's notice of the revised agenda for the yearly meeting of the Cormallon council. It was marked with a family seal, and the notation PRIVATE. The meeting was scheduled for later in the week, so Ran would probably want to get a look at this when he came in. I hadn't seen the last agenda list, so I used my privilege code to open it.

It read:

2nd of Kace

6th Hour	Breakfast/Welcome
7th	Financial Review
9th	Branch Reporting
10th	Midday Meal Served at Central Pond
12th	Particulars and Problems: • Mira-Stoden • Theodora • Andulsine alliance
15th	Recess
lst/eve	Supper, Wine, Entertainment

Does my name leap out at you there from the middle? It leapt out at me.

Notice there's no explanation listed for Mira-Stoden; everyone knows our branch in that city has been having problems. No explanation necessary for the Andulsine alliance either—people have been talking about it, off and on, for years.

And no explanation necessary for Theodora.

Damn, I didn't need an explanation either. When I asked

Ran a while back about how our House would handle my not producing any heirs, I had the Cormallon council meeting in the back of my mind. It might seem, to non-Ivorans, a little early in the marriage for anybody to be concerned on that topic, but the unfortunate tendency of males of the great families to get themselves knocked off has made the Houses prudent about succession rights. They like to have it all clear as soon as possible. I'd already seen what happened from one disagreement over succession, and I could understand wanting to avoid anything similar.

I did want children, but left to my own devices I'd probably have waited a couple of years. When the hints I'd picked up led me to conclude that I didn't have a couple of years, I'd made that check-in with the Selian Free Clinic. The big news was that my implant had indeed dissolved, months ago, and there was nothing standing between me and kids but random chance. And the unknown factors of our separate genetic heritage.

Not that I'd considered this anybody's business. But if you think the Cormallons won't jump right in and inquire about all kinds of personal particulars in regard to child-production, you don't know them. I noticed they'd left a lot of time for it, too; the whole long afternoon was reserved for their "particulars and problems."

Did they have the potential junior wives lined up already? I'd bet my House share that somebody, somewhere, had a written list. A nice neat one, like this agenda here.

Maybe with ratings next to each name. Gee, maybe when the branch reps showed up for the meeting they'd each get a copy.

I had only just reached that thought when the door opened, and Ran came in carrying a large bag. He put down the issue of that day's Capital News, and walked over to set the bag on the desk. "Be careful, it's hot," he said. He pulled the bag open so I could get to the bowls of food more easily, then he turned and went back toward the door to get the News again.

I let fly with the top bowl. It hit the wall just over his head, as he bent down to pick up the News. Chunks of red groundhermit slid down the wall and most of the rice fell in a lump on his sandals. He jumped.

"What the—" I sent the vegetables after them. He dove out the door.

"Theodora?" came his voice, tentatively, from the hallway.

I sat there, bubbling like a pot on a stove. You should understand that I am not, by nature, a thrower. That was more Kylla's speed. Perhaps nearly getting killed this afternoon had had an effect on my personality.

"Theodora?" he said again.

I said—good heavens, it was amazing how steady and cold my voice sounded—"Go upstairs and ask the Net for a copy of the council agenda."

There was a pause.

"Are you going?" I asked.

"Uh, Theodora . . ."

"You've seen it, haven't you?"

"Sweetheart, there's no need to take this personall—"

"How long has my name been on the list?"

"Listen to me," he said, still from around the corner of the hall. "I knew you'd be upset—"

"How long?"

"Um, it was on the first draft, but I had it taken off. But then so many people brought it up, I had to let them put it on again. It's not as though it *means* anything, Theodora."

I tested the pot again; it was still bubbling.

"Theodora?" came the voice from the hall, when I didn't answer. The left half of his face appeared in the doorway. "Are you going to throw any more bowls?"

I checked, but there was no immediate impulse. "Not at the moment."

He slipped into the room. "It's just a meaningless agenda item, you know. Nobody can make us take any action on it."

I said, "You don't want to talk about children with me, but you'll spend an hour on it in a full council meeting?"

"That's not fair. I don't want to talk about it with them, either. And if I can get the discussion of Mira-Stoden spun out long enough, I may not have to talk about it at all. They'll all have their minds on the wine and the gold-coin girls, they won't want to let the meeting run over. It's the only time a lot of them have in the capital all year."

Not forgetting the written schedule, I said, "You won't be able to cover the Andulsine alliance question then, either."

"What of it? It'll keep for another ten years. It's not like anything really gets done at these meetings, anyway; I've already seen all the branch reports, and so have you. If there were a real problem, we'd fly out to the people involved and go over it with them. Which we'll have to do in Mira-Stoden anyway, pretty soon. You can't settle anything in an hour, one day of the year."

I said, "But the others care enough about this to have it put on the agenda."

He sighed and pulled over a stool. He sank onto it, and I realized I'd managed to get hold of the real problem, right there; the simple fact that they'd gotten it on the agenda was a message to Ran.

And of course to me. What got said at the discussion was superfluous.

Ran was the First of the House. No doubt my body was a topic of discussion in Cormallon homes around the planet. "There is no privacy inside the House," the old saying has it, and it isn't said cheerfully. But for the first time it occurred to me that Ran's capabilities were probably debated just as freely. Did they check up on whether there were any bastards left around? Or would they simply insist on handing him another wife, like a sports player handed a new ball and told not to mess up on this round?

I looked at my husband sitting on the stool and said, "I begin to see why you never give any information to anybody. It's the only way you can keep any privacy."

He seemed reassured by this remark, and we sat there glumly. Red sauce dripped on the wall, which I would have to clean later. No wonder I'd never gotten into the habit of throwing things.

I said, "Ran, face it, our . . . mating . . . is an unknown quantity. Maybe Ivoran and barbarian have had children before, but I've never heard of it. There's no record of it. I can't get a straight answer from anybody on whether we're still one species. And what about sorcerers? Magic runs in families, you've got to believe there's something physical in that. Are you different even from the run-of-the-mill Ivoran? How different? Do you know? The gods know I don't."

He was silent.

"We might try for the next twenty years and not get

pregnant. Or it might happen next week . . . and then what? What kind of a child would we produce? Don't you see that I need some kind of answer to that, some hint, some clue?"

He said, finally, "I'm not as worried as you—"

"Thanks, you won't be bearing it!" I said, unable to stop myself from giving the age-old answer.

"Listen to me. You remember Grandmother left a message for me—"

I sat up straight, startled. Ran's grandmother had been a woman of surprises, formidable, a little scary, and impossible not to respect. For some reason she'd taken a liking to me, and I'd walked carefully the few times I'd met her. As everyone else did, I suspect.

He went on, "She was a great sorcerer. But I think we both know there were things she had in mind she wasn't telling us."

"I know." Grandmother was one who wrote her own agendas, which she didn't always share.

"I spent time in the library with her bluestone after she died. The psychic impressions were still strong . . . knowing Grandmother, they'd probably be readable if I picked it up today. When she wanted to leave a message, she made it crystal clear. She was fond of you, Theodora."

"I kind of liked her, myself."

"She told me—well, I guess you can imagine, she told me to stop fooling around and get married to you. She said you might take ship for home, but a good hunter doesn't quit when the sun goes down."

"Gods! You never told me this."

"I told you she'd said for me to stop being a fool."

"But not in these exact words. And how did she know I'd decided on shipping out? Her message to me didn't. . . ."

Ran looked thoughtful. "What was her message to you, anyway?"

"Hmm, she told me to stop being a fool, too."

Ran waited for more, then said, "Well. Anyway, she said I was an idiot if I didn't follow through, since you were just the sort of woman I ne— The point is, she said you were good for the family. She said relations among the Four Planets would be shifting, and you'd bring new blood and better awareness of barbarian thinking. I mention the new blood because she seemed to have great hopes for our offspring."

That made me drop the question I'd been hanging onto and pick up another one. "What did she say about these offspring?"

"Nothing specific, but she was always an extraordinary card-reader. She would never have worked so hard to get you safely into Cormallon if she hadn't thought you'd be valuable. That you, and me, together, would be valuable."

I sat there for a minute taking this in. The vague suggestions of an elderly relative, now deceased, would not generally have an effect for me on such a personal issue—except that if you'd known Ran's grandmother, you'd take her very seriously, too.

"You never mentioned any of this," I said again.

"Well, it was a personal message. Didn't anyone ever tell you it's not nice to look into other people's private correspondence? Like council agendas with PRIVATE stamped on them?"

I waved that away. "You toss the House business mail at me to open half the time anyway. Besides, my privilege codes exceed yours." This was true. I handled family expenses, like most wives, and had access to the House financial records. "They should have stamped EYES ONLY if they didn't want me to see it. Or BORING."

He shrugged. I said, "About your grandmother, though, I'm glad you told me. It's very reassuring." If also rather alarming in its suggestion that I had a mission.

"Good."

"But I'd still like to have us both looked over by a genalycist."

Now he looked disgusted. "First of all, I'm familiar with some outplanet history, and there haven't been any real, trained genalycists around for over a hundred and fifty years. Just cooks following recipes."

"Tellys claims to be making strides."

"Where did you hear that?"

"Around."

"Well, it makes no difference to us, anyway. We don't know any Tellysian genalycists."

Jack Lykon, I thought. Just call the embassy. All we have to do is do them a favor.

I was silent.

He said, "So we may as well consider the issue closed. Trust Grandmother, Theodora; she's a lot more reliable than some barbarian with a good line of talk."

I stood up. "I'd better get a rag and clean off the wall before it stains."

"I'd better get us some more food," he said, joining me.

"What are you going to say at the meeting, if the discussion comes around to me?"

"I'll think of something."

I considered that as we walked down the hallway. "Tell them that I had an implant when I was on Athena last, and it's only just wearing off. They need to give us another year."

He stopped, surprised. "Is that true?"

"Ran, I'm telling you what to tell them I said. Do you really need to know whether it's true?"

"No," he said thoughtfully. "Perhaps I don't. Would you like me to pick up groundhermit again?"

"Please. Extra sauce."

He left for the cookshop, and I went to hunt up a rag and do some thinking.

We made our report to Jusik the next day. He was sitting in the garden beside the pond, a small table beside him with a pot of tah on a warmer and an empty cup. He was wearing a silver outerrobe covered with tassels—funeral clothes.

Ran sat on a boulder to the left of the table, and I sat on one to the right. Jusik didn't acknowledge our presence; I'm not certain whether he knew we were there or not. He may just not have cared. After at least five full minutes, Ran said, "Our sorrow dwells with yours on this day."

He glanced up. "Thank you."

The funeral had finished an hour ago. Firebowls were still set around the garden, and an arc of silver metal rose from a black pedestal nearby. The arc was just a remembrance, left out for half a year after a death, to bring the thought of the dead person back to mind. Silver streamers hung from it, from today's ceremony, but they'd soon crumble or blow away. There are no cemeteries on Ivory, and no monuments, except for emperors.

Lord Porath showed no inclination to pursue the conversation. My husband, however, is not one to allow the exigencies of real life to get in the way of business. After what he considered a decent interval, he said, "Noble sir, we must speak with you regarding our investigation."

Jusik raised his eyes to Ran's like one performing a rote task. "You have arranged a meeting with your employer?"

Ran's right hand, half-hidden in his robes beside the low table, clenched, and by that I knew his temper had been scratched. His voice was nothing but courteous when he said, "Noble sir, I'm afraid you yourself are my only employer. It's for that reason we've come to you to present such findings as we have, rather than to one more closely concerned with them."

Mild interest flickered in Jusik's black eyes. "Who is more closely concerned with them than I?"

"The true target of the sorcerer who caused your son's death." Jusik sat up straight and fixed his gaze on us both. Now that he was assured of an audience, Ran hauled out his facts as though Lord Porath were any other client who'd asked advice on a matter of magic. "We know that the sorcerer who killed your son was a hired market mountebank with a stall in Trade Square. He was using the name Moros when last heard from. He initiated his attack from Catmeral Bridge, where he waited till the boat was within range and his victim in line-of-sight."

"And you allege this victim was?" Jusik rapped out the words.

"We haven't completed our investigation, but at the moment the likeliest victim seems to be one of your security guards—Loden Broca Mercia."

I broke in here. "We'd like your permission to warn him, noble sir."

Jusik glanced at me briefly, then said, "And how did you come by this farfetched theory?"

Ran said, "Are you familiar with a blue ring Kade was laid out still wearing? Your steward will confirm it if you're not."

Jusik looked startled. He nodded, and Ran told him the rest of the story, leaving out one or two details of minor interest. Jusik said eagerly, "So you traced this sorcerer to his lair! What did he say? Who hired him?"

Ran and I looked at each other. Ran said, "We didn't actually finish the trace. Moros seems to have left town."

"But you can follow him, can't you, now that you've got the ring?"

"I really don't think he's likely to ever turn up," Ran said firmly.

Jusik sat back. "I see." He looked at me. "You agree, I suppose, that this witness won't be back."

"I would be very surprised," I said.

Jusik had returned once again to being the First of Porath. He picked up the tah pot and poured a new cup, his eyes far away. Ran looked at me and shook his head. I really don't know how he knew I was going to ask about warning Loden again.

After a moment Jusik said, "Are you willing to stake your reputation on this? That Kade's death was accidental?"

Ran said, choosing his words slowly, "I would stake my reputation on what I've just told you."

Jusik put down his cup and smiled, as though a silver arc no longer hung behind his head. "Then there's no reason to believe my family is involved with this at all."

"One might say that the use of your boating party as a murder location was an insult to you," said Ran, tentatively.

The smile grew slightly broader. "An insult if I choose to regard it as such. I choose to be tolerant."

Behind Jusik, I saw the short form of Auntie Jace make its way across the garden. She approached the silver arc, folded her knees, and sat beneath it in an attitude of respectful meditation. I wasn't sure if she was scoring points with the family or just wanted to hear what we were saying.

Lord Porath leaned forward. "May I speak frankly to you, my brother First?"

"Please do," said Ran, in an absolutely toneless voice.

"My House is . . . distracted," said Jusik, spreading his hands. "We have our attention in other places right now. Coalis needs seasoning, experience; and then there's the matter of Eliana, and your brother-in-law."

"Yes," said Ran.

"If you had come to me with some other scenario—hypothetically, if you had come to me with some news of a House enemy, who had killed Kade deliberately—I would have met with this enemy and tried to accommodate him.

I don't want our name involved in this anymore. I don't want our attention on it, or our money poured into it. I want to cut free of it altogether."

"I see."

Jusik stood up, and manners required that we stand up too. He extended his hand. "You bring me good news," he pronounced, more loudly. Ran allowed his hand to be grasped for a moment in fellowship, then slid it away. Jusik bowed to me, and I inclined my head. "We will discuss some fair recompense in a few days, when the initial mourning is over."

It was a dismissal, but I lingered. "Noble sir."

"Ah—yes, gracious lady?"

"You haven't officially given us your permission to notify Loden Broca of the danger he's in."

He appeared mildly surprised. "Your task is over, is it not?"

"But he could be killed at any moment. And he's never done anything to you."

"I never said he had," he said, bewilderedly.

Ran took my arm. "My wife takes a different attitude to these things."

Jusik wore a look I'd seen before, a look of one at a loss before barbarian ways.

Ran smiled. "I hope you'll indulge us by granting permission."

"Well . . . of course. It's nothing to me. But make it clear to anyone who's interested that my House wants to stay out of this."

"Naturally," agreed Ran. He started steering me around the pond before I could say something else.

I threw a glance behind me as we left and saw Jusik standing, looking across the garden toward the distance, the tah service beside his feet. Behind him, I saw that Auntie Jace had finally gotten off her knees.

"He seemed thrilled to pieces to get rid of us," I said. We were standing by the door, waiting for the steward to accompany us down the path and out to the front gate. Our official leavetaking, and hopefully the last time we (or I) would have to step foot on these cat-consecrated grounds.

"Understandable," said Ran. "We're useless baggage tying him to an incident he wants put behind him."

"I'm surprised he even believed us, considering how set he seemed to have your guilt in his mind."

He made a face. "I'm sure he'll check up on his own to confirm." He sighed, ran a hand over the top of his head, and skid, "But he'll get confirmation. The case is over."

I stopped. "What do you mean, over? Who killed Kade?"

"Do we care?" he asked, in honest puzzlement.

"You care! You spent a quarter of an hour telling me what a useless excuse for a sorcerer he was."

"Well, and so Moros was. And now he's dead. Good for the profession."

"But who hired him?"

Ran paused with the look of one who is trying to translate each word into some obscure dialect. He said, "Jusik is satisfied. We've exchanged favors. He'll give us a break with this marriage business. I'm sure the question of who killed Kade is an interesting intellectual exercise—"

"This intellectual exercise nearly had us both knifed in Trade Square!"

"That wasn't anything personal, Theodora."

I'd taken it damned personally. I still have occasional nightmares about it. "What if they try again?"

"Why should they? Once word is out that the case is closed and we're no longer interested. It's really none of our business, sweetheart."

The last sentence came out in a slightly reproving tone. He sounded as though, if one weren't being paid for it, looking into a homicide was an invasion of the murderer's privacy. As though it would be *rude* to pursue it.

All right, this is an Ivoran, I told myself. Give him a reason that means something to him. "Won't it look bad for our reputation if people still think you're the one who knocked off the first son of Porath? While a guest in their house?"

He bit his lip. "Jusik won't support that rumor."

"Some people will still believe it."

He said, "Look, Theodora—"

The door opened. Eliana, Coalis, and Leel Canarol piled out. I took a step or two back.

Coalis' eyes went at once to mine. "Theodora! Is it true? You found Kade's murderer?"

Eliana, meanwhile, had zeroed in on Ran. But still affecting modesty (or maybe it was real), she didn't want to leap on him and shout for his attention, so she tugged urgently at her chaperone's sleeve. Leel Canarol stepped forward and addressed Ran (she was, I saw, slightly taller than he was): "Is it true, gracious sir? Kade wasn't the victim at all, it was meant to be that nice-looking guard on the boat?"

Ran winced slightly at the latest woman in his path to comment on Loden's looks. Kylla had had more than a few things to say on that subject in his hearing.

"Fast work," I murmured. We'd only left their father and Auntie Jace about four minutes ago. She must have raced inside and flew upstairs to pass the word.

"You'll have to speak with Lord Porath about it," said Ran firmly. "I would not presume to comment on the affairs of your family—"

"Oh, come!" said Coalis. "He never tells us anything. And if it's not really anything to do with our family, shouldn't we know that we're not involved?"

Ran began, "I'm sorry—"

Coalis sniffed through his thin, aristocratic nose. He did that very well, I thought. "*Stereth* will tell me," he said.

"You're at liberty to ask him," said Ran, "if you think he knows."

Coalis said, "I think if he doesn't know, you'll have to tell *him* when he asks."

Looking as though he'd just swallowed something bad, Ran turned and went down the steps without waiting any longer for the house steward or giving his farewells. It was verging on bad manners, in which he almost never indulged; and saved from that only by the fact it was deliberate. A reply to what he considered presumption.

Eliana and her defensive chaperone seemed taken aback. I shrugged hurriedly, said "Sorry, noble lady; bad day," and clattered over the porch and down the steps after him.

There was a Net message from Stereth Tar'krim waiting for us when we got home. Ran put it on permanent hold, unread, with a privacy code beside it. Yes, I was *very* curious. But considering my recent adventure with privacy codes and Net messages, I thought it best to stay away from it.

Chapter 12

We duly warned Loden Broca that evening. His lodgings, in a cheap inn in a nasty part of town, were not on the Net, and this being the kind of message one doesn't like to give to a courier, we were compelled to visit him at home.

Climbing the dark and dirty stairs to his room, Ran said, "Theodora, whenever you get me involved in one of these affairs—"

Catch that?

"—no matter how high the birth of our client, we always seem to end up rattling around with the dregs of society."

I stepped up the steep stairs behind him, noting how airless the place was. "This time we have a nice house to go home to at night, and you're not wandering around penniless."

"Mmm, there is that." On the fourth floor the stairs ran out and we emerged into a hallway every bit as brilliantly lit. He counted off the doorways. "One, two, three, four—five." He hit the flat of his hand against the door.

We waited. He pounded again. I said, "He's probably not home. If I lived in this place, I'd spend as much time away as I could, myself."

"I refuse to come back here again," said Ran, making yet more noise, as though he would conjure Loden Broca home and available through force of will alone.

The door to number four opened. A woman in a night-shirt appeared, her black hair caught back in a long fall. She looked in her thirties, and she appeared unaware that her legs were on display from the knees down. Perhaps she didn't own a nightrobe. "Do you mind?" she said. "I'm trying to get a few hours' sleep."

It was still early evening, but Ran said politely, "I beg your pardon, gracious lady."

She blinked and peered at him in the dimly lit hall. I don't know if I've mentioned it, but my husband is one of the better looking creations in the universe. She said, "Oh," as though in reply to something. Then she said, "He's not home. And if he were home, he wouldn't answer. Nobody comes but creditors."

"You saw him go out?" asked Ran. I could tell he was trying to keep his gaze up around face-level. You don't often see legs on Ivory, except on performers in a few dance shows.

"Heard him. A couple of hours ago. He's probably at a tith-parlor, that's where he spends his time."

"Do you know which one?" I asked.

Her eyes went to me, then shifted back to Ran. "No, sorry, could be any of 'em," she said, as though he'd asked the question.

Ran said, "When does he usually come back?"

She shrugged and slowly wiped one hand against her thigh as though it had jam on it. "Depends on how much money his friends have on 'em. Or if he got paid today. Or if he meets somebody and goes to her place—that means he won't be back at all." She paused. "If the money runs out, he could show up any time. If you want, you can wait at my place—"

"Thanks for your help," I said warmly. "We'll carry on from here. Please don't let us interrupt you."

"No trouble," she assured Ran, still not looking my way.

It would be undignified to check and see where *he* was looking, so I confined myself to surreptitiously jabbing him in the ribs. I heard the intake of breath, but he gave no other sign. Then he smiled at our informant, bowed, and echoed, "We'll carry on from here. Please don't let us interrupt you."

She sighed, shrugged again, and went back into her room. Ran turned and looked at me. "What?" I said.

"I'll be black and blue in a couple of hours."

"I have no idea what you're talking about."

He took my hand. "You're not usually this hair-trigger. Does the council agenda have you that nervous?"

I was going to deny that, but he pulled my hand, and the next thing I know I had my head against his chest and we were holding each other in Loden's ratty hallway, and I was having trouble talking. *"Kanz,"* I said, finally, "I don't know. I don't know. It's just that—I don't have any place to go. I *left* Pyrene, and I *left* Athena, and I don't regret it . . . but this business with the council, somehow that's not what I envisioned when I took on your family."

"You're not leaving Ivory."

"I know."

Reassured as to my sanity—nobody leaves Cormallon, you get thrown out or you're in for life—he pushed back my hair and said, "Listen, this custom of multiple wives isn't the horror you seem to think it is."

"Kylla doesn't seem to be looking forward to it!"

"I wonder if it's the marriage she minds or the fact that she'd be junior wife. That's not the point, though, the point is that of course if it bothers you so much, we won't do it. Nobody can marry into a pair unless the senior wife accepts her in full ritual during the ceremony."

"People have consented to wedding ceremonies before, who didn't want to. Because of pressure."

He smiled. "I'd like to see them pressure you, foreign-barbarian-without-manners."

"They'd pressure *you*, that's the problem."

He was silent. I said, "Should I wait while they figure out sneaky Ivory ways to make your life as difficult as possible? And while all the time you know yourself that any confusion over succession rights is not a good idea for the House."

Finally he said, "The marriage is young. The council is overconcerned. We have plenty of time."

"We only have the time they're willing to give us—"

Footsteps on the stairs made us step apart. We faded into the shadows at the edge of the hall, aware that if Loden Broca had creditors his first reflex upon seeing anybody would be to fly down the stairs again. And if it weren't Loden, who knew how friendly this particular tenant would be?

That second one wasn't a problem. Loden appeared at the head of the stairs, walking easily but not quite as steadily as he had yesterday morning on duty. The smell of bredesmoke accompanied him.

We waited till he had his door open and then Ran stepped forward on one side of him, and I took the other.

He started to bolt inside—a bad move if we'd really been after him—but Ran got a foot in the door and grabbed hold of the shirt beneath his short outerrobe. A minute of undignified back-and-forthing gave Loden time to see who we were. He stopped, looking confused. "Sir Cormallon," he said. He peered my way. "Gracious lady. Uh, what are you doing here?"

"May we come in for a moment?" asked Ran.

Loden hesitated. Then he said, "Of course, gracious sir, but it's kind of a mess." He held open the door.

It wasn't kind of a mess, it was a total mess. Rolled-up piles of robes, shirts, and trousers were sitting in mounds over the floor. You'd almost think he was a university student back on Athena, except if he'd been Athenan books would have been mixed up with the clothes. A flute was on the tiny windowsill, beside a glass with something old and encrusted in it. A bag of half-eaten apples lay open on the floor beneath, the apples spilling out over the dusty floorboards. There was a bed and a stool, standard issue from the innkeeper; no other furniture or pictures.

Loden was fortunate in his choice of inn. It was the kind of housekeeping that asked for vermin, but there didn't seem to be any at the moment. I watched Ran to see where he was going to sit, but like me he apparently decided standing was the better part of valor. "Sir Broca Mercia," he began.

Loden made a sound like an unhappy laugh. "Maybe not Mercia for much longer," he said.

"Oh?" asked Ran, derailed from his path.

Loden sat down on the bed. "My supervisor isn't pleased with me. He isn't pleased with any of us who were there when Kade Porath died, but he's particularly not pleased with me. I wish you hadn't come to the agency, gracious sir. People get the idea that you wouldn't have paid so much attention to me unless I were involved in some way."

I said, "We think you *are* involved."

He glanced up at me. "I swear, I didn't even know Kade Porath that well—"

"No, you misunderstand. We think you might have been the intended target."

He opened his mouth, closed it, and opened it again, but nothing came out. Apparently the idea was so new he needed time to comprehend it. Then he said, "I think you must be mistaken—"

"Possibly," said Ran, "but listen to our evidence." He told Loden Broca the story of his ring. "Clearly it was the focus for the murder," he finished. "And you've already told us nobody knew you were going to give it to Kade."

You could practically see an invisible iron anvil settling on Loden's shoulders.

I said, "Have there been any other attempts on your life?"

He made some fishlike motions with his lips, then said, "No. And they know where to find me, it's no secret I live here . . . although I . . . generally don't answer the door. I like privacy."

The grave's a fine and private place, said the scholar's voice in my head. I didn't have a lot of respect for Loden Broca as a human being, but suddenly I felt sorry for him. His life, such as it was, was rapidly going down the chute. Maybe he was a bad gambler and hung out in tith-parlors, but did that mean he deserved to die? This dingy room was the best he'd done for himself, and now he was going to lose that, and possibly his job, and possibly a lot more.

Once I'd lived in a cheap inn, and gone hungry when I couldn't work.

I gave Ran a look which he met with alarm. "We've done what we can," he said quickly, walking toward the door. "We felt we should warn you. Come along, Theodora, we've got a lot to do."

"Wait a minute," I said, irritated. I groped for the moneypouch on the belt beneath my outerrobe, and pulled out two ten-tabal coins by feel. I stepped over to the bed and said, "Here." Loden put out a hand, still looking rather blank, and I dropped them into it. "Maybe you should leave the capital for a while. Do the Mercians have any branches elsewhere?"

"In Timial," said Loden. "But my supervisor would be more suspicious than ever if I asked for a transfer."

"Theodora," said Ran, from the doorway, with a trace of grimness.

"All right, all right," I muttered, and joined him.

"Best of luck, sir Broca Mercia," said Ran politely.

Loden nodded, sitting in the dark, that blank look still on his face. We left him there.

That night I woke up a few hours before dawn, and decided to go downstairs to get a drink of water. I stumbled down, half-awake, got the drink, and was making my way along the hall to the stairs to go back up, when I saw a shape in the dimness by the front door that shouldn't have been there. A large, bulky shape. A man-sized shape, lying on the floor.

My heart started going like a power drill. How could someone possibly have gotten in? Ran had the house spell-protected. Not that they couldn't get past that if they wanted to, but only a fool would deliberately bring down a curse on his head. Not to mention there were the locks and bolts to contend with. But there he was. My brain tried to figure out some other shape that could legitimately be hulking there in the darkness, but nothing came to mind. What the hell was he doing on the floor? Did he break in, get tired, and take a nap? Nerves of steel; or just stupid? Gods, what if this was another corpse? Which would suggest somebody else was likely in the house at this very moment. . . .

These thoughts stampeded through my head, one after the other, like a crowd that's just heard "Fire!" It was only about three seconds since I'd first seen his shape there in the shadows. It was too dark to make out his face; were his eyes open or closed? Well, we were going to have to assume they were closed because otherwise we were in the deep kanz. I kept moving forward, very gently, till I reached the stairs. Then I started backward up the first couple of steps.

The shape heaved itself up, shoving my heartrate into the stratosphere. I'd half-convinced myself he was dead. I flew up the stairs yelling, "RAN!"

With a yell like that and let me tell you, I put my heart and soul into it—you'd think he'd get the pistol from its compartment in the headboard before he did anything else. And you'd be right.

In nonemergencies he's hard to get up, but he was already standing in the doorway to the bedroom, armed, by the time I got there. "There's somebody here," I panted.

Probably right behind me, in fact. I threw a look over my shoulder, saw a moving shape on the stairs, ducked past Ran and went for the knife hanging from yesterday's belt on the corner of the bed. Then I turned around.

Lights snapped on. We all blinked. Ran said, "Sim? There's not anybody else here, is there?"

A rumbly voice said, "No, none I saw. I think I startled the lady."

I'd reached the doorway. At the end of the hall, looking slightly embarrassed, was a man of about forty, wearing a conservative street tunic with a nightrobe over it. There was a holster showing beneath the nightrobe, but his hands were empty. I looked at him, then back at my husband. I said, "Ran?"

He turned and laid the pistol on the sleeping platform. He said, "Theodora, this is my cousin Sim, from Mira-Stoden."

One of Ran's innumerable cousins? I decided it would be better for my marriage if I put down my knife also. I opened my mouth to say something telling to Ran, then closed it and turned to Sim. "Honored by this meeting." I turned back to Ran. "What's he doing here in the middle of the night?"

"You went to sleep early," said Ran. "He got in after you went to bed. I was going to tell you in the morning—I didn't know you'd go downstairs. Or if you did, I thought I'd wake up when you left the bed."

"I don't know why. You never wake up when I leave the bed. I do it every night."

"You do?—Anyway, breakfast would have been plenty of time to reintroduce you properly."

"*Re*-introduce?"

"You must remember Sim. He was at our wedding party."

"Everyone in the known universe was at our wedding party." I glanced toward Sim, who looked silently uncomfortable. "Hello, Sim. Sorry if I startled you."

"Quite all right, lady Theodora. Sorry I gave you such a shock."

Fortunately he was too embarrassed by the whole incident to call attention to himself by opening up the long exchange of complimentary apologies we might have gotten trapped in. "Please drop the 'lady,' since we're definitely introduced. Ah, may I ask why you were lying by the door? It seems an eccentric place to choose to sleep. Not that you aren't welcome to bed down anywhere you like, of course."

I felt Ran's fingers on my arm as he stepped in to relieve Sim of further explanation. "It's the traditional place for bodyguards to sleep, Theodora. I asked Sim to come stay with us for a while. After what happened in Trade Square, it seemed prudent. My cousin's worked in security before."

"I . . . see." I scanned Ran's face, which as usual was giving little away. "You left me with the impression that you didn't consider us as still in danger. Now that the case is closed."

"It's possible that not everyone has heard yet that the case is closed. You know I like to be careful, Theodora."

"Yes, I do know that." I paused. "Will Sim be accompanying you to the council meetings? It'll cause a little talk, won't it?"

"Well, actually I thought that when I went to the meetings he'd stay with you."

"I see," I said again.

"I thought it might give you more sense of security," he added.

I felt my chest, which was thumping the exhausted rhythm of a mount that's been ridden hard for the day and needs wiping down. "You thought it would give me a sense of security." I walked past Ran and back into the bedroom, tapping the back of his hand where it rested on the doorway. "We'll discuss that further in the morning." I pulled open the coverlet and slid into bed.

I heard Ran's voice say, "I guess we'll see you at breakfast, Sim."

"Sorry about the excitement," came the reply.

"It's all right."

"Say, do you folks have tri-grain in the larder? I always have that for breakfast."

"I wouldn't worry about that right now, Sim."

I heard steps going down the stairs, and pulled the coverlet over my head. "Gods of fools and scholars."

"Did you say something?" asked Ran.

"I said good night."

* * *

So four days later I was sitting in the arboretum of the Taka Hospitality Building, just down the river from the Imperial Park, with a hulking shadow named Sim waiting by the entrance. The Taka had gone up a mere ten years ago, a durasteel tower with weapon-proof glass and endless suites of rooms, providing conference facilities for all persuasions—polished mahogany tables, seating twenty at a time, with full Net facilities, for the more democratic meetings; polished marble bowls with a raised podium in the center for more arena-like get-togethers; polished stone group baths, with or without pleasant Taka personnel to scrub your back while you discuss business. There were also group beds, for when the intellectual and physical aspects of discussion became blurrily entwined. I know all this because they had a brochure in the lobby.

I was not, you see, invited to the Cormallon council meeting, taking place at that moment on the twenty-first floor. (In a room with a table, Ran assured me.) This was a branch-heads-only meeting. I had been invited to the financial controllers' conference, that takes place in the spring; since women traditionally handle the budget, that one is heavily female. Supposedly the branch heads meeting is more policy-oriented, although as Ran pointed out, nothing can really be settled in a day. But just in case anyone was tempted to make any promises he couldn't keep, each delegate would have been primed by his sister, wife, or mother before coming, as to what he could give away and what he couldn't.

It occurred to me suddenly that I had done the same thing with Ran, when I told him to tell the council I still had an implant.

I sat in the arboretum among the sprays of flowering plants, listening to the three fountains plash in the background. Ran hadn't asked me to wait, but I had no immediate responsibilities and my thoughts were too unsettled to take on any. What was I doing on this planet, anyway? What in the name of heaven had come over me? Things would be *safe* on Athena. As long as I followed the path the university had laid out, my future would have been financially assured, though never rich. And nobody could have hurt me too much.

Nothing is for life on Athena, not like marrying into the

Cormallons; when things go wrong you move to another cluster and make a half-hearted commitment there instead.

I didn't even feel competent to raise a child, and here I was fighting the council for the opportunity, swearing it would be no problem. Not that they'd require much from me in the actual bringing up; my duties ended with the actual physical production. I was free to lie in a chaise all day and dine on lemon ices, as far as the House was concerned; there were plenty of people available to watch over children and see to their education.

But the truth was that I was having more problems with the idea than I'd been able to tell Ran about. More problems than I was totally willing to look at, myself. Ever since that little event in Trade Square, every fear I'd ever had about bearing children on this crazy planet had magnified enormously. Had nearly getting killed made me more intuitive, more aware of the skull on the other side of the mirror? Or just more nervous? Was I seeing things more clearly now, things I hadn't wanted to face? Or was I reaching new levels of cowardice?

Admit it, Theodora, this *physical production* thing scares you. Somewhere in the back of your mind you suspect it might kill you. But even if we're too far apart genetically—even if the fetus wasn't compatible—surely the odds are far better that it would die rather than you would? Hire an offworld doctor to be with you day and night, if you're so nervous. This isn't the beginning of historical time, there are techniques available. . . . You took this on when you agreed to stay.

Human bodies are such complicated, pathetic bundles of apparatus. Addressing the huge pink flower in front of my arboretum bench, I said, "Why can't I just plant a seed in a pot and come back in nine months?"

"I don't know," said a voice behind me. "Why can't you?"

I whirled around. Stereth Tar'krim stood behind my bench, his spectacles making him look like an intellectually curious rabbit. He pulled them off and wiped them on his blue silk outerrobe. "The moisture here is fogging them up," he complained. "You'd think we were back in the Northwest Sector."

I saw Sim approaching from behind Stereth, and waved

him back. I became suddenly aware that except for my new friend at the entrance we were all alone in this big, empty, plant-infested room. And Stereth probably knew a lot more dirty tricks than Sim ever had. Still, there was no reason Stereth should be mad at me. Was there?

"Hello," I said.

"Hello, Tymon. Can I sit next to you?"

I moved over on the bench. He settled down, smoothing his robe, and said, "You never used to talk to yourself back in the Sector."

"I was never alone there," I pointed out. "You always had people checking on me."

He smiled reminiscently. "Great days, weren't they? Remember the night you and Des rode in after ditching half the provincial militia?"

"What is it you want, Stereth?"

"Funny you should ask, Tymon, because I was just going to wonder what you wanted. You're sitting here making mournful remarks at lysus plants. I'm surprised you chose that big pink one to converse with—you never struck me as someone who went for the flashy type."

I felt my face getting red. "They keep this room too hot," I muttered.

"Yes, I noticed that," he agreed courteously. "But in regard to your happiness, my friend, is there anything I can do? All well with your love life? You're not quarreling with Ran again, are you?"

"We're doing fine, thank you. Why this interest in my personal life?"

"Can't think what brought it to mind," said Stereth, gazing out over the enormous pink blossom in front of us. It was a flamboyant junglelike flower, with a central stamen rising from the heart, flushed a deeper pink at its base, and resting its flaccid length on the jumble of petals around it. It was an embarrassingly lush piece of nature, and I had to keep checking the impulse to throw a cloth over it.

"Ran's upstairs," I said, changing the subject. "Having a meeting."

"I know. I called the Cormallon estate, identified myself as an Imperial minister, and asked if they could put me in touch with you or Ran. They said I could leave a message with the staff here if it was urgent. So I strolled over, and here we are. —You know, I left a message on the Net for you both a few days ago."

"Uh, yes. Sorry about that, we've been busy."

"We shall let it pass. More to the point, my friend Coalis tells me that you seem to have decided that one of the security guards was the real target. Is that true?"

"You take a sharp interest in this affair, Minister Tar'krim."

"I *do* take a sharp interest. That's why I'd like to be kept informed if you pursue it any further."

"Why should you care what happens to a hired guard?"

He pushed his glasses back up the bridge of his nose and let out a sigh. "Coalis and I are in partnership over some of his inherited business interests. I'd just like to know they're safe. Is that too much to ask of an old friend?"

I pulled a curling leaf off the mutant plant irritably. "You know, I can't see you and the young monk getting along on a long-term basis. Particularly in the loan-shark business."

"Coalis is a good boy at heart. He reminds me of Lex na'Valory."

I turned to stare at him. He looked innocently back at me. Lex na'Valory was one of Stereth's old outlaw band, avoided for his tendency toward psychotic violence. "*Coalis?* I *like* Coalis."

"I always liked Lex," he replied equably, "though one had to give him extra room."

"Gods." I returned my mind to the issue at hand with an effort. "Well, if you think Loden Broca Mercia is the target, I guess you might consider the Poraths out of the picture."

"Not necessarily. Broca did owe Kade a fair amount of coin, so there's an established connection with the business."

I felt my eyes widen. "You have Kade's client book!"

He smiled.

"Where did you get it?"

"I won it in a contest. Come on, Tymon, you know I don't reveal my sources. If I did, you and Ran would have been beheaded by now." This was the closest Stereth had ever come to reminding us how much we relied on his discretion.

I said, "Maybe you can do a favor for me, old friend."

He looked expectant. "A market sorcerer named Moros was involved. We can't discover much about him. If you can find out where he lived, or who his friends were . . . "

"Lived," he repeated. "Were. Do I understand that Moros himself won't be showing up?"

"That's a safe assumption."

He grinned. "My old barbarian comrade . . . I'm impressed. How did you dispose of the body without gossip? Do you travel with a corps of private guards now?"

I nodded. "Won them in a contest."

Snorting sounds were coming through his nose. After a moment he said, in a steady voice, "I'm sorry I didn't look up you and Ran earlier."

"Frankly, I'm surprised you claimed acquaintance with us on the boat. I thought you wanted us not to acknowledge you if we met."

He appeared genuinely hurt. "Only until some time had passed. That was for your sake, not mine, Tymon. You couldn't afford to have your sorcerer husband linked with Stereth Tar'krim's outlaw band. But now a full year's gone by, time enough that I could have met you both legitimately here in the capital."

"Then I apologize, Stereth. That was very considerate of you."

"Damned right it was." He glanced irritably around, then said, "Let's leave this pink fellow." He gestured toward the immense flower. "I don't feel I can compete with him for your attention."

We moved farther into the arboretum, settling beside one of the fountains. The entrance was exactly opposite now, half-hidden by leaves though it was, and you could just make out Sim in the distance. Splashing water backed the rest of the conversation.

Stereth said, "By the way, who's the large gentleman who takes such an interest?"

"A cousin of Ran's. Here to see the capital." Sim came stolidly forward a few meters to keep us better in view.

"Ah." Stereth smiled toward him in a friendly way. "I take it he's only interested in those parts of the capital you happen to be in." Perhaps coincidentally, Stereth placed his hands in plain sight on his knees. Then he turned to me and said, "So tell me now, old comrade. Don't make me get you drunk, like in the old days."

I was startled. "Honestly, you know as much as I do about Kade Porath—"

"Damn Kade Porath. He's a passing business matter. He lived long ago and in another country. Not even his family will miss him in six months." His glasses gleamed in the overhead light. "I want to know why you have that pinched look on your face. I don't believe it's from a case of sorcerous assassination."

The trouble with being on your guard all the time is that when you hear a kind voice it starts to unravel you. As you may have gathered, our relations with Stereth are complex, to say the least, but I had reason to believe he was genuinely concerned about my welfare. As concerned as he ever is about anything; he's a little bit dead in some ways. But he was always true to his troops, as long as he knew they were dependable.

"Now, you see what I mean?" I heard Stereth's voice continue. "There your expression goes, screwing itself up again."

I wasn't near tears, but I was having a hard time maintaining equilibrium. "Oh, gods," I said finally. "It's nothing important to an Ivoran."

"An Ivoran? Don't try to categorize me, Tymon, it won't work for you. Just spill it."

I took a deep breath. "Ran's upstairs trying to explain to the council why we don't have any children yet."

He blinked. This was obviously nothing he'd expected to hear. Then he put a hand on my shoulder and said, "You're barren, is that it? Tymon, there are ways around this, in terms of House heirs. You can—"

"No, no, no. That is, I may be, with Ran, but we don't know yet. Look, it's a complicated issue, but the thing that really bothers me is that I'm scared of getting pregnant." A sudden thought hit me. "Cantry!"

"What does my wife have to do with this?"

"She's part-barbarian, isn't she?"

"Actually, she's full-barbarian. Both her parents were Tellysian."

I was crestfallen. "So we still don't know. But wait a minute, Stereth, what about your kids?"

I saw a surprised look come into his eyes. Stereth had had a child, but that was a long time ago, by subjective reckoning; it was dead now. I said, quickly, "I mean, what if Cantry gets pregnant?"

Anyone else would have been annoyed with me by now, but Stereth is incapable of annoyance when he's after something he wants. Even if it's only a whim to find out what's bothering his old companion of the road. He said, mildly, "That's not an issue with us. My wife can't have children."

"Oh. I'm sorry."

"It's a long story, Tymon. And isn't it time now to tell me why you're so interested?"

I started to explain the species problem to him, and he held up a hand.

"I see." He thought. "You took a chance when you decided to marry into an Ivoran house, didn't you."

"We both took a chance. But I keep having this feeling—I don't know what it is, I'm not usually that intuitive—that if I try to have Ran's child, I'll die doing it."

Intuitions like this are not dismissed on Ivory, even by my gangster friend Stereth. He sat there thoughtfully, laying his chin on one fist. "This is serious," he said finally. "What does the council say?"

"Oh, gods, I don't want to tell the council! They'll make him marry somebody else!"

Why could I tell all this to Stereth, when it was so hard to say to Ran?

Stereth lifted his chin. "Ran doesn't respect your feelings in this?"

"I haven't told him."

He shook his head. "Tymon, tymon."

"You know how he is about duty; I don't want him to think I'm a coward."

He chuckled. "Given your past history, I really don't think that's something you have to worry about."

"This is different. This is . . . more personal, more . . . immediate. Stereth, a few days ago in Trade Square somebody tried to knife me. I was closer to death, in terms of seconds, than I've ever been in my life, and that includes the Sector. It threw me."

"Normal, Tymon."

"It wouldn't have thrown you."

"I'm not normal." We both knew this to be true.

I said, "I don't know . . . I feel as though I came too close to the other side of the mirror. Maybe I'm being oversensitive to think Ran would lose respect for me, but I'm not exactly filled with respect myself."

"You're dwelling too much on a simple physical reaction. The body wants to live. You can't help feeling it."

"So it might just be a simple case of the jitters? I've been hoping that's all it is."

"Take advice from your Uncle Stereth, sweetheart. Tell Ran about your doubts. Get drunk if you have to. Gods, he's a sorcerer; he ought to have a better idea of what's good intuition and what isn't. Why struggle along by yourself, when expert knowledge is available?"

I was quiet, and Stereth let me be for a minute. Then I said, "You know, I'm not usually the sort who gets agonizingly introspective. I guess I expect to screw up my own life to some extent, but in cases like this, where the consequences go beyond myself—it's like I'm letting the team down. That's why I hate responsibility."

I thought he'd have something to say to that, but he didn't. I found myself going on. "And what if I don't die? What if I produce some kind of monster? Or a baby that'll suffer for the rest of his life because I decided to take a chance? Do you know, when I learned to pilot an aircar, I found I could go ahead with the thought of crashing and dying, but the idea of crashing into somebody else and killing *them* totally paralyzed me?"

I was coming up with thoughts I hadn't fully acknowledged until now. "You're very good at this, you know?" I said, with a trace of anger.

"You're only telling me all this because you really want to tell Ran," he said mildly. "Don't blame me for it. And please don't look upset with me, or the large fellow over there will come over to see what I've done to you."

I said suddenly, "Gods, I hate the idea of every Cormallon on the planet pinning their hopes on me!"

For some reason this made him smile. Having said all he was going to say, Stereth sat there with me by the fountain, holding my hand. We must have sat for a good quarter of an hour, at least, following our own trains of thought, when he remarked out of nowhere, "The other side of the mirror . . . There's a saying in the empire; 'Sons and daughters are what we have instead of cemeteries.' The continuation of the House, affirmation of life, that kind of thing. You know, having kids could be the best thing for you; it's easier to be brave on someone else's behalf than on your own." He smiled. "Or so I've heard. We can't go by my reactions; they're too idiosyncratic."

"Huh. That's certainly the truth." I turned to him. "Stereth, what's all this business about the Tellysian embassy? Why are you building connections there? Loansharking to the ambassadorial staff will only get you in trouble."

He smiled, pulled off his glasses, and polished them again. Then he put them on.

I said, "And what's all this about the Tolla? Did you know they were involved?"

He got up, leaned over, and kissed me on the cheek. "The Tolla," he said, "are a figment of the imagination of barbarian newscasters." Then he bowed like a gentleman—the first time he'd ever taken leave of me in such a fashion—and turned and walked the length of the arboretum out to the main lobby.

I spent the day in the park—Sim trailed me at a discreet distance, and I did not invite him closer because I wanted to think—and returned to the arboretum in late afternoon. I left a message at the lobby desk to have Ran paged when he came down, and that's where he found me, by the fountain. "You waited here all day?" he asked. He sat down beside me on the bench where Stereth had sat.

"No, I was up the street in the park most of the time." Walking about the fine grounds and considering those topics a virtuous Ivoran woman ought to think about: Murder, loansharking, outplanet terrorism, and whether to have children. "You don't look happy."

"No," he agreed. He took a breath. "They insisted on discussing our marriage. I told them the implant story, but they said there was no harm in having a backup plan ready. One of my cousins pulled out an unofficial list of junior wives."

Well, I couldn't complain that he wasn't telling me everything. "What did you do?"

"There's a breakfast meeting tomorrow before we break up. I said I'd discuss my position then."

I'd done a lot of thinking in the park. "Here's what I want you to do. When you see them tomorrow, tell them that your wife says any further action is unnecessary. Tell them we'll have a child by next year's meeting."

He looked at me.

I said, "Tell them if I don't know, who does?"

Chapter 13

I dreamed of tombs again that night.

In the morning I slept late and heavily, and woke up disoriented. Ran had already left for the breakfast meeting, so I got up, pulled on a nightrobe and puttered around getting some fruit and a roll. Usually I wash up and dress right away, to get the morning routine over with, but today I gave myself a little slack, as though I already felt like an invalid.

At my suggestion, Sim had gone along with Ran to the Taka Building. I'd told them last night that I'd be home all morning, with no need for a bodyguard, and why waste his cousin's talents? I hoped Sim would hulk discreetly.

I brought my cup of tah over to the Net link and asked for messages. Stereth's old message still lay there with its privacy code intact, unread, like something dead. A message from Kylla saying to call her. And a message from Loden Broca Mercia.

Loden Broca Mercia? I wouldn't have thought he even had a Net code. I read:

Gracious lady:
Your kindness was much appreciated. Something has happened that forces me to beg your help again, much as I would wish not to. Please come to my room as soon as possible. This is an emergency. I need to see you right away. Every minute counts.

Loden Broca

Heavens! It was timed as half an hour ago. Barbarian that I am, a direct appeal for help seemed to me to call for an answer, and I couldn't say that the message hadn't hit a desperate note. Clearly some action needed to be taken immediately. My imagination started to race. What the hell was going on at Loden Broca's? In my mind's eye I saw men trying to break down his door while he cowered inside . . . in which case, how had he gotten to a Net terminal? All right, scratch that vision.

But damn it, what was I supposed to do about his problem? Surely I'd been through enough lately. Suddenly I recalled my embarrassing flight through the house the other night, pursued by Cousin Sim. . . . Two days later, alone by the Net link, I felt my face get warm. I had not, perhaps, been comporting myself at my best these past few days.

I abandoned the remains of my breakfast, splashed water on my face, and pulled on my clothes. Enough of the invalid life.

Now . . . should I call Ran before I go? I really didn't want to interrupt his breakfast meeting when he was busy bringing the council around to where I wanted them to be. I penned a brief note saying where I was going and hurried to the door. Then I paused. All right, you don't want to act like a coward, but there's no need to act like a fool, either, is there? I went back to the trapdoor in the closet by the stairway, opened it, and took out one of the pistols and a new charge. Then I wrapped a green silk scarf around my head, tucking up my red-brown hair, and set a sun hat over it. The picture of Ivoran normalcy, if a little on the small side. The bulge under my robe would not be seen as unusual by anybody.

I arrived at Loden's inn sweaty and breathless, about twenty minutes later. There was no one out front. I slowed down, checking the doorway and the nearby buildings. Paranoia is always helpful. Maybe I shouldn't have come, it wasn't really my business what trouble Loden got into . . . but the man did appeal for help.

It was daytime, so the main door was unbolted. I was wondering whether to just cross he street and try pulling on the handle when it burst open in front of me. Loden appeared, hauling a dirty mattress. As he pulled it down the steps a skinny, gray-haired man strode up and stood in the doorway behind him. "And don't leave your kanz on my steps," he yelled. "Put it in the road! And you've got one more trip, and I lock the door behind you!"

I took my hand off the tip of the pistol, where it had

apparently gone without my command. The gray-haired man slammed the door. Loden wrestled the mattress down to the edge of the road. He didn't appear to see me.

I walked over to him and tapped him on the shoulder. He jumped slightly. "Gracious lady!" he exclaimed. "Thank you for coming—"

"That was your landlord, wasn't it," I said.

"Uh, yes. He seems to have gotten himself excited—I didn't do anything—"

"You had me run over here because you're being evicted."

"He's throwing me out on the street! I have nowhere to go—"

I turned and started walking away. He ran after me. "Wait! Wait, noble lady, please—you haven't heard the whole story. Just give me a few seconds—you're here anyway."

I stopped and waited. He pulled out a handkerchief and wiped his brow. "Look, it's more serious than you think. I'm suspended without pay from the Mercia Agency. Len's throwing me out here because I'm a couple of weeks late. I'm not on the job any more, so I don't have guards around me; I'm not even behind shelter at night. You're the one who told me my life was in danger! What am I supposed to do?"

He did have a point. The odds on his getting killed had gone way up. "Looks like it's time for you to leave town," I said.

"But if I do that, they'll never take me back into the Mercians. It's the only thing I'm trained for. And I owe them the rest of my journeyman duty."

I sighed. He did seem to be painted into a corner. "I don't see what you think I can do."

"I don't know either, but . . . isn't there something?"

Suddenly Loden seemed very young. In standard reckoning, he must have been less than twenty—inexperienced, from the provinces . . . and a trouble-seeking idiot. Ran would never agree to take this kid in, and I didn't blame him. Where else could we tuck him away? Kylla's? I'd never saddle her with this. "I suppose I could lend you some money for an inn," I said reluctantly, knowing the House of Cormallon would never see that money again.

He pursed his lips. "Uh . . . if there's any other way . . . there's no security in an inn, gracious lady. Not from somebody who really wants to get you. I haven't been able to sleep a full night here since you warned me."

"Well, what is it you want?"

"I don't know."

We stood there on the edge of the dusty street. I said, "All right, what's left in your room?"

"Clothes," he said eagerly. "Robes and uniforms, boots and sandals."

"Get what you can carry into a sack. Don't get a second sack for me—I'm not carrying anything." I glanced at the dirty mattress suspiciously—heaven knew what was living in it—and said, "and throw that thing away."

He dropped it at once into the street and went back indoors.

As it turned out, when he took a long time upstairs, I went up and helped him go through his possessions. And I did end up carrying a sack, of course. You probably suspected I would.

We marched through the streets with our respective loads, and I thought, What a sucker you are, Theodora.

I had him drop off the two sacks at a street laundry, which I paid for. Then I led him to the road outside our house. He put his foot onto one of the four concrete steps that lead to our front door, and I said, "Wait a minute, sonny."

Sonny? Where had that come from? Suddenly I felt like a grandmother. He stood down again and waited.

I said, "I'm not bringing a stranger onto the territory of my husband's House. I don't know you, and you haven't impressed me with your reliability." A trifle harsh, but my real opinion of him was that the only reason I absolved him from suspicion in Kade's murder was because he struck me as having no ability whatsoever to plan ahead. Granted that Ran felt the murder was poorly executed, if Loden had been involved I strongly doubted it would have come off at all. On grounds of incompetence alone, it was far more likely he was just what he seemed—a person in deep trouble.

I circled around to the back of our steps, by the wall,

and tapped a square durasteel plate about a meter and a half high. "This is our security station for receiving parcels. Nobody can see inside, and its walls are six centimeters thick, pure weapon-proof material. It's ventilated, because in olden times a Cormallon retainer used to sit in there to receive and open the mail." I grinned suddenly. "A very brave retainer, I assume. Anyway, there's room to sit up or lie down in it, and we can give you a slops bucket for your personal needs. That's no worse than some inns. It's a safe enough place to sleep."

I looked at him. "Or if you feel it offends your dignity, I can lend you that money for another inn."

He said at once, "No, this will be fine." Then he hesitated. "You are serious, right?"

"Look, I went to your place today to risk my life for you, and I'll do what I can for you otherwise, but I'm not bringing you on Cormallon territory. So make up your mind—"

"No, no—I didn't mean—I'll be happy to stay here. Just till I figure out what to do next."

Yeah, the Emperor will step down from the throne and start sailing paper boats in the park before you come to any intelligent decision. —Nasty, Theodora. Be fair. The boy is under a lot of pressure.

I said, reluctantly, "I'd better give you food money. Don't eat it inside there, it'll stink the place up."

"All right." He took without hesitation the new ten-tabal coin I gave him.

Then he went to the cookshop, and I put up a brief note on the station to the effect that it was out of order, and all parcels should be diverted to the Shikron villa.

When Ran came home, I hoped he would be in a tolerant mood.

"I put him in the mail box," I said to him as Sim discreetly left the room.

"I beg your pardon?" said Ran. *"Mail box?"*

"The one out front. I figured he could sleep there till he gets his life a little more in order."

"Mail box?" he repeated.

"I put a note on it," I said, "telling any messengers to

shuttle deliveries over to Kylla's. And I cleaned out what was in it this morning."

"Theodora, you're telling me that Loden Broca is spending his nights in our parcel receipt?"

"Well, it's not a Taka hospitality suite, but it is weaponproof, and we've both slept in worse places—"

He sat down on the divan in our parlor. "Great bumbling gods." He looked up. "Do we have any tah on hand?"

I went to get him a cup of the pink kind, because that's the most soothing, and he clearly hadn't had a good morning. I spooned it in, let it boil, and took him out the square tah holder with two empty cups. After he'd drunk a little, I said, "So how was the breakfast meeting?"

"Are you going to tell me the rest of this Loden Broca story?"

"I want to hear your story first."

"Gods. All right, I told them what you'd said."

"And?"

"They're a polite bunch. They couldn't attack the word of a Cormallon lady, so they agreed to table the entire matter till next year."

"Hallelujah!"

It wasn't an Ivoran word, but he recognized it. "Theodora, what are you going to do next year?"

"Let me fill you in on Loden," I said, and I did.

When I'd finished he said, "What an idiot he is."

"I know."

"I'd just as soon not even have him in our parcel receipt. But I suppose he took advantage of your soft barbarian heart."

"He did appeal to us for help, Ran."

"What of it? Let him appeal to the Mercians for help. And why didn't you have me paged at the Taka? I could've sent Sim back to you."

"More likely you'd have told me to let him appeal to the Mercians."

"Well, yes." Ran does not deny the obvious truths. "But I would have sent you Sim just the same."

"There wasn't time. Besides, why would you want me to wait for Sim when you've said we're not targets anymore? *Are* we in danger?"

He looked pained. I said, "Just what is Sim's purpose in life, anyway?"

"He's here on a holiday," Ran said. "Show him the capital."

We looked at each other. He sighed. "All right, what's done is done, I suppose. If anyone trails Loden to our house to pick him off, at least we've got Sim on hand to aid in the defense. —Mind you, that's if we look in the least degree of danger, Theodora. If the danger's only to Loden, he can deal with it himself."

"Well, naturally."

"I mean it. I don't want you taking any chances because his cute brown eyes are in jeopardy."

"Kylla said that about his eyes. I didn't."

"Yes, I recall now. You simply said they were remarkably fine."

I smiled. "Thank you for your understanding." I kissed him on the cheek.

Sim stuck his head in the door and said, "Do you have an extra pair of slippers? And did I see the Gossip Gazette somewhere this morning?"

I whispered to Ran, "He's adapting very well."

"And do we have any hard bread and jam?" asked Sim. "I'm very fond of bread and jam. Cherry would be best. Though I don't want to put you to any trouble."

The Cormallons had all gone home (except for Sim); our assignment for Jusik was officially over; and with Loden turning out to be a quiet guest, I had to agree with Ran that our attackers from Trade Square had probably lost interest when the case was canceled. He and Sim had gone to Ran's robemaker to get new suits for the two of them, and I'd pushed them out of the house gladly, looking forward to a few hours of peaceful reading.

Naturally the doorbells began to jingle. I checked the plate, saw it was Coalis, and let him in.

"You've interrupted Kesey's *Poems*," I said. "I may never get through that damned book."

"What a welcome, gracious lady." But he smiled; and I could see my way of greeting him pleased his na' telleth heart. "We should exchange volumes before I go. I'm carrying the *Erotic Poems* in my wallet, and *I* can't get through *them*."

"Importunate strangers keep interrupting you, too?"

"No, I just don't like the poems. Though I shouldn't prejudice you against them." He stooped to pass through the hanging that separates the parlor from hall, took off his sun hat, and whirled it expertly onto a table; narrowly missing a wildly expensive vase in the process.

He plopped himself down on a cushion and grinned up at me. "I'm glad you're home. Sit down, I've come to show you something."

I dragged a cushion over and sat beside him. He said, "Stereth asked me to come."

"He did?" It did take me a little by surprise, but then, I had no other good reason for him to visit.

"He wanted me to set your mind to rest on an issue." Coalis reached into the pocket of his inner robe, and pulled out a slim, worn book held together by a piece of string tied in an untangleable schoolboy knot.

"I hope that's not your volume of Kesey," I said, sensing it wasn't.

He slipped the string off and flipped forward, then backward a few pages. "Here," he said, and handed it to me.

Loden Broca Mercia had a page to himself. I whistled. "Six hundred tabals. That's a lot of money for a journeyman guard to owe."

"He wasn't very consistent in paying it back, either," Coalis pointed out.

I read the notations in green ink, payments of twenty to thirty tabals at a time. No wonder the boy had been living on scraps and tap water in that inn. Still, Coalis had a point; Loden often skipped a week or two, letting his interest rise dangerously. Even on his salary, he ought to have made higher payments at the very beginning. The figures were clear about that, particularly the figures done in black ink by a neater hand, near the bottom of the page. I said, "Is this true? He's up to twelve hundred tabals?"

"That's what happens when you miss payments," said Coalis. "He's barely scratched the principal at all."

I closed the book and returned it to Coalis for him to re-string. This all served to confirm Loden's story. Though he'd lied about how much he owed, which was, I supposed, understandable. It's hard to admit you've been that much of a fool.

I said, "Stereth asked you to show me this?"

"He said he wanted to limit the uncertainty in your life. He didn't tell me what he meant by that."

Who ever was sure what Stereth meant? "How well do you know the minister, anyway?"

"Me?" The question seemed to surprise him. "I told you, we met on a na' telleth retreat. I was impressed with his talent for concentration. We've been spending a fair amount of time together lately because of the partnership, but I suppose once I'm settled he'll have other things to be working on."

"So he's been helpful to you in the partnership. Worth bringing him in."

"Oh, definitely! I wouldn't have had any guidance at all in this, if not for Stereth." Coalis's face shone. "He's been wonderful."

"Does he talk to you much about . . . about before, when he was an outlaw leader?"

"I wish he would. He said those days are past."

I breathed a tiny sigh of relief at that. Not that Stereth was a gossip, by any stretch of the imagination, but it was good to hear.

Coalis was going on. "He shows me all kinds of things now, though."

"Oh? What kind of things?"

"All kinds. He's got a lot of friends, and he introduced me to some of them. They were able to help me a lot in the business."

"I thought you were mainly handling the business as a one-man operation. Isn't that what Kade was doing?

"Well, yes, but you need to know what to do . . . you need people to run the operations end of things. I'm too small to do it all myself."

Too small? Oh— "You're talking about the beating-people-up, leg-breaking end of things."

"Well, it *is* part of the business, Theodora. Otherwise no one would pay us back. They don't have regular collateral."

"No, I understand the concept. So you . . . direct the operations now, is that it?"

"Not yet. So far I've just watched. It's very interesting.

"I'm sure," I said noncommittally, thinking, *So this is why he reminds Stereth of Lex na'Valory.*

"But Stereth's promised me a chance to direct."

"Well, that sounds . . . promising."

"I'll be supervising everything myself, once Stereth gets us on track."

"Really." I wondered how to change the subject. I said, "I guess Kade's death opened up a whole new world for you. Maybe missing the monastery wasn't the worst thing, after all. It seems more of a liberation."

He looked slightly shocked. "How can you say that, Theodora? The field of moneylending is an interesting one, but it's only an illusion. Like any other lender, I'll be teaching that fact to my clients. Not that it takes much deliberate teaching. I can assure you, practically all of them eventually realize that the money they wanted in the first place was not that important."

"I see. You'll be bringing na' telleth philosophy into ordinary life."

"Of course; that's where it belongs. Naturally I'd advance further in the monastery, but I intend to follow the path as well as I can."

"That's very, uh, admirable of you. I'm not far advanced in the na' telleth way, myself."

"You're only a barbarian," he said tolerantly. "And I'm sure you've learned more than you think. One can't help getting lessons in na' telleth-ri, just by living."

"You may have a point. I've been thinking a lot about 'the other side of the mirror' lately."

"Excellent," he said happily. "That's exactly what I mean. But don't be afraid of it. Look the skull in the face. That's the na' telleth way."

I laughed. "The barbarian way is to avoid."

"That way the skull finds *you.*"

Look the skull in the face. Easier said than done. Coalis was reaching for his sun hat, gathering his robes together as he got to his feet. "I'm afraid I must hurry," he said, apologetically. "I'm expected at home. —Oh! Let's exchange books," he added, holding out his volume of Kesey. I gave him mine and took his. We stood at the front doorway for a moment and he smiled, an innocent smile for a sixteen-year-old nobly born loanshark monk. "I'm glad this business with Kade is over," he said suddenly. He turned to go out into the sunlight. Then he turned back and said, confiding, "I couldn't make head or tail of the Kesey. If you do, you must promise to explain it to me."

"I promise."

He tied his sun hat, took our front steps jauntily, and went off down the street under the row of spindly mirandis trees.

It was a rather ordinary day, that day, the sixth of Kace. I did some chores that needed to be done, went through some records, thought about organizing the paper files and decided not to. When Ran and Sim came home, I listened to their lengthy descriptions and duly admired the sets of robes they'd ordered.

That night I lay in bed listening to one of the rare summer rainfalls. I'd been interested in what Coalis had had to say during his visit; somehow the story of Kade's dunk in the canal wasn't finished with me, whatever Ran might think. If I did pursue it, it would be on my own time, that much was clear.

Why pursue it? I couldn't presume to any claim to justice; I didn't even know Kade, and what I did know of him did not impress me. Was it just because I hated not knowing how stories come out? I had to admit that the thought that I would never know did offend my scholarly sense of neatness. Or was I just getting desperate for what Stereth called "certainty in my life"?

It would be good to have something to concentrate on, something outside myself. Lately I couldn't even concentrate on that damned book of poetry, even when I was alone and without any distractions. In fact, being alone and without any distractions was the worst of all.

What was my problem, anyway? Why couldn't I just tell Ran the idea of carrying our child scared me? But I was a product of the Athenan University. I had no evidence to offer, just nerves, and that was insufficient reason to avoid something that had to be done. *(He'll lose respect for you, Theodora. —Oh, shut up.)* I'd known our marriage would be complicated when I agreed to come back, but somehow I thought we could just dance around this issue.

A bad assumption for a scholar.

Ran was lying next to me, propped on one arm, looking through some papers. Minutes of the council meeting. I'd been quite interested in them till I found there was no mention of the "Theodora problem" in there; the issue had been debated "off the record." Out of respect for my privacy, no doubt, but I'd have liked to have gotten hold of a transcript so I could arm myself for the future.

I heard the papers being put down. He stretched. "You're quiet tonight. And you don't even have a book in your hand."

"I'm thinking."

"Oh?"

Perfect opportunity to bring it up— "I was thinking I'd better get my hair cut. It keeps falling in my face, unless I pin it back with ten thousand pins."

Ten Thousand Pins. The Biography of Theodora of Pyrene and Her Basic Lack of Organization. Ran rolled over a little closer. "Don't get it cut. This is the longest it's ever been."

What is this thing men have about long hair? I said, "Desire is a reflex, physical appearance an illusion."

"You've been talking to Coalis again," he said simply, making a connection that impressed me.

"He was here today. Showed me Kade's loan book, which confirmed Loden's story."

"Let's leave Loden in the mail box for tonight. Don't get your hair cut."

"It's more convenient short, I won't need to do anything with it. Have you ever noticed how in plays the hero pulls out a single pin and the heroine's hair tumbles down in a sensuous mass, just before they make passionate love? If that was me we'd be searching and pulling out pins for the next twenty minutes."

"But Theodora. I rather *like* searching for pins." He'd rolled over and was looking down me with all sincerity. "Let's count backward," he said. "Nine thousand, nine hundred, and ninety-nine." He slipped one out. "Nine thousand, nine hundred, and ninety-eight. You know, if you're going to laugh at me, we'll never get this done."

It was still raining near midnight. I lay awake, wishing for fire, flood, or earthquake; something solid and awful in the outside world that I could concentrate on. Something other than myself.

Look the skull in the face. Easy for you, Coalis.

I got out of bed and wandered into the upstairs study, bringing the leather pouch I keep behind my pillow. I sat on the carpet, opened the pouch, and took out the deck of cards Ran inherited from his grandmother.

Maybe this was a waste of time. I'd run the deck when we took on Jusik's case, and it had given straight business answers to a business question. The pack was tuned to Ran's concerns and safety; when it came to answering my personal doubts, the odds were that it would be less than helpful.

But if Coalis could look things in the face, so could I. I shuffled quickly, before I could change my mind, and started laying out cards.

The Band of Brothers. The card showed a table of six men drinking themselves into quite a happy state of inebriation. I kept my finger on the card and watched it dissolve into a room I'd never seen, a room with a huge thick glass window showing blue sky, a mahogany table, and over a dozen men wearing respectable robes sitting around a curved bench with cushions. Ran was by the window. *The Taka Hospitality Building,* I thought. Ran was answering something, giving short replies while one man after another made excited comments. Damn, if only the deck gave me sound as well as visual! Finally a short man with a rainbow holiday tunic under his street robe stood up and gestured wildly. Ran strode from the window, eyes blazing, spitting out words, and ended by smashing his fist on the table. The short man drew back, and everyone stopped talking. Heavens—I'd never seen Ran hit his fist on a table in his life.

I took my finger off the card when I shifted position, wondering if there was any way in the world I could get a transcript from the Net. The card turned back into the Band of Brothers, ink and color, vine leaves under the table.

An interesting window, in its way. Still, this wasn't what I was looking for, it was just a slice of an old reality. I needed better data.

A wild and grim impulse came over me. Enough of this

shilly-shallying. I shuffled the card back into the pack, placed it on the floor, stood up, and went into the bathroom. There I took the beveled mirror from its hook over the sink and carried it back to the study. I laid it on the carpet, facedown.

I was looking at the plain wooden backing with its twist of wire stretching across. Once or twice in the past I'd experienced a deeper and stranger kind of card-reading; scarier, more symbolic, not just a window into normal reality. I tried to keep away from that kind of thing, generally . . . could I call it up now? I crossed to Ran's desk and took out an old brush-pen, and brought the inkstone he used as a paperweight to the bathroom sink to grind and wet it. When the ink seemed sufficient, I knelt down by the mirror, dipped the brush, and drew a skull-shape over the back.

It wasn't hard. The old waterstains on the wood seemed to suggest a skull before I even began, though I tried not to think about that too closely. When I completed it, I carried the pen back to the sink to wash so I wouldn't get ink on Ran's desk. I left it there to dry.

All responsibilities taken care of, I sat cross-legged by the mirror. I picked up the cards and shuffled them over it, trying to disengage my mind from the circle of daily tasks that keeps us all nose-to-the-ground until we die. It was death I was looking for . . . a sighting from a distance, nothing nearer, and with luck even that might be a phantom.

I waited until I didn't care whether I put down one card or another, and so I put one down. It was The Old House, a stone place in the forest, half in sunlight and half in tree-shadow. Why in the world did that turn up? A reference to the House of Cormallon? In an ordinary configuration it might suggest regrets or nostalgia. . . . Before I could ruin the reading by analyzing it, I put my finger on the picture.

And I was standing in an old passageway, in a place half-familiar. I started walking down the passage. My footsteps made no sound. Why did I know this place?

A moldy, tattered hanging was in one doorway. I passed by and went down a staircase, feeling a terrible sense of abandonment about the building with every step I took. There was nobody living here, I was sure of that. At the end of the staircase there was a short hallway and a massive wooden door. Some kind of old moss was growing on the side of the wood. I pulled it open with an effort—and remembered suddenly how Stereth had pulled this door open once, days ago.

I was in the Poraths' house in the old quarter of town. What did this have to do with me and the other side of the mirror? I walked out onto the low wooden porch with its lacquered pillars . . . rotting now, with great gaps in the floor that I had to inch around. No sound of bird or insect came from the garden, overgrown and abandoned. I stepped off the porch in the unnatural silence.

I took the remains of the path through the garden to the place where we'd spoken with Jusik Porath. The silver arc in memory of Kade was gone, but there was a white marble statue in its place. And somebody was sitting where Jusik had sat, in a tangle of silk robes. He stood up, looking past me. It was Ran.

He turned toward the statue. I called "Ran!" and heard the sound echo in my head as though it only existed internally. It was the kind of sound you hear through ear coverings, though my ears were open. I walked toward him.

The statue was of me! That was somehow the most horrible touch of the night, and I felt shivers run up my arms. It wasn't a classical statue, there was no noble look on my face; it was me in one of my street outfits, looking as though someone had tipped a thin sheathing of white over my head and trapped me in a passing moment. Ran put a hand on the crook of the statue's elbow. A surface of red pooled up beneath it.

The statue was bleeding. I was vaguely aware that I was watching this from some other place, and was sorry that I'd come. More wounds appeared. Ran stripped off his outerrobe and his shirt, and tried to clean the statue off. But the blood was inexhaustible. It pooled at the statue's feet, soaked through the shirt, and left stains on Ran's face and hands and clothing.

I wanted to leave here. I wanted to leave here *now.* I didn't live here, right? I came from some other place. This was just a picture, I could go back if I wanted to! . . . If I could remember how.

I started yelling. It echoed in my head without disturbing the air around me. I was completely alone.

Chapter 14

I woke up in my bed. The room was light. I looked around; Kylla was dozing on a cushion by the wall, the long gold string-earring in her left ear curling on her chest where the robe fell open.

I still felt unreal. I was afraid to take a step out of bed, not knowing if the floor would open beneath me or the walls would start to bleed. Somehow I'd lost control of normalcy.

Kylla's eyes opened. "Theo," she said, not that awful silence of the symbolic world of the cards, but "Theo," like any summer afternoon. The world righted itself, as quickly as waking up from a nightmare and suddenly *knowing* what was true and what wasn't. "Are you all right?" she asked, getting up and coming over to the bed.

"I guess. What happened?"

"Wait." She walked to the door and called, "She's awake!" Then she came back to the bed. "Theo, darling, I understand you've been messing with magic that you shouldn't."

"I've done it before—" I began to protest, but she put a finger on my lips.

"Save it for Ran. I'm sure he'll have lots to say."

I supposed that he would. Ran is not one of those people who are above second-guessing you. Kylla busied herself putting the cushions back on the cedar chest, then picked up a glass of water she had ready and waiting on the side of the sleeping platform and handed it to me. I drank it to please her, though I wasn't thirsty.

Ran appeared, fully dressed. I wondered what time it was. He came over and sat on the side of the platform. He took my hand. Then he said, "What in the world did you think you were doing?"

By all means, let's not waste time on being sentimental. "Come on, Ran, it was just a normal run of the cards."

"I don't have to carry you, unconscious, out of the study after a normal run of the cards. You don't start screaming during a normal run of the cards."

"All right, I grant you, you might have a point—"

"During a normal run of the cards," he said, "you *maintain control.*"

Oh-oh. The lecture on "the most dangerous thing"—

"The most dangerous thing you can do with magic is to let it have the least bit of random freedom! You have to define and control every variable! Sorcery is not a place to have a na' telleth attitude!"

This is the one topic I never fool with Ran about. I made myself look attentive and embarrassed, and in fact it was not at all difficult.

He said, more quietly, "Theodora, I hesitate to say this, but—were you asking an open-ended question of the cards?"

"I've asked general questions before," I said, trying to recall exactly what my state of mind had been last night—death, children, memories of the assassin in the marketplace, all mixed up together. Perhaps I *had* been a little too open-ended in my worries.

"You've asked general questions before, but not when you use that na' telleth technique, that wipe-your-mind and see what happens *thing* that you do. You know I don't like it when you experiment. The cards are a perfectly reasonable source of information when you use them as a simple window. So *use* them that way, Theodora. Half the time when you use this off-the-wall method we get symbolic answers we can't even interpret!"

"I'm sorry if I worried you."

He sighed. "What where you so curious about, anyway, that you had to get up in the middle of the night and do dangerous experiments to find out?"

I was not up to opening that discussion now. I felt wrung-out, as though I'd just recovered from a long illness. "Can we go into it later?"

He hesitated. His face went expressionless. "Of course," he said stiffly. "We can discuss it some other time. I have to call Mira-Stoden anyway and arrange to postpone my trip."

"What trip?"

"We decided in council that I'd arbitrate Jula's dispute in person. It'll probably take a couple of days, it's not the sort of thing to try over the Net."

"Why are you postponing it? Did something else happen?"

"Yes, Theodora, I picked you up off the floor of the study."

"Oh." He really did not look pleased with me at all. "Look, you don't have to stick around for me, I'm fine."

"I'll stay."

"Honestly, I'd prefer it if you went."

He was silent. I said, "I'm perfectly well."

Finally he said, "You want me to leave."

"Well, why get the council any more annoyed than we have already?" And I didn't want to face all the questions I knew he'd have as soon as he got off the Net.

He stood up. "As you wish." He certainly didn't sound any happier about it or me. "I'll see that it doesn't last beyond noon tomorrow." That last came out almost like a warning. He added, "Sim will be here, and Kylla will look in on you tonight."

Belatedly, it seemed to occur to him that he might ask Kylla how she felt about that. "Ky, you won't have any problem dropping over, will you?"

Before she could answer, I said, "It's not necessary, Ky. Last night was a fluke. I'm all right now, really."

"I'll come by this evening, just the same," she said.

So Ran left, looking dissatisfied.

To give you an idea of my state of mind as we approached High Summer Week, I suppose I should mention that at least once every few days I found myself sharply reliving those seconds in the sorcerer's tent in Trade Square. I'd heard of people flashing back to traumatic moments, and I don't know if this was what was meant by it or not. I was never in any doubt as to where I really was, or what was really happening, but in the midst of walking down the street or opening up a food container, or—most often—lying in bed waiting to fall asleep—I would suddenly find myself, double-vision-like, inside an amazingly vivid memory of those few seconds. I could feel the grit under my hands when I hit the ground, see that knife looming up, and sense the horrible twisting in my stomach that had taken place at that moment.

I experienced it again, after Kylla and Ran had left and I was sitting in the larder spooning jam onto a piece of bread. *Interesting,* said a detached part of my mind, as jam dribbled onto my fingers. It didn't do a lot for the appetite, though.

"Are you finished with that jam?" asked Sim's voice.

I turned around. "Oh. Sorry, yes, here you are."

"Thank you, my lady."

"You know, you can call me Theodora. We *are* cousins."

He took a big bite of bread and jam.

As he chewed away, I said, "So you're taking a holiday. Have you been to the Lavender Palace yet?"

He shook his head.

"The Lantern Gardens? The Imperial Park?"

"No, my lady."

I didn't correct him. "Well, do you want to go out? I'm tired of being a burden on society. Go on, see the sights."

"No, thank you, my lady."

"There's a flyer race in Goldenweed Fields today."

"No, thank you."

It was clear that Ran had gotten in before me. He, on the other hand, felt free to go off to Mira-Stoden by himself, while not bothering to ask my permission before chaining this babysitter to me. I pried the jam pot away from Sim and spooned out another sliceful, thinking vengeful thoughts. It was nice to be angry at somebody else for a while.

The doorbells rattled furiously and I put down my breakfast and went to see who it was. Sim was already checking the spyplate. "Nobody I know," he said to me.

I looked for myself. It was Trey Lesseret, Loden's coworker from the Mercian agency. "We'll let him in," I said. "But stick around."

Sim nodded. He approved of paranoia. I hit all the locks and opened the door.

Trey Lesseret bowed quickly, saying, "Gracious lady. May I speak with you a moment?" He wore the trousers and tunic of his profession, and looked to be either on his way to work or on a break in midassignment. His expression was unhappy, and a little desperate.

He ignored Sim. As soon as he was inside, he turned to me and said, "Forgive my imposition, but do you know where Loden Broca is?"

"Why should I know where sir Broca is? Surely he's at work. Why don't you ask your supervisor?"

"Excuse me, but Loden already told me he was staying here." Well, Pinnacle-of-Discretion Loden. "I have good reason for asking, you see—a Net inquiry was made this morning at the agency—someone wanting to know where he is. Loden's only family is in the provinces, and none of them would use the Net."

"I see." I hesitated. "Are you aware of Loden's situation?"

"He told me someone's trying to kill him, if that's what you mean. That's why I figured I'd better find the young idi—why I'd better locate him. It's the first time, ever, that anyone's tried to reach him at work. Anyone who's not a girl, I mean." He paused and ran a hand through his sparse grayish hair. "Now, I only know about this because I overheard the secretary talking. I haven't got details. But I think he's damned lucky he was sent off till his probation's over. Otherwise he'd've been locatable within minutes—we're all supposed to be constantly locatable, it's part of our coverage strategy."

I considered this. "Did Loden tell you exactly where he was staying?"

"In your parcel receipt. But there's no answer when I hit the entrance with my knife butt."

"Wait." I ran and got my overrobe, tied on my belt and pouch, and slipped on a pair of sandals. "Sim, come with me."

We all filed outside and down the steps to the parcel receipt entrance. While Sim watched to make sure Lesseret was looking elsewhere—as he was, in all politeness—I keyed open the entrance. Metal slid aside and a man-sized opening formed to the right of the locked delivery tube. It struck me suddenly that this was the place, in one of those old puzzle-stories, where the second body would be found.

A strong smell of bredesmoke assailed us. I started to cough, and Lesseret looked a little embarrassed. I stooped and peered through the drug haze to the interior; empty, but for a pallet of old cloaks and half a nutcake. Getting that close made me cough some more. "You could get high just sitting in there," I said, as I stood up straight and topped the entrance. "Evidently he isn't worried about ventilation."

"Please help me," said Lesseret.

I was surprised. "What can I do? You see he's not here."

"He needs to be warned. But I can't look for him, I have to be back at my assignment in twenty minutes. I'm on probation, too, but they're letting me keep working—I can't afford any black marks."

"I'm sorry, but I don't see what it is you want me to do."

"Look, he's not at work and he's not here. He's almost certainly at a tith-parlor."

I glanced at Sim, who was expressionless. "Are you suggesting I call every tith-parlor in the capital . . . ?"

"No, of course not. They'd never tell you the truth about whether a customer was there. You'll have to go personally and look."

I would, would I? "Sir Lesseret . . . you seem like a nice person, and it's good that you're concerned about a friend, but this is getting out of hand. I don't even *know* Loden."

"He could be killed! He could *die* today! I don't know who else to go to. Look, I don't have a lot of money, but I could pay you a little a week—"

I winced, thinking of Kade and Coalis. "No, wait." I said to Sim, "Do you have any idea how many tith-parlors there are in this city?"

"I'd figure, thirty or forty," he said.

"It's not that bad," said Lesseret eagerly. "He always goes to the gambling quarter, and there are only about twenty there."

"The gambling quarter" is a five-block section of town where tith-parlors and cardhalls and things I still don't know about seem to have congregated; there are a lot of pretty colored lights there. At least it was a relatively small distance to cover.

A small distance for Loden's enemies to cover, too, if they figured out that that's where he was.

I sighed. "I take it he doesn't have a favorite place."

"Not really. He usually goes to Red Tah Street, there are five or six places there . . . but sometimes he goes somewhere else."

"Terrific." I suppose I'd accepted responsibility for him when I'd stuck him in our mailbox. I should have let him find his own way out to the provinces in the beginning. Appropos of nothing, I pointed to the half-eaten nutcake on the floor. "You know, I asked him not to bring food in there."

"The boy doesn't listen," said Lesseret worriedly, echoing my own thoughts.

"No," I sighed, "he doesn't." I looked at Sim. If you can't trust your husband's taste in bodyguards, what's the point of being married? "Are you game for this? We're not under obligation."

"It's not for me to say," he replied primly. "If you go, I go with you."

"Cousin Sim, this is the time for you to raise objections. We can go back inside and have lunch, if you want. If there's any danger in this, you'll probably get hit first, and I won't take you into something you'd just as soon avoid."

"It's up to you," he said stubbornly. The Cormallon sense of duty. I gave it up.

"Go back to your job," I said to Trey Lesseret. "We'll see if we can find Loden."

"My thanks," he said happily, going so far as to take my hand and bow over it.

"Never mind. We probably won't run across him anyway."

But he was too thrilled with having dumped his problem in someone else's lap to let me dampen his spirits. He hurried off down the street before anyone could change their mind.

Red Tah Street has closer to a dozen parlors on it, counting the cardhalls and smoke dens on both sides of the road. I'd never stopped in this little part of town before; it had no attraction. Aside from an occasional card game to pass the time, gambling has always been a closed book to me. The more random chance rules a situation, the more I tend to avoid it—probably because I lose. It's amazing, in fact, how consistently I lose. Back on Pyrene, when I was a kid, there was a little arcade off the recreation hall where we could bet study-tokens on a wheel with six numbers. I was the only child in the crèche who never won even once in all the years I was there. Winners got to pick from the bakery products left over from that day's kitchen detail. It was understood that our crèche-guardian would have to bring hard currency and purchase one for little Theodora, since she was incapable of winning any.

It was a good inoculation against gambling fever; all I associate it with is disappointment.

Red Tah Street was packed, even in the afternoon, so obviously others don't have the benefit of my bad luck. We were standing on the edge of the neighborhood, beside the first hall, under a painted wooden sign that showed a giant wheel with kings, princes, and beggars falling off into the mud as it turned. Clearly not an establishment that made great promises. "We could split up," I said to Sim. "Take different sides of the street."

He shook his head.

"I won't tell Ran. It's not as if these people were looking for us. It's Loden they're after."

He shook his head.

"Fine. Let's try the Wheel of Illusion first. I look forward to seeing a gambling parlor with a na' telleth name. You think maybe they don't play for money?"

He held the door patiently for me, not responding. Sim has standards when he's on duty. Inside, the place was cramped, dark, and not very well cleaned; it took about ten seconds to ascertain that Loden wasn't around. There was a numbers wheel in back and a set of card tables and benches in front, with fanatical looking men and women of all ages. A twenty-ish woman in a gold-threaded robe sat opposite a man in his sixties with a ragged tunic and no teeth. Their attention was solely on the game. I began to realize that gambling creates an equality of citizenship societies have toppled trying to achieve.

"He's not here," I said, intelligently. Sim grunted. I considered the arithmetic of our hitting each parlor on the street; it would be a shame if Loden ambled from one to the next, just missing us. I nudged Sun. "Let's see if we can find the manager."

"It's not really a tith-parlor," said Sim. "Just cards and wheel."

"No harm in asking," I said.

The manager was a middle-aged woman of great politeness and no expression. She wore a green robe and carried a pipe. "Young men come in here all the time," she said, when I asked. "Old men, too. Everyone comes here."

"He might be wearing a security guard's outfit. Trousers and tunic. And his name is Loden Broca."

She paused, then tapped her pipe against the wall. Soft gray ash fell onto the floor, where it vanished in the dirt and shadows., "Loden Broca. Yes, I know the name. I know the name of everyone on the debit side of our ledger, gracious lady. I seriously doubt if Broca will come here today. He owes us quite a sum of money."

"I thought he'd paid off all his debts," I said, remembering the loan he'd taken from Kade for that purpose.

"He paid some. Not all." She pursed her hard little lips. "Should you locate him, I hope you'll bear in mind we pay a ten-percent finder's fee for notifying us where we can find recalcitrants."

"Well, I'll certainly consider that." I started backing away. "Come on, Sim."

No one from the Wheel of Illusion made any move to follow us, and I was glad when we reached sunlight again. "What a jolly street this is. I can see why it's so popular. Let's try the Green and Gold."

The Green and Gold was better-lit than its predecessor, but not more helpful. At least Loden didn't have a tab there. We went through six more halls in the next two hours; fortunately Sim and I were well-dressed enough to receive courteous treatment from the managers.

At the Rainbow Enchantment Palace, a particularly small and no-frills place, I sat down for a moment by one of the machines. My feet hurt. Sim stood beside us, surveying the customers. A chubby girl about five years old ran up to me at once, wearing a pink ribbon; she bowed and offered me a cup of tah on a round silver tray. I was thirsty, so I thanked her and took it.

She ran off again before I could pay her. "Now you'll have to light up the machine," said Sim. "Drinks are only for players."

"You seem to know a lot about these places," I said. I stuffed a few kembits into the slot and watched the board take form, then read the instructions idly as I drained my cup. "Say, I think I know this. It's a variation on Solitaire."

Sim greeted this remark with his usual interest, so I tested my theory by using the button to move a few tiles around on the screen. My score started to climb. It wasn't quite like Solitaire, but it was similar; the strategic element had a little more influence, otherwise I probably would have experienced my usual losing streak. Instead I won two games out of three.

I was going for four when Sim tapped my shoulder. "Isn't this fellow in danger of his life, or something?"

"Oh. Yes." I swiveled the seat around and stepped off, feeling my face get hot. "I was only resting my feet for a few minutes."

"It was a quarter of an hour."

"You're joking."

I should know better than to accuse Sim of joking. He pointed out, in all seriousness, the information on his own timepiece, the clock over the machine rack, and (when we got outside) the sun in the sky. By the time we reached the doors to the Inner Courts of Heaven I was sorry I'd said anything.

Heaven was jumping. It was a big place, noisy and scrupulously clean, with the kind of lighting that tells you more about people than you wanted to know. Specifically, it was Tithball Heaven; there were a dozen ranges built against three of the walls. The fourth wall had racks of smaller machines with brightly lit tiles, like the addictive one I'd just left behind at the Rainbow. The center of the building was filled with tables and benches where people who were waiting for a range to open up could pay for food and drink. The Courts of Heaven provided everything; a customer could spend days here and never have to set foot outdoors.

There were well over a hundred people present already, and their busy time probably wasn't till evening. Sim and I made our way past the ranges, aiming for the back, where a raised platform would provide a better view of the room. Three brawny-looking gentlemen, their sleeves tied back, were too intent on their game to see they were blocking our progress. I watched as one with a jeweled bracelet clamped around his wrist threw his arm back and let the ball fly down the range. It hit the floor near the far end, bounced, and tapped the wall marked "east."

The player laughed. A bronze phoenix head over the range opened its mouth ponderously, displaying a score of 450. The tithball bounced three more times on the floor, hitting a tilted slope in back. Jeweled Bracelet stared; his triumphant look changing to that of a child whose bottle is being unfairly taken away. The ball rolled down the slope and disappeared. The score in the phoenix's mouth rippled and changed to 10.

His companions laughed. "You're right," said one of them. "Your playing has really improved."

Jeweled Bracelet glared. He clapped his hands, muttered, and pointed to the crack where the ball had vanished.

It popped up again and rolled down the range to his open hands.

The score in the phoenix's mouth changed back to 450.

"Hey, that's not fair," said one of the other men.

"An act of the gods," said Jeweled Bracelet. "If a server had bumped into me while I threw, we would have counted *that*."

"This is different."

"I don't see why."

"Look, sorcery is not allowed!"

"The rules don't say anything about sorcery one way or the other."

Sim finally managed to push a route through them, and they were far too busy arguing to take issue with it. We hadn't quite reached the platform when Sim stopped short and pointed.

Loden was sitting at one of the tables in the center. He was wearing provincial trousers, but with a stained silk robe over his shirt. Two empty winebowls were in front of him, stacked one atop the other, and a small plate of something that had had reddish sauce. A light-haired girl of about eighteen was in his lap.

"The prodigal," I murmured. Sim started his dignified progress through the crowd once again, and I sailed in his wake. When we reached Loden's table, he looked up and smiled happily.

"Theodora!" he cried. "Have a seat, gwacious—gracious lady. Let me introduce you. This is Pearl," he said, slapping his lapful's fanny gently.

She giggled. "Ruby," she corrected.

"She's a jewel, anyway. And this is Rickert." He waved an arm toward the third person at the table, a young man with his sleeves still tied back from the game. Rickert nodded sourly.

I said, "Loden, we need to talk."

"Sure, that's what I'm saying. Have a seat. Move over on the bench, Ricki, and let Theodora sit down." He grabbed the robe of a passing server, and the woman stopped. "Two more bowls here, all right? Thanks, sweet one." He winked at her.

The server's gaze met mine briefly. She rolled her eyes.

I said, "Loden, we need to talk. Privately. Right now."

Rickert stood up. "We have to go anyway. Come on, Ruby."

Ruby didn't look at him. "We've got hours yet, sweetheart. I'm fine where I am."

"No, you're not," said Rickert, in a tone that got even Ruby's attention.

She turned to him slowly and blinked. "It's still early—"

"Now."

She got up from Loden's lap, taking her time, a pout forming on her face. I noticed that Loden still had a hand under her robe. I couldn't tell if Rickert could see that from his angle. She moved away slowly, her robe trailing.

Rickert took her hand and pulled her in the direction of the door.

"I don't know what you're so excited about all of a sudden," I heard her complain as the crowd swallowed them up.

I looked at Loden, who returned my gaze with happy obliviousness. Sim sat down next to me.

"It's good to get out, isn't it?" asked Loden. "I have to say, that parcel receipt can get on your nerves. Not that I'm not glad to have it to go home to."

With Loden, it was hard to tell how much was drunkeness and how much was his normal lack of discernment. I hoped he wasn't too far gone to pay attention.

"Listen," I said, "your friend Trey came to see me today."

"Trey! A great guy. Was he looking for me?" Loden's two new winebowls appeared on the table, and he reached for one. Sim, bless him, pulled it out of reach.

"Loden. Trey says that someone's been asking for you at work. You know what that means?"

He looked blank. "Who would ask for me at work?"

"I don't know, Loden, this is the point. But considering people are trying to kill you, Trey thought you ought to stay under cover."

The idea was still making its way through the outer courts of his brain. I saw it hit center.

"Ohh," he said, in simultaneous comprehension and pain.

Thank the gods for that. Now maybe we could get him out of here quietly.

Sim stood up, clearly expecting we would leave now. I don't know what it was—the effects of the crowds, the constant sense of money and danger, the impersonal desperation all around me—but suddenly I didn't believe at all that Loden didn't know who was after him.

I said, "You're involved in something, aren't you?"

He managed to look both crafty and ashamed at the same time.

"Oh, Loden." I sighed. "How can you manage to make such a mess of your life?"

I spoke at that moment from pure sadness at the waste, and he put his hand across the table over mine. "Theodora—" he began.

"Here he is," said a voice.

It was Jeweled Bracelet and his two friends. "I thought you were going to give us a rematch," said one.

"Oh, sure," said Loden, "you wait till I'm eight winebowls down—"

"You haven't had time to drink more than three. And I thought you said you could beat us playing with your feet?"

"How much did you have in mind?" asked Loden, apparently forgetting Sim and me entirely.

The men looked at each other. "Twenty tabals," said Jeweled Bracelet.

"Thirty," said Loden.

I waved a hand to get his attention. "We were leaving, weren't we?"

He blinked at me slowly. "I'll only be a few minutes."

"That's right, gracious lady," said one of the men. "It shouldn't take us that long to pound him."

They started toward the far wall of tithball ranges. Loden paused to tie back the sleeves of his robe. I stopped next to him. "What were you about to tell me, a minute ago?"

"What?"

"A minute ago. You were going to tell me something about what you're mixed up in."

"Oh, that." He seemed to be turning his mind back to something that had happened years ago, and in another country. "No, I was just going to explain why I was here. I don't usually throw back this many winebowls in the middle of the day, but I had a fight with my girlfriend and I guess I was upset."

"You had a fight with Ruby?"

"Ruby?" He frowned.

"The girl you were with, Loden."

"Oh! Her. No, no, I had a fight with my *girlfriend*."

How many did the boy have? Jeweled Bracelet called, "Are you coming or not?"

"Don't get your shorts in a wad," said Loden cheerfully, fussing with his sleeves. He reached the edge of the range. "If I go first, you're never going to get a shot," he told Bracelet.

"Right," said his opponent, in the voice of one who humors an idiot. He put a ball in Loden's hand. "The phoenix has been fed."

"For the score," announced Loden, and he threw straight to the north wall, hitting the "thrower's choice" stripe. He grinned. "I'll go for eight hundred."

There was a murmur at this. I looked around and saw that a few people had already begun to gather, scenting blood. A woman in an orange robe shook her head at what she clearly saw as foolhardiness. Sim's voice, beside me, whispered, "If he can't make his points in three throws, he'll lose. And at two hundred a wall, he'll need a lot of luck."

I knew nothing at all about tith stakes, but I knew that Loden and I were very different people. I would never make a bet like that, regardless of how good I thought I was.

Loden rolled the ball around in his hand, tossed it, caught it, and extended his arm experimentally. More bystanders gathered.

He threw. The ball bounced on the range floor, hit the north wall, ricocheted off the west, hitting scorable territory each time, and flew over the trap to return down the range to Loden. He smiled.

The bronze mouth of the phoenix opened, displaying a 400.

A pleased buzz came from the crowd. Someone had taken a wild chance and surprised them by pulling it off, and that was entertainment. Loden's popularity was probably hitting 400, too.

But they held back. They were an Ivoran crowd; and he still could screw it all up. Loden glanced at Jeweled Bracelet, whose face was carefully blank, and smiled again. Without preliminary, he let loose his second throw. East wall, north, bounce over the trap, and home.

The phoenix hit 800. So did the crowd. Loden was clapped on the back, congratulated, called everything good. His three betting opponents were the only unhappy looking people in the room. Jeweled Bracelet made his way through the knot of people around Loden; he put a hand in his robe to pull out his money.

The hand came out with something slim and shiny . . . I frowned. He slipped next to Loden and touched it to his wrist.

A hotpencil. I yelled, "Sim!" and tried to push through the crowd.

Jeweled Bracelet had taken hold of Loden's hand and held it in a vise grip. I saw panic rising in Loden's eyes. Then Sim took hold of Bracelet's shoulders and pulled him bodily away. Bracelet fought back with the weapon he had so conveniently handy, the hotpencil. He jabbed it in Sim's arm and kept it there while Sim's other arm reached for his neck. Sim sank to the floor.

I had once undergone training in how to fight, but unfortunately it was responsive training; I had no idea how to jump someone from behind. But I'd managed to get close to Bracelet, and I kicked him in the right knee joint. It buckled, and he lost his balance.

He let go of Sim, whose body was now splayed on the floor. He turned to me, looking angrier than I've ever seen anyone look.

Uh-oh. The crowd had withdrawn somewhat, but there

were still too many pressed around us to run. I jumped onto the tithball range.

A forfeit bell sounded. Apparently I'd crossed the boundary and would have to lose points. I ran down the middle of the range toward the back walls.

Now sirens were going off. I looked back and saw Bracelet had climbed onto the range after me. What in the name of heaven had possessed me to run into a dead end like this? North, east, and west walls enclosed me.

I knelt down, reached into the trap, and started pulling out balls lost earlier in the day. I threw one, missed. The second hit Bracelet on the side of the head. That gained me about half a second, and considering my aim it was all I was likely to get.

By now lights were flashing and hefty-looking parlor employees were approaching from all over. *This* was why I'd run into a dead-end—thank you, subconscious. An expression of uncertainty came over Bracelet's face. His companions had already fled. He turned and ran, jumping off the range into the crowd, who very quickly made way for him. Ivorans do not like to become involved in danger they feel rightly belongs to other people.

The Courts of Heaven bouncers helped me off the range, none too gently. One of them had turned Sim over and was feeling for a pulse. "Is he all right?" I asked, as they dragged me past him toward the manager.

The manager was a little man in an impeccable set of robes, about forty years old. He was nearly my height, amazing in an Ivoran male. When I reached him, he started to scream in a thick provincial accent. "What do you think you're doing! Tracking dirt all over my range, interrupting paying customers! Are you drunk? Are you crazy? Never, never do I want to see you here again! You owe us money! Money to clean the range, money to make up for lost time! We are a respectable business! Money to compensate for harm to reputation!"

I bowed deeply twice, to reassure the bouncers, then reached slowly into my belt pouch and took out a handful of ten-tabal pieces. I bowed again, held out my hands toward the manager, and started to count from one hand to another. "Ten, twenty, thirty, forty . . . " My voice was low, and his tirade drowned it initially, but by the time I reached fifty he'd trailed off and I was speaking in silence.

"Sixty," I said, holding it out to him.

He looked me over suspiciously. I said, "Though a barbarian, I, too, am from a respectable House. Please accept my apology, unworthy as I am, for the trouble I have caused. To harm the shining reputation of your business is the furthest thing from my mind."

I bowed again. The bouncers looked at a loss. The manager said, at last, "There should be a fine." But his voice had lost the conviction of righteous anger.

"Please send your bill to the House of Cormallon," I said. "If there is any disagreement at all in our compensation, we will be happy to submit the matter to any House of arbitration you like."

Sixty tabals was twice what he'd get in any arbitration. He bit his lip. "So be it," he agreed, taking all my money.

I looked toward the bouncers. "Is my companion all right?"

Sim. My responsibility.

"The player?" asked one of them. "He's all right, just a burn mark and a little shook up."

The hell with Loden. "No, the other one."

"The big fellow," said one man to the other.

"Oh. Lon's called for help to, carry him across the street. There's a healer lives over the Green Rush Light."

"He's alive?" I said.

"He's alive. Had a longer exposure to hotpencil than the other one, though. Don't know how he'll do."

I turned to the manager. "Cormallon will pay for any medical aid. He's one of our House. We want the best."

"Kat's all right," he told me. "She must see six pencil burns a week, in this neighborhood. Not to mention knife and pistol wounds."

He'd calmed down considerably, and I was just starting to get upset. I could feel the adrenaline tide receding in my veins. Should I ask to have Sim taken to an outplanet clinic? But time was important with pencil burns, and if this Kat were really experienced. . . . I nodded. "Cormallon would be grateful if you'd see to his welfare." He smiled and bowed, understanding that I'd committed my House to looking kindly on his bill.

At once he said, "Kery! Jin! Make sure he gets to the healer's in one piece, and stay with him when you get there."

I dearly wanted to sit down. But if I did that, I might not get up again. I moved to where I could lean against one of the tile machines.

Loden was a few meters away, sitting on the floor, white-faced. He was holding one wrist, looking down at a red mark that traveled up his arm. If I were a better person, perhaps I might empathize; I'd felt much the same that day in Trade Square.

The manager followed my glance. "Come," he said, and motioned for me to accompany him to Loden's side. Speaking above his head, the manager said to me, "This one is not of your House?"

"Absolutely not," I said.

"Cormallon takes no responsibility for him."

"None at all."

"Then he must pay a fine, too, for his involvement."

Fairness is not an issue here, in case you haven't gotten that point. Loden seemed oblivious to us, still staring into the other side of the mirror. The manager nudged him with one foot.

"Youngster! You owe a fine to the Courts of Heaven."

I couldn't commit Cormallon to paying for him later; that would link us publicly, and whatever Loden was involved in I didn't want it leaking over onto our House. And I had no money left, myself.

In any case, he seemed deaf. The manager squatted by his ear and shouted. "Do you hear me? You owe a fine!"

His head turned slowly. "I didn't do anything."

They'd never let him leave till he paid. I squatted down on his other side. From that proximity I could smell his cheap perfume. "Loden," I said, speaking slowly and distinctly. "Pay him, or I'll kill you."

After a moment he nodded, still slowly, and took out his money pouch. His movements were those of a hundred-year-old man.

The manager grabbed it from his hand in disgust and searched through it. He snorted. "Eight tabals." He threw the empty pouch back in Loden's lap and pocketed the money.

They left us alone then, and I peered into Loden's stricken face. I bit back the angry tone I'd been going to use and said softly, "Don't you think you should tell me about it now?"

Still staring into some blank awfulness, he started to cry.

Chapter 15

He was not in any shape to communicate on the way home. I helped him as we walked back to the house, through street after street, but I couldn't help much. I was near the end of my strength myself, and wished that I'd had money for a carriage or wagon. I kept jumping at noises, staring around to see if Jeweled Bracelet and his friends would reappear; probably it was nerves that kept me going.

When we got to the front door I had a decision to make: accept him, however temporarily, in the house, or dump him back in the parcel receipt. An ethical dilemma. Bringing him in was bringing danger officially, onto Cormallon territory; on the other hand, the boy was a mess.

I suppose the fact that Ran wasn't home that night decided me. I'd let him stay until tomorrow morning, and kick him out before Ran got back from Mira-Stoden. In arguing with a spouse, it's always easier to justify something that's already happened.

So I tucked him into a spare room with a cot, where he promptly went to sleep. It was early evening by then.

The doorbells startled me. I ran to check the spyscreen, and saw it was Kylla, carrying a bag of something from the corner cookshop. I'd forgotten she was coming this evening.

"Hello, Theo," she said, when I let her in. She dropped her bag on a table. "I've brought soup and rice and lots of sugar candies. We can stuff ourselves all night. Did you hear from Ran? How are you? Are you any better since this morning—" as she whirled and got a good look at me. "Theo, darling," she said at once. "You look terrible. What happened?"

"Oh, Ky. It's been a long day since yesterday."

"Sweetheart! Sit down. I'll do everything. I'll bring you tah and candies and you can tell me all about it." And she led me to the divan, sat me down, and fussed over me in a very satisfactory way.

She brought me soup first, insisting I put my feet up as I ate. As she went to get the other containers open, she called, "I'm going to check for any messages on the Net, all right?"

"Fine," I said. Kylla'd spent half her life in this house. I always felt a little funny when she asked for permission to use the Net.

Kylla likes her soup hot and spicy, and that's what we'd gotten. I could feel my eyes start to water as I sipped it, and the sting was comforting. I was well prepared to be catered to for the rest of the evening . . . though I ought to check on Loden at some point, I thought vaguely.

Kylla returned without the rest of our supper. "What is it?" I asked, seeing the look on her face.

"The steward at home says I've just gotten a written invitation for tah and cards tomorrow morning—at Eliana Porath's."

Well, that took nerve, possibly even raw courage, on Eliana's part.

Kylla looked at me. "Did you hear what I said? It's an invitation to Eliana Porath's!"

"I heard. You don't have to go, Kylla."

"The hell I don't. If that little pasty-cake has something on her mind, I want to know what it is. What do you think I should wear?"

I started to chuckle.

"This isn't funny, Theo!"

"No, of course not. Uh, your mint robe is very nice."

We talked clothes for about half an hour, while the food got cold, and shortly thereafter the bells sounded again and the Poraths' messenger appeared at our doorstep. She was a girl of nine or ten, with a set of robes in three shades of red. She bowed and offered Kylla a small sky-blue envelope. Kylla then vanished into the downstairs office to compose her reply, and I offered the girl sugar candies. I ate one first, as etiquette required, then gave her three extra to put in her pocket and take home.

When she'd left with the acceptance and the candies, Kylla came and sat next to me on the divan. "Want to finish our supper?" I asked.

She shook her head. "I'm not hungry."

I was starved to the marrow, so I opened a container of rice and steermod beef. The smell filled the room, and Kylla started to pick at it. "I'm sorry!" she said suddenly, putting down her fork. "You were going to tell me what happened today."

"It's a long story—" I began.

She frowned. "Do you really think the mint robe is all right? It's got a shawl collar."

"It's beautiful, and it suits you."

She looked at me, blushed, and we both started to laugh. I patted her hand. "It's all right, it's an obsession. I understand."

She fussed with the supper bowls, and her eyes fell on a copy of the Capital News. The delivery people hadn't wanted to trouble to send them on to Kylla's house, so when they found they couldn't get the slot open they'd been dropping them outside the parcel receipt. For the last few days Loden had been stepping blindly through them, scattering them in the gutter. This morning he'd actually thought to leave them in a pile by our door.

"I didn't know you got Court Follies," she said. Court Follies is a scurrilous, politically oriented sheet, less acceptably illegal than the Capital News.

"I don't," I said, looking at the address on front. "The neighbors on our left do."

"How did you get it?"

"Loden, the idiot." I spoke from the heart, without thinking.

Of course, Kylla wanted an explanation. It was a long one. Finally she turned to me, eyes shining. "You've been letting that gorgeous security guard stay with you?"

"Trust me," I said. "It's an overrated experience."

When I got up in the morning I made the same call I'd made before I went to bed the previous night: to the Inner Courts of Heaven. The healer they called Kat didn't have Net access. Both times the manager sent someone across the street, and both times he gave me the same answer: Sim was alive, and his recovery looked promising. "We'll notify you at once of any change," the manager said. "But

Kat keeps saying he should be all right. The exposure wasn't long enough for permanent damage."

I thanked him and cut the connection. As far as I was concerned, Sim could have all the cherry jam he wanted, as long as he came back in one piece. Another message appeared on the Net just as I was getting up: from the Porath code, the Net said.

The Poraths again? Why would they call me?

I accepted it and found Eliana Porath's face looking out of my wall. Inexperienced at Net customs, she blatantly used the visual circuit. "Lady Theodora," she said, "I'm so glad you're home.

"Uh, lady Eliana. Nice to see you again."

"I have a favor to ask."

"Oh?"

"I've got, ah, a bit of a problem. My father seems to have asked your sister-in-law to join us today for a tah and card party. I only found out this morning, and we're racing to get everything ready."

"Oh."

"Yes. Well, this is very awkward . . . at this late hour it will seem too much like an afterthought . . . but would you consider attending as well?"

"Me? I don't really know any card games."

"That's *fine,*" she said, with fervent eagerness. "It doesn't matter. It's just that, you see, right now Kylla is the only guest, and even with Auntie Jace or Leel to make up the table, it really wouldn't be much of a game. You see my point?"

"I do indeed." There's safety in numbers. Eliana Porath was no fool.

"I would truly be most grateful if you'd come. And it will only be for a couple of hours. We can have a nice meal afterward, in the garden—our cook is a wonder—"

"It's all right, Eliana, I'll come."

"You will?" She let out her breath in relief. "Thank you so much. It's at the sixth hour, and I'll tell the gate to expect you. I'd better run now and see if we can get the table . . . thank you." And she was gone.

Well, chance in all forms was clearly to be my lot. Raucous machine-play and tithball yesterday, and genteel gambling with tah-and-cards this morning. I was about to sign off when it occurred to me, belatedly, to check for any messages.

There were two, both dated yesterday afternoon: one from Ran, the other from Stereth. I accepted them both.

Should arrive home by noon tomorrow. Hope you're feeling better. Where are you?

Ran

Your market sorcerer named Moros isn't named Moros. He used to be Bril Savin, but the Savins disowned him. He had a hut outside the city, on the west bank of the river. I hope this knowledge provides more certainty in your life.

Stereth Tar'krim

The one from Ran was characteristic. I would hear about that "where are you" when he returned. And good old Stereth and his provisions for certainty in my life. I wouldn't count on it, old friend. His message was intriguing, as messages from Stereth so often are. Presumably the hut was abandoned when Moros died. No mention of any wives or children. . . . disowned persons rarely find mates. It had been days since his death, and there was no reason to believe anybody would be there now, even assuming they knew where he lived. No harm in poking around a bit . . . Damn. I'd have to do it before Ran got home. He'd be quite capable of calling up three more cousins from out of town to keep me within the city walls till I lost interest.

I told myself there was no reason to follow up Stereth's information, except curiosity, powerful in itself, and a desire to get Loden out of trouble and out of our lives. Speaking of out of our lives— I woke the boy up, fed him, and told him I was throwing him out before my husband got home. He accepted the phrase as though it were one he'd heard before.

"I want to see you later today, though," I told him. "So start working on your story now." He nodded, looking sheepish. At least he didn't seem to be as harrowed as he'd been last night. "I mean it, Loden. The carriage stops here."

"I know," he said. He went off down the front steps and into, I thought, the gods knew what further trouble.

Good heavens! I hope Ran didn't feel that way about *me.*

It was nearly the fifth hour. I ran upstairs and awakened Kylla, where she lay sprawled over the bed in my room. She had her family's way of taking all the mattress space. "Ky, you've got to get up. We'll be late. Ky!"

She squinted at me blearily. "What time is it?"

"An hour till Eliana's party."

"Oh, gods, no." She let her chin fall back on the pillow. "It can't possibly be. I've barely slept!"

"You've been out since the reign of the last emperor—out like a light, I might add. I figured you'd want the time to paint over any circles under your eyes, before you see Eiana."

This call to war got her attention. "Ohhh . . . why, why, did you let me drink that whole bottle of Ducort?"

"You insisted, Ky. You told me you could handle it."

She dragged herself out of bed, moaning as she did. "Can't you see how I'm suffering? At least you could take the blame."

"Yes, Ky. I'm sorry I forced you to drink all that wine last night."

"That's better." She tottered to the bath and locked the door. I went to get ready myself, knowing she'd be at least half an hour.

I changed into one of my best robes, thought about it, and took the jade and caneblood necklace Ran had given me last Ghost Eve from its box underneath the bed. This was a social call, after all. I'd check with Kylla on whether it was too dressy for daytime, but with discreet earrings it might work.

I took it out of the box, remembering that Ghost Eve. I looked into the mirror as I held it up, and saw my eyes had gotten visibly misty. "You should be taken in hand, girl," I said to the reflection there. Then I went to the upstairs office and left a Net message for Ran, telling him I'd probably be having lunch at the Poraths' when he got back, and pointing him toward Stereth's message for what I intended to do after. Manipulation works two ways, you know. At least I'd have companionship in ransacking the hut, since I had no doubt at all Ran would show up there to make his displeasure known.

I was reassured to see the silver arc in the Poraths' garden. The last time I'd seen this garden was two nights ago in my card-driven hallucination, and my statue had bled rivers where the arc now gleamed with such a reassuring lack of organic properties. Ran was right, I thought uncomfortably, that had been my own fault; mixing up the stories of Kade and the Poraths and my worries about the Cormallon council, leaving open-ended questions floating around in my head. Keep that up, Theodora, and you'll be almost as good with magic as the late Moros was. The Poraths' house loomed ahead of us, full of family, servants, cats, and lizard; not at all empty or abandoned. Do you good, I told myself, to spend a little time with quiet, respectable people, after the excitement of yesterday. Folks here may get murdered, by the gods, but they're always courteous.

Kylla and I were heading for the central porch, wearing our finest—including the caneblood necklace, by the way—when the tall jinevra bushes around the blue pool rustled.

A head looked out at us. "Hello, Theodora."

"Coalis! What in the world are you doing in there?"

"Ah, excuse me for not stepping out. I just wanted to mention, I was out on business with Stereth last night, and he asked me to let you know he's left a Net message for you."

"I know," I said, puzzled.

"Well, when I told him you might be visiting today—since your sister-in-law was coming—he said to tell you it's about your market sorcerer. He said he thinks you sometimes don't read his messages."

"It's kind of you to pass this on, Coalis. May I ask what you're doing in the jinevra bushes?"

Shouts came from the direction of the house. Coalis winced. "Please let this matter by," he said.

The shouts were louder now. It was Jusik's voice. The front door was flung open and Lord Porath emerged, in white-hot temper, hands in fists. You could practically see his veins throb from here. "Where is he?" he cried. "He's still in the compound, don't tell me he's not! The gatekeeper didn't pass him out!" He strode down the steps, followed by Leel Canerol, Auntie Jace, Eliana, the steward, and three others I didn't recognize. They poured through the door and over the porch after him, like a scared litter of kittens.

Coalis' voice came urgently from somewhere below my ear: "Move away from the bushes!"

Jusik was stalking across the garden. I looked at him, looked back at the bushes, and then hastily stepped away.

Too late. I'd drawn his attention, and there must have been some movement behind the leaves. "There! Don't move, you fool, you disgrace, or I swear I'll beat your organs out of your skin! Don't you *dare* move!"

He was at the bushes in twenty strides, and yanking Coalis out by the arm. There wasn't really room between the thin branches of jinevra for him to exit on this side, but Jusik paid no attention to that. The recently created First Son of Porath emerged branchwhipped and scratched.

He at once threw himself into the dirt at his father's feet, the way they tell me the Six Families do when they need to impress the emperor with their sincerity.

"You vermin!" yelled Jusik. "You river toad! Disappointment of all our hopes! Get up!"

Coalis scrambled immediately to his feet, still saying nothing.

"Out all night! Drinking and gambling, I have no doubt! But what do you care? Why should it matter to you if the House of Porath depends on you? Do you think being first son confers the right of pissing away your time and money?" He paused for half a second, as though waiting for Coalis to convict himself further, but no one spoke. The other members of the household had gathered around in a half-circle, with identical appalled looks on their faces. "If only you were more like your brother! I wish to heaven it were you in the canal, and not him! Do you think anybody would have missed *you?*"

Coalis continued to stare at the ground. "Enough!" yelled his father. "Against that tree! Now!"

Coalis walked to the tree where Ran had once stood and waited for me to finish with Stereth. He placed the palms of his hands against it. I now saw that a leather strap dangled from one of Jusik's tightly clenched fists.

"Take off that robe!" cried Jusik. "Do you think to fool with me?"

Coalis stripped off his outerrobe and pulled down his white cotton shirt.

I thought that he would make some protest—shout back, at least, since meekness was getting him nowhere—but he didn't. And appalled though the rest of the family looked, no one made a move to interfere. Obviously they didn't want that temper turned on them, but even so—

The strap hit. Coalis's back arched and a sound came out of his mouth—not a scream and not quite a groan—a sound that convinced me that even though I'd never seen or felt a whipping before, it was an exquisitely painful event.

I was horrified. I was rooted to the spot, grotesquely fascinated, but mostly horrified, and not just by the pain. There is no corporal punishment of minors on Pyrene, and it is strongly disapproved of on Athena. This was stepping back into some kind of dark age, a stage-lit theater event somehow dropped into real life, but even worse, this was a thing so clearly taken for granted by my contemporaries.

The strap struck, and struck again. And nobody moved. Jusik was the First of Porath, he could beat the hell out of his son if he wanted to.

Alien. I became aware of Kylla standing uncomfortably beside me—embarrassed at her presence at a private family moment, sympathizing with Coais, disapproving of Jusik—but without that extra layer of repulsion, of incomprehension, that I was watching through.

Eight strokes. I wasn't counting at the time, but I can still hear the slap of the strap reverberate. Eight strokes, not even cruel by some standards. He could have beaten Coalis to death and not been held legally accountable.

He raised his arm a ninth time and threw the strap past the tree, onto the ground. "I want you in my library tomorrow morning! I want to hear you recite the Twenty Lessons of a Dutiful Son, and you'd better not have a word wrong! Studying, that's what you should be doing, not out on the street mingling with all the riffraff of the provinces—" He choked in a couple of breaths with difficulty, trying to keep himself from working up to another crescendo of anger. He stepped back from the tree, and Coalis immediately threw himself to the ground again in dutiful fashion—more dropped than threw, this time. Jusik made a disgusted sound, turned away, and stalked back into the house.

Everyone else at once ran to Coalis and tried to help him up, murmuring comforting sounds and inspecting his back. Auntie Jace was sent to the kitchen for wet cloths, Leel Canerol had him turn around for her as she tsked-tsked and gave him advice about keeping his shirt off till tomorrow. Eliana sniffled and kissed him.

Kylla and I exchanged looks. Should we walk on into this? We were more or less being ignored anyway . . . maybe this would be a good time to slip away.

Eliana looked up and met our eyes. "Our guests," she said to the others, like a hostess reminding someone to serve the canapes. Kylla and I came forward.

Coalis was facing us, so I couldn't see what the strap had done to his back. There was a fine grain of dust on his cheek from where he'd pressed it against the bark of the tree, with tear tracks cutting through the dust. His eyes were still moist and his skin was paler than usual, but his expression was no different than it had been ten minutes earlier in the jinevra bushes. I searched his face, looking for something I could get hold of, but there was nothing. He didn't, quite, look *calm* . . . he looked held-in, self-contained.

"I'm sorry," I said, meaning that I was sorry for calling attention to him in the bushes.

"That's all right. It's bound to happen, from time to time."

Auntie Jace ran back with her handfuls of dripping cloths. Coalis was made to sit, and she knelt behind him and helped Leel Canerol in applying them. Water ran down Coalis's back onto the dirt. He winced whenever Leel touched him.

Auntie Jace was muttering. "What's gotten into your father, anyway? He never used to beat you."

"Co, here, never used to spend his nights out," said Leel dryly.

"It's not that." said Coalis. "Ow!"

"Sorry."

"It's just that I've got to expect that with Kade gone, he'll be . . . giving me a lot more of his attention. After all, he used to beat Kade all the time. With me, he probably never thought it mattered."

"So now you're important enough to correct," said Leel. "Lucky you. I'm glad I'm a provincial commoner."

Eliana said, "It's so unfair. You weren't out spending House money—you were making it."

"Will you keep your voice down?" said Coalis, frowning. "If we're going to start letting Father in on everything we do in our spare time, I know a few things I could share with him."

His sister made a face—but dropped the subject.

Kylla stirred. "We seem to have intruded at a bad time," she said. "Perhaps we should postpone our visit for another day."

Eliana straightened up. "No, please . . . if this is when Father asked you to come, we'd better stick to it. I'm sorry things are so—disorganized." She put a hand on her forehead and seemed to be trying to recall what she would be doing for an ordinary visit. "We only just got the table set up," she apologized. "Father didn't tell us he was inviting you, the messenger only mentioned it in passing this morning, so we've been running around trying to get things ready."

She considered this and seemed to feel it lacked a certain graciousness, for she at once modified it. "Not that you aren't both very welcome. I just want to excuse our lack of preparation. Really, we're very happy you agreed to come." She sighed. "This hasn't been a good morning. Let's try to start over again."

"We're happy to be here," said Kylla, who knew what was expected of her. "Is there anything we can do to be of help?"

"I'll be all right," said Coalis. "I'm just going to lie down for a while. Don't change anything on my account."

"He'll be fine," agreed Leel, looking up from her cleansing of his wounds. "Why don't you go on upstairs, and I'll be there in a couple of minutes."

Perhaps it was a trifle over-direct of me, but I hadn't had a good morning either, so I went ahead and asked: "Did your father have any particular purpose in mind? Anything he wanted us to discuss during this party?"

Eliana took no offense. "We wondered the same," she

said frankly. "But he's been upset ever since he found out Coalis was away all night, and we really didn't think this was quite the time to inquire."

I wouldn't have brought the matter up, either. We followed Eliana upstairs to her room, where a small black table had been set up with a deck of playing cards in the center. Cushions surrounded it. The mattress had been taken off the sleeping platform and leaned against the far wall, and a portable tah burner with pot and cups had been set up in its place.

We filed in and sat down, to rather an awkward silence. "Leel will be up in a moment," said Eliana, who knew as much about that as we did. I looked around the room, the first daughter of Porath's world. No different from last time; clean, small, well-tended. A flute sat on the windowsill beside a stack of notepaper.

"You play?" I asked.

"I'm learning," she said. Auntie Jace made an embarrassed movement.

Fortunately Leel arrived before the conversation languished, and we could begin arguing about what game to start with. Sometimes I think card games and dinners just give us something to pretend to do while we all figure out how we stack up against each other in the human social web.

But as I'd said to Eliana on the Net, I don't know many Ivoran games. "I know how to play Sleeping Dog," I offered.

There was a strained silence at this; apparently it was considered a vulgar game. I'd learned it from some Sector outlaws the previous summer.

"We can play Flush," Eliana announced.

"It's *always* Flush," said Leel Canerol. "It's the most monotonous game on earth."

"We'll play Flush Thirty-Six," said her mistress, with a trace of temper. "*That's* not monotonous, it's the most complicated game there is. You can keep score, Lely. Since you find it so easy."

Leel Canerol made a face, but stretched her lanky frame against the wall until we all heard something crack, then grinned and walked over to the windowsill where she retrieved pen and paper. The paper, I noticed, was a textured, pastel kind, that came in short sheets, suitable for young ladies' personal notes.

Leel pulled out a stool and threw one leg over it. "Shoot," she said.

"Would you care to deal?" Eliana asked Kylla.

"Many thanks," said Kylla. She took the deck, an old-fashioned one of red and black oval cards, shuffled them grimly and dealt out seven cards to Eliana, Auntie Jace, and me.

I said, "Uh, excuse me, but somebody's going to have to show me how to play."

Kylla and Eliana were staring at each other, expressions of determined courtesy on their faces. I don't think they heard me.

Auntie Jace threw down two cards and took two from the pile. Eliana smiled prettily at Kylla and said, "I'll stand pat with what I have, dear."

I decided my best move would be to blindly participate, so I traded in one card.

Kylla took two without any comment. We went around several times doing this, then Auntie Jace said, "Flush," and put down her cards into three sets. They made no particular order that I could discern. We all put down our hands then and Leel Canerol walked around examining, counting, and writing.

It went on like this for about an hour. I kept a low profile and stayed away from the less understandable moves, as when Eliana suddenly laid a card at right angles across the discard pile and cried, "Block!" Fortunately, nobody seemed to expect me to do anything. Of course my nose started to go critical about forty minutes into play, and I kept my handkerchief in my fist, transferring the cards from one hand to another as I sniffed and blew as quietly as I could. Auntie Jace gave me some funny looks from time to time, but the others were too well-bred to take official notice.

Auntie Jace turned to me after one round and said, "Why in the world didn't you declare? You had a perfect hand!"

I shrugged, hoping I looked coolly above it all. Leel said, "She doesn't have to declare if she doesn't want to. Maybe she's working on a strategy." In fact I was. Keep my head low and hit the floor if the shots started to fly.

"Where do we stand?" asked Eliana suddenly, pushing her long dark hair back over her shoulder.

Leel consulted her paper. "Twenty-six on this last round for you, which puts you six under Kylla, twelve over Auntie, and eighteen over Theodora."

"Six under Kylla?" She frowned. "Are you including my bonus points for a perfect flush?"

Leel held out her paper. Kylla, looking a trifle irritated, said, "Perhaps you'd like to check the math, dear. I'd hate to take advantage of a schoolgirl."

Eliana took the paper, looked it over, and stated, "This is a nine, not a six, Leel. Raise me three points."

Kylla bent her head to peer at the scribbles. "It looks like a six to me," she said.

"Advanced age can have that effect on one's eyesight," replied Eliana. "Take my word for it, *elder* sister, it's a nine."

Leel Canerol and Auntie Jace began talking very quickly. "Would you like another hand?" asked Leel, gathering the cards without waiting for an answer.

"That would be delightful," said Auntie at once. "Or maybe we should all get some tah. Theodora, what do you—"

Kylla said, "Possibly those long sleeves of yours brushed the figure and smudged it, beloved sister. I meant to compliment you on that robe when I first walked in, by the way; it would have been very fashionable, let me see, about six years ago?"

"Look at the time!" I said. "Ky, shouldn't we—"

"I suppose you *would* be the expert on antique fashions," agreed Eliana.

Kylla's aristocratic nostrils were starting to flare, not a good sign. Eliana went on, "And it's true, these extra-long sleeves do get in the way. Perhaps you can lend me one of your lace bands to tie them back."

Ran's grandmother had worn lace sleevebands. I rose to my feet. "We *must* be going," I said.

The two of them sat without moving. I said, *"Kylla,"* through gritted teeth. Finally, finally, she stood up.

Eliana smiled at her and said, "So sorry you have to go. I did enjoy our game, and I must compliment you on your calligraphy when you accepted our messenger's invitation. So very elegant. Who wrote it for you?"

"I'm glad you enjoyed it, dear. Who read it to you?"

Kylla turned to leave just as a snarling sound erupted from Eliana's throat and she sprang to her feet. The little card table crashed over and Eliana grabbed Kylla's arms from behind. It looked as though she were trying to climb up Ky's back.

Kylla whirled around, knocking her away. Leel Canerol made a dive for her charge and missed. Eliana scrambled up and aimed an enthusiastic but poorly taught blow at Kylla, which she blocked. I threw aside the door hanging and yelled, "Assistance! Steward!"

Coalis was standing in the passage. I heard a loud slap from behind; somebody had made skin contact. Coalis strode past me and got between the two contenders just as Leel managed to imprison Eliana's arms. He raised his hands, palms up, to Kylla, looking vulnerable with his shirt off. "Our apologies. Our apologies," he got out. There was a red hand-shaped spot on Kylla's cheek and she was breathing hard. "Our apologies," he said again. "We humbly beg forgiveness."

After a moment, she nodded. Her eyes swept over the room like those of an heir who's just inherited a piece of land too poor to be impressed by. She turned and strode out.

I followed. A hand tugged at my robe in the passage to slow me down, and Coalis said, "That was something, wasn't it? I had no idea this would happen when I sent the invitation!"

I stared. "*You* sent the invitation?"

"Why not? I'm first son now, I don't have to ask permission to invite people home."

"Coalis . . . does the phrase 'asking for trouble' mean anything to you?"

"Oh, but it was splendid, wasn't it? What entertainment!"

I stopped, looked him in the eye, and said, "You are fooling with things you don't really understand."

"Come on, Theodora, I only wanted to see what would happen. What do you think they would have done if there'd been weapons at hand?"

His face wore its usual calm, but his eyes were glowing. "This family has even more problems than the Cormallons," I muttered.

"Pardon?"

"I said I have to go now. Kylla will need company home."

"Oh. Well, you're always welcome back. Kylla, too, of course."

"Our thanks," I got out, bowed my stiffest bow, and ran after my sister-in-law.

Leel Canerol caught up with me in the garden. "Please, gracious lady, I'd like to ask you not to mention this incident to Lord Porath."

I stopped short, remembering this morning's exhibition. "Would he beat her?" I kept my voice low. Kylla was ahead of us, at the gate, and I didn't want to put the idea into her head.

"He never has before, lady. But he can make things very difficult for everyone in the house when he's unhappy."

"I see."

"And—I couldn't help overhearing Coalis—if Lord Porath finds out his son is responsible for this, there could be a second lesson with the strap for him. Now, Grandmother was in her room with a headache this morning, but if she finds out Coalis got beaten, she'll make Lord Porath's life a misery. And if *his* life is a misery, we may as well all move to the provinces and change our names."

"Yes, I do see your point. Look, I see no reason to mention anything to Lord Porath, but I can't answer for Kylla."

"You might speak with her . . . when she's in a better frame of mind."

"Umm. I'll do what I can, that's all I can promise."

"My thanks," she said, and bowed, giving a wry smile when her head came up that suggested she knew very well I was wondering why she worked for the Poraths.

I shook my head. The smile became a grin. "Oh, it's not so bad," she said. "I've worked around, and they're probably the least trouble of any of the Six Families."

"Heaven help us all," I said.

She threw me a casual salute and loped back to the porch.

Chapter 16

I gave Kylla my caneblood necklace for safekeeping, explaining that I needed to go somewhere right now and didn't want to wear it. I didn't trouble to be specific, since she clearly wasn't listening to me in any case; but I watched to make sure she put the necklace safely in her wallet.

Then she took the carriage we'd come in and rode away, looking abstracted, leaving me to start a long trek across the city to the remains of the northwest wall. It took a good hour and a half in the midday heat, and five minutes into the walk I was sweating freely into my party clothes and thinking about a cool bath. The North Gate, where the groundcars and wagons pass through, was several streets to the east, but I'd remembered seeing a footpath for pedestrians near here that ought to lead out a door in the wall and along the east bank of the river.

So it did. Wildflowers and garbage lined the bank. Once past the wall there were very few people around, and I was glad I'd given Ky the necklace. Still, at least I could see far enough ahead and behind me to know I wasn't being followed. The path branched into two routes here, one well above the bank, among the red and blue flowers, and one leading down to the muddy path beside the water. I took the drier and prettier way. There was a shed set back from the banks, where a sorrel dog barked and laundry flapped in the breeze off the river. The dog, working himself up to a pitch of excitement few manic psychotics could match, gave me to understand that, if it were not for the inconvenience of a wood-and-wire fence, he would have been happy to lunge at me and tear off a few limbs. He threw himself at the fence several times, in fact, and I wondered just how sturdy it was.

Other than that, there were no human habitations, not

till one got out several kilometers into the country and the farms began. But about a quarter of an hour from the wall I came on a section of field and riverbank that the city was using, whether officially or not, as a junkyard. Old tables lay sunken halfway deep in river mud; cracked pottery, broken glass in rainbow colors, and metal parts covered the ground. There were stacks of old used paper with government officialese on the portions that could still be read. River rats prowled, looking interested. And down by the bottom path, a but had been made of wood boards and junkyard metal; the hut, if Stereth were right, of Moros, the sorcerer who'd killed Kade from Catmeral Bridge.

Well, I knew for sure that he wasn't home. That didn't necessarily mean the hut was empty, of course. A route had been cleared through the junk and garbage down to the hut, and I followed it past an old solo wagonseat, a set of broken tah-tables, three benches, and part of a bed.

There was a tiny window near the door, shuttered over. I pulled the door handle, then pushed, then gave as good a kick as I could. It opened.

The hut was empty. I stepped inside and found myself in a one-room home with cluttered shelves, a stove in the middle of the door with an iron railing around it, a tiny old-fashioned desk stuffed with papers (out of place in its baroque elegance), and a small wooden counter with covered jars of foodstuffs. Some unidentiable piece of meat hung by a string from the ceiling; it was just beginning to go bad. A sort of hammock arrangement had been egged in one corner with a sleeping pallet and a pulley.

All just waiting for Moros to return. One would think that if anyone else lived here, they would have taken down the meat by now. I pulled off my outer robe and pitched it onto the sleeping pallet. This would be a potentially boring task, but not dangerous, I decided; and I went through the food jars first.

No, I had no idea what I was looking for. I was following the "ask questions, gather data; and maybe something will turn up" school of investigative thought. Food jars were my first choice because they seemed logically least likely to contain anything of interest; this being Ivory, I assumed secrets were more likely to be there than anywhere else.

Moros had sugar, rice, and dried fruit. Not a man on a

high budget. I opened the stove door; it was empty. I poked around beneath it for a while, then started inspecting Moros's endless collection of bottles, labeled neatly on his crowded shelves. Herbs and oddities, bits of this and that—a recipe book for sorcery, but nothing that meant anything to me.

I stripped the bedding and looked under the mat. I knocked on floors and walls. I pulled down the oil lamp from its ceiling hook.

Which left the desk. At least the padded stool in front of it would give me a place to sit.

We would start clockwise, I decided. I began opening the folded papers stuffed on the far top right.

A bill for a new robe, recent and unpaid.

A torn employment notice for a sorcerer willing to travel to the provinces.

Sorcery notes, apparently unrelated to drowning.

Interesting: A series of hand sketches of the river and the junkyard outside. A family of rats sat atop the old wagon seat, looking bright-eyed and very funny. Moros was in the wrong line of work.

Had been in the wrong line of work, anyway.

A letter. Aha, I thought, now we get to the good stuff!

Dearest Gernie,

Of course I haven't forgotten you. This just isn't the ~~right~~ ~~proper~~ most convenient time for you to join me. Things are all up in the air here; it wouldn't surprise me if there was fighting in the streets before long.

It would have surprised me. So far the summer had been pretty dull in the way of Imperial goings-on.

So stay where you are, I implore you. Meanwhile, please accept this little help of ~~25~~ ~~12~~ 10 tabals. I hope it will ease things for your mother and sister.

Give my best wishes to everyone. Truthfully, my client list isn't growing quite as quickly as I'd hoped, but I'm doing very well . . .

I put down the letter. Gernie, whoever he or she was, would wonder when there was no more correspondence.

Maybe Gernie would come to the capital to see what was the matter.

For Moros' sake, I hoped they never tracked him as far as this place and saw how he'd been living.

Come on, Theodora, you're getting involved again. You'll never get through all these papers if you stop and speculate on every one.

—A review of the chakon theater-dance season, torn from the Capital News.

—Three letters from Gernie, folded and unfolded so they were brittle with usage; Gernie's sex was still unclear but his/her passion was not. Gernie kept pleading to come to the capital to be with Moros. Some of the letters were explicit; as a strait-laced Athenan I was a bit shocked, but I must say, fascinated—

Still, it was getting late in the afternoon. I returned the packet to its cubbyhole. A carved wooden box sat atop a pile of papers; I opened the box and turned it over.

A mass of ticket stubs from fortune halls in the gambling district. Points for just about any kind of game I'd ever heard of and many I hadn't. Moros, like so many others, hadn't been immune to dice fever, but at least he'd accumulated a stash of tickets to be cashed in at the appropriate halls later. Of course, there was no way of telling how much of his own money he'd had to lay out to win all these. I flicked through them idly: Cloud Hill, Wheel of Illusion, Patens of Bright Gold. The man must have worked his way through every establishment on Red Tah Street. I turned over the crimson ticket from the Red Umbrella Tith Parlor: "IOU 85 tab. L. Broca."

I froze.

I turned over another. "IOU 32 tab. L. Broca."

I started to flick them all over. Most were blank, but about half the ones from the Umbrella and the Silver Shoe had Loden's signature below an amount.

The idiot! Giving a signature to someone you were linked with in a criminal act—

That was an Ivoran reaction. My next one, which was Athenan, went: Wait a minute, what evidence do we actually have here? So Loden owed Moros money. Loden owed everybody money, apparently. What light could this shed on Moros's assignment on Catmeral Bridge?

Well, as long as Kade was around, Loden's money was pretty much spoken for. Moros really didn't have a prayer of seeing any of these IOUs cashed. Probably Loden had pointed that out in self-defense.

Would they really get together to murder Kade just to get Loden out from under? But they couldn't be sure someone else wouldn't pick up Kade's account book, as in fact someone had. Still, Stereth Tar'krim made the tossing of monkey wrenches a way of life. And given Coalis' monkish background, the odds would have seemed pretty good that once Kade was gone, the debt would vanish too.

I sat on the stool, clutching a handful of tickets, thinking.

Another possibility: Loden out-and-out hired Moros to kill Kade, and the IOUs were not gambling losses at all, but a plausible means of contracting to pay him after the deed.

The world was full of options, wasn't it?

But how did this get Moros dead, with his throat cut, that day in the market? And who were the thugs who tried to get Ran and me? And Loden was just, well, such an *idiot*. . . . Even a screwed-up sort of murder seemed beyond him, frankly.

I wished that damned dog would stop barking back at the shack down the path; I could hear him from here. I emptied the next cubbyhole of papers irritably. The prolific Gernie, with more to say on the same subject: More sketches. A hand-drawn map of the city; nicely done, I thought. I scooped up the gambling tickets and emptied them into my belt pouch, replaced the latest set of papers, and pulled out another.

That psychotic dog! Finally he seemed to be calming down. His impulse to murder was transitory, probably whoever was walking by the shack had passed out of canine sight.

I got up suddenly and went to peer out the small, dirty window. Two figures were silhouetted at the top of the bank.

Loden Broca and Trey Lesseret. There was *no reason* they should show up here and now, with all the hours and days since the murder to pick from. Oh, the unfairness of the gods! This went beyond coincidence, this was the malign nature of the universe revealed. I looked around the room as though expecting a solution to present itself, like a clown jumping out of a closet in a slapstick farce; but physical law remained physical law. One room. One exit. No place to conceal anything as large as a human being.

Behind the stove—too small. Behind the desk—too small. The counter. Wait—the bed? I heaved on Moros's pulley arrangement and lowered the pallet. Then I tossed my outerrobe up there again, put one foot on the railing around the stove, and rolled myself up after it. Would I be able to pull the bed up higher from this position? —Yes. With difficulty. I strained on the ropes until the pallet was so close to the ceiling I was practically plastered against it, then lay there in a sweaty, clinging tangle of robes. For a second I flashed back to that moment in Trade Square when I'd looked over at the knife. Probably Loden and Trey wouldn't need to bother with knives; Trey would still have his Mercian-issue pistol. I didn't feel concealed at all. You could probably market the hormone smell I was putting out then and sell it to sadists.

They took forever to get to the hut. It was several centuries before the door opened.

"Kanz," said Trey's voice. "Look what I stepped in."

Loden laughed.

"You think it's funny now," said Trey, "but I'll track it all over the floor, and you'll have to smell it."

"We're not going to be here that long," said Loden.

Footsteps on the wooden boards. Trey said, "Where should we start?" Without waiting for an answer, he went on, "You take the desk and I'll take the canisters."

The sound of jars being opened, lids tossed on the counter. Papers at the desk being thrown to the floor. Then what I assumed were the shelves of bottles being checked. Trey must have finished first and joined Loden at the desk, because I could hear both of them going through the papers.

"I don't think they're here," said Trey.

"They have to be here."

More papers scrunched and tossed. The sound of boots partially muffled by discarded letters on the floor.

"I don't think they're here," said Trey again, in the sort of voice a father uses to say: Your birthday present didn't arrive on time; be a man about it.

"He didn't live anywhere else, this is where he lived!

They've got to be here somewhere, we just haven't looked hard enough."

"Could someone else have gotten here ahead of us?"

"Who?"

"I don't know. Your Cormallons, maybe. You said they'd been told the address."

"Cormallon's not working for Lord Porath anymore. And anyway—there wasn't time. Nobody even knew where Moros lived till yesterday. He kept a closed hatch, that one—didn't matter how drunk he was, never a word of personal information."

"You should've tried harder to find out. Your little girl was right, Loden, you can't just leave stuff with your name on it lying around."

"Don't lecture me. If I wanted to be lectured, I'd still be living at home. And what could I have done about it, anyway? Nobody knew where he lived!"

"Somebody knew."

"Nobody in the halls of fortune. Minister Tar'krim tracked down a whore he brought out here once, otherwise nobody would still know."

"Huh," said Trey, in a cynical tone of voice. "If nobody's investigating, how come Stereth Tar'krim bothered to track down the whore?"

Silence. Finally Loden said, "I'm not responsible for—"

"I know. You're not responsible for *anything*."

"That's not fair! Nobody understands what I've been going through. Especially the last few days. The agency throws me out, I have to live in a kanz *mail chute*, for the love of—and what about the Courts of Heaven, huh? Two high-tones try to kill me with a hotpencil during a tithball duel! I practically died of shock on the spot. Nobody warned me that was going to happen!"

"Made your reaction all the more believable, didn't it?" said Trey, with cold humor.

"I don't need that kind of help," said Loden firmly. A second later he added, "Though the barbarian feather did seem more sympathetic, afterward."

Feather is not a term you hear much in the circles Ran moves in. It means female—in usage, generally a female of childbearing years. I'm not going to tell you the derivation. If you're ever on Ivory, don't use it.

"There you are," said Trey. "Be glad you've got Velvet-Eyes and me to look after you." He was crumpling papers as he spoke. "Kanz! They're not in the desk, Loden, face it."

"So what do we do?"

"Hope you're right. Hope they're here someplace. Because if they are, they'll go up when we set fire to the hut."

What?

Trey said, "Get the cans. I set them down outside."

Wait a damned minute here—

Loden's boots went out, returned, and there was a sound of something heavy and metal being set on the floor. Somebody unstoppered a can, maybe Trey, for he began gossiping as he worked. "So tell me," splash, "did you spend *all* your time in the mail chute?" Splash. "Or is it true what they say about barbarian women?" Splash, splat. "Ugly to look at, but wild animals on the mattress?" A chemical smell filled the room.

"I don't kiss and tell," said Loden.

"The hell you don't." A can was set back on the floor, now with an empty, hollow ring. "Your pants have seen more activity than an Imperial legion in the field."

Loden chuckled. Trey said thoughtfully, "Speaking of mattresses—"

"What?"

"That one up by the ceiling."

I froze, completely, as though that would somehow take the idea out of Trey's mind.

"What of it?" asked Loden.

"Well, we haven't looked there. Maybe Moros liked to take out his tickets in bed and gloat over 'em."

"Who cares? We're going to burn the whole place down, anyway."

"Loden. My boy. We want to *know* we burnt them, don't we? We don't want to worry about them for the rest of our lives?"

"Nobody cares about Kade anymore. By next spring they'll have forgotten he ever existed."

"Loden, people hang themselves on loose ends. Take the pulley."

With a rusty, squealing sound, the bed began to lower. I turned onto my right side and elbow and brought my left knee up. I got lower; the shelves of bottles came into view. I took my left foot off the mattress and brought my leg back. They would both be standing next to the pulley, on my left. I pivoted in the bed, hoping that the swinging my movement caused would be seen as a natural consequence of hauling the thing down.

I'd been taught a few tricks once by a dirty fighter, an ex-member of the Imperial Guard. I hadn't practiced them in a long time, not having any heavily padded partners on hand to try to maim and kill—the circumstances under which I'd been taught had been unusual. But when your options dwindle down to a precious few. . . .

Surprise, I could hear my old instructor say. *Surprise is your friend. Most fights are over in three seconds, if you're going to win them at all.* And she'd had us count the seconds to prove that it was true.

Trey and Loden were trained guardsmen with weapons. They knew what to do better than I did. But they weren't expecting Loden's barbarian feather on the pallet, and they wouldn't expect her to do much beyond cower. Time was on my side; it was the only blessed thing that was.

A hand on a rope was visible. In a second, there would be a head—

Trey's head. I kicked out my left foot with all my might, imagining there was a melon behind Trey's skull that I needed to burst. I could feel the heel of my sandal penetrate the softness of his face. He stumbled backward, without even time to look shocked.

But the swinging bed hadn't provided enough purchase. I jumped off it, ran up to Trey, as close against him as though we were lovers, pulled down the bloody face he was grasping between his two hands, and smashed his forehead against my knee.

He sank to the floor. I kicked his head one more time, being cautious. Probably about two seconds had passed. Loden was standing near the pulley, having taken a couple of steps back, looking horrified and at a loss. There was no belt holster; he wasn't armed, at least not with a pistol—maybe he'd had to turn it in when the Mercians put him on probation.

I looked down at Trey, ready to grab his pistol and point it at Loden. No holster here, either? What was wrong with the world when security guards went around unarmed? Didn't they let them out with the ordnance when they were off-duty?

Kanz. This left hand-to-hand, and the element of surprise was draining rapidly from the situation. I might be able to beat Loden on an IQ test, but he was a good twelve centimeters taller than I was, not to mention stronger and in better condition. Did I leave out better trained?

Quickly, Theodora. Do it now, before he has time to assess the situation. He's still of balance. I launched myself at him.

He backed away, arms out, not letting me close with him. "Theo," he-said, "wait a minute."

Don't let them start a conversation, I could hear my instructor say. *Nothing they say is of any interest to you.*

He moved farther away, behind the stove. "Relax, dammit, will you? Look, I'm unarmed."

By now he should be willing enough to fight; he'd had time to get himself together and realize he could beat me to a pulp. The fact that he wasn't doing it lent him some credibility.

I was starting to shake. Oh, kanz, if I'd missiled right into him, I could've finished before the aftershock hit.

His gaze went to Trey on the floor. "Theo," he said, "we're here for good reason." He locked eyes with me and wiped sweat from his brow. "Could you just, please, give me a minute to tell you about it?"

"What? What is it?" My voice came out on the thin edge of endurance.

He was being awfully polite to somebody who wasn't a threat. Maybe he had a problem psychologically with doing the killing himself. Morally slippery, Loden. The responsibility drops onto the person who arranges it, not just the person who carries it out. Not a boy who thinks things through, are you?

"Well?" I said again.

"I was going to talk to you about this tonight . . . you have to believe me." He pulled a silk kerchief from a pocket and wiped his neck. I could smell his cheap perfume from here, even over the chemical scent from the spilled cans; a musky, repellent thing that reminded me of nothing so much as wet dog. The parcel receipt had reeked of it when we'd opened it up. The two smells twined together nauseously.

The possibility existed that I might faint. I put one hand on the edge of the stove and let as much weight onto that as I could without seeming obvious. "So talk."

"Look, uh, Theo, you've been really nice to me, and I appreciate it. My family's a thousand kilometers away. I didn't have anybody but Trey I could turn to."

Probably so. And bad sense in gambling and bad taste in perfume don't make you a murderer. Now let's see you explain the IOUs. I shifted a few steps back; he was still between me and the door.

"I owed money to half the halls on Red Tah Street. I just wanted to get them off my back, you know? So I put all my debts together with Kade." And used the new cash flow to hit more parlors, instead of paying his back debts. I was beginning to grasp the picture. "Don't tell me you've never done anything crazy in your life. Never took any risks? Never threw any dice?"

Shook off two planets and married into alien thinking, magic, and unreason. Apparently I didn't waste my time gambling with small painted counters.

"Come on, Theo. Cut me a little slack."

"What about Kade?"

"I told you, I didn't do anything to Kade. I'm not a sorcerer, I'm just an agency hire-out. Besides," he stepped closer, gesturing, "don't tell me you care kanz about him."

I didn't, to be perfectly honest, as a good Athenan should be. But that wasn't the point.

He said, "Be reasonable. I'm just trying to get along. How great can my life be, sweetheart? I'm living in a mail box." I didn't need to be called "sweetheart" by Loden Broca. He was standing right next to me by then, his blue kerchief spilling out of his outer robe pocket. He put one hand against the wall behind me. "Am I asking so much?" His voice had gotten low and throaty.

Had Ivoran-style culture shock finally reached some cumulative level where I'd lost my senses, or was Loden making a play right here in Moros's hut, with his friend Trey sprawled on the floor? He leaned over and kissed my cheek, gently. "I'm just asking," he said, moving down toward my mouth, "for some understanding." Then he pulled back an inch and scanned my face.

I must say, I was utterly absorbed in morbid fascination. Never had I seen such unjustified nerve and ego married to such folly. It must be terrible to depend on *glamour* and have none. The situation was repulsive, yet riveting in a sick way. It seemed distant from my own life, like a scene from a melodrama, with the stage in lights and me way back in the tenth row caught up in watching somebody else's reality. I had a sudden suicidal urge to go along with him, just to see what he'd do next, and had to stop myself from returning the embrace.

But common sense broke into my wonderment, in the form of a voice, or rather the memory of a voice.

My old combat instructor: *He's standing right next to you.*

So he was. Wide open.

Well? You know what to do.

Regretfully, I did. At this point I was beginning to consider Loden as a minor child, in need of guardianship, or possibly institutionalization. But I knew what my instructor would expect me to do. And Ran. And Kylla. And every other non-Athenan soul on this planet.

I put my arms around his neck to position them better. He bent down again.

I brought up my knee sharply. As he doubled over he came out with an odd sound, something like a groundhermit whose neck has just been twisted for the pot. I took hold of his head, shoved it farther, and brought up my other knee to meet it.

He fell to the floor. His eyes were closed, but I heard a low, involuntary moan. He didn't move.

Give him a kick to make sure he's out, said my instructor's voice.

Come on—he's not armed. And he's in no shape to come after me without weapons.

It's proper procedure.

But he's an idiot. Can't I just let him go?

No answer from my internalized coach. I walked the other way around the stove, opened the door, and left.

I should have enough adrenaline to make it back to the city, I thought, climbing up the slippery bank. But I'd probably be out of commission for the rest of today and tomorrow. I passed the stack of broken tah tables, lying in muddy splendor, the green-lacquered sides cracked. They looked rather pathetic. Once somebody had placed them proudly in their house. Oh, well, we'd all die eventually, just like the flotsam here.

—Oh, for heaven's sake, Theodora. Go home and pour yourself out a bottle of Ducort—one bowl will put you out, the way you are now. Ran will be there, and tomorrow you'll be all right.

Good idea. I climbed past them. Something seemed to glitter past the edges of my sight, some trick of sunlight; I turned and looked behind me.

Loden was standing in the doorway with a pistol in his hand. The charge must have gone over my head.

How in the name of the gods did he get that? I dived behind the broken wagonseat. He hadn't been wearing a holster. Trey hadn't been wearing a holster. Why would either of them tuck a pistol away anywhere else? The wagonseat wasn't going to make it as protection, I thought.

Loden started up the hill, awkwardly, one hand going to his head. I crawled through the mud behind the wagonseat and into a pile of old boxes. I didn't know what was in them, but they stank.

This was terrible. I was going to be killed by somebody I didn't even respect.

And it wasn't right, either! I pulled myself under an overturned carton. Not that I expected fairness from the universe, but this was like one of those tile-machine games that nearly laid itself out perfectly for you, then missed by a single tile. Theodora the barbarian had just taken out two fully grown security guards. Two! Trained. And after that . . . shot in the mud by a libidinous, egotistical fool without sense to come in out of the rain.

Loden reached the wagonseat. I don't know why it bothered me to be killed by Loden, particularly, but it did. It's not that I looked forward to being taken out by an honorable and intelligent enemy; I looked forward to dying in bed. Or better yet, not dying at all. But this was just so, well, lacking in dignity.

Told you to give 'im the extra kick.

Oh, shut up. I burrowed beneath the pile. Kanz, I couldn't see Loden from where I was any more. Risking death seemed preferable to suspense. I came out on the other side of the cartons and raised my head—very, very slightly.

The wagonseat had been cut cleanly in two, on the diagonal. The ground behind it was dry, no longer muddy. Loden was nowhere to be seen.

There was a wardrobe with a door missing standing farther up the bank, tall enough to hide a man. Unless Loden had chosen to crawl behind one of the piles of junk . . . but his present headache would probably make crawling unattractive. Still, he was so clearly enraged with me that he was working hard to scare me to death otherwise he would just step out again openly with the pistol.

I did have a knife, but it can be more dangerous to pull that out in a fight than not. Knives can be taken away from little female barbarians and then their throats can be cut with them, which is a poor use of irony in one's life. But he was far enough from me now that I could throw it . . . though not as fast as he could use a pistol.

Kanz. Ran was never even going to know exactly what happened.

I am not a person of action! I thought desperately. I'm just a scholar! I *collect* things, I write things down. . . .

Movement on the periphery of my right eye. I whipped my head around. Far down the bank, on the path beside the water, two figures. . . . A red and white robe I recognized. A walk, a gesture, in the person beside him. *Ran and Stereth.* What were they doing here together? *Who cared?* I smothered a dangerous impulse to jump up and wave my arms.

They were still a good distance away. If Loden saw them, he'd shoot me quickly, pick them off, and get out of here. No. Keep him occupied, don't let him know the game has a time limit. Go on, Loden, torture me some more. Toy with me, scare me, remind me that you've got the pistol and I don't.

I crawled around the cartons and behind a table. If Loden saw any movement, it would take his eyes farther from the path below. Was that the edge of a sleeve hind the wardrobe?

"Lady Theodora!" His voice came over the empty air, the open silence around us, and the faint sound of the river.

If I answered, he'd know for certain where I was, if he didn't know already. "Why are you doing this?"

Why am I crawling through the mud and stink? If you'd seen the look on your face, you wouldn't have asked.

"Come on out and talk to me, like a normal person," he called.

I'm sorry I can't reproduce his tone of voice here. What it was saying was: Come out so I can shoot you and get on with my life. I don't know if he had any idea how transparent he was.

I glanced down the bank: Still too far away. Shame to die now, with possibility so close, but that's the way some of those tile-games end—when you're one tile down, you lose the whole pot. I turned back. Loden had emerged from behind the wardrobe. "You know, I really have nothing against you personally," he assured me, walking forward, toward my hiding place. "I was angry at you a few minutes ago, but I realize you were scared." His voice sounded more sincere now. Possibly he meant it as an apology for shooting me.

"Trey's not dead," he added. Why he wanted to share this with me, I don't know. I let myself roll down the slope toward the garbage sacks just below.

My roll stopped and my face bumped into something hard sticking out of one of the garbage sacks. A chair leg. Hardly any chairs on the entire planet, and I bump into one while escaping a lunatic. My nose started to bleed enthusiastically.

The sack in front of me parted, cut neatly in half, the surfaces of the cut smoking faintly. Loden's voice, pleased, said, "You left a trail when you slipped down there, Theo."

So much for hiding. I jumped to my feet. He blinked, startled, at my sudden appearance. I turned quickly to check for my potential rescuers, and Loden's glance followed mine. My beloved husband and the Minister for Provincial Affairs were well within sight; Loden goggled. As I recalled from the hut, he did not react well to surprise.

But he pulled himself together. He turned to me, raising the pistol. I faced the lower bank, took in the biggest lungful of air I'd ever taken, and yelled, "STERETH!"

The two figures on the path turned. Loden's arm pointed

straight at my face. Ran's pistolcut hit his shoulder—a full second after Stereth's cut cleaved his skull in half.

Feeling too shaky to stay on my feet, I sat down in the mud in my party robes and waited for them to climb the hill. Ran reached me first.

"There's blood all over your face," he said, breathing hard.

"It's just a nosebleed. I bunked into something."

He glanced briefly at what was left of Loden and then gave me a look that said we would talk later. Then suddenly he was kneeling in the mud next to me, looking shaken as he gazed at the pistolcut in Loden's shoulder. Stereth came a few seconds later, extending a steady hand to me that showed no trace of nerves whatsoever. "I'd prefer to sit for a minute," I said.

He stepped back obligingly and took a pipe from the pocket of his outerrobe. He packed it, lit it, and turned to Ran with an air of courtesy. Ran was still kneeling by Loden, his face pale. "Thank you," he said, without looking up.

Stereth smiled. "Well, sir Cormallon," he said kindly, "it would seem that you owe me a favor."

Chapter 17

Well, they debated debt, obligation, and what to do with the bodies for a good quarter of an hour, apparently forgetting me entirely. (In fairness, I must say that I encouraged them to ignore me while I angled my head back in an unbecoming fashion, waiting for the bleeding to stop.)

Then they hauled Loden's remains down to the hut, where it would have taken a while to find him, even if my two rescuers weren't discussing the merits of throwing a match on the spilled chemicals—no point in being asked any administrative questions by the city. When they returned, about forty minutes had passed, and my nose was gushing more violently than ever.

They fell to arguing again. "Ran!" I said. Oops. Raising my voice increased the flow. "Ran. Stereth." They didn't seem to hear me. I kicked out with my foot and landed one on Ran's shin.

"What are you—" he began, then frowned, looking down on me. "You're still bleeding."

"No foolig. I'b begidding to suspect I bay deed bedical help." Breathing through my mouth seemed the best option.

Stereth squatted down beside me. "I saw a lot of wounds in the Northwest Sector," he said kindly. "Try pinching the bridge of your nose."

We all hunkered around in the mud, pinching my nose and replacing one sopping handkerchief with another. Fortunately I'd laid in a good supply when I'd heard I was invited to the Poraths that morning. Damn the Poraths anyway. The insides of my nose had probably gotten weak from all that blowing.

After a while Ran said, "It doesn't seem to be stopping, does it?"

Stereth considered it thoughtfully. "It's getting *worse*. Coming out like a young river. We seem to have broken in on an artery."

I must have made a pitiful-sounding moan, because they both leaped to reassure me: "But you'll be fine!" —Sorry about the moan, but if you'll look back, I think you'll agree that this hadn't been a good day for me. It's not easy being the hero of your own story. We all do our best.

Anyway, my pathetic sound must have finally prodded them to action. "She's losing an awful lot of blood," said Stereth. "We'd better get her to a healer.

I said, through the mess of handkerchiefs, "Ad outpladet doctor." I have great respect for Ivoran native healers, but they're better at prevention than cure, in my opinion. Not that I wanted to debate the issue then.

Ran said, "A healer could handle this, Theodora."

"I wat a doctor."

He threw another couple of fresh handkerchiefs on my face and said, "Suppose we just take you to whatever is closer."

That made a lot of sense. I let them lead me down the bank to the path, and up the edge of the canal. I ran out of handkerchiefs around then, and Stereth took off his robe, removed his shirt, and gave it to me to hold over my face. I could barely see where I was going.

I mean, I'd just fought off two attackers and seen somebody who tried to kill me shot before my eyes. This would be the time when a real storybook heroine would be gracefully accepting accolades before marrying the prince. And there we were: A ragged line of three grimy people, with me being led along with my head tilted back and an old shirt over my face. And it wasn't even because I had a wound from fighting the dragon, a swordscrape taken in battle; no, it was a *nosebleed*. Life takes no notice of our wish for dignity.

We went to a healer in Dart Street. She was a cheerful-looking, intelligent woman with a sensible, motherly smile; just what you'd want in a healer. Of course, I couldn't see her at first through the cloth I was holding over my face. She very carefully stuffed my left nostril with enough cotton gauze to make curtains for all the conference rooms in the

Taka Hospitality Building, packed it tight and covered my nose with a bandage. I can't say I was enthusiastic about it at the time, but the outcome was more than satisfactory. About ninety percent of the bleeding halted immediately.

What a simple solution. What excellent results. Perhaps I should stop fooling around with the more arcane legends of Ivory and study basic first aid.

She was pleased that I was pleased. "How do you feel?" she asked.

Under the circumstances, it was a question I needed to think about before answering. Finally I said, tentatively, "It's nice not to have blood running all over my face."

She burst out laughing. "Everything is relative, isn't it?" She helped me up off the table and we went to the next room to see Ran.

"Stereth said good-bye," Ran told me. "He was late for an appointment." He looked at the healer. "Will she be all right?"

"Help her to take it easy for a few days." She turned to me. "Don't do anything strenuous. Don't bend over. Try not to laugh too hard. And if you have to shit, don't strain on the pot," she added, with the complete lack of embarrassment Ivorans have about bodily functions. "And don't try to take the dressing off yourself; come back in two days for that. I want to have my cauterization equipment ready in case it starts bleeding hard again."

"Your what?" I asked.

"Have you ever had the inside of your nose cauterized?"

"Uh, no, I don't think so," I replied, vowing silently that I would go to one of the outplanet clinics to have the dressing removed. I smiled. "Thank you for your help, gracious lady."

"Not at all," she said, "it's a treat to have a barbarian to work on. Everyone in this neighborhood seems to be from the same province."

We sat on the steps outside her office and waited for the carriage Ran had sent for. After a moment he said, "Stereth told me I'm to go to the medical clinic of my wife's choosing."

"—Ah." I was glad suddenly not to have won my point about the outplanet doctor. He might consider the obligation discharged. "You know this healer here doesn't count as my choosing."

"I know that. Why did Stereth make that particular requirement?"

"Uh . . ." Such verbal ability as I had was deserting me.

"Theodora? My wife?"

"Well. You know I want us both to have a genalysis to see whether we can have a viable child—"

"I've told you it would be grossly irresponsible for me to allow the Selians to examine my genetic structure."

"I wasn't planning on going to the Selians."

He digested that. "Share this with me, then. Who were you planning on forcing me to see?"

I said quietly, "I thought we might both go to the Jack Lykon Free Clinic."

"There's no clinic by that name in the capital . . . although the name is familiar."

"He's the man I met at the meeting with the Tellysian junior ambassador. Ah, the Tolla representative."

He turned to me slowly. "Are you telling me you consider the Tolla a safer repository for secret House information?"

"Ran, I have an idea." The concept of using the Tolla had shocked him into temporary silence, and I took advantage of it. I brought up the anecdote about the brewers, their adoption, and the enforced silence placed on them. I said, "Why can't we adopt Jack Lykon into Cormallon? There haven't been that many good genalycists around since Gate 53; the knowledge that you think makes him dangerous could make him useful to our House. The Tolla will be glad to lend him to us in return for our help with their weapons problem."

"Their weapons problem might be insoluble by sorcery."

"I have every faith in your ability to come up with something."

"And I doubt if this Jack Lykon would be willing to put himself in our power once the situation was fully explained to him."

"If he's really Tolla, he'll do his duty. And he seems like a nice guy, too."

Ran was silent, and I stopped myself from pressing the matter. Finally he said, "Let me think this through."

I said, "Of course," and congratulated myself for not bringing up the fact that his consent was required to repay the obligation to Stereth. It would work better if I didn't mention it.

Then Ran said, "Theodora?" His voice had changed.

"When that fool was trying to shoot you why did you call for Stereth, and not for me?"

Oh, gods. I'd been afraid he would ask that. I didn't have a good answer.

"You know, Ran, everything happened very quickly. I don't know why I yelled for Stereth; maybe I thought there was a better chance of his being armed."

"You know I've been carrying a pistol everywhere since that business in Trade Square."

"I . . . guess I forgot. I wasn't thinking clearly."

He fell silent, not fully satisfied, but not pursuing it. I've given the matter a lot of thought since then, because I didn't understand it myself. Did I trust Stereth more than Ran? Not that I was aware of. Didn't I love Ran; didn't I know he would act to protect me if necessary? Didn't I know very well he was carrying a weapon? There's no higher professorial power to hand me the answers to this quiz, but I think that in the end, the simple fact was that when I needed a natural killer my mind went automatically to Stereth.

I was in no shape to analyze the matter so thoroughly at the time, however. Ran looked troubled, and I was troubled myself.

After a moment he said, "Did you know that fool Loden"—it was always "that-fool-Loden," as if it were one word—"was using an attraction spell? Of course, *he* probably called it a love spell."

"You're joking."

"It was in his perfume. He was drenched with it. I had to suffer through the stink when we dragged him down to the hut."

It would in fact stink to Ran, if it was designed to attract females, which I assume from Loden's reputation is what he would ask for. Except that I hadn't much liked the smell either, though perhaps "stink" was a little strong.

Ran said, "He must have bathed in it. You didn't . . . notice anything?"

"I assure you I did not."

"No sudden urge to make love on the floor of the hut?"

"Perhaps he was given a hate potion by mistake. The only urge I felt was to knee him in the nuts, which I did."

"Interesting," he said, shifting from the husband to the professional sorcerer. "We'll have to analyze the situation when we have time."

I was about to suggest that barbarian genes might be different, but thought I'd pushed my luck enough with that topic.

No wonder he was uncomfortable. I'd spent my time hanging around with ne'er-do-wells armed with love potions, and then called on Stereth for rescue from the consequences of my visit. It wasn't surprising that my husband was a little miffed.

Only partly changing the subject, I said, "Stereth owed me a favor. For going to see the Tellysian ambassador."

"I see."

He was back to that stiff note, the same withdrawal I'd heard when I told him to go to Mira-Stoden.

Oh, hell. I'd just disgraced myself thoroughly, sliding around in the mud and bleeding all over my robes, from a situation I might have avoided with quicker thinking—since if I'd dumped Loden's IOUs back in the desk before I hid, they never would have bothered to haul down the bed. And it wasn't as if I'd needed the IOUs, the case was never going to court. Ran and I could have just told Lord Porath the story, and let him take it from there.

We may as well finish peeling the scab off any remnants of dignity and admit the whole thing.

"Ran, I'm scared."

He looked startled. "Loden and his friend are quite definitely out of the way, my love. Stereth and I made sure—"

"No, I'm scared of the idea of having a baby. I know I'm supposed to be some kind of rock-solid matriarch, passing the genetic torch down to the next stepful of Cormallons, but I keep—" I paused.

"Keep what?" His voice was quiet.

"I keep thinking I'm going to die. I keep having these dreams. I just find that, whenever I imagine having a child . . . I keep seeing him brought up posthumously."

"You never said anything."

"I'm supposed to be undeterred by this stuff, aren't I? Go bravely ahead and do my duty, count not the cost—"

"Theodora—"

"But fond though I am of your family, dying wasn't on my list of things to do when I came back with you."

"Theodora, we take intuition seriously around here. Why didn't you tell me this?"

I was silent. Finally, I said, "How do I know how much is intuition and how much is nerves?"

He sighed. Then he put an arm around my shoulder. "I suppose we could go to one of these outplanet medical clinics and inquire."

Have you lost respect for me? Come on, Theodora, go for two tough questions in a row. "Ran?"

"What?"

"What were you and Stereth doing out at Moros' house?" *Chicken. Buck-buck.*

"Oh! I got your message. I decided to call Stereth to see if he thought anybody else knew where Moros had lived, and how long they'd known. If the place was cleaned out, you know, there was hardly any point in going. While we were talking, I mentioned I was joining you there. It was his idea to come along."

I grinned. "Stereth doesn't wait to be asked."

"Lucky for us both he doesn't. At least in this case." Then he smiled. "So this is why you've been going around even more tymon-crazy than you usually are."

"Perhaps you should rephrase that, my husband."

"Sim will be relieved," he said, ignoring my suggestion. "I couldn't give him any indication as to what troubles you might be getting yourself into. Now I can tell him to relax and take his holiday. He's straining to go to the Lavender Palace, you know."

"You mean he actually converses on topics other than food?"

"I've known Sim for years. It takes him a while to lose his natural reserve."

"Ah. I'll look forward to chats with him, twenty years down the line."

I looked forward to seeing him off to the Lavender Palace, too—after a prolonged period of bedrest on his part.

I decided to wait for the opportune moment to fill Ran in on that escapade.

And so we sat there, waiting for the carriage, tucked up against each other like two winter birds. He must have had some idea what was on my mind because at one point he kissed the shoulder of my messy robe and said, "Come on. Don't worry about it."

I heard the faint sound of carriage wheels, and touched a finger to my cheek, checking for any dirt we'd missed. The healer had asked me whether I had any sensation in certain parts of my face; now the question seemed full of sinister implications. I touched my left cheek again. "Ran, I can't feel anything on my face when I touch it! The whole texture of the skin feels strange."

He said, "Theodora, you're touching the bandage."

Oh. I was glad Stereth wasn't around to have witnessed that.

"Here's the carriage," he said, and a minute later he was helping me to climb in.

Look, when it comes to adventure I do the best I can. Some people are born to dazzle rooms with panther-grace after receiving the plaudits of the crowds. Some people are born to wear sensible shoes, and I'm one of them. After this encounter, I spent a few days at home, taking it easy and being pleasantly spoiled by Ran and Kylla. I had time to consider that a clear-thinking individual might have been more on top of the Loden situation if he or she had stopped to think how quickly those hired thugs in the market had swung into action—only a couple of hours after we gave Loden a description of Moros.

I also had time to think about Loden's, well, impotent perfume; probably he'd gotten it from Moros. Ran had seemed to feel it was the genuine article. Why then had I looked upon it with such justifiable contempt? Here are some of the mitigating factors I came up with:

(1) I'm a barbarian; what the effects of this heritage may be in terms of magic has never been thoroughly studied, but at its most physically mundane I don't believe my sense of smell is equal to a native Ivoran's; (2) my nose had been operating at a deficit ever since the Night of Cats; and (3) Loden, like many people, was ignorant of how an attraction

spell works. It's a cheat, a bit of pure deceit that produces an array of physical symptoms which, in the right circumstances, convince the victim he (or she) is in the grip of sexual fever. When what they're really in the grip of is a list of medically determined effects, checked off coldly by the sorcerer-chef: Raised heartbeat (check one); dry mouth (check one); sweaty palms. . . . Statistically, a good attraction spell will work about eighty-five percent of the time. The other fifteen percent are people who through circumstance or sheer eccentricity can divorce their symptoms from what they've been led to believe is happening to them.

Just as a hypothetical example, I might point out that somebody who considers herself in danger of immediate murder has reason enough for a raised heartbeat and sweaty palms without ascribing them to any other source. True, there are a few symptoms caused by an attraction spell that are not on the list of, say, a fear spell—but again, somebody in immediate danger of death is going to have their mind on other things.

Loden was an idiot to have tried it. But then, as I think we've all agreed by now, Loden was an idiot.

Several days later found me waiting nervously in the courtyard of Cormallon itself. I paced the length of the pool, past the columns, turned and paced again. For the sake of his sanity, Ran had left me alone and gone into the study.

Jack Lykon was upstairs, running his genetic scenarios on a locked Net terminal. Jack Lykon Cormallon, if you want to be technical about it; his adoption had taken place the day before yesterday. Papers were filed with the Tellysian embassy detailing his voluntary agreement to place himself under House authority, and absolving the embassy and any Tellysian group or organization from any responsibility in the event of his death or disappearance.

Jack had been very nice about it, actually. "Don't be silly," he'd said, when I apologized for what we were putting him through. "I can't wait to get my hands on you, Theodora. That is to say, on your data."

"You won't be able to share it with anyone," I pointed out.

Jack grinned. He seemed none the worse for being the

focus of an eight-hour, three-sorcerer spell that observers had been barred from, but which had left a very strange odor all through the top floor corridor. "Knowing the facts myself comes first; sharing is a distant second, I'm afraid."

"Hmm. No wonder you don't mind being a Cormallon."

He'd been running Net scenarios all day and night. By now he must have hundreds. He hadn't said it would take this long.

I'd been pacing, dinnerless, straight into the evening, when he appeared at the door to the dining room.

"Theo?"

I went straight to him. "What? Tell me."

He ran a hand through his sparse brown hair. His eyes were deeply lined, his casually tasteful Tellysian jacket long since discarded, his shirt rumpled and stained. "I asked—God, I'm thirsty." His voice had come out as a croak. He stared around at the dining room as though at a foreign land, then picked up a carafe of water from a sideboard and drank directly from it. He wiped his mouth with the back of his hand. "I asked your husband to join us," he said, more firmly.

"I can't wait. Tell me now."

"It's not the kind of thing you can boil down to a sentence—"

Ran entered the other end of the hall. He glanced at a bottle of Ducort on a rack by the entrance, evidently wondering if fortification would shortly be necessary. Then he walked down the length of the sideboard, took in my state at a glance, turned to Lykon and said, "Jack?"

"Can we sit?" asked Jack.

Ran motioned toward some scattered pillows by a corner of the dining table. We sat.

Jack said, "First you have to understand that we're dealing with a lot of unknowns here. One specimen does not a statistic make. I had to tag a lot of variables with question marks, so I'm not speaking with a high level of confidence in anything I say."

He looked at Ran as though wondering how a sorcerer would take this kind of talk. The funny thing is, that's exactly how sorcerers do talk. He peered uncertainly into Ran's eyes. "Do you see the point I'm trying to make?"

"I do indeed, Mr. Lykon. You're being very clear. Please continue."

"Uh, yeah. Anyway, I ran all kinds of simulations, using different guesses in different phases. They're educated guesses, based on what we know already, but they're still guesses. I haven't found anything that looks like a 'gene for sorcery,' by the way. I assume it's genetically based, but it's obviously more subtle than that. We'll have to dig harder."

"Why do you assume it's genetically based?" asked Ran calmly, while I tried not to bite through my tongue.

"Well, everything's genetically based, in the final sense," said Jack. The genalycist's version of the hand of destiny. "Anyway, that's not the question you two are interested in. It gets complicated here—"

"Are Ran and I the same species?" I cut in.

He looked pained. "Theodora, for your own sake, try to let me tell this my own way, or you'll only get half the story—"

"Can't you give me a yes/no? I'll listen to the whole story afterward; I promise."

"Nothing is ever that simple. The category of species is imposed by man—by our attempt to cut up the universe into pieces to better understand it. The categories were never really that hard and fast, though. We want yes/no, either/or, yin/yang, but it's all really a continuum even gender is a continuum. There are plenty of babies born each year whose sex isn't clear to the attending physician. They have to make something up on the spot, or the parents get upset, then all hell breaks loose twelve years down the road—"

"Jack, this is fascinating, but I need to know about my own kids here—"

"Theo, I'm trying to tell you why I'm not the oracle with the final answers."

"And I'm grasping for straws, Jack. Throw me a couple of uncertain hypotheses. Please."

He sighed heavily. "All right. The signs seem to indicate that you two can conceive."

Score one! I would have smiled, but I was waiting for the other shoes to drop. I say 'shoes,' because Jack was showing centipedelike tendencies.

He said, "As far as I can tell, my highest-probability guess is that the child would be a functional, viable being, with a strong chance of being sterile."

"What odds?" I said.

"Functional and viable? Seventy-two percent. Sterile, ninety-three percent. And I'm saying it with a confidence level of eighty-five, plus or minus five."

I turned to Ran, whose dark eyes had the slightly dazed look of someone who's been slapped but is trying to continue in proper social fashion. *The Cormallon council must never hear about this.* He took my hand.

"The functional and viable rating is based on out planet medical care being available at all times, as well as access to a proper environment for premature births. The odds drop substantially without those two factors."

I asked, "You think it'll be premature?"

He shifted uncomfortably on his pillow. "Not exactly. Well, yes, it probably would be. It gets complicated here because Theodora isn't a normal Pyrenese—"

"Whoa! Where did you get that idea?"

"Your genes say so, Theo. You've got a higher portion of tagged unknowns than is usual for a standard citizen. Not that that makes you a freak or anything; there are always a proportion of unknowns showing up in the general population. It keeps us boiling. You've got plenty of company, statistically, but it makes our job that much harder."

He wiped his face again and glanced around for the carafe. It was still on top of the sideboard. He shrugged, giving it up for lost, and said, "I had to run a lot of extra scenarios. That's what took me so long. I was hoping to get a better run of luck somewhere along the way, but it didn't happen. The vast majority of combinations ended in death."

I said, slowly, "You said the fetus was viable . . ."

"Yeah. The fetus lives. You die. Eighty-nine percent of the time."

Ran's hand had frozen into something metallic. I said, *"Why?"*

"Incompatibilities between you and any offspring you would have with Ran. They're quite survival-oriented little packages, though; whenever the scenario ended in death, it was usually yours."

"Huh." I felt a slight tremor of hysteria somewhere down on the ocean floor. "It's good to know I'd be producing high-caliber individuals."

Ran said, with no emotion whatsoever, "You're not sure about this."

"I'm not sure of any of it. That's what I'm telling you. You wanted an expert opinion, and that's what you've got—an opinion." Jack let his professional facade crack by a millimeter. "I'm sorry, Theo. This isn't what I wanted to tell you."

I saw that his insistence on keeping this on a theoretical level, his clinging to the role of detached expert, was born of his own discomfort with making me unhappy. I said, "It's all right. We wanted the facts, as well as you could discern them."

"I'm sorry," he said again. He looked at a loss, as though any words beyond those two had deserted him.

I turned to my husband, "Ran?"

He still had that slapped look. His eyes focused on me slowly. I'd wanted a child, for what I thought of as the usual reasons; but Ran defined his identity around his family. I don't think it had really, seriously occurred to him that he wouldn't live the same traditional life everyone else in his family took for granted. That this particular branch of Cormallon would come to an abrupt breaking-off because he'd married me.

"Ran?" I asked, uncertainly.

We'd been speaking with Jack in Standard. Ran looked down at my hand, still in his own. He raised it and covered it with both his palms. "Beloved," he said, in Ivoran, "we will think of something."

Maybe we would. But I couldn't see any good answers anywhere on the horizon.

Chapter 18

No answers presented themselves over the next couple of weeks, either. Ran retired to his Net terminal to work on some scenarios of his own, based on the weapons requirements of the Tolla. He estimated it as a four-month project, and said somebody would have to go to Tellys at some point to do preliminary testing. Meanwhile, Jack Lykon's gag-spell was tested within an inch of his life before he was released from Cormallon territory. And our Sim was discharged from the care of the Red Tah Street healer and given a nice bonus to play with in the capital before he returned home.

And what was I doing? I wasn't studying tinaje healing; I didn't need to read the cards on new clients, as we weren't taking any new clients; I wasn't required to accomplish much of anything, at the moment, so I had plenty of time to brood. The day after Jack's talk I returned to the Dart Street healer and came out fitted with a thing she called a "cap," a gadget to prevent fertilization. Not that Ran and I had been showing any great talent in that area, but I decided not to take any chances. At the same time, you'll notice I didn't go to an outplanet clinic and pay the much higher price for an implant. Implants last for a couple of years, a length of time I felt unable to deal with at that point, despite Jack's warning. I'm not saying this made sense, I'm only telling you what I did.

Having accomplished this one errand, the days stretched before me, an open invitation to depression. So I decided to return to scholarship, the one thing in life that could be counted on not to rise up and bite you in the neck. Or not often, anyway. One day when Kylla was taking refuge in our parlor after an argument with Lysander, I sat down in the shade of the courtyard and cracked open Coalis' copy of Kesey's *Erotic Poems.*

I'd been swimming in and out of gloomy thoughts ever since our talk with Jack. Before this I would never in a million years have thought of myself as someone who found any part of their self-definition in fertility—the very idea was primitive and insulting. This misconception was rudely adjusted. I felt a failure as a Cormallon member, as a wife, possibly as a woman. Coming on top of all this, that remark of Jack's about my "unknowns" must have rankled more than I realized. I started to feel abnormal, out-of-place . . . the most distorted view of "barbarian" seemed to fit me, when I thought of who I was. Whoever I was. The word freak, in fact, was bobbing somewhere near the surface.

So it turned out I was really not in the proper state of mind to take on Kesey's view of the world.

Maybe you're familiar with the work. Kesey's *Erotic Poems* are about six centuries old, and there's been considerable language drift, but they're still understandable, and the book is supposed to be a classic. But despite an introduction full of lavish praise from all sorts of people, I became more and more disappointed. It mostly seemed to be about his trouble getting dates.

One of the poems was written from the viewpoint of a woman making love with him—he was supposed to be a veritable wonder at getting the woman's angle—and as I read it I found myself wincing.

I closed the book, marking the page with a finger, and stared into space. Maybe I really wasn't normal. Jack had seemed to imply it, Kylla often found my reactions to daily life amusingly odd, and Ran's occasional comments on the barbarian attitude toward sexual practices made me wonder. Maybe there was something wrong with me, after all. Maybe—

I walked into the parlor, still carrying the book. Kylla was looking out the tiny slit window that faced the street. "Kylla? Do you like the idea of a man pinching your nipples? I mean, do you find it erotic?"

Kylla, bless her, showed no surprise at the question coming out of the blue like that. She shivered in an involuntary response that reminded me of my own reaction. "Good heavens, no. You enjoy that, Theo? What's your chest made of, cast iron?"

"No, no, I find the idea exquisitely painful, myself. But in this book a fellow does it and the woman thinks it's terrific stuff. They both seem to take it as a normal part of lovemaking."

She smiled. "I'll bet a man wrote that book."

"He did, actually. . . . So you don't think I'm abnormal?"

"Certainly not."

I considered it. "Then where do men get the idea we enjoy it? This isn't the first time I've read about it; and I was starting to get paranoid."

She looked a bit sheepish. "Well, I suppose we have to take part of the blame. It's happened to me once or twice, and in the heat of the moment—well, I didn't want to hurt his feelings, so I pretended I liked it."

"Are you ever going to set him straight?"

She looked puzzled. "Who?"

"Lysander."

"Oh! Um, it wasn't Lysander who did it."

I stared at her. "Kylla! When was *this*—"

There was a sound of footsteps in the hall, and Ran walked in. He kissed us both. "Talking about anything interesting?"

"We were discussing literature," said Kylla, smoothing her outerrobe as she retook her seat by the window.

"Theodora, do we still have that seed-cake from yesterday? . . . Theodora?"

"Kylla," I began, as soon as he left.

"What book are you reading?" she said.

"What? Oh—it's Kesey's *Erotic Poems*. Ky, when did you—"

"Well, no wonder, then. My brother used to call it 'superbly humorless.' He said it was the most overrated piece of literature ever perpetrated on an innocent public, but at least you could use it to separate the pretentious from the true lovers of poetry."

I blinked. "I didn't even know Ran had read it. He didn't mention it."

"Actually . . . I was referring to Eln."

References to Ran's older brother were taboo, and came rarely, even from Kylla. "Superbly humorless." That sounded like Eln, all right. Maybe recalling the lover(s) of her younger days had brought him back to mind for her. I said, "Kylla, when did all this happen?"

"There's no seed-cake," Ran announced, reentering the room.

Kylla and I exchanged a glance, and let the topic drop. I'm willing to share most things with Ran—frankly, anything but openness gets far too complicated for me to handle in the long run—but Kylla's personal scandals don't belong to me. And he wouldn't want to hear about Eln.

My husband looked hungry. "Let's go out to dinner," he said. "How does the Lantern Gardens sound? Ky?"

She shrugged. I said, "I don't think I'm up to the naked floorshow tonight."

"We can take a table in the outside garden, by the pond. Listen to the music, watch the paper boats sail. I made a breakthrough today on the weapons project, I want to relax and let my mind empty out. Indulge me, Tymon."

I grinned suddenly. Maybe I owed him something for never trying to pinch vulnerable areas of my body.

"What's so funny, my barbarian?"

"Nothing. All right, let's go to the Lantern Gardens. But, Kylla, what happens when Lysander tries to call here and beg for forgiveness?" For this was how all her fights with Lysander ended. She had early set a precedent in their marriage that giving in would be based not on logic but on gender.

She smiled wickedly. "Let him call and be frustrated. Maybe he'll come by and sit on your doorstep. Let's stay out *late*, Ran."

He gave her a formal bow.

The outdoor section of the Lantern Gardens is huge. A shallow pond is on one side, and slender manmade rivers on high clay aquaducts extend out from it to curve around the tables. In the daytime, the trellises overhead are hung with cages, each containing a songbird. At night, the pond and its farflung tributaries bear an armada of colored paper boats, each carrying a candle. If you haven't gotten the idea by now, the Lantern Gardens is an expensive place to eat. It was Ran's favorite restaurant.

Kylla paid ten kembits and folded a small paper wish into a red boat, then dropped it on the pond.

"What did you wish?" I asked.

She smiled a smile that said she wasn't going to tell me. "For wisdom and discretion," she murmured, as we made our way to the table, "as every proper woman of good family wishes."

I looked around at the crowd: Wild tourists, showing bare legs and arms shamelessly, drinking down Ducort red as though it were fruit juice; sedate matrons, overdressed to the limit and beyond, dripping with gems; young men escorting conservatively robed young ladies and their chaperones . . . other young men escorting hard-eyed young professionals with no chaperones. One of them inched by us on the way to the lavatory, her belt of feathers brushing past me as she went—her illusionless eyes brushing over me as well. *Oh, yes*, I thought, *wisdom and discretion. I'm sure it's the wish on every boat here tonight.*

The Lantern Gardens makes what it claims is Pyrenese cheeseburger. I never saw a cheeseburger before with unidentified white sauce running down it, and hard toast instead of buns; but if it wasn't Pyrenese cheeseburger, whatever it was tasted good. I've ordered it there before. Midway through the meal, Kylla glanced toward the line of paper boats sailing on the miniature river just beyond us. "Here comes my wish," she announced, smiling.

The smile froze on her lips, even as it drained from her eyes. I turned my head to see what she was looking at. Three tables away, across the line of boats, sat Eliana Porath. Leel Canerol was on her right, a light meal in front of her and a glass of water. On Eliana's left was a young man in a robe of exquisite tailoring, edged in gold thread. He was chatting away happily . . . chatting quite a bit, in fact, apparently expounding-for-the-benefit-of-the-lady in the longwinded way some young men will, and some old men who never grew up. He had two forks set some distance apart on the table, and a knife at right-angles, and kept gesturing as he spoke, explaining . . . the mechanics of an aircar? His conception of government politics? A new addition to his house? At least he had a good-natured face, though, and there are worse things in the world than a tendency to be pompous. Eliana and her chaperone were clearly not required to do much beyond listen and make admiring sounds.

I turned back to our table and saw Ran watching them as well. "Well, life goes on," I said coolly. "I see her father's lending her out on a trial basis already."

"What did you expect?" asked Ran, taking a bite of Tellysian-style casserole. "The creditors won't wait."

I met Kylla's eyes. She shrugged and said, "It's over now. Why dwell on it?"

Why indeed? It was over and Kylla had won. Her life was safeguarded for the time being, and after all, how many times did a man outside the nobility, even one in Lysander's position, get asked to a marriage-alliance with the Six Families? I felt that my sister-in-law was quite up to handling any future approaches from commoner Houses.

I was drawn back to focus on Eliana, now turning to smile at her escort . . . a little tiredly? Did she have the illusion she was free and happy, or was she all too well aware of her cage? I could hear her grandmother's voice: *It takes the endurance of a warrior on the inside to make a fragile flower on the outside.*

Gods! I turned back to see Kylla contentedly digging into a sweet and sour ko-pocket. The same society, stirred only slightly differently—how can some people make a good and satisfied life within the confines of their cultural boundaries, and others end up smashed against the walls?

Of course, Eliana had a tyrannical father, while Kylla's father was safely dead . . . to the relief of his dependents, I sometimes suspected. But even if Lord Porath died tonight, it would only mean her custody would transfer to Coalis. And what alliances would her twisty brother have in mind? Stereth would no doubt have input into that. Everybody would but her, if she weren't extremely careful.

"A disappointing end to a disappointing summer," I said, cutting my soggy other-than-cheeseburger into neat squares.

"In what way disappointing?" asked Ran.

"This business with Kade. When I heard about foreign involvement from the ambassador, I guess I was half-hoping for some kind of political motivation—intrigue, scandal . . . ideals. And now to find that it's only money. . . ."

"Only money?" asked Ran, as Kylla's boat, now on the river to our left, finally caught fire. "Is this a Cormallon talking?"

I laughed and he covered my hand where it rested on the tablecloth. "I guess I don't know what I was expecting," I said.

Kylla's boat capsized, dousing the flames, and the other boats streamed on in a prism of colors. We finished the meal, leaving Eliana and her problems behind. When we got home, much later, we found Lysander asleep on our doorstep, his head propped against the front door. Kylla chuckled, knelt and kissed him tenderly, and took him away with her.

It was after midnight when I awoke. I lay there in bed, straining my ears; there was only silence, the deep, vibrating silence of the darkest part of the night. The very house seemed to be in coma, and what had brought me up through the waves? Sim was finishing his holiday at an inn closer to the center of town—the more freely to play and carouse, without the inhibiting presence of the First of Cormallon to observe him. The only other person here was in bed on my left. What had awakened me?

Had anything awakened me? I'd been having some kind of confused dream, some oddball thing about waiting in line for a manicurist in a body salon on Athena. Kylla had been sitting in the waiting room with me, but I knew that the people who went into the nail salon came out changed in some awful way—brainwashed or zombied or with some indefinable horror perpetrated on them. I tried to warn Ky, but she said, "Really, Theo, it's just a nail salon." Then I thought, maybe I should leave her here and save myself. But no, that would be wrong—I'd just have to try harder. I ended up hauling Ky down a set of stairs and out to the street, while she stared a look at me that said, Theo, you should be institutionalized, but if it means that much to you I'll come along, all right?

I lay there in bed, trying to review my little paranoic nightmare even as it faded. I frowned. Had that been Kylla in the dream or Eliana Porath? What was my subconscious trying to tell me? Did I believe Eliana was in some kind of danger?

Really, I wished if my subconscious had messages to send it would just use the Net terminal—

I froze. How had Loden known that Stereth sent me a Net message about Moros' hut?

Coalis had known. He'd told me about it, while he was hiding in the jinevra bushes.

I got out of bed and, taking my pack of cards, padded out to the upstairs office.

Three minutes later Ran's voice said, "I thought you weren't going to do this anymore."

I looked up to see him standing in the doorway.

"I wasn't going to try anything experimental. Just a straight card-reading."

"Is there some reason we need a straight card-reading?"

Aside from my curiosity? I sought around for an answer. "Well, do you want to still be held responsible for Kade's death?"

"Jusik's let the matter drop. He's satisfied of Loden's guilt."

"Is he really satisfied of Loden's guilt, or does he just want to close the book and get on with his other problems? An open matter of blood would be a great disincentive to any other potential bridegrooms they try to rope into the family."

He walked over and sat down, cross-legged, above the deck. "All right, granted, he probably still thinks I did it and that I gave him Loden the way people on a lifeboat toss over somebody to satisfy the predators. We will live down the reputation eventually, you know. And meanwhile, my beloved tymon, if you end up sprawled on the floor due to your nighttime rambles—in a most unbecoming position, I might add—"

"I said I wasn't going to do anything risky!"

"Then you won't mind if I stay and watch."

I hesitated. "You're not going to try and stop me?"

"You and the weather, tymon, I leave alone."

I dealt out a simple business configuration. "The Man of Substance"—satisfied, fat, and well-dressed—had to be Jusik Porath. There was no card to denote membership in the Six Families, and this was as close as we were likely to get. Beneath him, in a legitimate blood relationship, was The Daredevil, walking a tightrope between two poles as he balanced his way with a stick. And to the right of that, The Fool. I stared down at the Fool and back at Ran. "Guess who," I said.

"It's on the *right* side of the configuration."

Meaning a legitimate relationship of some kind. I hesitated. "You don't mind if I check," I said. "I'll keep it to the normal paths."

He made a half-bow, as though to say, after you.

I touched my index finger to The Daredevil and waited. Then I grinned at Ran. "Bingo," I said, in Standard.

The emerald lizard stuck its skinny tongue out at me as I climbed up the step to the porch. I was feeling brave, and was about to stoop to scratch it behind the ears when I noticed its meter was a little high.

"They ought to milk that thing." I said to Ran.

He glanced at the half-filled poison sac. "It's very tame," he pointed out.

"Yeah, that's what they always tell the neighbors the morning after the bodies are found."

Ran tapped the hilt of his dress-knife against the front door. It was pulled open almost immediately; the steward must have been told to expect us.

"Sir Cormallon," he bowed. "Gracious lady. Lord Porath has asked if you will accompany me to the library."

And so we did. The steward took us to a cheerful room, not really what I'd expected of Jusik, full of books and papers, overlooking the back courtyard for privacy, and decorated with pictures that reflected a personal taste not at all subordinate to the current rules of aesthetics. There was an actual wooden door, not just a hanging, to enforce his voluntary solitude. When we entered, Jusik was sitting on an old pillow of royal blue, evidently a favorite, beside a low writing table with an ornate brush-pen that gave every appearance of being an heirloom. Eliana, Coalis, and Leel Canerol sat a short distance away. They all looked up when we came in.

Ran's stride faltered. "I thought this was to be a private meeting," he said, addressing Lord Porath.

Jusik touched the edge of his heirloom pen and said, "I would prefer it this way."

Ran looked at me. I gave him my best right-back-at-you look; he would know better than I would if pursuing the matter would be politically correct in these circumstances.

He sighed, took a few steps forward, bowed, and spoke firmly. "Lord Porath, your judgment is of course the only proper one. At the same time, I feel obligated to point out that what is not said in front of witnesses, may be later agreed upon not to have been said. I mention this only to give you the option that rightfully belongs to you."

Jusik rolled the pen back and forth on the table. As he switched from his right hand to his left, I saw that the new hand was shaking. His voice was clear and direct, though; he said, "We may consider you've given me that option, like a gentleman, sir; now let's sit and talk, all of us."

I was already sorry we'd come. At the same time I had a conflicting desire to see everything out in the open, to see what people would say about it; an Athenan desire.

An Athenan desire with Ivoran consequences. Next time think about it a little longer, Theodora.

We sat. There was a knock at the door.

"Enter," said Jusik.

It wasn't the steward. It was Auntie Jace, white-faced, and she scurried in as though she feared someone would stop her. She knelt and bowed to Jusik with an alacrity I could envy even at my age. "Lord Porath, I hope my service has been satisfactory—I've been with your family for sixteen years now—I've never thought of anyone else, never lived for anything else—"

"Yes; yes." He softened his tone slightly. "Nobody has any complaint about you, Auntie. This matter doesn't concern you at all."

"No, yes, I know—that is to say, I beg to be allowed to stay. Please, noble sir. I've never asked any personal favors before."

Lord Porath looked as though he might debate that, but after a slight hesitation, he said, "Why not? Everyone else is here. Why pretend you can get the wine back in the bottle after it's been spilled? Sit down, Auntie, find yourself a seat."

She took a place at once, at the far perimeter of the cushions, as though if she weren't noticed she couldn't be thrown out. Her bright, birdlike eyes went back and forth, taking us all in.

"And now, gracious sir," said Jusik, turning to my husband, "perhaps you will enlarge on that topic we discussed during your Net call. The topic of my family's involvement in the death of my son."

Eliana, Coalis, Leel Canerol, and Auntie Jace—four heads swiveled as one to stare at Ran.

He cleared his throat. "Loden Broca, the actual agent who paid a hired sorcerer to dispose of Kade, is dead. But before he died, he went through the sorcerer's house in a search for incriminating evidence. Now, not many people knew where the sorcerer lived, or knew that the Cormallons had just been informed of the address. But Loden knew." He hesitated. "Coalis also knew."

Coalis froze. But his father did not rise up, grab a whip, and beat him to death. Jusik merely raised an eyebrow. "Is this an accusation? A case of treason within my House is a serious charge, far more serious than murder."

"Uh, not quite. You see, Eliana would also have known. At least, your two children seem fairly well informed of each other's activities." *Those activities you are so carefully not included in, Lord Porath.*

Eliana went as white as her robe. "Father," she began, horrified.

"Shush, Eli. Let's allow the gentleman to finish."

Ran inclined his head to acknowledge this courtesy. "The lady Eliana could very well have overheard Coalis' talk with . . . whoever informed him about the address."

Jusik's gaze went to spear Coalis. His son said, "Stereth Tar'krim mentioned it to me."

"I thought I told you not to keep company with that lowlife—" began his father. Jusik cut himself off. "But we'll discuss that later. I hope it will not be eclipsed by any worse matters you may be involved in."

Coalis swallowed hard, but said nothing.

I'd have felt a lot better if these things were being presented to a court of law on Athena rather than to the tender mercies of their natural parent.

Ran said, "Theodora, perhaps you should take over here. You noted the relevant points for us."

No, no, no . . . that's your job, Ran. The gazes all swung to me.

"Uh," I said. My mind went totally blank.

I felt Ran's hand touch mine beneath the folds of our outerrobes. "The IOUs," he prompted.

"Yes. The IOUs." I swallowed. "I overheard Loden and his friend say that it was Loden's girlfriend who sent him to sweep up the evidence. Loden told me straight-out earlier that he'd had a fight with his girlfriend—at the time I thought he meant the tootsie in his lap, but—uh, in any case, from the timing, the argument could have been on that very matter. The IOUs. She was probably having trouble getting him to do the intelligent thing. Uh, she's probably somewhat brighter than Loden was." Like the majority of people in the capital. "But as soon as she got the address, she called him and told him to get out to the hut and burn the IOUs. And then she called and invited me to tah and cards so I'd be occupied for most of the day." The invitation didn't come till that morning, after Stereth's message.

"Father," said Eliana.

He held up his hand. "Continue, gracious lady."

"Well, we don't have any hard evidence." And this isn't a court of law.

He said, "Are you saying my daughter would profit by her brother's death? Frankly, I can't even see how Broca would come out ahead."

I looked at Coalis, who went blank. What a family. Evidently Jusik still didn't know about Kade's profession. I said, slowly, "I believe Kade was good enough to lend Loden some money."

Jusik snorted. "I fail to see where he got it from, if he did. Look around you; you see how we live."

Coalis spoke up, in self-defense. "Father, Kade did mention something to me about loaning some money to a security guard."

Jusik looked at him in surprise. He didn't ask why Kade had shared this information with his brother, and not his father; apparently he was used to being left out of his family's information loop. He scared them too much. "Very well, son, I take your word for it. But this still doesn't give Eliana any motive." He smiled at his daughter. "Her life is as pleasant as those who love her can make it. She would not profit by alteration."

Right. I said nothing. Jusik waited, then said, "Gracious lady? You see my point. I prefer to believe that you and your husband have simply not thought this through logically, rather than that you harbor some grudge against my House. Although there are those who might feel that, after half-destroying my family through one death, you seek to put the survivors in disarray—"

"We think they were lovers," I said.

He pulled up short. "I beg your pardon?"

"Loden and Eliana. In bed. Lovers." *—What word didn't you understand? —Shut up.* Jusik was turning a fascinating shade of violet.

"First of all," he began, forcing the words past some obstruction in his throat, "my daughter is constantly chaperoned, by not one but two respectable women. She would have no opportunity for the kind of behavior you describe. Though considering the sort of society you must be accustomed to, I suppose it's understandable you would not grasp that."

"Noble sir . . . it's been brought forcefully home to me, very recently, that elegant young ladies with constant chaperones can find opportunities for gaining worldly experience should they wish to. At least, the intelligent and discreet among them can; and I think Eliana is fairly intelligent, and fairly discreet." Her dark eyes were fastened on me. I forced myself to look at Jusik, so I could continue talking normally. "In the case of your daughter, the connivance of at least one of her chaperones is all that would be necessary. All we really need is the opportunity for the two to meet and get to know each other. Loden was here often enough, your House employed the Mercia group before—and I have reason to believe that Loden was very . . . well-equipped when it came to attracting women. I'm sure the options presented by an alliance with a young lady of the Six Families wouldn't escape even him. He would have gone out of his way with your daughter."

He would have, too. The more I thought about it, the more I couldn't imagine him *not* going out of his way. It seemed so obvious, in hindsight. Self-interest was the only thing that got Loden's intellect racing.

Jusik's neck was still the color of a summer sunset. He growled, "Meeting and exchanging a few words, as youngsters will, is hardly the same thing as being lovers. The only door in this house is on the entrance to this very room; the opportunity simply did not exist."

"Oh, I'm sure there were a number of chances. The very night I had the honor of staying with you in this house," I'd almost called it "The Night of Cats," "I spent the early morning hours asleep on the chaise on your central porch. Auntie Jace was very unhappy to see me there. At the time, I thought she was overly touchy, but I realize now that she didn't want me to be so close to the entrance when she returned from having collected Eliana from the gatehouse. Where she had most likely spent the night with Loden Broca."

Auntie cried, "A disgusting lie! And only what one could expect from a barbarian! Lord Porath, you're too generous with these people, letting them into your house—"

"Auntie, please. I take it you deny these charges."

"I certainly do! I wasn't even near the gatehouse!"

I said, "I saw you well down the length of the garden, heading that way. What else is in that direction?"

"I don't recall going there, but if I did it was only to offer a cup of tah to whoever was on duty!"

"You weren't carrying any tah with you."

"I would have sent a kitchenmaid! Lord Porath, won't you protect me from this slander?"

He looked thoughtful. Her sudden change of course in mid-story had not been to her benefit. But he merely said, "Lady Theodora, you saw my daughter return to the house that morning?"

"No. I was asleep by then."

"Then you have no proof of this fantasy."

"Perhaps not. But it would be interesting to use your influence to get a look at the Mercian group's log for that night. I'll bet Loden Broca was in the gatehouse."

A silence descended on the group with that suggestion. Finally Lord Porath said, "I will do so. Eliana, have you anything to say?"

Her face lifted, paler than the creamy color young ladies who aspire to fragile flowerdom generally paint there. "I rely on your protection, Father."

He glanced at Leel Canerol, who said slowly, "While your daughter was with me, she did nothing that you would find inappropriate."

A careful choice of words. How much did the lanky fighter know?

Jusik glanced at Auntie Jace again, causing her to actually flinch. He was about to speak when he stopped and shook his head. An indulgent smile forced its way over his lips. "No. This is simply out of character. My child is sheltered, young, exposed to only the best and most proper things. It's simply inconceivable that she could be involved in anything of this sort. I'm sorry. For one thing, she wouldn't have the vaguest idea what to do—even if the thought of murder could enter her head, which I can't believe."

Ran said, "She's fairly experienced for her age." I turned to him in surprise. Ran had spent a couple of hours on the Net just before we came over, and I'd had no chance to ask him about it, but I hadn't been expecting any great surprises.

He went on, "My gracious wife informed me that a couple of confederates, whom Loden didn't recognize, were asked to make an apparent attempt on his life in a gambling hall. A show for our benefit, to drive home his role as victim. Not a bad idea, in fact; I don't doubt it was his lover's, and she showed the good sense not to warn Loden in advance." He actually smiled. "She couldn't know we would have a bodyguard, or that he would involve himself so enthusiastically." The smile disappeared. "The confederates were well-dressed and wore jewelry beyond what most people in the capital could afford to own. The lady Theodora has a scholarly mind; her description of a bracelet was quite exact." He paused for emphasis. "It belongs to Kas Sakri, a well-known player of the game of murder within the Six Families. No doubt they were doing a favor for—an ally? An opponent? A fellow player, at any rate."

Jusik had the appearance of a man who's dodged too many flying missiles. He said, "My son Coalis was briefly involved in that nonsense when he was younger. I put a stop to it. Son, have you been—"

"I haven't, Father, I swear!"

"He hasn't," agreed Ran. "I made inquiries. But Eliana is a well-known novice player."

"Females simply do not play!" Jusik thundered.

"She's acted as an accomplice in the murder scenarios of at least two friends. It's true, I haven't yet discovered a game where she was the chief player. But heaven knows she must have observed enough."

Jusik was silent. Ran said, "All this can be easily checked."

Coalis spoke up. "Father, even if it's true, it doesn't mean—"

The paternal glare swiveled toward him. "How much do you know about this?"

"Me?" The voice was a squeak. "Nothing, sir! Nothing at all."

"I doubt he knew about the murder, anyway," put in Ran helpfully.

Jusik turned to Auntie Jace, who looked as though an anxiety attack was not far away. He said, "Auntie, I've relied on your discretion for years. You haven't failed me. I must warn you, if you've been involved in any twilight dealings now, you'd best say so; for I promise you, if I find out later the tiniest part of this is true, there'll be no mercy for you."

His tone of voice was scary even to me. It must have been much worse for someone dependent on his good will. She looked horrified.

"No mercy whatsoever," he added.

She began to make a wheezing sound, as though she were trying to get air. She started to rock back and forth, gasping.

"Auntie's not well," said Eliana, accusingly. "These two have made her ill, Father." She crossed to Auntie Jace's pillow and put her arms around her chaperone's shoulders. "Let me get her to her room—"

"Stand away, Eliana," said her father.

Looking startled, she let go. "Get hold of yourself, Auntie," said Jusik sternly. "Breathe slowly. Slowly. In and out. There now, just calm down, and if you have anything to say—say it now."

She gasped some more, then cried, "It wasn't my fault, Lord Porath! I tried to talk her out of it!" Gasp, gasp. "But she's all grown up now, she won't listen to me!" Gasp, gasp. "No, she has a *defensive* chaperone now! What can I do to make her behave? I have no authority! I'm just, I'm just a retainer!" She burst into tears, her gasps becoming louder. "I brought her up, and now I'm *nobody!*" She buried her face in her hands. "You can't blame me. It's not *fair!*"

Eliana's lips were pursed, and a disgusted look was on her face; her neck was angled back, as though to put more distance between her and Auntie. She gazed at her chaperone with a kind of fascinated repulsion. Finally she turned toward her father.

Jusik's face had lost all expression. "Speak, daughter. Speak now. If the Mercian log confirms that Broca was in the gatehouse—"

"No doubt it will," she said. "But this one—" She cocked a head toward Auntie Jace—"is showing her usual backbone. She pushed and prodded and encouraged all the way. If I believed the sordid version these people tell, I'd think Loden bribed her to introduce us, that's how enthusiastic she was. Full of stories about court ladies and secret lovers—"

Auntie Jace started to wail. Clearly she would've denied it if she were still capable of speech.

"You admit to treason against your House," Jusik said tiredly.

"What treason?" she inquired with scorn. "Loden and I were *married*."

Ran and I looked at each other, startled.

She said, "I acted for the House of Broca. We all know that legally, when a woman marries, her obligation passes to her new family."

Jusik seemed just as surprised. He addressed Auntie: "Is this true?"

She nodded vigorously, her head still buried, her shoulders shaking.

"Great bumbling gods! When did you have time to exchange the marriage cakes? How long did you know this piece of garbage, anyway?"

"I won't listen to you talk about my husband that way."

"House of Broca, indeed! Who ever heard of the Brocas? A two-kembit guard, who had to borrow money from—wait a minute! Did Kade know you two were married?"

"Of course not. Why would he have wanted me to marry Shikron if he knew?"

Jusik paid no attention to this flippant contradiction on the part of his daughter. He said, "Did Coalis know?"

Coalis looked up, guilty knowledge blazoned across his face. "Certainly not!"

She said, quietly, "I never told Coalis. I never told anybody."

I could imagine Leel Canerol breathing a sigh of relief at that. It's not only his offspring that a First Ranked of the Six Families has the right to kill.

Jusik said, grasping for understanding, "I can't believe you would help to kill your own brother to settle a debt for this guardsman trash—"

"I had to stop the marriage arrangements," she said defiantly. Under her breath, I heard her add, "and Kade was no great piece of work, either."

Truthfully, I liked her for that addition. Naked honesty has always excited my admiration, apparently even in owning up to hatred and murder. What splendid self-possession for an eighteen-year-old, I thought. And what a pathetic view of her unworthy husband, what eighteen-year-old dreams of romance. Court ladies. Oh, gods protect us.

In a way I envied her, though. I'd had no romantic illusions at all at eighteen; the ones I had now had bloomed late, and took constant watering. If I'd never met Ran, I doubted I would have had them at all.

Jusik said, heavily, "So be it."

Coalis leaned forward, looking alarmed. "Just a minute, Father. We probably don't have the whole story—"

"Be silent." Coalis subsided, his eyes scared. So much for our na' telleth monk, removed from caring. Jusik said, "For the death of your brother, the First Son of our House—"

He hesitated. Eliana still knelt in the center, not far from Auntie Jace, with her back straight and her head raised. A Guinevere at the tribunal. And not an Arthur or Lancelot in sight.

"—You say you are no longer of Porath. So be it. Leave here now, never come back. Don't stop in your room for clothes or jewelry—"

"Father, *please,*" said Coalis. "She can't live! She can't possibly live! How will she survive?"

"She's of the 'House of Broca,' " he said coldly. "Let the Brocas care for her. If they choose to. And if she can find them."

Eliana stood up, trembling slightly, from fear or anger or both. She still displayed that self-possession drilled into her from childhood: The discipline of a warrior on the inside, to make a fragile flower. . . .

She touched the silver bracelet on her arm and for a moment I thought she was going to pull it off and throw it to the floor, in keeping with the level of high tragedy. But this was the woman who told Loden Broca to go back and burn the IOUs. She pulled the cuff of her sleeve down over it, turned, and bowed to her father for the last time.

Let the Brocas care for her.

Self-willed or not, there are damned few jobs in the capital for someone without family pull. I know this very well. And what was she trained in, but being a cultured and elegant young lady of the Six Families? A position no longer open.

So the cage was opening, now that there was no place to fly. She would never again have to placate Jusik, satisfy her chaperones, wear satin slippers in the snow and laugh delicately at the witticisms of wealthy suitors.

She turned, smoothed the wrinkles from her outerrobe with a gesture, and—quietly, carefully, gracefully—she left the room.

It felt as though a hurricane had passed. I looked at the others; they seemed as wrung-out as I felt. We all sat there for what must have been a good five minutes, like people dazed, before Jusik blinked and said, "Sir Cormallon. Gracious lady. We may consider this incident closed, I think. I would thank you to discuss it no further."

Ran bowed.

My mind still followed Eliana mentally, out into the garden, past that gatehouse for the last time. She must be well aware that that silver bracelet wouldn't last her very long.

So she'd taken her dignity and her dream of independence and turned to the nice-smelling security guard, Loden Broca Mercia, screwing up her life beyond any hope of redemption. What irony. She'd have been happier marrying whatever wedding card her family slapped down before her, regardless of age or temperament. She'd have had her brideprice rights, her divorce rights, her children with their duty to obey and defend her—she could have carved out a bearable, compromised life for herself. It's what I would have done. I mean, there are always books.

And plays. And sunsets. The way the capital looks from an aircar early in the morning when you're approaching from the west. I'd have taken the chips I had and banked them, and not risked all that on a question mark.

But I'm a prudent little soul, born to buy insurance. My own wild chances were always forced on me; Eliana was made of more splendid stuff. She'd have been happy as a man in this culture, or as a woman on, say, the sane part of Tellys. She chose Destiny with a capital D, chose the madness (an Ivoran phrasing) of sexual love over self-interest, recognized her enemies for who they were, regardless of family name. I admired and disliked and pitied her all at once.

I think I was the only one in Jusik's library who felt that first emotion, though.

Ran stood and helped me up. "Thank you for your time, noble sir," he said, and nudged me into an awareness of my manners. We both bowed.

There was a scream, loud and piercing, from the other side of the house. The garden side.

Everyone got to their feet. Ran looked at me. "The lizard," I said.

I must not have been the only one who thought so. Ran and I turned and started running, down the hall, down the stairs . . . behind Coalis. With Leel Canerol gaining on us, and Jusik just beyond.

We tumbled out onto the porch. At the far end, a shining patch of blue and green. . . . We raced over.

The emerald lizard stuck his narrow tongue out at us all, his calm eyes gazing at this sudden invasion of madmen. His poison sac was still half-full.

"That's as full as it was when we came in," said Ran, puzzled.

I said, "I know. And where—"

Another scream, from beyond the jinevra bushes. We ran through the garden, Leel easily outdistancing us all.

An old woman in tattered servant's dress stood at the edge of the blue pool. Eliana floated in the center, surrounded by a pink halo. Beyond the long waving curtain of her black hair, you could just make out her knife on the bottom.

Chapter 19

Eliana had kept a flute on her windowsill. I'd seen one exactly like it in Loden's room at the inn. From such little things are suicides made.

Twelve days later I got an unexpected invitation from Coalis, and on an unseasonably cool late afternoon, almost early evening, I went to the Poraths' for the last time.

The garden was crowded. A closed wagon was parked near the east wing porch, crushing the flowerbed, and as I watched I saw Jusik's writing table being carried out and placed inside. Were they so hard up they were selling off the furniture? A thick hose ran from the blue pool to a groundtruck nearby. The truck was vibrating, making a woompah-woompah sound, and a workman stood beside it peering down into the pool. I peered, too.

It was nearly empty. Old leaves and dirt eddied in the shallow remains. The bushes around the edge looked mournful and precarious of life. Maybe they'd always looked that way and the pool just took your attention from it. Or maybe all the truck activity had upset their growth.

Coalis waited by the front step, one of the Scythian yellow toms in his lap. He stroked it absently. He glanced up at me as I approached.

"They're draining the pond," he said.

"So I see."

"The ferocity of feeling in violent suicide must be expunged. The emotion would leave its shade behind, fouling the pool. It has to be drained."

"Ah."

He ran his hand gently from the tom's forehead to the tip of its golden tail. "They tell me you barbarians don't believe in that kind of thing."

"You're a na' telleth. What do you believe?"

He smiled humorlessly. "Maintaining a distance from violent emotion is always wise. Besides, the pool would be a shame to my father. People would point to it and say, 'There's where Eliana Porath slashed her own throat, when she was rejected by her family.' Probably what she had in mind when she did it. She should have known Father would have the spot drained."

"Can he avoid the social shame that way?"

"Oh, no. The shame will last for years. Eliana's last gift." He smiled again. There was no blame in his tone, only a light affection. "That's why we're leaving the capital."

"You are?" He'd taken me by surprise.

"Father has a gentleman's farm, out in Syssha Province. It's one of the last pieces of property my family managed to hang onto. That's where we're going." He nodded toward the wagon. "Father's sending the heirloom pieces on ahead with the servants."

Father this, Father that. "What about you, Coalis? Are you going, too? Your tutors are here in the capital, aren't they?"

"Oh, yes, I'm going, too. Father made that very clear. That's why I invited you over today, Theodora, to say good-bye. You're one of the few people in this town I wanted to say it to formally."

Thank you, I think. "But what about your studies? Couldn't you stay with one of the other Six Families?"

"I am no longer to be exposed to the corruption of the city," he said. "We are to return to a simpler, more moral time, learning the lessons of the harvest and the seasons among good-hearted country folk."

"I see."

"Father blames the capital for what happened. He believes his children have lost touch with the true virtues. He's dropped his hobbies to concentrate on the important aspects of life. *I* am to be his sole focus now; me, the cats, and any farm stock."

"I'm very sorry."

"Yes." He grimaced. "He fired Leel Canerol for suggesting his concern was a bit late. He invited her along with us at first, you know. To protect the goods on the way, and to help on the farm."

"Not her speed, I would think."

"Well, you never know who harbors these unsuspected rural longings. Perfectly innocent looking people, sometimes." *Not you, though, apparently.* "Anyway, Leel was wrong to have mentioned it, even if she was upset. Besides, if Father had piled the weight of his full attention on Eli before this—"

She might have suicided that much sooner, I filled in. Coalis closed his mouth firmly. There were limits even a na' telleth did not pass in speaking of one's parents; at least, not on Ivory.

I steered back the subject. "She's all right, then? He just fired her, nothing else?"

He rubbed the cat under its chin and a low purring sound began to gain strength. "You think he might have blackballed her in the capital? Beaten her before throwing her past the gate, without any clothes?"

"Well . . ."

"The fire's gone out of him, Theodora. Except for this farm scheme. You don't dare say a word against that for your life. Not even Grandmother." He sighed. "*She's* taking it better than we all thought. After her breakdown when Kade died, we assumed she'd lose control entirely. Father was even afraid it would kill her. But she's handling it better than he is. And she was closer to Eli, too—figure that out."

I sat down beside him, keeping a distance from the cat. "And what about Auntie?"

"Fighting a guerrilla campaign." He chuckled. "Holding on for dear life. I don't think she has any family left, and she doesn't dare ask for references. So she keeps to the corners and doesn't say a word. Father hasn't officially asked her to accompany us to Syssha. I'm betting she'll slip into the wagon and come anyway."

What a life. What a family. Jusik appeared at the other end of the east porch; he directed a workman to load a small cabinet of inlaid marble into the wagon. He glanced over at me where I sat and then turned back to his chore, as though dealing with anyone unnecessarily was more than could be expected of him. What in the world was Coalis going to do way out in Syssha Province? Loan-shark the sheep and cows? Collect three or four kembits a day from the peasantry?

The choice was not his, any more than the choice was Eliana's, though she'd tried to make it so. Possibly in the back of his mind Coalis was hoping for an early paternal heart attack and an early return to the capital; what was love and what was duty in his attitude toward his father, I certainly couldn't determine.

"I thought you'd like a souvenir," said Coalis, drawing my attention back.

I could not possibly conceive why he would think so. But he reached into a pocket and drew out a tiny bluestone globe trisected by a silver triangle. He put it in my palm. I'd seen the symbol before, over the entrance to a na' telleth monastery. No doubt I had more chance of seeing that monastery again than Coalis did. Even if Jusik died, no decent Ivoran boy would go into a monastery when he was the last of his family.

The woompah-woompah sound stopped and I saw the workman by the truck disengage his hose. He started hauling it back from the dry pond. In my mind I saw Kade, bully and loanshark; Eliana, going over the line in her plan to escape her father's house; Coalis . . . I wasn't sure exactly what Coalis' problems were, but he wasn't the boy next door. Just a typical Ivoran family, I thought, a little hysterically. Save this planet, people. Start a crèche, ban family names, the way we did on Pyrene.

. . . And Jusik, tyrannizing over the rest. Except he didn't look like much of a tyrant right now.

I said to Coalis, "Does this mean you've given up monkhood forever?"

"It's not a profession, Theodora, it's a state of mind."

One you would do well to emulate, I heard unspoken. He was probably right.

I stood up. "Farewell, and good fortune. Your acquaintance has been . . . unforgettable."

"Oh, Theodora." He stood and bowed over my hand. "Believe me, your acquaintance has made quite an impact."

Indeed, and it was courteous of him not to kill me because of it.

I walked past the dry pond, the crushed flowers, and the still-tall jinevra bushes. It would be good not to come back here.

Behind me, the bones of a dying family stirred themselves for the move.

I thought of Coalis sometimes and his quest for achieving the true state of "na' telleth-ri"; a quest whose cold arm reached into the most normal, taken-for-granted moments of life. The last line of a disagreement with one's husband, for instance: "What do you want me to do?"

An interesting word, *want*. Close enough to care to make the na' telleths nervous. What do you *want?* A chair, a bed, the salt passed? I ask to be polite; I'm human myself, I know how we are. Any desires hanging on your back, pinching your toes, stirring your drink for you so it no longer tastes good? Justice, vengeance, sexual satisfaction? Feel free to speak up, we're all siblings here.

It's how we deal with each other, the basic web of civilization. We start with barter, move on to a system; we're no fools. Here, have some money, you can buy what you *want*. Should we go to the play tonight? If that's what you want. Me, I only want you to be happy.

Jack Lykon had returned to Tellys, but his specter remained. And as I snapped at Ran, "What do you want me to do?"

Not that he had asked me to do anything.

At the end of the month we went to the fair in the Imperial Park.

Twice a year the lowest level of the park, beside the river, is given over to craftspeople and farmers from the provinces who bring in every old piece of crockery and wagonload of fruit they think they can unload on city folk. Mixed in with them are acres of riches: Unexpected delights in the way of painted bowls showing mythological creatures drawn out in fiery symmetry; handblown goblets; finely patterned paper to use for decoration; and all manner of dishes, pipes, tah-burners, ceramic flowerpots. . . . The park, needless to say, is crowded on such days. Stuff that would be auctioned off at a fine arts house on Athena can be picked up for a smile and a handful of old coins.

We'd wandered around for half the day to our artistic and monetary satisfaction, and toward late afternoon we started to aim for the food and spice wagons, to bring things home for supper. Today countrypeople were free of the spice monopoly's prices and could bring their whitemint and pepperfall direct to the consumer—and the consumers were lined up, happy to wait for bargains.

I stopped to look at a row of candlestick holders. A man went by in a yellow brocade robe, a little girl on his shoulders, giggling. Two others followed behind him, sucking lemon ices. Lately it seemed that everywhere I went there was a high tide of children. And the families all looked so happy. What happened to the harassed mothers, screaming red-faced at their kids, smacking them as they wailed and making passersby feel uncomfortable?

"Excuse me," said a voice. I turned to see a young woman in very plain standard dress, a fellow barbarian. She looked about twenty, verging on pretty, and out of place. "I'm sorry to bother you," she said, uncertainty in her voice, "but you look like you know your way around here. Do you think these—" and she extended her hands, each holding a cheap brass candlestick, "look all right?"

"Well . . ." I said, not sure how to respond; actually, I've always found brass candlesticks quite ugly, and the pair she had chosen had to top the list in that department.

"You see, I'm having a guest for dinner, and I want it all to look nice," she said.

"I've never been fond of brass," I said.

"They're about all I can afford," she said frankly. She gazed at them with dissatisfaction.

They were the cheapest pair in the row, I saw. I picked up one of the less expensive looking crystal holders and glanced at the vendor. He raised four fingers. My fellow barbarian followed the exchange and her face fell.

"Is your guest Pyrenese?" I asked hopefully. A Pyrenese would hardly notice or care about the artistic merits of his dinnertable. In fact, it would be considered morally beneath him to take note of such things.

"He's Ivoran," she said.

"Oh, dear." And you don't know what you're letting yourself in for, my child.

Ran appeared then; he'd been lingering over a set of marble paperweights two wagonloads back. A true Ivoran, an aesthetic question engaged his interest at once.

"Why don't you buy one of those bowls with the phoenix-griffin design? —You remember them, Theodora.

They're down by the water's edge—the craftsman was packing to leave, and selling them for almost nothing. Then you can fill it with scented water and put a few of those floating candles in."

"I never heard of floating candles," she said doubtfully.

"It would look splendid," he insisted. "Come on, I'll point you in the right direction. —You'd best get a spot for us in line, Theodora. I'll be back in five minutes."

An appeal for aesthetic judgment will get Ran's attention where an appeal for mercy may leave him cold. He pulled his victim/charitable object after him, and I filled up a string bag with fruit and pastries, and went to stand in line at the spice wagon.

Several people had brought their own carts, now piled high with loot from the day. Good gods, there were eight—no, nine—children in line in front of me, and a tired woman with the voice of a drill sergeant watching over them. Wasn't she young to have— One of the older children's robes rustled as she moved, and I saw the character for "property of." I watched till she turned around, and read, "Kenris Training School."

Trocha children: Orphans and "superfluous offspring" brought up to be sold into trade apprenticeships. Even they didn't look unhappy. They demanded attention of their guardian freely, constantly tugging on her sleeves, and she gave it to them as their due.

All a facade, I thought, standing there, remembering the Poraths and wondering about what had gone wrong in my own past.

I remember once talking to one of the therapists on Athena about the strangeness of "family" to a Pyrenese crèche-graduate like me. I'd been saying nice things about the Cormallons, thinking of the relationship between Kylla and Ran, and the therapist had grinned and remarked that the older he got the more he felt the phrase "dysfunctional family" was redundant.

He had a point. But is it just families? Is the Pyrenese system really better? It didn't give me a happier childhood. And would I have found the same painful rubbing-together, one wound against another, in any group that had to live with each other, even nonrelatives on Pyrene? I never gave it a chance, so I suppose I'll never know.

I have my suspicions, though. What is it about us human beings, anyway? How can we possibly hurt each other as much as we do and still feel so put-upon while we're doing it? I sometimes feel we would all benefit greatly from having our lives recorded and played back, so we could see every wrong move we make from a spectator seat; every harmful remark and then a close-up on the eyes of the person we're talking to.

So far Ran hasn't blossomed into any super-neurosis, and the quirks he has are ones I'm prepared to live with. His distorted view of family, distorted in its way as mine, is like an anchor; he's unreasonably prejudiced in my favor, just because I had the good sense to marry him. So he's willing to put up with a great deal, too, and just assume that my intentions are good.

That's an attitude worth gold. It's not why I married him, but I'm beginning to see that people get married for reasons that are different from the reasons they don't get divorced.

All right, Theodora; you don't want anybody to take these treasures away from you. But what are you going to tell the Cormallon council next year?

Not to mention the ghost of Ran's grandmother. I wished she'd been as forthcoming in her message to me; I wished I knew her exact words. I'd heard this "new blood" phrase before, but how I could be responsible for it was beyond me. Was I supposed to trust Grandmother, unstopper the healer's cap (I felt like a bottle of old wine in someone's cellar), and go for the marginal odds as Jack Lykon had laid them out? Grandmother must have been crazy. Because if there's anything to this heredity business at all, this hypothetical offspring wouldn't be getting any terrific genes for the manipulation of magic, not from me. And yet I was the item she wanted factored into the plan. Did this make sense?

All right, assume I reported in to the council next year as barren. I'd chiseled the information out of Ran as to what would follow:

"We'd adopt," he said.

"Then what's all this about a second wife?"

"Well . . . that's who we'd adopt from. It can be done on an entirely friendly basis, Theodora. You could even help pick her out—probably one of the Ducorts or the Cymins. Then when she, uh, produces, we write her a bank order, get a divorce—"

"Forget that idea."

"It's a purely businesslike arrangement, Theodora—"

I'd given him a look that must have had more power than I'd realized because he shut up.

I reexamined that exchange from a scholar's point of view: I didn't see how a child of Ran and one of Cormallon's usual allies would satisfy Grandmother's requirements for a new genetic infusion.

I wished the old lady were alive. I wished I'd known her a little longer. I wished the Cormallons weren't so damned secretive.

The cart belonging to the Kenris Training School was piled high with goodies, and with live cargo, too; a very small member of the school sat atop, facing backward, staring directly into my face. He looked to be about two or three years old, wearing a short quilted jacket of royal blue that somebody had buttoned for him right up to the neck.

When he saw me focus on him, his dark eyes came alert. He zeroed in on my string bag, resting on the edge of the wagon.

"What's that?" he said, pointing to my rose nectarine.

"That's a rose nectarine," I replied.

"What's that?" he said, pointing to a bundle of handwoven napkins.

"They're dinner napkins," I replied.

"What's that?" he rapped out, pointing to my pellfruit—then to my phoenix-griffin dish—then to my colored papers.

Each time I answered him he moved on to the next item. Is this kid making fun of me? I wondered, uncertainly. He can't even know what half these things are, but he keeps asking for more.

Finally his exhausted looking guardian started to pull the cart away. The boy turned to me quickly and the words tumbled out. He jabbed his finger toward each item to illustrate his fact-checking. "That's a rose nectarine. That's dinnernapkins. That's a pellfruit. That's feenixgrif'n-dish.

That's festival paper. That's red oranges. That's a penholder."

"Yes!" I said, delighted.

He didn't smile, but the solemn eyes looked pleased at his success.

The cart moved away, past the spice line, out onto the path toward the park exit. I stared at it.

Gracious lady?" asked the spice vendor. "You're next."

"I'll be right back."

I left the string bag on the wagon like any fool tourist and galloped after the shaky cart of the Kenris School troop.

"Excuse me! Excuse me, gracious lady." The young woman stopped, with a facial expression that suggested she was too tired to even try to understand why I was bothering her.

"Yes? Can I help you?"

"I was just wondering. Are these children . . ." I searched frantically for the right word. What we usually translate into Standard as "adoption" refers to a series of ways people are taken into Houses, usually with a task in mind; I had no task in mind here. "Uh, are these kids available?"

She said, politely, "If you require any sort of trade experience, we can probably supply it. For short-term assignments, we have contracts of even a day at a time. You have only to call on our registrar's office—"

"No, no. Are they . . . for sale?"

This phrasing she grasped. "Of course," she said.

And they call us barbarians. "I'll have to get back to you on this," I said, "but meanwhile, can you tell me the name of the kid on top of the cart?"

"Tirjon. We don't have any last names, of course, but there's an ID number: 428791."

Numbers instead of surnames, just like my birthplace. I was practically nostalgic. "Four-two-eight-seven-nine-one," I said. "Many thanks. Four-two-eight-seven-nine-one." I walked away from the Kenris guardian and back toward the spice wagons. Four-two-eight-seven-nine-one. I needed a pen.

Ran was waiting, having rescued my string bag. "Did I miss something?" he asked.

"Ran, I've been thinking." As we spoke we started clean-